LEGACY OF SECRETS

By Elizabeth Adler

LÉONIE
PEACH
THE RICH SHALL INHERIT
THE PROPERTY OF A LADY
FORTUNE IS A WOMAN
LEGACY OF SECRETS

ELIZABETH ADLER

LEGACY OF SECRETS

DELACORTE PRESS

Published by
Delacorte Press
Bantam Doubleday Dell Publishing Group, Inc.
1540 Broadway
New York, New York 10036

*For
Richard*

"Life can only be understood backwards;
but it must be lived forwards."

—Søren Aabye Kierkegaard (1813–55)
Stages in Life's Way (1845)

"For the Irish have not the heart to baptize their children completely,
they want to preserve just a little paganism and whereas a child is
normally completely immersed, they keep his right arm out of the
water so that in afterlife he can grasp a sword and hold a girl in his
arm."

—Søren Aabye Kierkegaard
Journal, 1840

"Thousands are sailing
Across the Western Ocean
To a land of opportunity
That some of them will never see
Fortune prevailing
Across the Western Ocean
Their bellies full
And their spirits free
They'll break the chains of poverty
And they'll dance"

—Philip Chevron, *The Pogues,* 1988

CHAPTER

⁓⁓⁓⁓⁓⁓⁓⁓ 1 ⁓⁓⁓⁓⁓⁓⁓⁓

MAUDIE

Ardnavarna, Connemara

SINCE THIS IS the story of the past as well as the present I finally have to admit to being an "old woman." Though if any of you were to call me "old Maudie Molyneux" I'd probably set the dogs on you—the dalmatians, stuffed behind me in this big old chair like two spotted oversize cushions.

Let's get this subject of age out of the way so that we don't have to consider it again. I never think of myself as "old," but I've been lying about my age for so long I can't really remember how old I am anymore, though Faithless Brigid in the kitchen refuses to let me forget. "How could you tell Georgie Putnam you were only seventy?" she demanded just the other day, "when he knows he's ten years younger than yourself?"

"It's a woman's privilege," I told her haughtily, though I confess to a blush of shame.

Now, Faithless Brigid is by way of being my good friend. We were born more or less around the same time, and when she was young she came to work at the Big House, and she's been with me ever since. You want to know why she's called "Faithless" Brigid? It was the name the villagers gave to her in her younger days. She was a handsome girl, big and buxom, and she flitted from man to man, one after another, and married nobody. I always tell her I suspect it was because she was a bit of a tart.

"Will ye be shuttin' yer mouth, madam," she shouts at me when I tease her with this. "You'll have the world believin' yer slander. I was niver a tart, as you call it. More like the other way around, from what I recall." And she may have a point there.

As a girl, I could never have been called beautiful; even pretty would have been optimistic. I was like my mother, Ciel Molyneux, small, skinny, and redheaded, with a face like a mischievous cat and a laugh my pa always complained was too loud. My freckles were the bane of my life. Except when I was twenty and I met Archie, and he used to count 'em. Oh, and that can be a dangerous game, let me tell you. Or maybe I shouldn't. Mammie always said I should learn the art of discretion, as well as to know when to stop talking, but I've never managed either and I'm not about to change my ways now.

What do I look like now, you may ask? In truth, not that much different. Fragile, bony, piercing blue eyes, and red curls that are dyed and maybe a bit too girlish, but that's the way I like it. I always wear my favorite broad-brimmed black "Jack Yeats" felt hat crammed on top, and since I'm horse-mad like most of the Irish, I'm usually wearing fawn jodhpurs, circa 1930, the sort that bag at the thighs, with a "hunting pink" jacket, faded it's true and fraying at the seams, but if I have to be old, then I'm damned well going to be comfortable with it. These boots, now, fit like gloves and are still exquisite. They were made by the most famous bootmaker in London. Oh, it was "nothing but the best" for the Molyneuxes in those days. Nothing but the best for years, for centuries.

And we never threw anything away; I've got every frock I ever owned, except the real favorites that simply wore out with too much use. In my wardrobe, if you move the orange cat, Clara, who has just had her kittens in there, you'll find original Chanels from 1930 and Dior's New Look from 1947. Rummage further and you'll come across Schiaparelli, and Mammie's Poirets and Doucets and Vionnets. There's Fortuny and Fath and Worth in there, too, and I love to wear them all. We still dress for dinner here. One has to keep up some sort of standards you know.

It's the same with this house, Ardnavarna. It's awash under a sea of possessions covering the past hundred and fifty years, and shabby as it is, it's still the most enchanting house I've ever set foot in.

"You're prejudiced," you may say, and you are right, but it's still beautiful. It's Irish Georgian, not too big, not too small. The white paint is peeling, sweet-scented summer roses climb wildly all over it as I write, and the lawn outside my window is a tall carpet of daisies surrounded by a riotous battleground of gaudy flowers and flamboyant weeds, though I'm inclined to believe the weeds are winning.

The tall sash windows are flung open to catch the late afternoon sunshine and pungent peat smoke drifts from our chimneys. The front door is a perfect example of the best Georgian, flanked by a pair of tall, narrow windows and topped with a delicately scalloped fanlight, and as usual it stands wide open to welcome friends, which goes some way to explain why Irish country houses are notoriously cold.

Myself, I've always thought Ardnavarna was like a jewel, gift-wrapped in green: the lawns, the borders, the shrubs, and the tree-covered hills climbing behind it and swooping protectively around it. And to the right, in a dip between the hills, there's a glimpse of the sea.

Indoors it's all faded eau de nile wallpaper and frayed chintz. Nothing has been touched for years, not since Mammie ran out of money in the forties. But we still have the remnants of grandeur and our memories: silver horse-show trophies in need of a polish jostle for space on the sideboard alongside twenties chrome cocktail shakers and Georgian silver ice buckets. Threadbare Persian rugs cover the oak floors and enormous Chinese vases are crammed with dried hydrangeas and roses, all color faded from them into a delightful pale buff that blends so well with the patina of old wood.

There's a wide, creaking oak staircase that was a dead giveaway in my reckless youth, when any ideas of hanky-panky could be shattered by one wrong foot on the second step from the top, and the gold brocade curtains are so ancient you are forbidden to draw them in case they crumble to dust in your hands. Peat fires slumber constantly in the ornate iron grates, blackening the marble chimneypieces and adding their pungent aroma to the delicate scent of potpourri and the delicious smell of fresh-baked barmbrack and scones coming from the kitchen, and the everlasting dust. And, as I look, every chair seems to contain a pile of books and about a million old copies of *Horse and Hound* and *Irish Field,* and maybe a cat or two.

But, despite my love for the place, I wasn't born here. I came into this world on a summer day, half sunshine, half rain, in 1910, not more than a mile away. At the Big House.

My father had already put down the good port I drink of an evening now; he was expecting a boy, you see, and that's what they always did for boys, put bottles of fine port in the cellar to mature for drinking when the son came of age at twenty-one. Of course, when I came along he just looked at me and shrugged and said to my mother, "Well, if that's the best we can do, at least we'll see to it she rides like a man."

And he did. Other people remember being in their prams, but I remember the stables. The smell of horses was my first memory. And, praise be, I took to them the way other girls took to dolls. I never had any fear. I had my own little Connemara pony, dun-colored and docile, and by the time I was three Papa had forgiven me for not being a boy. I think he was quite proud of his fearless little equestrian daughter.

Now, Pa and Mammie were great travelers and they always took me along, right from the year I was born. Mammie said she wasn't going to stay behind and Pa said he wouldn't dream of leaving her, so off we all went. To Paris, of course, and Deauville for the racing. The casinos at Monte Carlo and Biarritz—Mammie adored a flutter. Back here for the hunting and fishing, and then to London for the social season, Ascot and Goodwood, and sailing at Cowes. Oh, and the parties. They'll never give such wonderful parties again. Or maybe that's just youth talking and all parties are good when you are seventeen. Then there was Baden-Baden and the Black Forest, and skiing in Saint Moritz.

Oh, I was a travelin' child all right, with a governess and a trunkful of toys and a pair of doting parents. At ten I was quite used to taking the boat train from London's Victoria Station across to Paris. And by fourteen I was quite the little habitué on the Blue Train down to the Riviera. I made the journey so often I could easily have done it by myself, though of course I was never allowed. And all the concierges in the best hotels knew me: Claridges, the Lancaster, the Hotel de Paris, the Gritti Palace.

To you young things, with your blue jeans and cowboy boots, your colleges and careers, this probably sounds as faraway in time as another planet, but when Mammie and Pa decided I was getting out of hand and sent me to finishing school in Paris, I thought the end of my world had come. Banished from Ardnavarna, I was, just like the notorious Lily. But I'll tell you about Lily later—"all in good time," as Mammie used to say when I was impatient. Still, it's odd how the conversation always gets back to "Wicked" Lily Molyneux, but then, she was the kind of woman you never forgot.

Anyhow, I was banished for a year. And I fought against it, ooh, how I fought! I cried buckets, but to no avail. And when I got there I enjoyed it—though I never let them know it, o' course. Kept on complainin' right to the end. Just to keep 'em on tenterhooks.

They sent me there expecting me to emerge a "young lady," but nobody was surprised when it didn't happen. Mammie said I was an

individual, and she had never encouraged me to be anything but myself. I was bright and lively and full of fun, with my flaming red curls
and a funny little face and the Molyneux blue eyes. And I was just
seventeen and immensely popular with a ton of friends. Then I came
home and I had to be a debutante. Can you imagine me, fluffed up in
white tulle with feathers in my hair like an overblown cockatoo?

When I was in my twenties all I thought about was horses and men.
In that order. Except in Paris, and then it was the other way around:
men first and then horses. Now, *you* know I was never beautiful, but
they said I was amusing because I had an endless flow of chat and this
soaring laugh I'd inherited from Mammie that made people want to
join in.

"There's no side to Maudie Molyneux," people used to say. "She's
nice to everyone regardless." But I have to admit I enjoyed a good
gossip almost as much as a good hard ride across the fields on a misty
autumn day. I also adored Paris and clothes and I would hate, even
now, to tell you how much money I squandered on hats. Especially
those little cocktail hats we wore in the thirties. There was one woman
on the Faubourg St. Honoré, what was her name? Oh, yes, Madame
Simonetta, who did these little wisps of spotted net and feathers that
cost an absolute fortune. But they were divine, worth every penny. I
have them upstairs still, along with all the rest of the stuff.

Who dreamed, in those carefree days, what was to happen next? I
always say I had ten good years, and then all we silly young things had
to grow up. And come 1939, too many of them had to die.

My friends were scattered throughout Europe as well as England
and Ireland. Some were even fighting on the other side. It bewildered
us all: one minute we were all romancing and partying, the next we
were supposed to hate each other. But I suppose that's what wars are
all about, the infamous evil few leading the good and the brave into
battle, to serve their own ends.

My special young man was one of the first to go. Archie Herbert.
The freckle counter.

Oh, Archie was so good-looking. Tall, black-haired, very aristocratic
with a little dark mustache and soulful brown eyes. And he looked so
divinely handsome in his khaki uniform with all those burnished brown
leather straps and belts and polished gold buttons. Of course, I was
madly in love with him. He was a professional army officer on a mis-
sion to Paris when war was declared and he stayed to see what he
could do. He was taken prisoner and sent to Germany—his family was
quite high up, you see, so it was a feather in the Nazis' cap to take him.

I had one letter from him, if you could call it that . . . a few lines, half of them crossed out by the censor. And then nothing more. I continued to write to him, hoping he was still there and that maybe he was getting my letters. And then, after the war, they traced him. He had died in the POW camp in 1942. They had starved that fine, handsome young man to death. I don't think I ever got over that.

Of course, we all did our bit in the war. I joined the navy, the Wrens, mostly because they had the smartest uniform. I would have liked to join the cavalry but they didn't take women, and anyway, they didn't use horses anymore. The Wrens made me an officer, not for my grand education, for God knows I never had one. But I did have three languages. I never saw a ship the entire war, but I had the time of my life driving the officers around London. Then they transferred me to the Admiralty, shifting those little models of submarines and destroyers around on big relief maps of the oceans of the world.

Oh, my dears, war was a very flirtatious time. God knows we had little enough of the mortal pleasures in London: no silk stockings, no perfume, no clothes—and damned little food. Though you could still get a decent drink at the Café de Paris before it got bombed. And the good hotels, Claridges and the Savoy, did their best with what they had, to put on a decent lunch for a few shillings. The nightclubs kept on going, and the pubs. There was music and we danced and laughed a lot—and cried a lot too. And then the end of the war came, and when the euphoria wore off we saw how few of our friends came home. The young men we had laughed and joked with, the boys we had played tennis with and danced with. And made love with. Our world was never to be the same again.

After the war I came home to Ardnavarna. Mammie was still here, tending her chickens and her sheep and her cows. Mammie had become quite the little farmer. It wasn't until later that I understood why. She had had to become more self-sufficient. Money wasn't anything any of us ever thought about much. When you had it you spent it, and when you didn't, you just made do. But the Molyneuxes had always had money and we weren't grand spenders—no yachts and gambling away fortunes in Monte Carlo or wild extravagances on famous mistresses or fabulous jewels. The money had always been there, for centuries. Only now it wasn't. Or at least, not that much of it.

You know how the eldest sons always inherit the houses and the money, well, my father was the second son, so he hadn't inherited anything much. All he had had was a little money from his grandmother, but I suppose we had gone through most of it by then. Mammie's fortune had been invested overseas, in German steel and in now-defunct shipping lines and bankrupt rubber plantations—all the wrong stuff.

Half from the shock of it, I got married. He was an Irishman. A nice enough fella whom I'd known all my life. But after Archie, I couldn't settle. He bored me silly, so within a year I upped and left him. And then I met another man. Remet him, I should say. A naval officer I'd known from the Admiralty. I used to drive him around a bit in the official car in my early days in the Wrens. I'd liked him then and I liked him now.

Of course there was a problem because I was still married, so we just lived together at Ardnavarna. No one minded that. It was when I was going to get a divorce and marry him that the trouble started. Oh, it was all right to live with a fella, they could turn a blind eye to that. But to divorce? In those days? God forbid. And he did, via the bishop himself.

So it was either get the divorce and marry the man and live in exile, or stay home, at Ardnavarna. I chose Ardnavarna and I've never regretted my decision, though in any case, the first husband died a couple of years later and I was a free woman again. I became the Merry Widow Molyneux—because like all the Molyneux women, I didn't take my husband's name. By the way, it's pronounced Moly*noo,* just so we get it straight.

Life went on. I had a ton of friends scattered across continents, and I finally came into my grandfather Molyneux's trust money, so I could visit them as often as I pleased. I had my horses, Paris was back swinging again with American jazz and fashionable people . . . oh, I had myself a wild old time.

Then I went on a trip to India with Pa and Mammie. Pa took a bad fall from a polo pony and a few days later he developed tetanus. He was dead within a week and I had to bring Mammie home. She was devastated without him, and of course I was too.

Mammie stayed quietly at Ardnavarna, tending her gardens—oh, they were a picture in those days, you can be sure, and after a while I picked up my old ways again, flitting from London to Paris to Dublin like a butterfly. But I always returned to Ardnavarna for the hunt season. Our stables were among the best in the country, our dalmatians the best of the breed, fine descendants of the notorious Lily's own dogs, and our gardens the most beautiful in Connemara.

And then, when Mammie finally died, I came home to Ardnavarna for good.

But I'm talking about myself again, the way Faithless Brigid always says I do, and all the while I meant to tell you about what happened just yesterday, about all the excitement, and my unexpected guests.

CHAPTER

∻∻∻∻∻∻∻∻∻∻ 2 ∻∻∻∻∻∻∻∻∻∻

IT HAD RAINED that morning, and the dogs were tired because we had already been for our usual ride along the strand. That is, they run and I ride. On my fine bay hunter, Kessidy, or on mad Malachy, the chestnut who can go like the wind and often does, whether you want him to or not. He's a tricky old beast and you have to be trickier and let him know who's boss, and then he'll give you a grand ride. Fearless and fast and built like an ox, that's Malachy.

Most days we go through the bridle paths in the woods and down to the strand and we race along the edge of the water, with me hollerin' and laughin' like a mad creature, I'm enjoying myself so much. And the dogs running hell-for-leather alongside, barking their heads off from the sheer joy of it. *That's* the best part of my day. The wind whistling in my ears, the surf pounding hard as my heart and the horse fairly singing with speed beneath me. It's the next best thing to making love, I can tell you. Ah, and there I go, spilling my secrets again like wine from an overfull glass. "That's enough of yourself," as my mammie, God love her, would say to me when I talked indiscreetly. And you can see she was right.

Have you never been to Connemara? Well then, you have a treat coming, because to see Connemara for the first time is like having God's own country revealed to you in a dream. Every few miles the landscape changes: one minute it's all bleak and desolate, with bare blue-green mountains and maybe a rushing crystal stream carving a passage from on high down to a fast-flowing brown river. Then you'll leave the sparse, rocky landscape behind and there's miles of peat bogs the color of bitter chocolate, and mysterious, reedy silver lakes encircled by trees. Where the land dips toward the ocean you will see tiny, rugged whitewashed stone cottages with their thatch roped down against the harsh winter gales.

The Connemara sky brings artists from all corners of the world. It's the color of moonstones and opals and sometimes it's exactly the same mother-of-pearl gray of the sea, and it makes me wish I could paint. As you go, you'll maybe see a lone caramel-colored cow sitting on a rocky outcrop, placidly chewing its cud, watching you. And maybe a little Connemara pony will trot past you along the road, unattended, with its tiny foal, white with a curling wind-tossed mane and a plumed tail like a pony in a fairy tale, clip-clopping at its side. Some say it's lonely scenery, but to me it's just about as peaceful as you are going to find anywhere in this tired old world.

Anyhow, the afternoon was sunny and warm. I was mounted on Kessidy, but for once the dogs did not come with me. I left the lazy creatures behind, sleeping on the front steps, and trotted for a change, out of the grounds and down the leafy lane. After a while I saw this little Fiat nudging its way down the boreen toward the Big House with a young red-headed girl driving it.

Now, it's not easy to find the House; the old signpost was run over years ago but it was never much of a thing anyhow, just a hand-lettered weatherworn bit of wood, and now it tilts drunkenly toward the ground as though no one would ever need to know the way to Ardnavarna. It's a quick little turn off a secondary road, and with the broken signpost and all, it's easily missed. So I knew right away this was no ordinary tourist, lost and bewildered and looking for the entrance to the national park. This redheaded young woman was a person with a purpose.

Curiosity is another of my failings, so of course I followed her, only I went the easier way through the trees because over the years that lane has become little more than a rutted track that's almost impossible to traverse when it's raining and muddy. Long gone are the days when the carriage road led to Ardnavarna, maintained in perfect order by the Molyneux family. I felt sorry for her, jolting along for more than a mile until she stopped at the crumbling stone gateposts of the Big House, with a couple of lions atop holding our heraldic shield in their paws. The ornate iron gates are permanently wedged back with heavy rocks, and what's left of the once famous drive is just weeds and more ruts, and now the beech trees have grown so big they block out the light. It looks gloomy and oppressive, even on a sunny day.

She turned into the drive and jolted on toward the house and I walked Kessidy along behind her, lurking in the trees so she wouldn't see me. That drive is a mile long and it curves through the trees offering tantalizing little glimpses of gray stone turrets and driving you mad with impatience to see the place. And as you emerge from the leaves there it is, silhouetted in front of you, the afternoon sun at its back, looking for all the world as though it were still lived in.

The girl climbed from the car and put her hands in the pockets of her jeans, staring at it, and I saw her shoulders sag with disappointment. Because it's nothing but a blackened shell. The roof has fallen in in a dozen places and there's ivy climbing through the gaping window sockets. Of course, there are still vestiges of its former grandeur: the imposing portico with its four Corinthian pillars and the huge front door, wide enough to ride a horse through, which it's said my great-grandfather took delight in doing every New Year's Eve, sitting on the horse's back in the stone-flagged great hall, quaffing a glass of champagne. "To bring the Molyneuxes luck," he said. In which case the man was sadly mistaken.

I dismounted and walked a few steps toward her. "Come to view the old ruin, have you?" I called.

She swung around. "It's meself I'll be referrin' to, not the house, of course," I said, exploding with laughter at my little joke. "And who might you be, that's trespassin' on my land?"

"*Your* land?"

"Well, o' course it's mine," I retorted impatiently. "Everybody knows that. I expect you'll be a foreigner though. Nobody around here would even want to look at the old pile."

She stared speechlessly at me and I could see from her amazed look she was taking in my age and my girlish red curls with the battered black felt hat crammed on top, and my faded hunting pink, my ancient baggy fawn jodhpurs, and my smartly polished boots.

"If you were looking for Ardnavarna Castle, this is it," I said cheerily. "Or rather, what's left of it. It was a rabbit warren, fifty-two rooms, one for every week of the year. Cold as hell frozen over—even colder than Moscow in winter, my mother always said. And that with forty fireplaces going full blast—they never let 'em go out, even when the family was away. Heating that house was like fueling a ship and it cost ten times as much to run.

"But you'll be wantin' to know what happened. Nineteen twenty-two, it was, when we Irish had 'the Troubles,' and *the boys* paid us a little visit. They were local lads, I knew them all despite their masks. They said they were *very, very* sorry but they had instructions to burn it.

'Go ahead,' says I angrily. 'It's the first time since it's built the damned place will be warm.'

"I was only twelve years old and I was alone, but for the stupid governess, who had run to hide in the greenhouses. The servants all knew what was to happen, of course, and they had disappeared like leprechauns at dawn. *The boys* gave me fifteen minutes to take what I wanted and I thought quickly. There were the Rubenses, the Vandykes, the family portraits, and the silver. *And* my mother's pearls . . . all priceless, all irreplaceable.

"In the end of course, I ran into the stables and got the horses out and the dogs. I turned the chickens free and shooed 'em away, but the rest all went up in smoke, and I never regretted my decision for a single minute." I laughed, remembering Mammie's face when I'd told her. "But my mother never forgave me for the pearls."

The girl just looked at me, shy and big-eyed, not knowing whether to say she was sorry for me or glad, and I switched my riding crop impatiently against my thigh, waiting for her to introduce herself.

"Well?" I demanded. "So who are you?"

She straightened up, the way she might have done in front of the school headmistress, self-consciously smoothing her crumpled white cotton shirt. She had wildly curling copper-red hair and cool gray dark-lashed eyes, and she had freckles like my own. I softened toward her immediately. And then she said, "I'm Shannon Keeffe."

"An O'Keeffe, are ya?" She couldn't have told me anything more surprising and I laughed again, vastly amused this time. "Well, well," I said. "I always wondered when one of Lily's bastards would show up."

She blushed a fiery red with confusion. "But that's partly why I'm here," she exclaimed. "To find out about Lily. *Who* was she?"

"*Who* was Lily? Why, Lily was notorious. 'Wicked Lily' they called her around here, and maybe they were right. Lily had the kind of beauty that trails legends in its wake; she dangled men from her finger-tips and caused havoc wherever she went. She divided families, and brothers, sisters, lovers, and husbands and wives. Even children. And if you're wondering how I know all this, Shannon Keeffe, it's because my mother, Ciel Molyneux, was Lily's younger sister."

Her eyes widened with interest. "Oh," she said, sounding thrilled, "then you can tell me all about her?"

"That depends on why you want to know," I replied smartly. After all, I wasn't about to unveil the skeletons in the family cupboard to a total stranger. I put my fingers in my mouth and whistled and Kessidy trotted through the trees toward me. "But I'll tell you this," I added, leaping agilely astride the mare, "you're not the first to be on Lily's trail." As I cantered off down the driveway, I called, "Follow me, Shannon Keeffe, down the boreen."

She maneuvered the Fiat behind me down the lane to the left of the driveway. It was little more than a horse trail, so narrow that the brambles threatened to take the paint from the car and the fronds of bracken almost closed over it. Then suddenly the trees thinned out and the bracken parted and we were looking at Ardnavarna.

Sunlight glittered on the tall sash windows, pungent peat smoke drifted from the chimneys, and the dalmatians sprawled picturesquely on the steps. The door stood wide open, as usual, and in the green hills behind, the young stablelad was playing a plaintive little tune on his reed pipes, sounding exactly like a nightingale.

Scenting a stranger, the dogs lifted their heads, then they rose as one and bounded toward us. I dismounted and gave Kessidy a slap on the rump that sent her ambling toward the stables where the lad would take care of her, then I pushed the dogs back down again with a wave of my hand. "Down, you damned creatures," I yelled angrily at them, and they subsided, sitting on their haunches wagging their silly tails knowing I didn't mean a word of it. "Blitherin' idiots," I said to Shannon Keeffe, "but I'm dashed fond of 'em all the same. Truth is I couldn't live without 'em."

The girl was staring at the house with that rapt expression on her face that meant she had fallen in love, and I smiled, pleased. "Let's have tea," I said hospitably waving her inside. Her lovely eyes were wide with pleasure as she stared around the cluttered hall and the dusty old rooms, breathing in the scent of it. And I knew then that I liked her.

"It's the most enchanting house I've ever been in," she said in a soft, trembling little voice as if she were quite overcome by it. "It's as though it were alive." She laughed. "You can almost hear it breathing."

" 'Tis true," I agreed modestly, sweeping her in front of me to the kitchen, for there's nothing nicer than a bit of flattery when it's about something close to your heart.

Now, Faithless Brigid is as plump and big-boned as I am delicate and sparrowlike. She has a round face with three chins and her gray hair is parted straight down the middle and anchored just above each ear with a white plastic hair band. Her pink overall is usually hiked up three inches shorter at the back, showing the underside of her plump knees, and when she's working in the kitchen she always wears a pair of old green Wellington boots on her impossibly tiny feet. "For comfort," she says, with no thought for how it looks.

"That's Faithless Brigid," I said, sweeping layers of newspapers and books and a couple of sleeping orange cats to the far end of the table. "I've brought Shannon Keeffe to take tea with us, Brigid," I added loudly. The old girl has become a bit deaf these last few years.

"Then it's as well I've just brought out a batch of scones," she retorted tartly. "Next time, *madam*, if you'll be invitin' a person to take tea, will you be lettin' me know sooner, so I can prepare properly." With that she took a giant plate of fresh scones and banged it down on the table. She trotted over to the cupboard and brought out a huge pot of jam.

"Fresh raspberries, I picked 'em myself," I whispered conspiratorially as Brigid slammed the pot of jam onto the table in front of us. Then she took a blue pottery bowl of cream and slammed it onto the table next to the jam.

"The brack's not yet cooled, so you'll have to be makin' do with that," she grumbled, trotting back to her stove.

Knowing how to rile her, I told Shannon the story of how she came to be called "Faithless." She flung me a furious glare, and I grinned.

Jostling the dalmatians from the chairs where they sat like expectant-looking statues awaiting tidbits, I poured strong black tea into delicate Spode cups. "Here's yours, Faithless Brigid," I called mockingly, knowing exactly what her answer would be.

"Ah, and y'know I'm always takin' mine from yer fayther's old shavin' mug," she grumbled, trotting quickly over to the table. She's a creature of habit, my Brigid.

As long as I've known her, and *you* know that's a lot of years, Brigid has seemed to be in perpetual motion—just as I always seem to be in perpetual mid-sentence—trotting here and there, as light on her feet as a bantamweight boxer, despite her bulk and her old Wellingtons.

I said to Shannon, my mouth full of scone, "Brigid's older than me, of course. She used to look after me when I was just a wee slip of a girl. She must be over a hundred by now."

"I niver did," Brigid retorted heatedly, brandishing a bread knife in the air over the sticky, rich brack. "We're the same age and you know it. It's just you niver admit to it."

I fed the encroaching ginger cats and the dalmatians bits of scone and winked at the girl. "You'll be after forgivin' Brigid," I said loftily. "The old woman niver did know her place."

Brigid scowled but said nothing, and I smiled brightly at Shannon, thinking it was time I found out her story. I peered closely at her. I could see she was a beauty, though she had yet to grow into it. She had the magnificent copper hair I used to have myself, though mine was never half as luxuriant. And those divine gray eyes, so cool and clear, I knew one day they would drive men wild. That is, if they hadn't already.

I leaned forward, inspecting her freckles. "I've got this cream," I whispered, "made up from my mother's recipe in a village the other side of Kylemore. 'Tis miraculous with the freckles. Probably from its proximity to the holy nuns over at the abbey, my mother always used to say."

"Humph!" Brigid commented loudly from the stove.

"Ignore her," I said, moving my chair closer, "and tell me about yourself."

"Well," she said hesitantly. "My father's name is Bob Keeffe."

Behind me, I heard Brigid turn to listen, but she said nothing. Neither did I.

"I wondered if you knew him?"

"Why should I?" I asked cagily.

She stared at me, nonplussed. "But you know the name, O'Keeffe. And you said I was one of Lily's bastards!"

I nodded, sipping my tea, waiting to hear what she had to say before giving away the family secrets.

"It's a long story," she said with a huge sigh. "So I guess I had better begin at the beginning."

"It's as good a place as any," I agreed, as Brigid pulled up a chair and we settled down to listen.

CHAPTER
3

SHANNON

"I GUESS IT all began three months ago, on my twenty-fourth birthday," Shannon said. "My father gave a big party that weekend, at our country house on Long Island, to celebrate my engagement as well as my birthday." She smiled, a wry little half smile that failed to reach her lovely gray eyes. "Actually, it was my third engagement in two years. Dad asked me, 'Will it stick this time?' And I told him confidently, oh sure, this is for keeps. He was so relieved that I was happy, though I think Buffy, my stepmother, was just glad I was finally off her hands.

"Everybody knew 'Big Bob' Keeffe," Shannon said with a proud little smile. "His story was written up in every magazine for years, even though he was reluctant to talk about himself. But when you have the kind of success he had, you somehow become public property, and there are no secrets left anymore. Or at least, that's what I thought.

"He never talked to the media about his personal life, only about his business. He was a self-made man, a millionaire many times over, and everybody wanted to know how he had done it.

" 'Rags to riches, that's me,' he would tell them. But that's all he would say.

"They said he dealt in property, but he just laughed at that. He called himself 'a builder,' and he always wanted to build bigger than anyone else. His skyscrapers dominate the skylines of a dozen American cities and he was building his own dream, the one hundred and twenty-five story Keeffe Tower on Park Avenue, designed by I. M. Pei.

"People thought it was strange that he never talked about his past, they sneered at him and said it was because he was ashamed of his orphanage background. But it wasn't true, he was never ashamed to confess he had once been poor.

"Sometimes when I saw him on television talking about his projects, it would take me by surprise how handsome he was. The media described him as 'a burly, silver-haired, sixtyish man, who could charm the loose change from the pocket of a beggar and the clothes off any pretty woman.'" Shannon smiled wryly, remembering him. "And I guess maybe they were right. He had piercing light-blue eyes and thick silver hair that had once been as black as only the true 'black Irish' can have, and he was always immaculately dressed. But his hands were a workingman's hands; big and powerful. He said it was his inheritance, and that he was descended from people used to hard labor, farming stony Irish fields for centuries."

She sighed, remembering. "There were so many stories about him, and there were terrible rumors about his infidelities, but I'm sure there weren't that many and I know he always tried to be discreet, for my sake. And I guess for Buffy's. And I know for certain he'd never forgotten what it felt like to be poor and alone; he gave a lot of his money to charities, always anonymously, because he hated publicity. But fame —and notoriety—seemed to seek him out."

EVERY MAGAZINE AND newspaper in the U.S. had covered the story of how Robert O'Keeffe had started out a poor boy, an orphan who had labored on Boston construction sites for years to pay for his studies at M.I.T. And how, with an engineering degree finally in his pocket, he had married Mella, an Irish girl from Limerick. They said she was slight and red-haired, a gentle beauty; the love of his life and as alone in the world as he was himself.

He had found a steady job as a construction engineer and they had bought a little house in the Boston suburbs. A year later, when Shannon was born, he felt life could offer him nothing more. They were happy and content, a perfect little unit.

Then it all fell apart: Mella took sick with cancer that had gone undetected until it was too late. She died when Shannon was two years old, and Bob stayed home, drinking himself into a stupor every night, alone with his grief, while worried neighbors looked after the baby.

After a month, he later said, his grief turned to anger at the world for keeping on turning without his beloved Mella and then his anger turned to rage at himself for not being able to help her. He stopped drinking and he buried his frustration and rage in work. He left the baby in the care of a friendly neighbor while he worked all hours that God sent, filling his head with nothing else but blind ambition.

He said he was lucky: he was always the right man in the right place at the right time. Success came quickly, in a minor way, but he wasn't content with just that. He borrowed huge sums from bankers who were charmed by his silver tongue and impressed with his dedication as well as his knowledge of his business and his foresight. And within four years he took his small company into the big time. They said he was a man who knew what he was doing and what he wanted and that he was determined to have it. The banks were quick to spot the qualities of a winner. They gave him what he asked and they never lived to regret it, because Big Bob O'Keeffe never let them down.

When Shannon was six he bought an apartment on New York's Park Avenue and employed a fancy decorator to do it up. He installed her there with a housekeeper and a nanny and enrolled her at the Ursuline Convent School. They said that in return for his good fortune, Bob offered his services and a portion of his money to various charities and then he began to be seen around the smartest parties in town.

He met Barbara van Huyton—Buffy—at the very first party the very first week. She was tall and slender in a black velvet dress, with perfectly cut shoulder-length blond hair, a chiseled nose, and confident hyacinth eyes. Her family had an important name but no money; she was his image of the perfect upper-class girl and he married her six months later.

Buffy's friends said that when she married him she had traded her social advantages for his money. And they were right. He gave her a million-dollar marriage settlement with an additional one million dollars for every year they were married, to be paid into her account on their wedding anniversary. She was as cool as her husband was volatile, as clinical as he was passionate, and the gossips said that within a year of their marriage he had taken a lover. And they later said she was only the first of many.

SHANNON SAID, "I KNEW about my father's latest mistress, Joanna Belmont, though I guess not many other people did, except Buffy. And that was only out of self-interest." She added bitterly, "She just wanted to protect her investment. Obviously she couldn't have considered Joanna much of a threat. She probably thought she was just some actress.

"At least she used to be an actress, because I know for a fact that Joanna hasn't worked since she met my father. She's beautiful, you know. Thirty-five years old, six foot two in her heels, blond, and I guess you could say she's flamboyant. Her theater bios said she had the smile of Doris Day, the body of a young Ginger Rogers, and the legs of Shirley MacLaine, and I guess my dad found that an unbeatable combination. And maybe Joanna really cared about him, too, because with her flashy temperament it couldn't have been easy for her to keep a secret."

She shrugged wearily. "Anyhow, that was the way things stood the night of the party."

CHAPTER

CHAPTER
4

~~~~~~~~~~~~~~~~~~~~~~~~~~

LONG ISLAND, N.Y.

THE NIGHT WAS HOT and humid. A lavish dinner of caviar with scrambled eggs, Maine lobster, raspberry chocolate marquise, and vintage champagne had already been devoured by the four hundred guests under the lantern-lit trees, and on the long terrace with its distant view of the lake. Now they were dancing in the sumptuous swagged green-and-white silk marquee. Its billowing curtains were looped back to catch any breath of breeze, and elegantly gowned women strolled the lawns, fanning themselves with the long-handled Chinese paper fans Buffy had provided in anticipation of the heat. She had also provided umbrellas and tented walkways in the event of rain: Buffy was a woman who left nothing to chance, and Shannon thought her stepmother would have made a good corporate attorney. Buffy hadn't approved of the cabaret that was about to start, though. Her father had insisted on it against all her protests. "It's so Irish," she had complained.

"Well, for God's sakes, I am Irish," he'd bellowed. "And so is Shannon, despite all your efforts to tame her." And he had gone ahead and booked a traditional Irish band and a troupe of Irish dancers and singers to teach his guests to jig.

Pushing his way through the happy crowd of dancers, Bob Keeffe grabbed his daughter's hand and led her onto the stage. Silencing the band with a wave of his hand, his big voice boomed across the lawns without the aid of the microphone. "Ladies and gentlemen, my friends," he called, and the young people gazed obediently up at him and the strollers outside the marquee turned to listen.

"As you know, this party is a celebration of Shannon's birthday," he said. "But *these people* are a celebration of her Irish red hair and her smiling Irish eyes." Amid laughter he took the mike and announced, "Ladies and gentlemen, the fiddles and flutes and the squeeze-box will play for you, and these lovely young people"—he waved to the dancers standing behind him—"will show you how to *really* dance."

The music started up, and Bob put his arm around Shannon and whirled her away. Within minutes the floor was bouncing and the guests outside on the lawns drifted back to the marquee, drawn by the magnet of the different music.

Later, as she danced with her fiancé, Shannon saw her father make his way alone to the edge of the marquee. Leaning against the struts, one hand in the pocket of his immaculately cut white dinner jacket, he watched the dancers, and she thought how strangely lonely he looked for a man with so many friends.

Buffy was watching him too. She gave him that cool "Buffy" look and Shannon knew just what she was thinking. She could read her stepmother like a book. There always were only two things on her mind. Money and position.

Buffy had always hated being poor. At twenty she had pictured herself growing older, struggling to maintain her social position and beauty on a pittance, just the way she had throughout her girlhood, and she had decided to marry money. She knew what she needed was an "entrepreneur," a New Age man who made money as though he had just invented it. She had found him in Bob O'Keeffe.

She had been twenty-six and Bob was in his forties. The wedding was a lavish one, with all her family and her many friends as guests, and his daughter, eight-year-old Shannon, as flower girl. The *O* was discreetly shaved from O'Keeffe and she became Buffy Keeffe and Shannon became her stepdaughter. She was the perfect hostess; she knew everybody who counted on first-name terms and she was beautiful. And yet she knew that within a year of their marriage her husband had taken a lover and that there had been others since. Yet Buffy and Big Bob Keeffe remained a social legend, the smartest couple in New York and Palm Beach.

Shannon stepped back from Wil Davenport's arms. She said, laughing, "Give me a break, Wil. I'm all out of breath. I need water and fresh air."

"I'll get you both," he said gallantly, escorting her out onto the lawn and going in search of a glass of water.

Shannon smiled as she watched him go. She had known him exactly three months and she couldn't wait to spend the rest of her life with him. He was tall and dark and as handsome as any young man had the right to be. He was romantic—he sent flowers *all* the time. He wooed her with words and small presents. He wasn't very rich, he'd told her, impressed by her father's wealth, but she knew that didn't matter, her father had not started out rich either.

She didn't remember her own mother but she did remember when her father had married Buffy, and herself as a bridesmaid in lemon silk taffeta so stiff it crackled when she walked down the aisle. She had stood still as a statue, afraid to move in case her noisy skirts drowned out the holy words. And after that Buffy had simply taken over their lives.

By the time she was eleven years old Shannon was too tall for her age, skinny as a jackrabbit with a mop of fiery red hair. She had freckles she despised and teeth that protruded so much she just knew they'd need years of braces. And her knobbly knees stuck out of the hateful short, pretty frocks Buffy liked to dress her up in, which made her look exactly like Raggedy Ann. She had huge dark-lashed sweatshirt-gray eyes and an offhand manner that was a cover for her insecurities. Her face was wide-boned and symmetrical and her nose slightly dented from the time she'd fallen off her pony at the age of eight, a defect her stepmother insisted must be corrected later.

Buffy saw that she attended the right schools and had the proper friends, and that she went to parties with children "of her own sort," but the truth was the two had little in common except her father.

Still, her childhood had been happy enough, because she was the apple of her father's eye. But even though Bob Keeffe adored her, he was not an attentive father; he was far too busy making money for that. Yet he always made sure to show up for the main events, and he was proud of his only daughter.

"You've got it all, baby," he would say admiringly. "You can be anything you want, just like your dad. But remember this, little darlin', you've got to go after what you want and you've got to want it real hard. That's the difference between us Irish and these old-line rich folk. They came over on the *Mayflower* and we came over on the coffin ships. And just look at us now." And he had roared with laughter at the idea of exactly where he was now, so high and mighty and richer than the men next to him, with a wife as snobbish as theirs and a daughter on whom he could lavish his love and his money.

Yet, oddly, whenever she asked, "But who are our Irish ancestors, Daddy? Why don't we have any aunts and uncles?" he always closed up tight as a clam and told her not to be bothering her head about that, and that maybe he'd tell her when she was older. And then he would hurry her off to tea at some smart hotel.

Shannon grew up sheltered from the "real world" by their money and smart private schools. Her summers were spent in the company of boring grown-ups on Mediterranean yachts and her winter vacations were spent being bored with more grown-ups at villas in Barbados. The best time of the year was summer camp with the other kids, where for a few weeks they all ran wild and talked about boys.

As the years passed, her teeth were straightened, her knees unknobbled themselves, her limbs grew long and sleek and her body supple, but she kept her pony-battered nose, ignoring Buffy's instructions to have it fixed. She grew curves in the right places and was properly slender where it counted. But her hair was still a flaming red and her freckles were still the bane of her life, and to her embarrassment, her eyes were truly the windows on her soul, gray as a deep lake and reflecting every passing emotion. She knew it was impossible for her to keep her feelings to herself; they were right up there in her eyes for everyone to see.

She had been fourteen when she first saw her father with his mistress. She had sneaked out of her Boston school with two other girls and they had gone shopping and for tea at the Ritz-Carlton. He was with a pretty, youngish woman. She had dark hair and pale skin and he was holding her hand under the table. Shannon had felt the blush sting her cheeks with heat. They were unaware of her, wrapped up in each other. As she watched, her father had run his finger gently across the curve of the girl's cheek. He touched her full lips and she kissed his hand, clutching it for a brief moment. Shannon had turned and fled, followed by her friends. "It's okay," they told her comfortingly, "all men do that!"

Her father later realized something was wrong when she couldn't look him in the eye, and finally she told him what she had seen. He paced angrily back and forth on the Aubusson rug in the library of the Fifth Avenue penthouse.

He looked pleadingly at her. "I was going to say you are too young to understand these things. But obviously you are not. You understood what you saw." He shrugged. "I won't ask your forgiveness because you are my daughter, not my wife. And I can't tell you it's all right, because it's not. All I can do is ask you to try to forget it, and hope that some day, when you are older and know better, you will forgive me. *And remember this, daughter. Never trust a man.*"

At her party later, on the dance floor once again with Wil, Shannon saw her father leave his lonely place on the edge of the crowd. His eyes met hers, and the weary frown etched between his brows disappeared as he made his way toward her through the laughing crowds.

"A dance for your old dad?" he asked. His eyes were full of love as she stepped into his arms, slight and delicate as a breeze.

"Thank you, Daddy, for a wonderful party," Shannon murmured, her head against his chest.

He sighed ruefully. "I always wanted the best for you, right from the day you were born." He hesitated, then said sadly, "I know I wasn't around enough, when you were growing up." He shrugged his big shoulders helplessly. "I missed so much. I was always too busy, pursuing a dream. But I needed to do it, Shannon. At first to make something out of our existence after your mother's death, and then for the hell of it. I enjoyed my work, I got a kick out of making money. But sometimes I sacrificed you."

She hugged him happily. "No, you didn't, Dad, honestly. You were always there for the important things. Remember the time I fell off my pony and got a concussion? When I opened my eyes in the hospital you were holding my hand. And the time I sang and danced so badly in the school play? You were right there in the front row applauding like mad. Oh, and always on Christmas mornings and on those boring grown-up vacations."

He pulled a wry face and she laughed. "And you'll be there to walk me down the aisle." She rested her head affectionately against his broad shoulder, feeling the smoothness of his jacket under her cheek. With her father's arms around her she had always felt safe from the world.

There was a tap on his shoulder. A good-looking young man grinned at him and said, "Can't monopolize her all night, Mr. Keeffe. Give the other guys a break, won't you?"

Bob stepped back, watching for a moment as the young man swept her off, then he made his way to the side of the marquee. He looked at his young daughter, so happy, so carefree, so at ease in her world, her short skirts whirling and her long hair flowing like a gaudy, brave, copper-red banner. Then he turned away, and leaving the carefree world behind, he walked alone and unnoticed to where the edge of the velvet night sky touched the silver of the lake.

CHAPTER
5

LATE THE NEXT MORNING Shannon drifted drowsily from sleep to consciousness. She stretched her arms over her head like a lazy cat, running her hands through her tangled copper hair, smiling as she recalled the previous night. She only wished she could have her party all over again.

She laughed, remembering everyone dancing Irish reels in their chic clothing, and the men stripping off their dinner jackets as the music got faster and they got hotter. They had quenched their thirst in iced champagne and danced until dawn, though the "old folks," as her friends laughingly called them, had long since departed for their beds.

She lay back against the pillows, thinking about her new fiancé, Wil, asking herself if he wasn't the nicest, most handsome, most charming young man she had ever met. Except for her father, of course, because Big Bob Keeffe was in a class of his own when it came to charm, looks, and niceness.

She closed her eyes, imagining herself walking down the aisle on her father's arm in a cloud of white silk and lace, and Wil waiting for her at the altar with that look of love in his eyes, and she sighed with contentment.

She threw on a robe and drifted lazily downstairs, filled with a happy feeling of well-being. The servants had been working all night and the huge house was immaculately tidy. There were fresh flower arrangements on the tables and sideboards and no hint of last night's cigarette smoke. No one would ever have guessed there had been a party, were it not for the green-and-white striped marquee still on the lawn.

Fresh coffee bubbled in the machine on the marble console in the breakfast room, and she helped herself to a cup, adding a guilty spoonful of sugar and sipping it thankfully. Through the window she caught a glimpse of Wil on the tennis court. She guessed he was playing the local pro and she groaned, admiring his stamina.

Taking her coffee, she strode down the hall to her father's study and tapped on the door. There was no reply and she peeked in. The room was different from the rest of the house: it was small and crowded, and Shannon smiled; her father's study described his personality.

Big Bob Keeffe could never have been called "neat" and he spread himself and his belongings over every possible surface. The old-fashioned rolltop desk was stuffed with papers, architects' cabinets bulged with plans, a table was heaped with drawings, and a pair of battered red leather armchairs was piled with files. Two of his most prized paintings from his collection of Irish masters hung on the walls: an early Orpen portrait of a pale-skinned, red-haired woman in a pink satin gown that he said reminded him of his first wife; and a harsh Yeats landscape that only he admired.

On his desk was an inexpensive multipicture frame filled with photos of Shannon through the years, and on the wall was what he said was his greatest treasure and achievement, Shannon's framed diploma from Harvard. "Now I know you'll never starve," he had told her, laughing, at the boisterous celebration at Lock Obers restaurant after the graduation ceremony. "Brains as well as beauty, that's my girl."

The phone rang, shattering the peaceful silence, and Shannon caught it on the first ring. It was her father's partner, Brad Jeffries, and he sounded startled when she answered. "Just calling to say thanks," he said quickly. "Great party, Shannon."

Shannon had known Brad almost all her life. He and his wife had both been at the party last night, though she hadn't noticed them dancing a reel, and now she thought about it neither of them had looked as though they were enjoying themselves.

Her father's other partner, good-looking Jack Wexler, had been there, too, with the latest successful New York model on his arm, but she thought he hadn't been doing much dancing either.

She scribbled a quick note to her father asking him to ring Brad, added "Love you, Dad—and thanks," and signed her name with a flourish. Then she went in search of her stepmother.

But Buffy was not in her room either. The bedroom with its fresh blue-and-white sprigged wallpaper and crisp blue taffeta curtains was empty. So was her vast dressing room with its ranges of neat closets and her pale-paneled bathroom, and when Shannon finally found the maid she told her that her stepmother had left early for the city.

She went back to her room, put on a bathing suit and shorts, and went back to the tennis court to find Wil.

She stared, surprised at his tennis partner. It wasn't the club pro: it was Jonas Brennan. Sorry, she corrected herself, grinning, she meant Jonas *K.* Brennan. Or "J.K.," as he preferred to be known.

J.K. was her father's protégé. He had taken him into the business straight out of a hick southern college. Young Jonas had shown up at his office, clutching his degree and a minuscule CV, haunting the place for three days until the exasperated secretary had threatened to send for the police. "I'm not going until I see Mr. Keeffe," he'd said stubbornly, and he had meant it.

Finally, admiring his persistence, Bob had seen him. He had inspected his papers and his degree and thrown them contemptuously onto the desk. He'd said, "You've got nerve coming to see me with these."

"Goddam it, sir, I had no choice," the young man had roared back angrily. "I was raised in that town. I know it's hicksville and so is the college. My grandparents were sharecroppers, my father was a drunk, and my mother sold beer in the local saloon—and herself on the side whenever the moon was right. What other college could I afford? But that's no yardstick of my ability."

Silenced, Bob had studied him. Jonas was of middle height, stocky and strong, with smooth brown hair and nervous, angry brown eyes behind gold-rimmed spectacles. He remembered himself at that age: poor and full of rage and defiance. He hadn't been dissimilar from this boy.

That had been ten years ago. J. K. Brennan was now thirty-two years old and there was nothing he didn't know about the Keeffe businesses. He was Bob's right-hand man and Keeffe would have trusted him with his life.

Not Shannon; she had laughed when J.K. had awkwardly come courting her. "I could never date anyone called Jonas," she had teased, and to her horror, J.K. had actually blushed, before turning abruptly away. Since then he had kept his distance, and she had felt ashamed of her petty cruelty and had gone out of her way to make him feel at ease whenever their paths crossed. Still, there was a distance between them; there always had been and always would be. He was what he was, and she was what she was, and they were as different as chalk and cheese.

The sky was an overcast gray and the air was still and humid, and both Wil and Jonas were sweating.

"Morning, J.K.," she called as Wil swung himself over the net and deposited a kiss on her cheek. "You guys must be feeling pretty good this morning."

"As well as can be expected," J.K. said seriously, and she laughed. J.K. always took everything literally.

"Let's go for a swim in the lake," she said to Wil. "There may be a breeze down there. It'll cool you off." Smiling, she turned to Jonas. "You too, of course, J.K."

He shrugged, his clean-shaven face coloring. "Thanks, but I guess you must have a lot to talk about. After all, you haven't seen each other for at least a couple of hours." And turning abruptly, he strode toward the house.

Shannon sighed. She said irritably, "Why is the man always so darned awkward? He makes everyone feel uncomfortable. Except my dad."

"He's a clever bastard, though," Wil said, stripping off his T-shirt. "Come on, let's take that dip in the lake. I sure could use it."

The approach to the lake was through an avenue of plane trees, Bob Keeffe's pride and joy because it reminded him of Provence, and of the van Gogh landscape that hung in his office at Keeffe Center in Manhattan.

"The whole world lights up for me every time I look at that painting," he had told Shannon. "I used to keep a postcard of it pinned to my wall at college. I never dreamed I would ever own it. I just thought maybe I'd get to see it in a museum one day. And now it's on my office wall. That's what success means to me, daughter. The ability to make dreams come true."

But today the humidity had brought out the midges and gnats, and Wil and Shannon ran, shrieking with laughter, down the avenue's shady length, waving their arms frantically over their heads.

"Look," Shannon exclaimed, peering at the ornamental wooden gazebo overlooking the water fifty yards along the bank. "Someone is there. And still in his dinner jacket!" She laughed. "I guess he never made it home."

They strolled hand in hand to the gazebo, giggling like children at their find. They drew nearer and saw the silver hair and broad shoulders and Shannon stared for a moment, puzzled. She ran, alarmed, to the gazebo, stopping suddenly on the steps, clutching the wooden rail. Her hand flew to her mouth to stifle the scream that refused to come. Her eyes grew round with horror and blackness swirled around her. A gun lay on the floor. There was blood all over her father's white dinner jacket and a bullet through his brain. Bob Keeffe was dead.

CHAPTER

〜〜〜〜〜〜〜〜〜 6 〜〜〜〜〜〜〜〜〜

THE LITTLE LOCAL COURTROOM where the inquest was held a week later was packed with newspapermen. TV cameras waited outside, but Buffy, beautiful and haggard in a black suit and wide-brimmed black hat, averted her face. And Shannon, in a black linen shirt and skirt and wearing sunglasses to hide her tear-reddened eyes, trembled as the coroner discussed her father's wounds and the circumstances of his death.

The coroner said the star-shaped wound around the bullet hole was caused by gas blown out of the muzzle, proving that gun had been held directly against the head. Taking into account his business difficulties, the coroner could only conclude that Robert Keeffe had killed himself. He pronounced the death a suicide.

"It's not true!" Shannon shouted wildly. "It's just not true. My father would never take his own life. Never, never. You don't understand . . . you don't know him like I do. He just . . . he just wouldn't leave me like that. . . ."

Buffy put a restraining hand on her arm. "Be quiet, Shannon," she whispered coldly. "The man is only doing his job. And you are only giving the reporters more ammunition for their scandal sheets."

Her hyacinth eyes commanded Shannon to follow, as she swept from the room without a glance to left or right. Her face was cold and calm, but inside she was boiling with anger at Bob Keeffe for dragging her good name and her reputation through the tabloids and leaving her to sort out the mess. Because there was no doubt it was a mess.

The truth had started to emerge the very day after his death. About the troubles his businesses were in. The banks were rumored to be on the verge of calling in their massive loans: They said Keeffe was over-extended; there had been a dip in the property market; they had lost confidence in his dealings. GOTTEN TOO BIG FOR HIS OWN GOOD, the newspapers had said in bold black headlines.

Bob Keeffe was buried the day after the inquest. Buffy was the perfect widow, beautiful and veiled in black at the graveside. It was a dark, dripping wet day and Shannon thought desolately that even God had deserted her father in his final moment. Like the courtroom, the graveyard was filled with reporters and TV cameras, but the ceremony was private. Just Buffy and Shannon. No one else was permitted. And when it was over she and Buffy rode silently back home in the limousine.

Their footsteps rang hollowly in the black-and-white tiled hall. It was as though with Big Bob gone the house was completely empty.

Flinging her hat and gloves onto a pretty French Provençal loveseat, Buffy strode into the little morning room. As Shannon followed her it occurred to her that though Buffy had been married to her father for sixteen years, she had no idea of her true feelings about his death.

A fire had been lit in the grate and Buffy went to stand in front of it. She leaned her arm along the marble chimneypiece, staring at herself in the beautiful Venetian mirror. "My God, I look awful," she said disgustedly, touching the faint lines under her eyes with a careful finger. "Not surprising, after what your father has just put me through. And it's not over yet. Oh, no, not by a long shot."

Shannon sat on the edge of the squishy floral sofa, her hands clasped tightly together, looking anxiously up at her.

"I should have known when I met him," Buffy said viciously. "People warned me. But I took no heed. 'An upstart Irishman,' they said, 'stay with your own sort, Buffy. Leave the likes of him alone.' But I was stupid, I admired his get-up-and-go. I liked the fact that he made his money instead of inheriting it. What I should have known is it was 'easy come, easy go.' " She turned and glared at Shannon, her hyacinth eyes wild with anger. "Goddam it, it's all *his* fault."

Shannon pushed her hands nervously through her hair. "But it's not his fault that he died, Buffy. He didn't kill himself. I'm sure of it. Dad would never do that. He would never shirk his responsibilities. If the business was in trouble he would have found a way to get it out again."

"Oh, don't be so stupidly naive. He *had* no other way out." Buffy turned from the fireplace and flung herself into a chair. Shannon stared worriedly at her. She had never seen her like this before; she was always so controlled and in charge. Buffy's eyes were hard and her face was tight with anger. Suddenly, she looked her age.

"I had a meeting with the attorneys yesterday," she said, taking a cigarette from a silver box and tapping it thoughtfully against the edge of the table before lighting it. Flinging her blond head back against the cushions, she drew smoke luxuriously into her lungs, staring at the ceiling, noticing even as she spoke that the paint on the plaster cornices needed retouching. She shrugged. That was no longer her concern.

"Everything has to go," she said abruptly. "This house, the penthouse, the antiques, the paintings. The attorneys have been working day and night to see what they could salvage for us personally, but it will all have to be sold to repay the banks and the creditors." She turned her head and stared at Shannon. Her pale hair gleamed in the lamplight as she tapped ash from her cigarette with an immaculately manicured fingernail. Her voice was level and calm and she might have been discussing the menu for the next dinner party with the cook.

Shannon watched numbly as she went on. "Thank God I had the sense to protect myself with my marriage settlement. At least they can't take that," she said, satisfaction creeping into her voice. "And my jewelry, of course. That was always put into my trust."

Shannon knew all about the marriage settlement, her father had always considered it a good joke. With a million each year, plus the first million, and all of it invested well, Buffy was probably sitting on a lot more than fifty million dollars now, as well as jewelry worth several more. Buffy was a very rich woman.

The maid came in with coffee, depositing it on the small table next to her mistress. Buffy picked up the silver pot and poured two cups, handing one to Shannon, who placed it quickly on the floor by her feet. Her hands were still shaking and she felt as though a deep well had opened up inside her, a yawning gap where there used to be a heart and warmth and love. She was sitting here with the woman who had been her stepmother for sixteen years. Her father's wife. And she was talking as though their lives together amounted to a bunch of dollars.

"You'll have more than enough to live on, Buffy," she said worriedly. "You could even buy back this house, and the penthouses, then nothing will change."

Buffy laughed, a small, tinkling, mirthless sound. "Shannon, when will you realize that *everything* has changed? Your father is dead. His business is in ruins and he has left us to pick up the pieces. Well, I, for one, refuse to do that. I'm leaving tomorrow for Barbados. I'm going to stay with Janet Rossmore until all this dies down. And then maybe I can get on with my life again."

"But what about me?" As soon as she said it, Shannon wished she hadn't. The childish words hung in the silence between them and her stepmother turned her head away, avoiding her anxious gray eyes.

Buffy shrugged, a delicate movement that barely lifted her thin shoulders. "I scarcely think that is my problem now, Shannon. After all, you are a big, grown-up girl. You should be grateful for all I've done for you. I saw you through school and college. I made sure you met the right people. And now you are engaged to Wil, I consider you his responsibility."

She stood up, straightening her skirt. "Quite honestly, Shannon," she said, allowing the anger to flood her voice again, "your father has turned out to be nothing but a cheap thief. After what he's done to me, I'm finished with the Keeffe family. For good."

Viciously stubbing her cigarette in a large crystal ashtray, she turned on her heel and walked briskly to the door. Shannon's stunned eyes followed her but Buffy did not turn to look back. "I'm going to pack," she called over her shoulder, her voice growing fainter as she strode, high heels clicking, across the marble-tiled hall. "I suggest you do the same, Shannon. The bailiffs will be in here before you know it."

Shannon stared uncomprehendingly after her. The scent of Gauloises Blonde cigarettes mingled with Shalimar perfume trailed in her wake. And though Buffy had not yet actually departed, Shannon knew she was as good as gone. And she was on her own.

CHAPTER

7

∼∼∼∼∼∼∼∼∼∼   ∼∼∼∼∼∼∼∼∼∼

SIXTY-FOUR-YEAR-OLD Brad Jeffries had been Bob's partner and president of Keeffe Holdings for seventeen years. He had started as an on-the-line construction supervisor and worked his way up.

He was addressing a meeting of the representatives of five major American banks and four international ones. He coughed and straightened his tie nervously. Fiddling with his reading glasses, he read the prepared statement, asking that they give Keeffe Holdings more time to sort out the tangled corporate and financial web Bob Keeffe had left behind him, before they called in their loans and the FBI.

"Let us, the remaining partners, who have been left this legacy of trickery, do our honorable best to get you back your money, gentlemen," he said finally, staring expectantly around his stony-faced audience.

A derisive smile crossed J.K.'s face. If ever a man looked guilty, Brad did. Though as far as he knew there was nothing they could pin on the old fool; nothing at all. Now it was Jack Wexler's turn. Jack was an architect; he was a forty-five year old bachelor, good-looking in a smooth, strong-jawed Dick Tracy kind of way, with a powerful sense of his own importance and his talent *and* his attraction for women. He had designed several award-winning buildings for Bob and he had been his partner for ten years. Now J.K. watched him beg for the financing to finish Keeffe Tower.

"Put this building in my hands, gentlemen," Wexler said, "and I promise to bring it in under the projected final budget. As you know, the top twenty office floors were already leased preconstruction to EuroNational Insurance as their new corporate headquarters, and the rest of the building is seventy percent leased, including the atrium shops. If we do not meet the projected completion date, then these companies have the right to void those contracts and demand the return of their money. As you also know this amounts to a very large sum —money that at this moment we do not have." He didn't say "thanks to that crooked bastard Bob Keeffe," but he allowed his angry face to say it for him.

"If you pull out of the deal now, Keeffe Holdings loses every cent it put into the building of Keeffe Tower, and you gentlemen lose all your money. Of course, you can take the property and sell it, but it will be bargain day on Park Avenue. A half-finished one hundred and twenty-five story skyscraper everyone knows has been plagued with problems will not be an easy sale in today's disturbed economic climate. What I'm asking for is time, gentlemen, so that we all stand a chance of recouping our money. If you choose not to stay with us on this, then we all lose everything, because there is not another cent in Keeffe Holdings to pay the construction workers their next week's salaries."

J.K. watched the bankers' impassive faces as they scribbled notes on yellow legal pads. Now it was his turn. He straightened his jacket and glanced commandingly around the table, enjoying the feeling of power as they stared back at him, waiting for him to tell them how they were going to get their money back.

"Gentlemen," he said in the same smooth, assured tones he had learned from his boss. "Bob Keeffe was my friend. My mentor. I came to him as a boy straight out of college and everything I know about business I learned from him. But he couldn't teach me about finance because that was not what he was good at.

"Everybody knows Bob enjoyed being a rich man. That's understandable because, like myself, he came from a poor background. He worked his way up, and his was a quick ascent because he was a clever man and he was damned good at what he did. He built no-nonsense housing and office blocks; he gave folks what they wanted at the right price, and that's always a sound cornerstone for any business. But Bob also had that wonderful Irish silver tongue that could tell you what he wanted and why it was exactly right that he should have it, and within half an hour he would have you believing the most impossible schemes.

"I think we all fell prey to that silver tongue, gentlemen, and in the end so did Bob himself. His dreams became too big, but when he told them to you, you believed him because he had never been wrong before. He had proved himself right time after time. He was successful.

Or at least it seemed that way, because even those closest to him, his business partners, only knew what he chose to tell us.

"In fact Bob Keeffe was a man who never told his right hand what his left hand was doing. His grandiose schemes grew bigger and so did his borrowings. In the end he was forced to resort to trickery to cover his tracks and his repayments. Bob offered you stocks and bonds as collateral and on the basis of your handshake dealings he was never asked to produce those stocks and bonds. Ostensibly they remained in the safe of Keeffe Holdings, to be called on by you if necessary.

"In fact I now know he had disposed of half that nine hundred million dollars' worth of stock two years before he offered it as collateral. It belonged to Keeffe Holdings and he had a right to sell, but not without our knowledge. And he certainly had no right to offer something he no longer possessed."

He glanced down at his notes. "Fifty million to Switzerland, two hundred million to French banks, one hundred million to the British banks, and a lot more to the Americans. On the face of it, these were ironclad loans; nothing could go wrong, and if it did your money was secured. But Bob Keeffe took your money and he poured it into a dozen different projects, as well as into his own pockets.

"The company's monthly meetings, at which Jeffries and Wexler, and myself as secretary of the company, were present, and at which we discussed the work in progress and projected schemes as well as the use of financing, are all documented in the minutes, signed by Bob and myself. He was an old-fashioned man who kept a lot of information in his own head. We were often puzzled, but in the past couple of years when we asked questions we were met by silence. There were too many projects we didn't all know about and only one man running the lot.

"Gentlemen, Bob Keeffe was an adventurer. He was a showman. He enjoyed his role as a larger-than-life public figure. He liked the recognition and the respect and the glamour. It made up for all the rejection he got as an orphan kid who had to make it the hard way. He loved music and art and beautiful women, and all those things cost money. And he spent it like water on all three.

"If it had not been for his love of art, maybe this tangled web might never have been uncovered, or at least not for some years, and I truly believe that Bob himself believed that he could sort it all out. That one day he could stop robbing Peter to pay Paul, that this new skyscraper, and then the next, would be sold for the millions he owed and then he could sleep nights again. But Bob coveted a second van Gogh to hang on the wall of the new Keeffe Tower. It would be a tangible symbol, like the other he owned, of his dreams come true."

They stared at him: they all knew the story of Bob Keeffe's proposed bid of sixteen million dollars for van Gogh's "Garden of the Asylum," which had been painted in St. Remy. The Keeffe Tower was the jewel in the crown of his career. He had wanted the world to see what he had created from nothing. He had wanted to show them how rich and powerful he and his company were. And how splendid a Park Avenue building Keeffe Tower would be with a famous van Gogh hanging in its atrium.

"Every tourist—every *person*—in New York will pass through Keeffe Tower's atrium just to look at that van Gogh," he had told them. "And each one of them will stop for a cup of coffee in the café, or a drink in the bar, or to buy a book or scarf, or a jewel in the boutiques. It will bring in a hundred times more business than it cost. And it will make the Keeffe name famous throughout the world. You'll see, before you know it, we shall be building Keeffe Towers in Sydney, in Tokyo, in Hong Kong. This is only the first of many."

That van Gogh, symbol of Keeffe's young dreams, had brought about his downfall. The banks were suddenly cautious, they were no longer rushing to lend him money. One by one they had turned him down. His credit had run out. Somehow the news filtered out that Keeffe was in trouble, confidence in his companies melted like frost in the sun, and Keeffe Holdings's shares tumbled. With the dramatic drop in the share prices the panicked bankers had demanded more collateral to compensate for the loss, and for a couple of weeks Bob had kept them all quiet, promising them that it was "all a mistake" and of course he had the money and everything would be all right, if only they would give him time to sort it out. But no more collateral had been forthcoming. And then Bob Keeffe had killed himself.

"My colleagues are asking for more time," J.K. said to the bankers, "but in all honesty I cannot." He felt their astonished eyes riveted on him. "Bob Keeffe left us a billion-dollar mess. I don't know what he did with all that money, but for a man like that, with a globe-trotting, flamboyant, gambling, plutocratic life-style, nothing was too big or too expensive. I know he overpaid by hundreds of millions on city building sites he insisted on buying and everything was bought with money he did not have, money he borrowed."

He lifted his shoulders in a weary shrug. "I knew nothing of Bob's private dealings. Whatever he was doing, he kept it to himself. I was as close to him on a day-to-day basis as his wife. I thought I knew the man. But I was wrong. And Bob Keeffe was not the man I—or you—thought he was. He betrayed our trust, gentlemen. And that is the truth of the matter."

The stunned eyes of the other two partners met his as he sat down again and the bankers shuffled their papers and conferred among themselves. There really wasn't much left to say. J.K. had just confirmed their worst fears and there was only one thing to be done. Keeffe Holdings was finished.

No one ever understood how the news of J. K. Brennan's hatchet job on his dead boss at a highly confidential meeting of the company's bankers managed to filter into the media, but it hit the press simultaneously with the news that the banks had foreclosed and after that it was a financial free-for-all to see who came out with any money. The FBI were involved as well as the Securities and Exchange Commission and all the company's books were being removed from the headquarters to be examined.

A week later J.K. was thinking of Shannon Keeffe's distraught, pale, wistful face at the inquest as he took a cab over to the Keeffe Center on United Nations Plaza to meet with his partners. With a verdict of suicide, Keeffe's insurers were refusing to pay out on the twenty-five-million-dollar life insurance policy that his daughter had been beneficiary of. She would get nothing. It was a pity, he thought with a sigh, that the innocent had to suffer in affairs like this, but there was nothing he could do about it now. It was too late.

Wexler and Jeffries were already there, standing by the window, their heads together in conference. They glanced guiltily up as J.K. strode through the door on the dot of eight, moving apart quickly like men caught in a conspiracy. J.K. smiled. Tossing his jacket onto the back of the sofa, he rolled up his sleeves and went and sat in Bob's chair.

"Well, gentlemen," he said, linking his hands together and leaning comfortably across Bob's desk as though he owned it. "Why don't you tell me what you have decided."

Wexler glanced at Jeffries and then he said angrily, "You can't wait to step into his shoes, can you?"

J.K. smiled a cold little smile. "Unlike you two, at least I waited until he was decently buried."

Brad said in a trembling voice, "Tell us the truth, J.K. Did you kill Bob?"

J.K. sat back, gazing impassively at them. He locked his hands behind his head and stretched, then he said with a weary sigh, "Why me?

What motive have I got for killing the man who helped me up the ladder?"

"Dead men's shoes," Wexler repeated grimly.

"I was better off with Keeffe alive, and you know it." He glared at them. "Maybe I should ask if you, Jack, or you, Brad, murdered our beloved boss. After all, you have far stronger motives than I do." He smiled grimly. "How much was it, Brad, that you've stolen over the years? Ten, twenty million? Maybe more? You knew Bob was a dreamer. He employed you to look after things in the office while he went out and got the jobs and the financing. And you nickeled and dimed him, right from day one, until after seventeen years your hand was in the till more often than it was out. And as the business grew so did your thieving.

"It was a good thing Bob never got to know about that secret expensive horse farm in Kentucky, eh, Brad? In beautiful bluegrass country, and with a string of beautiful expensive Thoroughbreds, *and* a beautiful expensive young lady trainer to look after them for you. Not even *Mrs.* Jeffries knew about her, did she, Brad?"

Brad retreated, pale-faced, to the sofa. He poured himself a glass of whiskey and sipped it silently.

"And you, Jack," J.K. said, smiling icily. "Don't you have an equally good motive for killing Big Bob? When I first started to work for Bob I asked myself right away, how come a man like you—an architect working for Keeffe Holdings, earning good money to be sure, but not *that* good—how come a man like you managed to live in the style you lived in? Sure, later you became a partner, but you already had the town house on Sutton Place and the Aston-Martin and the Bentley. You already had the art collection; it was in a different style from Bob's because you were men with vastly different tastes. But Warhols and Rothkos go for a pretty penny at auction, just like van Goghs, and you could almost have matched his, dollar for dollar.

"You took kickbacks on everything, from the shipments of marble from Italy to the contracts for the steel girders. You made money on every aspect of the construction of Keeffe buildings, and you gave contracts not to the lowest bidder, or even the best man for the job, but to whoever paid you off the most. Even so, it was still a bit hazardous, with your flashy, expensive life-style. Still a bit hand-to-mouth. And maybe you wanted more?"

He sat back and smiled his genial smile at them again. "I am the one who knows where all the bodies are buried. I am the one who could turn either of you, or even both of you, over to the cops, the FBI, the SEC, even the IRS. You name it, I could do it."

Wexler's face was gray under his year-round tan. "You wouldn't do that," he snarled, standing menacingly closer to the desk.

"Maybe not. It all depends."

"Depends on what?" Brad Jeffries said wearily. "I'm getting too old for this, J.K. Tell me the worst. Am I a dead man, or what?"

"Brad, Brad! How can you say such a thing? There's only one dead man around here and we buried him last week. All I am here for is to remind you of your loyalty to Keeffe Holdings."

"I still don't understand why you said what you did about Bob at that meeting with the bankers," Wexler complained angrily. "We could have gotten them to give us time, we could have finished the Keeffe Tower and stayed in business. We could have arranged for it to be kept separate from the holding company mess, if only we had danced enough, begged enough, *sweated* enough. All those bastards wanted was their money back, and I know I could have at least swung it on the building. It was our one solid asset."

J.K. buttoned his jacket and walked to the door. "You're wrong there, Jack," he said pleasantly. "Keeffe Holdings no longer owned Keeffe Tower. Bob sold it just a week before his death to a company in Liechtenstein. At a considerable loss to us." He shrugged. "You can thank your leader for that one, Wexler. Bob never did have a good head for business and when the walls were caving in he just grabbed what he could."

"But how much?" Wexler gasped, stunned.

J.K. shrugged. "What does it matter? It all went to bail out whatever creditor was most pressing. And it's gone. When they sell off the remaining assets the banks will probably get about half what they are owed. The other creditors will get nothing. The employees will not even get a pension, gentlemen, including you and me, *and* his daughter, because that money, invested nicely and safely by me, went the way of all Keeffe money. Dwindled away personally by Bob, bit by bit."

He opened the door to leave and then he thought of something. He looked contemptuously back at them. "By the way, the SEC investigators and the fraud guys are down at the brokerage house now. I handed everything over to them. All you have to do is hope that I didn't keep extrazealous records about your own little activities. Goodbye, gentlemen. Have a nice day."

CHAPTER

8

SHANNON WALKED BLEAKLY through the eighteen-room penthouse overlooking Central Park. The rooms were bare, stripped of their beautiful antique furniture and ornaments. Little brass lights dangled over the blank spaces where her father's treasured paintings had hung; the lovely Sickerts and the Constables, the Picassos and the Monets. The parquet flooring was scuffed from the moving-men's feet, and the expensive silk curtains, soon to be ripped out by the interior designer doing over the apartment for the new owner, still hung forlornly at the windows.

Opening the door to her old room, she looked around for the last time. She had lived in this apartment most of her life. She had grown up in this room, as it changed first from childish pink gingham to teenage black and silver, then to simple white with an antique American patchwork quilt.

The only things she could call her own were the inexpensive paintings she had bought herself, the big doll house, her old toys, her books, her clothes, and a few bits of jewelry.

She had never been a "jewelry person," preferring fashionable costume glitter to real diamonds and pearls. But she had one wonderful necklace. Her father had given it to her when she was eight, on the day he married Buffy. She remembered staring, amazed at the pretty strand of diamonds tied in a love knot.

"Look how it sparkles, Daddy," she had said, thrilled.

"Not half as much as your eyes, little darlin'," he had retorted. "Now, you take care of that. It's by way of bein' a family heirloom." And then he had swept her into his arms and carried her off to help cut the wedding cake.

And of course, she had Wil's engagement ring. They had bought the fine, square-cut three-carat diamond from Cartier. She eyed it anxiously, knowing it had cost more than Wil could afford. He was still only a law student. His father was an attorney and she knew the family was comfortably off, but by her own father's standards they were not rich.

"Your family's money is the stuff dreams are made of," Wil had said to her admiringly. "I'll never be as rich as your father, Shannon."

"No matter," she had replied airily. "I'll have enough for both of us."

She quickly closed the outer door with a final click, shutting out a lifetime of memories. As the paneled elevator wooshed softly downward, she had to bite her lip to stop from crying.

She had known the doorman since she was a child, and he was waiting to say good-bye. "I'll never forget him, Miss Shannon," he said, folding her hands in his. His weathered red face crumpled suddenly and tears stood in his faded blue eyes. "He was a fine man. As good as they come, and nobody will ever say any different in my company. Best of luck to you, miss."

Shannon shook his hand and hurried away. She jumped into the little second-hand pickup truck she had bought when she had traded in her beloved black Mercedes 500SL, and headed out of town through the pouring rain.

The Long Island house had not yet been stripped of its furnishings, though the paintings and the finest ornaments had already been sent to Sotheby's, to be sold separately.

As she drove up, Shannon noticed the auction tent being erected on the big lawn and her heart gave a lurch, remembering the marquee for her birthday party only a few weeks ago. Officials were striding around the house affixing stickers to tables and chairs and ashtrays, which they confidently expected to bring inflated prices simply because they had belonged to Big Bob Keeffe. The house was on the market for fifteen million dollars, but the attorneys had told Shannon it was a drop in the financial ocean of what Keeffe Holdings owed.

"But how did it all happen?" she had asked Brad Jeffries. "Dad was always such a good businessman. How else could he have gotten where he did?"

"I only wish I had known," Brad answered nervously. "I've always considered myself Bob's anchor. Whenever his schemes got too grandiose, I was the one expected to bring him down to size. But he kept this quiet from me, Shannon." He shrugged. "I never looked at the books. Why should I? That's what accountants are for."

It was the same with Jack Wexler. He had come to see her, looking miserable and nervous. "I'm not good at this, Shannon," he had said tersely. "You know I care. And I wish to God I could have done something about it. But I didn't know. None of us knew how he was juggling things. If I had designed the new skyscraper I could have controlled it. But Bob didn't want me to design it," he added bitterly. "He wanted a big name. Bob didn't care what it cost either, he just wanted 'the best' and it seems he borrowed from everyplace he could to finance it. It's there now, on Park Avenue, half-finished, sticking up like a sore finger in the sky. Some monument! Jesus." He had groaned, putting his head in his hands. "I'm sorry, Shannon. If there's anything I can do, you know, money . . . well, anything. Just let me know."

"I will, Jack," she had promised, though of course she never would. In her view they had let her father down and now they were blaming it all on him. She would never take money from any of the traitors.

Surprisingly, though, it was J.K. who was the greatest source of strength. "Your father gave me everything I ever had," he had said simply. "Now I can repay my debt. If there's anything I can do, anything you need, it's yours." He had hesitated, staring down at his feet, his thin, pale face coloring. He'd fiddled with his gold-rimmed glasses and then said, "It seems ridiculous to be saying this to Bob Keeffe's daughter, but if you need money, count on me." He had pulled a checkbook eagerly from his pocket. "Name a sum," he'd said quickly, blushing deeper. "Anything. Ten thousand. Twenty. Fifty. Whatever you want, Shannon. It's yours."

But of course she had refused J.K., too, proudly telling him she had enough to get by on, that she would get a job, and anyway, she would soon be getting married.

And with Buffy gone and Wil back at Yale, it was J.K. who helped her with the packing. It was J.K. who had instructed Sotheby's on the sale of the houses and the contents. And it was J.K. who had personally overseen the crating and removal of her father's art collection.

He was waiting now in the hall, and his face lit up when he saw her. "I was worried about you," he said, glancing at his watch. "It's after two and you said you'd be back by lunchtime."

"You sound just like a nanny I used to have." She managed a smile. "There was traffic, rain . . . the usual Manhattan blues."

"I wondered if you could find time to go through this inventory?" He held out a daunting sheaf of papers, and she glanced helplessly at them and then back at him. "Must I? It all seems so pointless somehow."

"Of course not. If you trust me to take care of it."

She stared curiously at him, her gray eyes narrowing suspiciously as something occurred to her. "J.K. You were the man closest to my father. He always said you knew everything about him and everything about his business. If that's true, then how is it you didn't know about the mess he was getting into?"

"There were things he kept from me," he said, meeting her gaze squarely. "The company's finances were a complicated web with your father like the spider at the center. Only he knew the full facts and how out of hand it had all gotten. I was worried about certain things, but I never guessed how bad it was. He had never done that before and so I never suspected. Until it became obvious—the banks calling and so on. And by then it was too late." He stared at her a little desperately. "Believe me, Shannon, if there had been any way to save the situation, I would have found it."

"Of course you would." She walked sadly away, noticing that her wet shoes made track marks across the hall tiles. Buffy would have hated that. The silver tray on the hall sideboard held a couple of letters and she picked them up disinterestedly. She thought sadly that it was amazing how little the phone had rung since her father died. And, after the first official flow of condolence letters, it was surprising how few people had contacted her. She supposed they were all afraid of being tainted with the Keeffe scandal.

One of the letters was a statement from her bank informing her that she had exactly three thousand two hundred and forty-six dollars in her account, and that they were holding in their vault the title deed to the small piece of property in her name in Nantucket.

Recognizing the writing on the other letter as Wil's, she tucked it into her jacket pocket, smiling. Wil was the only bright spot on her horizon.

Tomorrow she intended to hitch the little trailer containing her worldly possessions to the back of her pickup and drive to New Haven. She would move in with Wil, then find herself a job in the town. And when Wil completed his studies next year, they would get married.

She glanced up at the sound of heavy feet tramping through the house. Workmen were rearranging the furniture in lots in different rooms and the house looked alien. She turned and hurried back along the hall, down the broad steps and across the wet lawns, along the avenue of plane trees to the lake.

It was raining hard, a gray, relentless day, but her space beneath the big willow tree at the edge of the lake was dry and safe. It was where she had always come as a child to lick her wounds, and she sat as she always had, knees hunched under her chin, arms wrapped around herself in her own soft green world. If she peeked between the fronds dipping into the shallows she could see the gazebo where her father had died, but instead she stared upward at the delicate tracery of branches.

"Oh, Daddy, Daddy," she whispered. "Oh, darling Daddy. Was there nothing any of us could do to help? Nothing we could do to stop you? Did all our love and caring mean so little that you had to kill yourself?" She shook her head. She would never believe it. Never.

Pulling Wil's letter from her pocket, she opened it, quickly reading the two brief paragraphs. *"Under the circumstances, I think it would be better if we 'postponed' our wedding. . . . I've decided to take a sabbatical at the end of this semester and take a trip to Australia, maybe work on a sheep farm. Dad says it'll be good character-building stuff. I hope we shall meet again sometime, when I return. . . ."*

Shannon stared blankly at the letter. The diamond on her finger felt like a lead weight as the awful reality of her situation confronted her. She was no longer the pampered, courted, protected princess, a rich girl. No longer the wild, headstrong, do-as-she-pleased Shannon Keeffe everyone loved and wanted to know. She had nothing and therefore she was no one.

CHAPTER

9

J.K. STARED WORRIEDLY after Shannon as she ran past him up the stairs. Her red hair was dark with rain and her freckles stood out against her chalky face. Tears ran unheeded down her cheeks and she seemed not to see him, though he moved to one side to allow her to pass.

She stumbled on the landing and fell, and he took the stairs two at a time to her side.

"Oh, God," he groaned, putting his arms around her. "You didn't go back to the gazebo? You mustn't, you'll only hurt yourself more."

She shook her head, sobbing helplessly against his shoulder, all her hard-gained self-control gone. He glanced down at her straggling hair and tear-stained face, thinking of all the times he had dreamed of holding her. And only now, because of what had happened, was it possible. Fate, he thought angrily, was a funny thing. His dark eyes glittered with emotion and instinctively he tightened his grip.

"It's Wil," Shannon gasped through her sobs. "He's going away. To Australia for a year. He thinks maybe it's better if we *postpone* our marriage." She lifted her head, staring piteously at him through her swollen eyelids. "How could he? Wil. Of all people. J.K., did no one love me? Or my father? Was it always just our money?"

She sat back against the wall, her long bare, mud-spattered legs sticking out in front of her, limp as a rag doll. "I'm sure that's not true." He took her hand and patted it comfortingly. "I guess Wil was just too young to . . ." He tried desperately to think of a reason. "He was just too young to take on the responsibility of marriage right now. After what has happened."

Her hand was freezing and he rubbed it briskly. "Look, I've got this little farm out at Montauk. Why don't you go there for a while. There's no one to bother you—no reporters, no TV cameras. Take one of your girlfriends for company, you'll need someone to talk to. It's always been a kind of refuge for me and maybe it could be the same for you."

Shannon eyed him solemnly. She had never seen J.K. in this caring role before. He had always been so brisk and businesslike, the perfect executive machine. But now he had turned out to be a machine with a heart. "I never thought of you as a person needing a refuge," she said, sniffing away her tears. "You always seem so controlled. So in charge of your life."

"Everyone needs an escape from something, even if it's only the day-to-day grind. But I mean it, Shannon. The place is yours for as long as you want it. And I promise I won't even come to visit unless you ask me."

Managing a half smile, she mopped her eyes and promised to think about it. He helped her up the stairs to her bedroom. "I didn't let them touch your things," he reassured her. He was still holding her hand, and she squeezed his gratefully. She closed the door behind her and he waited outside for a moment. He heard her soft footsteps on the carpet, and then the terrible sound of her sobs again as she flung herself onto the bed. He sighed as he turned away. Shannon Keeffe was going to find it tough to be an ordinary mortal, he thought.

Going directly to Bob's study, he picked up the phone and called the manager of Shannon's bank. Explaining who he was, he instructed him to allow her whatever funds she needed over the next few months, up to $50,000. He personally would guarantee the amount. Then, sitting back in Bob's old leather chair, now bearing a sticker proclaiming it to be in Lot 154, he thought wearily about his own future.

WHEN SHANNON WOKE it was dark outside. The rain had stopped and there was no sound. She was still in her rain-damp skirt and jacket and she stood up and wriggled out of them, then climbed back into bed. She wrapped the blankets around her, remembering that this was her last night in this bed. Her last night in this house. In this life.

Staring at the lighter square of blackness where the window was, she wondered whether to take up J.K.'s offer of the Montauk farm, but she knew it would only be a stopgap. She remembered her father saying to her all those years ago, *"You've got to go after whatever it is you want, little darlin'. And you've got to want it real bad."* But right now she didn't know what it was she wanted. She felt aimless, spineless, useless.

"You've got the blood of your fightin' Irish ancestors, Shannon," he had always told her, but it surely didn't feel that way now.

Sitting up, she turned on the lamp and glanced around her. Everything looked as it always had: simple, immaculate, and pretty. There were even fresh roses, pink ones, in a vase on her dresser. She would bet she had J.K. to thank for those. That strange man was turning out to be her rock in stormy waters and for the first time she understood what her father had seen in him. Nevertheless, she could not accept his offer. She had to stand on her own two feet. Her father would have expected it.

The two letters lay on the rug where they had fallen. She picked them up and read Wil's first. It sounded just as final as she thought it had in the first ten readings and she threw it bitterly back onto the floor.

The bank's letter proved more interesting. There was three thousand two hundred and forty-six dollars in her account. Most of it was from the sale of her car, and the rest was what was left from her month's allowance. She sighed, telling herself people had started life with less, including her father. She was young and able-bodied and well educated. She could darn well get herself a job and join the real world.

She read the rest of the letter, which said, *"We are holding the deed to your Nantucket property in our vaults for safekeeping."*

She read it again. *Your Nantucket property.* She knew about the cottage but she had never even seen it. Her father always promised they would visit it one day, but somehow he had always been too busy to take her, and she had never thought about going there alone. Yet it was the only true "family" possession her father owned.

He had told her the story of how, when he was fourteen, the head of the orphanage where he had been brought up since the age of five had summoned him into his office. He was a testy, impatient man, ill-suited to his life's work with children and they were all mortally afraid of him. Everything came from his hands: punishment and beatings, rewards and Christmas largess. He was God in their small, confined world and Bob had been shaking in his boots at having been summoned into "the presence." Shannon could hear his exact words as though it were a record playing in her head, he had told her the story so often—and it was *all* he had told her about his childhood. "O'Keeffe," he said, looking solemnly over the tops of the thick-lensed glasses that made his eyes look as bulgy as a toad's, "You are now considered a 'young man,' and therefore it is my duty to tell you that you are also a man of property. You were not left destitute, as most of the unfortunate children here were. There is the sum of five hundred dollars and a small parcel of land with a cottage in Nantucket. The property is almost valueless, because that part of the world enjoys little prosperity. Nevertheless it is yours, and one day you may wish to sell it for what little you can recoup.

"Meanwhile, I suggest you apply the goodly sum of five hundred dollars toward your education. You are a clever lad, and if you could only control your fiery Irish temperament, you could go far."

Of course her father had been excited, but it had been many years before he could afford to go and see his "property." When he finally moved to Boston, where he studied and worked as a laborer on construction sites, he took some of his hard-earned money and caught the ferry to Nantucket.

"Ah, Shannon, it's a special, magical place," he had told her, smiling reminiscently. "All sky and sea and the sound of gulls. Sometimes it's gray with no colors at all, then suddenly it's all blue and gold, the sea and the sand. You'll surely love it there, daughter, just as your mother and I did. It has a touch of magic about it. Since she died I've not been able to bring myself to go back, but one day we shall go. One day, little darlin'."

But of course they never had and now that day would never come. Or would it?

Shannon sat bolt upright in bed. The Nantucket cottage had been the place her mother and father visited together—"just as often as we could," her father had said. And it had "a touch of magic." Well, she could surely use a little magic right now! She had a place of her own, a roof over her head; somewhere to hide and be alone while she worked out what to do with the rest of her life. She would leave for Nantucket before the auction. Before they took away all her memories. She would look to the future, just the way her father would have wanted her to. A great feeling of relief swept over her, and she lay, exhausted, back against the pillows and was asleep within minutes.

When she awoke the next morning, there was a note from J.K. pushed under the door. *Let's have lunch?* it said simply. Shannon felt better; she would tell J.K. her decision and see what he had to say.

He took her to a little country inn a half hour's drive away. There were blue checked tablecloths and a bunch of white daisies in a yellow jug on their table. The place was crowded and there was a pleasant bustling air about it.

"It feels normal here," Shannon said, surprised.

"And that's just the way it should," he said. "I know it's going to be hard, Shannon, but that's what you have to do. Try and get things 'back to normal.' I asked you out to lunch because I was worried about you. You've had one blow after another: your father, your stepmother, Wil. Everybody seems to be deserting you, and I wanted you to know that I am not. Whatever you want to do, I'll help you."

She looked at him solemnly. He was wearing a blue polo shirt and a linen jacket and she knew he meant to look relaxed, but somehow it still seemed as if he were wearing a formal suit and tie. His brown eyes looked worriedly at her from behind his gold-rimmed glasses and she reached across the table and took his hand and squeezed it gratefully. "I never knew you were so *nice*, J.K.," she said. "Now I know why my dad didn't turn you down when you came for the job."

"When I came for that job he would have been perfectly justified in turning me down. I was brash, uncouth, and rude." J.K. laughed. "Thank God he didn't, I was down to my last ten bucks and no prospects. I'd banked everything on getting a job with Bob Keeffe. He had been my idol all through my teenage years: a man with nothing who had made a fortune. Your father had the American dream and I wanted it, too, or at least a part of it. I figured where better to learn how to get it than from the man himself. So there you are. Now you know the truth about me."

"I don't really know anything about you, J.K.," she said, surprised.

"Probably because you've never given me a second thought," he retorted, and they both laughed.

"Well, now I am, so why don't you tell me about yourself," she said coaxingly. "Where you were born, your family, your girlfriends, everything. After all, you know everything there is to know about me."

He thought for a minute and then said, "My father was a bastard." She stared at him, shocked, and he said, "He was a drunken bully who left his family more often than he stayed with it. Thank God, I barely knew him. I guess I didn't know my mother too well either. I was mostly brought up by my grandmother. She was a lovely woman, a doctor's daughter. I adored her. I would have done anything for her.

"But I'm sure you don't want to hear my sorry tale," he said with an apologetic smile, and she eagerly told him she did, so he thought for a minute and then said, "My grandmother married a charming rogue. She was a small-town girl who had never been more than forty miles from her Carolina home in her life. He was an older man, in his forties, and very good-looking in a different, rugged sort of way. She said he could charm the birds from the trees if he wanted something and he soon convinced her he had fallen in love with her. He admitted to being a hell-raiser with a fondness for the bottle. 'But that's all in the past,' he told her. And the poor girl believed him.

"She was twenty-three and plain and she was in love for the first time in her life. Her father, the doctor, threw her out of his house when she said she would marry, with or without his consent. They ran off together and she told me it was then that all her troubles began. They trekked from town to town, from state to state, always short of money. Sometimes he would pick up a temporary job and she would hope maybe they could settle down, but it never lasted.

"My grandmother told me that when she gave birth to her son, her husband took a long, hard look at them as though he were seeing them for the first time. He figured out loud how much it was going to cost him to take care of both of them, then he took whatever money he had in his pocket, every last cent of it, and laid it on the table. He said he was going out west, alone. He had heard there was money to be made there in oil. He would be in touch.

"For five years she brought up her boy alone, working in the local drugstore and making just enough to get by, though she told me she never had a new dress or a pair of shoes in all that time.

"She never expected to see him again and she was amazed when he returned five years later. He had money in his pocket and he swept them both off to the ranch he said he had bought in South Carolina. The ranch turned out to be a poor little farm and he didn't even own it. He was a sharecropper, a tenant farmer who paid his rent in a share of the crops. He put her to work in the fields and even the child was sent out, in his little sunbonnet, to help pick the poor crops."

J.K. sighed. "Of course, the inevitable happened: he left her again and this time he didn't come back. She had no money and no choice but to stay on and run the farm with the help of Noah, a young black boy she had befriended and helped.

" 'You ain't no better'n a slave yourself, ma'am,' Noah told her, watching her working alongside him in the fields. And he was right."

J.K. smiled grimly at Shannon. "They were a scandal, the white doctor's daughter and the young black living together in the four-room farmhouse, even though he slept in the wooden lean-to. She told me they were ostracized by all the God-fearing, right-minded folks around and that she barely spoke to anyone for ten years, except her son and young Noah. Her son, *my father,* grew up a barefoot poor boy, skipping school just as often as he could. He was finished with formal education by the age of fifteen and by seventeen he was raisin' hell in three counties.

"When he was eighteen, in about 1949, I guess, he was drafted into the army, and that boy hated it. He was already a heavy drinker and he ran away from the army just as he used to run away from school. After a few months he was discharged under a cloud. Grandma never did hear exactly why, but when he came home he refused to work on the farm. He roamed the country just like his father had, leaving her with only Noah for company. Every now and then he would return and hand her a wad of money, but after a couple of nights he would be off again, restless for company and drink. Arthritis was crippling her and she managed as best she could, but soon Noah was doing all the work."

The waitress came with their food and J.K. said to Shannon, "Are you sure you want to hear all this? It's hardly good lunch conversation."

She nodded. "It's good for you to tell someone. Besides, I feel now I'm getting to know you."

He nodded. "Okay. When my father was around thirty, I guess, he met a woman called Alma Brennan. Gran told me that back then she was a flashy hip-swinging kind of woman; she wore low-cut dresses and she could match him drink for drink. They quarreled violently all the time and he would disappear and leave her alone for months on end, without any money. Alma hated being stuck out on a farm in the middle of nowhere, but she was pregnant and she had no choice. As soon as I was born she got herself a job in a store in the local town, intending to save up to get the hell out, but every time she got her wages she would hit the high spots—if you could call the local saloon a high spot—and blow it all.

"By now my father was a serious drunk, and then one day, just like my grandfather, he left and never came back. My mother spent most of her time at the saloon, so they finally gave her a job. The customers liked her, she was jolly after a few drinks, big and blowsy, and she could give as good as she got. She prided herself on her smart mouth, my grandma told me, and she took her pleasures where she could find them."

J.K.'s eyes met Shannon's and he said bitterly, "I grew up in a small southern town, the grandson of a woman who they said lived with a black, and the son of the local whore. Can you wonder I was a loner? What kid's parents would let him be friends with a person like that?"

She shook her head and said compassionately, "Poor J.K. I didn't realize it was that bad."

"However bad you think it was, I can tell you it was worse," he said bleakly. "The only saving grace was my grandmother. She was an educated woman. She brought me up. She taught me to read and write, she told me stories and gave me dreams. And she told me to stay away from drink." He tapped his glass of water with his forefinger, and said, "I have never taken a drink in my life, not even a glass of wine. I'm afraid if I do, I'll end up like my grandfather and my father."

He laughed, lightening up a little. "I guess all of my dreams didn't come true. I never did become the football hero and win the scholarship to Notre Dame. I never did get that Mustang convertible, or date the pretty blond cheerleader. But I did get an education, of a sort. I worked hard and got a place at the local college. I kept pictures of your father pinned to my wall, the way he kept pictures of the van Gogh on his, as a symbol of what dreaming can get you. And as soon as I graduated, I headed straight for New York." He shrugged and smiled disarmingly at her. "You know the rest."

"And your grandmother?"

"She died a month before I graduated. My mother died four years before that. Cirrhosis of the liver. It was in the local newspaper, so everyone knew how they had scooped her up from the sidewalk one night, hemorrhaging from the mouth. Her liver was shot to pieces. I just gave the keys of the farm to my grandmother's old friend, Noah, and said that as far as I was concerned it was his. I was never going back."

He looked at Shannon and said simply, "And I never have."

"Poor J.K.," she said softly. "Poor lonely little boy. I get the feeling there are things you haven't told me. All the things that mattered so much."

"Maybe you're right," he said coolly. "But we were here to talk about you and now I've done all the talking."

His tone was suddenly distant and she thought maybe he regretted his sudden confession, and she quickly told him about the cottage and that she would be leaving for Nantucket.

He said, "Are you sure you'll be all right alone?"

"I'm not sure I'll ever be all right again," she replied bitterly. "J.K., I'm certain my father did not kill himself. He would never have done it on the day of my party. He wouldn't have hurt me that way. And he would never have left me unprovided for. Dad loved life, he had made his money once and he would have made it again. You know he wasn't a grandiose man, a man 'with an ego as big as a skyscraper,' the way the media is making him out to be."

He said, "Look, your father was in a lot of trouble. He was a proud man. Sometimes the fall from grace can just be too hard for a person like that to take. Besides, who knows what goes on in another person's mind? You think you know a man and then they do something you would call 'out of character.' Except maybe it's just they never showed you that other, darker, side of themselves before. It's happened to great men throughout history, Shannon. I don't want to upset you, but I don't think you should be thinking about how and why. You should be thinking about *you,* about picking up your own pieces and getting on with life again. And you know if there's anything I can do to help you, I will."

There was a friendly silence between them as J.K. drove Shannon back home for the last time. She knew he was right. Tomorrow she would put her past behind her and begin a new life as a new person.

CHAPTER
10

MAUDIE

Ardnavarna

"I WAS ON THE FERRY, on my way to Nantucket," Shannon said. "I was leaning against the rail staring into the green waves, thinking about my father. And then I realized I'd been so caught up in trying to convince myself and everybody else that he hadn't committed suicide, that I'd never even thought about who *had* killed him. Someone had cold-bloodedly shot him at close range and placed the gun where it would look as though it had fallen from his hand. *Someone had murdered my father. And I made up my mind to find out who.*"

Her voice trembled as she spoke the terrible words, and her face was so pale that her freckles stood out like confetti on a church porch after a wedding. I took her hand in mine, comfortingly. "You're a brave girl," I said quietly.

Brigid's heart was in her eyes as she stared solemnly at her. "I'll be getting some fresh tea," she murmured. "Aye, and maybe with a little touch of the whiskey in it, poor girleen, to bring the color back into your cheeks."

The dogs shifted their position, leaning against Shannon's knees under the table, and she bent to pet them. "I don't know why I hadn't thought of it before," she said quietly. "I guess I just hadn't allowed myself to. It was all too horrible, too frightening. I was so shaken that I don't really remember the journey to Sea Mist Cottage, but once I got there, I felt comforted. Somehow, it felt like coming home."

It was just a tiny gray-shingled cottage, foursquare and neat, like a dollhouse. There was a painted quarter board over the rickety porch with the name and the date, 1790, painted on it, and a straggling overgrown little garden, choked with roses and nasturtiums. And right next door, half hidden by the shrubbery, was a big white house with a veranda running all the way around its upper story, sort of topsy-turvy-looking.

But Shannon's mind wasn't on exploring. She unpacked her laptop and typed the word *Suspects* in bold. Then she remembered reading somewhere that most homicides were crimes of passion and that cops always looked closest to home for their suspects, so under it she typed *Joanna Belmont* and *Buffy Keeffe*. And next to their names she wrote *Motive—Jealousy.*

She thought about who else and then she added *J. K. Brennan, Jack Wexler,* and *Brad Jeffries* to the list, because they were the three men closest to her father and they were supposed to know what was going on in his business. Then she remembered someone telling her that men like her father didn't get where they were without making a thousand enemies for every friend, and her heart sank. Keeffe Tower had been plagued by strikes and walkouts and disputes, and any one of the hundreds of workmen, or the contractors or suppliers, involved might have had a grudge against him.

Or it might just have been a stranger; someone at the party, a barman, or maybe an intruder, a thief, a psychopath. It could have been almost anybody, she thought despairingly, and that was the trouble. She couldn't go to the police and say she "just knew" her father had been murdered. Cops would want reasons, motives, evidence, and she had none of those things. And she didn't know where to begin to find them.

She got herself a job as a waitress at Harriet's Fish Café in Nantucket. "Twenty bucks a night plus tips," Harriet told her, "and it's hard work."

It was, but at least it took her mind off her worries. Organizing Sea Mist Cottage filled her days, and her job at Harriet's took care of the evenings, but night was the time she dreaded most, when she was alone with just her thoughts. Even when she slept the terrible memories crowded her subconscious and she would wake crying, with tears in her ears and in her hair, soaking her pillow. And she hated her day off, when she was all alone with nothing to fill the long hours in front of her.

She walked the empty beach, hurling pebbles into the waves, thinking about her problem. The air was scented with salt and sea pinks and the only sound was the breeze rippling through the grasses and the purr of the waves along the shore, and she felt lonelier than ever, and she just wished she could turn back the clock and return to the past where everything was all right again.

Rain clouds were bunching overhead as she walked back to the cottage. She stared for a long time at her list of suspects on the computer, and then switched it off with a sigh of frustration, prowling the cottage restlessly, staring out at the rain and at the empty house next door.

Loneliness mingled with boredom, and she put a chair underneath the trapdoor leading to the attic and gave it a push. It hadn't been opened in years and it was stuck. She pushed harder. It creaked open and she hauled herself through the opening and stared around, disappointed.

She had hoped to find the attic piled with junk she could rummage through. She didn't know what she was searching for. Just some evidence that her parents had once been there, she supposed. But there was only a dresser against the wall and a few boxes of old kitchen stuff, chipped cups and saucers and old pots and pans.

On the gable end was a little round window and she stared out through the rain at the white house. She didn't know why, but the house intrigued her. It was different from the usual Nantucket saltbox. All shuttered up and silent, it was sort of exotic, mysterious almost.

Suddenly the silence was all around her. It was odd, scary, as though time had stopped and with it all sounds. There was a rustling noise. The hair bristled on the back of her neck and goose bumps popped up on her arms and she almost jumped out of her skin as something fell from a niche where two beams crossed.

She picked it up quickly. It was an old manila envelope and inside it was a bunch of letters tied with pink ribbon. The notepaper was fragile with age, crumbling at the edges; the ink had faded and the childish scrawl was almost indecipherable.

The address at the top of each one was *Ardnavarna Castle, Connemara,* and they began, *"Dearest Lily,"* and they were signed, *"from your loving sister, Ciel."*

"Papa has changed so . . ." Ciel wrote. *"He becomes red-faced with anger every time he sees me. Mama says it's because I remind him of you,*

though we do not look the least alike. . . . Darling Mama mourns so, and I worry she will drive herself to her own grave. . . . I am so lonely without you, and so is your favorite dog, Fergal, who has sired a new litter of pups, seven, and all as black-and-white spotted as can be, with the sweetest little pink noses. How I wish you could see them. . . ."

Shannon replaced the sad little letters in the envelope, wondering what they were doing in the attic of Sea Mist Cottage.

There was nothing of interest in the dresser drawers, just old linens, but as she slammed them shut she noticed a large rectangular object wedged behind, as though someone had tried to hide it. She tugged the dresser away and lifted it carefully out. It was a painting in an ornate gilt frame, a portrait of a young girl. She was a beauty. Her skin was creamy, her lips were red, and her glossy black curls tumbled prettily over her bare shoulders. There was an arrogant tilt to her chin and an imperious look in her deep-blue eyes. *And around her neck was the pretty diamond love-knot necklace that right that minute was in Shannon's own jewelry box.*

Shannon stared at it, stunned, as she read the name on the tarnished brass plate on the frame out loud. "Lily Molyneux, 1883."

"It's the same Lily from the letters," she exclaimed excitedly. "From Ardnavarna." She lugged the portrait carefully back downstairs, and dusted it off and propped it against the kitchen wall. *Who* exactly was Lily Molyneux? she wondered. And what was her portrait doing in *Shannon's* attic? *And why was Lily Molyneux wearing her necklace?*

First thing the next morning she hurried over to the village post office. "Any mail for me?" she asked hopefully, leaning her elbows on the counter and smiling at the gray-haired postmistress. But the mail wasn't the only reason she was there; she knew Mrs. Conrad's family had lived on the island for generations, since the old whaling days, and she was related to just about everyone on Nantucket. If anyone knew about Lily, Mrs. Conrad would.

"Two letters for you today," Mrs. Conrad said, beaming. "And from New York."

"New York?" Surprised, Shannon stuffed them in her pocket to read later.

"Mrs. Conrad," she said, "I was wondering if you know anything about Lily Molyneux?"

Mrs. Conrad always told people she never pried; she was just naturally curious. Had been since she was a child, and that's how she happened to know everybody's business, as well as their history.

"Lily?" she said thoughtfully. "Why, she was Ned Sheridan's ladylove, or so they said. The story goes that he built his house right next to Sea Mist Cottage so he could be near her. And that she darned near ruined him.''

"But who was she?"

"She was a foreigner. She came to the island as a girl and was befriended by the Sheridans. She lived here for a little while, alone in her cottage, and then she just disappeared. No one seems to remember much about her, except how beautiful she was. It's like a legend, her beauty, and no one who saw her ever forgot. Their memories were passed on to their children and then to their children, until it all became the stuff dreams are made of. Or ghosts.''

She laughed as Shannon stared skeptically at her. "Nantucket's always been a haunted island," she added mischievously. "I guess some folks who lived here liked it so much they just never wanted to leave."

Shannon shivered, thinking of the eerie silence in the attic. She leaned eagerly on the counter, her chin in her hands, listening.

"The Sheridans lived on this island for close to a century," Mrs. Conrad said. "Ned's father used to be a whaler, but with the coming of kerosene all that finished, and he set himself up in a ships' chandlery business on Steamboat Wharf. They had always been a seafaring family and good chapel-going Methodists, and it must have come as a shock when their only son, Ned, told them he wanted to be an actor.

"You can only imagine the consternation it caused; aye, and the trouble. Ned finished his studies all right, but he refused to take up a respectable profession the way they wanted him to, and he ran off to be an actor. Anyhow, he became famous. A star, you might call him.

"In those days theaters had no air-conditioning and in the hot summer months all the actors would take a rest at the shore. There was quite a famous actors' colony here at 'Sconset in the early part of the century, and Ned Sheridan came home and built his upside-down house, just like one he had seen on his travels to Hawaii, with the living room and veranda upstairs to catch the view.

"They said it was always full of friends—other actors and their children, and they'd often put on a show for the locals. Apparently they were genial, friendly folk, having a good time, and they were well liked. But later, with the coming of air-conditioning, when theaters began to stay open in the summer, they drifted away. I believe Ned would bring his children here occasionally, but after a while that stopped too.

"Anyhow, my dear, that's all I can tell you. The Sheridan daughters left the island, and none of them ever came back to Nantucket, so I don't know what happened to him. Only the story that Lily Molyneux was the true love of his life." She laughed. "And maybe that should have been his epitaph."

SHANNON WALKED SLOWLY back to the cottage, thinking about Ned Sheridan. She stared at the white house, imagining it filled with a noisy, cheerful bunch of actors, with children running in and out, and Ned gazing longingly next door, wishing he could be with his ladylove, Lily Molyneux.

On an impulse, she walked to the door and tried it. To her surprise, it was unlocked.

She glanced apprehensively over her shoulder as she climbed the twisting wooden stairs, mindful of Mrs. Conrad's references to ghosts, but when she threw open the shutters the big living room was filled with sparkling early morning sunlight and wasn't in the least bit ghostly. She stared curiously around. There were some old chairs, a table with one leg broken, and a worn Oriental rug. A few old theater posters in tarnished brass frames still hung on the walls, announcing Ned Sheridan as Hamlet, as the Count of Monte Cristo, and "The Sheridans" as Romeo and Juliet. In the corner, behind the broken table, half-hidden under an old rug, was a trunk crammed with old theater costumes, and hidden among them she found a photograph album.

She dusted off the stained burgundy velvet cover, turning the empty pages until she came across a single photograph. She knew it must be Ned. He was tall and slender. His thick blond hair slid silkily over his eyes and there was a devil-may-care expression in them. She thought Ned Sheridan was a very good-looking man, the kind you would call handsome, and that he and Lily must have made a dazzling pair.

"Lovers," she thought. Isn't that what Mrs. Conrad had said? Tucking the photograph album under her arm, she marched down the stairs again and back to her own cottage.

She had almost forgotten about the two letters in her pocket, and she took them out now to read. The first was from her bank saying she had the sum of three thousand and twenty-five dollars left in her account, and that she had a line of credit up to fifty thousand dollars, guaranteed by Mr. J. K. Brennan. And the second was from J. K. Brennan himself.

I know you'll get all upset when you hear from the bank, but I just want you to have the comfort of knowing that, should you need it, the money is there. Of course, if you don't then I shall be the first to applaud. But you are going through too many changes right now to have to worry about paying the rent and getting enough to eat. Believe me, I've been there. Use the money if and when you need it. It's the least I can do for you, and it's not nearly enough to repay what your father did for me.

She telephoned him right away. "I don't know how to thank you for the money," she said simply. "I'm not going to use it though. I have a job; I'm earning enough to get by." She wanted to prove to him that she wasn't just a spoiled little rich girl. She wanted him to know she was her father's daughter.

"It's there as a backup," he said. There was an uncomfortable pause and then: "So? What are you doing there on Nantucket?"

"I'm a waitress." She laughed, thinking of Harriet's. "And I'm pretty good at it."

"Great," he said, sounding astonished. "Let me know when you feel like company."

"I will," she promised. "And thanks, J.K. You are the only one who has really talked to me. The only one really to help."

"Not even Buffy?" he asked.

"Not even Buffy."

"Yeah," he said grimly. "Well, no need for thanks. I'm here when you need me, Shannon. Take care of yourself now."

HARRIET'S FISH CAFÉ was busy that night, but Shannon scarcely noticed, her mind was on Ned and Lily, and the puzzle of why she was the owner of Lily Molyneux's diamond necklace. How had it come into Bob Keeffe's possession? And why had he claimed it was "by way of being a family heirloom?"

THE ANSWER CAME to her in bed that night. One of the few things her father had told her about himself was that the O'Keeffes came from Connemara. And Lily Molyneux came from Connemara too.

She sat up in bed and switched on the lamp, staring at Ned Sheridan's photo propped against it, and the little packet of letters from Ciel, and the portrait and the diamond necklace. There was a connection between the O'Keeffes and the Molyneuxes, she just knew it.

She didn't think twice. The next morning she closed up Sea Mist

Cottage, gave in her notice to Harriet, took the ferry back to the mainland, and caught the first flight leaving for Ireland.

"AND THAT'S WHY I'm here now," Shannon finished her story breathlessly. "To find out about Lily and the O'Keeffes, and my family. I thought maybe it would help me find out the truth about my father."

"Maybe it will and maybe it won't," I said, "but one thing I can tell you is Lily's story."

"It's my opinion trouble always starts with a woman," Brigid said knowledgeably. "*Cherchez la femme* is what I say."

I stared at her, astonished. "I never knew you spoke French, Brigid."

"Oh, I've picked up a smatterin' over the years," she retorted crisply. "So tell us more about Joanna," she said to Shannon.

"I know my father really cared about her, and I guess Joanna really cared about him. Why else would she have kept so quiet all these years? After all, if she were just after his money, she would have been living in splendor and dripping with jewels, and making sure everybody knew about it."

She added quietly, "You know, I thought about Joanna a lot when I was in Nantucket. I thought of her, left all alone, just the way I was, and I couldn't help but feel sorry for her. She hadn't even been able to come to the funeral, and she had been the soul of discretion; her name never even surfaced in the press. She had no one she could talk to about him, no one to comfort her, and I knew just how she felt. Anyhow, I wrote her a little note, sort of from one wounded heart to another." She shrugged. "I thought it was the least I could do. For my father."

"So what about the cruel stepmother?" Brigid asked quickly.

Shannon smiled. "Buffy wasn't cruel. She was just selfish and . . . unkind."

"Mmmnn," I said thoughtfully. "I seem to remember hearing those very same words said about Lily."

"Anyhow, murder is just not Buffy's style. If she had wanted out, she would have gone for the glossy society divorce with its medals for valor under the strain of heavy social duties. She would have gotten her rewards for long service and a huge 'golden alimony parachute' at the end."

"Tell us about the partners," I said, while Brigid poured more tea.

Shannon thought for a moment. "I know Jack Wexler was jealous because Dad had a famous architect design his dream building instead of him. Dad once told me that he thought Jack fancied being in his shoes. But that doesn't make a man a criminal, does it?

"And I've known Brad Jeffries since I was a kid. It's impossible for me to think of him as a murderer. But maybe he secretly envied my father's high-profile image. Maybe he was tired of being the *invisible man* in Keeffe Holdings? Or maybe it was greed?"

"And J.K.?" I asked curiously.

She heaved a great sigh. "Who knows what lurks beneath his 'boss's right-hand man' image. But Dad knew J.K. was ambitious and he liked him for it. And I believed J.K. when he told me if there was anything he could have done to prevent the tragedy, he would surely have done it. Besides," she added, a touch defensively I thought, "he's been a good friend to me. J.K. was the only one who did anything to help me. Buffy had simply walked away, and I knew Brad's and Jack's offers of help were just lip-service." She shrugged, excusing them. "After all, the business had gone under and they had lost their jobs and probably their own fortunes too.

"And anyhow," she concluded in a small voice, looking wistfully at us with those large gray eyes, "here I am."

Mammie had always said it was impossible to shut me up, but Shannon's story had silenced me, and for once I had listened almost without a word. It was a wild story all right, of murder and millions and ghostly dreams. Then I thought of my other guest, away at the moment in Galway, and I smiled. Maybe there was more to dreams than I thought. And out of compassion as well as interest, I invited her to stay.

"ARDNAVARNA IS ALWAYS GOOD for people who are troubled," I told her, "and I can see you are that. There's nothing here to disturb your peace. Except maybe . . ." She stared expectantly at me, but I only smiled. I was keeping my coincidence, my secret, my *surprise,* for later. "Well now, we shall have to see what room you might like," I said briskly. "My goodness, is it six-thirty already? Supper's at eight, m'dear. And of course, we always dress."

I showed Shannon her room, the one that used to be Mammie's over the front porch and she seemed delighted with it, especially the big bathroom with the immense claw-footed bathtub set dead center and the Victorian brass shower fittings. I know the towels are thin with age and maybe there's a couple of holes, but no matter, they smell deliciously of the fresh salt wind and the lavender kept in the linen press. I warned her the bathwater may be brownish, but it's always that way after the rain, and it's only from the peat, and then I left her to soak in the tub.

I walked back along the first floor hallway to my own room on the southeast corner of the house. It's always been my room since I was twelve, and when Mammie went I somehow never had the heart to change it for her bigger one.

Now, *my* room is certainly not poky, though it is a bit too squarish in shape. There's an ornate Victorian brass four-poster with a mattress handmade by Heals forty years ago and still as firm as the day it was bought. The sheets are Irish linen; worn, of course, as everything is in this house, but there's nothing like linen next to the skin in bed. The rug is the same one that has always been there, Chinese, with faded bluish and greenish scrolls and a lotus blossom border. There's a wonderful big square dressing table with my usual clutter of silver and crystal whatnots: ring holders and pin trays and bud-vases and candlesticks, photos and old letters, brushes and mirrors. And on the carved pine chimneypiece there is a collection of spotted china dogs given to me over the years by family and friends who know of my devotion to the dalmatian breed.

There is a comfortable flowered cretonne easy chair in front of the fireplace with a little tapestry footstool worked by my grandmother, Lady Nora, who obviously spent endless hours on such things, filling our rooms with cushions and chair seats and bellpulls. My goodness, her hands were certainly never idle. The big window looks out over the back of the house toward the hills and that delicious glimpse of the sea, which is the first thing I gaze at each morning when I open my eyes. And the curtains are a bluish-pink flowery chintz to match the chair, and they are as old as the mattress, but not as old as me.

A pair of the famous wardrobes stand against one wall and there are more in the adjoining dressing room, all stuffed to overflowing with my lifetime of treasures. Oh, I do love clothes, even now that I'm in my dotage.

And I love this room. I remember when I was a child, I would look forward to being ill—not seriously ill, just a tiny malaise, but enough so I could stay in bed to be waited on with dainty trays of all the things I liked most, "to tempt my appetite." I would lie back against a mound of pillows staring out the window at the sea, feeling deliciously pampered and lazy, until someone, Mammie or Pa or friends, would pop their heads around the door and say, "Hello, young lady, and what have you been up to then?" And then my quiet little lair would be alive with laughter and gossip and huggings and kissings because nobody seemed in the least bit worried about catching my germs.

You know, it's my misfortune—and don't imagine I haven't regretted it all these years—that I never had children. God gave me a raw deal on that one because I surely wanted them: I wanted my first love Archie's child, but I never had the chance; I wanted my husband's child, but I never seemed lucky; and later I wanted the children of the man I loved and almost married, but it was not to be. I have thought many a time about how different my life would have been with Ardnavarna full of children and then grandchildren, the way most Irish houses are. Don't misunderstand me, I'm not lonely. Oh, no, I never was that. It's just that sometimes I get wistful about it, especially on long dark winter evenings. And that's why I was so pleased that night.

Because, you see, I had another houseguest. My "coincidence." He was away in Galway, but he would be back in time for dinner, and tonight it would be almost like having grandchildren around my table. I knew I had better bathe quickly and then check on Brigid in the kitchen. Two girls from the village had come to help, but still, she is an old woman, though she won't admit it, and I wanted to make sure she was all right.

I decided to wear the pink chiffon with the little shoulder-cape. "Shocking" pink they used to call it, and it's one of my favorites. I put the diamond arrows Archie once gave me in my hair and clipped diamonds in my ears; the setting is old-fashioned and maybe they are a bit dusty, but they're "good." Since my chest is now so scrawny there is no point in being décolleté, so I pinned my little shoulder-cape closed with my favorite enamel fox brooch, bought at a fair years ago. Silk stockings, of course—my biggest extravagance—then my silver high-heeled sandals, and a splash of Guerlain's L'Heure Bleue. I thought that should do it.

Downstairs again, I checked Brigid in the kitchen, then I dashed around lighting candles and lamps and plumping up cushions like a nervous hostess at her first party, because I was on tenterhooks about my little surprise. If it went the way I thought it would we were in for an amusing time. Or shall we say, "the mystery deepens."

The tall windows were flung open to the night air and I heard the sound of a car arriving, and then hurrying footsteps bolting up the stairs two at a time. I smiled reminiscently as I heard that fateful creak on the second step from the top. I busied myself with the bottles on the sideboard, pouring a little of this and a little of that into a 1920 cocktail shaker, just as the clock in the hall struck eight followed by a tinkling little tune. A few minutes later I heard Shannon on the stairs and then she entered in a cloud of Chanel No. 5.

I inspected her critically, the way I would a granddaughter, head to one side, eyes narrowed. She was wearing a column of black jersey with a deep V-neck and long tight sleeves with a tasseled belt clasped around her slender waist. With the light behind her, her red hair looked like a halo, and she wore almost no makeup and not a scrap of jewelry.

"Well, now," I said approvingly, "don't you look grand. A bit plain for my taste, girl, but then you are young enough, and beautiful enough to get away with it. I'm like my mother, I always had to layer on the flash to get noticed."

I saw her staring at my frock and my silver heels, which make my ankles look as fragile as a filly's, and my pink lipstick that matched, and the diamonds in my freshly fluffed-up curls, so I gave a girlish twirl and said, beaming, "Schiaparelli. 1932. Not bad, is it?"

"Wonderful." She sounded awed.

"I must have been about your age then. Ah, and hittin' the high spots I was, in London and Paris. I adored Paris. And clothes. Especially hats. Dearest girl, I would hate even now to tell you how much money I squandered on those frippery bits of net and feathers we wore in the thirties. But they did wonders for a girl's looks. I have them upstairs still. Remind me to show you later."

Brigid muttered something under her breath as she stalked past me carrying in a tray of nibbles. "What was that, Brigid?" I called.

"Much good they did you, the hats," she yelled back scornfully. "Y'should have saved yer money."

Now, saving money has never been my strong point, and she knew it. I said hastily to Shannon, "Here girl, make yourself useful, why don't you. My old arms can still control a fiery hunter, but arthritis is a funny ailment and I find they're too stiff to shake a proper cocktail anymore."

She shook the cocktails obediently and I saw her notice there were three glasses—all different because nothing matches anymore—arranged on the tarnished silver tray. "I'm expecting another guest," I said, just as the stairs creaked. We heard his footsteps in the hall and the drawing room door was thrown open and he walked in.

Shannon stared at him. The cocktail shaker crashed from her hands onto the silver tray, breaking the glasses.

The young man standing in the doorway stared back at her. A tall, handsome young man with silky blond hair.

"Shannon, dear," I said, ignoring the broken glasses with aristocratic panache, "I would like you to meet Ned Sheridan's great-grandson Edward Sheridan. Eddie, this is Shannon Keeffe."

My eyes narrowed as I watched them shake hands, warily sizing each other up. Obviously he knew who she was from all the terrible publicity, and, because he looked so like his ancestor, she thought she was shaking hands with a ghost.

"He's flesh and blood," I said with a grin, because I love making mischief. He looked at me puzzled, but I didn't enlighten him and Shannon glanced accusingly at me.

I tried to look bashful, but I'm no good at it. Instead I laughed. "Isn't it interesting you should meet here? And for the same reason? You both want to know about Lily." I poured the amber cocktails into one of the hastily replaced glasses and raised my glass. *"Slàinte,"* I toasted, smiling.

"Slàinte," they repeated, sipping cautiously. Shannon coughed as the drink hit the back of her throat, and I quickly admitted, "There's just a touch of poteen in there, darlin' girl. To set us up for dinner."

Eddie Sheridan laughed and I noticed that with every passing minute he was becoming more human and less of a ghost to Shannon.

"Another toast," I cried, enjoying myself hugely. "Here's to Lily Molyneux, who has brought us all together."

Then, with a grand wave of my arm, I shepherded them to the door. "Faithless Brigid's been tearing around like a tinker's coat all day in the kitchen, so we'd best go in for dinner before she begins to sulk. And a fine dinner it will be, too, I can promise you that, for whatever else, she's a marvelous cook."

I took my place at the head of the magnificent Regency table that had been my great-grandmother's when she lived here, when it was still the Dower House, long before the Big House was burned, and I thought what a lucky old trout I was to have two such charming young guests. As I rang the silver bell for Brigid I said mischievously, "I may never let the two of you go. I shall spin you stories of Lily, like Scheherazade, bit by bit so you'll be condemned to stay at Ardnavarna forever."

"I can't imagine a nicer sentence," Shannon said impulsively.

And of course she was right, because there is nowhere in the world quite like Ardnavarna. I glanced around the dining room. Its shabbiness was softened in the candlelight and a peat fire flickered in the grate, even though the tall windows were still open to the soft night air. And I counted my blessings.

Brigid staggered through the door with a loaded tray. She was wearing her posh "company" uniform: a dark dress and a little white organza apron meant for somebody half her size. She wore short white socks over her black stockings and her tiny feet were encased in little high-heeled lace-up boots. She threw Eddie a scornful glance as he leapt up to help her. "I've niver had ter ask anybody to carry a tray fer me yet, let alone a young spalpeen like yerself," she said, slamming the tray down on the sideboard and trotting back to the kitchen. I sighed. As you may have noticed, Brigid is good at slamming.

I heard Eddie asking Shannon why she wanted to know about Lily and she told him she thought she might be related through her father's family. "The O'Keeffes."

"And Eddie thinks he might be related to Lily too," I said. "Through *his* father's family." I beamed at them. I always enjoy making mischief and I was about to drop my second bombshell of the night. "Now, isn't this going to be interesting? To see which one of you it is, that's Lily's heir?"

Their astonished eyes met mine. "Lily's heir?" they said in chorus.

"Why, yes. Dear me, didn't I tell you? Lily left a pile of money behind her when she finally went. She didn't leave it to my mother, or to me. We had enough then, you see. She left it to her 'sole and legitimate heir.' "

"And who was that?" Edward asked.

"Well, of course, that was the mystery. No one ever knew who Lily's 'sole and legitimate heir' was. Or even if she had one. No one really knew anything about Lily, you see. She cut people out of her life the way other people cast out old clothes. But now I'm gettin' ahead of myself again. If I'm to be your Scheherazade, I'd best begin at the beginning. After dinner though, to be sure." I smiled craftily at the pair of alert young faces turned toward me. "Well, come on now, darlin's, enjoy your food," I told them, knowing I had them in my power.

Afterward, we settled ourselves in front of the drawing room fire. I sat on the sofa, the dogs on either side of me, and looked at the two young people gazing expectantly at me. It had been a long time since I had commanded so much attention and I was enjoying myself hugely. I knew it was mean of me to keep them in suspense, but the truth was I liked their young company. It brought back memories of my own youth and of my mother, sitting on this very sofa, telling me the very same story I was about to tell them now.

Mammie and I were so close, more like sisters than mother and daughter. Oh, how I loved her, and how I mourned her when she died. I ran away to Paris right after the funeral and for more than a year I found myself unable to return. The thought of Ardnavarna without her was unbearable. But when I finally came home again it was as though she were still here. Every time I walked in the gardens, I saw the beauty she had created. The vegetables and fruits she had planted still nurtured me, and her beloved hunter was waiting impatiently in the stables to be ridden again.

But life was never the same without her. Even now, so many years later, I miss her.

I sighed as I kicked off my silver sandals, tucked my feet under me, and began.

CHAPTER 11

THE PAST

"BEFORE I TELL YOU about Lily, you need to know about the Molyneux family. About how grand we were, so you'll know how we've come down in the world.

"Ardnavarna means 'the high place with the alder trees.' My ancestors planted hundreds of them on the hills around the house, all those you see today.

"In the old days people could always tell the importance of a big house by the length of the avenue leading up to it, and the castle was so huge and so grand that half a dozen men were employed full-time to rake the miles of gravel driveways so not a single wheel mark ever showed. A bos'n's chair swung permanently from the battlements to enable the workers to clean the hundreds of windows. There were forty indoor servants, a lamplighter, a candlesnuffer, girls who did nothing but keep the fires burning in the dozens, maybe hundreds of grates, and a tribe of small boys who kept the coal and peat coming up from the cellars.

"In my great-grandfather's day there were French chefs and English nannies, Irish nursemaids and German governesses, parlormaids, ladies' maids, valets, and laundresses, and cooks for the servants' hall. The footmen wore bottle-green tailcoats and striped black trousers, but the butler had a suit designed especially by my great-great-grandfather and made in Paris, in bright shamrock-green complete with gold braid. I told you, we Molyneux always enjoyed a bit of flash.

"The stables were the thing, of course. They always were, in Irish households. They could easily have accommodated five families and were built of the finest materials. There were dozens of horses and each stall was a model of cleanliness and each horse had his name on a brass nameplate, polished as bright as sunshine, on the door. There were hunters and hackers, carriage horses and the children's ponies, his lordship's four matched grays for his personal carriage, and a pair of pacers for her ladyship's special gig. Lord Molyneux was Hunt Master and the hounds were kept in kennels almost as palatial as the stables.

"As well as Ardnavarna, there was a town house in Fitzwilliam Square in Dublin, and one in London's Belgravia, and the family divided its time among them according to the season. They went to all the grand parties and receptions in London, and the levees and dinners and balls given by the Lord Lieutenant at Dublin Castle. And they entertained lavishly at Ardnavarna. Everyone came; their guest book must have read like a who's who of the era: royalty from half a dozen countries, all the nobility, artists, writers, celebrities. The fishing parties at Ardnavarna were famous, and an invitation much prized.

"Life was very grand then. And even by my own grandfather's day we were still rich. He was the youngest son and he only inherited the title himself by a series of accidents. His father had died, along with his two daughters, of typhoid on a visit to Italy. Then the eldest son, who had inherited the title, drowned in a boating accident two months after. And so my grandfather, Augustus Molyneux, inherited the lot: the title and the family money and Ardnavarna."

I stopped to catch my breath, glancing at my young guests. "Tell me if I'm boring you, darlings," I said half apologetically. "I get so carried away by the old stories, sometimes I feel I'm living them." I lit a cigarette and waved away the smoke, bracelets jangling. "Now. Where was I?"

"Your grandfather inherited," Shannon prompted me eagerly. The cat lying on her lap, shedding hairs all over her best black, stretched and purred. Shannon smiled and I thought that for the first time since she came she did not look tense.

I said, "Let me make it clear that I'm not telling the story of Ireland's Troubles, it's not about politics or the tragic brutal history. It's about the Molyneuxes and the O'Keeffes, and what happened to them.

"Now, August Molyneux moved his widowed mother into this dower house—this very one we are sitting in—and she devoted the rest of her days to developing the gardens. He had already met Nora Westmacott, the only child of a family of minor title with a poor little manor house down in Devon. But Nora Westmacott was pretty and she looked good on his arm, and despite the lure of other girls' titles and fortunes

August Molyneux chose her, and they were married three months later.

"Nora had black hair and pale skin and she was delicate. She gave birth to two stillborn children before William was born in 1866. And then, a year later, in 1867, a girl was born.

"The legend is that Nora took one look at her child and she was so overwhelmed by the baby's innocence and beauty, she named her for the purest of flowers, the lily.

"Then, seven long years after that momentous occasion, in 1874, when they had all but given up hope, another girl child was born. And this time they said she was named for the beautiful blue spring sky Nora saw outside her window as she emerged from two days of crucifying labor—*le ciel*.

"And, of course, it is Ciel's—my own mother's—memories I'm telling you now. Just as she told them to me, though with maybe a bit of my own imagination thrown in when it comes to who said what to whom." I laughed, knowing that my fertile imagination was more than capable of filling any gaps.

"Now, William was a quiet, studious boy. He hated hunting and outdoor pursuits, and it was the tomboy Lily who became her father's favorite. For seven years, until Ciel came along, she had his love all to herself. Oh, and she was a beauty, a darlin' little girl, all wind-tossed glossy dark curls and flashing fiery blue eyes—and a temper and sulky tantrums to match. Ciel said nobody could sulk as good as her sister Lily. And her father fell for that pouting lower lip, that stamped little foot in its pretty doeskin button boots, that mutinous shake of the head. And, at just the right moment, the perfect tear trickling down the cheek, the hint of a sob shaking her pretty little shoulders. Lily was expert at twisting her pa around her finger.

"Now Ciel, on the other hand, was a little redheaded mischief-maker with the face of a charming monkey. She had a grin that made everyone else smile and a laugh as loud as a fishwife's and joyous as a lark's. Her eyes were gray like her father's, she was small and freckled and always in trouble. And she adored her sister Lily.

"William was sent away to school in England, and the family divided its time between London, Dublin, and Ardnavarna. Their pa taught the girls to ride as good as any man. Lily took part in her first hunt when she was five years old—riding sidesaddle naturally, and looking delicious in a custom-tailored habit from Busvine's and perfect little boots made by Peal & Butley, with her curls drawn back in a net and the best bowler hat from Mr. Locke's in London.

"Anyhow, her father, Lord Molyneux, was a well-padded, handsome, arrogant man. Orders from him were uttered as commands and beware those who obeyed too slowly or, heaven forbid, disobeyed.

"Ciel said he always seemed fond of their mother, Lady Nora, but he was impatient with her delicacy, and he was also impatient with his son. William was a smallish youth, thin and pale, and he always had his nose in a book. He was completely uninterested in his father's passions: horses, dogs, hunting, shooting, and fishing, and, as you can imagine, he was a major disappointment to him.

"But Lady Nora was a kind, compassionate woman; if anyone on the estate was sick or in trouble she was the first to know, and she was always there with a basket of food and medicines. Lord Molyneux was proud of the fact that he knew each of his tenants by name, but it was Lady Nora who knew the names of their wives and children.

"Of course, Ciel was much younger than the other two. She was a funny, energetic child, always bouncing around and knocking things over. She was small and amusing, and always in trouble. She knew her father loved her, but there was no doubt Lily was his favorite.

"He had adored Lily since he first saw her in her mother's arms. She had a shock of black hair and sapphire eyes and a pretty pouting mouth that he said proudly, even as a babe, seemed to smile at him. Growing up, Lily was a daredevil, a tease and a flirt. She could get anything she wanted from her father just by climbing on his knee, linking her small arms around his neck and saying, 'Oh, please, Pa, please, please, please.' And she could get out of any punishment simply by drooping like the flower that was her namesake and allowing the tears to trickle sadly down her small face. He was always 'Pa' to her—never Papa like the other children. And she was always his 'darlin' girl.'

"Ciel said that in her whole life, Lily never thought of the consequences of any of her actions, though afterward her remorse could be truly terrible. Buckets of tears and howling like a pack of hounds, promising she would never do it—whatever sin *it* was—again. And at the time she meant it.

"Still, Lily adored her darling pa. She loved her brother, too, though she teased the livin' daylights out of him. And she truly loved her mother and her innocent companion in crime, her little sister Ciel.

"She would do miserable things—snatching William's silver-rimmed spectacles from his nose when he was engrossed in a book, knowing he could barely see without them. She would career around with them temptingly in her hand, dangling them just out of reach, out the window. Inevitably she would drop them, and there they'd be, smashed to smithereens on the gravel below, with her desperately trying to pick up all the pieces, crying she hadn't meant it, and she would do anything, *anything* to make amends. Later, he would find her favorite book, or one of her little model horses, or a chocolate stuck to his pillow, with a note saying *Sorry*.

"She would urge Ciel on to the daredevil exploits she found so easy, like jumping fences. But she didn't stop to think that they might be too high for Ciel's small pony, and Ciel fell off and got a concussion. She lay there like a stone with Lily on her knees at her side, keening and praying, making bargains with God the way Ciel said she always did. Saying that if He only let her beloved little sister live, she would never behave in such a stupid fashion again. That it was all her fault and God should take her instead. Naturally, even though she meant it at the time, she knew God never would.

"There were governesses galore, from every part of Europe, but none of them lasted. Lady Nora spent half her time in London interviewing new ones and she said that her terrible children's exploits were the talk of every drawing room and the bane of her life. Of course, she only half meant it, because she was a gentle, loving woman who adored her strong-willed offspring.

"Ciel said it was truly awful, the things they did to those governesses, simply because they knew if they were bad enough the poor women would be forced to leave, and then they would be free of lessons and discipline again until their desperate mother could find someone else to take her place. They put hedgehogs in their beds and mice in their milk and spiders on their pillows. They rigged ropes across the gallery to trip them and put roller skates on the polished floors where they would slip on them. And Lily always managed to get Ciel to do the dirty work so she could say innocently, 'But Mama, I never knew anything about it. I can't imagine how it happened.'

"Everyone for miles around knew Lily. The servants carried back tales of her latest exploits and the men laughed over them in the shebeen, and the women gathered around their hearths to gossip about her. To them, Lily was like a movie star would be now. She was beautiful and titled and rich, but she never talked down to them. She had charm, vitality, and an impulsive, reckless nature. She was always game for a dare and even if she was a mite too proud of her name and had the arrogance of her position as Lord Molyneux's daughter, she was never mean.

"Ciel said Lily was always kind to the village children. She never talked down to them and she would give them rides on her pony, and old sticky toffees covered in bits of fluff from her pocket. They adored her and would boast of her attentions for weeks. And she always went willingly with her mother to distribute medicines, or clothes and food to the poorest and most needy. Once she ran to her pa and told him desperately she wanted to sell her favorite horse and give the money to a poor homeless family she had encountered on her ride: a young man, his wife and baby, and two other small children. The man had lost his job and they had been wandering from place to place searching for work, sleeping rough in the hedgerows, rain and shine. Lily had galloped home and raided the kitchen for food for them. And that night, unable to forget the sad-faced children, she confronted her father. He looked at her proudly and said there was no need for her selfless offer and the next day the poor family had a new cottage and the man had a job as a gardener and the woman as a laundress.

"Naturally, Lily took the difference in her circumstances for granted; that was just the way it was. And giddy and wild though she was, as well as a terrible tease, she was also her mother's daughter, warm, tenderhearted, and easily touched.

"But, for any governesses that stayed the course, Lily was as elusive as the breeze. She was up and out at dawn, before they had even opened their eyes. Off to the stables and galloping away to the strand with Finn O'Keeffe."

I PAUSED AND GLANCED at my listeners. Their eyes were bright with interest, but it had been a long day and my age was beginning to tell on me. I decided I must go to bed and continue the next evening. "So now you know the background," I told my disappointed new friends. "And tomorrow, after dinner, I promise you will get to know Lily. And Finn."

And, leaving them dangling in suspense, I kissed them good night and drifted, joints creaking like the stairs, up to my bed.

CHAPTER

~~~~~~~~~~~~~~~~~~ 12 ~~~~~~~~~~~~~~~~~~

EDDIE

EDDIE SHERIDAN THREW ANOTHER log on the fire and turned to look at Shannon, curled up in a frayed armchair. One of the dalmatians had left Maudie and sneaked shamefacedly back downstairs to sit at Shannon's feet.

"Traitor," he said, grinning.

She smiled. "He just likes company, I guess."

Her face was pale and there were shadows under her beautiful dark-lashed light gray eyes. The lamplight behind her head made a halo of her red hair and she looked slender and frail in her long black dress. A sorrowful daughter in mourning for her father, he thought, remembering the headlines and the news reports. He said, "The last few months must have been really tough."

She nodded. "But Dad always said the Keeffes would survive, so I can't let him down now. Can I?"

They fell silent, gazing at the sparking log in the grate. Then he said, "Why did you think we had met before?"

Simultaneously she asked, "Why are you here?"

They laughed and Shannon said, "I own the cottage next door to the white house on Nantucket."

He shrugged. "No one has lived there for years. We only visited occasionally when we were kids. I grew up in California and we didn't come East that often. And later I was just too busy in college, first at Berkeley, then Yale Drama School. I guess I'm following in my great-grandfather, Ned Sheridan's, footsteps."

"You are the image of him." She blushed, embarrassed. "I've a confession to make. I took a look around the house. The door was open—and well, I just couldn't resist. I stole his photograph. I have it now.

Maybe I should give it back to you? After all, you are its rightful owner. Anyhow, that's why I knew you—I thought you were a ghost!"

He laughed. "So we are here for the same reason, to find out about Lily and Ned?"

"And to find out who murdered my father."

He stared at her, stunned. "I know you mean what you say, but is that possible? That he was murdered?"

"I think he was, but no one believes me. Except maybe Maudie and Brigid. And anyway, why are *you* so curious about Lily?"

"I guess because she's always been there, lurking in the background of the family conversation, like a skeleton in the closet. Anyway, I'm here to set the old rumors finally to rest."

"You mean the rumor that Lily ruined him?"

"Among other things." He leaned back against the sofa cushions, his hands behind his head, thinking. "The reason I always wanted to be an actor was because of the stories my grandfather used to tell me about Ned Sheridan. About how powerful and moving an actor he was. Gramps said he could hold an audience with just a movement or a glance, he could have them in tears one minute and in an uproar of laughter the next. He was a star, with his name up in lights on Broadway. But it had taken him years of playing the circuits in dusty little theaters in every one-horse town across America to get there. He met his wife in one of them. My great-grandmother, Juliet.

"She wasn't pretty—I've seen photographs—but Gramps told me she walked proud and flashed her enormous dark eyes; and on stage, she just transformed herself into a great beauty almost by an act of will. She was an actress in the *grand* tradition of Bernhardt and Ellen Terry, and Ned was the Olivier of the circuits, and both of them had voices that could mesmerize an audience. 'They had *music* in their voices,' Gramps used to say."

"I saw the posters," Shannon said guiltily, "hanging on the wall at the white house."

He laughed. "That's okay. I'm sure old Ned wouldn't have minded. Anyhow, the Sheridans were famous for almost two decades around the beginning of the century. I have all Ned's treasures: the stage clothes and props, the thigh boots and cavalier's plumed hat and sword from *Monte Cristo,* his doublet and hose from *Romeo,* her uniform from *Major Barbara.* And I pored for hours over those old playbills with their names above the title and twice as big. They played anything and everything. My grandfather said Ned always had a short attention span and when he went on tour he put his players through hell, a different play every three nights, a different theater every week. Travel on Sunday, open Monday night."

Eddie sighed regretfully, smiling across at Shannon. "Those were the days, at least for theater. Sometimes I think maybe I've been born in the wrong era, that I should have been around when great-grandfather Ned was.

"Anyhow, Gramps was their only son and he hated the life. He never wanted to be like them. He said it was all magic onstage, but off it was all traveling and turmoil, and fights with agents and managers and the other actors. He wanted none of it. All *he* wanted was a proper home of their own, one place where they all stayed together. And sure enough, later they got it. Two in fact. A lavish house on Long Island that became an extension of the theater: same people, same turmoil, same fights. And the white house at 'Sconset where Ned and his friends relaxed and had a good time.

"Gramps wanted Ned to have a normal job like the other kids' fathers. He would have liked him to be a banker or a stockbroker, though I think he could have settled for a plumber, just so long as they had a regular life. I guess he was a boring kid for two such artistic people to have, but those are the breaks. He was happiest when they sent him off to prep school. He said at last he felt like the other boys. Except his parents were 'stars,' of course. Funny, he could never understand why the other kids were so in awe of them. He thought their life was boring: all those trains and waiting around in cold theaters.

"And he told me that always lurking in Ned's background was this mysterious woman, Lily Molyneux. Juliet was a volatile woman and whenever she and Ned would have rows, which was often, he would hear his mother scream that it was all Lily Molyneux's fault. That Ned was still in love with her and if she called, he would go running. And he would. He knew it for a fact. And he said that was what led to his downfall.

" 'But how, Gramps, how?' I used to ask him. But he would shake his head and say, 'In ways too terrible for a young shaver like you to understand.' And that was that. He would never say any more.

"It drove me crazy," Eddie said. "I didn't even know what Lily looked like. And I never knew who she was because no one would ever talk about her. I promised myself that one day when I had the time, I would find out the truth, just to satisfy my curiosity finally. Because if there's a skeleton in the family closet I'd like to know what it is.

"I did some investigating in the family archives, and that's where I came across Lily's name, and an address in Boston, on Beacon Hill. I went there, but too many years had passed and no one had ever heard of her. The other address I found was on a letter written to Ned by Ciel. It was Ardnavarna.

"So." He shrugged and held out his hands. "Here I am."

Shannon said, "I can tell you what Lily looked like. She was a beauty. Maybe that's why your great-grandmother Juliet was jealous of her. She had long curling black hair and dazzling blue eyes and a passionate mouth. She looked spoiled and sexy and rich. And used to having her own way. At least she did when she was seventeen, when the portrait was painted."

"And is Miss Maudie going to tell us what happened? Or is she just going to dangle bits of the story in front of us, keeping us prisoner forever here at Ardnavarna?"

Shannon laughed. "I'm surely happy to be a prisoner at Ardnavarna. It's paradise in a time-warp." She stood up and stretched wearily. "It is odd how we have all talked around Lily tonight. She's there, at the focus of the conversation, but no one ever gets to the heart of her."

"Lily's heart," Ed said, checking the fire and standing the brass spark screen in front of it. "Are we sure she really had one?"

They walked up the stairs together and the second step from the top creaked loudly, making them giggle.

Edward took Shannon's hand and put it to his lips and said in an exaggeratedly actorish whisper:

"Good night, good night! Parting is such sweet sorrow.
That I should say good-night till it be morrow."

They smiled, liking each other. "Good night, Romeo," Shannon whispered, drifting tiredly along the hallway to her room.

"Shannon," he called in a loud whisper. She turned to look at him, and their eyes met. "About your father. You can count on me to help."

She nodded gratefully. She could use all the help she could get, but now that she had Maudie and Brigid and Eddie on her side she didn't feel quite so alone anymore. She was asleep almost as soon as her head hit the lavender-scented linen pillow, without even a thought as to who Lily's heir might be because her dreams were too full of Ned Sheridan. Or was it Eddie Sheridan?

Maudie

DESPITE MY LATE NIGHT, the sun streaming in through the open window and the scent of roses on the breeze woke me early the next morning. There was a faint whiff of ham and fresh-baked bread and I lay for a moment, completely relaxed, my eyes still shut. The old linen sheets were cool against my skin and I stretched luxuriously, feeling just as I did when I was nineteen. It's only when you get up and your joints creak that you remember you are old.

I glanced at the ancient tin alarm clock with the two big bells standing incongruously atop a perfect Regency rosewood cabinet beside my bed, and saw with a shock it was almost eleven o'clock. Hooves clattered on the gravel outside and I climbed from bed and hurried to the window and leaned out.

The stablelad, Colum, had let out my bay mare and she was nibbling happily at the daisies at the edge of the lawn with the dalmatians sniffing at her heels. I dressed quickly and hurried downstairs, eager for a ride on such a darlin' morning.

"Good morning, Maudie," Shannon called as I walked across the gravel. She was leaning from her window, her pretty face all smiles. She looked as though she were delighted she hadn't dreamed me up, and my heart warmed to her all over again.

"I feel I should be saying 'Top of the morning to ya,' but I won't," I said with a grin. "I'll wish you good morning instead, and ask if you would like to join me for a ride." Then I added doubtfully, because you never know with Americans, especially city folk, "Of course, you do ride, don't you?"

"I do. But you're all ready and I'm not even dressed yet."

"Then get yourself dressed, girl," I said, "and come on down. I'll join you for a cup of coffee in the kitchen first and then we'll be off while the weather lasts."

She raced downstairs five minutes later, dressed in a denim shirt, jeans, and cowboy boots. Her hair was tied back in a ponytail and she looked about fifteen years old.

Brigid was slumbering in front of the gray peat fire, her chin sunk into her chest. Soft snores came from her open mouth and an orange cat crossed the floor and leapt onto her knee, arranging itself daintily in her lap.

"Take no notice of Brigid," I told Shannon. "The old girl's just taking her morning siesta." I poured coffee into two huge blue-speckled mugs and pushed a big yellow jug of milk across to her. There was crisp fried ham in a covered silver dish, fresh soda bread, sweet butter, and my own raspberry jam.

"Food for the gods," Shannon said, contentedly munching a thick slab of bread and jam. "There's something about the air here, Maudie, that makes a girl want to eat."

"You could use a bit of flesh on your bones," I said critically. "Did your stepmother never tell you that men don't like skinny women? There's nothin' to grab hold of under the sheets." Shannon laughed; she said she could never imagine the elegant, wafer-thin Buffy ever telling her anything like that.

"Speaking of men," she said, casually, "where's Eddie?"

I glanced sideways at her; I know "casual" when I hear it, especially when it refers to a man. "You'll be wondering about him, I expect," I said. "He's driven off to Galway this morning." I was forced to smile at her downcast look. This girl's feelings were written in her eyes. "Of course, he did say he would be home this evening," I added craftily. "Though whether it's you or Lily who's luring him back, I can't say."

"It's neither," she retorted, gulping down the last of her coffee. "It's you, Maudie. He told me he finds you irresistible."

"Get away with you, girl," I said, pleased. I've always enjoyed a compliment. I squashed my hat over my curls and said briskly, "Let's be away then."

The stables are built around a cobbled courtyard to the left of the house, and Colum was already brushing a dun-colored Connemara pony. Colum was a small black-haired horse-mad village lad intent on a career as a jockey and a future as a trainer.

I told Shannon the Connemara pony was a champion. "Dun is the original color of the breed," I said. "And young Queen Maeve's already got three winning rosettes tacked up in her stall even though she's only a two year old. I'm expecting her to be Champion of Champions at the Galway Show this year, and she's bound to win at the Royal Dublin Horse Show next."

Colum led out Malachy and Shannon stared respectfully at him. "Seventeen hands and more powerful than an ox," Colum told her proudly.

"Think you can manage him?" I asked challengingly, half expecting her to say no.

"Sure." She swung herself onto the hunter and he shifted irritably sideways, blowing steam from his nostrils.

"You've got to show him who's boss," I instructed. "If he kicks up his heels just tell him not to be such a daft old beggar and he'll get on with it properly then."

The green avenues surrounding Ardnavarna closed over our heads as we walked our horses down the hillside toward the sea, followed by the eager dalmatians. The estate covers a peninsula bordering the Atlantic at Ballynakill Harbor. Small islands dot the sheet of silver water, and the sky can change in the blink of an eye from palest blue to mother-of-pearl, and from calm sunshine to a windswept squall. I led the way down the rocky path to the stretch of golden sand and then, digging in my heels, I set off at a mad gallop, as I always do. The dogs rocketed behind me and I heard Malachy give a high, prolonged whinny, then he was pounding after me.

I glanced over my shoulder to make sure Shannon was all right and that he hadn't run away with her. She was crouched low on his back and I could see she was laughing, but the wind snatched her laughter away and tossed it across the waves. Now, Malachy moves like a smooth, powerful steamroller; he covers the ground at a terrific rate, but they still couldn't catch me until I finally stopped my mad gallop a mile or so down the beach.

Shannon reined in the trembling horse. Her cheeks were pink and her eyes sparkled and she was smiling from ear to ear.

"You'll do," I said, eyeing her approvingly. "I thought I'd best throw you in the deep end with Malachy, but you can really ride, girl. I may have to keep you here until the hunt. You'd enjoy it."

We trotted companionably back to the path and cantered through the bracken-fronded trails leading to the ruins of the Big House. I wanted her to see the setting of Lily's story and I unlocked the padlock on the heavy front door and pushed it open. Beams of sunlight filtered through the broken windows, illuminating the crumbling stone walls and broken floors of the great Gothic hallway. There was a gaping hole where the wonderful sweeping staircase had been and a pile of dust where the elaborate plaster ceilings had crashed in ashes the night of the torching. Just looking at it brought back waves of nostalgia for my own childhood. "I lived here until I was twelve years old," I told Shannon. "Oh, and what a fun childhood I had. And I'm not sure it wasn't even better after the fire, when we went to live in the other house."

We left the house and walked through the walled garden with the espaliered pear and peach trees, shriveled now from neglect. "At this time of year," I told her reminiscently, "they would be casting a golden glow across that old coral-colored brick wall. The sun would be glinting off the glass houses where we would go to steal the figs and black

Moscovy grapes from the hothouse. They were so big the juice would run down my elbows and stain my dress and then I'd be caught and given a wigging."

Remembering, I could almost *taste* those grapes, and that's the way it was again later that night, after supper when we sat once again in front of the drawing room fire; I could almost *taste* the story I was about to tell, it was so vivid in my mind.

But first I must tell you I was wearing Chanel 1934; jade-green chiffon with a handkerchief-point hem and my dusty diamond earrings and bracelets. That young flatterer Edward told me I looked wonderful and presented me with a large bouquet of red roses and a big box of chocolates, bought in Galway.

"You don't have to resort to bribery," I said, pleased. "I promise to tell you more of the story tonight."

After dinner, I watched Eddie go to sit beside Shannon on the sofa and her soft welcoming smile as she made room for him. Now, wouldn't it be interesting, I thought, if they were to fall in love? But I daresay I'm getting ahead of myself again, the way I always do.

I said, "Just remind me dears, where we left off."

"Lily was riding at dawn with Finn O'Keeffe," Shannon prompted eagerly.

"Ah, yes. Finn. Well, why don't we begin at the beginning?" Propping my feet comfortably on one of Lady Nora's little tapestry footstools, I began to tell them the story of the past, just as I had heard it myself.

CHAPTER
13

CONNEMARA, 1879

PADRAIG O'KEEFFE HAD WISPY carrot-colored hair and a pasty complexion peppered with freckles and warts. His jaw hung slackly and his ever-open mouth displayed a few remaining stubs of yellow teeth. His chest was concave from years of smoking, his short legs were bandy and his arms long as a gorilla's. Everybody said Paddy O'Keeffe was the ugliest man alive.

And then how was it, they always asked themselves, marveling, that such an ugly man had two such handsome sons?

"Why, 'tis me breeding," he would boast, after a few jars. "My ancestors go back to Brian Boru and the High Kings of Ireland." He would ignore the fact that his wife came from an exceptionally good-looking family, and that he was the runt of the O'Keeffes. "Brian Boru was a handsome fella, even for a king," he would add, as though that explained it.

Of course he was no more descended from Brian Boru than anyone else in the village, and people laughed at him and his crazy ideas. But they didn't laugh at Daniel, tall as an oak and strong as an ox, with a fine head of curly red hair; or at young Finn, two years his junior, as straight and slender as a sapling, his hair as black as night and his gray eyes the color of the skies over Galway Bay with the sea mist drawing in. Dan was intelligent and methodical, and quick with his fists, but Finn was mercurial and sharp-witted, quick to learn and quick to laugh. If Dan was good-looking, then Finn O'Keeffe was beautiful. He was also a charmer. His only problem was being born poor.

Paddy had worked in the stables at Ardnavarna all his life. His wife had been employed at the Big House as a laundress and her younger children often accompanied her to work, playing in the kitchen yard or helping around the stables, knowing, even as tots, to hide out of the way if the lordship came by.

Their childhood was scarred by poverty and deprivation. The area had lost almost half its population forty years earlier in the Great Famine and the resulting exodus to America on the fearsome coffin ships. Then, when Daniel was twelve and Finn ten, their mother died, along with six of their brothers and sisters in one of the influenza epidemics that regularly swept through the countryside, decimating the poor population overnight. It left Finn and Daniel to be brought up by their father, Paddy, who cared more for drink than he ever had for his wife.

Their thatched whitewashed stone cottage consisted of a single room with an earthen floor. It had a sleeping loft over one end and a "cupboard" next to the enormous hearth where the eight children all slept, crowded in together like a litter of noisy pups. A peat fire smoldered constantly in the grate, and a black iron cauldron of watery soup bubbled over its sullen glow. A line of fish, caught by Daniel in the bay, was strung across the hearth to smoke, adding an indescribable odor to that of the peat and of the chickens scratching about in the straw in one corner of the room.

The smell clung to the boys' hair. It permeated their clothing and even their skin; it was so much a part of them that they were no longer even aware of it. That is, until the day twelve-year-old Finn was helping out at the Big House, hauling great buckets of coal up the steep back stairs and along the miles of richly carpeted corridors, and later fueling up the big stoves in the kitchen.

"God save us, boy," the housekeeper cried in front of the giggling maidservants, throwing her apron over her head and hurrying past him. "Y've the smell of a wild animal about ye. Git out o' here and take yer odor with ye. And don't come back till y've had a bath."

Bitterly ashamed, Finn dropped his empty buckets and ran to the stables where Daniel was helping his father muck out the stalls. Flies buzzed around them as they raked out the dung-matted straw and Finn stopped and stared, taking in for the first time their position in the world of the Big House. He and his father and brother were the lowest on the scale, the shifters of muck and haulers of coal and ashes.

"What's wrong with ye?" Daniel asked, leaning on his rake, looking at his brother. Finn's eyes were wild and angry and his cheeks burned with color.

"Are ye sick, boy?" Dan demanded, striding over to him. Memories of his mother and six brothers and sisters on fire with the fever that had carried them off crowded his mind as he clapped a large hand to the boy's forehead, inspecting him anxiously. It was cool and he breathed a sigh of relief. With his mother dead and his father drunk more often than not, Daniel had taken over the role as head of the ramshackle household and he took his responsibilities toward his younger brother seriously.

"It's an old head on young shoulders ye'll be after gettin'," the neighbors said of him. "And you only fourteen years old." But they thought proudly that he looked nearer eighteen with that height and those broad shoulders. Everyone knew Daniel O'Keeffe would grow into a fine strong man and make a good husband for one of the village girls, but young Finn was a different matter. With those looks and that blarney you could expect woman-trouble, they told each other darkly over heady draughts of poteen, thinking they must remember to lock up their daughters when Finn O'Keeffe came into his manhood.

But right now Finn didn't feel much like a potential threat to any woman. All he felt was a deep burning shame and a rage with himself for not even knowing that he stank.

"Why didn't you tell me?" he demanded, kicking viciously at the pile of dung. "Why didn't you say I stank as bad as the horse shit? Worse. Like a wild animal, she said. And everybody laughed." His gray eyes were black with anger and Paddy stared, astonished, at his son.

"Jayzus boy, ye only stink like all the rest of us. What's wrong with ye?"

Daniel felt the blush of shame sting his own cheeks as he stared at his brother. It was all his fault. He was the one in charge. He should have known to keep the house clean, to make sure they washed themselves thoroughly each day and that their clothes were laundered.

"We niver stank when our mammie was alive," he shouted angrily. Throwing down his rake he grabbed Finn's arm and marched him over to the pump. "Strip off yer clothes, lad," he bellowed.

Finn hesitated. There was an edge to the wind and he knew the water would be icy.

"Now," Daniel commanded, his voice echoing around the cobbled yard so loudly that the grooms and stablelads turned to look. They grinned as Finn quickly shed his clothes and crouched like a martyr next to the pump, his hands over his private parts, shriveled to the size of a peanut in the cold.

Daniel filled the galvanized tin bucket and threw the icy water over him. Finn howled and the stable yard rang with mocking laughter as

Daniel filled his bucket again and again with stinging cold water and threw it over his shivering naked brother.

"Y'll find clean sacking in the tackroom," he said finally. "Wrap yerself up in it and be away home with ye. Tonight we'll wash yer clothes, and then tomorrer no maidservant will be able to complain that me brother stinks."

Finn ran through the woods to the lane that led to their cottage. He shivered in the wind, lurking by the hedgerow afraid someone might see him half-naked and blue with cold, wrapped in nothing but a bit of scratchy old sacking. His heart sank as he heard the clip-clop of hooves along the rutted lane and he peered around the corner, afraid of who it might be.

His eyes widened with horror and he groaned out loud, hurling himself into the ditch beneath the hedgerow. The horses hooves clipped-clopped toward him and he pressed his head deeper into the mess of brambles and stinging nettles, praying they wouldn't notice him. Then he heard them slowing.

"Why, Ciel, what do you suppose we have here?" a silvery, imperious voice said loudly.

Finn shrank even deeper into the ditch until his nose was almost in the rank green water at the bottom. He heard five-year-old Ciel giggle.

"I do believe it's a wild animal," she said. "Maybe it's a bear, Lily. Do we have bears in Ireland?" she added doubtfully.

"Of course we do. *Dancing* bears," Lily retorted. Then, inspired: "I know what, Ciel, shall we make this one dance?"

"Oh, *Lily.*" Ciel, as mischievous as her sister, squealed excitedly.

Finn heard the clatter of hooves as the horse was nudged around. He felt the gentle jab of her riding crop as Lily leaned from her horse and poked him in the ribs. "Come out, come out, whoever you are," she sang. He heard the laughter in her voice and smelled the clean soap smell of her hands as he turned his head slowly up to look at her.

"Come on, little bear," Ciel trilled, bouncing impatiently up and down in her saddle. "You're going to dance for me. Isn't he, Lily?"

Finn climbed slowly from the ditch, seeing Lily's blue eyes widen with surprise and then amusement as she stared at him. He hung his head in shame, clutching the sacking closer, praying to disappear. Of all the people in the world he had not wanted to see right now, she was the one.

"Why," Lily said triumphantly, "it's Finn O'Keeffe. And I do believe, Ciel, that under that sacking, he's as naked as the day he was born."

"Naked. *Oooh.*" Ciel's voice was shocked. Baby though she was, even she knew you did not walk around Ardnavarna unclothed.

Finn's chin sank lower into his chest. "I . . . my clothes got dirty," he mumbled. "My brother put me under the stable yard pump . . . I was walkin' home when ye caught me."

Twelve-year-old Lily stared at him interestedly. She had known Finn O'Keeffe all her life. They were born in the same month in the same year, and he and his brother had always been around, working in the stables or the gardens, hauling and lifting and fetching and carrying. She had accompanied Lady Nora to his cottage when his mother and all his brothers and sisters had died, carrying the great basket of food for the three-day wake that was to follow. She knew his ugly father, Paddy O'Keeffe: "a drunken lout" her father always called him, "but a fine man with a horse." Paddy O'Keeffe couldn't tell when his own boy stank, but he knew what to do when a horse went lame or off its feed. And there was the big brother, Daniel, a true bear of a lad. Not skinny like this one. Even though he had a handsome face. She had heard he was full of blarney, too, and as much of a tease as she was herself.

She glanced sideways at her sister and said, "Do you really want him to dance, Ciel?"

"Oh, yes, yes. Yes, *please.*" Ciel pushed her red curls from her eyes excitedly. "Can he do it now, Lily?"

Lily sat tall and straight-backed in her saddle. She lifted her chin to an imperious angle. Tickling his ribs again with her riding crop, she said, "Dance, Finn O'Keeffe. Dance like the wild bear you are for my little sister."

Anger flared in his eyes. "I'll not be dancing like a bear for Miss Ciel nor nobody," he shouted.

"Oh, yes, you will," Lily leaned teasingly forward. "I *command* you to dance."

"Dance, dance, dance," Ciel chanted, beside herself with excitement. "Dance, my little bear."

Finn stared at her, relenting. She was just a baby. Aye, and she was the lordship's daughter, what harm could it do to please her? Clutching his sackcloth safely over his loins he turned slowly around and around in the middle of the lane.

Ciel clapped her hands and Lily laughed. "Faster," she cried. "Faster, dancing bear."

"I'll not be dancing anymore," he said, hating her for laughing at him. "I only did it to please the wee girl." They stared at each other, her so immaculate in her London riding habit, her white silk stockings and the little bowler hat over her black curls. Her so fresh and clean, so pink and white with her mocking blue eyes. And him, barefoot in a piece of stable yard sackcloth having just had the stink washed out of him.

He turned angrily away to avoid her mocking eyes and started to walk down the lane toward home.

"I did not dismiss you, Finn O'Keeffe," Lily called after him.

"I told you I'll be doin' no more dancing," he shouted angrily back over his shoulder.

He heard the sound of galloping hooves and he glanced up just as she drew level with him. Leaning sideways in the saddle, one arm extended, she grabbed the sacking and dragged it away, leaving him stark naked in the middle of the lane.

"Jayzus," he screamed, clasping his hands over his private parts again while Lily twirled the piece of cloth triumphantly over her head. "Jayzus, me lady," he screamed again, bending double and running as fast as he could away from her, down the lane.

"Oh, Lily, look at the dancing bear's bottom," he heard Ciel shout. And then Lily's peals of mocking laughter, each one like a nail of humiliation in his heart as he ran to the safety of his home.

"DON'T EVER TELL what happened," Lily warned her little sister as they trotted back into the stable yard.

"Why not?" Ciel demanded innocently.

"Because Pa wouldn't like it," Lily explained, slightly shamefaced.

A groom in the Molyneux uniform of green-and-white striped shirt, green vest, and beige britches ran to help her dismount, but Lily ignored him. She swung herself easily from the saddle and strode across the yard with Ciel running behind her. She frowned as she passed the mountain of dung.

"What a stink," she said angrily. She glared at Daniel, dirty and unkempt, leaning on his rake staring at her. "See that it's moved at once," she ordered, "or when my father returns I shall tell him that the stables are a disgrace." She walked away and Ciel stared doubtfully at them and at the muck pile, and then she hurried after her sister.

"That's the second time today somebody's complained of a stink around us," Paddy said with a toothless grin.

"Aye, and it'll be the last," Dan vowed, staring angrily after them, thinking what a high and mighty little princess she was, and that if he were her pa he'd give her a kick up the arse.

Ciel turned to wave at him as they went through the stone archway dividing the stables from the rest of the property and he waved back, grinning shamefacedly. "Aye, and the little one's only a baby with a load o' charm about her. And Lady Lily's only a wee slip of a girl," he said forgivingly, forgetting for the moment that she was only two years younger than himself, who was already expected to behave like a man, and the same age as his brother Finn who also worked a man's hours, and with no mother to look after him. Hefting a shovel he began to shift the muck into the wheelbarrow to be carted away.

Lily strode through the stone-flagged hallway with Ciel at her heels, the way she always was—as though she were attached by some invisible link. Up the great curving staircase to the second floor and then left down the long gallery, lined with pairs of mahogany doors so tall that they reached almost to the lofty ceiling. Marble plinths with carved busts of Roman emperors and Greek warriors were placed between each set of doors and enormous oil paintings covered the dark-green watered-silk walls. A long red carpet stretched the length of the highly polished oak floorboards, all the way to the pair of double doors at the far end that led to the children's wing.

The doors were suddenly flung open and a harried-looking thin-faced woman peered out. "There you are," she cried angrily. "I've been looking all over for you."

"We just went out for a ride, Miss Nightingale," Lily said, smiling ingratiatingly at the governess. "Did you want us then?"

Miss Nightingale snorted angrily and her eyes misted over with tears of frustration. "You know perfectly well you were supposed to be here for your lessons. Now look at the time. The morning is wasted."

"Not for me, Miss Nightingale," Lily sang out as she ducked around her and ran, lightfooted, along another, narrower corridor to her room. She flung herself onto the bed, kicking her heels in the air and shrieking with laughter as she thought of Finn O'Keeffe dancing like a bear to her command and then fleeing down the lane naked as the day he was born.

"Did you see him, Ciel?" she demanded as Ciel bounced, laughing, on the bed beside her. "Did you just see him? Oh, he'll never forgive me. Never. I'm sure of it."

"To be sure, he will," her little sister said, gazing adoringly at her. "Everybody always forgives you, Lily."

And, of course, he did. She saw him the next day helping his brother polish the glistening coachwork of the carriages.

She and Ciel had been to the hothouses to steal the Moscovy grapes intended for the dinner table. There were telltale purple stains around their mouths and Lily tried to wipe them away with a corner of her pink cotton skirt. She glanced sideways at Finn. He was watching her out of the corner of his eye though he was pretending not to, and she grinned conspiratorially at Ciel.

She thought he had an interesting face, now that she got a proper look at it instead of at his bottom. A handsome face too.

"Was I really rotten to him, Ciel?" she whispered, and baby Ciel nodded her red curls emphatically.

"Oh, yes, Lily," she whispered loudly. "You were very rotten."

"Was I mean?" she asked, biting her lip.

"You were mean." Ciel repeated positively.

"Well, then. I suppose there's nothing else to do."

Smoothing down her skirt, Lily strode purposefully toward him. Sticking out her hand she said sweetly, "My sister says I was mean to you yesterday and I've come to apologize." She gazed at Finn, her hand held out, her brilliant-blue eyes innocent, and he stared back at her thinking that today his tormentor looked like an angel from heaven.

"Well?" Lily demanded impatiently. "Are you going to accept my apology or not?"

"I am so, me lady," he retorted, wiping his hand on his pants' leg and taking hers gingerly. It felt soft as dandelion down and he smiled at her, his whole face lighting up.

"I like you better when you smile," Lily told him. "Better than when you're wailing like a banshee." She grinned at him, and leaning forward whispered, "I won't tell anyone what happened. At least not yet. Just so long as you do what I tell you."

He backed off warily, his gray eyes full of suspicion. "And what's that ye'll be havin' in mind?"

Lily sighed exaggeratedly. "There's no need to be afraid . . ."

"I'm niver afraid of you," he shouted, his face reddening with anger again.

"Oh, you are impossible, Finn O'Keeffe." Lily stamped her foot, glaring back at him. "And all I was going to do was ask you to ride with me tomorrow."

"Ride with you?" He stared at her, saucer-eyed with amazement.

"They tell me you are a fine horseman. Almost as good as I am myself. I thought we would put it to the test. A race along the strand. Tomorrow at dawn." She shrugged her slender shoulders. "But naturally, if you are afraid . . ."

"I can outride you any day o' the week."

She had got his back up again and she knew it. Finn saw from her eyes she was enjoying it and he cursed himself for rising to her bait. He looked at her, tall and slender, still a child in her pink cotton frock with grape stains around her mouth, her glossy black curls tousled, her blue eyes set like jewels in her lovely face, and her baby sister clutching at her skirts. His heart did a double flip, then sank somewhere into his belly. "You're only a girl," he said with a cheeky grin. "And tomorrow you'll find out you're no match for a man like me."

"A man?" Her chin tilted upward and her eyes flicked over him from head to toe and back again. "We'll see whether you are a man or boy, Finn O'Keeffe. Tomorrow at dawn."

She flounced off holding Ciel by the hand and he watched her, a happy little smile on his face, already seeing himself racing neck and neck along the strand with her.

"And what was all that about then?" Daniel demanded, polishing the barouche's always-gleaming bottle-green bodywork. "And what's that silly grin doin' on yer face?"

"Sure and it was nothin'," Finn said airily. "Just a bit of chat between me and the Lady Lily. And none of yer business with it."

THE NEXT MORNING Lily was up and dressed before dawn. She glanced affectionately at her still-sleeping sister. Ciel's mouth was open and her eyes were shut tight and her dark-red lashes looked like little curtains on the curve of her plump cheeks.

Lily smiled as she slid silently through the door with her two best-beloved dalmatians, Fergal and Mercury, trotting at her heels. Her four other dogs slept in the stables and as she walked through the archway into the yard they barked joyfully and bounded to greet her.

Finn was leaning nonchalantly against the door of a stall, looking as though he had been there for hours.

She stared at the waiting horses and then back at him. Her own favorite, a fast five year old, was already saddled up alongside an old hunter, good in his day but well past his prime. "You can't ride that hunter," she said bossily, marching over to the mounting block and swinging astride her own mare, held for her by a groom.

"Sure and is it yer little sister's pony you'll be wanting me to ride so ye can have an easy win over Finn O'Keeffe?" he demanded truculantly.

"He's an old hack. Tell the groom I say you should have Merchant Prince."

Merchant Prince was her father's favorite horse and Finn knew it. He said forcefully, "I'll not be riding his lordship's best horse. Not for anything. It'd be more than me life is worth if anything bad occurred to that beast."

Lily scowled; she had thought he would rise to the bait again, but he had had more sense. Merchant Prince was a stallion and the only man who could control him was her father. He was a valuable horse and Finn would risk neither her father's anger nor damaging the beast. But if he didn't have a good horse, it would be no fun.

"Oh, all right then. Ride Punch," she said as she walked her mare under the stone arch and onto the gravel driveway toward the bridle path that ran behind the house down to the sea.

Finn was on Punch in a flash, cantering next to her between the avenue of trees. "My father's in Paris, you know," she called to him. "He wouldn't have known about Merchant Prince."

"No, Lady Lily, mebbe he wouldn't." He reined back his mount to keep pace with her. "It's meself would have known."

She threw him a teasing glance. "Then it was a matter of integrity? Not fear?"

He glanced angrily at her. "Oh, damn ye, think whatever ye like," he yelled, and pounded off along the avenue and down the rocky path to the beach.

"This is where we start," Lily said, lining up her horse next to his. "Here, by this piece of driftwood. We race all the way to the end, then we turn and come back again."

He measured the distance. "That's over a mile."

"It is." She smiled and shouted quickly, "Ready, steady, go."

She shot forward like a bullet from a starting gun and Finn grinned as he dug in his heels and galloped after her.

Lily galloped astride like a man, feeling the horse move smoothly beneath her. The morning was cool and misty. The sand was hard under the horses' hooves and the air felt moist on her skin and she yelled out loud with happiness. She felt in tune with her world and nature and as close to God as anyone could. She turned quickly to look for Finn, just as he shot past her.

He was crouched low on the horse's neck like a jockey, keeping his weight off the beast to gain an extra burst of speed. She galloped madly after him, laughing and screaming as they swung around together and started back up the strand, neck and neck. It was only in the last ten yards that he pulled away from her to win.

He grinned triumphantly at her, waiting for her to berate him or accuse him sulkily of cheating. But she surprised him.

"They were right after all, Finn O'Keeffe," she said breathlessly, an admiring gleam in her eye. "You do ride like the wind and twice as good."

As they walked the horses back up the path she said, "Will you ride with me again tomorrow? At dawn?"

There was none of the old mocking tone to her voice and when she smiled at him it was with genuine friendliness. Her cheeks were pink and her damp black hair stuck close to her head. In her navy jersey and man's britches he thought she looked like a young boy. And when she stared at him with those wide, innocent deep-blue eyes, he would have happily ridden every dawn of his life with her.

"Tomorrow," he agreed, feeling as though life could offer him no greater pleasure.

CHAPTER

〜〜〜〜〜〜〜 14 〜〜〜〜〜〜〜

LILY'S PARENTS WERE AWAY on a visit to the Continent and there was no one to stop her from befriending the most humble of her father's servants. Anyway, she had always played around the stables, and she felt quite at home with him. She had picked up the stable yard language, to her mother's horror, and she even called her mother "Mammie," the way she heard the village children do. It was her own special term of affection for her mother, though it was only said in private, among the family. In society she and Ciel used the formal "Mama," and even Pa became "Papa."

She was out of her bed and into her jersey and britches, rain or shine, every morning before the sky was even pink.

"Where do you go all the time?" Ciel demanded jealously, waking up and catching her dressing.

"Out for a ride with Finn," she whispered, a finger to her lips as she crept from the room they shared because Ciel had refused to stay in the nursery. She always wanted to be with Lily.

It wasn't only the ride she enjoyed. She also liked it when they tethered their horses and sat companionably on the rocks, gazing out across the bay at the ocean pounding against Ireland's western shores, talking of this and that.

"I remember you from when I was very small," she said to Finn, lying on her back, gazing at the gray sky and twisting her braid around her finger. "You were always in the stable yard lurking behind the door of the tackroom or hiding in the hayloft, watching."

"And I remember you on yer pony when you were mebbe three years old. Your father had tied yer hands behind your back to teach you balance and the groom was walking you around the marshy bit of paddock where it would be soft if you fell off, and you were laughing as if it were all a big joke. There was no fear in you at all," he added admiringly.

She gazed silently at the sky for a minute, then she said, "And I remember when your mother and all your little sisters and brothers died. I came to your cottage. My mother had brought a big basket of food for the wake and I remember the tears on her face when she looked at the two of you." She sat up and looked into Finn's eyes. "I remember how you looked, your face so white and tight, like a mask in the light of the candles set on top of each little coffin. I tried to imagine how you must feel, losing everyone you loved like that. But I couldn't imagine it because I didn't know. I wanted to tell you I was sorry, and I just couldn't. But now I can."

Leaning forward Lily planted a kiss on his cheek. "So there," she said defiantly.

Finn put his hand to his face where she had kissed it, feeling as high as if he were flying with the seagulls overhead. His heart did that funny little leap again and then settled somewhere deep in his belly. "That's very kind of you, Lady Lily," he said shyly.

"You are never to call me that," she said crossly. "You are my friend and you shall call me Lily."

He thought he wouldn't dare call her by her name for ages, maybe even years; it just seemed too impertinent. But as the summer weeks passed they easily slid into being Finn and Lily, and they told each other things they would never tell anyone else.

He told her the truth about the way his heart was rent in two when his mammie and little brothers and sisters had died, and Lily told him she had cried for weeks when the dog she had had since she was five years old had been caught in a poacher's trap and she had found it, broken and bleeding. The poor thing had had to be shot and she would never forget it. He showed her where the faerie glades were in the woods and told her the old country stories of leprechauns and pixies, and tales of banshees and goblins. And she showed him the drawing she had made of him, sitting astride Punch with the wind blowing his black hair into his eyes. "You have nice eyes," she added shyly.

The long days of freedom were quickly over. Her father and mother returned from their trip abroad and Lily and Ciel ran around the flagstone hall, screaming with excitement when they heard their carriage on the gravel. William, thirteen and solemn as an owl in his wire-rimmed spectacles, watched them disdainfully. "You're nothing but a pair of ragamuffins," he said scornfully.

The butler marshaled the smiling staff into a line in the hall and went to stand on the steps to welcome his master and mistress, and Ciel and Lily darted under his feet, even giddier than the excited dogs who were already racing toward the carriage.

"Darling girl," Lord Molyneux boomed as he swung Lily into his arms, kissing her fondly. "I missed you. *And* you," he added, planting a kiss on top of Ciel's curls. "Now, come and tell me all you've learned since I've been away. And all you've been doing."

"Aye, and she's been doing more than she's been learnin'," the butler muttered under his breath as Lord Molyneux strode past him into the hall. All the servants knew about Lily's rides with Finn. Sure and wasn't Paddy O'Keeffe himself boasting about it in the shebeen every night, though it wasn't something any of them approved of. Friendliness was one thing, but even though Lady Lily was just a child, they knew she ought to keep her place.

Lady Molyneux greeted her staff warmly. She shook hands with each one as she walked down the line and asked after their families, and they smiled affectionately back at her. But it was a different matter with his lordship. He walked briskly past them with barely a nod. With him it was all deference and respect. Sure and it was only his rightful due, they conceded later. But they knew there would be no more long relaxed dinners in the servants' hall until the family packed up again and were back to Dublin for the Christmas holidays.

With Lord Molyneux in residence the Big House took on an air of tension and bustle. The first thing he did was to inspect his stables.

"Your mama is in charge of the house," he said to Lily, "but this is my world, darling girl. And yours, because I know you are like me."

His blue eyes, which were a match for hers, smiled at her and she smiled adoringly back, thinking how lucky she was to have such a wonderful man for her father. Especially when she spied Paddy O'Keeffe, cringing like a spider in a corner of the yard, shrunken and ugly, with his red boozer's nose and his pale, watery eyes. She thought of Finn and Daniel and she marveled that he had such good-looking sons.

Her father spoke pleasantly to Paddy, as he did to all his tenants— that is, if you ignored the harsh note of authority in his voice that made them tremble.

"Padraig O'Keeffe," he called. "Come out here and show your face."

Lily laughed as Paddy ambled over on his short, bandy legs, his long arms dangling, looking for all the world like an old chimpanzee. Her father turned to frown at her. "Never do that, Lily," he admonished with a flicker of anger. "These people are our tenants and we have a responsibility toward them. They are not as fortunate as you but that does not mean they are objects for your amusement."

"I'm sorry, Pa." Lily hung her head meekly, glancing at him out of the corner of her eye. He patted her arm comfortingly.

"Never mind," he said with a smile. "No need to get upset. I know you didn't mean anything wrong. You just never think."

Standing in the door of the tackroom, Finn watched the little performance silently. He stared at Lily, sitting sidesaddle today on Jamestown. She looked every inch the lady next to her lordly father. Their dawn rides along the strand seemed like a dream, and Lily had not looked his way once, though her father had nodded at him as he listened to Paddy's rambling tales of dogs and horses and poachers over the weeks he had been gone.

"This will be your son?" Lord Molyneux asked, pointing his whip at Finn.

"Aye, yer lordship, that will be Finn. And my other boy, Daniel, is the strapping fella yonder in the yard. Only fourteen, yer lordship, and will you be only lookin' at the size of him."

"I expect he gets it from Brian Boru," Lily said straight-faced, and her father glanced exasperatedly at her, a smile lurking at the corners of his lips.

"Mebbe, Lady Lily, mebbe," Paddy agreed eagerly.

"Bring the lads over here," Lord Molyneux ordered. "I would like a word with them."

Paddy waved his sons over and they came and stood, caps respectfully in hand, in front of their lord and master. Finn could feel Lily's eyes on him, but he dared not look at her. Instead, he stared boldly at Lord Molyneux. Even in a tweed jacket and cap his master looked every inch the all-powerful land-owning aristocrat and he knew this man's power over his life was complete.

"Without him we don't have a roof over our heads," his brother had explained to him when he had grumbled about their poor food and their ragged clothes in the cold of winter. "Without him we don't eat. We don't have peat in our hearth. We don't have clothes on our backs. Without Lord Molyneux and Ardnavarna we don't exist." There had been a gleam of anger in Daniel's eyes. "That's the way it's always been for the Irish," he had muttered bitterly, staring into the smoking peat fire as though he were seeing a bad dream.

"You have two fine-looking boys here, Paddy," Lily's father said, looking them up and down, noting Daniel's ox-like build and Finn's wiry thinness. "I hear the young one is a fine horseman."

Finn pushed a lock of dark hair from his eyes. He glanced quickly at Lily, wondering if it was she who had told him, but she looked coolly back at him without a flicker of recognition. He stared back down at his boots, his face burning. Sometimes he wished he had never met Lily Molyneux.

"How would you like to be personal groom to my children?" Lord Molyneux asked Finn. He did not smile but his tone was genial and his offer was certainly generous.

Finn lifted his head proudly. "That would be grand, me lord." Daniel dug his elbow quickly in his ribs and he added hurriedly, "And I'll be thankin' ye, sir, for the job. I'll do me best for the young ones, sir," he added, though in fact only Ciel was younger than himself.

"I would like you to help Lord William," Lord Molyneux continued. "My son needs someone closer to his own age to give him confidence. I look to you, Finn O'Keeffe, to make him into a horseman, for I surely have not succeeded."

"I promise you I will, sir," Finn said eagerly. He liked William, and he thought he knew how to help him get over his fear and dislike of horses.

Lord Molyneux studied Daniel. Though he held his cap respectfully in his hand, he met his eyes boldly, and there was no doubt the lad's physique was remarkable for a boy of only fourteen. He said, "Daniel, you will work with O'Dwyer, the head gillie, and when I have guests you can help him. And you can also work alongside the gamekeepers. Learn all you can about the job so you can help on the shoot."

"Yes, sir. Thank you, your lordship." Daniel's face lit up. He was being taken from the menial drudgery of raking muck and polishing carriages to learn a skill. It was a big step up in the world for a lad like him and he knew it.

"Speak to the land agent about uniforms," Lord Molyneux commanded as he trotted off with his daughter at his side.

Finn watched longingly as they turned through the arch. Lily had been his friend but she hadn't even looked at him. She seemed so remote, so different. He was turning dispiritedly away when she glanced back at him and winked. A huge grin split his face. She hadn't forgotten him after all. And he knew what that wink meant. That now he was to be her personal groom, he could be with her anytime she wanted. They could still have their dawn rides together. Nothing had changed—except for the better.

His heart soared and he looked eagerly at his brother. Daniel grinned back at him. "We've cracked it, Finn," Daniel shouted excitedly. "We're on the way to success."

CHAPTER 15

CIEL MOLYNEUX THOUGHT growing up as Lily's sister was the best thing in the world, yet they were as different as they could be, both physically and temperamentally.

Ciel was smaller, more robust-looking than her tall, slender sister. She was full of fun and energy but always biddable, whereas Lily had a fiery temper and was a rebel. And Ciel's childish naughtiness was always tempered by caution and a fear of what might happen to her if she were caught, while impetuous Lily simply never even stopped to consider the consequences.

Growing up, Ciel was Lily's partner in crime, although sometimes it seemed to her that Lily was the one who came up with the ideas and it was always she who got to do the dreadful act. Lily caught the mice and the spiders, but it was Ciel who put them in the governess's bed; Lily thought of it, but it was Ciel who actually hitched up the governess's skirt at the back while Lily distracted her, leaving the poor woman walking around the house with her bloomers on display.

It was Lily who thought of putting mothballs in the visitors' bathwater instead of French bath salts, and Lily who dressed them as maidservants, waylaying the proper maids on the stairs and carrying the jugs of water for their parents' important visitors' baths. It was Lily who dreamed up the notion of sneaking from their beds to dress up as highwaymen in plumed hats with scarlet silk handkerchiefs hiding their faces, galloping at breakneck speed through the sleeping village, shooting off a pistol and raising folks from their beds in alarm. And it was Lily who decided they should creep out at night in search of the local still to find themselves a jug of poteen.

Ciel remembered with a shudder taking just one swig of the powerful stuff: it had burned her throat like fire, tears had sprung to her eyes, and she had coughed until she was sick. Not so Lily: a couple of stolen mouthfuls and she had been merry as a clown, laughing scornfully at Ciel's plight.

There had been the time Lily had dared her to jump the stepping stones at Travelers' Leap, over the rushing, gushing, deep icy waters. Ciel had slipped and would have drowned that time if Lily hadn't leaped in and, at mortal danger to herself, rescued her.

Lily had been terrified and full of remorse as she half dragged, half carried her back home through the woods. "I promise I'll never dare you to do anything again, Ciel darling," she had vowed, tears streaming down her face. "It's all my fault. I forgot you were just a little girl and I am so much older."

"I'll be more responsible in the future," she promised her frantic mother, though of course Ciel never told of Lily's dare. She never snitched on Lily. No one ever did, not even the servants.

Loyal Ciel didn't even tell when Lily thwacked her pony on its rump, sending it bolting across fields and hedges with her clinging grimly on and Finn O'Keeffe galloping frantically after her, shouting and cursing until the pony finally threw her and she lay, still as a dead person. Lily had flung herself screaming at Ciel's side while Finn ran for help.

"Oh, Ciel, Ciel, don't die," she cried, distraught. "I love you. Come back to me, Ciel. I'll never do anything so stupid again. Oh dear, oh dear. I just didn't think." But that was always Lily's cry.

Lady Molyneux burst into tears when she saw Dan O'Keeffe with her little girl lying limply in his arms. After the doctor had been in and pronounced eight-year-old Ciel to have only a mild concussion, Lord Molyneux had summoned Finn O'Keeffe to his study. He stared contemptuously at him, purple with anger. "I trusted my children to your care," he shouted, his voice echoing from the rafters. "And look what happens to them. How dare you pretend to be a responsible groom when my youngest child—the very one who merits your attentions most—falls from a bolting pony and is injured? She might have been killed. *And it would have been your fault.*"

Lily's tear-stained face turned even paler. She sat on the edge of her chair staring down at her tightly clasped hands, avoiding Finn's glance as she let him take the blame, praying he would not tell on her. She simply couldn't bear to have Pa and Mammie angry at her, and after all, she was truly sorry. Anyhow, Ciel was going to be all right, the doctor had told them so, and she would make it up to Finn later.

But her head shot up when she heard her father tell Finn he was demoted to stablelad and he could thank his good work with William for the fact that he was not dismissed. "William is doing well," he told Finn coldly, "and you will continue to work with him. But for God's sake, lad, this time keep your wits about you."

Lily felt Finn's angry eyes on her as he walked past her to the door. After all, it's only a job as a groom, she told herself guiltily, and she promised herself faithfully she would make it up to him. Once Ciel was better and the crisis had faded from her father's mind she would soon talk him into giving Finn his job back.

She heaved a sigh of relief that Pa wasn't angry with her. He held out his hands to her and said, "Come here, Lily," and she ran to him. Holding her close he said emotionally, "I know it's a terrible thing for a father to favor one daughter over another, but all the time I was thinking it might have been you, Lily. It was you I was seeing, half dead in O'Keeffe's arms. That's why I wanted to kill that lad. For what might have happened."

Lily rested her pretty head against her pa's fine worsted jacket. She could smell his bay rum cologne and the freshness of his linen shirt, and a faint hint of the fine cigar he had been smoking. "You mustn't worry, Pa," she said sweetly. "I'm as good a horseman as Finn O'Keeffe. And from now on I'll keep my eye on Ciel. I promise you her pony will never bolt again."

Lady Nora was waiting for her in the hallway. She knew her daughter only too well, and her pretty, fine-boned face was drawn into severe lines as she caught Lily emerging from the study smiling.

"I want to speak to you, Lily," she said crisply.

"Yes, Mama." Noting her mother's coldness Lily used the formal "Mama" instead of her usual affectionate Irish "Mammie." She knew something was up and she walked apprehensively behind her mother to her little private sitting room.

"Close the door, Lily," Lady Nora said. She sat down wearily in the brocade-and-gilt chair by her desk. Frowning, she indicated that Lily should come to stand in front of her.

"I don't know what the truth of this matter is," she said severely, "but I can guess. I am quite sure it was you who was responsible for Ciel's fall, just as you always are. Though there's no use telling your father that, because he would never believe you could be so wicked."

Lily stared at her, shocked. Her eyes widened with horror. "Oh, Mammie, I am not *wicked*. How can you say that?" She flung herself, in a torrent of tears, at her mother's feet. "It's not true, Mammie, it's not true that I'm wicked." She sobbed, clutching her mother's knees and gazing piteously up at her. She couldn't bear her mother to be angry with her, she adored her almost as much as Pa. She clutched her mother's knees tighter. "Please don't say that. It's just that I didn't think."

"You never *think* until it is too late, Lily," her mother said coldly. "It is a serious flaw in your character and one you must endeavor to change."

"But how can I change?" Lily demanded tearfully. "I am what I am. A stupid, silly girl who never thinks."

"No one is only *what they are*," Lady Nora said, relenting a little. "We are also what we make of ourselves. Otherwise we would all be savages, no better than unlearned children."

"Yes, Mammie."

Lily hung her head and Lady Nora sighed, staring down at her perplexing young daughter. "You are almost thirteen years old now, Lily," she said at last. "I'm wondering whether it's not time to send you away to school in England for a year. Maybe the teachers could put the fear of God into you, because I certainly cannot."

"Jayzus, Mammie." Lily leapt to her feet. "You can't send me away to school."

"Kindly do not use the language of the stable yard to me," Lady Nora said icily. "And I shall have a word with your father this very day on the matter. In the meantime you will apologize to your sister and you will spend every minute of your time by her bedside in the sickroom, attempting to keep her from dying of boredom if not from the fall off the pony. You will eat all your meals in the nursery and you will not leave this house for an entire week. Is that clear?"

"Yes, Mammie. Of course." Lily accepted her punishment graciously; after all, she deserved it. "But about school, Mammie . . ."

"You may go now, Lily," her mother said, turning to the papers on her desk. "And remember, I don't want to see your face down here for another week."

Lily trailed despondently from the room. Not that she minded keeping Ciel company, and she certainly didn't want to go to the stables and face Finn O'Keeffe's white-hot anger, but this business about the English school terrified her. She resolved to speak to her father as soon as possible, even though it would mean breaking the promise she had just given to her mother not to show her face downstairs again for a whole week.

Lily waited until after dinner. For once there were no guests at the house, and she knew her mother would have gone to her boudoir, where she would be making yet another needlepoint seat-cushion for the set of forty Sheraton dining chairs. "A lifetime's work," she called it, choosing a different flower for each one, and a motto running like a ribbon along the edge.

Ciel's freckles stood out like spots against her milky white face and there was a big bandage around her head. She sighed as she watched her sister open the door and peer out.

"Oh, Lily," she breathed anxiously, "this time you'll be whipped for certain if you're caught."

"I won't be caught," Lily promised, closing the door silently behind her.

Lamps blazed along the corridors, as they always did throughout the entire house with no thought of economy, because there was simply no need for any. Lord Molyneux liked his house lit like a Christmas tree. "It's like a beacon, so anyone who wants me knows I am here," he would say proudly. "Just the way they know I am in residence when they see my standard flying from the roof."

Lily crept cautiously along the bright corridor, past the rows of doors and down the stairs to the first-floor landing. The servants had been warned that she was not allowed downstairs and she glanced apprehensively along the corridor to her mother's boudoir. But she had chosen her time well; the servants were eating their supper and her mother's door was firmly shut.

She ran noiselessly down the last flight of stairs, across the hall and along the corridor to the west wing and the library, where she knew her father went every night after dinner, to smoke his cigar and drink a glass of port and read the *Irish Times*.

She pushed open the door a crack and peeked in at the shelves of leather-bound books and the set of globes of the ancient world, and the heavy, claw-footed tables and deep club chairs of green leather. A fire glowed in the grate and a curl of blue smoke wreathed into the air over her father's head. He was sitting in his favorite chair in front of the fire wearing his dark velvet smoking jacket and reading the newspaper, just as she had known he would be. His back was toward her and he had not heard her enter.

She crept up behind him and put her hands over his eyes. "Guess who?" she whispered.

He turned around, astonished. "Darling girl, you are not supposed to be here. Your mother told you."

"I know, Pa, I know. I was just so upset. Not about being punished, because that's right. I know that. But about the English school. Oh, Pa, dearest Pa, please don't send me away. I couldn't bear it. What would I do at school all day? Alone? In England? I would be so miserable. I'd never get to see you, and I would miss you so very much."

She knew instinctively which words to use to persuade him. It would have been no good saying, "I don't want to go to school, I don't want those strict teachers telling me what to do." Instead she had told him exactly what he wanted to hear: that she couldn't bear to leave Ardnavarna and she couldn't bear to leave him. And she meant it.

Lord Molyneux looked affectionately at his daughter and she looked anxiously back at him. "Besides," Lily added with an upward glance at him through her lashes, "I would be so bored there I'd probably be even naughtier."

He laughed, easily won over. "I'll have a word with your mother tomorrow," he promised. "Now, off back to bed with you before she catches you."

"Good night, dear Pa. And I'm truly sorry about Ciel." She threw her arms around him and kissed him affectionately then tiptoed exaggeratedly across the room. She turned at the door, a finger to her lips and a mischievous gleam in her eyes, and he laughed.

"Little monkey," he said indulgently, turning back to his paper as she closed the door softly behind her.

CHAPTER
16

WILLIAM RODE AT A SEDATE TROT alongside Finn. He stared into space, thinking instead about his new telescope and the pattern of the stars in the heavens. William was no athlete, and though his pale face was attractive, like all the Molyneuxes, he could never have been called handsome. He was tall and thin like Finn, but the resemblance ended there. Finn's shoulders were wide, his belly was concave and his hips narrow; Finn had a vital, wiry strength and he carried his head proudly. "More proud than a peasant had the right," some grumbled, envying his progress up the ladder at Ardnavarna. And Finn was more than handsome, with his thin face and prominent cheekbones, strong features and wide, sensual mouth. And those cloud-gray eyes and dark lashes that turned every girl's head for miles around, even at barely thirteen years of age.

It was William who looked like the peasant, not Finn O'Keeffe. His fair hair was rumpled, his glasses had misted over in the rain, and his amiable fair-skinned face was smooth as a baby's. As usual he had been late and he had thrown on his riding clothes in a tearing hurry. Some buttons were buttoned wrongly and others not buttoned at all, and though he had got his boots on the right feet—at the second try— he had forgotten his hat.

He slumped bonelessly in the saddle, his shoulders stooped and his head sticking forward. Glancing at him, Finn sighed deeply. There was no way he was ever going to turn Lord William Molyneux into a horse- man, no matter what he did. All he could hope for was to keep the boy in the saddle and make sure he didn't break his neck.

The thought brought him full circle again to Lily, and he groaned out loud. He would kill her one day, he swore to God he would.

William did not even notice: he was there in the flesh, but in spirit he was back at school. Not that he was the most popular boy at Eton; he was too introverted and academic, but he loved English literature and poetry and was passionately interested in astronomy. And he loved being near the river, even in the bitter winter cold, because he was an avid bird-watcher.

He could lose himself—and all sense of time—lying on his stomach with his binoculars clamped to his eyes, watching for birds; and he was equally happy slumped in a chair with his nose in a book. He wrote treatises on the birds he saw, and on the stars and the planets, and he also wrote poems, though he had never shown them to anyone. Especially Lily, whom he knew would tease the life out of him.

William was a dreamer. He hated all the so-called "gentlemanly" sports—hunting, shooting, and fishing—and he was terrified of horses. His impatient, horse-mad father had forced him onto the backs of ponies since he was little more than an infant, and when his daughters proved fearless it had only made him more impatient with his son.

"The boy is always in his room," he would complain to his wife. "Always with his nose in a book. He should be outdoors, like a proper gentleman, riding with the hunt as befits his position, not watching damn-blasted birds!"

William stared down at the back of the horse's neck, seeing only the twin opaque circles that were his misted spectacles. The fact that he couldn't see through them didn't bother him; he wasn't even thinking about where he was going or what he was doing. It was simply a chore he was forced to undertake.

"Y'll be needin' to sit better than that, sir," Finn admonished him. "Straighten your back, Lord William, and take control of the beast. Else yer fayther will be onto me again for not teachin' ye right."

"Sorry, Finn." William straightened up obediently. "I wasn't thinking."

"Aye. That's what they tell me is your problem. But I could make a good horseman of you, if y'd only concentrate. Now will you just look at yerself, sir, trailin' along like a soppy girleen. I'm tellin' you, sir, your fayther is determined to keep you in the saddle, so it's better for yerself if you just makes up your mind to do it right. You've a fine brain in your head, sir, or so I've heard. It can't be difficult for you to learn something if you really want to."

"That's just it, Finn," William said sadly. "I don't want to. And I don't see why I should have to."

"Look at it this way, sir. You have yerself a fine home here at

Ardnavarna, and a fine life. One day it's going to be yerself takes over this place, and everyone around, from the other lords and ladies to your own tenants, is going to expect you to act properly, the way your fayther does. It's only right, sir, that you accept your duties the way we all have to, and make your fayther a happy man. At no great cost to yerself."

"What do you mean?" William rubbed his glasses with his sleeve to get a better look at Finn.

"Well, sir, and don't you have the finest teacher in the whole of Connemara in meself? Place yerself in my hands, sir, and with a bit of concentration we'll have yer fayther pattin' yer back an tellin' ye what a fine lad y'are, before this very month is out."

William stared interestedly at him. "One month, Finn? Is that really all it would take?"

"One month—of *concentration,* sir. And it is."

William thought it over carefully; if he sacrificed exactly one month of his life he could make his father a happy man and buy his freedom to do whatever else he wanted. "Then it's a bargain, Finn O'Keeffe," he said, offering his hand. "My time is yours for the next four weeks. After that I never want to see another horse again."

He told Ciel and Lily that night, warning them to keep it a secret from his father. "I want to surprise him at the end of four weeks," he said cheerily.

Lily stared jealously at him. Finn still hadn't spoken to her, though she saw him all the time in the stables. Now he was no longer her groom, he no longer had the right to wear the smart green uniform, and he was back in his old flannel shirt and cord pants. He wore a blue-and-white spotted handkerchief tied around his tanned throat and he looked handsomer than ever, and twice as angry as she had ever seen him before. There was a permanent scowl on his face whenever he looked at her and he went out of his way to avoid having anything to do with her.

She asked William what time his lesson was, and the next morning she was there before him. Finn was in Punch's stall, preparing him for the ride.

"It's like old times, isn't it, Finn?" she said, leaning across the stable door, smiling beguilingly at him.

"I don't know what y'mean, me lady," he said.

His voice was so cold she could have skated on the ice of it. "Sure and y'do," she said anxiously. "The two of us riding at dawn along the shore. Nothing there, just you and me and the seabirds."

He refused to look at her, tightening the girth and checking the bit. Anything rather than meet her treacherous eyes.

"I'm sorry, Finn, if I've hurt you. Truly sorry. But you see, it was you or me. Pa would have sent me away to school in England if he knew I had anything to do with Ciel's fall. We would never have seen each other again."

"All I know is it was my job was lost," he said tersely, brushing past her into the yard. "It was my livelihood you were playin' with. *My* job, *my* earnings, food in *my* belly. Not yours, miss high-and-mighty Lady Lily."

Lily stared at him, shocked. She hadn't realized what it would mean to him . . . that he might even have to go without food. She had thought it was only a temporary thing, that when her father calmed down she would easily get him reinstated.

"Oh, Finn," she said shakily, "I truly didn't realize what I had done. I thought it was just for a few weeks, and then I would talk Pa back into making you my groom again. I didn't even consider what it meant to you." She hung her head, twisting her hands together in an agony of remorse.

"I'll go right now to Pa. I'll tell him what a terrible thing I've done. I shall confess it was all my fault, and tell him he must reinstate you right away. Oh, God, I just know you'll never forgive me. Never. And you will be right."

Turning quickly, she ran across the cobbled yard. Finn ran after her and grabbed her by the shoulder. He stared into her face, into her brimming dark eyes, all their brilliance lost in her despair.

"You would do it, sure enough," he said, amazed. "Y'd go to your fayther and confess to the crime just to get me my job back."

"Of course I would. And I am. Right now." She twisted from his grasp and ran under the stone arch. He caught up with her and grabbed her by the arm again.

"Ye don't have to do this for me, Lily. It's enough to know you wanted to. I'll take the blame for young Ciel, and it was partly my fault anyways. I was in charge of her and I should have stopped you from smacking her pony."

She smiled tremulously at him and he gazed adoringly back at her, completely forgetting that she was to blame and that it was not his fault at all.

"Then are we friends again?" she said.

"Friends." He nodded.

"And I can come along with you and William on the ride?"

He hesitated. "It's concentration he'll be needin', Lily. And y'know well enough there's nobody can concentrate with yerself around, plotting yer mischief."

"No mischief," she promised, gazing up at him through her lashes. "I just want to be with *you.*" She added softly, "I've missed you so, Finn. You are my *best* friend. Don't we always tell each other everything? Things we would never say to another person, not even Ciel or Daniel. About how we feel and what we wish and . . . oh, all our secrets?"

The sparkle jumped back into Finn's deadened eyes as his spirits soared. "Sure, and we're friends again. But mind y'behaves yerself, Lily, I'll not be responsible for another accident."

"They really wanted to send me away to school in England," Lily said, flirting with him with her eyes, "but I refused. I stamped my foot and told them I would not leave Ardnavarna. Never, no matter what they did. They could drag me from here screaming and I'd just run away and somehow find my way home again, the way lost animals do. Oh, Finn, how could I ever leave Ardnavarna? How could I ever leave my horses and my dogs, and the sea and the woods, and oh . . . all the beautiful things I love about this place? And how could I leave my friend?" she added, meeting his eyes solemnly.

He looked at her, saying nothing. He knew exactly how she felt and Lily knew that he knew. There were moments when they were as attuned as twins, each thinking the other's thoughts almost before they had thought them themselves.

"Race you to the end of the strand," she called, running to the yard and leaping onto her bay mare, held by the waiting groom.

"I can't be doin' that, Lily," Finn said seriously. "I'll be spendin' all me time with Lord William. On the instructions of your fayther."

"Oh. *William.*" Disappointed, she stared at him. "Well then, I'll just ride along behind you. And I promise and promise I will not be any trouble at all."

He thought exasperatedly that of course she would be, but she was the mistress and he was the servant and he could not forbid her, best friends or not. But he still did not trust her to keep her word.

William walked under the archway, reluctance in every slow step he took across the yard to where Finn stood, holding Punch. "Good morning, Lord William," Finn said, a sigh in his voice as he looked at him. "We're after making a grand horseman of ye. Just keep that in mind, sir, and y'll do fine."

William glanced suspiciously at Lily. "What are *you* doing here?" he demanded as he clambered laboriously onto the horse.

"I'm coming along to help." Lily's mare suddenly skittered sideways over the cobbles and she laughed as William's mount reared nervously and he clung desperately on.

"That'll be enough of that, Lady Lily," Finn shouted authoritatively. "Right, sir," he said to William. "I'll ride alongside you. If you would only straighten your back and grip with your knees, sir, and your thighs. All horsework is in the legs, and that's where you need the strength. Now, come on, sir, a straight back, a loose rein, and a good firm leg. That's all it takes to master a horse."

"And letting it know who's boss," Lily called mockingly, leading the way out of the yard to the bridle path.

William gritted his teeth. "One month," he said grimly. "Just four weeks, Finn?"

"Four weeks, sir. And that's a promise."

Lily cantered ahead, turning every now and then to look back at her brother trotting unevenly along, completely out of rhythm with his horse. She turned and trotted back toward them. "Like this," she called, showing him how easily it was done. "Don't be such a ninny, William. It's only a horse." Finn shot her a wary glance. "Oh, he's just so *slow*," she said impatiently.

An hour's boredom lay ahead of her like a yawn, so giving her mare a switch with her crop, she set off at a mad gallop through the green avenue of trees toward the rocky path to the beach. Waves pounded the shore, the sunlight turned the spray into a glittering rainbow, and the wind tugged at her hair. It was a glorious day.

"Oh, dammit, dammit," she shouted angrily, turning her mare and galloping back again to collect Finn. The day was so wonderful, they should be racing along the strand together instead of fussing with silly old William, who would never make a horseman even if his life depended on it.

She galloped toward them, ducking low in the saddle to avoid the overhanging branches, eager to hurry Finn for their ride. He saw her coming and so did William's horse, Punch. It stopped dead in its tracks, then with a whinny of fear it reared up, dancing on its hind legs like a circus pony. Then it suddenly pounded down hard on its front legs and bucked William off, prancing up and down, whinnying with terror, its hooves dangerously close to his head.

Finn was off his mount in a flash. Shouting curses he grabbed the horse's reins, and calmed it with a few words. He tethered it to a tree and looked down at William, lying stunned on the grass, and then up at Lily, still on her horse, circling self-consciously around them. "You bloody little fool," he yelled angrily. "Don't you ever think about what yer doin'?"

"He's not hurt, is he?" she asked anxiously, her face as white as her brother's.

"No thanks to you I'm not," William said, sitting up and rubbing his head.

"The horse might have trampled him to death and you know it," Finn said ferociously. "Now will ye be away? And only thank your lucky stars I'll not be tellin' your fayther this time. Just stay away from me and Lord William, that's all."

Lily stared blankly at him for a second and then without a word she turned and galloped off. Finn looked anxiously at William still sitting on the grass, rubbing the back of his head. "That sister of yours'll be a terror, sir," he said, helping him to his feet.

"More than that," William retorted. "She's a menace. How she gets away with what she does is beyond me. Except, I suppose, she never really means any harm." He glanced ruefully at Finn. "Anyway, Finn, that's the end of me and horses. I've had enough."

Finn thought of Lord Molyneux and the orders he had given him to turn his son into a competent horseman. . . . "The only reason I'm not dismissing you," he had said, "was because of your work with my son." He knew if he failed in his duty now, this time Lord Molyneux would surely dismiss him.

"I've got to teach you, sir," he said angrily. "Your fayther will flay me alive if I don't. Or worse, he'll sack me."

They stared at each other and William saw the fear of the poor in Finn's eyes. The fear of no job, no wages, no food in his belly. William was his father's son; the concept of duty had been bred in him and he knew where that duty lay now. He sighed. "Very well then, Finn, a horseman I shall become."

Finn sagged with relief. He knew what it had cost William to say that, after such a dangerous fall. His face shone with admiration as he helped him remount. "I'll look after y'sir," he promised. "I'll see you niver have to fear another horse in your life again."

LILY STUDIOUSLY AVOIDED being anywhere near the stables when her brother was with Finn. She would lurk around the house and as soon as she saw William walking wearily across the hall, mud-spattered from yet another long cold rainy morning in the saddle, she was at the stable yard in a flash.

"My turn," she would say laughingly to Finn, and they would be off through the woods, oblivious of the rain and wind, happy just to be together.

At the end of the four weeks Lord Molyneux came to inspect William's progress. He watched his son with hawklike eyes, looking for faults, but William sat properly upright in the saddle, his jacket neatly buttoned, his hat firmly on his head, and a look of grim resignation on his face.

"The boy has done well," Lord Molyneux said approvingly to Finn, watching as his son crouched low in the saddle to take a hedge and then galloped off across the fields. "I would never have thought it possible." He looked appreciatively at Finn, mounted on a black hunter beside him. "I have you to thank for that," he said, a touch of warmth creeping into his voice. "Because despite your other failings, Finn O'Keeffe, you are indeed a fine horseman."

"You may resume your old duties as groom to my children as of today. And there will be an appropriate increase in pay to take into account your good work. Speak to the comptroller about it later."

He looked severely at Finn. "And let this be a lesson to you, my boy. Always concentrate on what you are doing. I am trusting my children to you. You are responsible for them. Never—I repeat, never—take your eyes off them. And if anything happens to any one of them I'll have you strung from the nearest tree."

TWO DAYS LATER the dozens of trunks and boxes were packed; the lady's maid, the governess, and his Lordship's valet were sent on ahead, and the family prepared to leave for their usual sojourn in Dublin.

The staff lined up as they always did to see them go, and Finn's heart was in his boots as he watched the gleaming bottle-green carriages set off briskly down the mile-long gravel driveway. He peered after them, his eyes narrowed against the sunlight. He thought he saw Lily turn her head to look at him as they passed and he raised his hand in a sad farewell.

But it wasn't only Finn that Lily turned to look at. It was Ardnavarna. The blue-and-gold standard that flew over the Big House had already been lowered, signifying the family was no longer in residence; the sun glinted from its numerous windows and its massive stone walls looked as though they would stand for all time.

With a sigh of happiness she turned her head away, thinking excitedly of Dublin and the parties and the new dresses and all the treats in store for her, with never a thought for her best friend, Finn O'Keeffe.

CHAPTER
17

ARDNAVARNA, 1883

FOR LILY, IT WAS ALWAYS a case of "out of sight, out of mind." Finn belonged to Ardnavarna and when she was away, she scarcely gave him a passing thought. But it was all very different for Finn. He thought Lily Molyneux was the most beautiful girl in the world. She lived in his dreams and in his heart. She was a part of him. Quite suddenly, when he was sixteen and no longer just a lad, he fell passionately in love with her. And then everything changed between them.

Little Ciel was nine years old when Lily was sixteen. William was away at school in England most of the time and the two girls muddled along at home with their succession of harassed governesses. They learned to speak French and went several times to Paris so that they might have a chance to perfect their accent. They acquired a modicum of history and geography and they read whatever books were in their library. They could play the piano well enough, Lily better than Ciel, and they could sing a pretty song for their guests' entertainment after dinner in the grand drawing room. They played tennis and croquet and were demons on the hunting field. They were friends with royalty and nobility and shared their parents' wide social life in Dublin and London, as well as at the shooting and fishing parties their parents often hosted.

They were a happy family. William was too often the butt of Lily's teasing, but he knew that she loved him and she could be counted on to protect him from his father's impatience and anger by diverting his attention.

They were proper young ladies. Ciel was what she always was: loud, bubbly, and joyous. She had such a zest for life and her laugh was irresistible—people simply had to join in. She was guileless, with none of Lily's subtle lingering glances and flirtatious ways. With Ciel, what you saw was what you got.

And Lily was just Lily. She grew up a beauty. Everyone adored her, no matter what she did. In London and Paris and Dublin, she drew eyes wherever she went. She was like a bright shining star, trailing magic in her wake, with young Ciel basking in her starry glow.

Finn watched her change from an impetuous, willful child into a beautiful young woman. Like his passion for her it seemed to happen overnight. One minute she was just a girl riding along the strand in men's britches and a fisherman's navy blue jersey; the next she was a young woman, gowned in pale pink silk with pearls at her throat.

She was standing at her parents' side, greeting their guests for a ball they were giving to celebrate Lord and Lady Molyneux's twenty-fourth wedding anniversary, and Finn's hopes sank to zero when he saw her. It was his first night as a footman and he was dressed in green livery, taking the guests' fur wraps and silk hats and scarves.

He often helped out when the family threw their grand house parties. Whenever nobility and foreign royalty and celebrities came to stay, he and Dan acted as gillies or gamekeepers, or followed the hunt. And he often worked as a porter, hefting bags from carriages and carting them upstairs. He had noticed with awe the grandeur of the rooms and compared them with his own bare earthen-floored, smoky cottage. He had observed how different Lily was then, no longer the laughing high-spirited companion of their dawn gallops along the strand, now the young lady of the house. But he had never seen her as she was the night of the anniversary party.

She was an elegant grown-up young woman, gleaming with jewels and just as haughty and proud as her lordly father. And he was Padraig O'Keeffe's boy, a crack horseman who knew the best beat on the river for the salmon, and where trout were to be found in the lough any time of day or night. He was the hefter of bags and the footman in too-tight breeches and white gloves to prevent his peasant's hands from soiling the plates these lordly people ate from.

That night Finn finally understood the distance that separated him from Lily and her life at the Big House. It was a chasm he could never hope to cross.

Lily could feel Finn's burning eyes on her. She sipped her very first glass of wine and made a little face at its dry taste. She smiled at him, but he did not smile back and she wondered what was wrong. She glanced down the long table at her parents' sixty guests and the twenty liveried footmen serving them. The vermeil service kept for grand occasions was being used and the table glittered with fine silver and crystal. There were tall candelabra and bouquets of flowers and showy silver ornaments, and a dozen five-tier epergnes cascaded with exotic hothouse fruits, including the Moscovy grapes and fat purple figs she used to steal from the greenhouses when she was a child.

Lily smiled to herself as she realized what she had just thought. *When she was a child.* Because there was no doubt that tonight she felt different. And from the admiring glances the men gave her, and from the way their eyes held hers and the way they lingered over her hand as they bent to kiss it, she knew she looked it. She felt heady from the wine and her new sense of power. Men would do her bidding, they would dance to her tune, all for a special smile, a flirtatious glance, a touch of her hand. She felt that sweet ripple of excitement in the pit of her stomach. But promising what? She sighed impatiently; she could hardly wait to find out, and she consoled herself with the thought that soon she would be seventeen. She would make her debut, meet her Prince Charming, and marry him. And then she would know all the womanly secrets.

From the underground gossiping at tea parties and the social events she attended she knew that, like her, none of the girls her age knew what "it" was all about. And neither would she until the eve of her marriage and even then she might just be told to "be kind" to her new husband, and be reminded that "men had different needs" and that as a good wife she would be expected to take care of those, and naturally, to bear his children.

Of course, she was always around the stable yard and the paddocks and fields and she just couldn't help noticing the dogs and farmyard animals copulating. They looked so silly that she laughed, along with the stablelads, when she saw them. Until one day Finn had caught her and he had dragged her angrily away.

"You're forgettin' yourself, Lily," he had hissed, red-faced with anger. "That's not for your eyes, so don't you go sniggerin' with the stablelads."

"And what do you think you are then, if not a stablelad," she had retorted angrily. "Don't I laugh and talk with you?"

"That's different. And you know it," he had shouted as Lily stalked away.

She sipped her wine again, throwing a troubled glance at Finn. The fact was, though, Finn had changed. He had become serious, quieter, and he flinched from her touch as though it were a red-hot poker. She could feel his burning eyes on her back and she turned and winked mischievously at him, but he pretended not to see. She glanced irritably at the boring old general sitting on her left, and then at the man on her right.

Dermot Hathaway was twice her age and the handsomest man in the room, barring Finn, of course. He had a wide, fleshy face, prominent dark eyes, a curving mustache, and smooth dark hair brushed back from a widow's peak. He was the tallest man there, with massive shoulders and a muscular body. He was attractive and different and he had a bad reputation with women.

Dermot was descended from a family as old and noble as her own; their great-grandparents had been friends, and their grandparents and parents. But Lily had never met him before tonight. She knew he owned great tracts of land in Wicklow and County Clare and that he had business interests abroad that kept him constantly on the move, traveling to exotic places like China and India and America.

He hadn't yet spoken to her, except to say "good evening." Glancing covertly at him she realized that though he was quite old, at least thirty-five, he was rivetingly attractive. She batted her eyelashes flirtatiously at him and said, "I can only imagine how disappointed you must be, Sir Dermot, to be placed next to the daughter of the house. And she only sixteen."

He turned to look at her. For a long few seconds he said nothing; only his eyes absorbed her, sucking her in as though he were printing every inch of her onto his memory.

"The thought had crossed my mind," he said drily, at last.

She felt herself blushing. No one had ever looked at her like that before. Besides, she knew he had seen past the pink silk and the pearls and the upswept hair to the silly flirtatious child she still was. Well, damn *him*, Lily thought, sticking her chin arrogantly in the air.

"Then I can only apologize for my mother's error in seating me next to you," she said stiffly. "And hope that you won't be too bored."

"Indeed I shall not," he agreed, turning to speak to Margaret Donoghue on his right, who was, Lily knew, twenty-six and married. *And* she had skin like velvet. *And* she wore rouge and scent. *And* she was rumored to be bolder than she ought to be. Dammit, she groaned inwardly, the woman was gorgeous.

She stared resentfully back at her plate, ignoring every course until the sweet, which she demolished with childlike intensity.

Dermot watched her, a half smile on his lips. *She's going to be a little bitch*, he thought, but what he said was, "I see you like chocolate, Lily."

She glanced sideways at him. She had thought he was so busy with Margaret Donoghue that he hadn't even noticed her, and now she wished she had remembered to toy with the dessert, like the young lady she was supposed to be.

"I only ate it because I was bored," she said, meeting his eyes. Again they seemed to devour her, just the way she had devoured the sweet.

"Then if you were bored it's my fault. I apologize." And then he turned back to his companion, leaving her to talk to the old general on her left who was, she thought despairingly, even more boring than she was herself. She stared resentfully down at her plate again, smoldering with rage at Dermot Hathaway.

She remembered her mother saying he was a rich bachelor and that all the women were after him, but that only made him more intriguing.

She toyed in a proper ladylike fashion with the cheese savory on her plate, sneaking little glances his way every now and again, assessing his progress with Margaret Donoghue, wondering how it was though they never touched, they somehow looked as though they were touching.

On the other hand, she decided, with a hot little quiver of excitement, it might be fun to have handsome Dermot touch you. It might even be fun to be married to a man like that. To be the one finally to capture him. She stared down at her plate, seeing herself walking down the aisle, radiant in white duchesse satin just like her cousin Kate who had married last year. Except with dashing Dermot Hathaway waiting for her.

She imagined how people would talk, marveling that young Lily Molyneux had married such a catch when women had been trying for over a decade to pin him down. She caught Finn's eye again across the room and blushed, hoping he could not read her thoughts.

When dinner was over her mother rose and led the ladies to the drawing room, leaving the men to their port and cigars and masculine stories.

Dermot stood politely for her to pass, but Lily barely glanced at him. Yet later, when French champagne and coffee from Brazil and tea from China were served with candies and sugar-frosted fruits in the yellow drawing room, she contrived to sit near him. And when her father called on her to play the piano and sing for their guests, it was Dermot she saved her beguiling, long-lashed glances for, as she sang a sweet little French love song.

Standing at attention by the drawing room door, Finn closed his eyes, imagining she was singing just for him.

Then it was Ciel's turn. She had been allowed to stay up late because it was a special occasion, though she had not been allowed to attend the dinner because her mother thought it would not be fair to sit any of her guests next to a nine-year-old child. "Lily is child enough for one night," she had said firmly.

Ciel climbed onto the piano stool, gave a too-brisk rendering of a simplified Chopin étude, and clambered hastily off again to laughing applause. "Lily," she said in a loud whisper so that Dermot heard, "who is that man you are making eyes at?"

He turned to look at her and Ciel stared back at him with an engaging smile. He said, "I think it is the good-looking young footman."

Then he laughed as a hot blush of humiliation burned Lily's face and she turned and fled with Ciel, as always, at her heels.

Finn hurried after them, but Ciel turned to him, her finger to her lips.

"No, Finn," she whispered. "Not here. You can't."

He stepped back. Even little Ciel understood. Of course he couldn't be with Lily. He was Paddy O'Keeffe's lad and he knew his place.

CHAPTER
18

As HER SEVENTEENTH BIRTHDAY drew near, Lily spent more time in Dublin, shopping in Grafton Street with her mother and Ciel for lacy stockings and satin slippers and the long white kid gloves she needed for her double debut: one in Dublin and one in London.

Mrs. Simms, who was as famous in Dublin as any French designer in Paris, was making her presentation gown and half a dozen other ball dresses, in shades of cream and lemon and rose, ice-blue and nile-green. Only the presentation gown would be white, with a tight duchesse satin bodice and a sweeping skirt, as pure and virginal as a bride's. Except, as Ciel said breathless with envy, twice as much fun.

Her mother hurried Lily off to London to sit for her portrait, and for a round of tea parties, and then it was home to Ardnavarna, and the Big House crammed with friends, with roaring fires and enormous dinners. And long rides with Finn through the woods or along the beach.

"Do you niver miss me when yer away there in the big city?" he asked moodily one morning.

They had tethered their horses and were walking through a sheltered glade in the woods. Lily kicked at the soggy mulched leaves around the base of a tree, thinking about it. The truth was she didn't miss him: she was just too busy; and besides, Finn belonged to her life at Ardnavarna. Still, she couldn't bear to hurt him. "Of course I think about you sometimes," she said. "It's just that there's so much to do: shopping and fittings for my dresses, and luncheons and tea parties. You can't possibly understand what it's like there."

"That's true enough," he said bitterly, "since I've niver been to the city. I'm stuck here at Ardnavarna."

"Sometimes I wish I were too," she admitted, "when there have been too many late nights, too many people to smile at and make conversation with. Too many dowagers with questions to ask, and too many mamas with eligible sons consulting my mama. Oh, it's all lists, Finn, lists of people who may be invited and lists of people who may not."

"Like me."

She stared at him, exasperated. "There's nothing I can do about that. But it doesn't stop us being friends."

"Aye. When you remember me, that is." Finn flung himself back onto his horse.

"Oh, you'll never understand," she yelled.

"And nor will you," he retorted, galloping off and leaving her staring bewilderedly after him.

LILY'S SEVENTEENTH BIRTHDAY fell the day before the Lord Lieutenant's levee, which marked the opening of the Season, and her parents hosted a grand celebration ball at their house in Fitzwilliam Square. A green-and-white striped awning was erected to protect their guests from the inclement weather and a red carpet was laid over the front steps and across the sidewalk. The footmen wore green livery and powdered wigs, the champagne was pink, and the grand house bloomed like a garden under a mass of creamy hothouse lilies.

Her mother's maid laced Lily into a tight corset and then slipped the cream dress over her carefully upswept hair, fluffing out the delicate gold lace overlaying the rich satin skirt and exclaiming how gorgeous she looked.

Lily turned this way and that in front of the long mirror, and watching her, Lady Molyneux smiled a little regretfully as she realized her tomboyish little girl had suddenly become a young woman. She said, "Sometimes I am so used to you, Lily, I forget how lovely you are." She bent to kiss her. "This is a wonderful time for you, my darling. A girl's debut is something she never forgets, all the dresses and the parties and the excitement. It's the beginning of a whole new life, when everything still lies ahead and childhood is left behind. Enjoy it all, Lily. The next great event will be your wedding."

Ciel sat on Lily's bed watching enviously. Her dress was also made by Mrs. Simms, out of stiff blue taffeta that matched her eyes. It had a wide velvet sash and she wore matching blue satin ballet slippers. Her mother tucked a flower into her hair and said gaily, "Am I not the lucky woman to have two such gorgeous daughters? We shall be the talk of Dublin tonight."

"Only because you are so pretty, Mammie," Lily said, hugging her.

Lord Molyneux was standing with his back to the drawing room fire, holding up the tails of his coat and toasting his backside awaiting them. William stood nervously by the window. He would rather have not been there, but like his sister, he was now expected to take part in the Season's social events.

Lord Molyneux smiled proudly at his women as they came in. A montage of Lily's childhood flickered through his mind as, with head held high, she walked regally across the room and stood before him. He stared silently at her, remembering her as the black-haired blue-eyed infant; as a toddler with tousled hair; as a young daredevil on her first pony, and as a tomboyish adolescent. And now his darling girl was seventeen and a full-fledged beauty.

Music drifted from the ballroom and he held out his hand to her. "May I have the pleasure of this dance, Lady Lily?" he asked, formal as you please.

Picking up her gold lace train, Lily smiled into her father's eyes. "I should be delighted, sir," she said. And he swept her, laughing, into his arms and around and around the drawing room in a waltz.

"I'm claiming my dance now because I shall obviously not stand a chance of getting near you once your guests arrive," he said as the music stopped. "And I just wanted to tell you that you are beautiful and will be the belle of your own ball."

"And you are the handsomest and dearest father of the birthday girl," she whispered, flinging her arms around him.

"Gather around, Nora, children." Lord Molyneux waved his family closer. He took a square blue suede box from a nearby table and handed it to Lily. "It's time to give Lily her present."

Lily held the box in both hands. She looked down at it and then up at them. "I almost daren't open it," she said, her eyes brilliant with excitement.

"Oh, for goodness' sake, open it, Lily," Ciel yelled impatiently. "I'm dying to see what it is."

Lily laughed and snapped open the box then stared at the diamond love-knot necklace. "Oh, Pa," was all she could say.

The diamonds sparkled in a ribbon of light as Lord Molyneux clasped the necklace around Lily's neck. The love-knot's bow fitted exactly into the hollow of her young, creamy throat and he said, "I chose it myself. I wanted to find exactly the right gift for my dear daughter on her seventeenth birthday."

"Oh, and you have," Ciel cried impetuously. "It's wonderful."

"I feel like a queen tonight," Lily told him. "Thank you, Pa and darling Mammie. This is truly the most wonderful night of my life."

"Until, of course, you get married," her father replied. His eyes clouded at the idea of losing her, and seeing it, Lady Molyneux quickly reminded him that guests would be arriving any minute.

A crowd had gathered in the street outside to watch the ladies in their satins and furs and jewels as they arrived, and some of them were dancing to the music that stole like a breeze across the misty square. An hour later the big house was alive with laughter and noise. The crystal chandeliers glowed like rainbows with a thousand candles, the pink champagne flowed and the knowledgeable white-haired dowagers, in their dark lace dresses and many rows of pearls and diamonds, nodded approvingly as Lily danced by in the arms of one fascinated young man after another. "She is bound to make a fine match," they told each other, knowledgeably. "A beauty like that, and with her pedigree."

"Isn't she wonderful?" Ciel said, dancing with her brother. "I'm just so proud of her tonight, aren't you, William?"

She tripped over his feet and he winced. "It's your fault," she said. "I'm a better dancer than you, even if I am only ten."

"You're right," he admitted ruefully. "And you'll still be a better dancer than me when you are twenty. I hate dancing."

"More than horseback riding?"

Her little monkey face had an impish gleam and he laughed and said, "You know what, Ciel? When it's your turn for your debut, you will be just as gorgeous as Lily."

She shook her head. "No one in the whole world will ever be as beautiful as she is."

Lily tossed a smile in their direction as she whirled around in her partner's arms. Her cheeks were flushed, her upswept black hair gleamed and her diamond love-knot necklace glittered expensively around her neck, a tangible token of her beloved pa's love and esteem for his eldest daughter.

"I didn't know *he* was invited," she whispered to Ciel, when she spotted Dermot Hathaway among the other young men.

"You mean the one you were trying to flirt with at the party?" Ciel asked innocently.

Lily threw her a withering glance. "You're like an elephant, Ciel. You never forget. At least not the things you are supposed to!"

Dermot cut in on her at the next dance. "I know it's not done," he said, unsmiling, "but it was the only way to claim a dance with the girl of the moment."

"Really?" she said, throwing back her head and meeting his eyes boldly. "But I'm sure there is 'a girl of the moment' for you every day of the week."

"Maybe," he acknowledged, holding her closer than anyone had ever held her before.

Lily's heart was pounding so hard she thought he must surely hear it. She could feel the warmth of his white-gloved hand on her waist through the stuff of her dress, her breasts were crushed against his chest and she could hardly breathe as he swept her with a final flourish to the edge of the floor.

The white-haired ladies sitting on the gilt chairs along the wall eyed them disapprovingly, but Lily didn't care. She was on top of the world with excitement and the feeling of her own feminine power. She glanced flirtatiously at him through her long curling black lashes. "I'm giving you permission to cut in again," she said, twirling her little gilt pencil between her fingers while she pretended to consult her dance card. She struck out a name and wrote in his instead.

"Then you enjoyed our dance as much as the chocolate dessert, Lily?" His mocking voice caressed her name and she shivered inside.

"Oh, damn the chocolate." She pouted. "Will you never forget?"

"I might," he said consideringly. "But I think you had better reinstate that young man's name on your dance card. I seem to remember I am already booked for that waltz."

A HOT BLUSH BURNED Lily's cheeks as she watched him dancing. The woman he was with must be at least twenty-six, she thought scornfully. "Damn him. Oh, damn him," she muttered under her breath, glaring at the young man standing hopefully in front of her.

"My dance, I think, Lily?" he said, taken aback.

"What? Oh yes. Dammit, so it is."

Dermot did not ask her to dance again, nor did he sit near her at supper. Lily was having such a good time she almost forgot him, but every now and again she would glance longingly his way, and Dermot did not fail to notice the gesture.

The ball ended at two A.M. and Lily was up at seven to prepare for the Lord Lieutenant's levee, and the day after that she was presented at the ladies' drawing room. She looked regal and exhausted, dressed in white satin, elegantly managing her long train and making a sweeping curtsy. She wore egret feathers in her hair and her diamond necklace and everyone there agreed that Lily Molyneux was breathtaking, that she was destined to become one of Ireland's greatest beauties, and that she was guaranteed a wonderful match, for wasn't every eligible young man already in love with her?

Later she went on to London for her presentation at Court and another round of parties, and again the gay flirtatious Lily was a huge success. Lord Molyneux was fiercely proud of his lovely daughter and now dowagers in both countries predicted a splendid marriage.

Ciel watched longingly, waiting her turn, though she knew she would never be the triumph Lily was. And William dutifully attended every dinner and ball with his popular sister, stiff and uncomfortable, longing for the moment he could be back at Ardnavarna, alone with his books or his bird-watching.

Yet when they finally returned to Ardnavarna for the quiet summer weeks, the one memory that was engraved in Lily's mind was of Dermot Hathaway's hot eyes burning into hers, of his hand on her waist and her body pressed close to his. And of his mocking jibe as he left her to dance with someone else.

"One day, I shall make him pay for that," she vowed, safe again at Ardnavarna. And it was then she decided she was going to marry Dermot Hathaway.

CHAPTER

~~~~~~~~~ 19 ~~~~~~~~~~

DERMOT WAS A MAN'S MAN. He was a sportsman, like Lily's father, and a clever businessman, dabbling in growing industries, railroads and steamship lines, in America. His business often took him away from Ireland, but he was always back in the autumn for the hunt. He was a tall, strapping, handsome fellow in that fleshy sensual way that women seemed to like, but he was also very popular with the men.

"A good fellow," his contemporaries would describe him, "even if he has a bit of an eye for the women."

In fact Dermot had more than "a bit of an eye" for them, and the word was that no woman was safe within fifty yards of him, including some of his friends' wives.

And because he was the only man ever to seem indifferent to her girlish beauty and flirtatious ways—*and* the only one ever to put her in her place—well, naturally, he was the one Lily wanted. All the others, the handsome young sons of her parents' friends with their grand titles, lords and dukes and even, they said, a prince, were swept from her mind as if they never existed. Dermot Hathaway was who she wanted and she set out to get him.

Lily was crazy about him. She could think of no one else. She found out through her network of friends exactly which house parties and dances he would be invited to, and then she made sure to attend them herself, always looking her dazzling best, always the proper little lady, always chaperoned either by her mother or by the lady of the house in which she was a guest. She was rarely seated next to Dermot at formal dinners because he was so much older than she. He was a sophisticated talker and raconteur, far more glib than the poor boy who had thought all week about what he would say to the lovely Lily Molyneux after he had inveigled his hostess to put him by her side. He needn't have bothered. She saved her flirtatious looks for Dermot across the table. And when, after the third party they attended together, he had still not asked her to dance, she asked him.

Lily knew it was never done, but she didn't give a damn anymore. She knew she looked beautiful in the lemon silk dress with the sweeping tulle skirt. She patted her glossy black curls and wet her red lips with her tongue, then she made her way through the crowd to his side, and put her hand on his arm. She didn't even blush as she said, "Sir Dermot, you cut in on me at my own party, so I feel that it's quite proper for me to return the compliment, and ask you for a dance."

Dermot looked down at her, taking in her beauty and her youth and her deceptively innocent sapphire eyes. He had known a thousand women and he knew trouble when he was looking at it, and he smiled. "Why not?" he asked.

A shiver rippled down Lily's spine as he looked at her. There was a knowingness in his eyes she had never seen in any other man's. It was a hot, searching glance that left her bewildered yet excited. Even Finn, with his beseeching, adoring eyes, had never looked at her like this.

"The dance before supper, Lady Lily," he said, with a little formal bow. And then he turned and walked off to claim his next dance with his hostess.

Lily looked down at her dance card. He had scrawled out the name of the boy she was to have had supper with and substituted his own. Her spirits rose like a fresh soufflé. She had no pity for the scorned young man. Dermot Hathaway was taking her in to supper.

Dermot had no real interest in having supper with a girl as young as Lily, beautiful though she was. He was only doing it to pique the woman he was really pursuing. She was married, attractive, knowledgeable, and sexy, and that's the way he liked his women. So far she had resisted his advances but he knew she was interested, and he also knew the best way to gain a woman's attention was to feign indifference. He was especially adept at using one woman as a weapon to get at another and tonight gorgeous young Lily Molyneux was that weapon.

He felt Lily shiver as he put his arms around her to claim his dance. He glanced mockingly down at her and said, "Are you cold, my dear?" And Lily thought she would die from blushing as he swung her masterfully into the waltz. She was a wonderful dancer, graceful and confident, and she leaned away from him trying to concentrate on the music and not his nearness.

"I'm afraid you have caused me a little trouble," she said as the music ended and he took her arm to lead her to the buffet. "It took a lot of explaining to convince the man who thought he was taking me into supper that I had quite forgotten that I had already promised you. Now I'm afraid I've lost a friend."

He shrugged, uncaring. "No matter. You have a thousand others. They say you are the most popular girl of the Season."

She looked modestly down. "Oh, that's all meaningless gossip. And besides, it's so juvenile. I've put it all behind me now."

"Have you indeed," he replied drily.

She bit her lip again, glancing anxiously up at him. But Dermot wasn't laughing at her. In fact he wasn't even looking at her. His eyes were locked with those of the married woman standing alone by the dining room door. Lily stared from one to the other, her mouth open in dismay, but then, as quickly as if it had never happened, Dermot guided her to a table.

"Can we take it that, as you have put all things juvenile behind you, you will no longer be devouring dessert?" he asked, glancing across the room at the enormous buffet tables piled with golden platters of pink salmon and coral lobsters, orange shrimp and lustrous oysters; and silver platters of pheasant and woodcock and spiced mutton; and crystal cornucopias of fruits and quivering colored jellies and lacy confections of spun sugar, chocolate, and cream.

Lily's mouth watered as she looked at the display. She was starving and felt she could have devoured the lot. Instead she said in her most bored grown-up voice, "I would like a glass of champagne."

Dermot summoned a footman bearing drinks, then he leaned his elbows on the table, watching as she gulped it down quickly. Lily said she would like another and the footman placed the second glass on the table in front of her.

"Is this a replacement for the chocolate?" Dermot asked, bored with the idea of being in charge of a young girl who was bent on getting tipsy.

Lily banged her glass angrily on the table and the wine slopped over the sides. "Jayzus, Dermot Hathaway," she exclaimed angrily, "why did you ask me to supper if you hate me?"

His eyebrows rose in surprise. So, the beautiful bland fairy-tale princess had another side to her, after all.

He said, "My dear Lily, I asked you to supper because you are by far the most beautiful woman in this room."

A hundred men had already told her that, but this time all she could say, nervously, was, "Oh."

"I'm sure your father can look forward to a very successful marriage for you," he said softly. "Any man would be proud to possess a woman like you."

"Oh," Lily said again. Her lips were parted and her eyes wide with surprise. She had thought she was losing her fight for his attention, especially when she had seen that woman and Dermot lock glances like gladiators in battle. She thought maybe it was because she was acting more grown-up, drinking the champagne and all, and maybe pretending to be aloof, that had finally caught his attention. Now he knew *she* was a woman too.

"I'm going to get you some food," he said. "It's my experience that two glasses of champagne, a young girl, and an empty stomach do not mix."

She stared after him, thrilled, thinking how kind and thoughtful he was after all. Although she wished he would stop calling her "a young girl" when she felt as grown-up as the woman he was talking to this very minute. The same one, she realized jealously, who had eyed him so possessively earlier. But it was nothing, just a brief few words, a mere politeness she was sure, and then Dermot was back with a footman carrying a tray of food.

"Jayzus," she said teasingly. "I'm so hungry I could eat a horse."

His prominent dark eyes roamed restlessly around the room and he barely touched his own food, but Lily did not even notice. Her tongue and her inhibitions were loosened by the third glass of champagne she insisted on having and she chattered gaily about Ardnavarna and her hunters.

His eyes rested momentarily on her and he said with a flicker of interest, "I hear you are a fine horsewoman, Lily. Almost as good as your father."

"Did Pa tell you that?" she asked eagerly.

"I believe it was your brother."

"Oh, William." She shrugged her creamy shoulders, hitching up her satin bodice as it slithered perilously down her breasts. "He's no good on a horse. Never will be."

"I'm having a house party for the hunt the weekend after next," he said suddenly. "Your parents were invited. Why don't you come with them? You might enjoy it."

Her huge blue eyes shone with excitement and triumph. "Oh. I'm sure I shall."

The music had started up again in the ballroom and she saw the boy to whom she had promised the next dance standing by the door, looking for her.

"Oh, dammit, dammit," she muttered as he came to claim her.

"Thank you for the pleasure of your company, Lily." Dermot took her hand, but instead of bowing as was proper, he carried it to his lips, and Lily felt the world explode into a thousand stars as the tremor of excitement reached from his mouth to her breast to her loins. His hot dark eyes burned for a few seconds into hers and then with a bow he was gone.

Minutes later, she saw him deep in conversation with the beautiful blond woman. And then she did not see him again for the rest of the evening.

At midnight, dizzy from the champagne and with a pounding headache, she said good night to her hostess and wound her way slowly up the curving Georgian staircase to her second-floor room. The lamps were lit and a maid was waiting to help her out of her dress and to hang up her clothes. Lily washed her face in ice-cold water from a jug and held a compress to her head to stop it throbbing. She flung off the rest of her things and climbed into the flannel nightdress that Mammie always insisted she take, because, despite the roaring fires in every grate, Irish country houses were notoriously cold.

She flung open her window and hung her head out, taking great gulps of the icy air. Then, feeling stronger, she turned back to the cosy fire and picked up a small leather-bound book of Lord Byron's poems. She fluttered through its pages but she was really thinking of Dermot. She just couldn't forget him and she threw down the book with a groan of despair. The man was destined to haunt her for the rest of her life; she just knew it. She remembered that she had not seen him since supper. Perhaps he had felt ill? Maybe he was all alone in his room, just down the corridor from hers? Maybe he was feeling sick and lonely, with no one to take care of him? She looked at the book of poems. What better excuse than to take him a book in case he couldn't sleep.

Without stopping to think, she threw on her long blue woolen dressing gown, grabbed the book of poetry, and opened her door. The corridor was at least twenty yards long, and the candles in the wall sconces cast mysterious shadows. She peered anxiously from side to side. The sounds of music and laughter floated faintly up the stairs, but the servants were still on duty downstairs, and up here all was quiet.

She closed the door softly behind her. She knew Dermot's room was across the corridor from hers and four doors along because she had made it her business to find out, and she glanced apprehensively over her shoulder as she tapped on the door, wondering what she would do if she were caught knocking on a man's door in the middle of the night. There was no response and she knocked again. Suddenly she heard footsteps on the stairs. She glanced wildly down the corridor at her room, but there was no time to reach it. She opened Dermot's door, stepped inside, and closed it quickly. She leaned against it, her eyes shut and her heart still pounding. And then she opened them again and saw Dermot.

He was standing by the bed looking at her. He had taken off his shirt and she noticed the dark hair curling across his broad chest, and then the blond woman sprawled, naked as Manet's scandalous "Olympia," on his tumbled bed.

The book of poems she was carrying fell to the floor with a thud. "Oh," she gasped. "Oh, oh . . ." And then she turned and fled back out the door, not caring who might see her.

The sound of their mocking laughter followed her down the corridor, and she pressed her hands over her ears to shut it out, remembering the amusement in the woman's eyes as she lay there naked, uncaring who saw her in Dermot Hathaway's bed. And the strange, knowing gleam in Dermot's eyes as he had watched her staring at them.

She hurled herself into her room and slammed the door behind her. Tears streamed from her face as she flung herself onto the bed. "Jayzus. Dammit, dammit, dammit," she roared, pounding her clenched fists into the pillow. She just knew she would never forget the scene. And their cruel laughter. And the look in Dermot's eyes. Never. Never. Never.

CHAPTER
20

THE DAY BEFORE they were to go to Hathaway Castle for the hunt, Lord Molyneux came down with an attack of gout. Lady Nora said she had to stay home with him because he was like an angry bear when he was sick and only she could cope, and that the visit to Hathaway Castle would have to be canceled. Lily was devastated. Despite what had happened, she desperately wanted to see Dermot again, but her mother firmly said no. Still, when she pouted and stamped her foot, telling Pa she dearly wanted to see the famous castle and how disappointed she was, he finally agreed she could go. She would take her old nanny as chaperone, and Finn would go on ahead with the horses.

Hathaway Castle crouched malevolently on the top of a hill by the ocean in County Clare. To the east it faced the plains and valleys where, for centuries, the warlike Hathaways had been able to spy their enemies approaching.

The western facade of the castle faced the ocean and the Atlantic gales swept over and around and, some guests said, shivering, *through* the castle walls, howling like a banshee when the winter storms struck.

As she stepped from the carriage, Lily wished she had never come, but she had just not been able to stop herself. Dermot Hathaway lured her like a salmon to the leap in springtime. She was crazy for him. He was in her head, waking and sleeping. He was different from all the other young men she knew, and he had the fascination of the unknown. And the forbidden.

She followed the footman along stone-walled corridors and through vaulted archways, noticing the fine Persian silk rugs and the suits of armor in the hallways and the ancient battle weapons—axes, swords, and cudgels—displayed in glass-topped chests. Her room, entered through a creaking Gothic door, was enormous and looked out over the castle grounds to the sea.

She flung open the window while her nanny unpacked her bags, listening to the ocean hurling itself onto the rocks and watching the black clouds piling up in the windy sky. The weather did not look too promising for tomorrow's hunt and she crossed her fingers, praying the storm would go away because she so badly wanted to show off how good an equestrian she was for Dermot Hathaway.

The storm struck at eight o'clock, just as the twenty guests were congregating for drinks before dinner. Fires roared in the huge stone hearths at either end of the great double-height room, and charcoal braziers were placed along its length for extra warmth as the Atlantic gales whistled through the rafters, echoing down the chimneys and hurling a skyful of rain at the windows.

The guests, grouped on sofas or standing near the fires, chattered about how 'elemental' Hathaway Castle was, and debated the odds for the hunt the next day.

"Not good, I'm afraid," Dermot told them. "Still, I've no doubt if we are all confined to the house we shall manage to keep ourselves amused somehow. Until the storm blows itself out, that is."

Shivering in the castle's chill, Lily was wearing deep ruby velvet, high at the neck and tight at the waist, with long sleeves and a flowing skirt. She was the youngest person there and she felt desperately out of place without her parents. Until, that is, she found herself seated on Dermot's right at dinner and he said, "You look as lovely as the Lady of Shalott."

Her spirits rose, but they sank quickly again as he turned away and talked only to the woman on his left through two whole courses, completely ignoring her. She could have cried, she was so crazy about him. But she knew crying was not going to do her much good. She would have to play a cleverer game than that to beat out her rivals. After all, she told herself determinedly, she was here for a purpose—to snare Dermot Hathaway. To steal him from under the noses of these predatory older women and make an honest man of him. To turn him into "Lily Molyneux's husband."

Dermot came to sit beside her on the sofa after dinner. She could feel the warmth of his body and smell the faint lingering scent of his cologne. His hooded eyes were looking at her in that strange way again, as though she were the only girl in the entire world he wanted to be with. And yet she was sure she was not. Yet.

"So, Lily Molyneux," he said softly. "What are you thinking?"

"I was thinking how rude you were not to talk to me at dinner," she retorted tartly.

"You were quite right." He leaned closer and whispered, "And I confess, it was not easy to ignore such a young beauty. But you are a dangerous girl, Lily. Far too beautiful, and far too seductive, and far too young to be left alone with a man like me." And then, with a mocking smile, he went to organize a game of bridge.

Lily hated card games and she refused to be a fourth. She knew they would play for hours and, left alone, she said good night and stalked sulkily to her room. Old Nanny chattered on as she helped her undress —about how cold the castle was, and how she hated the eerie howl of the wind, and how dark and gloomy the corridor was to her room, and how far it was from Lily's—but Lily scarcely heard her. She was too busy wondering exactly what Dermot had meant by "dangerous."

Nanny kissed Lily good night and went off to her own quarters, and Lily huddled, shivering, under the eiderdown. Her icy feet were pressed against a stone hot water bottle wrapped in a piece of red flannel and she stared into the glowing peat fire, wondering what she could possibly do to keep Dermot's attention for more than two minutes at a time. As she drifted off to sleep with the sound of the wind still howling in her ears, she remembered that Dermot had thought she was beautiful—and seductive. The only thing he didn't like about her was that she was too young. So she decided she would just have to force herself to grow up quickly. Right away, in fact.

The next morning, Dermot was up and dressed and down at the stables before dawn, checking the nervous horses. He scanned the gray skies for a break in the weather. "The going'll be wet, sir, and slippery, even if the weather does take up," they warned him. Dermot was a restless, active man, keen for his day's sport and he decided quickly that the men would hunt but the ladies would stay behind.

Angrily Lily watched them ride off. Deprived of her chance to show how fearless she was on a horse, she sat in the drawing room, listening to the gossip of her fellow guests, answering their polite questions about her debut and mutual friends with morose disinterest. She spent the afternoon in the library, inspecting shelves of books that looked as though they had not been opened in centuries, glancing frequently out of the window to see if the huntsmen were returning. But the afternoon drew on and still there was no sign of them. Moodily, she returned to her room. Leaning her elbows on the stone window ledge, she stared out at the distant, leaden gray sea, thinking about Dermot.

She heard someone in the corridor and, hoping it was he, she ran to the door and peeked out. A tiny maid, no more than thirteen years old, in a blue-striped frock and white linen pinafore, stared back at her. She was carrying a huge enamel jug of hot water. Lily asked where she was taking it. "Why, to Sir Dermot, m'lady," she replied nervously.

"To Sir Dermot? Which is his room?"

"The master's room's in the tower, m'lady." She pointed to the end of the corridor.

Without stopping to think, Lily grabbed the jug from her. She said quickly, "This is too heavy for you. I shall take it myself."

"Oh, but m'lady, ye can't do that," the girl cried, "it's me job—" But Lily was already striding purposefully down the corridor, slopping water from the jug all over the priceless rugs. She was overwhelmed with curiosity about Dermot's room and what clue it might give her to the personality of its owner, and nothing was going to stop her from finding out.

The door was twice as tall as she was, and as heavy as if it were made of lead. She didn't knock, she just pushed it cautiously open and peered in. Her blue eyes rounded with amazement as she saw the piles of silk rugs that covered the floor, dozens of them, thrown one over the other like a thick, soft, crazy patchwork quilt; and the tall windows, swagged with dark plum velvet, and the vast carved four-poster bed with a baldachin of rich ruby brocade, fringed in gold. A coverlet of wolf's fur was flung over the bed and on a massive table along one wall was an open bottle of whiskey.

The room was empty and she breathed a sigh of relief that her spying trip would be unobserved. The soft carpets deadened her footsteps as she tiptoed across the room. The door to the dressing room was suddenly flung open. Dermot was standing there, half naked, a glass of whiskey raised to his lips. She stared, like a mesmerized rabbit, at his naked chest, at his loins where the wet riding britches he was still wearing fitted taut as a second skin, at his massive shoulders and powerful thighs. She thought she might faint from the sheer masculine scent of him, of sweat and cologne and whiskey.

Dermot stared back at her, unsmiling. He had had a long, hard day's hunting, the going had been treacherous and the wind had been a bastard, whipping in their faces and shifting the scent so the hounds hadn't known where they were. The ice on the wind had caused them to stop for frequent nips from their flasks; he had eaten nothing since their early breakfast, and he had been drinking steadily all day. He was more than half drunk and the whiskey hitting his empty belly crept like liquid fire through his veins.

He said nothing, watching Lily taking him in from head to toe. He saw her blue eyes darken and he knew what she was feeling. A smile lurked at the corners of his mouth. The little bitch was in heat for him, and he knew it. He took the enamel jug from her nervous fingers and set it down on the washstand. Then he took her in his arms and kissed her.

His mouth was hot on hers and his kiss too fierce, but Lily wanted more of it. He hadn't been immune to her after all. He loved her. She was drowning in his arms, lost in the new pleasure of her own body.

He ran his hands down her back and along her buttocks, pressing her urgently against him, shocking her back to her senses. She put her hands on his chest, pushing him away, but he merely picked her up and carried her across to the bed.

"No," she cried, terrified. "Oh, no . . . I didn't mean to come here, I only brought the water for you . . ." She slid from the bed to the floor and he forced her back onto the carpets.

"You want to be like the woman you saw me with," he whispered in her ear. "Of course you do, I saw the way you stared at her, envying her nakedness, envying that she was with me . . . you little bitch, you've been asking for this long enough. And now you'll get it. Oh, and you'll love it, your sort always does. I can tell them a mile away, smell them even, feel the heat of them . . ."

She was pinned beneath his weight as he struggled with her dress, and she screamed. He laughed. "There's no one to hear," he said. "This is my ivory tower. Nobody comes here, not even the servants, without being summoned. It's just you and me, Lily, you and me . . ."

He bent and bit her breast and she screamed again, this time in pain. Oh God, oh God, what am I doing here, she thought frantically, as he forced her legs apart with his knee. He flung back her skirts and she began to cry as he pulled at her undergarments. "No . . . oh no, please, don't. If you love me, don't," she whispered.

"Love?" He laughed again, bearing down on her. Oh God, Lily thought, remembering how she had giggled over the horses and the dogs in the stable yard. . . . oh God, this was far, far worse and it was something that shouldn't be happening. It was terrible. It was the worst thing that she could ever do.

She screamed with pain and fear, still fighting him as he forced himself into her. Dermot smiled. The little virgin tease had finally got what was coming to her. He flung back his head, groaning, his face contorted in the agony of fulfillment. And Lily lay still beneath him, as though she were dead.

He got up and walked back into the dressing room. When he returned he was wearing a silk robe and his hair was brushed smooth. He poured himself another glass of whiskey and sat on the edge of the bed. He stared thoughtfully at her. She was lying facedown, crying, great shuddering sobs that threatened to choke her. He sighed regretfully. If he had not been so drunk and she had not been so provocative, he would not have touched her. But she had come to his room at just the wrong moment, and she had offered herself to the wrong man. Now he would have to get her out of here and make sure no one ever knew. Especially her father.

"Get up, Lily," he said after a while.

But she just turned her face into the soft silken Oriental rug and wept.

"Get up, I said."

His voice was soft but there was a menacing tone to it, and Lily glanced apprehensively up at him. He walked across to her and took her hand, pulling her to her feet. She sagged against him, and he sat her on the edge of the bed and put the glass to her lips, forcing whiskey down her throat.

She gagged as the liquor burned its way down and he said irritably, "For God's sake don't be sick in here. Listen to me. You will not come down to dinner tonight. You will stay in your room and I shall have a tray sent up to you."

Lily just stared at him. Her eyes were wide with shock. He was acting as though nothing were wrong, as though it was all normal. . . .

She began to scream hysterically and he slapped her face hard. Her head snapped back and a red welt burned on her cheek. She stared at him, stunned into silence.

"Let us get this straight, Lily," he said. "You are a very knowledgeable young woman. Behind those innocent blue eyes lie a thousand unknown sins, and this will only be one of them. You knew why you came here. You've been haunting me for weeks, begging for me to touch you. You can't deny it."

"It's not true," she cried, shocked. "I only wanted—"

"To flirt with me, Lily? Oh, come now, you know that's not true. You got what you wanted, and, for the moment, so did I. And that's where it stays. You will go home tomorrow and we shall never see each other again."

Lily wasn't really sure of the facts of life, but she understood enough to know that what had happened was what married people did, and now marriage was her only answer, and her only salvation. "But you'll have to marry me," she cried.

His hand shot out again and this time he grabbed her by the throat. His face was livid with anger. "If that was your little game, my dear Lily, then you are very much mistaken. And if you think you can go home crying 'rape,' then let me inform you that if you ever tell anyone about this—anyone at all—then I shall kill you, Lily Molyneux."

Taking her arm, he dragged her, stumbling, across the room. He opened the door and looked up and down the corridor. It was empty. Lily collapsed in a sudden heap at his feet. He picked her up and carried her to her room and flung her impatiently onto the bed.

"I shall make arrangements for you to leave tomorrow," he said, looking at her with brutal indifference. "You can give my apologies to your parents and tell them the weather is too bad for hunting, and that you are coming down with a fever."

He walked out the door without a backward glance and Lily lay on the bed, staring after him, too shocked even to cry out.

After a while she stood up and dragged off her clothes. She stared, horrified, at her stained garments. Nanny mustn't see, she mustn't know. Nobody must ever know. She would hide all the evidence. She would lie and pretend, even to herself, that nothing had happened, and then, miraculously, it would be all right again. Surely it would. It must. *It must.*

Her body throbbed with pain and she was trembling from shock. She put on her warm woolen robe and rang for hot water. She waited, shivering, too numb to cry, for the maid to fill the bath in front of the fire, and then she sank into the water, praying for its heat to wash the feel and the smell and all the cruel evidence of Dermot Hathaway's body from her, so that she might be clean again. But even she, innocent as she was, knew it was not possible. She would never be the same again.

She had never even heard the word "rape," but she knew the very worst thing that could happen to a woman had happened to her. It was unthinkable. It was something that was never mentioned in polite society, not even within the family.

She thought desperately that she could never tell her mother, and certainly not her father. And Dermot Hathaway would not make an honest woman of her, but anyway now she hated him as passionately as she had admired him earlier. And besides, she was afraid of him. She shivered as she remembered his threat to kill her. She just wanted to get away, to go home to Ardnavarna, where she would be safe.

She arrived home unexpectedly the following day, driving through one of the worst storms of the decade, and her mother immediately exclaimed how pale she looked. She put a hand to Lily's brow and felt her fever, and she ordered her straight to bed. She considered sending for the doctor, but the terrified Lily said she didn't want to see the doctor and ran sobbing to her room.

Her mother stared anxiously after her, then sent the old nanny up to take care of her. She went to her own little pharmacy where she kept the bottles of patent medicines and pills she gave to her tenants when they fell ill, and she mixed a little potion and took it up to her daughter herself.

Lily was sitting up in bed in a high-necked white cotton nightgown. Her eyes were dark with misery and her face as white as her nightie, and Lady Nora sighed worriedly. "If you are not better tomorrow, I'm sending for Dr. O'Malley," she said firmly, spooning the medicine into Lily's mouth like a mother bird feeding her fledgling. "I remember Hathaway Castle from old; when that Atlantic gale blows there's nothing to stop it from whistling through those ancient walls. I should never have let you go."

"Oh, if only you hadn't, Mammie." Lily moaned, tears flowing again from her already swollen eyes.

"Darling Lily, whatever is it? Tell Mammie how you feel." She put her arms around her and Lily huddled in their safe embrace. She never wanted to leave her mammie again.

Ciel watched worriedly from the window seat. When her mother left she ran to sit on the edge of the bed. Lily's eyes met hers and she suddenly collapsed in a torrent of tears. She threw herself about the bed, pounding her pillows, stuffing the sheet in her mouth to stifle her screams. Ciel stared at her, terrified. Tears of sympathy sprang to her own eyes and her mouth was fixed in an O of distress. "Lily. Oh, Lily. Whatever is it? What happened?"

Lily stopped her pounding and screaming. She sat up and looked at her beloved little sister. Ciel was the only person to whom she had always told everything. Except for Finn, but he was different. And anyway, she certainly couldn't tell him about this. But Ciel was so young and so innocent—just the way she herself had been only yesterday. Yet if she didn't tell someone she would just burst with the horror of it.

She clutched her sister's hands, and in a few brief whispered words she told her what had happened. Ciel's innocence was tinged with knowledge. She knew what the sexual act was between animals, though she had never related the same thing to people, and the stallion covering the mare in the stable yard could not be compared to what had happened to Lily.

"Oh, I'll never tell, Lily, never," she promised, horrified. "But you will be all right, won't you? It's all over now, and if neither of us ever says anything, then nobody will ever know. And you'll just go back to being your old self again. Everybody loves you, Lily. Absolutely everybody. I certainly do."

She kissed her and the guilt and horror lifted a little as Lily wondered if she might be right. Maybe in a few weeks it would just erase itself from her mind, the way they said everything did with time. And then maybe she could go back to being the popular young debutante again. Only this time she would take those young men who were chasing after her more seriously. She would choose one quickly and make the grand match everyone was predicting for her. Hers would be the wedding of the year and she would live happily ever after. She would give up parties and dancing and flirting and live quietly with her nice young husband in whatever grand houses they owned. They would have children and she would be an exemplary mother just like her own darling mammie.

But somehow, even as she planned it so convincingly, deep inside she knew she would never be the same again. And she wept again, for the simple, innocent girl she had been.

A MONTH PASSED QUIETLY. Lily kept to her bed a great deal and rarely ventured downstairs. Pa came worriedly to see her. She managed a wan smile and told him she thought that her hectic social life had caught up with her, and she was suffering from exhaustion.

"Then you must rest, darling girl," he said affectionately, patting her thin hand and kissing her pale cheek. And he sent away to London for books and games to amuse her; he ordered bouquets of flowers for her room and instructed his wife to make sure she fed Lily any delicacy that might tempt her poor appetite.

When Lily finally came downstairs again she loitered wanly around, lying on the big library sofa in front of the fire, pretending to read while she stared worriedly into the embers. Eventually she was drawn to the stables again, and Finn O'Keeffe's eyes lit up when he saw her. A huge smile spread across his face. He said, "I've been worried about you. They told me you were sick but nobody knew with what. Will you be feelin' better now?"

He was her friend. He was so simple, so normal and familiar and undemanding, and Lily knew he would never hurt her. She thought of how complicated her life had become and for the first time she wished she were just a peasant girl so she might be with Finn forever.

"Let's go for a ride," she said, thinking she could turn back the clock and forget what had happened.

The horse felt like molten velvet beneath her as she galloped bareback along the strand. The wind tugged at her hair and the sun glinted off the waves and the golden sand kicked up with a soft thud from beneath the horse's hooves. Life felt good after all. Finn kept pace with her and she glanced sideways at him, laughing. They were young and beautiful and carefree as the wind, and deliriously happy in each other's company.

They reined in their horses at the end of the long strip of beach, and looked breathlessly at each other, laughing with the sheer joy of the hard gallop and the lovely day, and of being with each other.

"Oh, Lily, I do love ye so," Finn gasped impetuously. "I love you, and I always will." He stared boldly at her. "There. Now I've said it," he said with a sigh of relief.

The smile disappeared from Lily's eyes as quickly as the sun behind a cloud. She had known he loved her but not like this, not the way men "loved" women. "You were supposed to be my friend," she shouted angrily. "Oh, oh, dammit. Dammit to hell, now you've gone and spoiled it all." And she took off back down the strand, leaving him staring sadly after her.

Back in the stable yard, she flung herself from the horse and ran, sobbing, home to the Big House. Daniel O'Keeffe glanced angrily at his younger brother as he trotted into the yard. "Is it yerself has been upsetting Lady Lily?" he demanded, worried that Finn might have jeopardized his job again. "Will you niver learn, boyo, to keep your place?"

"And where's that, then? *My place*?" Finn's gray eyes spat anger at his brother but it was himself he was angry with.

"You know where it is, sure enough. And so do I," was all Daniel said. And Finn thought bitterly that he was right.

LILY'S OLD NANNY had been with her since she was a newborn infant. Now she acted as lady's maid and she missed nothing. Another month passed and the vital signs that she was hoping for still did not materialize. She stared worriedly at Lily as she stepped from her bath, glancing shrewdly at her slender body as she wrapped her in a huge fluffy white towel.

"I think we shall have to be seeing the doctor after all, Lady Lily," she said, rubbing her back briskly. "There'll be something wrong with you and we'd best find out what it is."

"No!" Lily grabbed the towel from her. She ran into her dressing room and slammed the door and the old woman looked sadly after her, shaking her head. Lily's terrified face had only confirmed her worst fears. There was nothing for it but to tell her mother.

Lady Nora was in her boudoir working on her tapestry. Sometimes she thought she enjoyed these quiet weeks alone with her family more than the great social whirl that took up the rest of her year. Ardnavarna was remote and life here was so predictable and tranquil, there was little to disturb her peace.

She was surprised when Nanny knocked on her door and told her she had better speak to her daughter, "for something's not as it should be, my lady," she said. She asked her whatever she meant by that, and when Nanny told her she turned pale with shock.

"She must be ill," she gasped, because anything else was unthinkable. And worriedly she called in Dr. O'Malley.

Lily lay on her bed like a terrified lamb to the slaughter while kindly old Dr. O'Malley made a brief examination. He asked her a few questions but she turned her head away, refusing to answer, and it was Nanny who furnished him with the replies. He suspected the truth but the patient would tell him nothing and it wasn't until various tests were made that he was able to confirm their worst fears.

Lady Nora sat alone in her boudoir thinking bewilderedly of her daughter, wondering how this horrifying thing could ever have happened. Had she not been a good mother? Had she not loved her daughter? Worried about her? Protected her enough? She had been certain she was chaperoned everywhere she went, made sure she met only the right people. She could think of no one, no one at all, who would take advantage of her beautiful young daughter in this bestial way.

A thrill of terror struck her heart as though she thought of what her husband would say when she told him, for tell him she must. She clasped her hand to the pain in her chest, wincing as it got stronger. White-faced, she rang the bell to summon the maid to bring her a glass of water and then she put her head down on her pretty worktable and she wept.

The young maid stood in the doorway holding the jug of water on a tray, open-mouthed with shock. She dithered on the threshold, uncertain whether to come in or go out.

"Yer ladyship," she said kindly, "will you not be feelin' well, ma'am? Shall I be callin' the doctor again?"

Lady Nora sat up. She dried her eyes on a tiny lace-edged linen handkerchief and straightened her back. Ladies were never supposed to show emotion in front of the servants and she thought wearily that the whole kitchen would hear about it within minutes. Her hand shook as she poured a glass of water and took a sip. "It was just a bad pain in my chest," she told the worried girl. "I shall be all right now, thank you, Mollie."

After a few minutes she walked along the corridor to Lily's room. Her daughter was sitting by the window staring out at the rainswept gardens. She did not turn her head to look, even though she knew her mother was there.

"Lily darling," Lady Nora said gently. "You know what the doctor said?" Lily hung her head and said nothing. "Are you feeling better?" she asked, but Lily still did not answer. Lady Nora sighed. Sorrow dragged at her heart as she looked at her beloved girl. "You must tell me what happened, Lily," she said. "I promise I will not be angry with you. But I must know who this boy is so that your father can deal with the situation."

"Pa?" Lily's shocked eyes met her mother's. "You mean you will tell *Pa?*" Two bright spots of color stood out on her pale cheeks as she realized that her father was going to know. "How can you say that, Mammie?" she cried despairingly. "How *can* you tell him?"

Her mother shook her head. "In God's truth, Lily," she said slowly, "I don't know how I can tell him. I only know I must, and that in order to help you, I have to know the truth."

"And what will happen to me then?"

"Why, then you must marry the boy, Lily. A quiet wedding, a long visit abroad . . . a premature child. We could keep it a secret somehow."

Lily's face would have turned paler if it could. She felt sick as she thought of Dermot Hathaway. Her father would make her marry him, but Dermot had said he would kill her first. And anyway she would rather die than marry that beast.

She stared silently out of the window and Lady Nora sighed. "I'm begging you, child," she said softly. "Tell your Mammie and I promise to do what I can to help you. You know how much I love you."

Lily shook her head, staring at the rain sweeping relentlessly down the windowpane in a solid sheet, just like her nightly tears. "I can't, Mammie," she said wearily. And she would say no more.

LORD MOLYNEUX WAS IN THE LIBRARY smoking a cigar and reading his newspaper. His wife sank wearily into the chair opposite him and he glanced at her in surprise. "You look tired, m'dear," he said with a flicker of concern. "I thought being at Ardnavarna would have been a good rest for you, but I suppose with Lily ill, it's been a worry."

The pain tugged at her heart again but she ignored it. There was no way to avoid what she had to tell her husband and she did not flinch in her duty. She was quiet, controlled, and brief.

He said nothing. His eyes, blue as Lily's, stared at her as though she had gone out of her mind. Augustus Molyneux was a big man, but as he rose to his feet in a colossal rage he seemed to tower over her. Lady Nora put her hand to her chest, wishing she might die before her beloved husband struck her down for breaking his heart and telling him about his errant daughter.

His face turned purple then gray, then his legs seemed to give way and he sank back into his chair. He said, "Dear God, Nora, there must be some mistake. It's not true, it's not possible." His eyes met hers beseechingly and she thought he was going to cry. "Not Lily," he whispered.

She said, "It is true, Augustus, though I wish with all my heart it were not."

He got up again and went to stand by the darkening window, staring out, like Lily, at the sodden landscape, while his wife told him hastily of the solution she had already told her daughter: a quick marriage, a long trip abroad, a premature birth . . . "You will have to speak to the parents. It could all be arranged, Augustus. If only Lily would tell me who he is."

Without turning his head he said, "Send Lily here to me."

Lady Nora got up and walked to the door. She glanced worriedly back at him. "You must be gentle with her, Augustus," she said. "Remember the girl's condition."

"Dear God, Nora," he roared, agonized, "how can I ever forget?"

WHEN HER MOTHER TOLD her she was to go down to speak to her father in the library, Lily ran to look for Ciel. She found her sprawled in front of the nursery fire, the dogs beside her, reading.

"How can you just lie there so cosily?" she demanded, close to tears, "when I am summoned to see Pa and I know he is going to kill me."

Ciel's huge gray eyes were full of pity as she ran to her sister. "Oh, Lily, Lily. What shall you tell him?"

"Nothing!" Lily's eyes flashed with contempt as she thought of Dermot. "I'll never tell and nobody will ever make me. I'll kill myself first."

"No. No. Oh, Lily, please don't. *I* love you. *I* will help you. And maybe Pa won't be too angry once he gets used to the idea—"

"Oh, *Ciel,*" Lily said with a despairing half smile at her ingenuous little sister. "You were always a foolish optimist."

She washed her face, brushed her black curls, and tied them back with a pink ribbon. She put on an old pink cotton dress and rubbed the toes of her muddy boots on the backs of her woolen stockings. Then, unable to put off the moment any longer, she walked slowly downstairs to face her father and her fate.

Ciel ran down the steps, at her heels as always, but even she didn't dare go into the library this time when Lily knocked and her pa called "Enter." Creeping closer, she put her ear to the door to listen.

Lord Molyneux was standing by the window, staring out, and he did not turn to look at Lily. He could not allow her to see his pain. He said, "What have you to say for yourself, Lily?"

His voice was aloof, impersonal, as though he were sacking a maid-servant, and whatever flicker of hope Lily might have had sank like a stone to the bottom of a pond.

"I'm very sorry, dearest Pa," she whispered, hanging her head. Her muddy brown boots stuck out from the bottom of the too-short cotton dress and she wished miserably she had changed them.

"Sorry? And is that supposed to be enough? Will being sorry absolve you from your responsibilities to your family? To your name? To your position in life? Will being *sorry* take away our disgrace?"

He swung around and stood with his hands clasped behind his back, staring at her as though he could scarcely believe she was the same beloved daughter. "I have given you everything, Lily," he said, and she could see his anger rising like steam in a boiling kettle. "Everything you ever wanted. And you betray me like this."

"Oh no, Pa, I didn't betray you . . . it was . . . it was . . ." She couldn't think of anything and she hung her head, silent again.

"It was *what*?" he demanded. "What *are* you, Lily? A peasant who knows no better? Bah! Even peasant women have moral standards." He paced the floor, controlling the rage she could still see simmering.

He gripped his hands tightly together behind him and she wondered, terrified, if he were going to strike her.

"Your dear mother has thought of a solution," he said finally. "You will tell me this blackguard's name and, though it means humbling myself to admit that my daughter is no better than a slattern from the streets, I shall speak to the boy's father. I intend to make sure he marries you immediately. Is that clear, Lily?"

She stared silently down at her boots and he said angrily, "There appears to be just one flaw in this plot. Your mother informs me that you will not tell her the boy's name. But you will tell *me*, Lily, and you will be married within the week. Is that clear?"

Lily still stared down at her boots, saying nothing. She told herself he would never make her marry Dermot, never. She had meant it when she said she would kill herself first. She hated him. He was a beast. With a shiver of fear she remembered how frightened she was of him.

Her father said warningly, "Lily, I give you exactly one minute to tell me his name. If you do not, you will pack your things and leave this house immediately."

Her head shot up and she stared at him, horrified. He stared implacably back at her, then he took out the gold half-hunter watch from his waistcoat pocket. He flicked it open and began counting off the seconds.

Lily searched desperately for some way to save herself. Maybe she should just lie, maybe she should tell him the name of any one of the hundred boys who had wanted to marry her so badly just a few weeks ago? But it wouldn't work and she knew it. Her pa would speak to the boy's family and they would scorn her as a liar and a slut just as her own family had. No. There had to be another way, there had to be someone so far beneath them socially her father would never dream of making her marry him. The name came to her like a ray of hope from heaven.

"It was Finn O'Keeffe," she said.

Outside the library Ciel clapped a hand to her mouth to stop the scream she was about to utter. Her ear still to the door, she heard her father say slowly, with a terrible flat anger in his voice, "*Who* did you say it was, Lily?"

"It was Finn. Finn O'Keeffe, the groom."

"*Dear God.*" Her father's roar of anger could have been heard in the very stables and Ciel leapt back from the door, terrified. "*I'll kill him,*" her father shouted. "*I shall kill the dirty bastard . . .*"

Ciel didn't wait to hear any more. She ran as fast as she could down the corridor, through the green baize door, through the butler's pantry and the kitchens, out the back door, and down the shortcut to the stables. The rain pelted down on her and the dogs splashed muddily along beside her, but she didn't even notice. She had to get to Finn O'Keeffe before her father did.

Because of the rain the stables were quiet and only a young lad was on duty. Ciel flung herself onto her pony and charged, bareback, across the cobbled yard, through the archway and down the lane that led to the O'Keeffes' cottage.

Daniel opened the door. He stared at her, astonished. Her red curls were plastered flat against her skull, her eyes were popping out of her head with terror, and her face was ashen. "What is it, Ciel?" he cried. "Has there been an accident at the Big House?"

Ciel shook her head; she started to cry. "Oh, no. No. It's Lily. She's having a baby and she told Pa it's Finn's and now he's coming to kill him. You must run away, Finn," she cried. "Pa means it. He was going to get his gun. You must go right now."

Daniel flung himself onto his younger brother, livid with anger. "Can this be true?" he yelled, grabbing his brother by the throat. "That you are to be the fayther of Miss Lily's child?"

A dagger of pain seemed to strike through Finn's heart, leaving a wound from which he knew he would never recover. His lovely, beautiful, perfect Lily had betrayed him. She had lied and cheated and gotten herself in trouble with one of her fancy friends and now he was to die for it.

"It's niver true," he shouted, throwing off his brother and grabbing hold of Ciel, ready to kill her for what she had said. But it was Lily he wanted to kill. He wanted to strangle her with his bare hands. "If it were true," he said, letting go of Ciel, "I'd willingly take me punishment. But it's not true, brother. That child will be none of mine."

"Oh, Finn, Finn, *please* go quickly," Ciel urged. "Pa will surely be here any minute."

"How could Lily do this to me?" he cried.

"I don't know," she said helplessly. "All I know is you must run."

"God save us," Daniel yelled, frenziedly. "The child's right. We must run for it, Finn. We must put an ocean between us and his lordship's wrath, for he'll surely never quit his search for ye." Grabbing his jacket, he thrust his brother out through the door in front of him. "Tell our fayther we've gone," was all he said to Ciel as the two of them fled into the lane. They leaped over the hedgerow and ran across the field into the woods.

Ciel watched until they were out of sight and then she climbed back onto her pony. Taking the route over the fields so she would not meet her father on his way to kill Finn, she rode back to the Big House.

CHAPTER
21

LORD MOLYNEUX DID NOT FIND FINN, but everyone for miles around knew that he had gone searching for him with his shotgun. They knew he was out to kill him and they knew why. The word went around like wildfire, everyone from the servants to the stablelads to the farmers and the fishermen and their wives knew that Lily Molyneux had claimed that Finn O'Keeffe was the father of the child she was carrying. And not one of them believed it.

"Finn O'Keeffe worshiped that girl," they said. "He would have killed anyone who touched her. *And* Finn, for all his blarney, knew his place. He would never, never have been crazy enough to take advantage of his lordship's daughter, no matter how wild he was for her."

They muttered angrily about her in the shebeen as Paddy O'Keeffe, who had been thrown out of the cottage where he had been born and lived all his life, drowned his sorrows in whiskey. It was whiskey he could no longer afford because he no longer had a job and two fine sons to look after him in his old age.

Nobody was surprised when a few days later Paddy O'Keeffe just upped and wandered off, losing himself in a place where nobody knew him and nobody had heard that he had a son named Finn. And it wasn't till months later that they heard his body had been found by a roadside in Westport, miles away.

Lily did not believe it when her father told her in a remote, ice-tipped voice that she was to leave her home and never return. "You will go to your aunt Mallow's in Cork City," he told her, standing with his back to her, staring out the window so he need not look at her beautiful face.

"You will be placed on the first ship sailing for Boston, and from

Boston you will journey to a distant relative, a cousin in New England. Your bags are being packed this very minute. You will take whatever fits into two trunks and the sum of fifty pounds. Your cousin will look after you until the confinement." He stammered over the word, then paused until he had himself under control again. "After that you will make your own way in the world. But one thing is clear, Lily. One thing is very clear," he repeated remorselessly. "You will never return to Ardnavarna."

LILY STILL DID NOT BELIEVE it when she saw her two hastily packed trunks waiting in the hall; she didn't believe it when her mother and her sister flung themselves weeping at her father's feet, imploring him to relent, and he did not. She didn't believe it when all the curtains were drawn and the mirrors covered with black crepe, like a house in mourning. She did not believe the grief and terror on her mother's face, nor Ciel's imploring screams as her father dragged her mother away and locked her in her room so she could not see her daughter leave.

Lord Molyneux shut himself in the library, pouring whiskey with a trembling hand as the wheels turned on the gravel, taking his beloved daughter, the child of his dreams, away from him forever. Then he put his head in his hands and wept.

The servants had been forbidden to watch her leave and they huddled together in the kitchen. The wailing women threw their aprons over their heads, and the men stood grim-faced and silent.

William was away at school and only Ciel saw Lily go. She climbed from her bedroom window and shinned down the tree outside. She ran wildly down the driveway after the carriage, screaming her sister's name, begging the coachman to stop. He looked back and saw her then flicked his whip at the black-plumed funeral horses, urging them faster.

"Lily," Ciel screamed, heartbroken. "Oh, Lily. Come back. Please come back." But Lily could not hear.

Everyone for miles around knew what was happening and they lined up along the lane, staring at Lily the traitor. They had known and loved her all their lives, but now their contempt for her showed in their grim, expressionless faces and stony eyes.

"It's going to be all right," Lily told herself shakily. "Pa will come after me any minute now." The roses on her extravagant little straw hat nodded as she stuck her chin haughtily in the air, staring back at everyone so they would not think she was afraid. Pa would never send me away . . . never . . . he's just frightening me until I come to my senses, or he comes to his . . ."

But the carriage had already reached the bend in the lane and still her father had not come. Even at this distance she could hear the dogs howling and she looked desperately back, searching for her father. But Ardnavarna was silent and shuttered. And her beloved pa did not come riding to rescue his "darling girl."

And, throwing back her head, Lily howled, too, a great wail of pain like the terrified dogs. Because she knew now it was true. She was locked out of paradise. She would never go home to Ardnavarna again.

Maudie

I GLANCED AT MY TWO YOUNG LISTENERS and saw tears in Shannon's eyes. I knew what she was thinking. "You are right to feel pity for her," I said. "She was raped by an unscrupulous man, a sexual adventurer who should have known she was different from his usual experienced women. She was just a silly child who didn't know what she was doing until it was too late. Her whole life changed because of it, and the joyous young girl was no more."

I sighed, pitying her, as I pushed off the dogs and stood up, shaking out my crumpled chiffon skirt. "Bedtime, my darlings," I called. "And tomorrow, after dinner, I shall tell you what happened next."

CHAPTER

~~~~~~~~~~~~~~~ 22 ~~~~~~~~~~~~~~~

MAUDIE

Ardnavarna

I WORE SAPPHIRE-BLUE Dior the next night, flirtatiously short to the knee, daringly décolleté with a flutter of marabou feathers flung over my shoulders, hiding my bony chest. I wore Mammie's huge sapphires dangling from my ears and I was astonished when Eddie assured me that if I were to sell them I could live out the rest of my life in grand style on what they would fetch! And Shannon told me what true *style* I had, and how pretty my legs still were and that my perfume seemed hauntingly familiar.

"L'Heure Bleue—Guerlain, dearest child," I told her when she asked. "It was all the rage when I was a gel. And Jicky and Shalimar. But L'Heure Bleue—such a naughty name—was always my favorite. Maybe because I enjoyed what it meant rather too often than was good for me."

Eddie laughed. "Tell us what it meant, Maudie," he encouraged me.

"Well, of course it was the wicked Frenchmen who gave it that name. It's supposed to mean the blue twilit evening hour when men were entertained by their mistresses after leaving the office and before going home to their wives. I don't suppose the French were the only ones to think of it, but they were certainly the only ones to name a perfume for it."

"I feel so plain next to you, Maudie," Shannon complained, "in my little black dress."

"And Lily's diamond necklace," I said.

"Dad said it was 'by way of being a family heirloom.' " She quoted his words exactly. "And that I should treasure it."

"Of course you should, dear girl," I said. "It's a vital clue." I tried to look mysterious and Edward smiled at me, pouring glasses of champagne.

"I know, I know." He laughed. "But we shall have to wait to find out why."

"Oh, dear, I'm afraid you've got my number, as you dear Americans would say." I sipped the champagne, heaving a small satisfied sigh. "Dear boy, pour a glass for Brigid, will you? She loves a tipple and she knows the good stuff from the mediocre. Many's the glass of champagne we've shared together after a party. I can't thank you enough, dear Edward, for such a treat. *And* you had to drive all the way into Galway to find it."

"My pleasure, ma'am."

I turned to Shannon. "I'm not just keeping you on tenterhooks," I told her. "You just have to know the whole story, all the many secret layers of it, for it to make sense. Though I'm not sure myself, dear girl, how it is going to help you find out who killed your father. But it's my belief that truth is always hidden under a dozen different veils of secrecy, and you must lift each one in turn to find it. So after dinner we shall continue with Lily, and the past."

Brigid, round and neat as a new pin in her best black with her white ankle socks and little trotty-heeled boots, blushed as Edward made a toast to her. "To Brigid, the best cook this side of the Atlantic. Queen of her kitchen and without whom Ardnavarna would not be the same."

"Hear, hear," I agreed. "To me darlin' Brigid, without whom I should never be the same silly old woman I am."

"I can drink to that," she said wickedly, tossing back her champagne in a single long gulp.

"Mind your manners, woman, will you," I chided her. "You're supposed to sip the golden nectar and take your time about it."

"Not with my lobsters ready for the pot, I don't," she snorted, heading for the kitchen.

"Mind you don't go falling now, on those silly high heels. You are too old for them," I yelled after her, ignoring the fact that I myself was wearing my silver stilettos. "The poor old dear never had a head for drink," I added, "but I daresay the lobsters will be none the worse for it.

"Throw another log on the fire, Edward my boy, and Shannon, put a record on the gramophone. I'll just mix the doggies their dinners and we shall all be ready for our own home-smoked salmon, and then the lobsters . . ."

"And then Lily for dessert," Edward finished for me, and I laughed.

Shannon was sifting through a pile of dusty old 78 rpm records. She put one on the ancient gramophone and the strains of a Brahms violin concerto floated through the lamp-lit room. She looked suddenly sad and forlorn and Eddie went to stand next to her. He took her hand and squeezed it sympathetically.

"What are you thinking?" he asked.

"Just how much my father would have enjoyed meeting you both," she said. "And how much I would have loved him to see Ardnavarna."

"Oh, but your father knew Ardnavarna, all right," I blurted out. "I was going to tell you *all in good time,* but I thought it might comfort you to know he was here and that he knew the old place. But you'll have to wait for the full story later, at the right time."

Stunned, Shannon sank into a chair alongside a dalmatian who grumblingly moved over to give her room.

I looked worriedly at her pale, pretty face. Maybe I was an old fool to have said what I did, but the poor girl was grieving so, I'd just had to let her know her father had been here. I told her quickly that I had met him myself, just that once, and that he was a fine man. There was an integrity about him, and a strength. And that's why I had believed her without question when she told me her story. "A man like that gets on with life no matter what it brings," I said firmly. "I think all of us here in this room are agreed your father did not kill himself. And I think all of us"—I included Edward in my glance—"are agreed to find out who did."

After dinner, we adjourned as usual to the drawing room. Eddie poked the fire into a cheerful blaze and I settled myself in my favorite sofa. One of the dogs squashed comfortably in beside me and I propped my sparrow-boned ankles on a tapestry stool, and began the next episode of my story.

"Aunt Mallow in Cork City was a brisk, unquestioning woman," I said. "A poor relation summoned occasionally to the Big House for the Christmas and Easter festivities; the sort who sat in the chair farthest from the fireside, keeping to her knitting and remaining discreetly just outside the family circle. She knew her place and she knew what was expected of her. If she guessed why Lily was sent to her to be put on the S.S. *Hibernia* sailing for Boston on that very evening's tide, she knew better than to ask her question out loud. Or to let her pity show, as she said good-bye with a brief kiss on the cheek and watched the child walk slowly up the gangway to board the steamship."

~~~~~

LILY'S FACE WAS BLEAK as she walked to the rail, searching for her aunt in the milling crowd below. But the woman had already disappeared from sight, hurrying back to the small comforts of her own rooms in a genteel guest house paid for by her dear cousin Lord Molyneux out of the charity of his heart.

The old six-masted iron steamship was carrying a cargo of Cork's best butter and bacon and Irish whiskey, as well as a hold full of ragged immigrants. Lily lay on her narrow berth wedged against the varnished timbers in her stuffy little cabin with its single brass-rimmed porthole, as the rickety vessel slid from Cobh and lumbered through the choppy green waves of the notorious St. George's Channel. The next day they were hit by the full force of an Atlantic gale. Lily was too sick even to think about what had happened to her, but after a couple of days she got used to the bouncing rhythm and sat up in her little berth and took stock of her surroundings.

Huge gray-green waves slid past her porthole, but she did not feel frightened. She put on her old navy fisherman's jersey and breeches, pushed her long hair under a velvet cap and ventured out onto the deck. There was a little place near the prow where she could tuck herself away from view, and in between the worst of the storms she spent hours alone there, watching the green waves sliding by, listening to the cries of the seabirds and to the rigging tapping and jangling in the wind, trying not to think about her future or her past. Only about *now,* the very moment of time that she was living. Because that was all she could bear.

High up in her aerie, she could not hear the frightened cries of the unfortunate Irish immigrants crammed like cattle in the hold, heading for the new world and the riches and success they all dreamed were waiting for them. She could not hear the men in the hold shouting for help with the sick, and for food and water, and the women crying and the children wailing. Nor could she know that beneath them all, in the hot gritty bowels of the ship, Finn and Daniel O'Keeffe were shoveling great heaps of coal into the yawning fiery jaws of the boilers, working their way to America. Half naked and black as miners, they alternately cursed and prayed either to live or die, as the neverending storms threatened to capsize them.

There were a few other passengers, but because Lily kept to her cabin and spoke to no one, she immediately became the talk of the ship. Gossip rippled through the decks about the mysterious, aloof

young aristocrat who never joined her fellow passengers, even for dinner. The talk filtered down even to the steerage where, amidst filth and
disease, they condemned her to hell for her title, for her rumored
haughty ways, and for her rich family. The talk went even deeper,
down to the blistering engine room where Daniel heard, stunned,
about the beautiful and mysterious Lady Lily Molyneux.

He managed to keep his mouth shut when he was told, but afterward alone in the engine room he cried out angrily, "Faith and she's
chasing us! She'll haunt us for the rest of our lives." In the back of his
mind Dan hid the private memories of Lily that he treasured: of her
beguiling smiles, of her sapphire eyes, of the exquisite curve of her
slender young neck, and of the warm lingering glances for which he
had secretly yearned.

Of course she cared nothing for him. Finn and Lily had been thick
as thieves since they were youngsters and it was only natural that,
when they were grown, Finn would fall in love with her. Because simple love like his did not recognize the high walls and boundaries that
set them apart. Only Lily's sort knew the rules and how to sidestep
them when they wanted.

Still, Dan knew the child she was carrying was not his brother's and
he bent his massive shoulders to the mountain of coal, heaving shovelful after shovelful into the fiery furnace, wiping the sweat from his
brow with a blackened hand, wondering at the circumstance that had
placed Lily on this very boat, as though destiny itself were taking a
hand. He thought of Finn asleep in the dark cubbyhole that was their
"quarters," unaware that the cause of all his trouble was only yards
away from him. He guessed the family had sent Lily off to America to
have the baby and decided quickly that it was best his brother knew
nothing about it. Because if he did, he would surely kill her.

He kept Finn hard at work and away from the other stokers and
sailors. It wasn't difficult because Finn was no longer his usual convivial, talkative self. He worked silently, his face set in bitter lines, his red-
rimmed eyes staring blankly from his coal-blackened face.

They were never permitted on deck and as Finn rarely conversed
with anyone, it was easy to keep the gossip about Lily away from him.
The voyage progressed slowly, each day inexorably following the next
in a routine of heat-blasted filthy labor and exhausted dream-ridden
sleep.

They were forty miles off Nantucket when the gales really began to
blow. The captain consulted his barometer anxiously. He was a man
with fifty years seafaring experience and he knew exactly what was

coming. Ordering the first officer to tell the passengers they were confined to quarters and could expect rough weather, he battened down the hatches, locked the steerage passengers into their hold, and sent men down to secure the crates of Cork butter and bacon and whiskey so that the cargo would not shift dangerously under the new pounding they were about to endure.

Lily stared out of her porthole at the mountainous gray waves. The little *Hibernia* shuddered and shimmied under their impact, its timbers creaked fit to burst and her trunks slid from side to side across the cabin floor as though they possessed of a life of their own. The ship wallowed sullenly in a trough, and then a great blast of wind flung it toward the next wall of water. The *Hibernia* climbed and climbed until she seemed to be standing on her end and Lily clung desperately to the edge of her bunk, watching, terrified, as her trunks crashed against the cabin wall. The huge wave broke over them, forcing the *Hibernia* down and a sudden torrent of icy water roared down the companionways, flooding the ship.

Lily stared, fascinated, at the water flowing under her door. She began to pray. She didn't know whether she was praying to live or die but if she were going to die, then she did not want to die alone in her cabin.

She waded down the flooded corridors to the companionway leading up to the deck, peering, terrified, at the huge waves; angry, powerful watery monsters ready to drag her to her doom. She pictured herself drifting downward through a greenish miasma, her long black hair floating behind her, her dead eyes staring forever into nothingness as the water filled her lungs. And from the emptiness in her heart, she knew she did not care. She did not care about anything anymore.

Then the wind abruptly stopped and the waves slid glassily past, looking even more menacing in the sudden silence. The terrified cries of the poor immigrants in the hold filtered upward and Lily realized with horror that they were locked in. If the *Hibernia* went down they would not be able to get to the boats, or even jump over the edge and try to swim for it. Confined down there, they were all doomed.

She ran up the stairs to the bridgehouse and the captain turned to look at her. "There are women and children locked in your hold," she stormed. "If we are going to capsize, you must set them free like the rest of us, to face the worst."

The white-bearded captain eyed her angrily. "Dear God," he boomed, "don't I have enough on my plate without a useless woman do-gooder parading my decks in a storm?" He glared at her, then he softened a little, seeing she was so young. "If I let them out now they will only panic and fall overboard, and maybe a lot of them will die unnecessarily. When I feel the peril is imminent they will be set free to face their maker. I've captained a ship for fifty years now," he added grimly, "and I've never lost one yet and I'm not giving up the fight so quickly."

Lily realized he was right and offered an apology. He laughed. "You've got spirit, ma'am," he said, "and I like that. I'll tell you the truth of the matter: if this storm keeps up for another hour we shall be on the rocks off Nantucket and then we are all dead. If it stops, we might get lucky and drift through into Nantucket Sound. Either way, the *Hibernia* lost her rudder when we struck a shoal just now, so the matter is out of my hands. You can stay here," he added kindly, knowing she was alone, "if it's company you're after."

Lily curled up in a corner, her arms wrapped around her knees, watching, but no longer praying. The sky outside grew black as night again. The wind began to howl and the rain lashed down. Giant waves combed the ship, and tugged by the wind it floated off the shoal and drifted helplessly into the black night.

Down in the engine rooms the engineers and the stokers stood uselessly by as the great fires subsided in the boilers.

"We're at the mercy of the storm now, I reckon," the chief engineer said, lighting a cigarette. "Can ye just listen to them Irish bastards howlin' down in the hold. Sick as pigs and terrified as if they're heading for the slaughterhouse."

"They're no bastards," Finn spat back at him. "They've got mothers and faythers just the same as you. And wouldn't you be sick and afraid, stuck in that stinking hold with your children to care for?"

"Aye, aye, I reckon as how I might," the engineer said in a conciliatory tone. "I forgot you was Irish yerself. I'll tell ye somethin', I could use a bottle of that good Irish whiskey we've got in the hold, to steady my nerves. My mates abovedecks told me one of the crates had split open and we might just be able to help ourselves to a nice drink or two before the whole blasted lot goes to the bottom. And us with it most likely."

He swaggered off in search of his bottle and Daniel stared glumly at Finn. "Is she not listing as bad as she did before, Finn?" he asked, trying to assess their chances.

Finn shrugged. "What do I care? What future do we have anyway? We're just as helpless as those poor souls trapped in the hold." His angry eyes met his brother's. "Did y'niver stop to think what we might do when we reach Boston, Dan?" He stared helplessly down at the toes of his broken old boots. "We're a couple of ignorant Irish country lads with no money in our pockets and no prospects. We shall have to jump ship and steal our way into Amerikey without papers nor friends to welcome us. We should have stayed home in Ireland to die, instead of coming all this way in a god-blasted boat that's no better than an old fishing scow in a storm."

Dan shook his head despairingly. He knew his brother was right.

The engineer returned clutching four bottles of Irish whiskey. "Get this down you," he chortled, handing them out. "I guarantee you'll feel like new men before y've halfway drunk it."

They hunkered down on the floor by the fading glow of the boilers, gratefully swigging the whiskey. Soon they were joined by others. Daubed in coal dust and sweat with their red-rimmed eyes and mouths, Dan thought they resembled a circle of devilish gargoyles. The whiskey was finished and fresh supplies sent for. They discussed the captain and agreed he was a good man and if anybody could save them it was he, though with the rudder broken they were as good as gone.

"Barring a miracle," Finn said, his words tripping over his tongue.

"It'll be the passengers off first if there's any miracles to be had," the engineer growled blearily. "And the first will be the captain's new favorite. Walkin' around in her breeches she is, bold as brass. They say she's a lady, but I ain't never seen no lady looking like that."

"Ladies," Finn said contemplatively. "Let me tell you, boyo, ladies are not all they are meant to be. They don't think like you and me."

"They don't look like you and me neither, thank God," someone added amid laughter.

"No. This one's a real *Lady* lady," the engineer went on with drunken persistence.

The words penetrated Daniel's brain through a haze of whiskey. The hair bristled on the back of his neck as he sensed danger. Clapping his hand over the engineer's mouth, he said fiercely, "Shut up, ye stupid bastard."

The engineer fought him off. "Who are you callin' a bastard?" he yelled angrily. "Put up yer fists, ye damned Irish mick, and we'll see who's a bastard or not."

Finn leapt between them hurriedly. "Just look at you daft divils. Don't we have enough to worry us with the ship about to sink, without the two of youse fightin'? Besides, if the captain hears of it he'll have you both clapped in irons and arrested as soon as we get to Amerikey."

"If we gets there, that is," the engineer said sourly, throwing back his head and pulling hard on the whiskey bottle again.

"Bah, I'm going up to see what's happening," Finn said. "If I'm meant to die at least I'll not die down here, trapped in a coalhole with a bunch of fightin' drunks."

Stumbling from the drink, he hitched up his filthy pants, strode from the boiler room, and made his way up the winding metal stairs and across the galleries to the iron door leading onto the cargo deck. Daniel went anxiously after him. "Y'can't go up there, Finn," he said. "It's not allowed. Just look at the state of ye. What iver will the passengers say if they catch sight of ye, looking like a wild man?"

"I've as much right to die on deck as any passenger," Finn retorted.

Daniel thought about what he had said. "You're right," he decided hazily. "Don't they say that in our final moments God makes all men equal?" He marched after his brother, up the companionway onto the deck, just as the ship gave another almighty shudder. There was a terrible grinding, tearing noise and then, with a final shiver, the vessel fell silent.

"The ship just died," Daniel said in an awed whisper.

Finn stared at him and then he peered from the top of the companionway into the blackness outside. Waves were breaking over the stricken ship and the wind suddenly began to scream again, driving the rain in front of it. "There's women and children down in that hold," he said, suddenly sobered. "My God, Dan, what's to become of them? We've got to help them."

"How?" For the second time in his life Daniel felt absolutely powerless. "What are you going to do? Put them over the side in boats? Into a sea like that? Why, they'd not last two minutes. No, we'd best leave it to the captain. And to God."

They stared helplessly at the raging storm. The ship groaned like an animal in pain, and shaking their heads, they walked back again to the engine room and the comforts of the whiskey bottle.

The hours dragged by and still the *Hibernia* was afloat. Finally the long night everyone had expected to be their last was over and with it the storm. His ship was drifting into Nantucket Sound, but the captain knew their troubles were not yet over. They were in dangerous waters filled with shoals, and anticipating the worst he ordered the immigrants freed.

Two hours later they were drifting in a dead calm. A bank of fog crept silently toward them and the captain glanced at Lily, still huddled wearily in the corner. "When it lifts," he said encouragingly, "we shall send up flares. We should be close enough to Nantucket to be spotted and they will send boats. You can be sure you will be on the very first."

Lily had forgotten her own problems for the moment. She thought about the immigrants on the lower decks, frozen and wet and afraid, knowing nothing of what was going on. She knew there were women and children among them and she asked the captain to please send them down food and milk. He nodded. "I'll see it's done," he promised.

Suddenly exhausted, she waded back down the corridor to her cabin and lay on her damp bunk, staring at her straw hat with the roses floating past, wondering what was to become of her.

Down in the engine room the empty whiskey bottles that had rolled to and fro with the swaying of the ship were now heaped together in one corner. Finn eyed them warily. He wondered hazily if it was his imagination, or whether the movement of the ship had stopped. Yes, he could swear it had. His eyes met Daniel's and he said eagerly, "Let's go up top, Dan, and see what's happening."

"Don't waste yer breath and yer body," the engineer said sourly. "Ye'll still be the last off, even after the steerage. It is women and children first. That's the law of the sea." He took another swig of the whiskey and belched loudly. "O'course, our captain's favorite young lady will be piped ashore with all flags flyin'. No doubt she'll enjoy that, the Lady Lily."

Finn lifted his head. *"Lady Lily?"* he repeated.

"He means nothing," Daniel said desperately, grabbing Finn's arm and dragging him away. "He's just an old drunk, Finn, and don't you know it."

"The Lady Lily Molyneux," the engineer repeated in grand tones. "An earl's daughter, no less. Though she looks like a lad to me . . ."

Finn turned on Daniel, his eyes blazing. "You knew? You knew Lily was on this ship?"

"Only now. When he said so," Daniel lied. "It's just bad luck, that's all, Finn. Lily's nothin' to do with us anymore. Just leave it."

Finn flung him away and ran to the stairs. "Where are y'goin'?" Dan shouted, grabbing him.

"Where am I going?" Finn's eyes blazed at him. "I'm going to kill her, of course." He flung off his brother and was up the twisting iron staircase and across the galleries and through the doors before Daniel could even pick himself up off the floor.

Lily was standing by her open trunk. The fifty pounds she had been given lay on top and she was fastening the diamond necklace around her throat. The door suddenly slammed back against the wall and she stared at the coal-blackened wild man confronting her. She would have known those eyes anywhere.

"Finn?" she whispered, half joyful, half amazed. She didn't stop to think how or why he was here, she just knew that now everything would be all right. "Oh, Finn," she gasped. "Thank God. You've come to save me."

"Save you? You lying little bitch. I haven't come to *save* you." His strong hands were on her throat. He picked her up and shook her until her eyes bulged from their sockets and her face turned blue. "You've ruined me, Lily Molyneux," he muttered through gritted teeth, still shaking her. "You cheated on me, cheapened yourself like a street woman. Ah, God, I want to kill you for that more than anything. How could you, you bitch? How could you—"

Daniel sprang at him from the doorway. "Y'stupid bastard," he roared. "Do you want her to turn you into a murderer as well?" He pried Finn's hands from her neck and Lily fell against the edge of the berth, choking and retching.

"We'd better be out of here fast, before she has you clapped in irons," Dan yelled, dragging him away. "Godblast it, Finn, move yer great self."

Finn shrugged him off. He stood threateningly over Lily. "I wish I had killed you," he said grimly. "But you'll live to regret what you have done to me, Lily. By God you will." His hand shot out and he wrenched the diamonds from her neck. "I'm taking this to pay me back for what you've done." He grabbed the gold coins from the top of the trunk. "And the money as well. I'll come back though, Lily. I promise you that. One day I'll be back for the rest of what you owe me." He added in a whispered growl that only she could hear, "That which you've claimed I've already had." And then he ran from the cabin after his brother.

Lily fell back into her berth. She knew Finn had meant to kill her: she had seen it in his eyes, heard it in his bitter voice, felt it in the angry pressure of his hands on her throat. She shook her head in disbelief. "Oh, Finn, I didn't realize Pa would be so angry with you," she whispered hoarsely. "I never thought he would try to harm you. I thought it would just be me he would be angry with. And now look at what I've done." And she lay facedown on her wet bunk, and cried for her sins.

An hour later the captain inspected his ship anxiously. They were stuck firm as a clam on the shoal in a dead-calm sea with broken masts, and no rudder and a gaping hole amidships. They were listing twenty degrees to port, shipping water badly, and they were losing the battle even though they were bailing as fast as they could.

The fog had not lifted and he knew that if he sent up his precious flares now, the chances of them being spotted in this weather were almost nil. He thought of the two hundred and twenty immigrants in steerage, and of his other passengers and crew. He alone was responsible for their safety and he knew he could not wait. He would have to send up the flares and risk it. If there was no response to his SOS signals he would cram as many of the passengers he could into the four lifeboats and send them off into the fog toward the rocky shores and pray they made it to safety.

The first flare turned the fog pink and the captain searched the sky for an answering light. He sent up another, and another, but still there was no response, and his heart sank as he gave the order to lower the boats.

Lily followed the rest of the passengers onto the deck. She had lost everybody she ever cared about, including Finn. Now she did not care if she lost her life. She hung back, letting others go first. She had given up the fight. Now it was God's choice if she lived or died.

She hurried after the sailors who were rushing down the companionways to the steerage decks. They pushed the poor Irish immigrants roughly to the rail. "Get ready to jump," they yelled, thrusting them over the side and into the lifeboats bobbing below.

The first boat was soon filled with women and children, and rowed by four strong men it bobbed away into the fog. "Pray for them," a young Irish man who had been helping load the boat said bitterly, "for they will surely need it." Beside him, his wife crossed herself and her terrified children howled and clung to her ragged skirts.

The ship suddenly settled deeper in the water, hurling them all down the sloping decks. Terrified, Lily grabbed the rail, staring down at the final boat. It was almost full. She glanced at the young man who had been helping. He was standing next to her, looking despairingly down at his wife and children in the boat, and they stared, panic-stricken, back up at him. There was just one place left for Lily. She looked at the young wife, imagining her widowed with six mouths to feed, alone in a new country, knowing no one, possessing nothing, her man drowned and all hope gone.

"What good are they without *him*?" she cried bitterly to the captain. "How would they manage without a husband and a father? They might as well drown now as die of starvation when they reach Boston. His place is with them in that boat."

The young man looked longingly at his wife and then back at Lily. "Faith, I can't let y'do this, miss," he said quietly.

"You have no choice," Lily replied. "I'm not going." The captain knew she meant it. He stared wearily into the fog, telling himself she was nothing but trouble. Then, like a star from heaven, he saw an answering green flare. Help was at hand at last. He ordered the man to jump.

"God bless you, miss. We shall niver forget you," the young man cried. His wild blue eyes linked with Lily's for a split second and then he jumped out into the darkness after the others.

Suddenly the *Hibernia* began to shake like an animal in its death throes. It shuddered and jittered and the timbers screamed as they were rent apart and it began to slide slowly onto its beam ends. Lily heard the captain shout a warning, but then she was knocked off her feet and sliding helplessly toward the edge. She grabbed for the rail but it was too late. She plunged over the side into blackness.

The icy seas closed over her head. The waves sucked her down and down and her lungs were bursting. She realized she was dying after all. Fate had cheated Finn of that pleasure. This was the way it was meant to be. *This* was her terrible punishment.

CHAPTER

∾∾∾∾∾∾∾∾∾ 23 ∾∾∾∾∾∾∾∾∾

NANTUCKET, 1883

NED SHERIDAN WAS IN the first rescue boat, riding the swell and peering through the mist for the flares that would guide them to the sinking ship. Other boats bobbed behind, searching for survivors by the light of whale lamps high in their prows, and they roared in dismay as they saw the *Hibernia* suddenly list steeply, tossing people into the sea.

Ned tied a rope around his waist and plunged into the icy water after them. Lily bobbed to the surface near him, then immediately went under again, swamped by another wave. He grabbed her as she came up a second time and the other men hauled them over the side. They laid her in the gunnels, staring anxiously at her.

"It's a young girl," they said, shaking their heads, thinking she was already dead, though Ned turned her over and began to thump the water from her lungs. After a few minutes she began to cough and splutter and they went hurriedly back to rescue the others.

Wrecking schooners were already pulling alongside the ship, waiting for the captain to leave so they could claim it as salvage. The captain stood at the rail while they rigged a Manila hemp line, watching as his crew scrambled across to safety, clinging like monkeys to the wavering cable, cursing and shouting as they were dunked into the freezing ocean. But he had no intention of handing over his ship; he intended to sit it out until the fog lifted, and then get a tow to port.

The women and children and the sick and old were taken into the townsfolks' homes, while the men were billeted at the Pantheon Hall or the Hall of the Sons of Temperance, and given dry clothing, blankets, and hot food.

Ned carried Lily wrapped in a blanket to his own home on Main Street. A young Irishwoman walked behind him with her baby in her arms, while her six small children rode in a cart pushed by a sturdy lad. She wailed loudly at being separated from her man, and her children wailed noisily along with her.

Alice Sheridan was waiting at her door. She was a small, slender pale-faced woman, plainly dressed in the manner of her Quaker forebears. The simplicity of the Methodist Church had long since taken over from the strictness of the Quakers on Nantucket, but Alice Sheridan still followed the same tenets of sharing and giving and like the other townswomen she opened her home and her heart willingly to the refugees.

When she saw them approaching she hurriedly called her daughters, seventeen-year-old Abigail and ten-year-old Betsy, to fetch more blankets from the chests, and to search the linen presses for whatever children's clothes they could find. "For we shall have a full house tonight," she said, counting the ragged crying children. She scooped the baby from the tired mother's arms, urging her inside, and the children trailed in after her. It wasn't until Ned lay his blanket-wrapped bundle down on the braid rug in front of the roaring kitchen fire that she even noticed Lily.

Silence fell as they all stared down at her. Lily's long black hair trailed in a sodden mass down her back. Her face and hands were blue with cold and there were shocking bruises on her white throat. Ned looked at her fine bone structure, the dark level brows, and long curling lashes lying in perfect half-moons across her cheeks. He noted her beauty and her pallor and her absolute stillness and thought he had been too late. She was dead.

"Why, she's just a girl," his mother exclaimed, tears of sympathy springing to her eyes.

" 'Tis the lady that gave me husband her place in the boat. She saved me husband's life," the young mother cried, recognizing her. "And now the poor thing has lost her own." And she began to cry again, followed in loud chorus by her youngsters.

"Hush your wailing," Alice Sheridan said firmly. "The girl's not dead yet, and it would be nobody's fault if she were. Shipwreck is like love and war: 'everything's fair,' and you just do what has to be done."

While her elder daughter, Abigail, dunked the squalling children into a tin bath of hot water, Ned ran for the doctor. Lily's breathing was shallow; sometimes it seemed to stop altogether and they held their own breaths anxiously until there was a faint fluttering sigh and they knew she was still with them.

The doctor came quickly. He took Lily's pulse and listened to her heart and her chest, and he shook his head over the bruises on her throat. He said she was suffering from shock and exposure and that they could expect a raging fever that night. There was no saying how long it might last: one night, two . . . a week even. If the fever broke soon enough, she would survive. "If not," he said, lifting his shoulders in a helpless shrug, "there are already nineteen dead that we know of and a dozen others missing. The wonder is it wasn't more."

Ned was banished to sleep in the attic and Lily was tucked up in his bed with the brass warming pans and hot bottles and the fire roaring in the grate, because despite the fever the doctor had warned the room must be kept at an even temperature. Alice kept vigil over her while the others stole helplessly in and out.

In the early hours of the morning, unable to forget her, Ned left his attic bed and went downstairs. His mother was dozing lightly in a chair by the fire, and he stole across the room and looked down at the sleeping beauty in his bed. As he watched, her heavy lids fluttered and her eyes opened.

She was so young and so lovely and so mortally ill, Ned's heart somersaulted with pain and love. He wanted to wrap his arms protectively around her and tell her that he would never let anything bad happen to her, that he would look after her and cherish her forever. But then her eyes closed and she was back in her own twilight world again.

The fog cleared the next morning and the *Hibernia* could clearly be seen from the shore, sitting out on the shoal. Her captain was still aboard and the two wrecking ships were standing by. Ned and his father saw that the *Hibernia*'s list was even steeper than before and they knew the vessel was doomed and there would be no need for a tow.

The captain gave orders to remove his cargo and by the time night fell half her ballast had been removed and the *Hibernia* floated free. The wreckers moved in quickly to take what else they could before she swung onto her beam ends and went to the bottom.

Ned returned home that night with Lily's two water-stained burgundy leather trunks and the intriguing information that she was the Lady Lily Molyneux, aged seventeen and en route to visit a relative in New England.

His two sisters glanced at each other with amazed little cries. "Lady Lily," they exclaimed, impressed. They doubted a "Lady" had ever been seen on Nantucket before.

Like their brother they were blond, blue-eyed, and Nordic-looking.

They were quietly pretty and modest, brought up in a household that taught the simple values were what mattered; a love of God and a love of their fellow men. "Sharing, caring, and giving," had been their parents' watchword, and naturally it had become theirs, though it didn't stop them from eyeing Lily's matched trunks and wondering what they might contain.

"A Lady must surely have some pretty things," young Betsy said a little enviously, smoothing down her brown woolen skirt, imagining it was satin or silk and light as a moonbeam instead of coarse and heavy enough to keep out Nantucket's winter winds.

Lily's fever still raged, vaulting up and down, sometimes leaving her shivering and sometimes drenching her in sweat. Betsy and Abigail took turns with their mother, sitting quietly at the bedside, their eyes fixed anxiously on her. But with the storm over, Ned was reluctantly forced to return to Boston.

NED WAS TWENTY-THREE YEARS OLD; lean, young, and very handsome; with heavy straw-blond hair that slid silkily over his light-blue eyes. He was strong-jawed and clean-shaven and muscular.

When he had finished school he had run off to seek his fortune in the theater. He was working as a barman in a Boston saloon to earn enough money to get him to New York when one night a dramatic-looking man strode in. He was wrapped in a voluminous black cloak with a flowing silk shirt, a pearl-gray silk cravat and a wide-brimmed black hat. He tapped on the counter with the silver tip of his malacca cane and demanded brandy in ringing tones.

Ned's face lit up. He knew he must be an actor, looking the way he did and with a voice like that. He served him his brandy and respectfully asked him who he was.

It was a question de Lowry hated. He glared at Ned, his bushy black eyebrows meeting in a scowl. "Young man," he retorted coldly, "you should not need to ask *who* I am."

Ned apologized humbly, explaining that he had just left college and that his ambition was to be an actor. "A famous one like yourself," he added, taking a calculated guess.

De Lowry inspected the young barman with interest. He liked what he saw: with that face and that physique he didn't need to act. And he could see he was young and trusting and unwise in the ways of the world, and that suited the older man just fine. He immediately offered him a job. "Of course, the salary is almost nothing, dear boy," he boomed, "but I am offering you the invaluable opportunity to learn an actor's craft from a master."

It was the answer to all Ned's prayers. He gave up his job that same night and became a member of the de Lowry Famous Traveling Players. He was an actor at last. He got to play everything from a cabin boy to a French aristocrat as well as acting as general factotum to the de Lowrys, fetching and carrying for them; jugs of stout and bottles of whiskey mostly. He was also useful in arranging credit at saloons and cafés where his fresh-faced innocence worked better than de Lowry's shifty bravado.

The de Lowry Famous Traveling Players performed in chilly flea-bitten halls in cheap towns, and Jacob de Lowry, whose real name was Jacob Leech, wrote most of the plays with the unskilled assistance of his wife, the blond and overblown Sasha Orlov. They mostly were costume melodramas meant to show off de Lowry's aging and tightly corseted physique to advantage. With his flashing dark eyes, his po-maded black hair and twirling mustache, dressed in close-fitting breeches, high boots, and flowing silk shirts, he was quite a sight. The tear-jerking romances displayed Sasha's bosomy charms to the full. In her floating chiffons, she had acquired a reputation for "carelessness" with her draperies, allowing a little more of her flesh to be revealed than she should, and keeping her audiences on the edges of their seats in anticipation of more.

The de Lowrys had been arrested more than once on charges of indecency, but they had always managed to skip town.

For the actors, life with the de Lowry Famous Traveling Players was either spent on stage or on trains or on the run. From debt collectors, disillusioned theater owners, irate landladies, barkeeps, stores, and restaurant owners. They told each other that one day Jacob would run out of towns that didn't know about him and his "Famous" reputation and they would all be out of a job. Meanwhile they had work and ultimately they were always paid, though not very much.

Ned thought he was in heaven just being near a stage and he was bewildered by the professional cynicism of his fellow actors. Especially the "ingenue" Jeanette Foyle, whose ingenue days were long over and whose fading prettiness was edged with disillusion. She took him to her bed immediately and for a few weeks kept him in a permanent state of semiexhaustion. He only managed to get through his onstage performances and his chores for de Lowry on sheer youth and joie de vivre, and he was relieved when Jeanette found herself a new lover and he was free again to devote all his time to learning his craft. And from then on he followed the advice of his fellow actor Harrison Robbins, to keep his sex life outside the Players and save himself a lot of grief. "Because, old friend, 'a woman scorned is a fair demon,' " Harrison warned him solemnly.

And Ned thought Harrison should know. He was thirty-two, dark, mustached, and a winner with the women in the audiences. He was also a dedicated gambler, a fair-to-middling drinker, a bad actor, and good company. And he and Ned were friends. Or "companions in arms" as Harrison called it, because working with the de Lowrys was a constant battle: they battled to get a decent role because de Lowry insisted on playing all the leads regardless of his age; they battled to get new costumes and enough time to learn the lines of each new "play" de Lowry had dreamed up overnight; and they battled to get paid.

One night in a barroom in Worcester, Massachusetts, Ned told his friend about Lily. "She's the most beautiful girl I've ever seen. Can you imagine any reason a wonderful, young girl like that—with everything to live for—could *die*, Harry?"

Harry shook his head. "Forget her, Ned, that's my advice to you. She sounds like nothing but trouble."

"I can't forget her." Ned remembered her sapphire eyes, the curve of her lips, the way she felt in his arms. "I have to go back to her," he said, climbing from the barstool.

Harrison grabbed his arm. "Oh, no you don't. You have a show to do tonight, young fella, and an obligation to the rest of us. You can't go running off because some girl—a total stranger you just happened to have rescued from the deep—might die. Besides, she doesn't need a lovesick swain loitering at her bedside. Take it from me, women don't like you to see them when they are sick. Save it for when she's looking her best."

Ned Sheridan was no stranger to love. He was still only twenty-three, but there had already been several women in his life. And he had loved some of them too. He could still remember his first true love, as well as the first girl he had ever made love to. He recalled the trembling exhaustion of his passionate affair with Jeanette and the purity of his love for a professor's daughter at Brown. But he had never in his young life felt this heart-vaulting, all-consuming passionate love for any woman before, and he knew he never would again.

He sighed. Harrison was right, he couldn't let the Players down. He realized he did not know Lily, but it didn't stop him from thinking about her constantly and he told himself that one day when he was a famous actor, he would be rich and successful and he would give her the world on a golden plate.

THE HOUSE ON MAIN STREET was quiet. A beam of January sunlight dappled the green-and-white quilt worked by Alice Sheridan's grandmother over a hundred years before, touching Lily's face with warmth. She opened her eyes and stared at the crisp blue winter sky outlined in the glittering many-paned windows, wondering where she was.

Puzzled, she glanced around the room. The walls were plain white, there were rugged ceiling beams and wooden floors, a multicolored rag rug and a rocking chair. A model of a whaling ship in a bottle stood on a plain pine dresser, and over it hung an embroidered text in a dark wooden frame. It was like a room she had seen in a dream; she remembered it and yet she did not know it.

She looked at her plain cotton nightgown and her own hands lying limply on top of the coverlet and asked herself whether darling Pa had sent her off to school after all. And then she saw her two sea-stained trunks standing in the corner and the horrible events of the past flashed through her mind.

She stared at the cavernous cedar trunks, remembering the terrified maids cramming them with everything they could lay their hands on. What had not fit in, her father had ordered them to burn. Her hunters had been sold, her Connemara ponies banished to another county— because her father would never harm a horse—and her beloved dogs had only been allowed to remain because Ciel had flung herself weeping at Pa's feet, pleading that they belonged to her too.

All that remained of her past was in those trunks. Except for one thing. The baby. She ran her hands over the undeniable roundness of her belly, knowing that it was still there, leaching life from her like a parasite, and she knew that she would never be able to look at its face.

She pushed back the covers and swung her legs over the side and tried shakily to stand up. Her knees trembled and she sank back again, moaning as she remembered the shipwreck and Finn, with his hands on her throat trying to choke the life out of her. And then the icy waters closing over her head and herself sinking deeper, knowing she was going to die.

"And I should have," she cried pitifully. "I should have died for my sins." Flinging herself against the cool linen pillow she wept for the loss of her past and fear of her future.

Alice Sheridan came quickly up the stairs. She sat on the edge of the bed and put her arms around Lily. "It's all right," she said, patting her back soothingly the way she had patted her babies' backs when they were fractious. "You are safe now, and I promise you everything will be all right. We shall look after you. You may stay with us as long as you wish. You will be like one of my own daughters."

She could not have said a more comforting word. Lily stopped sobbing and glanced hopefully up at her through her lashes. She did not know who Alice was, but those were the first loving words she had heard since she had been banished.

Then she shook her head miserably. "No," she sobbed, "when you hear about my wickedness you will not want me either. You will throw me out just the way my own family did."

"Dear child!" Mrs. Sheridan exclaimed, shocked. "Of course I shall not throw you out. And you are far too young to have been very wicked."

Lily stared at her. She saw a slender, smooth-faced woman, plainly dressed and with work-reddened hands. Mrs. Sheridan's brown eyes were filled with sympathy, but Lily knew that when she told her the truth, she would send her away from this refuge.

Mrs. Sheridan plumped her pillows and tucked her back into bed. She said, "You have been so ill we were afraid we might lose you. But God sent you back to us and we shall not let go of you so quickly. You must drink some broth and we shall have you on the road to recovery in no time."

Her broth was delivered by a little blond girl who stared curiously at her and told her she was Betsy Sheridan and that she was ten years old and that she had been forbidden to say anymore.

Her next visitor was seventeen-year-old Abigail, blond, fair-skinned and pale-eyed like her sister, who came with a shy smile to take her tray away. "We are so glad you are feeling better, dear Lily," she said warmly, and tears of surprise misted Lily's eyes as she wondered why these total strangers should care whether she lived or died when her own father did not.

She lay awake all night thinking about what to tell them. The only thing the Sheridans knew about her was her name and that she was en route to stay with a relative in New England. She could tell any story she liked and they would believe her, and she spent the night reinventing her past so the Sheridans would not throw her out of their peaceful little paradise.

When Mrs. Sheridan came up the next morning with her breakfast tray, Lily said humbly, "I have no way to repay you for all your kindness, and I must explain why." Mrs. Sheridan sat on the edge of her bed to listen and she said, "You see, Mrs. Sheridan, I married young. I was just seventeen and he was a soldier in the queen's army. He was not much older than me and so handsome and kind and gentle."

She hesitated, as though it pained her even to talk about him, and then continued in a sad voice, "We were very much in love, but my father had an important title; he was rich, he owned big estates and grand houses, and my young captain had nothing. My father said I would be marrying beneath me and he refused his permission. But Mrs. Sheridan, love cares nothing for all those things. I know now it was wrong, but we ran away and got married and we were so happy. And when I found out I was . . . when I found I was going to have a baby, I felt sure my family would rejoice with us and welcome us back into the fold. But it was not to be. They hardened their hearts against me. And when, a month later, my lovely young husband was killed in an accident, they refused even to come to his funeral."

She gazed piteously at Alice Sheridan. "They refused to have anything more to do with me or his child. I had nothing left, just a very little money and these two trunks with my things. So you see, Mrs. Sheridan, there is no 'relative' in New England. It was all just a story. And that's why I was traveling alone and unchaperoned on that tired old cargo ship. I was coming to America, like the rest of the poor Irish immigrants, hoping to find a better life for myself in the New World."

She hung her head. "If it were not for the child my husband would not have taken the new commission. It meant more money but it also meant he had to travel abroad. And it was on that journey he was killed. So you see, it's all the baby's fault. Because of it, my husband died. I don't want this baby I'm carrying," she said passionately. "I would rather die than have to look at it." And though she was lying about what had happened, she was telling the truth about the baby. She couldn't bear to look at the child of the man who had ruined her perfect life.

Alice shook her head in shock. Then she said comfortingly, "Just remember this, my dear. A miracle happens every time a baby is born, and somehow love is born with it."

She put her arms around her and Lily rested her head against her shoulder. It was the first time since she had been banished that she had the warmth of human contact and affection, and she sobbed with relief. If she could not die, then at least the child would have a happy home with the Sheridans. She would be free of Dermot Hathaway at last.

Her heart sank as she thought of Finn and Daniel. But later Obediah Sheridan himself came to tell her that a total of twenty-one women and children had drowned and half were unidentified. "Our townsfolk took up a collection for the survivors," he said, "and a few days later they sailed off to Boston to begin their new lives." He sighed, sorrowfully contemplating their plight. "At least they had food in their bellies and decent warm clothes instead of their own pitiful rags. And a little money in their pockets to give them a start."

But Lily did not hear him. She was imagining the icy green waves closing over Finn's head, seeing him sinking deeper and deeper, his dead gray eyes wide open, staring at nothing. But she knew Finn could swim like a seal. *And* he was strong. He and Daniel used to go out in the bay in all weather to catch fish for their suppers, and he had capsized more times than he cared to remember. He just couldn't be dead. Not her friend. Nor her handsome, reckless Finn.

CHAPTER
24

MAUDIE

Ardnavarna

I WAS TIRED, and with all my characters about to begin new lives in the New World, I thought it appropriate to leave Lily's story there for the night. It had been many a year since I had had the company of young people and their energy amazed me. They talked all night, snatched an hour or two's sleep, and were off for a dawn gallop, just like Finn and Lily. Except that Eddie cannot ride a horse. Shannon has set herself to teach him and very smug she is, too, to have something over him.

But here I am, talking as though Shannon and Eddie were falling in love. Now, whatever could have put such an idea into my head, I ask you? I'm just dreaming, I suppose. Though it would be nice.

I climbed into bed and sank, relieved, against the pillows, listening to the nighttime country sounds. Town people always complain that country nights are too quiet, but there are always owls hooting and foxes barking, horses neighing and the wind sighing in the branches. Sometimes there's a cacophony out there.

I couldn't sleep, and when I woke it was raining. The morning air coming in through my window was chilly and my view of the sea was lost in mist. I thought anxiously about my roses and climbed from bed to take a look, but found my legs like jelly. Suddenly weak as a foal I sank back down again and leaned my dizzy head against the pillow. After a few minutes I was forced to admit that I felt odd: my heart was pounding and my hands were all a-tremble.

Irritably I pushed the bell beside my bed and a few minutes later I heard Brigid hurrying up the stairs and then her quick trot along the corridor. Her Wellingtons make a funny little slap and squish on the bare boards and I always know when it's her, but then, who else would it be these days?

"Ye've been overdoing it," she said, glaring at me, and I sank meekly back against my pillow, feeling like a child again. "Too much partying and too many late nights. Will ye niver admit yer an old woman and act yer age?"

I've never acted my age and she knows it and I don't intend to start now, but I could see the worry in her brown eyes and I knew the old biddy loved me as much as I love her. Whatever should we do without each other? My heart trembles at the thought. We are each other's lifeline, each other's link with the past and our memories. And when you are our age there is more past than future. We sit of a winter's evening in front of the kitchen fire, toasting ourselves among a clutter of dogs and cats with a glass of whiskey clutched in our hands to keep out the cold and fuel the memories, talking of "remember when . . ." Brigid knows all my memories as intimately as I know hers. Though I have to confess mine are more exciting.

Sure and she was a rock when some years ago I found that lump in my breast and the doctor said it would have to come off. I went home and took off my clothes and stared at myself in the mirror, at those twin round objects, always small but still firm and pretty, and always a woman's pride: the badge of her femininity, potential nurturers of infants and a source of more pleasure than I will ever admit to in company. And I confess I was filled with self-pity.

I ran down the stairs to Brigid in the kitchen and she read from my face that the worst had been confirmed and we clung together, crying. "Y've to be strong, Maudie," she told me and I knew how deeply moved she was to be calling me by my name instead of simply "ye" or "madam," which she only ever uses when she's mad at me. And for her to be showing me overt affection as well, which is something we never do. I told her they were going to cut it off.

"Ye've the heart of a lion, Maudie. Ye'll be fine," she said staunchly. And then she added, "Is there no other way?"

"Radiation and chemotherapy," I said. "A fifty-fifty chance. My hair will fall out, I'll be sick as a dog all the time, and I shall be too weak to ride a horse."

"Thems all yer options?" I nodded. She considered them. "I never was one for the knife," was all she said finally.

So I chose the chemo. But even then they couldn't take my vanity away from me. I went to London, to one of those persons called a "top stylist" and ordered myself the brashest red wig, long and curly—like

Ann-Margret, I looked. And I bought myself a dozen silk nighties and
fluffy bedjackets and a few hundred books so I could still pretend it
was like when I was a little girl and got sick. All my friends came, every
day. Even on those days when I was not well enough to see them, they
rallied around, the way we always had for each other. For almost two
years I took it on the chin, feeling like hell. But I can tell you I never
wanted to die. Dammit, no! I wanted to ride mad Malachy again and
besides, nothing was going to get me away from Ardnavarna so easily.

When they told me I had gone into remission, I went straight to
Dublin and I bought myself a pile of silk underwear that amazed the
salesgirls at Brown Thomas. "There," I told 'em, satisfied as they
added up my enormous bill. "Now I *feel* better."

Anyway, back to my rainy morning. Brigid kept me to my bed and I
slept the day away, but I refused to give up my nightly audience. I put
on my best nightie—satin, my favorite for night attire, and pink because it's flattering to the pale skin and anyway I like the way it clashes
so beautifully with my scarlet hair. I added a dash of pink lipstick and a
little scent, and fastened my old ermine cape around my shoulders. I
looked ready for a nightclub when the two young things trooped
through my door later.

They had dined together by candlelight on my instructions because,
after all, a little candlepower never did a girl's looks any harm and I
confess I'm encouraging any hint of romance between my "children."
They looked shy about seeing me in bed and I noticed they were
holding hands as they walked toward me. "Aha," I thought, but I said
nothing. Teasing is never good for a beginning romance; it's all so
serious.

I shoved the dalmatians over and made room for them on the end of
my big four-poster. Shannon sat cross-legged, looking rather anxiously
at me and I was touched to see that she cared. I liked her more and
more as each day passed, and now I wish I had known her father
better. One brief glimpse of a dynamic man like that was not enough.

Eddie pulled up the old armchair. He draped his long body across it
and flung his legs over the arm. He moves like an actor should, everything natural and unstudied, and graceful in a masculine way. He has a
sense of humor that I like too.

"Love your outfit, Maudie," he said with a grin, and I stroked my
ermine proudly. It always feels like bunny fur to me even though it
used to cost a fortune. When we still wore furs, that is.

"Thank you," I said, because Mammie taught me to always accept a compliment politely instead of brushing it off with "Oh, this old thing?" the way so many girls do.

I said, "Tonight, my dears, our characters begin their new lives, and we shall follow each of them and see how they make out. Let us begin with Daniel and Finn, in Boston."

Boston, 1883

JANUARY WAS BITTERLY COLD in Boston, but it seemed even colder in the miserable slums of the North End. The narrow cobblestones were slippery with a layer of icy sleet as Daniel O'Keeffe made his way dispiritedly back to the tiny windowless cellar where they were living.

The wooden shacks leaned against crumbling brick houses that had once belonged to the better-off merchants of Boston. Before the Irish came, that is, swarming close to the wharves where they got off the boats, into every nook and cranny that afforded them shelter. The immigrants came in such numbers that Boston's worthy burghers had been forced out of their homes up to Beacon Hill or Back Bay to find cleaner, more salubrious air, away from the Irish smells of poverty and sickness and despair.

And no one was more despairing than Daniel as he climbed slowly down the broken steps that led to his new "home." Their cellar was dark and damp. It was bare but for the piles of straw and sacking spread on the floor for their bed and the wooden crate that served as a table, and it was almost as cold inside as it was out.

He pushed the flimsy door closed, hoping to cut off the ice-edged north wind that promised a foot of snow before too long. Finn was not home and he lit the single candle and thanked goodness for the small reprieve. At least it meant he didn't have to tell him just yet that there had been more than a hundred other men after the same job he had hoped to secure on a road gang. He had pushed himself eagerly forward, hoping his brawny physique would attract the foreman's attention, but there were plenty of other brawny Irishmen and ten had quickly been chosen before he could get himself noticed.

The cellar's low ceiling forced him into a permanent crouch and he folded his hands around the candle flame to warm them. His belly growled angrily from hunger. It had been twenty-four hours since he had last eaten, if you could call the meager greasy stew, doled out in return for a few cents at the saloon on the corner, a meal. Another few cents had brought the solace of a shot of whiskey to send the blood coursing in his veins, trying to chase out the cold.

A flimsy partition divided their cell from next door, where a whole family, a man, his wife, and four children lived in one room no bigger than their own and to whom they paid their rent of a dollar a week. He could hear the children bawling and fighting and the distraught mother screaming at them, but he was so used to it he scarcely heard it anymore. The whole building—the whole *street*—was filled with tiny hovels where large families struggled to keep their dignity and their sanity in a space no more than ten feet by nine. And he wondered how many of them wished bitterly they could turn back the clock and exchange their old familiar poverty in Ireland for this terrible new kind.

He glanced at the pile of straw in the corner, knowing that beneath it lay a fortune that could change their entire lives. How many nights had he watched Finn rummage in his hiding place and bring forth Lily Molyneux's diamond necklace and run it through his fingers. Daniel had noticed how the jewels, like the people, seemed to have lost their sparkle beneath a layer of grime. He had listened to Finn repeat with venom how if he ever saw her again, he would wrap this same string of useless diamonds around Lily's beautiful white throat and strangle her. For the diamond necklace had proved as valueless to them as a cheap paste imitation.

When they first arrived Finn had walked eagerly all the way uptown to find a smart jeweler. Dressed in his cord pants and rough tweed jacket and a clean shirt, with a woolen muffler knotted around his neck, all donated by the citizens of Nantucket out of the charity of their hearts to the poor Irish refugees, he had felt grand enough for anything—until he stepped over the threshold of the plushly carpeted jewelers.

A hush fell as the eyes of the grand morning-coated salesmen fastened on him. They regarded him with such horror that he glanced down at himself to see that everything was all right and that he hadn't maybe left his fly undone by mistake. But everything seemed intact, and removing his cap respectfully he had walked cautiously across to the shining glass display counter.

He had said a cheerful good morning, smiling around for a response, but none was forthcoming. The smile slipped from his face as two of the salesmen closed quickly in on him, one on either side. "We don't want your sort in here, begging. Get out at once before we call the police."

They thrust him out onto the sidewalk with a vicious push and locked the glass-paneled door safely behind him.

The threat of the cops rang like warning bells in his ears as he ran back down the hill. He realized too late that, of course, they would not let people like him into grand shops, and he thanked God he hadn't shown them the necklace because they would certainly have thought he had stolen it and then for sure they would have had him arrested.

"But you *have* stolen it," Daniel said stubbornly, when he told him the story that afternoon. "And that's God's truth."

"No, it's not," Finn had retorted vehemently. "She owes it to us. Aye, and more!" And he had gone straight out again to the local pawnbroker, knowing he would get less money but at least it would be something. He told himself that later, when he got a job and was a grand success himself, he could retrieve it. Then, with his new respectability, no one would even think to question where he got such a valuable piece of jewelry. But the pawnbroker had glanced suspiciously at him and then said he didn't deal with anything as expensive as this. It would be more than his life was worth if the cops came ferreting around. "They sees me with this," he warned Finn, "I'll only end up in jail alongside you."

And so the necklace was thrown under the straw like a dog's bone, as useless as an empty whiskey bottle to be dragged out and mourned over after a few drinks. And now, six weeks after they had arrived, all their charity money was spent.

Daniel glanced up as he heard the ring of hobnailed boots on the icy steps and his brother came in. His handsome young face was pinched with the cold and covered with a few days' black stubble, but there was a big smile in his gray eyes and he clutched a few paper-wrapped parcels to his chest.

"Look at this, Dan," he cried, dropping the parcels onto the wooden crate. He rubbed his hands together and held them around the candle the way Daniel had, to warm them. "You'll find a fresh loaf in there— none of yesterday's rubbish for us. And the best Irish butter. *And* a half pound of German sausage from the delicatessen on North Street." He delved inside his jacket and pulled forth a bottle of Irish whiskey and planted it on the crate. "That'll warm you, old feller," he said with a grin as Dan stared from him to the whiskey and back again in amazement. "And before you ask, I'll be tellin' ya. I changed two of Lily's English sovereigns into dollars today."

He hunkered down next to the wooden crate while he told Dan what had happened. "I went into St. Stephen's Church to get out of the cold and to see if the old Holy Fellow upstairs could come up with an answer for us, seeing as we could not ourselves. But nothing was forthcoming and the sacristan was looking sideways at me, I'd been there so long. So I came out and walked along the streets for a while and then up the hill. And where should I find meself at the top?" He beamed excitedly at Daniel. "Why, brother, outside a bank, o'course. I thought to meself, *I have these fifty sovereigns strapped around me waist for safekeeping and doin' me no good at all, so why don't I just take meself into this bank and ask them, bold as you please, to change them into dollars."*

Opening the whiskey he took a slug and offered the bottle to Daniel. "They did it with niver a question. And do you know how much I got for those two little gold sovereigns, brother Dan?"

Daniel shook his head and Finn grinned triumphantly at him. "Ten whole Yankee dollars, old son, that's how much I got for them." He stared excitedly into his brother's eyes. "Do you know how much I have strapped around me waist, boyo? In value, that is? The equivalent of two hundred and forty dollars. *A fortune, Dan. A whole God-blasted fortune."*

Dan stared speechlessly at him. A working man was lucky if he earned ten dollars a week to house and feed and clothe himself and his wife and numerous children. *And they had sovereigns worth two hundred and forty dollars.* "We could live for two years and four months on that," Dan calculated quickly, suddenly as excited as his brother. He lifted the bottle to his lips and drank deeply. Relief and whiskey made his legs feel weak and he took another slug to steady himself.

"You've saved us, brother," he cried admiringly. "You've saved us from destitution, for I niver got that job today and I swear to you I was at the end of my tether and cursing Lily Molyneux to hell along with yerself." His eyes misted over as he thought of his homeland. "Aye, and I wanted to go home, Finn," he added mournfully. "I wanted to be back in Connemara. To be back in the woods chasin' the pheasant and the woodcock and grouse. Walking Boston's streets, I wasn't seeing them, Finn. I was only seeing meself pulling a salmon from the river in that quiet beat beneath the willows, y'know the one I mean?"

Finn shrugged. He had money in his pockets and he felt like a new man. He was ready to take on the whole of the North End, *and* the city of Boston, aye—*and all of Amerikey, too,* if need be. He closed his ears to his brother's mournful memories of Ardnavarna and said impatiently, "Ye forget we was as poor as the next Irishman. And that for one wrong look or word his lordship would have had ye back shoveling horse shit again." He patted his pocket and said confidently, "We've got more money in our pockets, now, brother, than we ever would have in Connemara. This is what they mean by 'a golden opportunity.' Those sovereigns are gold and this is our opportunity.

"I'll tell you what," he cried, inspired by the excitement of their newfound wealth. "We'll celebrate, Dan. We'll take ourselves out to the Italian's café and we'll fill our bellies with as much food as they can hold. And then after we shall go to the saloon."

Daniel nodded in agreement. He struggled to his feet, knotting his thin muffler at his throat in readiness and Finn said, "Wait though, I'll just get Rory from upstairs to go with us."

He darted up the steps into the tenement and ran three flights without stopping, then banged heavily on the wooden door. Silence fell as the family inside froze into immobility. Such a knock could only mean police trouble. "It's all right, it's only me, Finn," he called, and the door was instantly flung open and a young lad grinned welcomingly at him.

Rory O'Donovan was younger than Finn by a year, sixteen to his seventeen, and he lived with his widowed mother and brothers and sisters, all seven of them in two minute rooms. The windows had been boarded up against the cold and, like Finn's cellar, the rooms were always dark, giving Rory the characteristic waxy immigrant pallor. Rory was thin and frail-looking with sticklike arms and legs, brilliant dark eyes, and a hacking cough that sometimes shook his thin frame so badly Finn thought he would burst.

He had met Rory on his very first day in the North End. Fresh off the boat from Nantucket and jingling the islanders' pitifully few charitable coins together in his pocket, he had stopped to ask the boy if he knew where cheap lodgings were to be found. Rory had directed him to the cellar where the impoverished tenants had agreed, for the weekly sum of a single dollar, to divide their cellar into two and rent one half to the O'Keeffe boys.

Finn and Rory had been friends ever since and Finn flung his arm around Rory's shoulders now and invited him to come with them to the Italian's. "I've had a touch of luck, boyo." He added with a grin, "I'll be after tellin' you about it over a hot meal."

Rory went to fetch his cap and scarf, and Finn quickly took the opportunity to slip two dollars into Mrs. O'Donovan's hand, telling her to think nothing of it, there was plenty more where that came from. She stared gratefully after him as he and Rory clattered down the splintered stairs that smelled of cabbage and urine and unspeakable grime and poverty. The two dollars would pay off what she owed "on the book" at the grocery store, so she could get more credit and feed her family for another week, if she were careful.

"He's a fine lad, young Finn O'Keeffe," she told her clustering children. "He'll be going a long way in this world, y'can be sure of that."

The Italian's café was a decent walk away in Ward Eight, but tonight they didn't even notice the distance or the cold as they laughed and talked excitedly, caps pulled low over their eyes and chins tucked down into their mufflers out of the icy wind. A few flakes of snow whirled around, but somehow it didn't seem to matter as much as it had before and Finn felt that heady freedom of being a man of means for the first time in his life.

"I like it, old fellow," he chortled, slapping Dan on the back and grinning broadly at Rory. "I like this feelin' of having money. It makes a fellow feel grand. Aye, more than that. As though nothing can touch you; you're safe from all the trials and tribulations of the world." He patted the gold sovereigns in the leather pouch strapped to his waist under his jacket and sighed with satisfaction. "Maybe I won't have to kill Lily Molyneux after all," he said with a wink at Dan, and the two of them laughed as though it was the biggest joke in the world while Rory stared bemusedly at them.

"I'll tell you all about it when you're old enough," Finn promised him with another wink as they herded into the steamy little storefront café. The heady fragrance of herbs and spices and roasting meats filled their hungry mouths with anticipatory saliva, and they ordered a flagon of rough red wine and downed it along with slabs of salami and sour green olives while they waited for their food. And when the plates of roast chicken and savory polenta came they fell silent, concentrating on the food as though it were the only thing on earth that mattered. They finished in record time and Finn leaned contentedly back in his chair. He called for more wine and more food for his friends and thought life had never seemed so good.

His thoughts turned as always to Lily and he wondered again what had become of her. Her name had not been on the survivors' list put up in the Hall of the Sons of Temperance in Nantucket, but Lady Lily's name would not have been placed with ordinary mortals anyway. Somehow she would have ended up with the gentry like herself. He brooded over the story one of the sailors had told him, of how he had seen her thrown into the sea. He told himself it could not have been Lily, that things like that didn't happen to girls like her, there would always be some poor fool at her side ready to protect her. He told himself bleakly that Lily had survived. He just knew it. He felt it in his heart.

After the steamy heat of the little café the cold outside struck them like a blow. Their breath hung on the air and their hobnailed boots clattered on the black ice, sending them slithering and cursing over the cobbles.

"Too cold for snow," Rory said as the blood-chilling wind whistled through his thin jacket. This was his second Boston winter and he knew the score. Later, when the temperature rose a notch or two, there would be snow all right, tons of the evil stuff. He thought miserably of his five brothers and sisters, all needing new boots, and he knew he just had to get a job, somewhere, anywhere. He would do anything.

"You'll work with us, fella," Daniel said, answering his unspoken prayer, striding rapidly through the icy streets as though he did not even feel the cold. Hurrying along beside him Rory asked eagerly what he meant. "We shall go into business with this money," Dan boomed importantly. "Right, Finn?" He stopped and stared at their questioning faces and then he laughed. "Just ask yourselves, boyos, what do people need most? Why, food and drink, of course. And after that clothing. Pants, skirts, coats, boots. We shall open a store with our money, lads, and then one thing's for sure. We shall never go hungry. Not with our own shop."

"Y'think we've enough money to do it, Dan?" Finn asked eagerly.

"To be sure, but I'll go speak to the ward boss. He'll set me straight about what to do." He slapped Finn affectionately on the back. "It's all thanks to your quick-thinking brother," he said, forgetting he had ever accused Finn of stealing from Lily, and his big handsome face split in an excited grin as he thought of the money and their new start in life.

Standing at the counter in Brady's Saloon, Finn said, "It's a fine country, Amerikey is. They give you five times as many dollars as you have sovereigns, like money grows on trees." He glanced happily around the smoky room. As usual, it was packed with ragged men and black-shawled women sitting over a single drink they could ill afford, because at least the saloon was warm and the company took their minds off their woes. And it was a thousand times better than the dark frozen hovels they called home.

"Mebbe we should open a saloon instead," Finn said to Daniel. "It's certain we would never be short of customers."

"There's three saloons to every block in the North End," Dan retorted, "and all of 'em filled with folks with just enough left over to buy themselves one drink. The only money being spent in here is what's left over after feeding and clothing their families. No, boyo," he repeated, "a store is where the money is, I'm convinced of it."

Rory knocked back his whiskey and began to cough. The cough turned to wheezing and his face turned red. "Best have a brandy, Rory," Finn suggested as the boy slowly regained his breath.

Rory hung his head miserably. "Me dad died o' the drink. And me mother always said if I was after takin' after him she would nail me feet to the floor before she'd let me into a saloon."

"And 'tis right the woman was too," Finn agreed approvingly. "I'll have no drunk in my employ." He winked at his friend, flinging an encouraging arm around him. "Just think, Rory," he said, his face shining with seventeen-year-old wonder as he contemplated their sudden step up in life, "one day you and me and Dan will be rich men."

"Is it rich, you are then?" Jack Brady, the landlord, asked, leaning interestedly on the scarred wooden counter, along with the customers crowding around to hear who had made it big in Amerikey.

"It is," Dan said with a modest grin. "Me and me brother here. We've come into a fair bit of money and we'll be settin' ourselves up in business. A nice little store that we hope you'll all be patronizing, because we plan to offer you the best prices in the North End."

"Two hundred and forty dollars," Finn exclaimed proudly. A stunned silence fell over the room as he patted the bulge under his jacket. "And me and me brother would like to buy each and every one of you, our fellow countrymen, a drop of the best Irish whiskey Brady has on his shelf. To celebrate. And so you don't forget the O'Keeffe brothers from Connemara when yer next doing your shopping."

Forty pairs of eyes fastened wonderingly on them as Brady passed the glasses around and they lifted them in a toast to the O'Keeffes' enviable good fortune. Two hundred and forty dollars was more than any one of them had made in their entire lives and more than any of them could even conceive of seeing in one grand lump sum. The whiskey was downed with a cheer and then someone struck up "Irish Rover" on the accordion, and someone else on the fiddle, and then the pipes and penny whistles, and before you knew it Brady's was roaring with song. The whiskey kept on flowing thanks to Daniel and Finn, and Brady smiled happily at his sudden bonanza, though he said warningly to Dan, "You'd best not spend it all in one night on the booze, old fella, or you'll niver get your fancy shop."

Rory finished his whiskey and said, "I'll have to be gettin' back, Dan. Me mother will be wondering."

Dan was still mulling over Brady's words. He knew the saloonkeeper was right and he knew that, with him drunk, the money would float through their fingers in one grand wonderful raucous party unless he did something about it. He nudged Finn and whispered to give Rory the sovereigns. "You take our money home with ye, lad, so we're not after spending it all," he said. "Give it to yer mother for safekeeping, and we'll see you in the morning."

Finn fumbled under his jacket and passed the leather pouch with the sovereigns to Rory. He slapped him on the back and ordered a bottle of decent brandy. "Take that to yer mother, Rory," he said. "It'll come in handy when the winter cold brings the ills and fever. And God bless you, me old son. You're me best friend in the world, apart from me brother Dan, that is. And don't forget to tell yer mother of yer new job with the O'Keeffes."

He turned back to the bar, jingling the remaining coins in his hand. Flinging them down on the counter he said munificently, " 'Tis yours, Brady, for whatever else it will buy to keep my friends happy."

Another cheer went up and the music grew louder and the singing of the old songs more raucous as they raised their glasses, pouring the whiskey of warmth and forgetfulness down their throats, lost in the wonder and magic of the O'Keeffes' newfound riches. "Aye, Amerikey is a wonderful place after all," they told themselves, hope rising in their hearts, for if one of their countrymen could find success then surely there was a chance for them too.

Rory was not drunk. He tucked the leather pouch containing the O'Keeffes' precious sovereigns into his jacket pocket and pushed his way through the merry throng into the cold. The door swung shut behind him and the reality of the North End's mean stinking streets overwhelmed him again. Except now they were covered in a white blanket. Snow whirled around his head and he lifted his face to the blizzard, sticking out his tongue to catch the cold crystal flakes as he slithered back over the cobbles toward the cheerless room where he would huddle with his sisters and brothers, head to toe in the mess of straw that served as their bed, like a litter of frozen starving pups in a farmyard.

The snow deadened the footsteps of the man following him and he turned with surprise as he felt a heavy hand on his shoulder. The man's flat tweed cap was pulled low over his eyes and a curly black beard hid the lower part of his face. "What d'ya want?" Rory demanded, but there was fear in his voice because he knew from the gleam in the fellow's eyes and the shillelagh in his hand exactly what it was the man wanted. The blow caught him on the side of the head and he went down without a sound.

Flinging a quick glance over his shoulder, the man knelt over Rory, fumbling with frozen fingers under his jacket until he found the precious purse, still warm from his body. He stood up and stared for a second at the boy at his feet, his blood already staining the snow. A look of desperation and agony crossed his face. "I'm sorry, boyo," he said softly, "but I need this for me starvin' family." And then he ran off, skidding around the corner on the ice, running and running as far from the North End and his evil deed as he could.

CHAPTER
25

RORY O'DONOVAN WAS NEVER quite the same after that blow on the head. He spoke with a stammer and he stumbled over steps and tripped on the cobbles. The icy winter wind made his cough worse and he grew even thinner. His mother shook her head in despair over her eldest son. He was the only one who could work and put food into the mouths of her children and she did not know what to do.

"If only Finn O'Keeffe had held onto his own money." She sighed. "Nobody would have dared attack him and that big fella, Daniel, the way they did my son." And Finn and Daniel wished it a thousand times also, back in their dark cellar.

In his dreams Finn remembered the heady excitement of possessing money. He touched the gold coins again and watched them magically change into dollars, so many dollars he could scarcely count them. But in the harsh freezing light of day he faced the reality that they were kept alive by the unwilling charity of the people of Boston, who hated the Irish for bringing their poverty and sickness to their clean, prosperous city. Still, babies and children had to be fed and the rich Bostonians employed the Irish women as servants in their houses and the men as laborers on their new buildings. And those with no jobs were given a little food so they did not die.

Whenever Finn or Daniel found a day's employment unloading sacks of coal or flour at the wharves, or swinging a pick in the stony hills, or shoveling infill into the muddy flats of Back Bay, they would divide their meager pay in two and give one half to Rory's mother. "You'll not suffer, Mrs. O'Donovan," Dan told her gruffly. "My brother and I will look after you, never fear." And he sighed deeply because he did not see how in the world he was going to keep that promise.

It was a rainy April morning and Finn was walking past the Common when a horse pulling a smart little two-wheeler gig bolted. He swung around at the familiar sound of galloping hooves and flung himself instinctively at the horse's head as it came alongside. He clung grimly onto the traces, his legs dangerously close to the wheels as the horse pounded on, dragging him through the mud. Then it stopped; it reared up, pawing the air, and he knew he had it beat.

It was over in a minute and he grinned, pleased with himself as he held the nervous horse's head. It rolled its eyes and whinnied and stamped, but he soon had it calmed.

The woman driving the gig was Beatrice James, the wife of Cornelius James, one of Boston's richest men. She looked her rescuer up and down, frowning at his torn jacket, worn without the benefit of a shirt because that had long since disintegrated into rags, and at the muffler knotted at his bare throat. She stared at his muddy pants and his old broken boots stuffed with newspaper to keep out the cold, and at his wild curling black beard and into his hungry gray eyes, and she shuddered fastidiously.

But at the same time she noticed his confident way with the horse and she told herself that, after all, the young ruffian had just prevented a very nasty accident. She said gratefully, "I have to thank you for saving me, young man."

Finn shrugged. "It was nothing, ma'am," he replied, eyeing her. She was tall and aristocratic and though her clothes were plain he knew they were expensive. The little carriage was a beauty and must have cost a lot and he thought hopefully that she should be good for a dollar or two reward.

He ran his hand knowledgeably over the nervous filly, inspecting it for injuries, remembering the stables at Ardnavarna. He sighed longingly; he could almost smell the sweet scent of hay and feel the power of a good horse between his thighs.

The horse trembled nervously under his hand and he said warningly, "I'll be tellin' you now, ma'am, this little filly is too high-strung to go between the shafts."

"But my coachman chose her personally," Beatrice replied, annoyed by his presumptuousness. "He said she would make a fine little carriage horse for me."

"Then he's just been proven wrong, ma'am. She's too fast for you and too nervous. Even with blinkers she'll be dangerous. She's better suited to the racetrack than the streets."

Beatrice knew he was right and she shuddered, thinking of her fate had the carriage overturned. She took a dollar from her purse and handed it to him and he pocketed it eagerly. She said, "There's another dollar for you, my lad, if you will drive me home." Taking a white pasteboard card engraved with her name and address from her purse, she handed it to him. He stared at it and she realized, shocked, that of course he could not read, and told him quickly to take her to Louisburg Square.

Finn hopped nimbly onto the driver's seat and they set off at a brisk trot. The horse behaved perfectly for him and Beatrice thought how opportune were the ways of the Lord that had thrown the young Irish ruffian into her path.

Finn gave a low whistle of amazement as he drove into the yard in back of the Louisburg Square mansion. Four horses poked their heads inquiringly over the stable doors and there were two fine carriages in the coachhouse as well as a smart covered sleigh used when the ice and snow made the streets impassable for wheeled traffic. He vaulted lightly from the gig, then offered his grimy hand to help Mrs. James. Wrinkling her nose in disgust, she ignored it and stepped past him.

His face flushed red as he remembered the day, long ago, in that stable yard at Ardnavarna, when his brother had washed the dirt and the stink off him. "I'm sorry, Mrs. James," he said angrily, "but it's hard to keep as clean as a man would like when you are as poor as I am."

She turned to look back at him. He had called her by her name and she realized he must have read it on the card she had given him. "Then you do read after all," she said, surprised.

"Aye, I can read. And write as well. And I've worked with horses all my life. Lord Molyneux always said I was the best horseman he'd ever seen, and wasn't it meself that taught young Lord William to ride when they all said he niver would. I worked as groom for the earl, ma'am, and my brother worked as gillie and gamekeeper on the estate, until we came here to make a new life for ourselves."

"A city like Boston is hardly the place for a groom and a gillie to find constructive employment," she said caustically.

"No, ma'am, it is not," Finn agreed politely. "But our ship was wrecked. She went down off Nantucket and they brought us to Boston. And here we stay, for we've no money in our pockets to be goin' anywhere else."

Beatrice James smoothed her pristine gray kid gloves over her thin wrists, taking another long, critical look at her rescuer. He was certainly a clever lad with horses. *Lord* William he had mentioned, *and* a grand estate in Ireland. Of course, everybody knew the Irish were horse mad, but she had firsthand evidence that he was as good with them as he said he was. Besides, he had shown exceptional bravery.

"Wait here," she said, handing him the other dollar she had promised. "I shall have a word with my husband and see what can be done."

Finn pocketed his dollar. He jingled the two coins together, his spirits rising like the morning sun. "Jayzus," he said to himself, "I've fallen on my feet here." He ran to the pump in the middle of the yard and sluiced his hands and face with the icy water. He rubbed the toes of his boots on the back of his pant legs and took off his cap and smoothed back his hair. He reknotted his muffler and tugged his jacket over his naked chest and he paced anxiously up and down the cobbled yard, inspecting the horses who hung their heads over their stable doors.

Cornelius James observed him silently from the steps of the house. He was smaller than his wife and older, with gray hair and shrewd brown eyes. His family was originally English and they had not always been wealthy. Of course, they had never been as poor as the Irish and they had always been cultured and lived in old houses filled with books and paintings, and naturally they were educated. He had made himself rich with the clever invention of a patented device used in the Massachusetts cotton mills. And when he was rich enough he had married Beatrice, a daughter of Boston Brahmins, and then he had taken those riches and used them to make himself millions on the New York Stock Market.

Cornelius and Beatrice James were God-fearing Presbyterians, regular Sunday churchgoers, with prayers said morning and evening in their home for the family and the staff. Mr. James prided himself on being a charitable man and he was prepared for his wife's sake to take on the lad who had risked his life to save her.

Of course, the fellow was Irish and he had not believed a word he said about working as a groom on a fancy estate in Ireland, because everybody knew the Irish could wrap up the truth in a colourful tissue of blarney to suit any occasion. But after watching the lad with the horses he took it all back. He could see he knew what he was doing and what's more, he cared. He could tell by the way he was *talking* to the beasts.

"Young man," he called, and Finn sprang to attention, whipping his cap from his head and staring wide-eyed and eager at him.

"Young man, I am Cornelius James," he said striding toward him. "My wife has told me what happened and I am grateful for what you did to help her." Putting his hands behind his back, he teetered back and forth on his heels, inspecting Finn with piercing brown eyes. "You are even younger than I thought," he said, guessing, "sixteen, seventeen?"

"I'll be almost eighteen, sir," Finn said anxiously.

Mr. James nodded. "Fair enough. Then I'm offering you the position of stableboy. You will be in charge of seeing that the carriages are kept clean and you will make sure the horses are taken care of and exercised daily. Is that clear?"

Finn's face shone with joy. "Oh, yes, sir. Yes, indeed it is, sir." He thrust out his freezing hand. "And God bless you, sir, for givin' me this chance. I'll not let you down, y'can be sure of that."

Cornelius was forced to smile as he shook the lad's hand. He liked his enthusiasm as much as he liked his way with horses.

"And what about the pay, sir?" Finn asked, getting down to basics.

"Your pay? Ah, yes. Twelve a week to start, with a raise after three months if you prove satisfactory."

"Twelve *dollars,* sir?" Finn said, wanting to dance a jig of joy.

"And your meals, of course," Mr. James added, striding back into the house. "You can start tomorrow."

"Yes, sir. Yes, sir, yer honor," Finn shouted back. "I'll be here, sir, at dawn I will. You can count on me." And then he ran home to tell Dan and Rory the good news.

Dan swore that now their luck had changed he would get a job too. "Luck's like that, Finn," he said confidently. "When she's with you, she's with you all right."

Hunger led Dan to the logical place—Corrigan's food store on Hanover Street. He loitered outside, hands in his trouser pockets and shoulders hunched against the wind, peering longingly through the window at the brimming barrels of flour and sacks of potatoes, at the chests of tea and boxes of cabbages and onions. Every time the door opened the aroma of boiled ham almost drove him crazy and he busied himself picking up the scatter of cabbage stalks and leaves from under the trestles in front of the store. He took a rag from his pocket and polished the window, smiling through the glass at Corrigan's scowling face. Every day for a week he was outside Mick Corrigan's, whistling cheerfully, picking up the litter, opening the door for the customers, doffing his cap with a smile and a pleasant "good morning" to them. Though Mick's window had never been cleaner, he exasperatedly told Dan several times to "be off with yer," and each time Dan just met his angry stare with a smile.

"Sure and I'm just helping, Mr. Corrigan," he replied politely.

After a couple of weeks the sight of Dan's thin young face and his hungry eyes fixed longingly on the slab of ham compelled Mick to invite him inside. And once inside Dan talked. In no time at all he had told Mick his life story, except his reason for leaving Ireland, and without mentioning the Molyneux name, and he soon had Corrigan won over.

Corrigan was getting older and he told himself he had earned the right to take it a little easier. If he employed Dan he would not have to close up shop when he went off to the saloon to meet his cronies at midday, and he could stay open later at night. Dan would pay for himself in the extra business gained.

"I'll offer you the job as my assistant," he told Dan magnanimously, "at six dollars a week. And a discount on all the groceries you buy."

"Seven," Dan said firmly.

"Done!"

They shook hands and Dan became assistant manager at Corrigan's Corner Store on Hanover Street selling everything from beans to buttons and bacon to boots, working six and a half days a week for seven dollars' pay and cheap groceries. But he was no longer one of the unemployed and he felt as though he had just conquered the world.

He bought himself a new shirt and pants on credit from Mick to be deducted at a dollar and fifty cents per week from his pay. He had a haircut at Flynn's barbershop and a bath at the public bathhouse; and smart and clean and youthful, he stood behind Corrigan's battered counter. The irony of working in someone else's store when it might so easily have been his own made his stomach churn with resentment. He burned with ambition, imagining himself standing proprietorily behind his own shiny counters, watching the money come in.

The simplicity of the formula never failed to amaze him: you undercut your competitors and you offered folks the goods they wanted at the right price and they paid you their money. It could not fail and he watched with frustration as the dollars and cents flowed into old Corrigan's pockets instead of his own, knowing there was nothing he could do about it.

AT HIS NEW JOB, Finn's only problem was the head coachman, Skellern. He was big and loud, and when he drank he became truculent and argumentative. He walked around shouting orders and laying out with his fists when he considered they were not carried out fast enough, and he grumbled constantly about Finn. He did no work himself except for driving Mr. James to and from his office and madam to and from her various social events in the afternoon, and sometimes to their friends' houses in the evenings. He always washed out his mouth with a strong-smelling cleanser first and sucked on peppermints to take away any trace of liquor on his breath, but Finn knew he was dangerous and he didn't know what to do about it.

Finn took pride in his work. He liked the way the carriages gleamed after he had polished them and he always took special care with Mrs. James's own little gig, and there was never a hint of mud on the wheel-spokes when she left the house. It was such a joy to be back working with horses again, he would almost have done the job for nothing. But when a month later Skellern found out it was on Finn's advice that the frisky little Thoroughbred who had almost caused the accident was sold, his drunken anger boiled over.

He was a big, stocky man, built, as Padraig O'Keeffe would have said, "like a brick shithouse." He grabbed Finn by the collar and swung him around. Thrusting his face next to Finn's, he demanded, "And who's the little paddy bastard has been sneaking behind my back to the boss, then?"

Finn eyed him uneasily. He knew Mr. James trusted Skellern and that he would listen if Skellern said Finn was not doing his job properly. Skellern had total power over him and Finn writhed in his grip, longing to punch the drunken bastard in the nose but knowing he could not.

"I don't know what yer talking about, Mr. Skellern," he stalled.

Skellern pushed him up against the stable wall, pinning him with one ham-fist. He thrust his face so close, Finn's head reeled from the sour stench of liquor on his breath. "Ya blasted little mick," he whispered, driving a vicious punch into Finn's belly. "I'll teach you to be after my job. You'll be out of my stable yard as soon as I've had a word with the boss; don't think you won't." And he heaved another rib-crushing punch at Finn.

Like a drowning man, Finn's life swam before his eyes: he saw himself penniless and without a job again, and he gathered himself together and hauled off at Skellern's vengeful face with a punch that seemed to come from his very boots. Skellern fell to the ground as though he had been poleaxed and Finn stared down at him. Then he turned his head and vomited violently into the corner.

The cook was Irish and had a soft spot for young Finn O'Keeffe. She watched from the steps, drawn like the other servants by the sound of raised voices. She went immediately to her mistress and reported what she had seen. "And I think it's time somebody told you, ma'am, before he kills you both, that Skellern's an old drunk and not to be trusted with the carriages. We've none of us liked to say anything, but I'll not see that good lad treated with violence, not even if it means my job too."

Beatrice James stared at her cook with astonishment. Mrs. O'Dwyer had worked for her for three years. She usually kept to her place and that's what she was expected to do, and so she understood immediately that what the woman was saying must be serious. She sent the butler and some other servants out to take care of Skellern and asked Mrs. O'Dwyer to tell Finn to wait in the kitchen until the master came home.

Skellern was carried into his quarters over the stable and a doctor sent for. Finn crouched on a stool staring into the kitchen fire while the cook plied him with cups of hot tea and unwanted slices of cake. His belly ached so bad he thought his guts were broken and his head swam and he felt faint, though he wasn't sure whether it was from Skellern's punch or his fear of what was to come.

The doctor came to inspect him and said if he vomited blood he should go immediately to the hospital. "If not, I daresay you'll survive," he said, impatient at having to deal with brawling Irish workmen. In his opinion if the worthless immigrants wanted to kill themselves by fighting, they should let them get on with it.

Finn hunched gloomily over a mug of tea waiting for Mr. James to return and the ax to fall. When he was finally summoned to the study he had already accepted the fact that he was fired and that he would be lucky if he were not sent to jail for assaulting the coachman.

Mr. James was sitting behind a big desk and he stared severely at Finn over the tops of his horn-rimmed half-glasses. "You had better tell me the truth of this affair," he cautioned.

" 'Twas not Finn's fault," Mrs. O'Dwyer said, folding her arms belligerently over her plump, apron-clad bosom. "He's a good lad and a good worker and old Skellern's nothin' but a drunk. I told the mistress before and I'm tellin' you now, sir. And I only wish I had spoken up earlier so that every time you went out I wouldn't be worryin' whether you'd be coming home on a stretcher."

"Thank you for your concern, Mrs. O'Dwyer," he replied drily. "And now I would like to hear what Finn has to say."

"I knew I would lose me job for doing it, sir, but I just couldn't help it," Finn said miserably. "Skellern swore and cursed me. He was going to tell you lies about me not doing my job. He was angry I'd warned you about the little mare he'd bought being too dangerous for the mistress. He wanted me sacked for it and now he's got what he wanted." He shifted nervously from foot to foot, his cap clutched in his hands, a flush of shame on his cheeks and a look of bleak disillusionment in his eyes. "I just wanted to say my piece first, that's only why I waited."

Mr. James said severely, "I will not tolerate liquor in my house and certainly not with my servants. I have already fired Skellern and I am offering you his job, O'Keeffe, at the same salary. Twenty-five dollars a week and you will need to hire a new fellow to take over your old job as stableboy." He waved them away. "You may go now, and just remember, there'll be no more fighting."

Mrs. O'Dwyer beamed, her rosy face filled with satisfaction. " 'Tis an honorable fellow you are, sir," she told her employer. And Finn's spirits soared again as he thanked him. "I know just the lad, sir, to take over as stableboy," he added, thinking of Rory.

Limping painfully back through Beacon Hill's elegant gaslit streets to the North End, he imagined Rory's excitement when he told him he had a job for him at twelve dollars a week with meals. "Sure and it was worth a punch or two," he told himself with a triumphant grin as he went in search of Daniel to tell him the good news.

CHAPTER

~~~~~~~~~~~~~~~ 26 ~~~~~~~~~~~~~~~

LILY FELT AS THOUGH she were living in a dream. Nantucket was held
fast in the grip of an icy winter and she shivered the months away by
the fireside in the Sheridans' parlor. She had no idea what she would
do after the baby was born because she had no money. She had never
had to think for herself, and she had never needed to contemplate
employment.

Abigail Sheridan told her about the Irish maidservants in Boston.
"The rich Bostonian women like them," she told Lily. "They say they
make very good servants and the poor things work all hours God sends
without so much as a word of complaint."

But Lily was not going to be anybody's servant. The very idea was
ridiculous. She told herself there must be something else she could do,
but when she thought about it she was astonished to find that she
could not think of a single useful thing. She could not cook, sew, or
clean. She could speak French and was well-read and could play the
piano a little, but because of her silly pranks with the many governesses her education was missing great chunks. She was socially adept
and well dressed enough, but none of those trivial assets mattered one
jot when it came to applying for a position as a governess, or a children's nursemaid, or even, she shuddered at the thought, as a cook.

Meanwhile, Alice Sheridan's kindness wrapped her in a temporary
cocoon of security and she shut away all thoughts of the future. She
lived one day at a time as dreary gray month passed into dreary gray
month. The only real bright spot on her horizon was Ned. To his
family's amazement he suddenly took to coming home as often as he
could.

"Of course, he's coming to see Lily," Abigail whispered to her mother, and they smiled conspiratorially, glancing at Lily listening wide-eyed to Ned's tales of life on the road. Alice Sheridan thought what a fortuitous solution it would be if her son forgot his wild ideas of becoming an actor and came home and married Lily instead. Then the baby would have a father and Lily would be able to love it like a good mother instead of wishing it dead. And Ned would take over his father's chandlery business the way Obediah had always wanted. She heaved a little sigh of satisfaction. It was such a perfect resolution.

March came and with it blustery blue skies and a faltering early spring sunshine, and for the first time Lily felt strong enough to venture outdoors. She walked through the town on Ned's arm and he introduced her proudly to everyone from the owner of the Union Stores where they stopped to purchase sugar and flour, to old Bill Clark, the self-appointed town crier and newspaper vendor, and all the Sheridans' neighbors and friends. Everyone knew about her and they wished her well, and Lily thought maybe Nantucket was not such a bad place after all.

They rode on the little train to Surfside and walked hand in hand along the beach and Lily told him about Ardnavarna. She talked despairingly about her father and how much she loved him, and how she was destroyed when he sent her away, though of course Ned thought it was because she had run off to marry her young captain.

He squeezed her hand sympathetically and said, "You have me to rely on now, Lily. I'll always help you." He glanced yearningly at her and she smiled, recognizing the look in his eyes. "You should think about becoming an actress," he said. "People would stand in line just to see you onstage."

She glanced at him in astonishment. She had heard all about actresses and she knew it was not a respectable profession. Especially not standing onstage to be stared at by beastly horrible men with only one thing on their mind. But each time Ned came back he mentioned it again, embellishing on his idea to the point they were stage partners, he as Romeo and Lily as Juliet. "We shall become a 'theatrical legend,'" he announced triumphantly, already seeing them onstage accepting thunderous applause with magnificent bows. And when she pointed out that she could not act, he just smiled and said it didn't matter.

He said, "With your looks an audience would be content just to watch you." And Lily smiled gratefully at him. At least now she had one true friend and admirer.

With each month that passed Lily felt the baby growing inside her. It often kicked her awake at nights and she would groan out loud with despair. When Ned came to see her in May she complained of feeling tired. She refused to go out though the day was warm and sunny and it would have done her good.

"Don't you understand," she cried, when he tried to coax her. "I don't want things that are *good* for me. I don't want anything except not to have this baby."

He knelt and took her hands in his. "Lily," he said, "I haven't spoken before because I thought you would just laugh at me and tell me I was a fool and that we don't even know each other. But when you were lying in my bed, burning with fever and about to die, I vowed I wouldn't let you. I promised to look after you. I fell in love with you that very first night, Lily, and I haven't been able to get you out of my mind since."

She tried to pull her hands away but he gripped them tighter. "Listen," he said. "In the Orient, where they understand such things, they believe that when you save a person's life you become responsible for that person's soul. That means I am responsible for you, Lily, and I always will be. I know I'm still young and I've nothing to offer you except my love. But one day I shall be a great actor, and I'm asking you to share my life. I promise to be a good father to your child and I promise to look after you."

It was an easy way out and Lily was tempted. But if she married Ned she would be forced to keep the baby. And she knew she could never even look into the face of the child who had ruined her life.

"At least say 'maybe,'" Ned pleaded, "and I shall return to the Players a happy man."

"Maybe later; I'll think about it," she said.

He flung his arms around her and kissed her soundly. "Ah, how I love you, Lily Molyneux," he said with a triumphant smile. "And don't you ever forget it," he added.

He danced across the floor holding an invisible partner in his arms and Lily laughed. "You see," he cried happily from the door, "I'm the only one that can make you laugh!" As he disappeared into the hall she could hear him singing and then calling cheery good-byes to his family before dashing off to catch the paddle-wheeled ferry back to New Bedford.

Two weeks later Lily woke in the middle of the night and knew that the dreaded thing was happening. She called urgently to Mrs. Sheridan, who wrapped herself hastily in a woolen dressing gown and came running.

"It's not going to be so bad," Lily told herself bravely at first. "It's really not too bad. I can bear it." But the hours dragged on and the pains grew worse and more frequent and she screamed with anger, wishing the baby dead and herself with it. After fourteen long hours the child was finally born and she lay as limp as the corpse she wished she were. When she heard it cry she clapped her hands over her ears in horror. It was real. The baby was there.

Mrs. Sheridan wrapped the infant in a soft blanket and held it out for her to see. "It's a boy, Lily," she said, her voice filled with the wonder of birth, "and such a handsome little fellow with hair as black as your own."

Lily shut her eyes tightly so she would not see it; she pressed her hands harder against her ears so she would not have to hear it, and when Mrs. Sheridan tried to lay the baby next to her she pushed it away.

The doctor said that her agitation would upset her milk, but it turned out she had no milk for the child. "It's as though she had willed it," Mrs. Sheridan said somberly as she gave the baby a bottle.

"Better not upset her anymore," the doctor warned. "Just keep the child away from her until she comes to her senses."

Lily lay in bed with her face turned to the wall, speaking to no one. Now the baby was gone from her, she knew she would have to leave as soon as possible. And therefore she must eat and get stronger so she could run away.

Still refusing to look at her baby, she remained in bed for two weeks forcing down the nourishing meals prepared for her by the anxious Sheridans. She knew the times of the sailings to the mainland, but she had no money to get there and nowhere to go when she did.

The baby's loud cries echoed through the house and though Mrs. Sheridan never said anything to her, she would look hopefully at her and Lily knew she was thinking that soon she would come around and accept her own child.

She decided to go to Boston. It was the nearest big city and the Sheridans would never find her there, and now she knew where to get the money. She waited until everyone was in bed and then she stealthily opened her trunks. She stared at the heaps of useless silks and satins that seemed to have belonged to another girl a lifetime ago and then she packed a few of the more practical things into a straw basket. Tucked away down the side of the trunk she found her valuable set of silver hairbrushes, and with them, in a monogrammed silver frame, a picture of the family, grouped on the steps of the Big House. She held it under the lamp, gazing tearfully at them. She could remember the day the photograph had been taken as though it were yesterday.

She and Ciel had been ready to go out in the little jaunting cart. Pa and Mammie had come to wave them off when suddenly William had rushed out with his new photographic equipment, tripping over his tripod and the mysterious black box. It had taken him ages to set it up and even then he had stuck his head under the square of black cloth and fiddled about for so long that Pa had roared furiously at him to get on with it! And, oh God, yes, wasn't that Finn holding the pony's head, smart in his striped groom's waistcoat and brown breeches. She could almost feel the warm morning sun on her back and Pa's hand clasping hers and hear the pony crunching the apple Finn had given it to keep it from dancing impatiently around while William took his picture.

She placed the photograph carefully in her straw basket along with the silver brushes that she was certain she could sell for a vast amount of money. After she got to Boston she would figure out what to do. But she certainly was not going to be a maidservant. Not she, Lily Molyneux.

She knew Alice Sheridan kept the money she saved from her weekly housekeeping in the old brown teapot on the dresser shelf, "for use in emergencies." Telling herself this was an emergency Lily took five dollars from the teapot and wrote a little note saying she was sorry but it was the only way. She promised to send the money back as soon as she could and said that she would also send money for help pay for "the child," and that she hoped they would care for him and give him the love she never could. She thanked them for their kindness and said she would never forget them.

That morning, before dawn, when the house and even the squalling infant were still quiet, she took her straw basket and crept silently down the stairs and out the front door, which was never locked, and hurried on shaking legs through the sleeping town to the wharf.

There was a ship sailing for Boston on the dawn tide and she parted carefully with three of her five dollars for the fare, putting the rest safely away in her pocket. As she watched the island disappear into the swirling morning mist she knew that a chapter of her life had finally closed and now a new one could begin. And surely, she thought, it could not be any worse.

CHAPTER

27

MAUDIE

Ardnavarna

I COULD SEE EDDIE was listening, fascinated, to my revelations of the past. He glanced at Shannon, sitting beside him on the sofa. An orange cat purred on her lap and she stroked its soft fur automatically. She looked sweet and vulnerable and very young, and I knew what he was thinking: that Lily must have looked the same way.

Eddie knew she was looking for the truth about her father and was hoping that the story of her family's past would help her find it, and I could see how much he wished he could help her.

"Maybe I should fill you in on Ned's background," he said, "if you think it will help find the truth about Lily."

We sat up and took notice. "Oh, please," Shannon said, "I'm dying to know more about him, he sounds so . . . so in love with her, and so nice."

"Maybe he was, I don't know. But he was young and naive and crazy about her."

Eddie's arm slid along the back of the sofa behind Shannon's shoulders, and I saw their eyes meet in a long, intimate glance. It was one of those private looks between two people no one else is meant to see and I turned and threw another log on the fire, kicking it into a blaze with my silver-sandaled foot.

"Better get on with it," I said briskly.

Eddie laughed; he knew what I was thinking. "I'll tell you the story as my grandfather told it to me," he said with his beautiful deep actor's voice that must have been so like Ned's. Somehow it brought the past to life for us again.

THE DE LOWRY PLAYERS WERE PLAYING New Jersey when Jacob de Lowry told Ned angrily, "You either stay or you go!" His ferocious black brows formed a straight line as he glared at him. "How can I be expected to put on a successful show when one of my actors is so moonstruck with love he cannot keep his mind on what he is doing? For God's sake, lad, aren't there enough women for you in every town we play?"

He would have fired him there and then except he knew the audiences liked him. Ned got the most applause of anyone, including himself and Sasha, and it was for more than just his looks. Ned Sheridan had talent.

Jacob was looking sixty in the face. He was tired of traveling, but he could see no way out, with his company floundering from one weekly financial disaster to the next. He often thought of how pleasant it might be to retire to a nice little house on the bluffs above the Hudson River where he knew many stars had homes. It was within striking distance of Broadway's bright lights, and he could join the Lambs Club and attend first nights with Sasha on his arm, both of them dressed to kill. But how to do it? That was the problem. There was no money in the kitty and there wasn't likely to be any soon.

Sitting in front of a spotted mirror in a chilly room in a cheap New Jersey boardinghouse, Jacob studied his profile, turning to the left and the right, tilting back his head to escape the jowls threatening to overhang his high collar.

"You're getting old, Jacob," Sasha said from the bed where she was ensconsed in a nest of fluffy satin pillows that always traveled with her. Like Jacob, she was not good-looking, but she was handsome and, like him, she knew how to flaunt it. Only each year it somehow got harder. She was younger than her husband, in her late forties, but she was also thinking longingly of a cosy cottage with roses around the door and maybe a cat curled up by the hearth. They often talked about retirement, endlessly figuring out ways to come up with sufficient money, but it always depended on the next month's engagements, and then the next, and each was always as unspectacular as the last. Except lately, with young Ned Sheridan in their troupe, people were beginning to sit up and take notice.

"You should give Ned a bigger role," Sasha said suddenly. "Let him play the lead."

Jacob swung around, staring at her, astonished. He said angrily, "I have always played the leads, Sasha. My audiences expect it."

"Not anymore they don't." Sasha lit a cigarette and blew a perfect smoke ring into the chilly air. Snuggling deeper into her pillows, she said cruelly, "Let's face it, Jacob, it's Ned the audiences are looking at in his tights, not you. In case you haven't noticed there's something about him that draws their eyes like a magnet." She patted her fluffy bright blond hair and yawned. "It's not just you, Jacob, it's me too. The men are looking at Ned instead of at my tits. And you know what that means, Jacob? It means he's got star quality."

Jacob decided to ignore her jibe about getting old and concentrated instead on the new thoughts springing into his mind. He had seen every stage star there was and he knew talent when he saw it. He knew they were lucky to have Ned. His threat to fire him had been bravado on his part because he knew the boy would be taken on by any actor-manager with eyes in his head and even half a brain.

There was no doubt Ned had talent and looks, but he was also naive. *"The hick,"* Sasha had dubbed him when she had first seen his eager straw-blond handsomeness and gentle manners. Of course, he was an educated hick, but he was naive in the ways of the world. Ned was still blinded by the glamour of the theater and he hadn't been around long enough for reality and disillusionment to set in.

"He needs good management if he is to become a star," Sasha said, yawning, "and he'll never get that working with us, Jacob, so you needn't worry he'll run off and leave us in the lurch."

Jacob thought about what she had said and he suddenly saw a whole new, easier world opening up to him. A world where he need no longer be the aging actor-manager, trailing his underpaid ragbag of artistes. Ned Sheridan depended on him for his employment. He believed every word he said, and Jacob had said plenty, telling him grandiose tales of theaters he had never played, dropping names of the stars and famous theater managers he claimed he knew. Ned Sheridan knew no one else in the theater world. And Ned Sheridan trusted him.

Jacob canceled his own appearance for the next night and told Ned he was to go on in his place. "It will do you good, my dear boy," he said, throwing a friendly arm around Ned's shoulders. "I have some business to attend to in New York. There have been offers for my services. . . ." He waved his cigar airily, giving the impression that a dozen New York theater managers were standing in line for him. Then he sighed and said, "How I wish I were your age again, Ned. There are so many great roles out there, perfect for a young good-looking leading man like you." Ned looked eagerly at him and Jacob tapped ash from his double Corona reflectively. "Of course, a person needs *connections* to get those tip-top parts. And naturally, after all these years, I have those connections."

He stared coolly at Ned. His piercing dark eyes were unfathomable and Ned did not even wonder why, with his "connections," Jacob was still playing seedy little theaters in the sticks. He was his only contact with the big time and he wanted it badly. "Do you really think there's a chance for me in New York, Mr. de Lowry?" he asked eagerly.

"That would mean deserting the Players, my boy." Jacob scowled. "Have I not been a good employer? A good *friend* to you? Has not Jacob de Lowry taught you everything you know?" He threw his hands in the air and cried dramatically, "And now you want to desert me."

"Oh, no! No, sir, I don't!" Ned would have begged de Lowry on his bended knees for even the smallest chance with one of his "connections." "But you said yourself there were so many good parts for men my age. And I just know I have the talent to prove myself. All I need is the next step."

"*If* I were to provide that step, then naturally I would expect to be recompensed for my loss," Jacob said, twirling his cigar between his fingers and looking thoughtfully into the distance. "There must be some suitable way, of course. There always is. . . ."

"Anything, sir," Ned offered as the bright lights seemed to creep closer.

"Then I have the perfect answer," Jacob said quickly. "I shall become your manager. I shall handle your career, dear boy, and with my connections and your talent you will go far. To the very top, I don't doubt. And believe me, there's no better place to be," he added importantly, as though he knew all about how it felt to be on the pinnacle of success.

"There's just the matter of my fee, of course. Now, let me think. . . ." He twirled his cigar again; he knew exactly what it was going to cost Ned Sheridan and he could already see the country place with the roses and the cat, and the Lambs Club and the opening nights. Ned Sheridan would be his entrée into the big time for the first time in his life. "Of course, as your manager I could ask for more, but I think fifty percent would be appropriate, considering our friendship."

"Agreed!" Ned grabbed Jacob's hand and shook it enthusiastically. "When do we leave for New York?"

"*You* do not leave, dear boy. *You* are going onstage to play my role—

the lead—while I shall travel to New York and consult with my friends on your behalf."

Jacob departed the next morning, dressed in his flamboyant best—gray pinstriped trousers and a black broadcloth jacket, greening at the seams with age. He wore a flowing silk foulard knotted at his neck and a voluminous black cape and broad-brimmed black hat, and he carried his silver-topped malacca cane.

He swore Ned to secrecy and did not tell Sasha why he was going to New York. She watched him go, wondering what exactly he was up to, because the wily old bastard was up to something, she knew. She noticed young Ned Sheridan was seething with excitement, too, and she was sure it was not just because he was to play the lead tonight instead of Jacob. She sighed as she emerged from her nest of pillows and began to prepare for the performance. Whatever Jacob was up to, she surely hoped it was successful because she was getting too old for this.

That night Ned gave everything he had to his role as a French count in love with a dying courtesan. It was Jacob's version of *Camille* and the meager audience lapped it up, calling for an encore.

Sasha gazed at them, stunned. She had not heard a call for an encore in years and lately she was only too glad to get off the stage so she would not hear the horribly personal insults hurled at them by the departing patrons. Ned stared across the flaring footlights at the few dozen people applauding him and he felt that heady rush of power and exhilaration that only success could bring. He told himself excitedly that with Jacob's help he would soon be playing to audiences of hundreds of people, and he couldn't wait for Jacob to get back with the good news.

Jacob's "connections" in New York's theater world were real enough: he knew them all right, but they did not want to know him. Still, with Ned's studio portraits clutched in his hands and his own bravado he managed to bluff his way into the office of famous producer Charlie Dillingham, who just happened to be casting a new play, and there just happened to be a role for a handsome juvenile lead. Dillingham told Jacob to send Ned to audition. "But he'd better be as good-looking as his picture," he said, tapping the studio portrait of Ned with a warning finger.

"He's more than that," Jacob replied confidently. "My client has talent, Mr. Dillingham. The kind of talent that brings in audiences. *Ned Sheridan will put arses in your seats,* Mr. Dillingham, make no mistake about that."

The next day Ned and Jacob went to New York together. And Ned, bareheaded, handsome, and confident, strode into Dillingham's office as though he owned the place. He told Dillingham what a good actor he was and at the auditions held later in the Fifth Avenue Theater he proved it. Ignoring Jacob's urging to repeat his previous night's role in *"Camilla by Candlelight,"* (written by J. de Lowry), he read cold from the script Dillingham handed him.

It was a lighthearted play; there were no hidden meanings and deep thoughts. It was meant purely to entertain and Dillingham knew that Ned Sheridan was the man for his juvenile lead. The women would adore him for his looks and the critics would not be able to say a bad word against him. But he was a hard man and he struck a hard bargain. One hundred dollars a week was a long way from the five hundred Jacob had hoped for and he saw he would have to wait awhile for his rose-covered cottage. Still, he asked for a week's salary in advance and he handed fifty dollars to Ned with a flourish. "Don't spend it rashly, dear boy," he cautioned. "The play doesn't open for another month and there's no guaranteeing how long it will last. One week's pay may be all you get."

Ned did not give a damn. He was walking down Broadway, the street of dreams, and his own dreams were about to come true. He went straight into a jewelers and spent it all on a pretty amethyst ring for Lily. It might be awhile, but when he could get back to Nantucket he would ask her to marry him again, and this time he would seal it with an engagement ring.

He worked out his final two weeks with the Players, playing the leading roles because Jacob said it would be good practice for him. But in reality it was because the word about Ned had gotten around and for once the de Lowry Players were playing to a full house, and Jacob wondered with a pang of regret whether he had done the wrong thing after all, sending his protégé to New York.

"He would have gone anyway," Sasha said with a shrug. "It never takes long for an actor to know when he's got the upper hand, because he's usually been at the bottom so long. Didn't I tell you the boy had talent?"

"This is just the beginning," Jacob said, happily smoking his Double Corona. "Ned Sheridan will buy us our cottage in the country, *and* our entrée into New York stage circles. Fifty percent!" He laughed. "And the boy never even questioned it."

Sasha glanced disparagingly at her husband. "He will, Jacob," she promised. "Soon enough, he will."

Two weeks later Jacob and Sasha escorted Ned to the railroad station, warning him that the city was full of thieves and con men, telling him to find himself a respectable boardinghouse and to watch his money. Just as the train was pulling out Harrison Robbins hurtled along the platform, a valise clutched in his hand. The train was already moving and he ran alongside, flung the valise on board, then swung himself up after it. He turned to wave as they steamed past the de Lowrys. "I just quit, Jacob," he yelled, laughing at their astonished faces.

"After all, I couldn't let my greenhorn friend go off to Broadway alone," he explained to Ned. "It would be like sending an innocent lamb to the slaughter." He sat back and folded his arms and grinned at him. "I'm sick of de Lowry," he said. "And I'm sick of second-rate plays and third-rate theaters. I'm an actor. I can dance and I can sing. I can play the fool or the suave seducer with the best of them and I'm taking my chances in New York with you, Ned. Besides, I know this terrific landlady. She serves the best Sunday roast you and I will have tasted in a long time *and* she'll keep her motherly eye on both of us. Believe me, Ned, it'll be a lot better than the crappy lodgings we're used to. I've got three hundred and fifty bucks to my name and if I don't have a job by the time it runs out, I swear I'll become a traveling salesman. It's make-or-break time, kiddo. That's what it gets down to when you've been an actor for twenty-five of your thirty-two years and you still haven't made it."

Ned leaned across and shook his hand. He said, "Thanks, Harry, for coming along. And it's make-or-break time for both of us. If I flop, I'm going back to Nantucket to run my dad's chandlery and marry Lily."

"And if you win?"

Ned laughed. "I'll still marry Lily."

"I knew it. Hark to the voice of experience, old son. Forget her. There's a hundred pretty chorus girls just longing to be seen on the arm of the handsome young lead in Broadway's latest success, *Tomorrow's Man*. You are tomorrow's man, Ned. And Lily is the past. Forget her, I say."

"If you knew her, you would never say that," Ned said stubbornly. "No one who met her could *ever* forget Lily."

Harry lit up a cheroot and stared out the window at the passing scenery. "I only hope you don't waste yourself on a memory," he said thoughtfully.

The boardinghouse was on West Fortieth Street and the landlady, Eileen Malone, carefully inspected the two young men ringing her bell.

"It's you again, Mr. Robbins," she exclaimed. "I haven't seen you in an age. So who's your friend?"

"My friend is the next big Broadway star," Harry said, introducing him. "He is starting rehearsals for a starring role, Mrs. Malone. Not, I admit, *the* starring role, he's a little too young for that honor. But the ingenue is good enough to start, especially working with the famous Charlie Dillingham and I don't doubt he'll go on to even bigger and better roles from there."

Mrs. Malone looked at the handsome, eager blond young man with the expressive pale-blue eyes and thought Harry was probably right. But then, she was a sucker for a good-looking fella anyway. She showed them their rooms, they paid their rent in advance, and Harry told Ned he was taking him out to breakfast.

"We may not be able to afford dinner at this place yet," he said, sweeping grandly into the men's café on the Broadway side of Delmonico's, "but for the grand sum of forty cents you can partake of boiled eggs, toast, and coffee. Add another dime for a tip, and for a total of fifty cents you can sit with the greats of theater land, reading the reviews in the morning papers just like they do. And when they look up you can catch their eye and nod and smile and after a while they'll start to think they must know you." He raised his shoulders in an exaggerated shrug and rolled his eyes to heaven. "And then, dear boy, you can ask them for a job."

"Does it really work?" Ned asked glancing eagerly around to see what famous faces lurked behind the raised copies of the *New York Herald* and the *Tribune*.

"I sure hope so," Harry said, ordering boiled eggs and toast for the both of them. "But even if it doesn't at least you'll be able to drop their names to other people. You know, the sort of thing . . . 'When I was in Delmonico's having breakfast this morning with A. L. Erlanger, I mentioned to Lillie Langtry and David Belasco that I thought Ned Sheridan would be perfect for the starring role. . . .' "

Ned threw back his head and laughed out loud. Newspapers were suddenly lowered around the room and a dozen pairs of eyes fastened speculatively on him. "See?" Harry said triumphantly. "It's working already." Ned laughed again, but Harry was quick to notice that one or two of those newspapers remained down and that there were thoughtful looks on the faces of a couple of the readers. His idea had not been a bad one after all: Ned Sheridan was already being noticed.

"You'd be much better off with me as your manager than that old ham, Jacob," he commented, slicing off the top of his egg.

"But he got me the part," Ned protested. "A hundred a week, and that's five times more than I've ever earned."

"Only because de Lowry didn't pay you enough. He never paid *any* of his actors enough. So, what's he charging you for the favor? Ten, fifteen percent?"

"Fifty." As Harry's stunned eyes met his, Ned added quickly, "He deserves it; without him there was no job."

"The dirty low-down little crook," Harry said slowly, leaving his egg untouched. "Ned, you're like a babe on Broadway. Ten percent would have been more than enough from such a small salary. Agents, managers"—he shrugged—"they get anything from ten to twenty-five and that's tops, when they've really *made* a star." He glanced suspiciously at Ned. "Have you signed a contract with him?" Ned shook his head. "Good. Then there's nothing that binds you to pay him a cent. *The hell with acting!*" he said suddenly, slamming his fist on the table, and again the newspapers were lowered to stare. "*I* shall be your manager, Ned Sheridan, because if I'm not you'll be working every night of your life for a thief like Jacob de Lowry."

"It's a matter of honor," Ned said stubbornly. "We shook hands on it."

"Okay, so pay Jacob his fifty for the run of the play. But after that, I'm looking after you. Agreed?"

"Agreed," Ned said, relieved, thinking that he hadn't even set foot on the stage of the Fifth Avenue Theater yet and already he was in trouble.

Rehearsals started the following morning and after a leisurely breakfast at Delmonico's he and Harry wandered over to the theater around eleven. Mr. Dillingham and the rest of the cast were already assembled on the stage and Ned hurried through the darkened auditorium to join them.

"Thank you, Mr. Sheridan, for being good enough to give us the benefit of your company," Mr. Dillingham said scathingly. "You have just kept my stars waiting for fifteen minutes. You will be on time in future or I shall be looking for another second lead."

Mumbling embarrassed apologies, Ned took his place on the stage. He had memorized his lines and everyone else's as well, and he had no need of a script but he held it open, like the others, while the director put them through their paces. It was a long, hard day of rehearsal, and so were all the others leading up to opening night.

"There's terrific advance booking," Harry told him, examining the newspapers over their regular Delmonico's breakfast on the morning of opening night. "The word is it's not a bad play—not great, but not bad. And look here, Ned, it says 'Watch out for Dillingham's secret weapon, a handsome young actor in the role of Marcus Jared, the "Tomorrow Man" of the title.'"

Harry's mustache fairly bristled with excitement. "It's your first notice in the Broadway columns, old son, and it'll not be the last."

Ned was nervous. He was made-up and in his costume hours too soon and he prowled backstage, muttering his lines, his fingers clutched around the little box with the amethyst ring he had bought for Lily.

He had not told her or his family about his big chance in case it was a disaster, and if it was he had told himself he would quit; he would go back to Nantucket and marry Lily and maybe that's what he should have done anyway because he sure as hell couldn't remember a single line.

The opening-night audience was already filing into their seats, and he could hear them laughing and chattering as though nothing was wrong. Harry strode, beaming, toward him.

"Dillingham's filled the orchestra with celebrities," he said happily. "Everybody who's anybody is here tonight. You've got it made, Ned. Just go out there and give 'em your best. Oh, and by the way, Jacob's out in front with Sasha. I left instructions he wasn't to be allowed backstage until after the performance, okay?"

Ned nodded miserably. He went back to his dressing room and sat hunched in front of the mirror, thinking of the fool he was about to make of himself in front of New York's most glittering celebrities and Broadway's harshest critics. He was finished, he just knew it.

The call boy yelled "five minutes" and he went to stand in the wings. The very first lines were his and for the life of him he couldn't remember them. He smoothed back his pomaded blond hair and straightened his jacket. The curtain rose to a polite ripple of applause and somehow he managed to stride out onto the stage. He stared into the glaring footlights, sweating with their heat and his own panic, his mind a total blank. From somewhere he heard his own voice saying, "Well, where is everybody? I thought we were supposed to meet at three . . ." and suddenly he didn't have to try to remember his lines, they were just there. All the exits and entrances, the directions up stage and down, were second nature.

There was a burst of enthusiastic applause as the star, Marion Javits, appeared, and then another for Maxwell Dunlap and suddenly everything was going with the kind of swing that meant a good troupe of actors was working well together.

The audience laughed at Ned's lines when they should have and he stared gratefully into the auditorium, waiting for the laughter to die down before continuing. Then the first act was over and the applause came again. Solid, reassuring applause.

The stars disappeared to their dressing rooms and so did he. Harry was waiting for him. "It's going good, old son," he said enthusiastically. "They're laughing as though they've been cued for it. And they're sitting up and taking notice of you, Ned."

He played the second act like a man in a dream and when the final curtain came down the applause echoed around the theater. Marion Javits shrugged elegantly. "Those are the free tickets you can hear. The balcony's where the truth is. *And* tomorrow night, when the paying customers come."

She took her bows alone and so did Maxwell. Then they took several together. Then they beckoned Ned onstage and Harry gave him an encouraging little shove. Ned bowed, listening to the special swell of applause that was his alone. Lifting his eyes he beamed gratefully at the invisible people who liked him.

After the curtain calls came the first-night party at Delmonico's and this time when he walked in the waiters smiled respectfully and said, "Congratulations, Mr. Sheridan, sir. The word's already out the play's a success." Jacob was waving his cigar and looking important as only he knew how, and Sasha, in a daunting black dress that exposed a lot of bosom, gave him a big wet kiss and whispered breathily in his ear, "You were magnificent. But then I always knew you could be."

Innumerable beautiful women kissed his cheek, and important men of the theater whose names he had only heard mentioned with awe before tonight looked approvingly at him as they congratulated him on his performance.

"It wasn't a performance," he told Harry, bewildered. "I *was* Marcus Jared onstage tonight."

Harry knew exactly what he meant, but he thought regretfully that in his thirty years as an actor he had never once felt that way onstage. He knew Ned had a special talent and he knew he deserved the best and he wasn't about to let him be ruined by de Lowry.

He cornered Jacob by the bar and signaled a waiter to give him another drink. "More champagne, Jacob?" he asked with a masked smile.

De Lowry glanced suspiciously at him. "What are you doing here?"

he demanded. "I didn't think you would have the nerve after walking out on me the way you did."

"Speaking of contracts," Harry said, crowding closer. He leaned one arm against the wall, trapping Jacob between the bar and himself. "Ned tells me that he has not signed a contract with you."

"Oh, but he will. I have it right here for him to sign tonight. It's a simple little thing, a mere formality."

He patted his pocket with the document and Harry held up his hand. "Don't bother to show me," he said coolly. "Ned understands how you tried to fleece him. He's more of a gent than I am, so he's agreed to keep his bargain and pay you fifty percent of his salary for the run of the play. After that you're through."

"You're talking nonsense," Jacob blustered. "Of course he'll sign. I got the boy the job, didn't I?"

Leaning closer, Harry grabbed him by the lapel. "Sure you did, Jacob. And then you told him it would cost him half his money. Not ten or fifteen or even twenty-five percent. You were *greedy*, Jacob."

Sticking his face closer he whispered menacingly, "You're nothing but a cheap old thief and you know it. I'll bet that 'simple little con-tract' in your pocket ready for Ned to sign ties him up neatly for the rest of his life at fifty or even sixty percent to Mr. J. de Lowry." He grinned; he could see from Jacob's blustering purple face he was right.

"Forget it, Jacob," he said, letting go of him. "You've fleeced too many actors for too long. Stay away from Ned or I'll see you in jail for a thousand-and-one little frauds the length and breadth of the country. I'll wire you your fifty percent every Monday for the run of the play. Don't bother to acknowledge receipt, and 'don't call us, we'll call you.' " With a final menacing glance he sauntered off to rescue Ned from the gaggle of young women surrounding him.

The early editions of the morning papers were carried in by a jubi-lant Dillingham. "They liked it," he yelled into the sudden nervous silence, and a cheer went up.

Amusing, the critics said, and, *Delightful, if slight. The acting speaks louder than the words,* said another. *Especially the new face on Broad-way, Ned Sheridan, as good-looking as he is capable of pulling your heartstrings, a fact that most of the women in the audience were quick to notice. This does not mean that Mr. Sheridan is not a fine actor. Indeed he is. His command of his small role made him stand out on a stage of fine players. His is a career to be watched.*

Harry hugged him and so did Mr. Dillingham. Marion Javits kissed him sulkily—his notices were longer and better than hers—but her costar Maxwell was more generous. "It was a damned fine performance," he said. "Make the most of it because you can take my word for it, the play won't last more than a month."

He was almost right. The play did close after a month, but Dillingham sent it out on the road and this time Ned had his name in equal billing with two stars. He wrote to Lily from whatever town he happened to be in that week but he knew he could not expect a reply on the road, and the ring stayed in his pocket until the summer's heat closed the theaters at the end of June and he was able to go home again.

He bought up all the lilies in every florist on Broadway and hurried downtown to catch the Fall River Line boat. He prowled the decks half the night, unable to sleep for thinking of her. He disembarked at Fall River and prowled the hot windy platform of the railroad station until the train took him to Myricks, and then he prowled that station restlessly until another train took him to New Bedford. When he finally boarded the paddle-wheel ferry for Nantucket he was numb with weariness and the bouquet of lilies was wilting badly, but when they passed the Cross Rip lightship he knew he was almost home.

He breathed in the cool, salty sea air, and the world of the theater and the weariness and strain of the past months seemed to drop away behind him. He felt like a new man as he hurried from the wharf up Main Street to find Lily at last.

His mothers and sisters ran to the door to greet him, stopping when they saw the significant lilies clutched in his arms. A baby wailed in the background and he stared uneasily at their somber faces. Fearing the worst, his heart skidded to his boots. "Lily's dead," he said, looking from one to the other.

"No, son. Oh, no, she's not dead," his mother said. "But she's gone, Ned. She ran away after the boy was born. She asked us to look after him. And we shall never see her again, you can be sure of that."

Ned threw his bouquet to the floor. He paced into the kitchen and stared at the squalling red-faced infant in the straw basket. After a while he said soothingly, "Don't you worry, son. We'll find her. I promise you. And when we do, this time we shall never let her go."

CHAPTER
28

MAUDIE

Ardnavarna

BRIGID WAS KEEPING AN EAGLE EYE on me but I'm feeling better today despite the late night. When I was small Mammie said I used up all my week's energy in one go and then I would wilt like a dying flower and she would have to put me to bed for an entire day to recover. You should try it sometimes. A long lazy day, away from the telephone and the television and the newspapers, just dozing and reading and nibbling on a little something, chocolate or cold chicken or bread fresh from the oven spread with sweet butter. Even good hot porridge does the trick, though maybe you'll need Brigid to fix it for you. I can tell you, my dears, that a lazy day in bed pampering yourself does as much good as a week at one of those expensive new health spas.

I went once with my friend, Molly Arundel. It was *ghastly*. First of all, it was all women. Then they starved us and made us eat lettuce leaves and what they called consommé, but I told Molly it was chicken-crap watered down. They trapped us in mud baths and sweating machines so we couldn't cause any trouble and sneak off to the village pub for a "G and T" and a ham sandwich and to check out the men. And those brawny Swedes pummeled us unmercifully on the massage tables.

"Maudie and Molly, the Terrible Twins," they called us, because we caused so much trouble, always complaining and always sneaking out of the grounds in our bathrobes. Did you know they take your clothes away from you, just the way they do in prison? And I can tell you it's a dead giveaway when you show up at the local pub in your powder-blue terry-cloth robe.

I miss old Molly. She was my special chum, you know. We were girls together and at a dozen different schools together because neither of us were what Mammie called "stickers," meaning we never stuck to anything for more than a few weeks at a time. That included men, of course, especially in Molly's case. It was a man who killed her, you know.

Now, unlike me, Molly had been a beauty in her day, dark-haired and green-eyed and slinkily glamorous. She rode like a man, smoked like a chimney, and cursed like a trooper, and yet she was the most feminine woman I have ever met. Apart from Mammie, that is, because Mammie with her funny gamine little face was eternally feminine.

Anyway, Molly had been married three times and widowed three times and she had also enjoyed what she called "playing the field," so even though she was getting on in years when she met this fellow, and despite a fondness for gin and tonic and black olives, she was in good shape and she was still lovely. She had a silver streak in her dark hair at each temple. "Just to let the men know I'm not as young as I look," she told me. And she'd had a good face-lift and her boobs done, too, because she was living in Palm Beach then, and you know the way things are there.

And that's where she met him. Palm Beach. At one of those charity balls they seem to have every night so they have somewhere to wear those wonderful couture dresses they all seem to be able to afford. Of course, Molly had as much as anybody, maybe more. Her father was in steel and he did better than my mammie at it, I can tell you. Mammie lost all her money in German steel in the war, if you remember, whereas Molly's father simply coined it in armaments. Armored tanks to be precise, though he went on to bigger and better and more modern things, so old Molly had enough to do whatever she liked. And she liked to play.

But I'm digressing again. She was sixty-fivish and he was thirty years old, blond and handsome, a man straight out of a Ralph Lauren ad. Slicked-back hair, strong jaw, lean body, and a pair of horn-rimmed specs to give him an "intellectual" look. Truth is, without 'em he looked a bit vapid and I often used to wonder whether he kept them on during . . . well, you know. I never did ask Molly because she might have thought I was making fun of him, and she was crazy about him. I could see that. Anyone with half an eye could. He moved in with her and she bought him all the smart clothes he wanted until he looked as though he had stepped from the pages of a glossy catalog. He accompanied her everywhere, to all the lunches and the dinners, and the dances.

She telephoned me here at Ardnavarna and said, "Maudie, you simply have to meet him. He's so wonderful."

So I flew out there and went to stay with them in her villa by the sea. It was one of those gorgeous American houses, modern with a bit of Mediterranean and a touch of the tropical, with jewel-colored pools set in astonishingly green lawns and tropical lanais and that awful air-conditioning. "For God's sake, turn it off, Molly," I used to say, even though the temperature was eighty-five outside. "There's nothing wrong with a bit of honest sweat. It's good for the pores."

Anyhow, as far as I could see, she and this fellow spent most of their time in bed. In between the parties and the dinners, that is. I saw very little of them privately. I asked her how I was supposed to judge him when I hardly saw him. "You're not here to judge, darling Maudie," she said, astonished. "You are here to *admire.*"

Pleased as punch she was that she, a merry sixty-five, was keeping this good-looking youngster on his mettle in bed. But of course, you see, that's what killed her. They were in bed and she had a heart attack and that was that.

"What better way to go, darling Molly," I said over her coffin at the funeral. Ah, she loved life, my friend Molly. And didn't she enjoy it right to the end?

Well, back to business. I got up the morning after my lazy day in bed, bright as a button again, and I collected Shannon and the horses and the dogs and we went for a long ride over the mountains. Jayzus, did I feel good. Like a new woman. The rain had cleared and the air smelled as though it had been washed and dried, the way laundry does on the line. "How are things with Eddie?" I asked Shannon when we paused to let the horses drink from an icy mountain stream.

"Fine," she said cautiously. I caught her eye and she grinned. "He's really nice, now I'm getting to know him better," she said, blushing shyly. Now, I always approve of blushing. More women should do it. It's so charming.

That night we gathered around the fire again after dinner. I was wearing emerald-green taffeta, long and formal, bought in 1974 for a grand Palm Beach ball that I had been to with dear old Molly. Now, who was the designer? Oh yes. Bill Blass. The American designers have such a sense of style when it comes to the grand occasion.

Shannon was in black silk pants and a white silk shirt, very simple and understated, but with her youth and good, rangy body, she can get away with murder. Oh dear, that's not the right thing to say, is it? Eddie was in jeans but he wore a tie and jacket and looked incredibly handsome, as always. I cannot believe how privileged I am to feast my eyes on two such gorgeous young things, night after night.

I racked my brains to know where to begin my story. I decided to continue with Lily.

Boston

THE NORTH END BAKED under a hot July sun. Ragged children played tag on the littered streets while their mothers sat limply on their door-steps watching them. It was even hotter inside their hovels than out and besides, they knew that this weather bred germs so they kept their young outdoors, hoping the "fresher" air would save them from the epidemics that swept through the tenements every summer.

Lily could feel their hostile eyes on her, taking in every detail of her silk skirt and the white lawn blouse that had started out that morning so fresh and crisp and now was stuck to her like a second skin. Gritting her teeth she trudged on, clutching her straw bag tightly, glancing nervously around, afraid any minute she would be set upon. The smell of sewage hung nauseatingly in the air and she quickened her pace, heading away from the wharves and the devastating poverty.

A grim smile crossed her face as she thought about that. She was as poor as they were, even poorer. She had exactly twenty-five cents left in her pocket and she had no idea what it would buy, but she was certain it wouldn't be much. She needed money quickly and she was searching for a pawnbroker where she could pledge her silver hair-brushes. Her throat was parched and the sun was beating on her head, and she was beginning to feel weaker with each step.

She stopped and leaned tiredly against a wall and a young woman sitting on the steps watching her said, "Will you be feelin' ill, miss?"

Lily looked at her. She was young and haggard and looked as ex-hausted as Lily felt. Her children came running, clustering around her knees, staring up at the rich-looking stranger.

Lily sank down onto the step beside her. "I'm just tired," she sighed. "Is it all right if I sit here a while?"

"Suit yerself," the woman said, "but if yer ill then you'd best go around to St. Stephen's, they'll help you."

Lily shook her head. "It's not a church I need, it's a pawnbroker. I've got twenty-five cents left to my name."

The woman shrugged. "Then you have more than the rest of us."

Lily stared at her and then at her many children. "But where is your husband?"

"Out. Searching for work. Him and a thousand others for one job."

The woman's voice was matter-of-fact. She was beyond emotion, even bitterness. "There's a pawnbroker on Hudson Street," she suggested. "Maybe he can help you."

Lily thanked her and said she would be on her way. She walked a few steps, thinking of her expensive silver brushes and how much they would bring—twenty, maybe even thirty dollars—and then she turned quickly and pressed her twenty-five cents into the woman's hand.

"You need it more than I do," she said, hurrying away from her thanks.

THE PAWNBROKER STARED at her through his little brass grille. The beautiful sterling silver hairbrushes, the ornate matching mirror, and the comb were amazing. He looked again at the girl. Her face was as white as her blouse and she had the same look of desperation he had seen so many times before, because nobody ever came into his shop that wasn't desperate. "The Last Resort," they called him bitterly. But this girl was different. And the brushes were worth a small fortune.

Lily sank into the wooden chair by the counter and put her aching head in her hands, waiting for his decision. If he didn't give her the money, she didn't know what she would do.

The pawnbroker looked doubtfully at her, hoping she wasn't ill. All he needed was a sick woman in his shop. He hurriedly fetched her a glass of water and watched as she drank it. He had to get her out of here before she collapsed. "I'll tell you what," he said quickly. "I'll let you have five dollars on the lot. And remember, you must pay me back within six weeks." He knew she would never come back and he also knew a fence who would take them off his hands immediately for thirty or forty bucks.

"I'll take it, and thank you," Lily cried gratefully. She glanced more hopefully at him as he counted the money into her outstretched hand. "I need a job," she said eagerly. "Can you tell me where I should go?"

He tucked the silver brushes away under the counter and glanced indifferently at her. "Where your sort always go," he said disparagingly. "To the Irish Maids Employment Agency over on Tremont."

Lily's heart sank at the thought, but five dollars was much less than she had expected to get for the brushes and she knew it would not last long.

Mrs. Richardson at the Irish Maids Employment Agency had been a governess herself until she had discovered there was a more lucrative trade in selling poor Irishwomen to the rich Bostonians. The Irishwomen made good servants: they were neat, clean, honest, and virtuous. They worked hard and took pride in what they did, and they did it well because their mothers had taught them how to cook and wash and clean. And they all had a dozen brothers and sisters, so they knew about looking after children. The unheated attic cubicles they lived in were better than anything in the North End and, for room and board and five dollars a month, they worked seven days a week and only asked for time off for Sunday Mass.

Mrs. Richardson knew from her own past experience the trials of living as a servant in a rich household, and she also recognized class when she saw it. She looked Lily up and down and the girl looked straight back at her without flinching. She told her crisply, "The first thing you have to learn is that a servant does not look her employer back in the eye as if she were her equal. She lowers her head and says, 'Yes, ma'am, and thank you, ma'am,' and she always remembers that."

"Yes, ma'am," Lily said, quickly lowering her eyes.

Mrs. Richardson's Irish girls always had rough red hands and strong brogues, but the young woman standing on the other side of her desk had none of these badges of office. "You don't look very strong," she said critically.

"Oh, but I am," Lily cried anxiously, pulling herself straighter and managing an eager smile. "It's just that I had to walk such a long way in the heat. But I'm as strong as the next girl."

Mrs. Richardson leaned on her desk, her hands clasped in front of her. "May I ask exactly what is your background, my dear?" she said more sympathetically. But Lily just shook her head and said quietly, "Like everyone else, I left my home in Ireland to find a new life. My husband died on the voyage over. I'm all alone."

"Are there any children?"

"No. Oh, no. No children," Lily replied positively.

"I have a position in a rather fine house on Beacon Hill. On Chestnut Street." She checked her list. "They need a general maid immediately. I was going to send someone else but it's a grand household and it would suit your sort. The wage is five dollars a month, uniforms provided and room and board. And of course, the first month's wage is payable to me, for my commission."

She handed Lily a card with an address on it and told her to see Mrs. Janssen, the housekeeper. "One other thing," she said, looking Lily up and down again, "you had better not go wearing those clothes. Servants do not wear silk and Mrs. Janssen is going to think you're an uppity girl who's no better than she ought to be." Lily's face flamed with guilty color and Mrs. Richardson added mildly, "I'm not saying that's the case, my dear. It's obvious you have come down in the world, but if you want to work as a maidservant, then you must look like a maidservant. There's a secondhand store at the bottom of Court Street. They buy and sell. I suggest you take yourself there before you apply for the job."

Clutching the card that would lead to her future, Lily climbed wearily back down the stairs and onto Tremont. The secondhand store was a long walk. Her back ached and her legs ached and her head ached, but the woman in the dusty secondhand store was kind.

Taking one look at Lily's pale face she hastily brought a chair. "Sit down, my dear," she said kindly, "and catch your breath. You never know which is worse in Boston, the heat of summer or the bitter cold of winter." She gave Lily a glass of lemonade and said, "Now what can I do for you?"

She nodded as Lily explained her predicament. "And what else have you to sell?" she asked. "Besides the clothes off your back."

Lily rummaged eagerly in her bag and brought out the cloak with the fur trim, her little fur jacket, two other velvet jackets, her fawn woolen skirt, and her fur muff. She said eagerly, "They are all of the best quality."

The woman nodded. "I can see that, my dear. I'll take this and these," she picked out the velvet jackets and the fur and the muff. "But you had better keep that cloak and that good woolen skirt. You'll be glad of them when January comes around, believe me." She looked consideringly at the little pile of pretty clothes, knowing she could get a very good resale price, especially for the fur. "I can offer you twenty dollars, my dear, for the lot. Plus I'll give you a fair price on a suitable dress for your interview."

Lily almost fainted with delight. Twenty whole dollars plus five for her brushes. And just this morning she had been down to her last twenty-five cents. The storekeeper brought out a gray cotton dress, long-sleeved and buttoned high at the neck, and she took Lily into the back to try it on. Lily was too thin and the dress hung on her, but she told her cheerily, "They eat well at some of those houses on the Hill, you're sure to put on weight. Besides, that dress is a bargain. The woman who owned it died, so it's scarcely worn."

Lily's skin crawled at the thought of wearing a dead woman's dress. She wanted to rip it off her back but she knew she could not. With a pang she remembered shopping with Mammie at Mrs. Simms in Dublin, and the feel of cool soft satins and silks next to her skin. Now she was wearing a dead woman's clothes and she hung her head in shame, wondering what her mother would think if she could see her.

"You'll need a sturdier pair of boots than those you're wearing," the storekeeper told her, bringing out a pair in stiff black leather. "And a shawl for when it's cool."

Lily laced up the boots, hating the way they felt. She wrapped the shawl around her shoulders and gazed sadly at herself in the mirror. She looked exactly like the hollow-eyed young woman she had met on the street this morning. Without her fancy clothes she had become a poor Irish peasant, just like all the others.

"That'll be three dollars the lot," the storekeeper said briskly. Lily handed over the money and the storekeeper wished her well and she walked slowly out onto Court Street as a new woman.

She plodded wearily up Beacon Hill's steep, charming streets. The houses were large and well kept, there were trees and gaslights and a feeling of quality and assurance that spoke of solid money and cultured people, a world away from the North End slums. As she climbed the steps at the house on Chestnut Street and rang the front doorbell, Lily told herself wearily that at least it was pretty.

A butler in a white linen jacket opened the door. An expression of horror crossed his face as he looked her up and down and she blushed. Tilting her chin in the air she said, "Would you tell Mrs. Janssen that Lily Molyneux is here to see her."

He grabbed her roughly by the collar and marched her back down the steps. "And who do you think you are, ringing my front door and asking for the housekeeper? If the mistress ever saw you she'd have Mrs. Janssen's job—and mine too." He gave her an angry thrust in the direction of a steep flight of basement stairs. "That's where your sort belongs, my girl, and don't you forget it. And I never want to see your face in my front hall again."

Lily fled down the basement steps to the servants' entrance. She turned to look at him. He had taken out a handkerchief and was wiping his fingers, a frown of disgust on his face as though he had just touched something dirty. Anger boiled in her and she was tempted to go back and tell him exactly who she was, but then she remembered she was no longer that person. She was what he thought she was. A maidservant and less than nothing.

A cheerful young Irish girl opened the door at her knock. Her black hair was half-hidden under a cap and she wore a blue-striped cotton dress and a voluminous clean white apron. "I'm to see Mrs. Janssen about the job," Lily said, her cheeks still burning with shame and anger.

The girl grinned. "To be sure," she said, "it'll be the new general maid we was expectin'. I'm Kathleen. And yourself?"

"Lily." She glanced nervously at the girl. "I've never done this before. What's it like being a maid?"

"Sure and it's not too bad. You have a roof over your head and decent food in your belly. Mrs. Janssen's an old tyrant, but they say all housekeepers give themselves airs. And o' course she's not from the old country. She's Swedish and she thinks she's better than we are. And she's right, because she's the boss and we all work for her."

She shepherded Lily through a dark corridor into a servants' hall, and said, "The mistress of the house is so high and mighty y'hardly dares to look at her. Keep out of the mistress's way and in Mrs. Janssen's good books and you'll be all right. There's four of us," she added. "I'm the kitchen maid, and there's the parlormaid and the upstairs maid, they've got the best jobs. And you'll be the 'general,' which means you get to do everybody else's dirty work, scrubbing the pans and the floors and steps, and helping with the laundry. It's hard work," she added with a sympathetic sigh.

Lily's heart sank as she watched Kathleen go off in search of Mrs. Janssen. She had imagined herself carrying in trays of tea and dusting and maybe arranging flowers, not scrubbing steps. Kathleen returned. "Herself will see you now," she said, shepherding her to the housekeeper's sitting room.

Mrs. Janssen was white-haired and red-faced and Lily could tell from her piercing stare that she did not like her. "Whatever does that woman at the agency think she's doing sending me a frail creature like you," she cried exasperatedly. "Surely with all the Irish in Boston she could have come up with something better!" Lily shriveled under her angry gaze. She had no answer and Mrs. Janssen said grimly, "If we were not in dire need I would send you right back to her, but you'd better start immediately. There's a dinner party for thirty tonight and Cook needs all the help she can get. And you had better be a hard worker, girl, or you'll be out on your ear."

Lily remembered Mrs. Richardson's words of warning and with her eyes carefully lowered she muttered, "Yes, ma'am. Thank you, ma'am," and she followed Kathleen back into the corridor and up endless flights of bare wooden stairs to the attics under the mansard roof.

Even though the tiny dormer windows were wide open, the attics shimmered with a breathless heat that had them gasping and clutching their throats for air. " 'Tis no better at night neither," Kathleen said, fanning herself. "The heat gathers itself up here, and here it stays. And in winter you'll be breaking the ice. You can hear the steam heating chugging away down below but there's niver a blast of it reaches here." She sighed, mopping her brow. "It just seems we can niver win," she said, resignedly accepting her lot.

There were five flimsily partitioned cubicles for the servants under the mansard roof and Lily's was no different from the rest: a splintery wooden floor, a black iron bed, a pine nightstand with a cheap washbasin and jug and a square of unframed mirror over it. There was a battered chest of drawers and a brass peg on the wall.

"At least there's a mattress," Kathleen said, looking at Lily's glum face, "though sometimes I think it's stuffed with gravel, it's so lumpy. Not that we get much time for sleep anyway. But you'd better hurry or Cook'll have yer guts for garters."

Lily dumped her basket quickly onto the bed. She smoothed down the dead woman's gray dress and tightened the ribbon holding back her hair. Kathleen smiled encouragingly at her. "It'll be all right once you get used to it," she said, whisking her back down the stairs to the kitchen.

Cook was standing at the scrubbed pine table busily mixing something in a bowl. She was big and dark-haired with brawny arms, fat jowls, and a bitter expression. "And where have you been?" she asked Kathleen, harshly cuffing aside the young girl standing at the table peeling potatoes. The girl went on steadily peeling the potatoes, but tears of pain rolled down her cheeks. She could not have been more than thirteen years old and Lily thought she seemed too frightened even to glance up from her task.

"And who might you be?" Cook asked. And, like Mrs. Janssen, she rolled her eyes exasperatedly to heaven when Lily said she was the new "general." "My Lord, what will they send us next? An old woman fit for the junkyard maybe. Well, get an apron on, girl, there's a sinkful of dirty pots and pans. And Kathleen, you can butter the soufflé dishes and be quick about it."

The afternoon flew into evening as Cook piled task after task on Lily and Kathleen and the little girl, whose name was Teresa. The parlor maid and the upstairs maid, grand in their black "afternoon" dresses and frilled organza aprons and caps, flitted in and out for cups of tea and a gossip, and later Lily was sent running upstairs with a tea tray for the children's nanny.

Back in the kitchen Lily was set to work again scrubbing vegetables. She went from one chore to the next in a daze of exhaustion and when the dinner was finally served Cook said with a sigh, "Thank the Lord, that's another one over." And then she headed for her own room, leaving them to clean up.

They sat at the kitchen table and devoured cold meat pie and slabs of bread and butter and mugs of hot cocoa like ravenous little animals. They washed the dishes and scrubbed the table and swept the floor, and then, at one-thirty when everything was clean and tidy again and with Cook asleep and snoring long ago in her room, they climbed wearily up the gloomy back stairs to their hot little attic.

Lily slept the knocked-out sleep of total exhaustion, blissfully unaware of the heat and her aching back and her problems. But the next morning she was wakened with the birds and told to hurry. She was given a blue print frock and a vast wraparound apron, and after a hasty breakfast of bread and tea, she was sent outside to scrub the front steps. As she carried her heavy tin bucket of water and big scrubbing brushes up the basement steps and along the street to the front, she hid her face in shame. Her tears fell into the soapy water as she sank to her knees and began to scrub. Hatred and resentment clawed at her heart. She was learning that there were more subtle ways for the Almighty to exact his punishment for wickedness than an easy death.

Despite Kathleen's cheerful friendliness Lily was lonely. She was different and the other girls knew it: her voice was low and cultured and she did not speak with their own heavy brogue; her undergarments were of fine linen—they knew because they saw them hanging on the washline next to their own; and she was not used to hard work—anyone with half an eye could see that. Still, Lily tried hard; she remembered to keep her eyes lowered at all times and to keep "her place." When the others went off to Mass on Sundays she walked by herself on the Common, feeling lonelier than ever. And at night she lay in her lumpy iron bed unable to sleep for the heat, thinking longingly about home. But she tried never to think about her baby and Dermot Hathaway. She wanted so desperately to be free of them, because of what they had done to her.

The days dragged by in a haze of scrubbing and sweeping and polishing and peeling. Her hands were as red and chapped as Kathleen's and Teresa's and her life seemed settled in a routine of endless dreary tasks.

One Sunday morning, a few weeks later, Mrs. Janssen summoned Lily to her study. The rich smells of roast beef wafted up from the kitchen as Lily tidied her hair and made her way nervously to the housekeeper's sitting room, wondering what she wanted. She stood with her hands behind her back and she kept her eyes down, waiting.

Mrs. Janssen stared severely at her. "It has been pointed out to me that you do not attend Mass on Sundays with the other maidservants," she said coldly.

"No, ma'am, I do not," Lily replied.

Mrs. Janssen's eyes flashed with anger. "You know that the girls are only granted time off to attend their church. And since you do not choose to attend, then you are not entitled to the same privilege. From now on you will be on duty all day Sunday."

Lily's eyes opened wide at the injustice. "Oh, but—" she began.

"But what?" Mrs. Janssen's eyes blazed at her. "Are you daring to contradict me, girl?"

Lily's chin shot up and she looked her angrily in the eye. "Jayzus, ma'am, yes I am!" she shouted, stamping her foot. "That's my time off and you know it, and little enough it is too."

The housekeeper's red face turned purple with rage and astonishment that anyone would presume to answer her back. "Why, you little Irish slut," she shouted, banging her fist on her desk. "I've never in all my life heard such language. You will pack your bags and get out of here immediately. *And* you'll forfeit your wages. Don't ever let me see you in this neighborhood again or else I'll have the police onto you."

It was an empty threat but Lily did not know it, and she scurried terrified from the room. Her old impetuousness had cost her her job and now she also had the threat of police trouble hanging over her.

She fled up the back stairs to the attic and began flinging her things into her straw bag, afraid that if she were not gone quickly Mrs. Janssen would have sent for the police. Kathleen hurried after her. "The old woman's crazy," she said sympathetically. "But listen, Lily, I met Mr. Adams's parlormaid at Mass the other week and she told me they needed a girl. It's a lovely house on Mount Vernon. Why don't you try there. Maybe you'll be lucky."

Lily thanked her gratefully. She took the steep winding stairs two at a time and ran as fast as she could down Chestnut Street. The agency had taken her first month's wages and Mrs. Janssen had kept the second. She had scrubbed and cleaned for two months, seven days a week, eighteen hours a day for nothing.

The Adams house was one of the biggest and oldest houses on Mount Vernon. Still panting from her mad escape, this time Lily knew to go down the basement steps to the servants' entry. Another little Irish maid let her in and conducted her to the housekeeper, Mrs. Hoolihan. She looked her briefly up and down and said disinterestedly, "You'll do. You can start right away."

Lily hurried thankfully off, relieved that she had not asked about her previous employment. She would have had to lie again and her life had become a bewildering tissue of untruths. Sometimes now it seemed to her that the lies were taking over and becoming the truth.

The little maid, Emer, was subdued as she showed Lily her room. "There's six of us altogether," Emer said. "I'm the general and you'll be kitchen. Mrs. Hoolihan and Mrs. Bennett, the cook, are queens of this household," she added bitterly. "They have their own sitting rooms and they do hardly any work. Mr. Adams is a bachelor. He's an older gentleman and he travels abroad a lot. He's away in France until October, so there's no entertaining to be done and they have it easy. It's the likes of me and you who get to do all the work around here. Still, we've enough to eat and there's a bit of money and I'm hoping to become a cook meself one day, or maybe a children's nurse." She sighed again. "It's a quiet household all right."

Lily remembered to keep her eyes lowered and to act respectful. She had learned her lesson and she was determined to keep this job because she had to repay Mrs. Sheridan the five dollars she had taken, and she had to send money to pay for the baby. But fortunately the housekeeper seemed disinterested and the cook was the housekeeper's friend and they spent all their time closeted together in Mrs. Hoolihan's sitting room. The parlormaid and upstairs maid put on airs and kept to themselves, and young Emer's garrulous gossiping tongue grated on Lily's nerves.

She lay in bed one sleepless night, feeling hopeless, as she always did, about the past and the shame she had brought to her family. A sense of her own wickedness overwhelmed her. She wished for the thousandth time she had never met Dermot, and she cursed her own confident, reckless stupidity. Desolately, she wondered if Ciel ever thought of her. She decided to write to her. She didn't know if she would ever get the letter, but Ciel loved to collect the mail and there was just a chance.

She sat up half the night writing her letter and the next morning she asked Mrs. Hoolihan for ten minutes off. As she handed over her letter in the post office, she thought it was like the Manila hemp line sent out to rescue the sailors from the sinking ship. Only her sister could save her from drowning in loneliness.

CHAPTER

29

MAUDIE

Ardnavarna

TELLING LILY'S STORY brings back my own memories of what it was like to be a child at the Big House. Remember, I lived there until I was twelve years old and a gloomy place it was, too, with just the three of us rattling around in it like peas in a drum. But as you know in Lily's day it was a palace, perpetually filled with visitors and guests, relatives and friends and shooting and fishing parties, Christmas dances and hunt balls.

By the time it got to my turn many of the Molyneuxes friends and contemporaries had lost their sons in the wars. And by then most had lost their money, and a great many of them had also lost their big houses. Those that hadn't still lived in crumbling old mansions that half froze them in the winter, with the damp creeping up the elegant Georgian wallpaper and jam jars scattered around the rooms to catch the rain dripping through the holes in the roof.

I remember those freezing drawing rooms when we went to visit. Our hostess would be sitting in her fur coat, serving whiskey with her gloves on while her husband jabbed futilely at the smoldering peat fire with a gigantic iron poker and the wind whistled down the enormous chimney with a draft that lifted the corners of the rugs and sent the heavy old brocade curtains aflutter.

"But why did they stay?" Shannon asked.

"It was simple. They had nowhere else to go. Their big houses were often mortgaged to the hilt, two or three times over, even though their bank managers did their best to keep them within the narrow confines of a budget. But of course, the very word 'budget' is alien to the Irish nature, and they had never been taught to live any other way, so they just carried on doing what they were doing. There were always a few good horses in the stables, and always bottles of gin and whiskey and sherry on the sideboard; there were fresh salmon from the river and trout from the loch and pheasant and snipe and rabbit from the woods and fields, so they never went hungry. The servants never asked for their wages and the local shopkeepers extended them credit the way they always had, only this time the credit lasted for years, even though the bills were presented every month. A pound or two here and there toward it kept the tradesmen happy and life went on almost as normal, with the parties and the hunt balls."

Maybe reducing them to penury was God's punishment on the landed gentry for the terrible things some of them did to their tenants. I sighed. Ireland has always been plagued by poverty and troubles. And by the English, I daresay.

But I'm digressing as usual, and all I started out to tell you was that though the Big House was gloomy when I was a girl, it was not for lack of money in those days. It was just that the Gothic stone hall was like a cathedral, so lofty a child's shrill small voice echoed around it, and so cavernous there were a hundred places to hide when we played party games. Sometimes I wonder whether we ever found all the "hiders" in hide and seek, and all the "sardines" shut away in those vast cupboards. Who knows? Maybe one day we shall open a door and there will be a pair of children perfectly preserved in their party frocks, like babes in the wood.

But the old house was full of life and merriment even if it was damned cold, and however much we traveled it was always good to come home.

But as I told Shannon and Eddie, after Lily left the Big House nothing was ever the same again. First, though, you'll be wanting to know what I was wearing that night for our after-dinner story. I think it's important, how a woman looks. Call it vanity if you will, but as you know frocks are my passion and that night it was 1952 Chanel, a long navy silk jersey that always clung so much it was impossible to wear undergarments. But that's another story. And in case you are wondering, yes I did wear them that night, those miraculous silk bloomers they sell in America that don't show what they call your "panty line." But anyhow, back in 1952 we didn't have them.

So. This is what I told Shannon and Eddie that night.

Ardnavarna

WHEN TEN-YEAR-OLD CIEL MOLYNEUX watched Lily being driven from Ardnavarna in the carriage pulled by the black funeral horses she knew without a shadow of a doubt that her own life had just changed for the worse.

Her father locked himself away in his rooms and her mother took to her bed. William was away at Oxford University and nobody bothered to get Ciel a new governess, and left alone, she roamed the estate on her pony with Lily's dogs running at her heels. Tears rolled endlessly down her face as she mourned for her sister, because it was as bad as if Lily were dead. Worse, because had she been dead Lily would have been buried lovingly at Ardnavarna.

When her father finally emerged from his solitude a few weeks later, she stared horrified at his pallid face, at his dead eyes, his graying hair and stooped shoulders. In the space of a few weeks her proud, robust father had become an old man. Ciel followed him miserably around the house the way Lily's dogs followed her, but he rarely spoke. And when she tried to talk to him he turned his face away as though he could not even bear to look at her.

Lost, she ran to her mother for comfort and Lady Nora attempted to rouse herself from her lethargy to attend to her younger daughter's needs. Her *only* daughter, she reminded herself bitterly. Her husband was like a stranger now; he never smiled; he was taciturn, and flew off into a rage at the smallest thing: the coffee was not hot enough at breakfast or the wine had been decanted badly or the house was too hot or too cold and the servants slovenly. No matter how hard she tried to maintain the household as if everything were normal, she could do nothing right. Ciel watched Pa raging at her innocent mother and she did not know what to do.

When they got the terrible news of the sinking of the *Hibernia* and heard that Lily's name was not on the list of survivors, Pa departed immediately for London. He stayed at his club instead of at their town house, playing cards and attending race-meetings with his friends. He did not wear mourning and he forbade a memorial service. Everyone thought him callous and hard-hearted, but behind the cold facade, Ciel felt sure he was hurting as badly as she and her mother.

Lady Nora took to her bed again, a broken woman, and Ciel ran for her pony and rode along the strand. She stared at the crashing green waves imagining her sister drowning beneath their icy weight and she screamed her sorrow out loud. It cannot be true, she cried, it just cannot. Any minute Lily will come riding down the path between the rocks and the dogs will run barking like mad creatures to greet her. And Finn O'Keeffe will be with her, the way he always is, racing beside her.

Her mother stayed in bed and her father stayed in London and nobody seemed to care about her anymore. Ciel wished her mother would appoint a new governess and then at least she would have someone to talk to, but Lady Nora did not emerge from her darkened room. The doctor came and went and the servants talked in hushed whispers, while Ciel wandered from room to room, or rode her pony for miles over the bogs, sometimes not returning until after dark. But there was no one to ask angrily where she had been and why she had stayed out so long, driving them half out of their minds with worry. No one bothered that her hair was tangled and her dress grubby, and that now she ate her supper all alone in the vast icy dining room at the big table that seated thirty.

She would peek longingly in at Mammie on her way to bed and find her already sleeping from the potion the doctor had given her. And she would peek wistfully into the cozy kitchen where the maids were having their suppers, gossiping and laughing among themselves. And into the library where Pa always used to smoke his after-dinner cigar. It was cold and empty now, just the way her life was, with Lily dead.

Her mother became suddenly crippled with arthritis. She said with a sigh that the damp climate had finally penetrated her very bones and she took permanently to her bed. She no longer managed her household and dust gathered everywhere. And when her brother finally returned from Oxford for the holidays Ciel fell on him with tears of rapture and sorrow.

William held his sobbing sister close, wiping his misted spectacles, holding back his own tears. "We used to be so happy," Ciel sobbed. "And now look at Pa. And Mammie. Look at us and tell me if we will ever be the same again?"

The months dragged tediously past. Her father never came home, William returned to Oxford, and Ciel's only pleasure was riding by herself through the woods or up in the bleak mountains. In little more than a year the happy, mischievous little girl was reduced to a sad-faced lonely child.

The pile of letters lay on the silver salver on the round mahogany claw-foot table in the middle of the hall for months, gathering dust like everything else in the Big House, awaiting Lord Molyneux's return. One morning Ciel was walking through the hall with the dogs at her heels, as usual, when a mouse suddenly ran across the floor. The dogs were after it in a minute, leaping onto the table and sending the salver and the letters flying across the floor. Angrily Ciel grabbed them by their collars. The mouse disappeared under the oak wainscoting and she thought with a sigh there would be no use telling Mammie because her mother no longer seemed to care about anything except the next powerful dose of painkiller the doctor gave her.

She picked up the letters, glancing idly at each one, staring hard at the creamy envelope bearing her name. She would have known Lily's big bold handwriting anywhere and her heart seemed to jump into her throat and then back somewhere deep in her stomach. She grabbed the letter in both hands, holding it close to her chest, hugging it as though it were her sister herself. Trembling with joy, she knew that the precious letter meant Lily was alive.

She took the stairs two at a time and sped along the corridor to her room. She locked the door and climbed into Lily's bed with the dogs settled around her and tore open the envelope. Her hands shook as she smoothed back the folded pages and began to read.

Dearest Ciel,

If you should ever receive this letter I shall be the happiest girl in Boston. I think of you, my dear little sister, all the time. I miss you so, and oh, how I miss darling Mammie, though I am afraid to think of Pa as he was when I last saw him. Oh, Ciel, how could he be so cruel? How could he think that what happened was his darling daughter's fault. And was I really **wicked,** Ciel, to blame Finn? I think about what I did and I just don't understand. I didn't think about the consequences: I just thought Pa would not condemn me to marry him, though God knows it would have been better than being forced to marry that fearsome D.H. . . . And oh, Ciel, what do you think? Finn and Daniel were on the *Hibernia,* working as stokers. Ciel, he hates me so much, he almost killed me. And I should not have been bothered if he had. He took my necklace and my money instead—and said I owed him it. And I think he was right.

She wrote about the shipwreck and she told her about the Sheridans and the baby. She said she had not even been able to look at it and had left it to be brought up safely by the Sheridans. She told her she was working in Boston for a Harvard professor . . .

as a maidservant, dearest Ciel. Oh, how the mighty are fallen! Now I am seeing life from the other side of the awful green baize door. If you ever receive this letter, and I cannot be sure you will, then I just want you to remember that I think of you all the time. Oh, Ciel, how I miss you, and how I miss Ardnavarna. I am a penitent locked out of paradise with no hope of forgiveness. If only I could turn back the clock, if only . . . dearest little Ciel . . .

Ciel read the letter a hundred times; she held it to her lips and kissed it; she offered it to Lily's dogs so they could sniff her scent on it and they barked joyfully and wagged their tails.

She leapt from her bed and ran along the corridor to tell her mother the good news, but when she opened the door she hesitated. She remembered that this sad, silent, dark room had once been filled with flowers and light and the scent of powder and perfume, instead of the acrid odor of medicines and sickness. Drugged with the morphine that kept her terrible pain at bay, her mother would be too confused to understand that Lily was alive again. Sometimes these days she would even think Ciel was Lily, and that she was still a child, and she would scold her for tobogganing down the stairs on tea trays and tell her she must not be bowling in the long gallery. Her poor mother was permanently locked in a twilight past, so stuffing Lily's precious letter into her pocket, Ciel stole over to her bed and dropped a sorrowful kiss on her sleeping face.

She curled up in a chair by her mother's bed and the faithful dogs settled at her feet, snoring gently in the firelight. And she thought of the letter she would write to Lily that very afternoon.

But there was no time to write to Lily that afternoon and not for a long time after that, because as she sat there watching, her mother suddenly opened her eyes. She stared, puzzled, at Ciel. "Lily, dear," she said weakly, "I have such a bad headache. Could you go to my little pantry where I keep the medicines and get me some of those pills? You know the ones I mean, dear, they're white." Pressing her hands to her temples, she groaned. "Hurry, dear child, the pain is very bad."

Ciel peered anxiously at her. She knew that the doctor gave her mother morphine for her pain and he had warned that she must take no other pills. Suddenly Lady Nora sat up. Her back arched and she thrashed around on the bed, moaning. Then she fell back onto the pillows and lay still.

Terrified, Ciel screamed her name. Her mother's eyes were wide open and her lovely face was twisted into a horrifying grimace. Ciel screamed again and with a last panicked glance she ran for help.

The housekeeper and the servants flocked back up the stairs behind her. They gathered around the big brass four-poster, staring at Lady Nora, drawing in horrified breaths and shaking their heads when they saw her twisted face.

"I'm afraid she has had a seizure," the housekeeper told Ciel sympathetically. "I'll send the lad right away for the doctor."

The housekeeper stayed with Ciel while the other servants went back downstairs. They stood anxiously in the hall, talking softly, crossing themselves and muttering prayers for their mistress's recovery, though seeing her, none held out much hope.

" 'Twill be a happy release if the Lady goes," they told each other, "for she's niver been the same woman since wicked Lily was sent from home."

The doctor came and he shook his head. "I'm afraid we must expect the worst, dear girl," he said to Ciel, patting her consolingly on the shoulder.

Messages were sent immediately to summon Lord Molyneux and William back from England. Ciel sat on the little pink velvet boudoir chair by her mother's bed, awaiting their return, weeping over the cruel fate that had changed darling Mammie's sweet face into a frightening mask. The subdued dalmatians lay at her feet, heads flattened between their paws and their ears nervously back, as though they sensed death approaching.

Lord Molyneux arrived and this time his tears flowed freely for anyone to see. He stayed devotedly at his wife's side, sleeping on an iron cot. No one knew what he said to her in those long days and nights of waiting, but passing her door they could hear the low murmur of his voice. Ciel and William wondered bitterly if he was telling their mother it was all his fault she was dying. They knew if he had not so heartlessly sent Lily away, Lady Nora would have not become so sick. Now she had nothing to live for and so she was going to die.

A few days later, as the sun rose, Lord Molyneux looked at his wife and he thought a miracle had happened. Her twisted face had smoothed out and she looked like her old self. There was even a hint of a smile around her lips. "Nora!" he exclaimed joyfully, catching her hand in his. But he knew from its coldness that she was not there. She had crept away from life as quietly and discreetly as she had lived it.

Lady Nora's silver-handled mahogany coffin was placed in an open cart on a carpet of moss and flowers fashioned by the tenants. The same black-plumed horses that had driven her daughter away into exile pulled her to her final resting place through the misty gray drizzle. Ciel and William walked with their father behind the coffin. They wore black mourning clothes and they carried bouquets of their mother's favorite lilies plucked from the hothouses by the head gardener.

Pa walked slowly. He leaned heavily on his cane and the villagers shook their heads over him as they fell into line behind them. The Molyneuxes many friends had arrived in droves to pay their last respects and the small family chapel was filled to overflowing, and their tenants stood outside listening to the service, crossing themselves and offering their own prayers.

When the coffin was carried into the family tomb where generations of Molyneuxes had been buried and the great creaking stone door was finally pushed back into place and locked, Ciel threw herself, wailing, to the ground. She kicked her feet and drummed her fists on the gravel until they bled, screaming for her mammie. Lord Molyneux looked helplessly down at her and William hurried to pick up his sister. He dusted her off and helped her back down the winding path through the dripping trees and damp bracken to their empty home.

LORD MOLYNEUX REMAINED at Ardnavarna, but he was no longer the Pa that Lily would have remembered. His step was uncertain and he walked with the aid of a stick, carved specially for him out of hazelwood by one of his tenants. And he took to roaming the straggling village and the scattered farmsteads and fishermen's cottages, poking his head inquiringly into his tenants' doors and asking after their welfare. Suddenly paternal and philanthropic, he gave every man a pig and a cow as an Easter gift. He ordered new thatch on every roof for winter, and gave instructions for the cottages to be painted in bright, cheerful colors: coral and peacock, lemon and kelly green.

All except Padraig O'Keeffe's cottage. It stood out like a gray sore on the newly colorful landscape and he came and looked at it, and then he ordered it pulled to the ground, stone by stone. He commanded the stones to be cast into the sea so that no man might ever use them again. He ordered the land where the O'Keeffe cottage had stood plowed under and planted with brambles and nettles and thorny things so no one would ever walk on it, or grow crops on it, or build a house on it again. He cut the O'Keeffes savagely out of his world, blaming them for all his troubles, and the villagers knew it and they resented it.

Lord Molyneux looked bitterly into the face of his only daughter, really seeing her for the first time in many months. Her unkempt red hair straggled around her shoulders, her dress looked as though she had worn it for a week, there was dirt under her nails, and she was bare-legged. He hung his head in shame that a child of his had been reduced by his neglect to such a state, and he ordered her away at once to a school he knew of in Paris where they were used to dealing with wild young children and where, he sincerely hoped, they would take the responsibility of Ciel off his hands and turn his unkempt young daughter into a lady.

Ciel cried all the way on the train from London. She cried all the way across on the ferry to Cherbourg. And she cried on the train to Paris. But as she was driven through the beautiful springtime city, she dried her eyes and sat up and took notice. The sky was blue and the chestnut trees were in blossom, the streets were bustling and there was a snatch of music in the air.

She inspected the school cautiously. It was a beautiful white building on a quiet street near the Jardin du Luxembourg. The corridors smelled of wax polish and the dormitory was lined with narrow white beds, each one containing a child's doll. The teachers were smiling and gentle and she suddenly felt relieved. For the first time in her life she felt glad to be away from Ardnavarna.

She ate her supper of soup and bread and butter and drank hot chocolate from a wide flat cup, and she snuggled up in her own narrow white bed that night, glad of the company of the other girls. Before she went to sleep she took out Lily's letter, crumpled from endless readings, and read it yet again. Tomorrow, she promised herself, she would write to her sister and tell her all the terrible things that had happened since she left. And that Ardnavarna would never be the same again.

CHAPTER
30

BOSTON

THE JOHN PORTER ADAMS MANSION was even grander than the one Lily had just left. Designed by an eminent architect, Charles Bulfinch, the beautiful bow-fronted town house occupied a commanding position on Mount Vernon Street. It had dozens of rooms filled with treasures of all sorts, because not only was Mr. Adams a member of one of Boston's wealthiest old families, he was also professor of European literature at Harvard and a great collector. He traveled for much of the year and always returned home with paintings and books and rare manuscripts, as well as porcelain figurines and ancient statues and carvings. And with the house already full of inherited family treasures every room was bursting at the seams.

He was away on an extended visit to Europe when Lily started to work there, but the sloppy-looking young parlormaid told her that Mr. Adams was a bachelor and a "gentleman," and that he was so wrapped up in his books and his work he rarely even noticed they were there. "It's an easy job," she had said, lazily running her finger through the dust on the hall table as she showed Lily around. "All you need do is give the house a quick clean before he gets back, and he'll never know the difference."

Lily's room was the same as before, up in the attic, and her job was the same: scrubbing, sweeping, washing. Resentfully, she went from one task to another, though she noticed everyone else seemed to have plenty of spare time. The housekeeper, Mrs. Hoolihan, put on her coat and hat promptly every morning at eleven. She would fling a few orders at Lily and at Emer and tell them she was going to Mass, then she would disappear for a few hours.

"It's not Mass she's going to," Emer told Lily. "It's the saloon." And

Lily was sure she was right because Mrs. Hoolihan would return later in the afternoon, red-faced and aggressive, clutching a brown paper sack.

"Gin," Emer whispered, giggling, as the housekeeper waddled off to her room and slammed the door. In the evenings she would often be joined by the cook and they would hear the chink of glasses and muffled laughter and then Cook would begin to sing loudly.

Emer covered her ears. "She always sings when she's drunk," she told Lily. "And it's always hymns." And with no one to stop them, she and the other maids would sneak out to meet their friends, leaving Lily alone in the big house.

The first time it happened Lily sat in the kitchen listening to the ticking of the clock on the wall, watching the hands jump from second to slower second, minute to even slower minute. The silence and the loneliness stifled her. When she could bear no more she ran from the kitchen and up the stairs into the front hall. She looked around her. To her left was a vast chandeliered dining room and to her right Mr. Adams's library. A fine sweeping staircase led to the enormous drawing room on the second floor and beyond that was the music room with a beautiful Steinway grand piano where, Emer had told her, their employer often played melancholy Chopin études late into the night.

But it was the library that Lily liked most. The tall windows, hung with gold damask curtains, overlooked the garden at the back and Mount Vernon at the front. Three walls were lined with shelves of leather-bound books and locked cabinets held precious medieval illuminated manuscripts. Framed drawings by Leonardo da Vinci were grouped together on a wall covered in bronze silk, and a magnificent Japanese screen stood next to a seventeenth-century Aubusson tapestry. There were dozens of small glass cases filled with curios and treasures: a collection of tiny boxes in tortoiseshell and silver and porcelain and gold; there were ancient Roman coins; and prehistoric flint arrowheads and fossils and artifacts, and a thousand other fascinating things for Lily to wonder at.

When she stepped inside the room and closed her eyes and breathed in the scent of old leather with a hint of cigar smoke, she might have been home again in Pa's own study at Ardnavarna. She wandered happily around inspecting her employer's collections. She sat in his green leather chair behind his big desk, looking around the dusty room, imagining she owned the place. She pretended she was the real Lily Molyneux again and that these rich surroundings were rightfully hers, and then with a sigh she came back to earth again and the truth.

She ran from the library and up the wide sweeping stairs and flung open the great double doors leading into the magnificent drawing room. Dust lay everywhere, even on the keys of the open Steinway grand in the music room, and she cleaned it off impatiently with a corner of her apron. She ran her fingers softly over the keys but the instrument was badly out of tune, and she wondered angrily what Mr. Adams would say when he got back and found his fine house in such a state. He would probably sack all the maids, and then Mrs. Hoolihan, whose fault it was, would reign on at Mount Vernon like a drunken queen.

Lily knew how a good household was run; she had been surrounded by servants all her life; she had watched her mother giving the housekeeper orders, and listened to her arranging the week's menus with the cook. She had accompanied her to the hothouses to direct the gardener about flowers for the house and fruits for the table, and she had seen how she kept an eagle eye on the giddy young maids. Everything at Ardnavarna had run like clockwork and it was ten times the size of Mr. Adams's mansion.

Lily decided she would clean the library herself. She took off her stiff black boots so she would not dirty the pale rugs. Their softness felt good beneath her bare feet and she drifted around the lovely room, pretending she owned it. She carefully dusted all the ornaments and polished the glass curio cases, smiling with pleasure as their contents seemed to spring back into sharper focus. She clambered on a chair and shook out the great curtains, and swung herself nimbly around on the mahogany library steps to dust the books.

The parlormaid laughed at her. "Why waste your time?" she demanded airily. "When just this morning Mrs. Hoolihan had a card from Mr. Adams saying he has extended his tour indefinitely, and not to expect him back for several months." She grinned cheekily at Lily as she put on her coat and hat. "And when the boss is away the mice they do play," she paraphrased as she swept out the door.

Mrs. Hoolihan and Cook discussed the hard-working kitchen maid over a bottle of gin that evening, and they agreed that, with himself away, it seemed a pity to be wasting good money on a pair of upstairs maids who did no work anyway, when they had Lily willing and able to do it all. "We'll save two wages," Mrs. Hoolihan said firmly, "and that'll be extra money in *our* pockets, my dear."

The upstairs maids were sent packing the very next day and Lily was promoted to parlormaid. "There'll be two dollars a month more in it for you," Mrs. Hoolihan told Lily grandly, "and you get to wear a good uniform. You can think yourself lucky to be an upstairs girl, because you're young. And remember, I expect you to work hard, not like those other lazy little biddies."

"Yes, Mrs. Hoolihan," Lily said, eyes respectfully lowered, but inside she was smiling because now it meant she was free to wander anywhere in the house she wanted. She could borrow the books or play the piano. The house was hers.

But the housekeeper did not hire a replacement for Lily and there was just her and Emer to do everything. Still wearing her blue print frock and apron, Lily swept and washed and dusted, upstairs as well as down, and Mrs. Hoolihan pocketed the two maids' wages.

"She's spending it on gin," Emer said as they watched the empty bottles mounting in the cupboard in the hallway. "And Cook's stealing too. She's in cahoots with the grocer and the butcher. They give her receipts for stuff she's never ordered, she keeps the money and gives them a cut." She sighed, thinking of her chapped hands and aching feet. "If I didn't need the job so bad I would try my luck elsewhere," she said miserably.

"And so would I," Lily agreed. But hard though it was, she knew she would never get another job as a parlormaid. With every day that passed, she told herself she could not go on like this much longer. She was not meant to be anyone's servant—she had been a lady, and somehow one day she would be a lady again. She would wear silk again and never even set foot in a kitchen. She didn't know how she would achieve it, but she knew she would. Whatever it took. And she just gritted her teeth and kept on working.

She was dusting the hall one afternoon when the doorbell rang. Quickly wiping her hands on her apron she ran to answer it, staring surprised at the tall bearded man standing on her doorstep, and at the cabbie unloading a small mountain of baggage onto the sidewalk.

"Good afternoon," the man said, striding past her into the hall and up the stairs.

"Good afternoon, Mr. Adams, sir," Lily called after him, realizing at once who it was. She doubted he had even noticed her, let alone heard her, and she ran down to the basement to tell Emer to warn Mrs. Hoolihan and Cook. Then she scurried up the back stairs and changed quickly into her parlormaid's black dress and organza cap and apron.

The quiet house sprang suddenly to life. Lights blazed in every room, and thanks to Lily most of them were shining clean. Mrs. Hoolihan was sober again and Cook was back in her kitchen. Mr. Adams was home.

John Porter Adams was not a "social" man. He hated parties and especially boring dinners where the matchmaking Boston dowagers always placed him next to some eligible young woman guaranteed "to catch his eye." He was forty-nine-years old and so far they had failed. He knew that a woman would only mess up the perfect life he had created for himself: a world of art, books, and travel, and the undemanding company of good friends. He had an excellent wine cellar and the freedom to do as he pleased. He preferred conversation with learned men to the flirtatious small talk of women, and besides, he knew a woman would ruin his schedule.

He was a man in love with his work, and his lectures on seventeenth-century European literature at Harvard were the highlight of his year. He had earned a Ph.D. in classics from Oxford University and was also a linguist, fluent in French, Italian, Spanish, and German, as well as ancient Greek and Latin.

The Porter Adamses were an old Boston family of great wealth, and as the last surviving male heir John had inherited most of it at the young age of twenty-three. He was a fine-looking man, tall and a little stooped, with a Vandyke, dark eyes, and hair that had turned gray just before his twenty-sixth birthday. He was not a fastidious man: his clothes were good but there was a haphazard, forgetful air about him. He wore odd socks and mismatched jackets and pants. He would throw a muffler casually around his neck and go out into a snowstorm forgetting to put on his overcoat. He could never find the studs for his dress shirt, or his cuff links, and he couldn't tie his bow tie. One of the servants always had to do it for him, and whenever it happened he thought to himself that he really should employ a valet, but then a valet would want to "organize" him and he was a man who simply loathed being organized.

He refused to own a carriage and horses and instead walked everywhere, often forgetting there were holes in his boots until they almost fell off his feet. And at the end of a day there was nothing he liked better than a simple meal and to sit afterward by the open library window in summer, or in front of the roaring fire in winter, with his nose in a good book and a glass of excellent port on the table at his side. Whenever the mood took him he would wander upstairs and sit in the dark, playing the piano. It had a wonderful tone and the quiet sonatas and études he favored wrapped him in exquisite solitude. He was his own perfect companion and he needed no one. He was vague, erudite, gentle, and not quite of this world.

With the exception of Mrs. Hoolihan he never even noticed the servants, and Lily soon learned not to expect him to greet her if he passed her working around the house. He never even saw her. She was just part of the background, like a piece of furniture and far less interesting than a book or a painting.

There was to be an "entertainment" at the house the following Saturday evening to celebrate Mr. Adams's return. He had invited six of his Harvard colleagues, and Cook was in a turmoil of preparations. Mrs. Hoolihan flitted about in her good black silk, looking important and checking on Lily every two minutes as she set the table.

"I know where the glasses go, Mrs. Hoolihan," Lily told her impatiently, as the housekeeper shifted them around for the third time, putting fingerprints all over them, and Lily sighed because now she would have to shine them up again.

"How is it you know how to set a table, when you're nothing but a kitchen maid?" Mrs. Hoolihan demanded.

She was always aggressive after a few drinks and Lily said soothingly, "Sure and didn't I work at the Big House in Connemara, Mrs. Hoolihan. I was taught by the butler himself."

"Is that right?" Mrs. Hoolihan asked, impressed, departing for the kitchen to check on Cook.

Mr. Adams preferred simple food. "Nothing fancy and nothing sloppy," were his instructions to Cook, and she was preparing lobster bisque, baked sole, roast pheasant, lemon ice, and chocolate pudding. Mr. Adams himself had selected the wines and decanted them and now he called impatiently for someone to come and find his cuff links and his studs and to fasten his tie.

"He doesn't know we don't have the upstairs maid anymore," Emer said wearily. "And she was the only one who knew how to tie his tie."

"I'll go," Lily said confidently. Pa had often allowed her to help him with his tie when he was dressing for dinner and she knew exactly how it was done.

She ran upstairs, thinking worriedly of the hundred and one details yet to be taken care of, hoping Emer would remember to stoke up the fires and light the candles. The house smelled sweetly of the masses of flowers she had bought and arranged in huge vases, making Mrs. Hoolihan grumble loudly at the expense. "The master's not used to flowers," she had said acidly. "And what's more, he doesn't care."

Lily hurried into Mr. Adams's dressing room and took the stud box from where it was always kept, on top of the chest of drawers. "Here they are, sir," she said. "Let me help you put them in."

He stood to attention like a little boy, humming a complex tune and staring over her head into space while she fitted the gold-and-onyx studs in his shirtfront. "And your cuff links, sir," she said, and he held out his arms obligingly. "And now the tie, sir. If you could just sit down in front of the mirror it would make it easier."

He glanced in the mirror, seeing her for the first time. "You're not the same one," he said, astonished.

"No, sir, I'm not. I'm the new parlormaid. Lily." Standing behind him she tugged the tie into position and inspected it in the mirror. "I think that should do it, sir."

He glanced at it briefly and said, "Yes, fine, just fine. Thank you." And he wandered off still humming his tuneless tune.

The sound of Cook singing "Rock of Ages" came from the direction of the kitchen as Lily hurried back. She was hovering, red-faced, over her stove. A half-full bottle of gin stood on the table beside her and Emer caught Lily's eye and made a little face. "She's been at it for the past hour," she mouthed silently.

Lily nodded, worried. If Cook messed up the dinner, they would all be in trouble and maybe out of a job. She ran to Mrs. Hoolihan's room and knocked, but there was no reply. She knocked again, but the housekeeper still did not answer, and with a sigh she ran back to the kitchen.

She noticed thankfully that at least Cook still seemed to know what she was doing: the soup was ready, the baked sole was curled neatly into little twists ready for the oven, and the pheasant was already roasting. The game chips were prepared, the vegetables were ready to go on the stove, and the puddings were daintily arranged on a silver tray.

Lily crossed her fingers; with a bit of luck and no more gin they might make it through the dinner.

The doorbell rang, and throwing an anxious glance at Emer, Lily ran to answer it. She smoothed her apron, patted her hair neatly back under her white cap and smiled politely at the two gentlemen waiting on the steps. "Good evening, sirs," she said, taking their coats and showing them up the stairs into the drawing room where their host was waiting. The other guests arrived soon after and she offered them champagne, remembering not to look them in the eye, but it didn't stop her listening eagerly to their conversation about her employer's recent travels to Italy.

She announced that dinner was served and stood silently by the sideboard while they enthusiastically spooned up their lobster bisque, praying that the fish course would be ready in time. She collected their plates and sent them down in the dumbwaiter, breathing a relieved sigh as, like clockwork, the fish arrived.

She knew how it should be served and she went discreetly from person to person, offering him the dish. No one so much as glanced at her; they simply placed a portion on their plates and carried on their conversation. And Lily went back to stand by the sideboard, eyes lowered, listening to their talk of travel and art and books and academic gossip. It was so like evenings she remembered at home that it brought tears of nostalgia and regret to her eyes. She wiped them discreetly away with her fingers, but no one was looking at her and no one noticed.

She collected their plates and sent them down to the kitchen in the dumbwaiter, but this time only the platter of game chips and the brimming sauce boat joggled upward. She placed them on the sideboard and waited impatiently for the pheasant. After a few minutes she tugged on the rope to signal the kitchen to send it up, but still nothing happened.

The minutes ticked by. Mr. Adams threw a quizzical glance at her and passed the claret decanter around again. Panicked, she tugged on the rope again but still nothing happened.

Heavy footsteps sounded in the hall and the dining room door was flung open. Cook stood there, scarlet-faced, clutching the enormous silver platter with the pheasants. Lily saw young Emer hovering behind her, a terrified look on her face, and she knew to expect the worst.

Planting one foot deliberately in front of the other and humming "Rock of Ages," Cook marched drunkenly toward the table. An expression of mild astonishment crossed her employer's face as he looked at her. "I thought I'd show you it myself, sir," she said, holding the platter triumphantly aloft.

A blast of her gin-soaked breath wafted over him, the tray dipped unsteadily, and Lily's horrified eyes followed the pheasant as it slid slowly to the edge of the silver platter, heading for Mr. Adams's lap.

She leapt across and grabbed it just in time and Mr. Adams and his astonished guests watched the cook stumble tipsily from the room. "Rock of Ages" sung in a wavering contralto drifted loudly from the hall, and he said mildly, "My apologies, gentlemen. Let us hope this lapse on my cook's part has not impaired the excellent quality of her food."

The conversation picked up where it had left off and Lily hurriedly served them. She carried out her duties perfectly, but inside she was seething. The drunken cook and housekeeper had probably cost her

her job and she told herself angrily it wasn't fair. They did not deserve to work for a decent man like Mr. Adams. And besides, she knew they were robbing him every way they could. She stalked angrily back to the kitchen.

"Jayzus, Emer," she shouted, slamming through the door. "Cook's a stupid old drunk. And *we* shall be lucky if we have a job in the morning."

Emer finished the dishes and crawled wearily off to bed, leaving Lily alone. The kitchen door was open and she could hear the guests' laughter and booming masculine voices, and somehow she did not feel quite so lonely.

Cook and Mrs. Hoolihan had power over her and she knew that tomorrow they would use it, because they would be too ashamed to face her after what had happened. They would fire her and Emer. Maids were two a penny in Boston and they would be able to hire replacements the same afternoon. She decided there was only one thing to be done.

The next morning she knocked on Mr. Adams's study door and asked if she might have a word with him. She looked him straight in the eye and Mr. Adams stared back at her as though he were seeing her for the first time. But no, it was the second. "You are the one who tied my tie," he said, remembering.

"That's right, sir. I'm Lily."

He nodded. "But were there not two other maids?" he asked, bewildered.

"Yes, sir." For a moment Lily almost lost her nerve. He might fire her for saying what she was going to say, but if he did not, Mrs. Hoolihan surely would. She had nothing to lose and she quickly told him of the firing of the two maids and how the housekeeper and Cook had pocketed their wages, about the "arrangement" Cook had with the tradesmen and suppliers, and of Mrs. Hoolihan's daily sorties to the saloon and their nightly bottles of gin.

"You saw for yourself the state Cook was in last night, sir," she said finally.

John Adams threw back his head and laughed. "It's only thanks to your quick thinking the whole platter didn't end up in my lap. It's a good thing you are young and fleet of foot, Lily." He sighed, thinking of the disruption this would cause in his settled household. He looked hopefully at her.

"You say you are Irish, but you have no brogue." He twisted a silver letter-opener between his fingers, watching her.

"I'm convent-educated, sir," Lily replied, blushing at the new lie. "I lost my family on the voyage over," she told him hurriedly. "The ship went aground off Nantucket and they were all drowned."

He was shocked. "I'm so sorry." And then he got briskly down to business. "I shall fire Mrs. Hoolihan and the cook. You, Lily, are appointed as housekeeper in her place at the salary of fifty dollars a month, and you will hire a new cook and whatever maids are necessary to run my household properly. I can trust you, can I not, Lily?"

He smiled at her and she blushed with triumph. "Indeed you can, sir," she said.

She strode confidently from the room, dazzled by the thought of fifty whole dollars a month. It was a fortune and she knew for a fact it was ten dollars more than he had paid Mrs. Hoolihan. She would send twenty-five dollars each month to the Sheridans for the baby and still have twenty-five dollars left for herself. She could throw away the dead woman's gray cotton dress and the ugly stiff black boots. She could buy decent clothes, good French soap, maybe even some cologne. And she would have a proper room of her own, with a proper bathroom shared only with the new cook, whom she herself would appoint. There would be no more scrubbing steps for her. It would almost be like she was mistress of the house. Especially with Mr. Adams being a bachelor. The thought lingered speculatively in her mind as she hurried back to the kitchen where the mailman was just delivering the morning's mail.

And there, right on top, was a letter addressed to herself. A fat, bulky letter, from Ciel.

CHAPTER
31

DAN'S EMPLOYER, MICK CORRIGAN, was a bachelor, but as he told Dan many a time when business was slow and he fell to reminiscing, that did not mean he had never had a sweetheart. "My mistake was to leave her behind in Cork and come out here by meself, to try to make a new life for us," he said with a huge, sorrowful sigh. "Oh, she was young, Daniel, me boy—just eighteen and as beautiful as a sunset over Bantry Bay. Sure and didn't I survive the voyage on one of the first coffin ships sailing to America, when all else was dyin' from the typhoid? And wasn't my love the unlucky one, to stay home and die of the very same disease?"

Mick was in his sixties. He had wispy gray hair and rheumy eyes and the faded pallor of forty years of tenement living. Dan thought he was an unlikely candidate for youthful passion, but Mick still lit a candle in memory of his lost love every day in St. Stephen's. And he told his story endlessly to anyone who would listen.

Mick shook his head sadly, busily measuring flour into small brown paper sacks, twirling them between his gnarled fingers to seal them. "And the irony is that me, a starvin' Irish fella, built up a good business selling food to more starvin' Irishmen." Tears misted his faded eyes. "Sometimes, Daniel, I ask meself, will it never end?"

"And that's why, when I saw your hungry face outside me store every day, there was something about you reminded me of myself. Sure and it brought it all back again," he said mournfully. Placing his flat cap firmly on his head he grabbed his stick and hobbled to the door. "I'll be back at two," he called, heading as he did every morning at this hour for Hegarty's Saloon on the corner of North Street, where he met his cronies and reminisced endlessly about "the old days" over a jar or two.

Dan picked up a cloth and began slowly to polish the battered pine countertop. He replenished the barrels of sugar and tea and potatoes; he stacked the harsh carbolic-smelling blocks of soap, counted the candles and rearranged the kindling wood. He tidied the meager display of cabbages and carrots and onions set out in boxes on the trestle outside, and in between times he served a few customers, marking their credit in Mick's notorious ledger, because come Friday those who didn't pay had their credit immediately cut off until the account was settled.

And all the time he was thinking he should be doing this for himself. Frustrated, he glared at the man walking into the store carrying a satchel on his back. "We don't buy from travelers," he said stonily as the man deposited his satchel on the floor and leaned wearily on the counter.

"It's a glass of water I'm needin'," he retorted. Taking out a red handkerchief he wiped his sweating forehead. "I've been walking all night, and I'm just about beat. I spent every last penny on a 'bargain' and now I don't even have the price of a meal."

Dan brought him a glass of water and said curiously, "And so what was the bargain that's sending you into a pauper's early grave?"

The man bent down and opened his satchel. He took out a steel pocketwatch and laid it on the counter between them. "Two hundred of them I bought," he said mournfully. "From the customs seizure office. They were selling off confiscated goods dirt cheap and I thought I saw my opportunity. I paid fifty cents each one, a hundred dollars the lot. I saw myself selling them for a couple of dollars to the stores, but I guessed wrong. Nobody wants to buy. I put my own money *and* my wife's brother's money into the scheme, and now I can't even go home again for fear he'll kill me for losin' it all."

He looked hopefully at Dan. "You wouldn't care to purchase one yerself, would you?"

Dan stared thoughtfully at him. Figures with dollar signs jingled through his head like the ringing of a cash register and he said quickly, "I'll do more than that. I'll take the lot off your hands for fifty bucks."

"Fifty bucks?" The man glared indignantly at him. "And didn't I just tell you I paid one hundred for them?"

Dan shrugged indifferently. He turned away and began dusting his shelves. "Take it or leave it," he said. "At least you could count your losses with your wife, instead of dying of hunger here on the streets of the North End."

The man held out his hand. "I'll take it," he said.

Dan hesitated. "You'll have to wait till later tonight for the money, but to seal the bargain, here's four dollars on account." The man pocketed the four dollars and swung his satchel over the counter. Telling Dan he would be back at seven that night for the rest of his money, he stepped jauntily out the door heading for the nearest bar to partake of a large ale and a plate of Irish stew.

Seeing his jauntiness Dan wondered worriedly whether he had just been taken. He picked up the watch from the counter and put it to his ear. It ticked merrily away and he sighed with relief. Taking a coin, he prized open the back and looked at the little cogs and wheels swinging briskly to and fro and around and around, and this time he smiled. He knew a bargain when he saw one.

He thought out his plan while he waited for Mick Corrigan to return. He no more had fifty dollars to his name than the next man in the North End, but he thought he knew where he might get it. When Corrigan returned promptly on the dot of two, Dan told him something urgent had come up and he needed an hour off. Removing his tradesman's white apron, he put on his jacket and slicked his red curls down with a drop of water. Then he shouldered the satchel and stepped briskly away in the direction of Prince Street.

It was a double irony that the man he was going to see on Prince Street was also a grocer. Thomas Keany was the Irish "boss" of the North End and a power in local politics. He had started his grocery store twenty-five years ago and had built it into the biggest in the area. A small room in back of the redbrick store served as his political headquarters, where the immigrants knew they could come at any time for the benefit of his advice. He was a big, bluff man with dark wavy hair and a walrus mustache, and the Irish trusted him with their secrets. They brought him their problems knowing they could rely on his help, and in return all he asked was their loyalty and their votes in the local elections.

Dan knocked on his door and was bidden to enter. Keany was busy with two other men, and Dan dumped his heavy satchel on the floor and stood, arms folded, patiently waiting until they finished their discussion. Keany shook hands with the men and turned his attention to Daniel. "How can I help you, lad?" he asked genially.

Dan took a pocket watch from his satchel and eagerly began his story of how he had a chance to buy them cheap. "It's a steal," he said triumphantly. "Only fifty dollars. And himself paid one hundred for them."

Keany sat silently behind his big desk, looking at him over the steeple of his fingers. "A bargain is only a bargain when you can afford to pay for it," he pointed out.

"It is," Dan agreed solemnly. "But I'm a poor man and that's why I've come to you for help."

"Tell me about yourself," Keany suggested, settling back in his chair to listen. And Dan told him the story of the shipwreck and their struggle for survival and he explained what he meant to do with the watches.

"I'll become a tinker, going from town to town with a satchel on my back, selling my watches for profit—with no overhead except my own bootleather—so I can make enough to buy Corrigan's store from him," he said.

"And does Corrigan want to sell?"

Dan grinned confidently. "Not yet, he doesn't. But he will. Once I talk him into it and show him the color of my money."

"Even if you sell at a good profit, you'll not make enough to pay for Corrigan's store," Keany pointed out.

"Then I'll come to you for a loan of the rest," Dan said triumphantly.

Keany laughed. The lad's plan was as full of holes as a poor woman's stocking, but he liked his brash eagerness and his confidence.

"I'll lend you the fifty myself," he said, reaching into his pocket, "because you've got more blarney than I've heard for a long time. And if you pull it off you can come to me about the loan to buy Corrigan's shop. *If* Corrigan wants to sell." He laughed again, thumping his fist loudly on the desk. "Dammit boy, why in the world does an enterprising silver-tongued fella like yerself want to be a corner shopkeeper? You should be in politics."

Dan pocketed the fifty and shook Keany's hand. "Not me, sir," he said, "it's me brother Finn has the blarney needed for that game. But I'll not be the owner of a corner shop for long. I'll start with this one, then another, then another. I'll have a whole chain of 'em, in Boston and Philadelphia, Pittsburgh, Chicago . . ." His blue eyes stared into the future as though he could already see the chain of shops stretching into infinity across America, and Keany shook his head, marveling.

"You're a man of vision, and I wish you luck. Meanwhile you had better start selling those pocket watches so you can pay me back my fifty."

"Yes, sir!" Dan picked up his satchel and strode to the door. He hesitated, then he turned and came back again. He took out a watch and laid it on the desk in front of Keany. "That's for you, sir," he said gratefully. "A gift. And I promise you that one day Dan O'Keeffe will replace that watch with one of pure gold."

He strode back across the room and went out, closing the door behind him. He paused, then opened it again. "And I'll have it inscribed," he added grandly. "To Thomas Keany. With thanks. Daniel O'Keeffe." Nodding to himself, as though it were already an accomplished fact, he patted the fifty dollars in his pocket, shouldered his satchel, and strode back to Corrigan's to give in his notice. Tomorrow he would be the first O'Keeffe to become a tinker.

FINN WATCHED HIS BROTHER STRIDING confidently away the next morning, his cap jauntily atop his red curls and his long legs covering the ground rapidly. He thought worriedly that it was almost winter and it was the wrong time for his brother to be changing his profession and becoming a traveler. And the freezing weather was no good for Rory either. He was coughing like a kennelful of sick dogs and some days he barely seemed to have the strength to set one foot in front of the other.

Still, he managed to keep on working, and Finn and Rory kept the James's coaches shined and the horses groomed. When Finn put on his gray coat with the flowing shoulder cape and the gray top hat with the curly brim and drove Mr. James to his office or to the railroad station to catch the train to New York, he knew there was not a finer turnout in the whole of Boston.

With each week that passed Rory grew sicker. Finn told him he should stay in bed but it was even colder at home than the stable yard, and besides Rory was too afraid of losing his job. So Finn left him sitting by the fire in the tackroom, shining up the bits and polishing the leathers, while he took on Rory's jobs as well as his own. He came into work earlier and he left later every day, but the work was done and he made sure Mr. James had no cause for complaint against Rory.

Christmas came with no word from Dan, but Finn expected to see him walking back down the street with his profits bulging in his pockets any day now. On Christmas Eve he and Rory were invited into the house to sing carols and then each was given a hamper of food and a five-dollar cash bonus. His heart filled with gratitude at their generosity, Finn stared around the garlanded hall, seeing how a rich man of Boston lived, and ambition flared in his heart. He was suddenly no longer satisfied to be Boston's smartest coachman. He wanted a house exactly like this. He wanted to be a rich man even if he died achieving it. And in the season of peace and goodwill his heart burned with the desire for revenge on the Molyneux family.

Meanwhile, all he had besides his dreams were his job and a seven-by-nine-foot hovel in the North End that wasn't a great deal different from the hovels his forebears had lived in.

New Year's Eve brought a blizzard that obliterated the city overnight. The next morning Finn and Rory plowed knee-deep through the drifts, past unrecognizable white-covered landmarks. Rory coughed until he was red in the face and they stopped a dozen times to let him catch his breath. He was shaking with cold and sweating with fever, and Finn wrapped him in a plaid horse rug and sat him in front of the tackroom fire. He hurried to ask Cook for a mug of hot cocoa and coaxed Rory to drink it, and then he peeled off his jacket and set to tackling Rory's jobs as well as his own.

Each week Rory grew gaunter and thinner, perpetually shivering despite the warm jacket Finn had given him. Desperately Finn offered half his own wages if only he would stay home and get better, but Rory proudly refused.

"I can't take your money, and besides, I'm afraid to lose me job and never get it back again."

The day finally came that Rory could not face the long walk to Louisburg Square. He lay on his straw pallet with his sisters and brothers grouped silently around him and his mother clinging to his hand, crying. Finn went worriedly off to work but he couldn't forget him, and that night he hurried back up the stairs, afraid he might be too late. Rory's eyes were as shiny as two bright stars as he smiled at Finn. "Don't worry if Mr. James needs a new stablelad, Finn," he said. "I'll just have to look for another job when I'm better. In the springtime."

Finn sat with him through the night. Rory did not cough and he didn't toss and turn the way he usually did and he thought hopefully it must be a good sign. Just before dawn Rory woke and reached out for him. "You're a good friend," he whispered. And those were his last words.

Finn wept for his friend, but he was at work promptly as usual because he was too afraid of losing his job. He had the carriage waiting when Mr. James came down the front steps precisely at eight o'clock, as he always did.

"Good morning, O'Keeffe," Mr. James said, stepping into his carriage. He turned and looked sharply at him, noticing his reddened eyes and drawn face. "Is something the matter?" he asked.

Finn hung his head to hide his grief as he told him about Rory, and asked if he might have an hour or two off for the funeral. Mr. James nodded. "You can tell his family that I shall take care of the expenses," he said. "And now drive on or I shall be late."

Rory's funeral was a cold affair, but thanks to Mr. James's generosity at least he had a decent pine coffin and there was a wreath of evergreens to toss onto his grave. Finn and five other friends shouldered the coffin and carried it into St. Stephen's for the service. Afterward he followed it on the cart through the mean, frozen streets to the cemetery, wondering bitterly why his friend had had to die. He said a prayer for him and he also said one for himself. "God," he prayed silently, "I have to get out of the North End or it will destroy me too. I *have* to. There must be some way, please help me, God. Please. I'll never ask you for anything else again."

Cornelius James was an observant man. He had noticed in the last few months that Rory was rarely around and that Finn was working longer and longer hours, and now he knew the reason. He discussed him with his wife and they decided the boy was worthy of a chance of something better. "Call it a social experiment," Cornelius had said to his wife. "If he wins or loses is up to him, but either way it's bound to be interesting." He called Finn into his study and Finn stood before him, twisting his cap nervously in his hand, hoping he wasn't going to be fired.

"I have been observing you, O'Keeffe," Mr. James said calmly. "And I have seen you following the parable of the good neighbor. What you did for your friend was noble. It came from a good heart." He paused and Finn met his gaze anxiously, wondering what was coming. "A man like that deserves a reward," Mr. James added. Finn brightened up: he had promised Mrs. O'Donovan he would look after them and he could use a bit of extra money.

Mr. James paced the study, his hands behind his back. "You are an intelligent young man," he said, staring thoughtfully at him, and Finn's hopes rose as he saw the reward getting bigger. "But a man lacking in schooling," he continued, and Finn's hopes plummeted again. "Yet it seems to me you have an instinct, a shrewdness that could be turned into something better than merely looking after horses.

"I have analyzed your qualities, O'Keeffe, and I find you honorable, steadfast, a hard-worker, and a man capable of true friendship. Mrs. James and I have discussed you at great length. I have decided to give you the opportunity to better yourself. If you wish to accept, I am offering you a job in my New York offices, and an opportunity to learn the money business."

"The money business?" Finn said, his head still ringing with the magic words "New York."

"The Lord told us to help our brothers," Mr. James said, "and you have carried out his wishes. Now I am prepared to help you, Finn O'Keeffe, to become something better than a stablelad and a coachman. Do you accept?"

Do I accept? Amazed, Finn thought of his fervent prayer at Rory's funeral. He thought of Christmastime, singing carols in the hall and his vow that one day he would have a mansion just like this. He thought of his revenge on the Molyneuxes, imagining Lily's face if she ever saw the grand person he was about to become. "I accept," he said, beaming.

CHAPTER
32

FINN HAD NEVER OWNED ANYTHING new and he had certainly never owned a suit of clothes in his life. With Mr. James's fifty-dollar advance burning a hole in his pocket, he went to the local haberdasher and told the sales assistant he needed everything "from new drawers to new boots."

He chose what he imagined a well-setup young man about New York would wear: two white cambric shirts with four celluloid collars that the sales clerk assured him would save on washing; a stiff black serge suit and a cravat of sober gray. He bought big sturdy black boots, polished to a mirror gloss, and—a touch of extravagance he could not resist—a pair of mother-of-pearl cuff links and a matching stickpin. All he needed was a hat—in fact he would have two! A roll-brimmed derby for winter and a straw boater for summer.

He stared with satisfaction at the new Finn O'Keeffe in the mirror. The whole outfit had cost the grand sum of twenty-five dollars and the amount he had just spent dazzled him. It was a fortune, but the promised salary of twenty dollars a week made it seem like small change and he threw the money in lordly style onto the counter. The clerk wrapped his other things in a parcel and Finn strode confidently from the store to Hanover Street and Mick Corrigan's.

The only problem was that Dan had not yet returned from his travels. He had promised to be back within a couple of months. "With my profits in my pocket," he had said. But six months had passed and Finn was worried.

As he strode through the North End's teaming alleys, every head turned to look at the darkly handsome young Irish fella who looked as though he had come into a million. A crowd of small boys ran giggling at his heels, making rude comments, but he just grinned and good-naturedly flung them a handful of coins, remembering how he, too, would have scrabbled in the gutter for them not so long ago.

Mick Corrigan eyed him up and down in amazement. "Can it be yerself, Finn O'Keeffe?" he demanded, peering closely at him. "Sure and I can see now that it is. *And* dressed like a politician. Has your brother made his money then, the way he said he would?"

Finn shook his head, explaining his own good fortune. "I'll be writing you with my address so that when Dan comes back he'll know where to find me."

"When Dan comes back!" Corrigan shook his head and heaved a lugubrious sigh. " 'Twas the wrong time to be throwin' in his job and becoming a peddler," he said, shaking his head. "I doubt you'll be hearing from him for a long time."

Even more worried about Dan, Finn went to say good-bye to Rory's mother. He gave her some money and told her he would always look after her. She wished him luck and he headed for the station to board the train to New York.

THE WEATHER IN NEW YORK was unseasonably hot, the sky was a cloudless blue, and the sun blazed down. Finn emerged onto East Fortythird Street outside Grand Central Station, clutching the parcel with his underwear and socks, his extra collars and his other shirt. He felt stifled in his heavy suit but his step was jaunty as he set off in search of a room to rent. The very idea of a proper room of his own was heady stuff and he grinned as he inspected house after house with VACANCY signs in their windows. He chose a modest-looking place and rang the bell. The woman who answered the door glared at him as he said confidently, "Good day to you, ma'am. Sure and I'm after renting a room."

She stepped back a pace and pointed an accusing finger at the sign in the window. "Can't you read, you ignorant fellow," she cried angrily, and she slammed the door in his face.

Finn stared at the sign. It said VACANCIES and underneath, *NO ACTORS. NO DOGS. NO IRISH.*

He walked on down the street, and the next and the next, but everywhere he went he saw the same sign. With their reputation for drinking and fighting, no one wanted the Irish, and they rated even lower billing than the dogs. He sought solace in a saloon on Lower Broadway with the comforting name of Murphy's.

"You'll be all right around here, fella," Murphy told him when he explained his predicament over a glass of stout. "They'll take anything, Irish, Italian, Jewish, German, or plain old American—as long as they can pay the rent in advance. Try Eileen Malone's on West Fortieth, near Bryant Park."

Eileen Malone looked at the handsome young Irishman standing on her steps, neat and perspiring in his old-fashioned heavy black suit and derby hat. She looked him slowly up and then slowly down again. And then she began to laugh.

Finn shifted uncomfortably from foot to foot. "Will you be tellin' me what's so amusing?" he demanded, red-faced with heat and embarrassment. He was boiling but he didn't want to remove his jacket and spoil his smart new image as a *professional* man.

"Will you be only looking at that suit," Eileen hooted. "You'll not be tellin' me you're an actor, looking like that? Unless you're dressed for the role of an Irishman."

Finn glared furiously at her. He turned and strode back down the steps.

"You'll get nowhere in this city if you can't take a joke," she called after him. "Besides, I'm the only Irish landlady on this street."

Grudgingly, he walked back again and followed her into the hallway and up the brown oilcloth-covered stairs to the third floor. "I keep a clean house," Eileen pointed out, "and I expect the same of my tenants. Though I've no complaint with you on that score," she added quickly as Finn glared at her again.

He looked at the room. It had a window with a view of the treetops in the park. "The bed has a horsehair mattress," Eileen said proudly. "There's no straw here, young man. You only get the best at Eileen Malone's."

He felt the bed cautiously with his fingertips; he tested the dresser drawers and stared at his own amazed face in the cheap mirror. He noted the brass pegs along the wall and the upright wooden chair with the plush seat and tasseled edges. It was hard as a rock but it was a proper chair and it was his to sit on.

"There's a gas lamp," Eileen said. "And there's a water closet and a bathroom down the hall, shared with six other boarders." She eyed him thoughtfully. He had not uttered a word since he came in and from the look on his face, he might have found paradise.

"I'll take it," Finn said eagerly, and she sighed. She had known he was a greenhorn as soon as she saw the suit.

Taking pity on him she said sarcastically, "Spoken like a true Irishman. Only you're supposed to ask me the price first."

He took twenty dollars from his pocket. "How much?" he asked, shuffling the money through his eager fingers.

"You're lucky I'm an honorable woman," she told him severely. "Any other landlady on Broadway would have just doubled the price. It's five dollars a week. In advance paid prompt every Friday."

Finn counted the money into her outstretched hand and she said, "For an extra two dollars a week I provide an evening meal. *And* I'm a good cook," she added, patting her own ample hips as evidence. He quickly gave her the extra two dollars and she pocketed it and walked to the door. "Supper's at six-thirty sharp," she called. "Most of my tenants are actors and they have to be at the theater by seven-thirty. Those that's working, that is."

She closed the door behind her and Finn looked proudly around his room. He took off his jacket and hung it over the back of his chair, pausing proprietorially to admire it. He pulled back the net curtain and stared at his view of the park. Taking off his boots he placed them next to his bed, then hung up his hat on the brass peg. He unpacked his brown paper parcel and put his new things away in a dresser drawer. Down the hall in the bathroom, he washed his hands and face in water that flowed from a faucet, and he dried himself on clean white linen. He observed the shower and the big white tub and the water-closet. He padded back to his room, undressed, turned up his magic gas lamp, and then lay carefully down on the bed. The soft pillow cushioned his head and the clean white cotton sheets were cool against his body. He lay very still for a few moments savoring it all, and then he began to laugh.

He was like an ignorant child in a toystore. He had never had a room of his own before; he had never had a window, let alone a view; he had never had a real bed or a dresser, not even a brass peg on the wall. And he had certainly never had a bathroom before and a fresh clean towel to dry himself on. He had finally left behind the old world of straw pallets on bare earthen floors with a wooden crate for a table and a single candle to see by, and he felt like a king.

"Dan, old fella," he said out loud, still laughing. "If only you could see your brother now, you would never believe it. *And* I'm being served a cooked supper at six-thirty *prompt*." He was still smiling when he fell asleep.

Eileen Malone was famous among the struggling members of the acting profession. They knew that her house was clean, her food plain but good, and that it was served in generous quantities. "I'll not starve anyone," she often said as she handed out generous portions of mashed potatoes and cabbage and cutlets, and on Sundays, her special roast beef. "Not when my own family and countrymen have died from it," she would add feelingly, watching as her satisfied boarders cleaned their plates.

When her husband died seven years after they were married, Eileen found herself to be that rare phenomenon, a childless Irish widow with no sons to take care of her in her old age. She knew she would have to make her own living. Pulling herself together, she sold her small house and with the money saved and a loan from the bank she had bought a bigger one nearer Broadway where she knew she would always be able to keep her dozen rooms filled.

Life was not without its harsher moments: getting money out of actors was not easy, which was why most landladies snubbed them. But Eileen had a soft spot in her heart for a good-looking man and besides, they kept her entertained with their stories. She knew all the latest Broadway gossip and they made her feel a part of their world. She was forty years old, well endowed, and of a motherly disposition.

She supposed it was Finn O'Keeffe's innocence that appealed to her as much as his good looks, because even in that suit, he was a very handsome young man. There was just something about him, a lean, urgent hungriness—not just for food, but for life—that struck her heart a hammer blow.

"I have this instinct for talent," she would often announce, looking piercingly around the supper table at her boarders. "Didn't I predict my boarder Ned Sheridan's success? And wasn't I right? Isn't he at this very moment on tour with a successful play? Believe me, that's only the beginning. That young man is destined for great success. And when he returns he'll come back to stay at Mrs. Malone's again. Nowhere else will do."

Her boarders would stare at her, hoping her perspicacious gaze would mark them out for success in the same way it had Ned, but it was only Finn who gave her that same feeling. Not Maria Venturi, the young actress from the third floor back who was three weeks behind with the rent and would be out on the street come next Friday if she did not pay. And not the Marquand sisters who were French and flirtatious and played in reviews, kicking their legs and showing more than they ought—but at least they paid their rent on time. And not any of the other would-be playwrights, vaudevillians, and actors who lived permanently on the edge of "success," haunting managers' offices by day and the Broadway bars by night, eking out their money and always hoping for that lucky break.

"Mr. O'Keeffe is different," she told her boarders, introducing him when he appeared promptly at six-thirty for supper. "Mr. O'Keeffe is going into the money business." They glanced up interestedly at that magic word "money" and she gave Finn the seat of honor on her right, well away from the French girls who flirted automatically with any man, no matter how old or unattractive. "But does not everyone flirt?" Corinne Marquand had asked innocently when Eileen had warned her about it. Blond, pretty Corinne had her eyes fixed on Finn now and Eileen was watchful as the emaciated little maid deposited a brimming bowl of soup in front of each of the boarders.

"What exactly does it mean, 'the money business'?" Corinne asked, directing a charming smile at Finn. "It sounds so *masculine.*"

"It's to do with stocks and shares," Finn explained, returning her smile. "I'm to work for James and Company, the brokerage house."

Everyone had heard of it and they stared respectfully at him, wondering how much he would be earning.

"And what will you do there, Mr. O'Keeffe?" Eileen asked.

"I'm to learn the business, ma'am. Mr. James will be spending more time in New York and he is to teach me himself." Even Eileen was impressed then and Finn decided he had better not tell them he was just a jumped-up stablelad and coachman, and that out of the charity of his heart Mr. James was giving him an opportunity to better himself. And he had better not fail, he told himself grimly. This was his chance and he knew from bitter experience that opportunities did not come twice.

After dinner he went back to his room. He undressed and hung his clothes carefully on the brass pegs and turned down his gas lamp. With his head on a duck-feather pillow and clean cotton sheets against his skin, he drifted off to sleep as easily as if he had gone to heaven. And he didn't dream about New York or Eileen Malone or Corinne Marquand, or even about Mr. James and the brokerage house where he would begin his new life the next day. He dreamed about Lily, the same way he always did.

HE WAS UP WITH THE DAWN and ate his breakfast, cooked by the little maid-of-all-work, Peggy, at six-thirty. No one else was around, not even Mrs. Malone, and when Peggy put the huge plate of corned beef hash in front of him, he tackled it enthusiastically and asked her where everyone was.

"Actors keep different hours from the likes of us," she informed him. "They work nights—when they're working, that is."

She poured him some more coffee and leaned against the sideboard, watching him eat. Peggy was another redheaded, freckled Irish girl, the daughter of immigrants. She was painfully thin with sunken eyes and skin as transparent as skim milk. Eileen Malone had promised her family she would feed her, as well as pay her five dollars a month and her room—which wasn't really a room, it was just a wedge of attic partitioned off from the cheapest room in the house, which was occupied by Miss Venturi.

But, poor waif though she was, Peggy's city sophistication was greater than Finn's: she knew the working habits of actors and actresses, the names of the latest plays and musical shows and who was in them, as well as the price of the seats and the names and locations of every theater. "I'd like to be an actress one day," she said wistfully, filling his cup again.

"Well, good luck to you, Peggy," Finn said, getting up, satisfied, from the table. He had a full belly and a great day to look forward to. "Can you direct me to Wall Street?" he asked.

She looked doubtfully at him. "You'll not be thinking of walking? It's an awful long way."

"No matter." Finn shrugged. Hadn't he got his fine new boots to walk in? And wasn't the sun shining? Besides, he was intent on saving every cent he could. She told him the directions, and picking up a cane from the stand in the hall, he twirled it around his fingers and danced down the steps into the street.

The sun was hot and the humidity soared unseasonably upward and Wall Street was farther than he had thought. By the time he reached James and Company's palatial gleaming glass-and-mahogany front doors he was red-faced and sweating from the heat, his new boots pinched and he was nervous because he had lost his way and he was ten minutes late.

The top-hatted doorman looked suspiciously at him; but he was Irish, and when Finn explained who he was he wished him luck and showed him in.

The room was marble-floored and lofty. Chandeliers sparkled overhead despite the fact that it was daytime, and sunlight peeked in in colored ribbons through stained-glass windows. Polished desks with ruby leather tops were arranged along the length of the rooms. There was a green-shaded brass lamp on every one, and at every one sat a pin-striped young man.

The chief clerk at the big front desk had brilliantined hair, spectacles, a smart black suit, and paper-white hands. He looked as though he had never seen daylight and had been buried in an office his entire life.

He looked Finn up and down with a look of distaste as Finn explained who he was.

"*Not* a good beginning," the chief clerk said, glancing at the big round clock on the wall that said a quarter to eight. "In the future you will be at your desk by seven-thirty."

He showed Finn into Mr. James's office. Dazzled, he stared at the Oriental carpets and the oak-paneled walls hung with portraits of stern-looking men.

"Welcome, my boy. Welcome." Mr. James shook his hand warmly. "O'Keeffe is my personal protégé," he told the chief clerk. "Give him a desk outside my door, next to my secretary. Introduce him to all the staff and tell them I expect them to cooperate in helping Mr. O'Keeffe learn our business.

"All you need to do for the first few weeks is watch," Mr. James told Finn. "Wander around, look at everything. Be curious, ask questions. And if there's anything you do not understand, then come to me."

Finn sat nervously at his desk waiting for someone to tell him what to do, but the chief clerk had disappeared and everyone else had their heads bent over massive ledgers.

Remembering Mr. James's instructions, he got up and wandered through the aisles, looking from left to right at each desk as he passed, but no one even glanced his way. At least not when he was passing they didn't, but he knew they were watching him. He could feel their eyes on his back. Then he heard whispering and a ripple of subdued laughter.

He swung around and stared hard at them, but every head was bent industriously over a ledger and he turned away puzzled. He walked slowly on and then he heard that snicker again.

His Irish temper rose. Thrusting his hands angrily in his pockets, he hunched his shoulders and stalked the aisles threateningly. One more snigger and he'd punch 'em in the nose, each and every one of 'em. He'd take on the lot, so he would, and he'd show 'em. *"Jayzus, boyo,"* he warned himself, *"remember you've got one up on these miserable clerks. You are Mr. James's protégé and what you were before doesn't matter. This is your big chance! Keep your fists in your pockets and use your head for once."*

He swung around and confronted them. "I'll beat the lot of you, you pasty-faced little bastards," he said in a low, menacing whisper. "Just remember this. I am here at Mr. James's personal invitation, and you are not." Their heads shot up and they stared at him with astonishment. Whistling jauntily, he walked to the nearest desk and told the clerk to explain to him exactly what he was doing.

Mr. James's secretary reported the incident to him and Mr. James reported it to his wife over dinner that night. "The boy came in wearing a funeral suit, clutching his derby to his chest, and looking for all the world like the Irish country hick," he said, smiling. "And I threw him out there, just as he was, into the lions' den. 'Make or break,' I thought. They gave him that city-slicker treatment and the first thing he did was let them know that, greenhorn or not, he had the edge on them, because he was my personal protégé. Now *that's* what I call smart, Beatrice. Mark my words, he's a very clever young man and we'll make a gentleman out of him as well as a banker."

From then on Finn took a trolley to Wall Street and he was at his desk every morning before seven. He knew that all he had was his ability to read and write and his own intelligence, and that his fellow workers were educated. But to his surprise, as the first week passed and then the second and then the third, he realized that, in the world of money, his qualifications were all that were needed. *And* the right patron, of course.

"Money is important," Mr. James said, personally handing him his salary check for the first, exhausting month. "Obviously the money you have just earned can be exchanged for goods to that value. But, and I emphasize that *but*, O'Keeffe, as you have seen these past few weeks, money can also *make* money. *Every dollar you earn can earn money for you.* You don't have to manufacture anything. You don't have to create anything. And the more money you amass, the more money you earn. I have opened an account for you with James and Company's bank and suggest you put as much of that salary check into it as you can, so it can gain interest, and then we'll think about investing it properly."

Finn thought Mr. James's philosophy for making money was even simpler than his brother Daniel's about the shop, but he had other plans for his money. He had quickly learned that if he was going to play their game he would have to look like the players—only better. He went to the smartest tailors in Manhattan and boldly told them he was Mr. Cornelius James's personal protégé and that he wished to be measured for two fine suits of clothes.

"I am putting myself in your hands," he announced grandly, sinking into a chair while obsequious sales clerks swarmed over him, showing samples of worsteds and shirtings, silk ties and handkerchiefs, silk socks and fine leather boots, overcoats and smart hats. They measured him for everything and he told them that one suit and six shirts must be ready within a week, and no, he could not wait any longer. He told them authoritatively that he would pay forty dollars down and the rest on credit and they said they were honored to have his custom. And feeling like the million dollars he knew he was on the road to making, he strode from the shop.

He went to a barber on Broadway and had a decent haircut and a luxurious shave and then, smelling faintly of bay rum, his hair smooth and his mustache immaculate, he headed for Delmonico's, where he bought himself a celebratory drink. Then he made his way home to Eileen's.

"There's a gentleman waiting for you in the parlor," Peggy told him importantly. "I wasn't sure whether to let him in or not because he looked such a ruffian, but he said he was your brother."

Daniel was standing in the doorway, filling it with his bulk, and Finn's eyes almost popped out of his head with the shock. It was a wildman he was looking at: Dan's long, curly red hair mingled with his straggling beard, half hiding his face; his collarless shirt had burst its buttons and his old tweed jacket had holes at the elbows. His decrepit cord pants were held up with a pair of bright new scarlet suspenders and a scarlet kerchief was knotted flamboyantly around his neck. But the blue eyes twinkling from beneath his bushy red eyebrows were Dan's all right!

"Will you just look at yourself," Dan said, eyeing his brother up and down. "It's a proper little city gentleman y'are." They hugged enthusiastically and then they checked each other out at arms' length.

"You're a success all right," Dan said proudly. "I can tell from the suit."

"This is rubbish," Finn retorted. "Sure and haven't I just been to the finest tailors in all New York and ordered two new ones. *Made to measure*," he added proudly. "But I was worried about you, Dan." Dan just laughed.

Patting his bulging pockets, he said, "Didn't I tell you I'd be home with my profits in my pocket. Well, here they are, Finn." Glancing warily over his shoulder, he cupped his hand over his mouth and whispered, "Seven hundred and twenty-three dollars and sixty-five cents, brother. That's how much I've got in me pockets. Take away the fifty I owe Keany, and apart from boot leather and food and lodgings, there was no other overhead.

"Oh, I'll admit selling pocket watches to country rubes was hard work at first, but then I had a stroke of luck. I was in South Carolina when I hit on a county fair and I set myself up and took out one of the watches. I started talking about my pocket watch, how good it was, how precise a movement and what a great timekeeper. A small crowd gathered and there was one young fella I could tell was more interested than the others. He was jingling his money in his pockets and I could see from his eyes he coveted that watch. So it was him I was sellin' to because I figured at least I'd have the one sale.

"I said that nothing would ever go wrong with this fine watch because it was made in Switzerland." He glanced mystified at Finn. "I don't know, maybe it was the 'made in Switzerland' that did it—that and the fact that I opened it up to show them the works. The crowd had grown bigger and they passed it from hand to hand, marveling at all the little cogs and wheels doing exactly what cogs and wheels are supposed to do. 'There's jewels in there,' I told 'em, sounding very important. 'Rubies and diamonds.' I pointed out the little red and white bits you can hardly see. 'You can't afford not to have one,' I told them, 'and at three dollars and fifty cents, I'm giving 'em away.'"

Dan's red curls bristled with excitement as he grabbed Finn's shoulder and said, "The young fella said he'd take one and handed over his three-fifty. And then another fella, and another, and before you knew it, they were clamoring for them. I sold seventy watches in less time than it took the hands to move from twelve o'clock to fifteen after. And Finn, I knew I had found the secret: aim your sales pitch at the one fella who looks likely and it's ninety-nine percent sure he'll buy. And soon as he buys, the others figure he's gotten the only bargain. Then you tell 'em you just happen to have a few more but you were keeping them for the fair in the next county. Soon as they think they can't have one, they want it real bad.

"I went from country fair to country fair, and I sold all my watches. I had made three hundred fifty dollars, but it wasn't enough, so I knew I'd have to sell something else. I was sleeping in a haystack, the way I usually did, when I heard a rustling noise. It was dark and clouds were scudding across the moon. Brother, I can tell you, I was scared. I thought someone must have followed me, someone who knew I had money in my pocket and now they were coming to steal it from me."

He shook his head, shamefacedly. "I have to confess, Finn, that a terrible fit of rage took over me. A red mist swam in front of my eyes when I thought of what it had cost me, trailing through winter snow and spring rains, sleeping rough and eating as little as I could to save every cent, and I thought, 'Jayzus, I'm damned if I'm letting them take my money.'

" 'Come out you dirty bastards,' I yelled, grabbing me stick. 'Show yer faces and Dan O'Keeffe will take on the god-blasted lot of yer.' "

His face lit up with a sudden impish grin. "And what d'yer think came worming its way out of the straw? Just the littlest fella you ever saw, that's all. Dressed all in black, with a gray beard and a bright-red nose and a bottle of hooch clutched in his one hand and a peddler's old satchel clutched in the other.

"He was hiccupin' with the fright and the drink, and he put his hands in the air, spilling half his bottle, and said, 'Don't shoot me, Mr. O'Keeffe. I'm just a peddler, seeking a night's rest in the haystack, like yerself.'

"So of course I laughed, and we shook hands, and he shared his bottle with me, and we swapped stories. He told me he came from Russia, he was seventy years old, and had been a peddler all his life and he was tired of it.

" 'I've made a decent living,' he said, 'and I owe neither to man nor woman. I have decided this very night to quit and go back to my family in Chicago. But first I have to sell three hundred pairs of red suspenders that, to my eternal regret, I bought cheap, twenty-five cents a set, from a Jewish fella in New York City. And it may take me the rest of my life because they ain't movin', boy. They just ain't movin'.'

"We had another swig of the bottle," Dan said, "and it was just like it was with the pocket watches. I saw in front of my eyes all those guys at the country fairs, standing watching me, and every man jack of 'em with his thumbs hooked in his suspenders.

"We had another drink and the peddler showed me the red suspenders. They were wider than usual with clips that shone like gold in the moonlight, and in my minds' eye I saw all those rubes standing there, their thumbs hooked through 'em, and those good old dollar signs jingled in my head again like before. 'I'll take 'em off yer hands for the price you paid,' I said, quick as a shot. 'Then you can go back to yer family tomorrow. I can't see an old fella like yourself sleeping rough when you've a bed and a wife to go home to.'

" 'Done,' he says, even quicker than me. And we shook hands and I paid him seventy-five dollars cash for the lot. He and I finished the bottle and the next morning we wished each other well and went our separate ways."

He beamed at Finn, hooking his thumbs through his own scarlet suspenders. "And are there not now two hundred and ninety-nine rubes in Amerikey sporting a pair of the finest gold-buckled scarlet suspenders, extra wide, extra quality? And don't I have their ninety-nine cents each pair in my pocket right this very minute?" His laugh boomed through the house and the boarders drifting downstairs to supper stopped to stare at the big red-headed ruffian in a pair of scarlet suspenders talking with Finn O'Keeffe.

"Mr. O'Keeffe," Eileen Malone exclaimed, hurrying to get rid of the unkempt stranger cluttering up her hallway.

"That'll be meself, ma'am," Dan said, swinging around with a courtly bow. She stepped back a pace, nervously clutching a hand to her heart and he said politely, "I'm sorry for my unkempt appearance, ma'am, but I've been on the road for seven months now. I'm here from Boston to visit my brother, Finn."

Eileen glanced uncertainly at Finn and with his newly acquired manners, he said, "May I introduce my brother, Mrs. Malone. Daniel O'Keeffe. He'll be needing a room for the night and a bath, too, if you think you could manage it."

Eileen melted under Finn's smile. She noticed the haircut and the newly trimmed mustache, and thought again how very good-looking he was, and that maybe under all that red hair his brother wasn't a bad fellow after all.

"Will it be just the one night?" she inquired.

"Indeed it will, ma'am, Mrs. Malone," Dan replied. "I'm heading back to Boston tomorrow to buy meself a shop." He patted his pockets confidently, glancing at the boarders standing around in the dining room doorway, listening. "And I'll buy every one of you a drink after supper to celebrate," he said loudly, as a cheer went up.

Eileen sent him to wash his hands before supper and, like a blushing schoolboy, he did as he was told. At the table she gave him second pride of place on her left with Finn on her right, and afterward she even allowed herself to accompany them to O'Hagen's Saloon. To celebrate the O'Keeffes' good fortune.

CHAPTER

33

MAUDIE

Ardnavarna

IT WAS A FINE BRISK MORNING with the wind blowing, and since I had to go into Galway to the shops anyway, I thought I'd ask Shannon and Eddie to come with me. There's a wonderful old bookstore there, filled with all sorts of ancient treasures as well as all the latest, and I thought they might care to browse while I took care of my errands.

They had been out for a walk and they came drifting slowly back over the lawn toward me. It's almost waist-high now and scattered with wild irises and cornflowers and it looks as verdant as a meadow. Blue flowers grow wonderfully well in our soil, you know—you should see the hydrangeas in turquoise and purple and every shade in between. And the hedges lining our roads and boreens add a mass of pinks and reds as exotic as any jungle flowers. Add the rhododendrons in season, and my lilacs, and of course my beloved roses, and you have a gardener's paradise. Which is one of the reasons Mammie loved it so.

Anyhow. There they were, the two young things, not walking hand in hand but with their heads close together as they talked. I saw that her face was alight with interest and . . . and what? Was it admiration? Adoration? Hard to define, but it was certainly interest and I hoped for the rest. I'm an old biddy of a matchmaker, but I do like them both so much, and they are so "suited," as Mammie would have said.

My dogs were trailing at their heels with that soppy devoted-doggy look on their faces. If those two had stayed here much longer I swear the damned creatures would have defected from my bed to Shannon's. And only for her would I allow such a traitorous display of adoration on their part.

I called out to them that I was going into town and did they want to come along. Sure they did, they agreed.

"I'll drive," Eddie added, but I would have none of it.

"I'm doing the driving," I said firmly. "Come with me." And I took them around to the garages where in the old days a dozen smart motors had been housed and polished by the car-mad lad who had acted as assistant and who did all the dirty work.

When I was just a child we drove around in great style in Pa's special bright yellow Lagonda—long, low-slung and sporty, exactly like the one in Michael Arlen's novel *The Green Hat*. It was a fashionable book then and I suspect dear old Pa must have been inspired by it because he copied its dashing young hero, driving it all over Europe, feeling snazzy as a race-car driver.

Then there was Mammie's own motor—red, of course; with our hair we always went for red. A Bugatti it was, and so long in the front that when I sat in the backseat I could scarcely see the ornament on the hood. It was a speedy thing and Mammie drove it like it was a horse, shouting words of encouragement as she took a corner too fast. It's a wonder she never set it to jump a five-barred gate.

There were a couple of other, less favored, duller cars in ordinary plain black, and then there was the pièce de résistance, the Rolls-Royce Silver Ghost, a dream of a car that we all went jaunting off to the continent in, drawing admiring crowds wherever we went. Quite the little star that motor was, and Pa would never let the chauffeur near it except to give it a polish. It was his baby, his pride and joy, and he refused to let Mammie drive it. It seems to me that we never went off to France with any less than three cars; the Silver Rolls, of course, for when we all traveled together, which Pa drove; the Lagonda driven by the chauffeur, and the red Bugatti for Mammie to drive.

And then later we got the Daimler, sort of as an "extra" because the others were getting on in years, but we just couldn't bear to let them go. And that's the car I showed to Shannon and Eddie. It was about 1937, I think, with a canvas top that folded back like on a baby carriage, a long hood, wide running boards, a squared-off brass-rimmed windshield, and big brass headlights sticking out the front like two huge wide eyes. It was as shiny-black as the ace of spades, with red-leather upholstery, and I always considered it my own.

EDDIE AND SHANNON WERE THRILLED with it. They inspected it and were astonished to find it still in perfect running order. I told them about the mechanic in Oughterard whose hobby it was to keep it in trim. He just loved that old car so much.

We tootled off down the drive, along the boreen and past the entrance to the Big House, up the winding rutted lane that leads to the road. Eddie winced as the car bounced springily over the ruts, and I laughed. "'Tis no problem," I yelled to them in the back. "The car's been taking this lane for more years than you have been alive, and none the worse for it either."

We had the top down and the day was bright and cloudy by turns, the way it happens around here. They seemed to enjoy our leisurely pace, gazing around, admiring the wild scenery; and to keep them entertained, because it's a fair way into Galway especially in the old car, I began to tell them more of my story. Oh, and before I forget, I wasn't wearing my old jodhpurs and jacket. Dear me, no, Mammie would never have allowed that. One always dressed to go into town shopping, so I was in country green; a longish skirt and a matching jumper because it could get chilly in the car, and as I said the wind was blowing. With it I wore flat-heeled brogues and a jaunty little turban in a deeper green with my red curls just sort of peeking out of the front. Very 1940s. In fact I think I remember Betty Grable wearing something like that in the wartime movies. Oh, and weren't they fun, I remember . . . but there I go again. Anyhow, to the best of my memory, these garments had no designer name other than a shop label, B&T in Dublin, and they were newish. 1985, I think. All except the hat. That was Paris. Madame Simonetta, 1939.

And Shannon herself was in a cream Aran sweater she had bought locally and a summery flowered skirt, longish and swirling and worn with cowboy boots. An odd combination to my mind, but somehow on her it worked. Eddie, of course, was in the ubiquitous denim. So there we were, sitting on our red leather seats in our shiny black motor with the brass headlights like two wide eyes, bowling along the Connemara roads, mostly on the wrong side to avoid the potholes, talking as usual about Lily.

Boston

THERE WAS A NEW SPRING in John Adams's step as he hurried up Mount Vernon Street, heading home. And a new look about him too. Gone were the mismatched clothes and worn boots; now his clothes were set out each morning for him by his housekeeper and he was as smart as a vague erudite professor of seventeenth-century French literature could be expected to be.

He could not have said exactly when it was he began noticing his housekeeper, nor could he put his finger on exactly the reason. Lily had been in charge of his household for more than a year now and he supposed it must have happened gradually. She was the most discreet and self-effacing servant, but yet he always knew when she was there. Perhaps it was the faintly spicy hint of French cologne, or the sweet Parma violets pinned at her shoulder, or maybe, he thought guiltily, it was the rustle of taffeta petticoats beneath her dress when she walked. And he, who had never before noticed a woman's fripperies, knew he could describe those dresses exactly.

He told himself that of course it was only because they were so different from a housekeeper's usual nondescript gray garments. Lily wore soft silky velvets in winter, in a deep rosy violet or a dense forest-green. And in the warmer weather she wore a lighter silk faille in a sapphire-blue that darkened the blue of her eyes, or some other shade that reminded him of spring lilacs.

Naturally her dresses were discreet—high at the neck with long, tight sleeves—but a man could not fail to notice how their very simplicity set off her slender figure so delightfully, and how the rich hues brought out the creamy color of her skin and the wild-rose flush of her cheeks. And he could not deny that the charming way she wore her lustrous black hair, pulled back into a Grecian knot, emphasized the purity of her profile and the classical length of her neck.

"Delicious!" he exclaimed out loud as he strode up the hill and passersby turned to stare and smile. He strode on, oblivious to anything but his thoughts. "Can this be you, John Porter Adams?" he asked himself. "Thinking a woman's profile 'delicious,' instead of thinking about a Greek statue? Can it be you, thinking of the sensual rustle of a woman's silk petticoats and not the cold painted versions in a portrait by Gainsborough?" He stopped to consider the matter, unaware of the ripple of laughter from the passersby, while staring down at his boots—nicely polished boots now with no holes in them—thinking of his discreet, self-effacing housekeeper.

Lily was a paragon among servants: she was quiet and modest; she did her job well and his cluttered, dusty house seemed to have sprung to life beneath her slender white hands. He shook his head bewilderedly. Again, he could not have said why. Maybe it was the vases of fresh flowers in every room? Even in winter there were hothouse roses and lilies—her namesake, tall and pale and pure. He knew that he now employed fewer staff and yet his establishment cost him less to run than it ever had, and his house gleamed and sparkled and shone with cleanliness. His meals were exactly the way he liked them, simple but good. Every evening his velvet smoking jacket and his monogrammed slippers would be laid out ready for him, and a maid would hurry to run his bath. A decanter of the dry Manzanilla sherry he enjoyed would be set out on the library table, and best of all, Lily would be there to greet him.

John Adams hurried eagerly up the hill. He prided himself on being a truthful man and he had to admit that the reason he was hurrying was because he knew she would be waiting for him. And he told himself that tonight he would ask her to share a glass of Manzanilla with him before dinner.

She must have heard him coming, because she had the door open before he even got to the top of the steps. "Good evening, sir," she said with a demure smile. "Shall I take your hat, sir, and your scarf, though I hardly think you needed one on such a beautiful spring day."

"Was it nice?" he asked, beaming. "I'm afraid I didn't notice the weather." But he did now. The windows of his house were flung wide to the evening air; a slight breeze ruffled the curtains and the scents of the garden mingled with the vases of flowers on the hall table and Lily's violets and her cologne. "How delightful the house looks today," he exclaimed enthusiastically, smiling at her. "It's all your doing, Lily."

"Thank you, Mr. Adams," she said, lowering her eyes demurely. "It's kind of you to say so."

A young maidservant bobbed good evening to him and then scuttled upstairs to run his bath, and before he could change his mind he said quickly, "Would you be so good as to join me in a glass of sherry this evening, Lily? I . . . there are some things I should like to discuss with you."

Lily hesitated. He thought for an agonized moment she was going to say no. Then she replied, "Of course, sir. It would be an honor."

"In half an hour then," he said quickly. "In the library."

He stroked his short Vandyke beard, gazing thoughtfully at her, until she reminded him that his bath must be ready.

"Oh," he said, startled. "Of course. Yes, of course it will." He ran up the stairs two at a time like a boy, turning at the landing to look back at her. She was watching him, smiling, and he grinned as he took the rest of the stairs at the run. Even though he was a mature professor of fifty years, somehow he felt almost boyish tonight.

Twenty minutes later he was bathed and changed and pacing the library floor. "There you are," he exclaimed, relieved when on the stroke of the half hour Lily tapped on the door. She walked toward him, her blue silken skirts swishing, and he sighed happily. "Did I ever tell you how glad I am you do not wear gray?" he asked, handing her a cut-crystal glass of his best sherry. "It brightens up my household, to see you in blue and violet." He nodded, half to himself. "Yes, yes. You brighten my life, Lily."

"Thank you, sir. I've always liked bold colors, even when I was a child."

"And where was that?" he asked, intrigued.

"We lived in Connemara, sir." She smiled. "Maybe that's why I liked the bright colors. The landscape is so muted there, all silvered over by the clouds and the mist."

"Does the sun never shine?" he asked, astonished.

She laughed and he told himself it was surely the pleasantest sound ever heard in his big old house.

"Oh, sometimes the sun shines, sir," she assured him. "Some days the sky would be as bright as my blue dress and the sea would be turquoise and green. We would ride our ponies at the very edge of the waves and never want the day to end, nor anything to change." She paused and then said, "But of course, it did." She walked to the open window looking out onto the garden, and he stood next to her while she told him about her younger sister, Ciel, who was attending school in Paris.

"Ciel!" he exclaimed. "What charming names your mother chose for her daughters!"

Lily stared down at her glass of sherry. "My mother is dead, sir," she said.

"Oh, yes, of course. I remember now, you told me you lost your family on the way over. Drowned, were they not? I'm so sorry, Lily, it was clumsy of me to remind you."

"Not at all, sir." She stood up and said briskly, "I think dinner is ready, Mr. Adams. Thank you very much for the sherry. It was sweet of you to invite me."

He threw back his head and laughed. He said, "No one has ever called John Adams 'sweet' in his entire life."

Lily smiled at him. "Then you are obviously not moving in the right circles, sir," she retorted with a hint of her old flirtatiousness.

He watched her walk across the room, thinking how graceful she was: so simple, so slender, so feminine. "Lily," he called, and she turned at the door.

"Yes, Mr. Adams?"

"Would you join me for sherry again tomorrow evening? I've so enjoyed our little talk."

This time her smile seemed to come from her heart, lighting up her face. "Of course, sir," she said. "I should be delighted."

Taking a glass of sherry together before dinner soon turned into a little ritual. Dinner was put back permanently half an hour, and it became the highlight of his day. Spring drifted toward summer, and for once he did not plan a trip to visit Europe. "I have so much work to do on the book I'm writing," he explained to Lily. "It's already taken me two years and I'm afraid if I do not finish it, I shall be considered a dilettante by my peers."

"I'm quite sure no one could ever call you that, sir," Lily said indignantly. "You are devoted to your work—anyone can see that."

She seemed to have the feminine knack of finding exactly the right soothing phrase, and he added it to her growing list of attributes. "Why not join me for coffee after dinner in the library, Lily," he suggested. "It's lonely sometimes, of an evening, and I appreciate your company."

Lily looked at her employer. "Distinguished-looking," was how she would have described him, with his silver hair and his pointed beard, and his nice brown eyes hidden behind horn-rimmed spectacles. She never talked to anyone else, except her employer, keeping a distance between herself and the cook and the two young maids, but even though she buried herself in the thousand and one details involved in running a large house such as this, she was still as lonely as when she had first arrived in Boston. She had heard that John Adams was a genius in his field and she knew that his conversation would be stimulating. "Oh, I'd love that, sir," she said, meaning it.

His writing lay neglected on his desk and the pile of new books he had bought remained unread on the table, and the after-dinner conversation in the library became a nightly event both of them looked forward to. Lily talked a little about her home and her childhood, and she drew him out to talk about his travels and about art and books and his work. "The three loves of my life," he told her, "and the greatest comfort to any man."

Lily laughed. "My father always said a man's wife was that, sir."

He stared at her. "Would you do me a favor, Lily, and not call me 'sir' when we are alone together? I'm enjoying the rare company of a charming, educated young woman, and there is no reason for you to always address me as 'sir.'"

He showed her his collections and all his treasures, turning the fragile leaves of a fifteenth-century book of hours painted in transparent watercolors and gold leaf; and a very rare Gothic bible, and Persian and Chinese manuscripts. He talked at length about his favorite subject, seventeenth-century French literature, and she asked him to recommend some books to read so that she could understand all the points he was making. So he drew up a reading list and then each week he asked her questions on what she had read, treating her like a schoolgirl.

Summer drifted into fall, and fall into winter, but Mr. Adams did not entertain his colleagues anymore, the way he used to. He preferred the company of his housekeeper.

"You must have met a woman, John," they said jocularly. And they were astonished when he laughed and shrugged his shoulders. "Can it be true?" they asked each other. "Has some woman snared old Porter Adams at last? And if so, who is she?" None of them could remember ever seeing him with a lady.

The following year, on the first day of spring, as Lily was approaching her twenty-first birthday, Mr. Adams waited nervously for her in the library. He smiled, relieved, when he heard her tap on the door and she came in. He thought how beautiful she looked as she walked toward him, and he wondered with a pang of regret if he would ever see her walk into his library again. Because after what he had to say to her, there was a chance she might not.

"Come here, Lily," he said, and she stepped closer. Looking into her eyes he said, "Over these past months you have come to mean a great deal to me. I know that I am many years older than you, but still we enjoy each other's company, do we not? I have been thinking, Lily, that it would be a very pleasant idea if you would agree to marry me."

She stared at him, wide-eyed with shock, and he said quickly, "I can see my proposal has come as a surprise to you, but I'm not a man who knows how to show his emotions. I'm asking you to be my wife, Lily. I don't expect your answer right away, but please, think it over, take your time. . . ."

Lily said nothing. She just shook her head disbelievingly and turned away. He watched, agonized, as she walked to the door. "At least consider it," he called after her. "That's all I ask, that you think about it. Take a week, a month . . . take forever if you must."

Lily turned and looked at him. "Thank you very much, Mr. Adams. I shall think it over," she said, closing the door quietly as she went out.

Walking calmly as if nothing had happened, Lily crossed the hall to the back of the house. She looked around at the pleasantly furnished comfortable little sitting room and the small bedroom that she had called home for over two years.

She sank into the blue brocade chair by the fire and put her feet up on an embroidered footstool. She glanced at the table next to her with the little pile of books that were her "required reading" for Mr. Adams's personal literature course, and at her treasured silver-framed photograph of home.

"Jayzus!" she exclaimed, leaping to her feet and pacing her small room agitatedly. Why did he have to go and spoil it all by asking her to marry him? It had all been so nice, so civilized and pleasant. So *safe*. She had worked hard to get where she was; she had tried hard to put the past behind her. Most of the money she earned went to the Sheridans for the child, though she never said where she was or who it was from. She wanted no contact with them or her past.

She thought again about Mr. Adams's offer of marriage. She could become Mrs. John Porter Adams, the beautiful young wife of one of Boston's richest and most important men. She contemplated for a minute what it would be like to be married to him, and she wanted to cry. He was old enough to be her father. Oh, and she was still so young, so very young, and despite what had happened, there was always the hope in her heart that, somewhere on the horizon, someone would come to rescue her.

She flung herself onto the bed and began to cry as she hadn't in a long time. Not since she had received Ciel's letter with the terrible news that her mammie was dead. Later she dried her tears and told herself not to be so silly and that maybe, just maybe, it was possible that if she became Mrs. John Porter Adams, Pa would forgive his prodigal daughter and she would be able to go home again to Ardnavarna.

SHE AVOIDED MR. ADAMS for a week, sending the little maid to wait on him, afraid of his eager eyes, watching for an answer. Night after night she lay awake, thinking about what it would be like when she was his wife. She would be mistress of this house instead of a mere housekeeper. She would have the power of money and position. She could do what she liked with the somber old house, she could entertain and give parties. It would almost be like old times.

The following evening she went to the library. She knocked on the door and waited for him to call, Come in. He was at his desk by the far window overlooking the garden. He leapt anxiously to his feet as she walked the length of the room and stood before him, her head held up proudly, her back straight.

"Well, Lily?" he said.

"I accept your proposal, Mr. Adams," she said calmly. "I shall be very happy to become your wife."

THE MARRIAGE QUIETLY TOOK PLACE two weeks later, at the lovely Park Street Church. The bride wore a fitted jacket of deep-blue corded silk over a swirling cream silk skirt. Her straw hat was trimmed with silk flowers and she wore a bunch of violets tucked into her waist and a large sapphire and diamond pin, a wedding present from her husband, at her throat. No guests were invited and two strangers had to be summoned from the street to act as witnesses. Lily's hand shook as she signed the register. She looked so pale and nervous that her new husband put a steadying arm around her.

"You have made me the happiest man in the world," he said as they left for their two-week honeymoon in Vermont.

The old Colonial Inn was simple but charming, with a white-pillared portico and a shady porch overlooking the gardens and a fast, narrow river. The only sounds were country ones: the rushing of the river, birds' song, sheep and cows, and the occasional bark of a playful dog. If the proprietors were surprised by the obvious age difference between the bride and the groom, they did not show it as they conducted them to the two-bedroom suite he had reserved.

He left her alone in her room to change for dinner and Lily sat on the white counterpaned bed, thinking with dread of her wedding night. Panic swept over her and she trembled with fear as she remembered cruel Dermot Hathaway. She knew what was expected of her tonight and she knew she could not go through with it. It was all a terrible mistake. She should never have married him. Once again she just had not thought and now it was too late.

She wondered if it would have been easier if he were a young man, and she thought of Finn, so dark and vital and handsome, looking at her with those hungry eyes. But John was old. His hair was gray, his hands were pale, and his body . . . she shuddered, unable to think further. He is a gentleman, she reminded herself; it will be all right. Then she remembered the other Lily, the seventeen-year-old star of the debutante year who had been confidently predicted to marry well. She could have married any one of a dozen handsome young men and now, at twenty-one, just look where she was.

Her head ached and she ran to the window and flung it open, filling her lungs with the cool evening air. She told herself she had just married one of Boston's finest men, that he was clever and cultured and rich. She reminded herself that she would be one of Boston's great ladies, a pillar of society again, reprieved at last of her guilty past. She told herself she would give dinner parties for her husband and afternoon teas for the ladies, and maybe even a grand ball. Her new husband loved to travel and she would accompany him: she would buy wonderful clothes from the Paris couturiers, from Worth and Paquin and Doucet. And then the young Mrs. Adams would dazzle all of Boston with her beauty and her flair and her social grace. And maybe Pa would forgive her at last.

Keeping the picture of her glowing future firmly in the forefront of her mind, she dressed for dinner in a soft green gown of clinging mousseline de soie with a wide neckline that bared her shoulders. She tied the violet satin sash and tucked a bunch of violets at her waist. She put up her hair and anchored it with little pearl pins, and when her husband knocked on the door she lifted her chin, took a deep breath, and said she was ready.

They were the only guests in the white-paneled dining room, and Lily ate nothing. She stared silently out the window at the darkening view of trees and meadows, listening to the rushing sounds of the river and the late evening trill of the birds while her husband poured champagne that she did not drink.

John was no fool. He knew she was nervous and he thought he understood. But he was inexperienced in the mysterious ways of women and he did not know what to do. "Why don't you try the ice cream, my dear?" he said helpfully. "They tell me it's homemade."

Lily looked at him, her sapphire eyes spitting anger. "For God's sake, don't treat me like a child!" she snapped.

He stared at her with surprise. "I'm sorry. I just thought the ice cream might please you."

"Well, it doesn't." She turned her head and looked moodily out at the gardens again.

"You must be very tired, Lily," he said mildly, and she turned and glared at him again. He smiled, holding up a protesting hand. "And no, before you say it, I am not treating you like a child. I'm merely behaving the way I assume a concerned new husband would act under the circumstances." He took her hand across the table and said gently, "Lily, I think I understand what you are going through right now—all your misgivings and wondering if you have done the right thing marrying a man so much older than yourself. And all your fears about our honeymoon. I want to reassure you that I shall not disturb you. You have your own room and it will stay yours until you choose to invite me to share it."

Lily saw the sincerity on his face and she said, ashamed, "You are the very nicest man I have ever met. It's just that I haven't even had time yet to get used to calling you 'John,' instead of 'Mr. Adams.' It's all happened so quickly."

He smiled, relieved. "It didn't take too long to move from 'sir' to 'Mr. Adams.' About a week, as I remember. So I shall live in hope."

Lily knew that what she had said was true, and that he was the very nicest man, and that she was lucky to be his wife. Filled with shame for her outburst, she lifted his hand and pressed it to her cheek. "Would you mind if I left now?" she said quietly. "You are right. I am tired."

He accompanied her to the stairs, dropping a brief kiss on her cheek. "Sleep well, my darling," he said, watching her walk tiredly up the broad staircase. And he thought his new wife looked as beautiful and fragile as a naiad in her flowing green dress. Afterward, he went out to the porch to smoke a cigar, listening to the hoot of a barn owl in the woods and thinking contentedly what a very lucky man he was.

Lily unhooked the dozens of little buttons and let the soft dress slide to the floor. She walked to the window and leaned her arms along the sill, gazing yearningly into the soft darkness.

This should have been the most wonderful night of her life: she would have been married in the family chapel, and the Big House and all the grand houses in the area would have been filled to overflowing with her wedding guests. Pa would have walked her down the aisle, proud of his beautiful young daughter in her virginal white lace dress; and the handsome young man who, in her dreams always seemed to have the face of Finn O'Keeffe, would have been waiting for her at the altar. There would have been soaring organ music and wonderful flowers, Ciel would have been her only bridesmaid, and her mother would have shed joyous tears. Afterward, there would have been a magnificent ball, and later that night she and her lovely young husband would have linked hands and looked conspiratorially at each other, laughing, and they would have stolen away to their room, to be alone together at long last.

The familiar smell of John's cigar smoke drifted upward into the window and she thought of what her mother would have told her on her wedding night. "You must always remember your duty," she would have said firmly, and Lily knew she was right. She had "made her bed" and now she would have to lie on it, with her husband.

She put on the new white satin nightgown and brushed her long black hair one hundred strokes, remembering the lovely silver brushes she had pawned long ago. She told herself now she could buy more silver brushes if she wanted, as many as she damned well pleased. But she didn't want them. She did not want anything, except for this night to be over.

She walked across the charming little sitting room to her husband's bedroom. She turned down the lamp, climbed into the big brass four-poster, and pulled the covers up to her chin. Closing her eyes, she waited.

John finished his cigar. He lingered for a while, enjoying the cool night air and then with a pleased sigh he told himself again that he was a very lucky man. He had thought his life was full before, but now, with Lily by his side, it was complete. He said good night to his hosts and strode up the stairs to his room. He undressed in the dark, thinking how delicious the scents of the garden were coming in through the open windows. But there was another scent, the familiar sweet spicy smell of Lily's cologne.

He turned to look at her lying in his bed and he shook his head, smiling. "Can it be true?" he whispered, sitting beside her. He turned her hand palm-up and pressed soft kisses into it, and then he whispered, "Are you sure, Lily? I wanted you to have time. . . ."

"I am sure," she said bravely.

He climbed into bed and lay next to her and it was she who reached out and put her arms around him. He groaned and pulled her closer, trembling, and they lay quietly together. He stroked her hair and kissed her face; he ran his hand over the soft smooth skin of her arms and her naked back, and Lily clung tightly to him afraid that if she did not, she might change her mind and run away.

When John made tender gentle love to her it was all so different from Dermot Hathaway that she wondered why she had been afraid. He was sweet and considerate and she knew it meant a lot to him, though it meant less than nothing to her. It was her "duty," she reminded herself. It was part of the bargain in becoming Mrs. John

Porter Adams, because God knows, sinner and exile that she was, she had little else to offer him but her body.

THE HONEYMOON PASSED PLEASANTLY: they went for long walks in the countryside or lazed by the river; they read and they ate delicious dinners, alone in the dining room, the only guests. The night before they were to return home, John told her he wanted to hold a reception to introduce her to Boston society. "After all, you are now related to most of them," he said. "And I can't wait to show you off to all those old battle-axes who have been trying to marry me off to their grand-daughters and nieces for thirty years."

The invitations were engraved and hand-delivered and Lily threw herself excitedly into the preparations. Before her marriage she had fired the cook and maids and employed new staff, because she did not want anyone in her home who remembered when she was just the housekeeper.

She planned a buffet menu she thought would please her smart guests. Of course, there would be champagne and a dozen different cold dishes because the evening promised to be very warm. She unearthed the Adams's family silver and had the massive platters and candelabra polished and buffet tables set up in the big dining room. She hired a string quartet to play discreetly in a corner of the music room, and employed a florist to turn the entire house into a bower of blossoms. She wished she had had time to go to Paris to shop first but decided that she would wear her wedding outfit because it was the prettiest thing she possessed. And then John opened the big safe at the back of a cabinet in the library and showed her the family heirlooms, the diamonds and emeralds, rubies and sapphires, and told her that now they all belonged to her.

To say that the ladies of Boston were stunned by the announcement of John Porter Adams's marriage was an understatement. "But who *is* she?" they demanded excitedly over their teacups. "They say that she is a foreigner. He must have met her on his travels, because no one in town remembers ever seeing her." And they sent their acceptances by return of post, hardly able to hold back their curiosity until the night of the reception.

Lily thought triumphantly that the house looked a dream of perfection as she walked around making sure everything was in its place. The grand stairway had been turned into a rose pergola and a dozen footmen in deep blue silk livery lined the steps. There were flowers everywhere and the soft strains of her husband's favorite Mozart concerto drifted from the music room. The buffet tables were a wonderful sight, all crisp white damask and tall bouquets of lilies in silver vases, and the family silver. John poured the champagne and raised his glass in a toast. "To my wife, the most beautiful woman in Boston," he said solemnly, because he really meant it.

"And to Boston's most distinguished man," she replied, smiling back at him, because she also meant it.

There was the sound of a carriage outside and she glanced excitedly at him. "Oh! Here they are!" she exclaimed, and he laughed as she hurried to the top of the stairs to receive her guests. She looked so young and charming in her tight blue bodice and swirling cream skirt. She had flowers in her hair and she was wearing the diamond-and-sapphire earrings he had not seen worn since his mother's day.

The hired butler flung open the door and Lily watched puzzled as he came up the stairs holding a silver salver with a white card on it. "Mrs. Brattle White's compliments, ma'am," he said.

Lily picked it up and read it. The excitement left her face and she passed it silently to her husband. "Mrs. Brattle White regrets that due to unforseen circumstances, she will be unable to attend the reception tonight," John read out loud. "It's all right Lily," he said consolingly. "The old dear's probably got a summer cold. After all, she's in her seventies, you know."

Another carriage drew up and again the butler brought them a card. It said the same thing: "Mrs. James Adams regrets . . ." he read, puzzled. "But she's my aunt," he exclaimed. "She's been after me to marry for years. *Nothing* would keep her from meeting my bride. What's going on? Has Boston come down with some epidemic I don't know about?"

Carriage after carriage drew up outside, but no guests arrived, only the little white cards engraved with their names and their handwritten regrets.

The footmen waited impassively on the stairs and the hired butler paced the hall; the music played and the champagne and food waited in all their expensive glory in the dining room.

Lily straightened her back and stood tall. She tilted her chin in the air, and summoning all her dignity, she walked up the stairs to her room. She stood at the window watching the procession of smart carriages wending their way up Mount Vernon Street. And each time the coachman stepped out and climbed the steps to deposit his card on the silver tray. All those "regretful ladies," she thought bitterly, facing the truth. She was related by marriage to every good Boston Brahmin family. And received by none of them. She knew there would be no more parties in her house. No one would ever come.

John found out the truth from his aunt later that night. It was his ex-cook, now employed by Mrs. Brattle White, who had let the cat out of the bag on the very day of the party. "She's Irish, like meself," she had told her new employer. "*And* she used to be his housekeeper. She gave us all the sack though, when she decided to marry him and up her station in life. She always did give herself airs. Anyone might have thought she was a real lady, instead of an Irish servant like the rest of us."

The next morning Mr. and Mrs. Adams departed hurriedly for an extended "honeymoon" abroad, leaving behind a scandal that refused to go away.

CHAPTER
34

MAUDIE

Ardnavarna

AFTER I HAD DONE MY SHOPPING in Galway and Shannon and Eddie had finished browsing in Kenny's Bookshop and buying hazelwood walking sticks and gorgeously colored mohair lap rugs, and thankfully not purchasing a single thing with a shamrock on it, we adjourned for lunch. Over pints of Guinness and plates of oak-smoked salmon with rich soda bread, not as good as Brigid's but then none ever is, we talked about Lily. Eddie said he thought she was headstrong and selfish, though she had redeeming qualities. And Shannon said she was sorry for her because all she had been was young and spoiled and rather silly and it was not really her fault.

"Ah," I said, "but blaming it on Finn O'Keeffe, that was her fault."

"You're too soft-hearted when it comes to Lily," Eddie told her.

"No, I'm not," Shannon retorted. "Besides, if Finn and Dan had stayed at Ardnavarna, they would have ended up just the way they began, as a groom and a gillie. And just look what happened to them."

"Ah," I said again, mysteriously this time. "But you haven't heard the whole of it yet. You can see I have all my characters poised, all interlinked in some delicate way, their lives almost touching, but not quite. *Not yet.*"

They laughed at me. "We know," they chorused. "We have to wait. 'All in good time.'"

"No time like the present," I said briskly, pushing aside my plate and downing my Guinness in a practiced fashion. "And we shall continue with Dan."

Boston

DAN O'KEEFFE WENT TO THE BARBER and had his thick curly red hair cut short and his bushy beard trimmed to a reasonable face-framing fuzz, and he then bought himself a new outfit before he went to see Thomas Keany. Clean and neat again and with his money in his pocket, he felt on top of the world as he strode down Prince Street, greeting a dozen different acquaintances en route.

The ward boss invited him to take a seat, eyeing him searchingly, noticing his new clothes and his confident smile and also the new look of experience on his face. He said, "Well, O'Keeffe? Have you come to return my fifty dollars?"

"Indeed I have, sir." Dan laid the money on the table. "But not yet the gold watch I promised you."

Keany left the fifty lying on the table between them. He said, "Then I take it the venture was not a success?"

"Indeed it was, sir." Dan told him exactly how much of a success his venture had been while Keany listened attentively. "I made seven hundred and twenty-three dollars and sixty-five cents, Mr. Keany," he ended triumphantly. "I bought myself new pants and a jacket and a haircut and I gave a friend of the family, poor Mrs. O'Donovan, fifty dollars. With your fifty repaid that leaves me with six hundred and three dollars exactly. And that's more than enough to buy Corrigan's little old shop. I'm sure he'll sell for five."

Keany nodded reflectively and said, "Tell me lad, what makes you think you can do better with Corrigan's store than the man already has himself?"

"I'll smarten it up, sir. I'll paint the place, make it look fresh and clean. I'll stock better produce and offer more variety."

"And will you be charging more?"

"Well, I'll have to add a bit to the prices to cover the extra expenses. . . ."

Keany nodded. "And that's exactly where your scheme falls to pieces. Corrigan's shop is in Boston's poorest area. The people there barely have two nickels to rub together and every cent you add to the price of an onion counts. Corrigan's is a nickel-and-dime business in a nickel-and-dime area and it'll never be any different. Those poor women will look at your fancy paintwork and the extra cent on the onion and they'll go around the corner to the next grocer because he's cheaper. The only thing that matters to them is the price. Absolutely nothing else."

Dan stared glumly at him. His grandiose dreams of a smartly painted, neatly stacked shop flew out the window and a new image of himself appeared, wandering the open road with a peddler's satchel on his back until he was as old as the little guy he'd bought the suspenders from. And, like him, when he was seventy he saw he would still be sleeping in a haystack with a bottle of hooch to keep away the night's cold instead of with a good woman in a feather bed.

He took all the money from his pocket and laid it on the desk alongside Keany's fifty dollars and said miserably, "So there's my choice then. Become old and gray like Corrigan, selling two cents' worth of sugar to women who can't afford it, or wear myself out as a traveling man with only a bottle for company in me old age."

Keany rapped his knuckles emphatically on his wooden desk. "I've been behind this desk for twenty-five years, son, and I've had all sorts come to me for advice, or a loan, or help in sorting their problems. I've seen a fella desperate for the price of a coffin to bury his child; old men with nothing left in their pockets for a night's lodgings in the bitter cold; and families needing a roof over their heads. Men have come to me, like you did yourself, for money to set themselves up in business, and I admit I've made mistakes. But not many. A man becomes a pretty good judge of character under those circumstances."

He sat back again; putting his fingers together he looked thoughtfully over them at Dan. He said, "Did y'ever think of going up a notch or two, Dan lad? More of a carriage-trade business, in a smarter area where there's good money spent on food—and plenty of it. I happen to know of a lease going on a shop at the corner of Clarendon Street— only a small place, mind you, but it's a damn fine location. Most of the cooks on Beacon Hill are Irish women and they'll patronize an Irish grocer for sure. A fine-looking enterprising young fellow like yourself could do very nicely there."

Dan looked doubtful. Clarendon Street was alien territory, a place of nobs and snobs. His entrepreneurial confidence had been gained dealing with country hicks and he wasn't sure he was ready to tackle the grand ladies of Boston yet. "I don't know what they eat in rich houses," he said doubtfully.

"You didn't know who wanted to buy pocket watches or red suspenders either," Keany pointed out. "But you had enough savvy to find out. The lease on the property is two hundred and fifty for the year."

Dan looked at his six hundred dollars. It would buy Corrigan's shop and Corrigan's life-style; he knew he would not lose his money, but neither would he make any. Or he could take a gamble on a year's lease of the smart shop with enough left to do it up and stock it, and if he were lucky he would make money. *Real money.*

"Thanks for your advice, Mr. Keany, sir. I'll take that lease," he said quickly, before he could change his mind.

"If you are the fella I think you are, you will not regret that decision," Keany said, shaking his hand. "I've had plenty of men come to me with good schemes for businesses and the only flaw in 'em was their own character. I'm betting on you, Dan lad. But remember, only you can make it a success."

Keany arranged for the lease and Dan signed his name with a firm hand and paid his two hundred and fifty. His stomach clenched agonizingly as he watched his money disappear into the attorney's safe, and he remembered all those bone-chilling lonely nights on the road and all the hard-talking it had taken to amass it, dollar by dollar. Telling himself there was no going back, he went to inspect his new premises.

Keany had been right: the shop was on an important corner with a window onto Clarendon and one onto Boylston, and a doorway cater-corner in between at the top of two wide stone steps. The shop itself was twenty by twenty square, with a smaller storeroom in the back. There was a minute hallway and a dark narrow staircase leading to the two rooms over, and they were to become his new home.

"Just one year, Dan boy," he told himself seriously, standing in the middle of his shop. "That's all you've got. At the end of it, you've either made your money back or you've lost it all."

He walked through the tree-lined streets of Beacon Hill and Back Bay, noting the elegant redbrick houses and the gas streetlights and the leafy calm. There was a pleasant feeling of leisure about the area, as though it would be in bad taste to even think of hurrying, and he noticed even the smart shiny carriages clip-clopped past at a sedate pace.

Plucking up his courage, he went to the tradesmen's entrance of one of the grand houses and asked to speak to the cook. He told her he was opening a new grocery on the corner of Clarendon and asked if there was anything in particular she would like him to stock, and he made a careful note of her answer. He repeated this at a dozen or so houses and made a note of all the information.

He installed mahogany shelving in his shop and glass-fronted cupboards with solid brass fittings. He polished the mahogany counter to a high sheen and added a couple of bentwood chairs for his customers to take their ease while placing their orders. He had his shop front painted a rich deep red, the color of good claret, and had the name

DANIEL'S inscribed in brass letters on the fascia board and painted in gold leaf on each window, with HIGH CLASS GROCERS, SUPPLIERS TO THE CARRIAGE TRADE, written underneath.

He bought an old carriage for deliveries and had it painted in the same smart claret and gold as the shop, with DANIEL'S emblazoned in gold letters on the sides, and for ten bucks a week he employed a grateful young man called O'Dwyer, with Irish blue eyes and a family of six to keep, as stockroom assistant and deliveryman. He made early morning rounds of the markets, meeting suppliers and wholesalers, searching for only the best of everything. And "Country Fresh" were the bywords used on the flyer he sent out announcing the opening, in rich burgundy lettering even though colored inks cost a fortune, on thick expensive paper so that it could not be ignored. He had it hand-delivered to the kitchens of all the grand houses by a dozen scruffy little Irish kids eager to make a few cents, and he placed prominent ads in every Boston newspaper and journal.

Early the next morning, smart in a white linen coat, Dan inspected his shop windows proprietorily from the sidewalk. He unrolled his red-and-white striped awnings, watered the twin bay trees in neat tubs, one on each side of the steps, inspected the fresh fruits and vegetables set out in small wooden crates on green felt-covered trestles, each fig and peach wrapped in white tissue paper like a precious gift. The sacks of fresh coffee beans, chests of China tea, and jars of vanilla pods, saffron, and cinnamon perfumed his shop, as did the large copper bowl of fresh flowers on the counter next to the huge brass cash register that had cost him a small fortune. But then, everything had. He had gone for broke with the "Nothing but the Best for the Best" attitude that was to become his motto.

He stood behind his counter and waited confidently for those tip-top people to patronize the store he had created especially for their needs. He did not have to wait long. The cooks he had spoken to at the big houses on the Hill were the first in. They noted the cents shaved off the prices here and there, and the bigger reductions on the "Opening Specials," and they nodded sagely as they prodded plump-breasted chickens and succulent pears, testing the quality. They inspected the big brown speckled eggs with bits of straw still adhering to them, which had been laid that morning at a country farm, and the pristine vegetables and fresh herbs. And they bought. Daniel's little claret-colored carriage with the dapple-gray pony and young O'Dwyer driving it were kept busy trotting up and down the smart streets, delivering the orders.

At the end of the first day, when he counted his takings, Dan had over a hundred dollars in the till, more than he would have taken in in a week at Corrigan's. And by the end of that first week he had taken in a total of four hundred and fifteen dollars and thirty-five cents, and he thought, satisfied, he had made the right move. His customers were the cooks and chefs from the city's mansions; they had the purchasing power of very wealthy households who demanded "the best" and they liked the big, polite redheaded young Irishman who was always ready with a joke and always had a moment to pass the time of day with them.

Dan calculated that in one year he would have recouped his investment and would be able to pay Keany back the loan for the delivery carriage and the pony. His profit margin was twenty percent and he knew if he worked hard and was careful with his prices his store would make him a comfortable living, way better than at Corrigan's. But it wasn't enough. It would not make him a rich man.

At the end of a year he went to Keany, paid back his loan, and handed him a gold pocket watch. "It's inscribed, just the way I promised," he told him proudly.

"To Thomas Keany. With Thanks. Daniel O'Keeffe," Keany read. "That's a very fine gift, Dan, and I appreciate it, though there was no need for thanks. You've worked hard for what you've got."

"That's why I'm here, Mr. Keany," Dan cried, thumping his big fist enthusiastically on Keany's desk. "Once a man gets a full belly, Mr. Keany, he gets a hunger for something else. *Success. Power. Wealth.* I said at the beginning I wanted more than one store, and now that I've got the formula I want to expand. I want another store in Back Bay. And then a third one, in New York. I'll put my assistant, O'Dwyer, in charge of this one, and I'll open the new one in Back Bay myself to get it going. Then, when it's operating perfectly, I'll find another couple of young Irish clerks to run it for me. Then I'll go to New York and do the same thing. . . ."

"Let's start with Back Bay," Keany said practically. "But remember, two shops is twice as much work as one, Dan O'Keeffe."

"Sure and don't I have the energy and strength of a dozen," Dan exclaimed truthfully.

The Back Bay shop opened with a flourish and soon two claret-and-gold delivery carriages were to be seen trotting through the smarter streets of the city, and Dan's receipts for the week averaged over a thousand dollars instead of four hundred. Those dollar signs jingled like the cash register in his head again and he knew his theory was right. But he bided his time. When he had repaid all his debts and had money in the bank, then he would go to New York and speak to Finn, because he had a few other ideas brewing in his head.

Meanwhile, he was walking out on Sundays with a very nice young girl, a maid at a big house on Mount Vernon Street he had met at St. Stephen's Church. She was dark-haired and pretty with rosy cheeks and gray eyes and she came from County Wexford. He saw her once a week on her day off, and he looked forward to it almost as much as he did to counting up the week's receipts on Saturday night. Every other spare moment he got after work, he spent down at the Ward Six office, helping Keany with his complex political organization.

When the Irish immigrants had first begun arriving in America, they had started a system of local government specifically their own, intended at first simply to help the immigrants with their problems in the new country. Over the years the system had developed to where the Irish in the big cities like Boston and New York, Pittsburgh and Chicago, dominated the Democratic Party on the local level. The immigrant areas of the cities were divided into wards, and each ward had a boss. In Ward Six's case it was Thomas Keany, but there were other powerful men in Boston: namely George McGahy, who ran Ward Seven, and Martin Lomasney, the all-powerful boss of Ward Eight. All were strong-minded fellows who worked hard for their poor constituents and in return they all expected "loyalty," meaning *votes,* when the time came to elect the men they had personally chosen to run for the local council and for the state legislature and for Congress.

At first Dan worked for Keany as a "heeler." It was his job to go around to the saloons rounding up voters when the delegates for the nominating conventions were to be chosen. It was also the heeler's job to keep those who would vote against his boss's choices out of these meetings. Few chose to argue the point with big brawny Dan O'Keeffe and those that did felt the power of his fists.

But Keany soon realized Dan was too good for the job. "A man like you, with his own business, who looks the way you do: big, solid, reassuring, that's exactly the kind of man who can get votes," he told him. "A man with your gift of the gab and the knack of saying the right thing at the right time to the right folks—oh, don't think I haven't noticed," he added with a twinkle. "What I'm saying is, a man like you, Dan, is a natural politician. I'm moving you up in the world. You can start by making speeches in support of my nominees for the local elections."

After that Dan was often to be seen on street corners, urging the folks to vote for the Ward Six nominee. All his old verbal prowess gained selling watches and suspenders returned and he gave the best speeches in the area; everybody said so. "We would vote for you, young fella, any time," one woman called to him, and that remark was not lost on the ward boss.

Over the next couple of years Dan learned all the advantages as well as all the tricks of politics. He worked for Keany for the love of it, expanding his contacts into the many Irish societies and organizations as well as the church. He was a young man not easily forgotten, and with his towering height and massive physique, he gave the impression of a strong man who could be relied on. A man who always kept his word. And the people liked and trusted him.

He became a well-known figure in the North End, greeted on every street and welcomed in every bar, not as a heavy drinker though he could down a jar or two with the best of 'em as any Irishman could, but as a shaker of hands and a man who brought a smile to their faces and a ray of hope to the hearts of everyone he met. And he never considered himself too grand for any job; he was as willing to sweep the floor of the meeting room and help run the Catholic Orphan Society picnic or attend a local man's funeral and make sure his widow was helped as he was to attend the fancy fund-raising dinners and march in the parade on St. Patrick's Day.

"Your two shops make you a nice living," Keany said to him late one night, long after most people were in bed, when they were still in his office. "Yet you seem to spend most of your time here at the ward headquarters. I said it when I met you, Dan, and I'll say it again. You're a natural politician, and I'm proposing you run for office."

"Run for office?" Dan's expression went rapidly from surprise to interest. It was true that politics were gradually taking over more and more of his life, and he loved it: he liked working with the people, changing their lives, even if only in small ways, for the better. And he certainly wanted to see his fellow countrymen gain an equal place in America, the country of immigrants. But run for office . . . well, that was a different matter.

"I wasn't just thinking of the local council," Keany said, lighting up a cigar and watching Dan carefully through the smoke for his reaction. "It's the Massachusetts State Senate I'm thinking of."

Senator Dan O'Keeffe. A buzz of excitement ran through Dan as he thought about it, but he said cautiously, "I've my businesses to think of running. I can't just walk away and leave my shops. Besides, I'm too young. I'm only twenty-eight."

"You have already learned how to delegate responsibility. You've got good men running the shops and you can still expand, just the way you planned. And in this era, youth is an advantage. Don't forgo this opportunity, Dan. You are exactly the kind of young man we need."

Dan went away to think it over. He paced the floor of his small sitting room over his shop, wishing Finn were there to talk to. Only Finn could advise him what to do. The next morning he told Keany he was going to New York to speak to his brother and he would let him know his decision in a couple of days' time.

"Do it," Finn, smartly dressed, urged over a lavish dinner at Sherry's. "I envy you the opportunity."

"But what about my stores? I'd planned to open more, right here in New York."

"You're the brains behind the enterprise," Finn reminded him. "Like my boss says, let your money make money for you. Invest in more stores with the same formula, put a good manager in each one and it'll run itself. You can as easily have a dozen as two, now you know how it's done."

Dan went back to Boston and told Keany he was willing to become his nominee for state senator. On Keany's advice he stepped up his street-corner speechmaking, only this time on his own behalf, drawing bigger crowds than had ever been seen before. He marched at the head of parades, with brass bands blaring Irish tunes and fireworks blasting. He gave 'em razzmatazz like they had never seen before and the people loved it and showed up in droves to see him.

"I know I'm young," he cried, his thumbs hooked through his signature red suspenders, his black derby hat pushed to the back of his head and his feet planted firmly apart on the soapbox that was his platform. "But I've been through everything you have yourselves. Every insult, every degradation. The poverty and the hunger. I *know* how it feels. And I know how to help you. I'll not see you swept under the senate rug with the rest of the rubbish, nor dumped in the garbage can to rot. I will work for *you.* I will work for *all* of us. I'll put every ounce of energy I've got to fight for a minimum wage for every man. And for you women working all hours God sends, slaving for your rich employers, I'll fight to set a limit on those weary hours so you will no longer be exploited. And I'll do my damnedest to stamp out sweated labor. All you have to do is put your trust in Dan O'Keeffe and give me your vote."

But it wasn't only the neighborhood votes he needed, he also needed the other powerful ward politicians. With Keany at his side, he made the rounds asking for their support, and Keany finally managed to persuade the powerful Lomasney over to his side.

Finn returned to Boston to spend the crucial final days leading up to the election with his brother, and he was there when the results were announced. Lomasney's support had swung the extra votes his way and Dan was elected the youngest senator in the state of Massachusetts. Finn marched proudly beside his brother, sharing his triumph as they strode through the very same North End slum streets that had offered them miserable shelter in a freezing, windowless hovel when they arrived in Boston only eight years before.

"Eight years. Who would ever have believed, Finn?" Dan said, tears of gratitude shining in his eyes as he remembered. "You, the stablelad at Ardnavarna, now a rich businessman. And me, the gillie, owning two shops and with money in the bank; a senator, representing my own people. Only in a great country like America could a man's dreams come true."

FIVE YEARS WORKING for Cornelius James in New York had made a dandy out of Finn O'Keeffe, if not quite a gentleman. Corinne Marquand lay propped on one elbow in his bed, watching him dress for an evening out that did not include her, even though they had just made love. His evening clothes were the finest New York could provide, as were his shirt, his shoes, his velvet-collared black overcoat, and his white silk scarf. The pearl studs in his dress shirt were real and so were the solid gold and diamond cuff links, bought from Tiffany with the generous Christmas bonus that Finn told himself he had damned well earned, working twelve to fourteen hours a day.

He stayed on at Eileen Malone's because it would have been a waste of money to rent an apartment for ten times the amount she charged him, and besides, he only used it to sleep; he was at the office at six-thirty every morning and out all night, and there was always some pretty actress with her own apartment who was happy to take him into her bed and look after him. Corinne was just an ongoing habit both of them enjoyed occasionally. Nothing serious.

He wasn't vain about his appearance, but he had learned his lesson the hard way that first week in New York when everyone had laughed at his cheap suit and his celluloid collar. Now he always dressed in the best and he found it an instant badge of respect; doormen whose job he would have once coveted rushed to open doors for him; headwaiters bowed and scraped, and pretty women glanced admiringly his way. And most importantly Cornelius James's friends treated him, if not quite like an equal—after all he had two demerits in the Wall Street establishment, he was Irish and Catholic—then at least with grudging respect. Cornelius had proven to his wife and to his friends that it was possible to make a silk purse out of a sow's ear, and the ignorant greenhorn Irishman was now an astute businessman whose quick brain had pulled off several neat coups.

Finn had proven a master at the technique of "selling short," borrowing stocks and selling them, to be delivered at some future date, taking a chance that the price would fall before that delivery date. When it did he was able to repurchase the stock at a lower price, return it to the lender, and pocket the profit.

It was a gambling tour de force and Finn had taken to the concept as naturally as breathing. He could almost smell a new stock with the aroma of success about it, and so far he had never lost his bet. But he couldn't say he was a happy man and he did not know why.

Corinne yawned lazily. Finn was a prodigiously energetic lover and she would have liked nothing better than to have snuggled up against his lean body and slept the evening away. And then maybe, after a light supper and a glass or two of wine, made some more delightful love. But it was never that way with Finn: he ran several lives and, she suspected, several women on parallel courses, and the "real" Finn was a mystery. But still, he looked so handsome she melted with desire just looking at him. "You are very *élégant, mon cher*," she said admiringly as he buttoned his jacket.

Finn flung his velvet-collared overcoat over his shoulders and smiled his thanks. "I'm off to the opera," he said, dropping an affectionate kiss on her tousled blond head. "And thanks to you I'm late." He wrapped his long white silk scarf around his neck, brushed off his top hat, and quickly made for the door. He paused, smiling at her, naked and pretty in his bed. "Corinne," he said.

"Hmmm?" She rolled over to smile at him.

"You're beautiful. Thanks."

Her pretty laughter trilled after him down the polished brown linoleum stairs and he waved to Eileen Malone, standing by the dining room door.

"Not with us for supper again tonight, Mr. O'Keeffe?" she asked.

"Maybe tomorrow, Mrs. Malone," he called cheerfully, heading out the door.

As he hailed a cab, Finn remembered that first day in New York, when he had walked to Wall Street, sweating and with his feet on fire from the stiff new boots. No matter how much money he made, or how successful and well dressed he was, he would never forget how cheap he had felt when he heard their mocking laughter. It was more than just that, he told himself as the hansom dropped him at the Metropolitan Opera House. The mark of the slums would never leave him. Poverty and ignorance were like a wound that never healed, and the memory of a thousand humiliations and insults and degradations still festered angrily at the back of his mind. Making money, lots of it, more than he could even imagine, was the only thing that might one day heal that wound. But he would have to be a richer man than Lily's father for that.

It was his first time at the opera, a performance of Rossini's *Barber of Seville,* by the Italian company visiting from La Scala in Milan, and the glittering foyer with its sweeping marble staircase brought back memories of festive nights at Ardnavarna. But then, instead of his perfect evening clothes, he had been the footman dressed in his velvet suit and powdered wig, like the flunkies lining the staircase now. He had served glasses of champagne instead of drinking them, and he had watched lovely Lily like a jealous hawk, instead of being surrounded by women, gorgeous in lace and satin and glittering with jewels, who greeted him like a long-lost friend.

They had feathers and flowers in their shining hair and an eager light that he recognized in their eyes, and their perfume was as intoxicating as the champagne. Women would never be a problem for Finn. But he still kept the image of Lily in his mind, as perfect as any photograph, smiling scornfully at him as she prodded him with her whip and commanded him to dance naked like a bear for her little sister.

"There you are, my boy." Cornelius James came toward him through the crowd, his wife Beatrice, resplendent in black velvet and a diamond tiara, on his arm. The first-night audience was made up of celebrities and socialites, and plain man though he was, Cornelius James knew most of them.

"A man in a position like mine meets a lot of people," he told Finn solemnly. "People with family money, and the old guard socialites; people with new money, railroad and steamship tycoons and business entrepreneurs. They all have to invest it, my boy, and they trust a man like me because I never act richer or grander or more important than they are. They bring their money because they know I'm an honest God-fearing man with a nose for a good investment, just the way you are yourself."

He beckoned Finn into a quiet corner, and said, "There's something I wanted to say to you, dear boy. Beatrice and I have talked this over and we have both agreed that our 'little experiment' has proven more than successful. You are an asset to James and Company and in little more than five years you have transformed yourself from an ignorant lad into a successful and socially acceptable young man. We think you deserve a reward. I have purchased a seat on the New York Stock Exchange for you. After tomorrow you will be a member of one of the most elite business institutions in the country. I have no son to inherit my business and when I retire, if you continue to work hard, I intend for you to take my place as chairman of James and Company."

Finn stared at him with amazement. He shook his head disbelievingly and said, "Sir, I'm not worthy of such an honor."

"Not yet, you're not. You will have to prove it to me first." Cornelius patted his shoulder paternally. "The seat on the Exchange is just the beginning."

"I'm deeply grateful, sir," Finn said. "I'll try not to let you down."

The next morning he rented a fabulously expensive one-bedroom apartment on Fifth Avenue at Forty-second Street, which he could not afford, but who cared? One day he would be chairman of James and Company and that was all the reference he needed. He stocked his pantry with champagne and caviar, his closet with more fine clothes, and his bed with beautiful women. Finn O'Keeffe had finally come up in the world, temporarily blocking out the past. But was he a happy man? He shook his head, bewildered. He had no answer to that.

CHAPTER
∼∼∼∼∼∼∼∼∼∼ 35 ∼∼∼∼∼∼∼∼∼∼

NEW YORK

EIGHT YEARS AFTER HE LEFT Jacob de Lowry, Ned Sheridan's was a name to be reckoned with in the theater, though he was as often out of town as in it, traveling the length and breadth of America. There were performances in Canada as well, and half a dozen trips to Europe to play his favorite city, London, where they greeted him almost as rapturously as they did his costar, Viola Allen, a delicate beauty of the type the English adored. He was in demand by all the major producers and a dozen scripts of new plays were sent to him each week.

He rented a palatial apartment on Fifth Avenue at Thirty-eighth Street and filled it with splendid furniture, paintings, and books. He shared it with a sweet and adoring girl named Mary Ann Lee, whom he called "Lucky," because ever since he had met her one dark, rainy night in Baltimore four years before, he had had a phenomenal run of luck. His career had grown from ingenue lead to that of star, with his name in lights on theater marquees from New York to San Francisco.

Lucky Lee was twenty-two years old and, like Ned, she had always wanted to be an actress, ever since she was a little girl in Milwaukee. Her uncle had had the theater in his blood: his Argentinian mother had been a dancer, and he took his little niece to see every show that came to town.

Her uncle died when she was thirteen and after that there was no more theater, but little Mary Ann was already lost in that unreal world. She waited until she was sixteen to run away from home with twenty dollars and change in her purse, and joined up with George Tyler's Miss Philadelphia Troupe, who were staggering across the country on tour, barely breaking even, sometimes barely even squeaking through, and always a mere step away from financial disaster.

As untrained as the next girl, Mary Ann told Ned she was adopted into the chorus on the strength of her pretty face and even prettier legs, and the fact that she could kick them as well as anybody. Miss Philadelphia was short of money one opening night—there were no funds left, not a single cent—when suddenly it was discovered that someone had forgotten to buy the chorus men their patent-leather dance shoes. George Tyler, never a producer to be daunted by the mere temporary shortage of funds and never lacking for a bright idea, immediately sent across the road to the local undertaker. He made a deal for several pairs in assorted sizes of the patent pumps used in that profession. On opening night the chorus danced in dead men's shoes.

Show biz was like that, Mary Ann soon discovered, always on the brink of great success or total disaster, with not much in between.

When Miss Philadelphia finally folded, or more properly "collapsed," Mary Ann found another job in a similar touring company and for a while she was employed on and off.

She was just eighteen when a show she was appearing in folded unexpectedly in Baltimore, and the management promptly left town without paying off their debts and their players. She had five dollars to her name, several pairs of worn dance shoes, and a few clothes. It was not enough to get her to New York and she found a job as a waitress in the city's grandest hotel, serving breakfast coffee and eggs to prosperous gentlemen travelers. One morning Harrison Robbins had strolled in and ordered two fried eggs over easy, bacon, and toast and settled himself down to read his newspaper.

Mary Ann recognized him immediately; his photograph had been in all the local journals that week, alongside his client, the handsome and very famous actor Ned Sheridan, and she knew if anybody could get her a job, he could.

"Excuse me, sir," she said, standing hesitantly by his table, the coffeepot clutched in both hands.

Harrison glanced up from his newspaper, registering the fact that she was pretty, and he smiled. "I'll have tea, thanks," he said, thinking that a waitress with cornflower eyes and black hair and a shy smile deserved at least a dollar tip.

"Mr. Robbins, sir," she said all in a rush. "I'm an actress. Well, just a chorus girl right now. I got stranded here when the show I was in failed and the manager left without paying us."

"Too bad," Harry said sympathetically, "but that's show biz. There's good, but there's an awful lot of bad."

"I need a job, sir, and I was wondering if you might have something?

Anything. I mean, I'll even work backstage, ironing the costumes, or . . . or anything. . . ."

Her voice faded away and Harrison heaved a sigh, asking himself why young girls would never learn that, even with talent, the world of the theater was a gamble, and more often lost than won. Pretty though she was, he would bet she had no training, no experience, and no talent beyond her looks, which was why she had been working as a chorus girl in a third-rate show that couldn't even afford to pay. Still, he had been through too many harsh, unpaid years himself to be unkind, and besides, she was pretty and rather sweet.

"Come and see me this afternoon at the theater. Around two-thirty," he said, turning back to his paper. "I'll find something for you, though it might not pay as well as waitressing."

It did not matter: Mary Ann would have gone anywhere, anytime, just to be near the stage again instead of serving coffee and juice every morning.

It was a day of pouring rain; her shoes leaked and her thin coat was soaked through in the ten minutes it took her to walk to the theater. She told the stage doorman she had an appointment with Mr. Robbins and was sent, hair dripping into her eyes and shoes squishing with every step, to Mr. Sheridan's dressing room to find him.

She tapped on the door and a wonderful deep voice said, "Come in," making the mundane words sound profound as a poem. She opened the door and stood dripping onto Ned Sheridan's plush red carpet, completely tongue-tied as she gazed into the eyes of the most handsome man she had ever seen.

"You look like a drowned kitten," he said, amused. "Who on earth are you?"

"Mary Ann Lee, sir," she said, trying desperately to shake the rain from her hair and spraying him with water.

Harrison Robbins rushed into the dressing room just then, waving a cablegram in the air. "We've cracked it, Ned," he yelled jubilantly. "Frohman's gone for it. The whole Shakespeare tour. *As You Like It, Hamlet,* and *Lear.* Top money, a dozen top-notch theaters across the country, ending up on Broadway. The best set designer, and costumes made in Milan, and you get to choose your own cast. *By God, boy, we've gotten everything we wanted. You've finally made it all the way.*"

Ned stared at Mary Ann and explained, "They always said I couldn't play Shakespeare. Now I've got the chance to prove myself. Maybe it's because a little half-drowned black-haired kitten just walked across my path and brought me luck."

"She's hoping for a job," Harry said, laughing.

"She's got one," Ned retorted, "as my mascot. 'Lucky' is on salary from this very moment. *And* she's going on the Shakespeare tour with us." He looked at her again, more carefully, and added, thinking of Lily, "Besides, you remind me of a girl I once knew, a long time ago." With a sad little shrug, he headed back to his rehearsal as though he had already forgotten about Mary Ann.

So Lucky was adopted by the Sheridan company and given a job as assistant wardrobe mistress and the occasional walk-on part, and gradually, in those long, lonesome nights rehearsing in Philadelphia and later on the road, Ned Sheridan had found himself drawn to her. He told himself it was not just because she reminded him of his Irish Lily, she was also sweet and shy and adoring, and before too long they became lovers.

The Shakespeare tour was a huge success, elevating Ned to the stature of serious actor instead of just the good-looking light comedy player producers had cast him as previously. After a triumphant opening on Broadway they had become a hot ticket, even at three dollars a performance, an unheard-of amount at the time. And they played to full houses until the theater closed for the summer.

Lucky moved into the new apartment Ned bought and gave up her own acting ambitions to play the role of his mistress. She was shy but everyone around Broadway knew her, and knew she was Ned's mistress. He had not asked her to marry him, though he half expected he would at some point in the future; but whenever he was tempted, he always told himself, "Not now, you might find Lily again one day."

He had often met Lily's son, a dark-haired sullen lad who did not look anything like her and who never put himself out to be nice to anyone. But he had never found Lily, even though he had employed a private detective for over a year after she first left. Lily had disappeared without a trace; she had been gone eight years and the only contact with her now was a bank draft his mother received every year, for one thousand dollars to pay for the boy. It was mailed from a different city every time, from places as far apart as St. Louis and Chicago.

He and Lucky had been living together for four years now and tonight he had another big opening in a brand-new play. The tryouts on the road had not been without trouble. The leading lady had quit and been replaced only a week ago by a temperamental and fiery unknown, Juliet Scott, and Ned was wondering gloomily whether his luck had run out, as he made his way to the final dress rehearsal. For the first time in his life he was not looking forward to an opening night, and no matter what Harrison said, a feeling of foreboding clouded his entire day.

EVEN THOUGH IT FELT LIKE SPRING, with fat furry buds on the chestnut trees and the scent of lilacs in the air, Lily Adams wore her golden sable coat when she took her afternoon carriage ride around the charming streets of Back Bay and Beacon Hill. Her expensive barouche was lacquered her favorite shade of violet and upholstered in pale gray suede, and her coachman wore the same silvery gray, matching the pair of beautiful high-stepping carriage horses.

Lily went for the same drive every afternoon, rain, snow, or shine. Each afternoon before she left she tucked a fresh posy of violets behind her horses' ears, and into her coachman's hat, and she wore the same flowers pinned to her furs with a diamond crescent moon. They would drive for an hour past all the great Boston houses where she was never invited. A charming little half smile lit her face, but her blue eyes blazed with unquenchable anger as she glanced from left to right, looking for all the world as if she were a woman on her way to keep an appointment, when the truth was she had nowhere at all to go.

The fall and winter months were the hardest, when her husband was busy with his lectures and his meetings with his colleagues. Even when he was home, he was always immersed in his books. Occasionally he would invite visiting foreign academics to dinner. They did not know that Lily was "socially unacceptable," and for an evening she would play the gracious young hostess, wearing an expensive gown and good jewels. But there were never any other women at the party and afterward she would leave them in the library with their port and cigars and the stimulating conversation she would so loved to have shared.

Every winter she almost went crazy from boredom. Gloom would settle over her in October and it would not lift until June, when they would leave to spend the whole summer in Europe.

She had been in Boston eight years and she had been Mrs. John Porter Adams for six, and each year had been lonelier than the last. She was married to a cultured man, preoccupied with his own affairs, who assumed she enjoyed her own company the way he did, and that she was perfectly happy sitting by the winter hearth, leafing restlessly through a book or embroidering yet another tapestry cushion for the dining room, exactly the way her own mother used to. *Only her mother and Pa had been in love.*

During those long winters she lived for the letters from her sister, and she wrote reams back to her, carefully describing a life filled with entertaining and gaiety, friends and acquaintances. It was a life that did not exist. The only truths in her letters to Ciel were that she was married to a rich, kind, older man; that they had a fine house in the smartest area of Boston and that she was related by marriage to some of the country's best old families. "Though of course, dear Ciel," she wrote snobbishly, "what the Americans mean by 'old' is not the way we understand the word. They are speaking of three or four generations and we are speaking of several hundred years." But she did not write that the good old families did not speak to her.

Each time they went to Europe she schemed and plotted how she might meet her sister, but so far without success. They always went to Italy and France, but Ciel would have already been whisked back to Ardnavarna for the summer and Lord Molyneux never allowed her to go anywhere else.

During those Italian summers Lily was a different woman. Youth bloomed again under the warm Tuscan sunshine; she drank young red wine and ate rich green olives and tomatoes picked from the fields, and bread cooked in a big oven by the village baker and fished out on a long wooden spade. She wore low-necked blouses and thin cotton skirts, tucking them up even shorter when she climbed the green, thyme-covered hills. She walked barefoot, with her long hair streaming free, on cool marble terraces of fourteenth-century villas, and glided in a gondola under fairy-tale bridges on Venetian canals. She bathed in the cool green waters of Lake Garda and Lake Como, and sipped little cups of bitter coffee alone on awninged café terraces, looking coolly beautiful in simple white voile with a big shady straw hat trimmed, as usual, with her favorite violets. But she was always the outsider, longingly watching the passing parade.

On those summer trips to Europe, she became a girl again while her nice husband seemed to grow even older. He became more withdrawn, caught up in his search for rare first editions and manuscripts, while she was in search of life. Blood pulsed through her veins like the red wine of Italy itself and though she was too frightened even to flirt, every now and then her eyes would linger speculatively on some olive-skinned handsome young man, wondering who he was, what he would say if she spoke to him, what he would do if she said, "I'm lonely. Help me."

Her husband was not a passionate man and Lily told herself she must be grateful for that, but she was young, only twenty-six. She was beautiful and men admired her, the way they always had done. And she so wanted to be *loved.*

But, of course, she never spoke to the handsome young Italians, and October found her back in Boston. Once again she took her afternoon carriage rides trying to show society she did not care what they thought. And at night she lay awake, thinking endlessly of the mistakes that had brought her to this gilded prison. As dawn peeked through her window curtains she finally slept, and she always dreamed of Ardnavarna. It was the same old familiar dream, in which she was the adored, petted little princess at the center of her loving family, with her ponies and her dogs and her rides on the strand with Finn O'Keeffe. And only in her dreams was she happy again.

It was during the second year of her marriage that a young woman had applied to her household for position as a general maid. Lily did not employ a housekeeper; she knew perfectly well how to run her own household and she interviewed the job applicant herself.

The woman had been waiting in the servants' quarters next to the kitchen, standing nervously in a corner nearest the door as though she expected to be booted out for having the nerve to set her shabby foot in such a grand house. Her apron was clean enough, but her thread-bare dress was worn to the drab no-color gray of poverty, and the thin woolen shawl she had tied around her shoulders was held together by a cobweb of careful stitching. Lily knew it would do nothing to keep out the cold and even though the woman's boots were carefully shined, she would bet there were holes in them. Her heart melted with pity and she knew she would give her the job, even though she didn't look strong enough to lift a heavy zinc pail filled with water.

"I'm strong, missus, and a hard worker," the woman said anxiously, reading her thoughts. She had not expected to speak to the lady of the house. No one ever did, they always saw the housekeeper, and she kept her eyes down, staring at the toes of her worn boots.

"I understand you do not wish to live in," Lily said gently. "Why is that?"

"I've seven kids to look after, missus."

"And do you have a husband?"

"I have a husband all right. *And* he has a job. Twelve dollars a week he brings home, but it doesn't go far with seven mouths to feed. The eldest is only ten, and he's a newspaper boy. He doesn't have one of the best corners though, and he only makes a couple of dollars a week. Still, he tries hard." She added bitterly, "Of course, you wouldn't un-derstand such things, missus."

She glanced up at Lily and her eyes opened wide. She took a step closer, staring at her open-mouthed. "I don't believe it," she exclaimed. "It's her. Yerself. The one that saved me husband on the *Hibernia*." Sinking to her knees, she clutched at the hem of Lily's dress and kissed it gratefully, as though she were the pope himself. "I thought you were dead," she cried. "I was with ye at the Sheridans. Mary O'Dwyer's me name. 'She won't last the night,' they told us when they shipped us off to Boston. And I knew that I would never have the chance to say thank you for what you did. But I lit a candle for your soul, missus, in St. Stephen's. And I've kept you in my prayers ever since. And now there's been a miracle."

Lily stared at her, horrified. She thought at first she must know about the baby, but she quickly realized the woman could not have known that she was pregnant. No one had known, not even the Sheridans until she had told them herself. She breathed a sigh of relief. There was no danger of John finding out. But she remembered her own struggle to survive, and asking for a job just the way this woman was now, and her heart was touched.

"I don't want you to be my kitchen maid," she said. The woman looked disappointed and scrambled to her feet. Red-faced and clinging to her dignity, she said, "I'm sorry, missus, maybe I shouldn't have said what I did. I didn't mean to be impudent, I just wanted to thank you."

"Instead, I want you to be my personal maid," Lily said. "You will look after my suite of rooms. You will take care of my clothes and you will accompany me when I go out shopping. I shall provide a uniform and because of your special position and the fact that you will not be living in and getting the benefit of free room and board, I will pay you extra." She hesitated, torn by a dilemma. She wanted to help her but she knew she could not pay her more than her husband earned because the man would lose face. She said, "I will pay you ten dollars a week."

The woman stared at her, saucer-eyed. She would have thought herself lucky to earn five dollars a month scrubbing floors. She didn't know what to say, and she twisted her chapped hands together, fighting back tears of gratitude. "The Lord will surely bless you for your brave heart and yer charity, missus," she said when she could finally manage to speak.

Lily shrugged. She did not think the Lord would be that kind to her. "You will call me Mrs. Adams or ma'am," she said, giving her twenty dollars' advance on her wages and telling her to start the next day.

Lily had as much need for a personal maid as for a banquet chef, but at least she had done something for her countrywoman, and she felt good. John was a very rich man and she was in a position to help others. And who needed help more than her own people? The more she thought about it, the more she liked the idea, and she started planning how to get her husband's support.

That night, she wore John's favorite deep-blue velvet dress and the sapphire pendant earrings that had been his grandmother's. She had ordered the cook to prepare his favorite dishes and after an enjoyable dinner she coaxed her husband into donating ten thousand dollars each year to help her starving countrywomen. The money was divided between the Irish wards and a check sent to each ward boss, with the request that the Adams name not be mentioned and that Mrs. Adams had specifically requested that the Irish women receive help.

That annual ten thousand had brought aid to many destitute women for four years now. And during that time Mary O'Dwyer had turned into an excellent lady's maid. Her husband drove the delivery wagon for Daniel's on Clarendon Street and they considered themselves fortunate people. They rented a better house on the fringes of the slums and, thanks to Lily, their children were well fed and warmly dressed in winter and all but the youngest attended school.

But time still passed slowly and even though the sap was rising in the trees on this spring afternoon, Lily felt as though the blood were drying up in her veins.

THE SAME MORNING that Ned Sheridan was thinking gloomily about the prospects of his opening night, Lily read his name in the theater column of the *Boston Herald*. NED SHERIDAN FORGOES SHAKESPEARE FOR MODERN DRAMA, the headline ran. The newspaper shook in Lily's hands, so much so that her surprised husband glanced up and asked her if she was all right, but she scarcely heard him. She was too busy reading about what a great actor Ned was, about his superlative Hamlet, and his tragic Lear. "A star among stars," the article called him, "and a brave man to take a risk with a new play by an unknown young author."

Lily remembered his telling her that he would be a star one day. It was when he had asked her to marry him. And she had refused, because it would have meant keeping the baby.

She thought wistfully how full and happy his life must be compared to her own lonely existence, and she knew nothing on earth was going to keep her from seeing him.

She said, "I'm going shopping, John."

"Whatever you like, Lily."

"In *New York*," she added.

"New York?" he repeated with astonishment.

"There's a new designer, a woman from London, the latest thing . . . besides, the change would do me good. I'm bored. . . ."

He was immediately sympathetic, guilty about his own preoccupations. "Of course we shall go to New York. We'll stay a few days, do whatever you want. Next week perhaps, or the week after."

"I'm going now, John. Today. And I shall go alone. You would not enjoy trailing around shops and dressmakers. Besides, the change will do me good. I shall be quite safe, I shall stay at the best hotel." Lily added before he could say no, "And I shall bring you back a present."

Two hours later, she was on the train to New York, alone. She took a suite at the Fifth Avenue Hotel and asked them to send up a maid to unpack her things. Then she took a long, scented bath and dressed as carefully as if she were going to meet a lover, in silk stockings and high heels and a black lace dress with a low, wide neckline and long, tight sleeves. The maid hooked the dozens of tiny satin-covered buttons and gazed admiringly at her in the mirror as she swept up her black curls and pinned them with a scatter of diamond stars. She added long diamond earrings but decided against a necklace. She flung on a black velvet wrap edged thickly with black fox, checked her appearance in the mirror, then took a cab over to Broadway.

The theater foyer was thronged with noisy, laughing, expensively dressed people and she smiled, feeling in her element again. And people turned their heads to look admiringly at the beautiful woman all alone in the crowd. Of course there were no tickets. "Not for a Ned Sheridan opening night," they told her.

Undaunted, she made her way around to the stage door. The doorman eyed her up and down, then he took off his cap and stood up. "Can I help you, ma'am?" he asked respectfully.

"I am here to see Mr. Sheridan."

He shook his head doubtfully. "Mr. Sheridan doesn't see anyone, ma'am, not on opening nights. Not till after the show."

"He will see me," she said confidently. "Tell him Lily Molyneux is here."

"Yes, ma'am." Still shaking his head doubtfully, he pushed open the heavy black door and disappeared inside, leaving her shivering with cold and excitement on the sidewalk.

Harrison Robbins answered the knock on Ned's dressing room door.

When the man told him in an urgent whisper that Lily Molyneux was waiting to see Mr. Sheridan, he stepped hastily outside and closed the door quickly behind him.

"Lily Molyneux?" he repeated incredulously, even though he had always thought she'd turn up one day. And, true to his perception of her as "trouble," she had shown up at the worst possible moment, on a first night, twenty minutes before Ned was due onstage.

"Tell her Mr. Sheridan can see no one before the show." But then he realized Lily was not the sort to take "no" from a doorman for an answer. "I'll tell her myself," he said, striding purposefully along the drab corridor.

Lily swung around, a smile lighting up her face. "Oh," she said, disappointed. "You are not Ned."

She walked toward him and Harrison knew immediately why Ned had fallen for her. Though the theater world was full of beauties, Lily was easily the loveliest woman he had ever seen. There was an alluring feminine grace in the tilt of her head and the question in her wide eyes and the half smile on her lips. Even her voice was soft and musical.

"I was hoping to see Ned," she said, clutching the fur at her throat.

She was sure to be all the trouble Harrison had thought she would be and more, and he knew there was nothing he could do about it. He couldn't keep her away from Ned, and he knew when Ned saw her, the poor sap would be a goner. Lost in love for Miss Lily Molyneux. Again.

He said, "Ned can't speak to anyone before the show. You understand, don't you? He has a very difficult role. He needs to concentrate and you would only distract him."

"I'm an old friend," she said quickly. "But of course I won't disturb him. I would have liked to see the play but there are no tickets."

"At least I can take care of that for you." He escorted her back to the foyer and told the usher to put her in Box C, as his personal guest. He told Lily he would come for her after the show and hurried back to Ned's dressing room.

FINN O'KEEFFE HAD BEEN KEPT LATE at the office and it made him late for the theater. There were problems in the financial world, rumblings of bank failures and a recession and, unlike many others in his profession who claimed it was all scaremongering and that there was nothing to worry about, he was concerned. He had stayed late especially to speak to Cornelius James about a disquieting bit of information he had received from a fellow at one of the big banks, about the rumored insolvency of a major company, but Cornelius didn't seem too concerned.

"It happens every few years, Finn," he had said calmly. "Everyone gets panicked, the market goes wild for a few weeks, shares fall, and everyone predicts the end of the world. Then everything's suddenly 'all right' again, and all the smart fellows who've bought on a falling market sell again at the inflated price and make a killing. It's a good ruse, while it lasts."

But Finn still had an uncomfortable hunch that all was not well. When he picked up Jessica Tyrone, his date for the evening, at her family's mansion on Fifth Avenue, it was still on his mind, and he apologized for his lateness.

"I understand, boy," her father said. He was an Irishman from County Kilkenny who had made it rich fifteen years before, striking oil after spending half a lifetime scrabbling across deserts and rocks. Now he had built himself a grand mansion on Fifth Avenue, with fifteen marble bathrooms. He had three daughters of marriageable age and he looked very favorably on young Finn O'Keeffe.

Jessica was blond and pretty enough, though not a great beauty. But she was a "catch," and her father liked the fact that Finn was Irish and handsome and doing very well for himself in an area few of his countrymen had yet penetrated: the closed, narrow world of Wall Street and banking. And he also liked the fact that he was an Irishman who had made it with his brains instead of the sweat of his brow.

The auditorium was in darkness and the first act had already begun when Finn escorted Jessica into their box to join a group of her friends. All eyes except his were fixed on the star, Ned Sheridan, whose mesmerizing voice filled the big theater.

Finn simply could not concentrate on the play; he thought restlessly of what Cornelius had said and how he should believe him, but something in his gut was telling him no. He knew it would be going against Cornelius's rules and the advice he had just given him, but he was determined to gamble on his own hunch. That was the way he always operated and he had not been wrong yet. Tomorrow he would dump the shares of certain companies everyone but he himself believed were sound. If he were wrong, he would lose clients as well as cost his company a fortune: and Cornelius had just gone out of his way to tell him that he was wrong. But if he were right, he would save their fortunes.

The play seemed interminable and when the final curtain descended, Finn applauded with relief. The audience rose as one to give

Ned Sheridan a standing ovation. Jessica whispered to him about how wonderful Ned was and he nodded politely, though he had not heard a single word of dialogue.

He thought the audience would never stop clapping and let him go home. His eyes wandered restlessly over the auditorium, stopping interestedly to look at the woman alone in the box opposite. She was half in shadow, but there was something eerily familiar about her profile and the proud way she held her head and the curve of her long neck. He shrugged; she was just another beautiful woman; New York was full of them. But he liked beautiful women and he watched her. He caught a glimpse of her face as she flung a fur-trimmed wrap over her shoulders and turned away.

It was a face he knew intimately in his dreams, in all his lost hopes and in his memories. He told himself that it couldn't be, that it was just a trick of the light. He was looking at his dream. His love. His nightmare. He was looking at Lily.

"Is everything all right?" Jessica asked concernedly.

Finn stared blankly at her, as though he had forgotten she even existed. Then he remembered they were supposed to be going to Sherry's for supper. He told her quickly to go with her friends, that he had to get back to the office to take care of something urgent.

He pushed his way through the throng on the red-carpeted stairs down to the foyer, glancing urgently around. He grabbed an usher and, pressing ten dollars into his hand, asked him to find out quickly who the lady alone in Box C was, and if anyone knew where she had gone, but the man came back with the news that she had been given the box at the last minute and no one knew her.

Finn clenched his fist and slammed it into his palm. He could swear it was Lily, he *knew* it. She was in his heart, his head, and his guts, and he knew it was her just the way he knew about those stocks. He walked out into the cold night street, hands in his pockets, shoulders hunched against the wind, watching the departing crowd, hoping he might see her, but soon everyone was gone and he was alone on the windswept sidewalk.

He walked to Delmonico's and bought himself a glass of whiskey at the bar. His face was pale and tense and the barman, who knew him well, said concernedly, "Are you feeling all right, Mr. O'Keeffe? You look like a man who's just seen a ghost."

Finn's troubled gray eyes met his. "You are right, Mack," he said bitterly. "You are so right. Only it wasn't a ghost. It was a demon."

CHAPTER
36

HARRISON ROBBINS OPENED THE DRESSING ROOM DOOR, but Lily put her finger warningly to her lips and stood there for a moment, watching Ned. He was slumped tiredly in front of his mirror. Lucky was standing next to him, smiling with relief that the dreaded first night was over and it was another big success.

Ned lifted his head and looked in the mirror. He looked beyond his own face to Lily in her black lace gown, with the black fox-fur wrap slung over her elegant shoulders and diamonds winking in the light, almost as brilliant as the tears standing in her blue eyes. He did not say a word. He turned from the mirror, staring at her. Harrison saw their eyes link and it was as though there was no one else in the room, just Lily and Ned.

He glanced at Lucky, and could tell from the expression on her face what she was thinking: that in their four years together, Ned had never looked at her quite like that. As though no one else existed for him, no other woman in the entire world. Lucky put a hand to her trembling lips, on the verge of tears, and Harrison felt a rush of pity for her. He knew, just as she did, that it was all over for her.

Ned took Lily's hand. He put it to his lips and kissed it. He held both of her hands in his and stood looking at her, marveling. "You have come back," he said, his beautiful voice gruff with emotion.

"I had to see you," Lily said simply.

Without looking at either Harrison or Lucky, Ned took his overcoat from the rack and flung it over his shoulders. His dresser hurried across with his white scarf and his hat, and he put his arm around Lily's shoulders and they walked from the dressing room without a word of explanation or a backward glance.

Lucky watched them go, her hand still on her trembling lips, and a stricken expression in her eyes. She had looked pretty in a pale-pink silk dress, filled with excitement and animation, but with all the color gone from her face, she now looked washed-out and ill.

Harrison said hurriedly, "She's a very old friend. Ned's family have known her for years, but she has been . . . she's been traveling. I think Ned didn't even know if she were dead or alive. I guess he's so overcome by seeing her again, he just plain forgot about you and me and the opening night party." He picked up Lucky's little chinchilla jacket and helped her into it. She was stiff with shock and he had to bend her elbows to get her arms into the sleeves.

"We shall go on to Sherry's," he said, adding confidently, "I guess Ned will join us, if he's not there already."

But Ned was not at the party, and he did not show up later. In fact it was said on Broadway that it was the first time a star had not attended his own opening night party, and the fact that the play was such a huge success made it all the more curious.

Harrison made half a dozen different excuses: that Ned had succumbed to a bad headache, that he had a sore throat and was afraid of losing his voice, and that he was exhausted. He asked everyone's understanding and promised to throw another party the following night. Somehow, no one believed him and rumors flew about a bust-up between Harrison Robbins and Ned; about a fight with the author; about a row with the management; about a breakup with Lucky, who looked like a woman who had awakened from a bad dream and found herself still in it.

Ned and Lily clung to each other in the hansom cab, laughing and crying, murmuring, "I never thought . . . I can't believe it . . . How wonderful it is . . . I'm just so glad, so happy . . ." They did not need to finish their sentences, they only needed to look into each other's faces to see how happy they were to see each other again. Back in Lily's suite at the Fifth Avenue Hotel, she shrugged off her fox-trimmed wrap and stood smiling at him.

"I don't remember you like this," he exclaimed. "You were a pale, half-drowned waif. And now look at you." He shook his head, marveling at her in her black lace and diamonds. "You've become a great lady."

Lily laughed. "I was never humble," she reminded him.

"You must tell me everything." He grabbed her hands again and led her to the sofa.

He ordered champagne, and waving away the waiter, he opened it himself and poured her a glass. "A toast," he said, smiling into her exquisite blue eyes, "to the wanderer's return, to my darling Lily, to my wife-to-be."

Lily put down her glass with a sigh. "I think I had better tell you Ned, that I am a married woman." He stared at her with disbelief as she told him about John and her life. "I'm dying of boredom," she cried passionately. "Oh, Ned"—she flung herself into his arms, the pent-up tears of years of despair spilling from her eyes—"the blood is drying in my veins because I'm starved of youth and life and music and laughter. My life has shriveled to nothing. I'm still young. I need people and love and excitement. Whatever shall I do?"

Ned wrapped his arms around her, holding her in a grip so tight she knew he would never let her go. "I'll help you, Lily," he promised, kissing her scented black hair and her soft, wet cheek. "I shall find a way. You know I shall always look after you." Her skin smelled of violets and her lips were soft under his kiss and she melted into his arms like ice under the sun. And he undressed her and made love to her with the trembling, passionate adoration of a man who has at last found the woman of his dreams. And all Lily's old terrors faded, and the scars on her heart left by Dermot Hathaway began to heal under his tender kiss and his loving touch.

Only later, lying awake in his arms, did the guilt and tears return, because she knew her husband was a good man who adored her, and she was cheating on him. But as she always had done, she acted first and regretted later.

Still, she couldn't bring herself to return to Boston when she had said she would; she delayed her journey once and then again, telling her husband that she had met old friends and was enjoying herself. John thought about how he was always preoccupied with his work, and how badly his relatives and friends had treated her. And he smiled indulgently, just the way her father had, and told Lily not to hurry back.

Ned moved into the suite next to Lily's at the Fifth Avenue Hotel and Lucky packed her things and moved out of his apartment. When Harrison told him she had left, Ned felt pangs of guilt and told him to make sure she had a nice apartment and enough money. But Lucky was lonely; her hopes and dreams of being Ned's wife were gone. She had no friends of her own: everyone she knew was through Ned. Her life had revolved around him, his routine, his needs, his wants, and his work. Without him she had nothing.

A few months later, Lucky's body was fished from the East River. It had been in the water for several days, but no one had reported her missing or questioned where she might be. No one had even missed her. She was finally identified from the furrier's label on the little chinchilla jacket she was wearing, and it was traced to Ned Sheridan, who had bought it for her. Harry identified the body and the first taint of scandal touched Ned when the news hit the tabloid headlines: Ac-tor's Mistress Found Drowned In East River.

Ned mourned for his poor little "stray lucky black kitten" who had reminded him of Lily. He told Lily what had happened and how bit-terly he regretted her death. But he had promised her nothing and now he had Lily and she was all that mattered. Lily was horrified to learn that she was the cause of the girl's death, and she wished she had never gone to the theater that night, because though she loved being with Ned, she knew she didn't love him. Not the way Lucky had.

When he saw Lily at the theater, Finn O'Keeffe forgot all about his hunch that all was not well with a certain large public company, and the disturbing rumor of a bank failure. He did not dump his clients' shares in the company, and he did not remove his own or his clients' or any of James and Company's money from the bank. A week later the company crashed amid howls of pain from its investors, and simultane-ously the bank closed its doors and his clients lost a fortune and so did James and Company. Cornelius said gloomily, "You should have taken your own advice, lad, and not listened to me."

"I was going to," Finn said, staring morosely out of the window, his hands thrust deep in his pockets and his head bowed.

"Then why didn't you? Was it because of me?" Cornelius sighed deeply, regretting his words. "Maybe I'm getting too old, Finn. I'm losing my touch, my instinct for the market. Maybe I should be hand-ing the reins over to the younger generation."

Finn turned from the window and looked at him. Cornelius was offering him an unheard-of opportunity. If Cornelius left, he would become the youngest head of a Wall Street brokerage house. A few short weeks ago he would have felt on top of the world. He would have said triumphantly that life could offer him nothing more. That he had achieved his ambitions and all that was left was to make more and more money. Now he felt nothing. The position was being offered only because he had failed to do what he knew he should have done, and Cornelius was taking the blame.

And right this minute he did not care about the position. All he could think of, all he had thought of, all he ever wanted to think of, was finding Lily. Though what he would do once he had found her, he did not yet know. Make love to her? Marry her? Kill her?

He told Cornelius that it was not his fault. That he alone was to blame for the losses and that Cornelius should not think of quitting when the chips were down. "You've had a long and honorable career on Wall Street," he said. "You can't leave now, when things are bad. You have to leave on top, the place you've always been and the place you belong."

Cornelius knew he meant every word. He smiled paternally at him. Finn had turned out to be more than just a business and social experiment; he had more than fulfilled his potential and he had not lost his values on the way. So Cornelius agreed that it was better if he stayed on and he treated Finn even more like his own son than a clever young employee to whom he had given a chance.

FINN PUT A PRIVATE DETECTIVE ON LILY'S TRAIL. He was a thickset, red-faced, secretive-looking man and he came well recommended for his skill in seeking out errant husbands or wives for juicy divorce cases. The theater where Finn had seen her was his only clue, but it was more than enough, and the man was back before too long with the information that the woman in question was Mrs. John Porter Adams, that she lived in Boston, and that she was Ned Sheridan's new mistress. She traveled back and forth between Boston and New York, spending more time with Ned than she did with her rich upper-crust academic husband at their splendid home on Mount Vernon Street.

Finn paid the man off. He was alone in his office and he thought of Lily in the actor's arms and groaned out loud. Then he thought of Lily's unsuspecting husband, and he knew she had not changed her old selfish ways. But goddamm it, she was the woman in his head, the girl in his heart, the wound in his guts.

The name Lily was engraved on his heart, and it would be until the day he died. But that didn't mean he was not going to seek his revenge. It would take time. He had to plan it out carefully. First he needed more money. He needed to be richer than John Porter Adams. Richer than Lily. Then he would make his move.

STATE SENATOR DAN O'KEEFFE WAS SURPRISED to see his brother in Boston, because they were both such busy men leading such complicated lives that there was little time for family get-togethers. If Finn worked fourteen hours a day, then Dan worked the full twenty-four. He spent the normal working days at the State Senate, and put in extra hours seeing his constituents. Whenever he found free time he would make a surprise call on one of his shops, to check on how things were being run, and so far he had no complaints. As his fame grew, his business boomed. He had opened six more shops in different cities, the first two in New York. He stayed up thinking about politics and business when he should have been sleeping, and he often had his best ideas over a glass of whiskey at the Telegraph Inn, or immediately after making love to the particularly attractive cigarette girl, in one of the upstairs rooms set aside for such a purpose.

Dan was discreet: he never gambled though there was an illicit roulette wheel at the inn, nor did he ever make an overt play for any girl. He was a big, handsome man and there was no need; girls found his good looks attractive and his Irish blarney and fund of stories entertaining.

"It's like this," he told Finn, who had warned him to be careful because as a state senator he was a target. "I'm a fella who likes a drink and a fella who likes women. My problem is that all the girls I meet socially are 'good' girls. They come from good Catholic families and they all want to get married. I'm not ready yet to set my feet on the path to the altar. So what alternative does the Lord leave a fella like meself, virile and in his prime? But I'll tell you this, Finn, give me a choice between a woman or politics, and I would choose politics every time. Set me up with the most charming female in Boston and then tell me there's a caucus out in Pokestown, and I'll be at that caucus. I can take women or leave 'em. And when the day and the woman comes along that I cannot, then I'll marry her."

He glanced conspiratorially at Finn. "And I'll tell you something else, brother. A secret I've been keeping, but now you're here I can tell you; I intend to run for the congressional seat." He laughed at Finn's astonished face. "Your old brother is entering the race for Democrat candidate to the House of Representatives, boyo. Whoever would have thought it? 'The boy wonder' they're calling me over at the State Senate House. Sometimes I think maybe what our old dad said was true: that we are descended from the High King Brian Boru. Or where else are we gettin' our brains?" He grinned. "But I shall need your help, Finn. I'll need all the support I can get. Are you with me, brother?"

"I'm with you," Finn promised. He had come to Boston to catch a glimpse of Lily, because he could no longer keep away. He had been working twice as hard as he had before, throwing himself into the race to make money. He thought of little else but his goal, and when he took time off to play in order to keep his sanity, he no longer escorted the darling daughters of New York's rich men to the opera. Instead he sought out chorus girls and the dancers in cheap Broadway bars, who were jolly and happy-go-lucky and no strangers to hardship, and who were therefore eager just to party and make love and forget their problems for a little while. Exactly the way he was himself.

Finn drove through Beacon Hill and up and down Mount Vernon Street observing everything. The house where Lily now lived was very imposing and he thought of another time he had seen Lily, on the *Hibernia,* with nothing to her name but her clothes and the fifty gold sovereigns and the diamond love-knot necklace he had stolen from her. His fingers closed around it now in his pocket. The stones were cool under his fingers, as hard and bright as Lily herself.

As he watched, the door opened and a man came out. He stood on the steps for a minute or two, blinking in the strong sunlight, and Finn saw that he was older. He was well dressed but not in quite the same carefully smart way Finn was himself, yet somehow, with his very casualness, he bore the stamp of wealth.

Finn waited. The long, tedious hours ticked by, but still the black lacquered front door did not open. Noon came and went, then one and two. Just before three o'clock, a violet coach pulled in front of the house and on the stroke of the hour the shiny black front door opened again and Lily emerged into the sunshine.

Finn's eyes fastened on her like a hawk on its prey. She was exactly the way he remembered: tall, slender, graceful as ever. Just the way she turned her head, lifted her chin, smoothed her skirt, filled his head with a thousand memories. The look of delight on her face when she patted the pair of dapple-grays as she gave them a cube of sugar and, typically Lily, tucked a bunch of violets into their harnesses, made him smile. She stood for a while, gazing up and down the empty street, and then with a huge sigh she climbed into her open carriage and drove past him down the street.

Finn followed at a discreet distance. She drove to a jewelry store on Boylston and emerged half an hour later with a small parcel. She waved the coachman on and walked unhurriedly along the street, looking in shop windows, a little smile on her face. He was puzzled by the fact that she did not look like an unhappy wife embroiled in the throes of an affair with another man. Lily looked like a happy woman.

Then she climbed back into her carriage and drove through the streets of Beacon Hill back to her home.

As she walked up the steps the door was opened by a maid, then it closed. Finn was left on the outside once again. Shut out from her life, the way he had always been.

He stayed a few days longer in Boston, helping Dan plan his campaign and talking over the financing of the new shops Dan was planning on opening in Chicago.

Dan told him about his other new project. "I'll never forget, Finn lad, when we first came here, all those little Irish kids thronging the streets, trailing helplessly after their mothers, freezing in winter and broiling in summer, with no escape from the miserable disease-infested North End slums. Now I'm planning on doing something about it. I've raised the money and I'm building the Dan O'Keeffe Summer Camp for Catholic Children.

"They're nothing but simple wooden shacks on the shores of a lake, but it's a beautiful spot in the heart of the countryside. It's surrounded by farms and those poor kids will have enough fresh air to last them through the winter. They'll have good food in their little potbellies, because they are all potbellied from malnutrition. They will eat good fresh brown eggs laid that morning on the farm, and vegetables and fruits grown on the spot. Sure and thanks to the money I've raised, they may even have cake." He paused and looked at Finn, seeing he was impressed.

"And this is the clever part, old fella," he said. "The North End is no longer just Irish, there's every nationality now. Italians, Poles, Germans. You name it. All the immigrants are here. So I'm not doing it just for Irish children. It's for children of all nationalities."

Impressed, Finn looked at his brother. He admired not only Dan's dedication and his good motives in forming the summer camp, but also his good thinking in not limiting it only to Irish children. By opening it to all Catholic families, Dan would endear himself to every struggling immigrant parent in Boston and they would be sure to give him their votes. So he was doing good and gaining himself a place in Congress at the same time.

Finn did not tell Dan about Lily and he did not go to spy on her again, because he did not trust himself not to act like a fool. Instead, he went back to New York and flung himself into his work, dedicating himself to making money. Because it was the only thing that would make him Lily's equal.

CHAPTER
~~~~~~~~~~~~~~~ 37 ~~~~~~~~~~~~~~~

BACK HOME AT ARDNAVARNA, Ciel lived for Lily's letters. Especially now that they were filled with fresh excitement, all about her busy new life, dashing between Boston and New York, going to theaters and to parties and buying new clothes. And they were also full of Ned Sheridan, the handsome young actor whom she had remet quite by chance in New York. In fact Ciel thought it most odd that Lily's letters were more often about Ned and New York than they were about her husband and Boston.

Ciel was twenty years old. Her seventeenth birthday and debut year had passed without comment from her father. There had been no celebrations, no portrait, no parties. And no diamond necklace. She doubted he even remembered, he was so wrapped up in his own world. Ever since she had left the Paris school at sixteen, he had kept her firmly out of sight at Ardnavarna, while he spent most of his time in London, dozing the afternoons away on the red leather-covered benches of the House of Lords, or playing cards at his club.

Ciel minded not going to all the wonderful London parties and having the same kind of fun her friends were having, but it wasn't quite as bad as it might have been because at least now William was home, running the estate instead of their father. And she had her dogs and the horses and there was always the hunting season, when everybody came home to their big houses for balls and supper dances. She would make occasional forays by train into Dublin to buy new clothes, charging them to her father, and she was always smartly turned out, whether it was in the hunting field or at a dinner party, and she admitted to William with a grin, there were a few young men who seemed to enjoy her company.

William took his nose out of his book and really looked at his little sister for the first time in ages. They lived in the same house and ate all their meals together, but his head was too full of other important things, like the eclipse of the moon or the migrating habit of the Canada goose, to make polite conversation or listen to her girlish gossip, and he almost never really "saw" her. She was just there, the way the dalmatians were, underfoot and usually a nuisance.

"You're almost as tall as I am, Ciel," he said with surprise.

"Taller," she said promptly. "*And* I've got a good figure."

William was no expert on girls, but he thought his sister was fairly good-looking. "You're no beauty," he said honestly, "but you're not bad."

Her laugh rocketed from the rafters. "Well, that's a left-handed compliment if I ever heard one. But you're right, I'm not beautiful. Not the way Lily was. Still, men don't seem to mind. I think they quite like me."

She went to look at herself in the ornate gilt-framed mirror over the chimneypiece. Her red hair was long and curly, and usually tied back with a ribbon because that's as much as she could be bothered to do with it. And there was just so much of it, and it was so shiny and vigorous, it seemed to stand out like a halo around her small, pointed little face. Her eyes were large and of a dazzling blue with, thank heavens she thought, dark lashes, because she would have hated that pale-eyed look ginger eyelashes gave you. Her neck was long, her ears flat, her nose straight, and her mouth too big. Her skin was good but she had freckles, and she thought irritably that they made her look like a ginger-spotted dalmatian.

Still, there was no doubt she was a success with men; she had dozens of them as friends. They came to see her and they told her their secrets and who they were in love with, or sometimes they said they were in love with her.

She never would have thought it, but now she longed to get away from Ardnavarna. Since Lily had gone it had become a prison, full of bad memories. A place to escape from, though the only escape she could foresee was marriage. That is if her father would ever let her marry, because he seemed determined to keep her locked up—"out of harm's way," he said—so that she would not follow in her sister's sinful footsteps. And if marriage was the only escape, then she had not yet met the right man, because she was in love with nobody. Only life. And that seemed to be passing her by.

On a gloomy November Friday, wet with rain and mist, her father returned unexpectedly from London and informed them that they were going out with the hunt the following morning. Ciel and William glanced apprehensively at each other. Their father was frail and bent, he had not hunted in years, but there was an air of purpose about him they hadn't seen in a long time either.

"I have work to do, Father," William said quickly, hoping to get out of it.

"I'll take no excuses," Lord Molyneux said. "I want both my children with me."

He was at the stables early the next morning while Ciel and William were still eating their gloomy breakfast, the silence broken only by the crunching of toast. "It won't be too bad," Ciel comforted William as they strode to the stables afterward. "You can always say your horse went lame and escape early. I'll cover for you."

"William," their father roared suddenly, back in his old commanding form. "Why the hell don't you look after the horses properly? I leave you in charge and what do I find when I come back? Pegeen has a sore fetlock and Black Lad has a cough. Dammit, boy, can't you do anything right?"

He stormed around the stables inspecting the horses and decided William would have to ride a sturdy cob with a nervy disposition, while he would ride the massive chestnut hunter that Ciel usually rode. She knew from experience the chestnut was tough to handle; he had a fiery temperament and a tendency to take the lead.

"Take care, Pa," Ciel warned as he mounted the edgy beast. "He likes to run away with you."

"Don't be ridiculous," he said scornfully as they trotted from the yard and into the lane, heading for the meet at a neighboring estate. "No horse has ever run away with me yet and I'm certainly not going to allow this one to."

The air was full of mist, like floating rain and soft as silk, cutting the visibility down to a hundred yards. William glanced uneasily at the soggy ground; he knew the going would be treacherous and he sighed. He hated horses, he hated hunting, and he hated killing any living creature, but he could see his father was enjoying himself and he squared his shoulders and tried to sit properly upright, the way Finn had taught him all those years ago.

Ciel glanced back at her brother and smiled; after all these years he still looked awkward on a horse, and as they trotted around the long curving road through the parkland to their neighbor's mansion she noticed how eagerly her father rode, as though he were really looking forward to the hunt for the first time in years.

There were already a couple of dozen people milling around outside the house when they arrived. While drinking a warming stirrup cup they discussed the bad weather and the softness of the ground. The Hunt Master blew the horn, and with yelpings and shouts of excitement they scattered across the fields.

The horn sounded again; the dogs had a scent, and they were off at a gallop. Lord Molyneux was out in front, jumping the low stone walls like a twenty-year-old, with Ciel galloping eagerly behind him. William stopped to wipe the mist from his spectacles and his horse whinnied nervously. "All right, all right," he said impatiently, wondering why anyone would ever want to ride a horse. He jogged along behind, marveling at his father off in the distance, and at fearless Ciel on her own frisky hunter.

He saw someone attempt a ditch, he couldn't be sure who it was at that distance, but he saw the horse balk and the man vault over its head. "Jayzus," he exclaimed, praying it wasn't his father. He dug in his heels and set off at a gallop across the muddy field just as the riderless horse turned and charged directly at him. William veered to the left under a tree, but still the horse came at him. Then his own horse reared, throwing him backward, cracking his head against a heavy branch as he fell to the ground.

Ciel never knew what made her turn at exactly that moment: maybe it was just the old instinct to look after her brother when he was on a horse. Whatever it was, she saw the accident happen and she screamed to her father that William had fallen. "He would," was all he said.

She saw the villagers who were standing in the lane watching run toward him. As she rode quickly up they stood back, standing with heads bowed, unable to look at her.

"William," she screamed, throwing herself into the mud at his side. He was lying on his back. His eyes were closed, his round silver-rimmed glasses were still on his nose, and there was a big ugly bruise on his right temple where the branch had caught him. The soft mud had cushioned his fall but it did not matter; he had been dead before he hit the ground.

The other riders saw something was wrong and hurried back to them. They took the front door from a nearby cottage off its hinges and William was placed on it. Lord Molyneux sat astride his horse, directing the proceedings. In a bleak, unemotional voice he told them to carry his son back home to Ardnavarna.

Tears flowed down Ciel's face as she led the somber procession home, and every few minutes she looked at William, covered in a horse blanket, being carried by the villagers behind her. "I should never have let him ride that horse. It's all my fault," she said. But then she looked at her father, stern-faced and straight-backed next to her, and she knew it was all his fault for ever making William become a horseman. And she shook her head and wept for her brother.

The funeral took place the following week, on a dark, bitter winter's day with the rain turning to sleet. When William's body was placed in the family tomb and the heavy stone door finally pushed into place and locked, Ciel remembered her mother's funeral and William picking her up from the gravel where she had thrown herself. She remembered him drying her tears and brushing off her coat, and holding her hand all the way home. And she wept for her gentle, loving brother.

She wrote a long letter to Lily, telling her the awful news. "Pa bore up until after the funeral," she wrote, "but now he is in a wretched state. He sits in the library staring at the wall, saying nothing and looking a hundred years old, all stooped and with trembling hands, though I never saw him shed a single tear. But then, that was never his way, was it?

"I long to come to see you, Lily, but there is only me to look after Pa," she wrote. "You can have no idea how unutterably sad life is now at Ardnavarna. And poor darling William, who wanted nothing more than to live quietly, looking after his land, caring for his people, serving God and his country in his own unpretentious fashion; darling William is gone. Oh, why is it, Lily, that the good really do die young?"

CHAPTER
38

FINN WAS AT THE STOCK EXCHANGE before it opened and he was there when it closed, and he was in his office the rest of the time, apart from the minimum hours required for sleep so he could be up again when the world markets opened.

"He's obsessed," Cornelius James told his wife. "He thinks of nothing else. Maybe he's trying to make up for the debacle when the bank went under, and if so he is succeeding, because he has more than earned back what the company lost. He has an instinct for a good deal and money just seems to float into his outstretched hands. And that's all he seems to want. Money, money, money. He's lost his capacity for enjoying life."

"Don't forget, he was poor," she reminded him. "A man from a background like his will always think that only money can buy him happiness."

Finn took time off to help Dan with his election campaign in Boston, but he did not go to watch Lily. Still, he knew her every movement. The private detective he employed had earned himself a small fortune of his own, keeping daily watch on the beauteous and perfidious Mrs. Lily Adams, who cheated on her unaware husband, certain that he was so wrapped up in his work he would never find her out. And she was right, because John just seemed grateful that she was happy with her new interests and friends in New York. And naturally, he trusted her.

Lily fizzed with excitement when she was in New York, out and about at dinners and parties, on the arm of the good-looking famous Broadway star, but in private her guilt gnawed at her. And besides, she knew for certain that much as she liked Ned, she was not in love with him. At least, not madly, passionately in love, the way she wanted to be. It was all too smooth, too predictable, too easy. What was missing, she told herself, was *excitement.*

She kicked back the sheets late one night after they made love, and prowled, naked, to the window. She pulled aside the gold brocade curtain, peering restlessly out into the night.

"What's the matter?" Ned asked, leaning back against the pillows and lighting one of the Egyptian cheroots he had taken to smoking recently.

Lily wrinkled her nose at the pungent sweetish smell of the tobacco. "Do you have to smoke those things?" she said irritably. "You know I hate it."

"No, you don't. You always tell me how nice it smells."

"When did I say that?" she demanded heatedly. "Tell me when, Ned Sheridan."

"Oh, a couple of hours ago, I guess. After dinner at the restaurant. I seem to remember you even had a puff."

Lily stamped her foot angrily. "Jayzus," she said, "do you always have to be right? Can't we ever have a fight?"

"But I don't want to fight with you, Lily," he said, astonished. "I love you. You know that."

She pushed back her long black hair and glared at him. "Yes, but . . ." She stopped and turned back to the window again. She had been going to say "but it's so boring." And it was true. She *was* bored, and in a way she was glad that Ned was leaving the next day, taking his company on a tour across America. He had asked her to leave John, to come with him, to live with him, to marry him. He would settle for anything and she knew it. Ned would be glad of the crumbs of her love. Even when he made love to her his adoration made him treat her gently, like a porcelain doll who might break, when what she really wanted . . . Again she stopped herself, but this time it was because she did not know what she wanted. She only knew it was not this.

She saw Ned off at the railroad station the next morning. He had his own private carriage with a blue-carpeted bedroom and a brass bed, a mahogany bathroom, and a red plush parlor complete with armchairs and potted plants. "It's plenty big enough for two," he said hopefully, but she just laughed and shook her head and kissed him good-bye.

He followed her back down the steps onto the platform, reluctant to leave her, and she eyed him ruefully, her head to one side. "I shall miss you, darling Ned," she told him, thinking that she was a fool and that she should leave John and go with him after all.

"Not half as much as I shall miss you," Ned replied, then jumped back on as the train steamed and huffed and hooted and then rattled away from the platform. He leaned from the window watching, but Lily did not stay to wave. She turned and walked resolutely away down the platform, and out of his life. Again.

THE FOLLOWING WEEK, Cornelius James returned to his office after a hearty lunch taken with an old friend and colleague who had retired the previous year. "You should try it, Cornelius," his friend had said. "Look at me. Look how I am enjoying life. I have learned to play golf and lawn tennis. I go out with my son on the sailboat during weekends at Newport, and at last I have time for my grandchildren."

"You've got something there," Cornelius had replied thoughtfully. "The only thing is that I don't have a son, or even a daughter, and none of those delightful grandchildren, like you have. But Mrs. James is getting a bit frail—they say it's arthritis, stiffening of the joints and all that. Maybe she would be better in a drier climate."

Sitting at his desk he shook his head, thinking of the icy Boston winters with the snow and the rain that prevented Beatrice from setting foot outside for months on end. His sigh of regret changed to a gasp as a sudden pain in his chest took him by surprise. Telling himself he must have eaten and drunk too well at lunch, he summoned his secretary and asked him to bring a glass of water.

When the man returned with a carafe and a glass on a silver tray, Cornelius's head was resting on the leather-bound blotter on his desk in front of him. "Mr. James, sir," the man cried. He put down his tray and hurried to his boss's side and lifted him up, but he knew he was too late. Cornelius James was dead.

The funeral was held in Boston, but Beatrice could not attend because the wet weather had aggravated her arthritis and she could not walk; she could not even sit more than five minutes in a wheelchair without the pain becoming too agonizing to bear. She kissed her husband good-bye before they sealed the coffin, and watched from her bedroom window overlooking Louisburg Square as it was carried down the front steps by his pallbearers, chief of whom was her husband's protégé, Finn O'Keeffe.

Afterward, there was a reception for the mourners at the house, with sherry for the ladies and warming whiskey for the men, and small pieces of madeira cake and plain biscuits. Finn was asked to stay afterward for the reading of the will in Beatrice's sitting room.

The lawyer cleared his throat. He looked at the old lady and the young man sitting expectantly on the straight-backed Queen Anne sofa, and said, "My sole duty is to inform you of the contents of the Last Will and Testament of Cornelius James. It is very simple and straightforward." He glanced sympathetically at the widow. He had known her for many years and it was sad to see her become so quickly frail and old. "If I may be permitted, Beatrice," he said, "to offer you my deepest condolences. Cornelius was a good man and a good friend."

"And a good husband," she said with a quiet little smile.

Cornelius's will was brief and efficient.

To my dear wife, Beatrice Martha James, I bequeath half my fortune to use and dispose of as she wishes, for her comfort and enjoyment. I also bequeath her the house on Louisburg Square and all its contents and chattels to be used or disposed of as she may wish.

To Finn O'Keeffe, the young man who has endeared himself to my wife and myself by his dedication and his aptitude for hard work, his determination to better himself against all odds, his staunch friendship and the goodness of his heart, I leave the remaining half of my fortune. I also bequeath to him my business. He will take over James and Company and become its president and chairman. There are just two provisos to do with names: one is that he will never change the James and Company name and impose his own or any other. The second is that he will adopt my name on the day he becomes head of the company, and become Finn O'Keeffe James. In explanation I will say that it was the great misfortune of my wife and myself never to have a son of our own, and I would like the small vanity of allowing our name to be perpetuated through a young man we would have been proud to call our son.

"And that Beatrice, Mr. O'Keeffe, is all," the lawyer said, folding up the documents again.

Finn took Beatrice's gnarled hands in his. There were tears in his eyes as he said, "Mrs. James, I am deeply touched, but of course I cannot accept half Cornelius's fortune. The money is yours."

She smiled and patted his hand gently. "I don't need it," she told him calmly. "I have more than enough for my wants, and the Church will get what's left when I go to join Cornelius. He wanted you to have the money so you could live up to your position as chairman of his company. And he trusted you to carry on his name in the same honest and creditable way he did himself."

"I will do my best, ma'am," Finn promised.

"Another thing," Beatrice said. "I am planning on moving to a drier, warmer climate. To California. The doctors tell me it will be good for my arthritis and that I might not last another winter on the East Coast. I want to give you this house. I'm sure that is what Cornelius would have wanted."

A few weeks later she left for California and Finn found himself the owner of the house where he had once worked as the stableboy. "If only," he thought as he prowled the big, graceful empty rooms, "if only it had been Ardnavarna." But no matter. He, Finn O'Keeffe James, an Irishman and a Catholic, jumped up from the bogs and the North End slums, had achieved the impossible. He had penetrated that most exclusive old guard enclave, Beacon Hill. He was the owner of a grand house on Louisburg Square and the possessor of a fortune. And right around the corner lived his neighbor, Lily.

CHAPTER

≈≈≈≈≈≈≈≈≈≈ 39 ≈≈≈≈≈≈≈≈≈≈

JOHN ADAMS GLANCED UP from the book he was reading as his wife came into the room. It was a gloomy gray afternoon and he was surprised that she had been out on her usual drive, but she always seemed so bored nowadays. She almost never went to New York and he wondered guiltily whether he should make an effort to take her there himself. But dammit, he was so busy and there was still so much research to be done for his next book. Still, summer was just around the corner. He would whisk her off to Europe again, and maybe this time they could travel further afield, to Greece, or even Turkey. Meanwhile, at least for this evening, they would have company. That should please her.

"There you are, darling," he said, watching as she tossed her coat moodily into the waiting arms of her maid and walked across to the fire to warm her hands.

"Of course I'm here, John," she said irritably. "Where else would I be?" She turned her back to the fire and hitched up her long violet wool skirt, warming her backside, and he stared at her, amazed.

Lily laughed. "My pa always used to hitch up his coattails like this," she said. "Unladylike, I know, but it warms you quicker than almost anything I can think of." *Except lovemaking,* she thought yearningly.

"You never talk about your father," he said, surprised. "I don't think I know much about him."

"There's a lot you don't know about me," she retorted. "And none of it is the least bit important." She glanced at the French eighteenth-century clock on the marble mantelpiece, all gilded cherubs and sheaves of corn and flowers. It was very beautiful and the hands pointed to four o'clock.

"Is that all the time it is?" she exclaimed indignantly. "How can the hours possibly go so slowly?"

"Even you cannot change the passing of time, Lily," he pointed out mildly.

"And if I could I would put it back," she retorted.

"We are to have a visitor," he said. "A Mr. James. He's a relative of old Cornelius James. He just inherited his beautiful house on Louisburg Square, and along with it quite a library of rare books. He says he knows nothing about them and he wants my advice. So I invited him around for tea. At five."

"How exciting," Lily said scathingly.

"Yes, I thought so too." John beamed at her. "It would be nice for you to meet him, my dear."

Lily sighed. She supposed any old book collector was better than no visitors at all. "I'll be here," she promised as she drifted from the room.

John had to admit to himself that he could not resist the kind of challenge young Mr. James had laid at his feet. *"I know nothing on the subject of rare books,"* he had said in his letter to him, *"and I have heard, on the very best authority, that you, sir, are an expert. I beg of you, Mr. Adams. Educate me."*

He had telephoned Mr. James, glad for once that Lily had insisted on having one of the newfangled machines installed in the house, and invited him over that very afternoon.

He smiled, putting away his book as he heard the doorbell ring and the parlormaid hurrying across the hall. "Welcome, welcome, young man," he cried genially, shaking his hand and taking stock of him. He guessed James was around thirty, slender and dark-haired with a mustache and brooding gray eyes. He brought with him a breath of cold air from the street and a current of vitality and excitement, like a man going into battle instead of coming to consult an old fogy like himself about rare books.

"Glad to meet you, sir," Finn said, looking at the man who was Lily's husband, noticing his slightly shabby but good suit, his age, and the genuine warmth of his greeting. He tried to harden his heart against him.

He glanced around the room. It was lined with shelves of books and filled with drawings and paintings and dozens of glass-topped curio cabinets. Seeing his interest, John led him across and began to show him some of his treasures.

The maid came in with a tea tray and John smiled apologetically at

Finn as they went to sit by the fire. "I'm sure my wife will join us in a few minutes," he said genially. "Meanwhile, tell me about your books."

Finn told him that he knew they were old, and maybe they were even rare and valuable. But all the while he was waiting for the sound of Lily's quick familiar footsteps in the hall.

She must have had velvet soles on her shoes, because he didn't hear them, only the sound of the door opening. "Ah, there you are at last, Lily," John said. "Come and meet our new neighbor, Mr. James."

Lily thought she was going to faint; for a few seconds she was transported back to Ardnavarna and it was just she and Finn again, the two friends, inseparable as ever. She wanted to run to him, to throw her arms around him shouting joyously, "It's you, Finn. *You.* You did come back for me after all."

The color rose in her cheeks and she just stood there looking at him.

"Are you all right, Lily?" her husband asked, concerned.

"Perfectly all right," she said quietly. "It's just that Mr. James reminds me of someone I once knew. It is Mr. James? Isn't it?"

"Quite right, ma'am," he said, taking her cold hand in his. She was trembling and he smiled. "Finn O'Keeffe James, to be exact. It was one of the conditions of Mr. James's bequest," he explained. "He wanted the chairman to still be called James."

"You're very young to be chairman of a brokerage house," John commented.

"The youngest on Wall Street, sir." Finn threw a triumphant grin at Lily. He could swear there was a glitter of tears in her astonished eyes. This was his moment of triumph. It was what he had worked for, hoped for, waited for, all these long years. His heart and his belly clenched with love, even as he told himself that he hated her, that he would get even with her.

Lily's hands shook as she passed him a cup of tea, and he gave her a knowing little smile that said he had power over her. The power to tell her husband the truth and wreck her new life the way she had once wrecked his.

John talked enthusiastically about Finn's new library, but Lily scarcely heard.

"I am thinking of giving a small dinner party next week," Finn said later as he was leaving. "I would be delighted if you and Mrs. Adams would be my guests."

John quickly said that because of the pressure of work he would have to decline.

"Then perhaps Mrs. Adams would like to come alone." Lily threw him a furious glance and he smiled at her, amused. He knew that expression so well: the tightening of the nostrils, the quick glare, the feigned indifference. Oh, he knew when she was mad all right.

John glanced at his silent wife. "What a good idea—you'll enjoy yourself for once."

"On Friday then. At eight." Finn said.

Lily went to the window and watched him walking jauntily down Mount Vernon Street, and then she ran upstairs to her room and threw herself on her bed, trembling with excitement. Finn O'Keeffe was back in her life; he was living around the corner in Louisburg Square. He was rich and successful. And dammit, he was as devilishly attractive as ever.

She went over every detail of his visit, marveling at the contrast between the last time she had seen him and now. Then he had been a raving madman, black with coal dust, and now he was well dressed, suave, a man of the world on equal terms with her husband and an equal with her.

And she shivered with foreboding: she knew he was up to no good, could feel it in her bones. She had seen it in his knowing smile, in the lingering touch of his hands on hers that let her know he had the power to ruin her life. If Finn ever told John the truth, she knew he would divorce her. A Boston Adams did not suffer a trollop with an illegitimate child, no matter how well-born she was. Even her own father had thrown her out, and she knew she could not expect anything else from her husband.

She thought despairingly of all the lies and the half-truths she had told, and she sighed. It had all gone too far; there was no way to explain the simple truth anymore. The chance had gone long ago, when she was a stupid seventeen-year-old girl who thought she knew it all.

She told herself a hundred times that she would not go to Finn's dinner party. But, of course, when Friday evening rolled around, she just couldn't resist. She changed her mind about what to wear a dozen times, right up to the very last minute, tearing off the blue velvet dress she had just put on and ordering her maid to get out the red silk, telling herself if Finn wanted to see a scarlet woman, then he would get one. She put on a black corset that pinched her waist, red silk stockings, and matching gloves. She added the Adams's heirloom ruby-and-diamond earrings, necklace, and two matching bracelets. She flung a floor-length silver-fox cape over her shoulders, and then she was ready.

She glared at herself in the mirror, telling herself she was a fool for going to all this trouble for Finn O'Keeffe, and she kicked off her shoes, threw the cape onto the floor, and hurled herself despondently into a chair. She put her head in her hands, groaning. What was she doing? What was she even thinking of? She would not go. She definitely would not go.

She paced the floor, her arms folded tightly across her chest, her fists clenched. Anguished, she stared out of the window at the carriage waiting beneath the streetlight. It was a clear, frosty night and she shivered.

"Jayzus," she yelled, dashing impetuously back across the room and thrusting her feet into her shoes. She slung her fox cape around her shoulders, grabbed her little gold evening purse, and headed quickly for the door before she could change her mind.

The house on Louisburg Square was only minutes away. She walked slowly up the wide stone steps and rang the bell, shivering as she remembered arriving alone at Hathaway Castle that fateful day.

Finn threw open the door. "There you are, Lily," he said, taking her hand and drawing her inside. "Welcome to my home."

"Good evening, Finn," she said coldly. "Do I take it the pretense that we do not know each other is over?"

"It is. When we are alone," he said with a laugh. "I promise all your secrets are safe with me, Lily." He did not add "for the moment," but she read it in his eyes.

A butler came to take her wrap and she said, "It's good to see you have come up in the world. I hope you are grateful. After all, if it were not for me you would still be cutting peat from the bog and rotting your guts drinking poteen."

"So I would, Lily," he said with a quiet little smile. "And I'm thanking you now for the slur you put on my character. Thank God it took a finer man than your father to decide there was something worthwhile beneath the grime and the horse shit. I started out as a stableboy in this very house. Mr. James made me coachman, then later he gave me my chance. I never looked back. Except to Ardnavarna, in my memories. When it was just you and me together, Lily, riding our horses into the dawn."

He stared at her. She was even lovelier than she had been as a girl. Her black hair was piled in shining waves, a delicate strand or two curved around her face and at the nape of her neck, and her deep-blue eyes were brilliant with anger. His heart did the same somersault as when he was sixteen and had fallen in love with her. But he knew she had not come to beg him to forgive her. Lily had never done that, not even for her pa.

She stared around the empty drawing room. "Am I the first to arrive?" she asked, surprised.

"Why not sit here, Lily," he said, leading her to a chair by the fire. "And yes, you are the first." He gave her that old taunting smile. "And the last."

Shocked, she stared at him, then she leaned back in her chair with a regretful sigh. "I should have known it," she said. "You are still not a gentleman, Finn, despite your fancy clothes."

"And there are those of us, Lily, who suspect that despite your own fancy clothes, *you* are not a lady."

Their eyes blazed at each other for a minute, and then despite herself she began to laugh. "Jayzus, Finn O'Keeffe," she exclaimed. "Who ever would have thought it? *Just look at you.* Pa would turn in his grave if ever he saw you."

"Is your father dead then?"

"No, he's not dead, though he might as well be. But Mammie is. And William. In a riding accident."

He said, genuinely sorry, "Poor William. Even I couldn't make a horseman of him."

"Ciel stays home and looks after Pa now," she said. "He's become old and doddering. She says half the time he just sits and stares at the library walls. It's miserable for her, but she can't leave him all alone." Her eyes met his. "Oh, Finn," she whispered, "I dream every night about going back. Even though I know it can never be the same."

They gazed at each other, remembering the way things used to be. Then he stood up and said briskly, "Maybe your memories are better than mine. All I remember is the hard work and being at your pa's mercy. Whether I had a roof over my head, whether I had food in my belly, was a matter for his lordly whim. I remember when he promoted me to groom and I thought I had achieved the pinnacle of my ambitions."

He poured champagne and glanced coolly at her. "It took you to show me that there was more to my ambitions than to be a poor Irish stablelad, good with a horse and good for little else. Still, the past is the past. It's time we put it behind us, Lily. Let's drink to our future."

She looked warily at him. "Do you really mean that?"

"Oh, I mean it all right." He raised his glass.

"To the future then," she said.

"To *our* future," he corrected her, smiling as he noticed that telltale blush again.

The candles were lit in the silver candelabra and Finn dismissed the butler and said he would serve them himself. "After all," he said to Lily, "I know how. From my footman days."

"You'll ruin my reputation," she warned as the butler closed the door discreetly behind him and they were alone.

He grinned. "And then we'll be equal. An eye for an eye, a reputation for a reputation. Besides, Lily, you have no reputation to ruin in this town. I found that out soon enough." She glared at him across the table and he said, "Everyone in Boston knows about John Adams marrying his Irish housekeeper. Everyone who counts, that is, and it seems you don't count in this town. It must make quite a change for you, not being accepted."

She said defensively, "I have my own friends."

"Yes. I heard about him too." Her chin shot up and she stared at him. "Ned Sheridan," he added. "The handsome young actor."

"Ned's family took me in after the *Hibernia* sank. They looked after me like their own daughter. Ned's a good man, he's my friend . . . Oh, what's the use?" she said with a shrug. "I refuse to make excuses. I admit I married John because he was my only way out of a life of drudgery. What other way was there? And besides, he's a nice man, he's kind and gentle and I truly do love him. Only . . . ."

"Only?"

She stared pleadingly at him. "Need I explain . . . ?"

"You need never explain anything to me, Lily. I think I know you better than I know myself." He reached across the table and took her hand. "Lily, what happened to the child?"

Lily felt the blood drain from her face, from her veins, from her heart, which had suddenly turned to a lump of stone. She had trained herself never to think about the child—no one knew, except Ned, and he never spoke about it. She had buried her son in the depths of her mind, along with Dermot Hathaway. "I—I don't know," she said at last.

"You don't know? . . . But you must. Did you miscarry after the shipwreck? Did it die, Lily?"

She leapt to her feet and ran to the door, but he grabbed her by the shoulders, spinning her around to face him. "You'd better answer me, Lily," he said roughly. "We are talking of a child who almost ruined both our lives."

"I gave him away," she said limply. "I couldn't even bear to look at him. To me, he never existed."

He helped her into a chair and stood looking down at her. He said, "Tell me whose it was, so I can know who to kill for it."

She glanced up at him, frightened. She could see he meant it. "Then you must kill me," she sighed, "because I am the guilty one. I put the blame on you, the way I always did, thinking I would make it all right later." She put her head in her hands. "God, I was so naive," she wailed, "and so stupid."

Finn looked pityingly at her; she wasn't crying, and he knew it was because she had already shed her tears. He wanted to put his arms around her, but he didn't. Instead he took her hand and said, "I'm sorry. We just agreed to bury the past. Let's forget it, Lily. Let's just enjoy tonight, being together again."

She glanced at him, hoping he meant it and that she was reprieved, that he wouldn't tell her husband.

"Oh, Finn," she said tremulously. "I've missed you so."

"Aye, and I missed you. Did you ever think that you and I would be dining together like this?"

She smiled. "Never. And in your own grand house. You must be cleverer than I thought, to have achieved so much."

"I worked damned hard for it. And so did Dan. Ah, but I can tell you don't know about my brother. Surely you've heard of Daniel's stores? He started out with one and now he has two dozen, and growing all the time." He smiled proudly. "Did y'ever think Dan would turn out a businessman? You haven't heard the best bit yet. I thought you might have read about him in the Boston newspapers. He was a Massachusetts state senator, and now he's been elected to Congress. My big brother is down there in Washington, helping make policy and change laws." He looked challengingly at Lily, as though asking her to beat that if she could.

She remembered the two young Irish brothers, and how elated they had been that day in the stables when her father had promoted Finn to groom and Dan to gillie. "How clever you both are," she marveled. "I only married money, but you and Dan found the secret of success."

Finn forgot the past in the sheer pleasure of having her here, in his house, sitting opposite him, so close he could reach out and touch her. And he wanted desperately to touch her, more than anything else in the world. He sighed. Things would never change.

"Jayzus," she exclaimed afterward, flinging herself onto the sofa in front of the drawing room fire. "I'm so happy, Finn O'Keeffe, just to have found you again. My old friend."

He sat beside her and put his arm around her. "Is that all we were, Lily? Friends?"

Lily looked at his thin, handsome face close to hers, older now and with lines of experience on it; she felt his hard body against her breasts; and she looked into the eyes of the one man she knew she had always loved. The fizz of excitement traveled the length of her body from her toes to her loins to her belly to her breasts, and then to her lips as she kissed him. *"This* is what I want," she told herself, wrapping herself even closer to him. *"This is what I have always wanted. Ever since I was old enough to know about love."*

Finn's hands were caressing her and she never wanted him to stop. Dermot had almost destroyed her and Ned Sheridan had redeemed her, but Finn was the man she had always loved. She would do anything he asked, anything. Only not now.

She pushed him away. "I can't," she said shakily. "Not here . . ."

"Then come to New York."

"Tomorrow," she agreed quickly. "I'll be there."

He walked her home through the quiet, cold, gaslit streets, pausing often to kiss in the shadows. They said a formal good night at her front door and she tucked the card he had given her with his New York address into her purse.

"Tomorrow evening," she whispered. "At seven."

She saw the smile light up his eyes. "I'll be waiting," he promised.

IT WAS SNOWING IN NEW YORK, fat whirling flakes that made the sidewalks slick and decorated Lily's black hair like wedding confetti as she hurried into Finn's apartment building. She was wearing her golden sable coat and a matching Russian-style hat, and when Finn opened the door and saw her, he laughed and said that with her pink nose and pink cheeks she looked exactly like a little frozen golden bear.

"But it's you who were the bear," she said, laughing. "Don't you remember, when I made you dance for Ciel?"

"I remember," he said, unwrapping her from her coat.

"Did you ever forgive me for that?" she demanded, turning in his arms and smiling at him.

"I forgave you for that all right, and you know it."

"And . . . for everything else I ever did that hurt you?"

He shrugged. "You know everyone always forgives you everything, Lily. That's the way it's always been."

"Oh, Finn," she cried happily, reaching up and linking her hands around his neck. "I can't believe we are really here. Together again. Almost like in the old days."

"Only better," he murmured, his face in her hair, "because now you and I are equal, Lily. I can hold you in my arms. And I would never have dared do that—in the old days."

Her cold lips met his and they clung together, drinking each other in. Then she pushed him away, laughing. "I can't breathe," she complained. He began to take the pins from her hair. It reached her waist in a shining black wave and he ran his hands through it, marveling at its scented softness.

He took her hand and they walked together into his bedroom. It was dark and masculine with deep-green walls, and tall shelves filled with books. There was a Turkish rug on the parquet floor and a wide bed covered with a gold velvet spread.

Finn drew her into a circle of lamplight by the bed and kissed her again. He unbuttoned the dozen tiny buttons down the back of her soft violet woolen dress. It fell from her shoulders and she turned and slid her arms around his neck and began to kiss him. Her longing for him was like an ache inside her, she thought of nothing else, only his hands on her bare skin, holding her closer and closer.

She slipped off her chemise and stood in front of him, and he stared at her as though she were a vision. Filled with happiness, she said, "It's all right, Finn darling. This is the way it's meant to be." And she walked into his arms again and he kissed her and then lifted her up and lay her on the gold velvet bed.

Their eyes never left each other as he stripped off his clothes and walked toward her. He removed her undergarments as gently as if he were unwrapping a precious porcelain statue, and then he looked at her, naked in his bed. His eyes traveled from the tips of her pink toes, along her smooth legs past the slender curve of her hips, the deeper curve of her waist, and the delicious curves of her breasts. He saw the dusky rose flush of excitement on her cheeks and her cloud of glossy black hair spread like a cape around her. Her parted red lips waited for his kisses and her brilliantly shining sapphire eyes looked unashamedly into his as she flaunted her nakedness to him.

"You are the most beautiful girl I have ever seen," he said, taking her foot and kissing each of her perfect toes.

"And have you seen many, then, Finn?" she asked, suddenly jealous.

"Enough to compare."

She held out her arms and said passionately, "I think I have been waiting all my life for you."

They clung together, flesh against flesh, lips against lips, and she felt him tremble with desire for her. And when he finally made love to her it was with all the fire and passion she had craved from Ned. "God, don't ever stop, don't ever leave me, don't, don't," she screamed in passion, and he made love to her again.

Afterward they lay exhausted, still entwined. He lifted his head and looked at her. Their eyes locked, filled with new knowledge of each other, new intimacies, new savagery, new tenderness. "I always loved you," he said quietly. And he meant it.

She stroked his face and he kissed her hand. "And I have always loved you," she said. "I suppose I always knew it, but it was forbidden."

"No longer," he said, and she smiled.

"No longer," she agreed.

He sat up and took the love-knot necklace from the table by the bed. He dangled it in front of her eyes, smiling at her.

"Then you didn't sell it after all," she exclaimed.

"How could I?" he asked ambiguously. "After all, it belonged to you."

"And so," she reminded him, "did the fifty gold sovereigns."

He shrugged nonchalantly. "They always say evil comes to those who do evil. Somebody stole them from me."

She laughed. "Poor Finn. You just couldn't win, could you?"

"Not until now," he said, sliding the diamonds around her neck and fastening them.

She lay back on the pillows in her cloud of hair, naked but for the diamond necklace, and he smiled a satisfied little smile. "You will never know," he said softly, bending to kiss her again, "just how many times I have pictured you exactly like this." And he lay down next to her and took her in his arms, feeling like a man whose fantasies had all just come true.

CHAPTER
40

MAUDIE

Ardnavarna

WELL NOW, TODAY IS A DAY of slanting rain. The droplets running down the drawing room window obscure my view of the lawn, and I'm afraid my lovely tall daisies are being crushed beneath the torrent and the wind is wreaking havoc with the Gloire de Dijon roses, whose scent for the one month they blossom is worth waiting the rest of the year for. "Elemental," I suppose you might call our Irish weather. But it's nothing at all like that long, cold New York winter that Lily spent as Finn's mistress.

Lily told Ciel that they devoured each other with their passion that winter. Somehow she deluded her poor husband into believing she was doing charity work. She took a permanent suite at the Fifth Avenue Hotel, but she rarely used it. She was in Finn's bed in the morning when he left for his office, and she was in his bed, waiting for him, when he came home again at night. I don't know what she did in between. I don't think she ever said. It wasn't important. Except to Ned Sheridan.

Ned came back from his tour on a day when, quite by chance, Lily had just returned from a weekend in Boston and she was in her suite in the hotel. She knew she had to tell him and it pained her, but she was so wild for Finn, nothing else mattered.

She told him bluntly that it was over and his face turned gray with shock. "But I want to marry you," he said, bewildered.

"You know I would never be happy married to an actor," she said sadly. "I've told you often enough. It would never have worked, Ned.

You're always on tour, going from city to city—it's all trains and hotel rooms and cold theaters."

Stricken, he stared at her. He said, "But I am an actor. I can't change that, Lily. What else would I do?"

"Nothing, darling Ned," she said soothingly. "Your career is everything to you. It's more important than I am. And after all, who am I to deprive the theater of one of its brightest stars. Besides," she added, lying, "I must go back to my husband."

As he left she said, "We shall always be friends, Ned, shan't we? I couldn't imagine my life without you in it somewhere." And he, poor darling sap, grabbed as usual at the crumbs from her bountiful table.

"Always," he agreed, pinning all his hopes on that one little word.

But Lily had no time even for a friend, and she dropped Ned from her life again as easily as she had forgotten about her child, born on Nantucket ten years before, because all she could think of was Finn.

New York

A COUPLE OF MONTHS LATER, wounded and unable to forget her, Ned married his costar, Juliet Scott. Lily read about it in the *New York Herald.* "How could he get married?" she asked herself, bewildered. "When only a couple of months ago he was swearing undying love for me. Swearing he would always be my friend."

Then she forgot him, because she found she was pregnant. She had almost felt the moment of impact when their bodies had joined together to make their child. It was all so wonderful and so completely different from the fear and humiliation she had suffered the last time that she danced around the room with the sheer joy of it.

Their affair had been going on for five months. Spring was in the air and she calculated her baby would be born in October. She would have to divorce John and marry Finn. Because that's what she wanted. To be Mrs. Finn O'Keeffe James. She could see her life stretching before her in a thousand shiny warm days of happiness.

They would buy a house in the country, because she didn't want her son raised in the city, breathing all that dirty air. And she must find a good nanny for the boy and staff for the house, and oh, there would be a thousand and one things to keep her busy.

Once they were married they would entertain properly, and who knew better than she how that was done? They would have a host of friends and she and Finn would love each other forever, just as passionately and completely as they did now. She shivered with excitement, remembering their animalistic forays in bed. Afterward they were tender with each other, but when they made love she demanded his power and passion, and she got it.

They were such a perfect match, she told herself contentedly as she took a leisurely bath, preparing for Finn's return at seven o'clock. She put on a simple dress: white with tiny blue flowers sprinkled over it. She knotted the blue sash tightly around her waist, thinking with satisfaction that she would not be able to do that for much longer. She tied back her hair with a matching ribbon, splashed on her spicy oriental cologne, and pinned a bunch of violets at her shoulder. She stared at herself in the mirror; she looked like the seventeen-year-old girl she had once been.

She heard Finn come in and she ran from the bedroom to greet him, her face alight with her secret. She was enchanted by the new life she saw in front of her and she couldn't wait to tell him all about it. He was Finn: her childhood friend, her confidant, her morning-racer across the strand at Ardnavarna. He was the only man in the world who truly understood her, and their new life together would rise like a phoenix from the dead ashes of the past.

She told him excitedly about the baby and her plans for their new life and he stood by the window, staring down into the street as though she were talking about someone else. "And I'm sure it will be a son," she said happily. "I feel it in my bones."

Finn knew the moment of truth had finally arrived. Even when he was with her, he had never allowed himself to forget the wounds she had caused him. They festered like an old sore constantly picked at, and he deliberately kept them fresh to remind himself, when the time was right, of what he must do. He meant to get even with her, even if it killed him to do it.

"So," he said coldly, "then I have finally accomplished the deed I was credited with ten years ago, Lily. Now you can go back to your nice husband and bring up your child. It's as likely to be his as it is mine, and there is no way to prove otherwise. You've done a good job in keeping our little affair secret. He probably doesn't even suspect."

She stared at him, her mouth open and her eyes wide with shock, and he added the final knife thrust. "I'll not be marrying you, Lily Molyneux. You're too grand for the likes of myself."

She twisted her hands together, shaking her head in disbelief. It had to be some strange joke he was playing on her. It wasn't happening; it couldn't be true. She knew he loved her.

Finn watched her silently. He knew what she was like. Only when he had reduced her to nothing, just the way he had been, would he return to save her. And he had no doubt she would come running back to him. Then he would tell her how much he loved her, that he wanted her, that she was his and always would be. But not yet, because his wounds went deep. She always did exactly what she wanted to do, and she always got what she wanted. But not this time. Now Lily had to learn her lesson.

LILY TOLD CIEL MANY YEARS LATER that she didn't even remember how she got from Finn's apartment and back to the hotel. She couldn't even remember the journey back to Boston, only the terrible pain in her heart, and the new baby inside her. "Another bastard," she said bitterly, only this time she had thought it had been conceived in love.

She went back to her husband, her life reduced to rubble again. But somehow, being Lily, her old instinct for self-preservation asserted itself once more and she figured out a plan. She would tell John she was going to have a baby and he would naturally assume it was his. The only trouble was that since she'd been with Finn she had avoided her husband's attentions, and there was no way the child *could* be his.

She knew there was only one thing to do if she were to save herself, and she dressed in her prettiest for supper that night. She wore the perfume he liked and the blue dress and the sapphire earrings, and afterward she took him to her bed. A few weeks later she informed him, with an apprehensive little smile, that she was going to have a baby.

John Adams was delighted at the idea of being a father at his time in life—after all he was over sixty now. "They say it's never too late," he said jovially to Lily, and he wrapped her in a cocoon of comforts and presents and luxuries. He brought her armloads of flowers and huge boxes of Belgian chocolates and gave her a nightly glass of his best port wine to drink, because it was supposed to be good for the blood. He made her stay in bed late in the mornings and insisted she retire early in the evenings and he planned out her day so it was not too tiring, until she thought she would go mad from it all. And she never heard a word from Finn.

She read jealously about Ned and his new wife in the newspapers: about what a glamorous, sophisticated couple they were, a pair of glittering stars both onstage and off it. She flung the newspaper irritably to the floor. Dammit, she thought, she wished it were her. She should have married Ned, then she would have been the one basking in his fame, enjoying herself at all the parties and the opening nights. And the baby would have been Ned's instead of Finn's.

But she knew it wasn't true. She wanted Finn O'Keeffe's baby so badly she would have stayed prone in bed for the whole nine months if necessary. Because once she had her child their old battle for power would reverse itself. With Finn's son, she would be the one on top again. Burning inside with anger, she settled herself down to wait.

CHAPTER
41

NED WAS IN SAN FRANCISCO when he married Juliet. The play was a thriller and she played the murderess, stalking her prey clutching a bloodstained knife in her hand, looking like a beautiful Valkyrie with her blond hair flowing down her back. When they were together onstage their combined star-power dazzled the audience, which hung on their every word and applauded every entrance and exit.

Offstage, Juliet was not pretty: she had all the right components, but they were not arranged precisely right for prettiness. Her nose was fractionally too short and her brown eyes were just a little too small. Her mouth, though well shaped, was rather thin, and her chin a touch too pointed. Her marvelous hair was her claim to glory, long and golden and curling, with a dozen different shades in it that gave it a lively glow. When she wore it piled fashionably on top, it gave her extra inches and added a softness to her rather sharp little face.

When the tour ended, Ned took her to the island of Hawaii for their honeymoon. When they weren't fighting Juliet made him laugh, and he felt better, though he doubted he would ever be a truly happy man again without Lily.

He wasn't sure he was in love with Juliet, but he did fall in love with Hawaii and its warm tropical climate. Ned wanted to stay in Hawaii forever, but since he could not, he took his new bride home to Nantucket when the theaters closed for the summer break, and he arranged to build a summer house exactly like the one he had fallen in love with in Hawaii, on a plot of land next to old Sea Mist Cottage at 'Sconset.

He supervised the arrangements himself while Juliet fumed with boredom. She liked the Sheridan family well enough, though she thought their youngest son sulky and impertinent. "Boy" Sheridan had gone unnamed for so long after he was born that even after he was finally christened he continued to be know as "the boy," and somehow it had just stuck. The Sheridans had waited a long time, hoping for Lily to return, but eventually they had given him the name of a good Christian and the founder of the Methodist Church, John Wesley.

He was a tall, rangy lad of eleven years, with black hair and fleshy features and dark eyes that burned resentfully at the world. He attended the local school, although Alice Sheridan said he was a bad scholar and inattentive.

"Still, he's a good boy," she said, though Juliet thought she caught a hint of doubt in her voice. She told Juliet the story of how his own mother had abandoned him and that they had brought him up as their own. "Maybe we indulged him too much, the girls were always fussing over him, and I was no different," she said wistfully.

Juliet looked at Boy struggling with his homework. She could see it was a mathematical problem and she was good at math herself, so she said, "Let me have a look, Boy. Maybe I can help you."

He lifted his head from his book and stared at her. "I don't need your help," he said in a vicious whisper.

There was a such a strange, cold look in his dark eyes that Juliet hurried, frightened, from the room. Outside in the sunshine she told herself she was crazy to be frightened of an eleven-year-old. But still she shivered when she remembered the viciousness of his voice and the cold look in his eyes.

She and Ned were opening in different plays in October and Ned was in Boston for pre-Broadway tryouts when the stage manager told him there was a telephone call. He picked up the receiver expecting it to be Juliet, but it was Lily. She told him she was at home, and that she missed him terribly and would he please forgive her and come and have tea with her that afternoon.

He dropped everything, leaving the company limping through rehearsal without him, and rushed to her side. Nothing would have kept him from her, not fire, or war, or his wife, Juliet. Lily had called and so he went.

He felt on top of the world as he rang the doorbell and was ushered inside by a shy little parlormaid. She took him up a grand staircase to "madam's boudoir."

Lily was standing by the window. "I saw you coming up the street," she said, smiling. "You were almost running, as though you couldn't wait to get here."

"I couldn't wait to see you," he said. He looked at her swollen belly and he groaned.

"It's not John's," she said sadly.

He said, astonished, "Does he know that?"

She shook her head. "He believes it's his. It's better that way. It hurts both of us less."

She told him wearily about Finn and confessed what a fool she had been, and he took her hands and kissed them. He said, "Lily, it should have been our child. You would have made me the happiest man alive."

"And I would have made myself less of a laughingstock," she said bitterly. "Oh, Ned, why do I never think first? Why, oh *why*, did I have to fall for Finn? I'm such a fool. I'll just never understand love. I'll never get it right."

She glanced at him under her lashes. "Are you still my friend?" she asked hopefully.

"Forever," he said, kneeling at her feet.

The little parlormaid tapped on the door and came in carrying a tea tray. She paused, staring uncertainly at the famous actor kneeling at madam's feet. "It's all right," Lily said. "Just put the tray down over there, on the small table." They laughed as she scurried out to tell the kitchen staff what she had just seen. "I expect they are all agog to have you here," Lily said, pouring tea. "And so am I."

"When is the baby due?" He couldn't take his eyes off her, thinking that if only she were his wife, she'd be having his child.

"This week or next." She shrugged tiredly. "Though, of course, John thinks it's not for another month or so. This is going to be a 'premature child.'" She sighed, wondering bitterly when her lies and deceptions were ever going to end.

She poured tea and offered him cake and asked about his wife. "Juliet is a wonderful actress," he said, "but she has a sharp tongue." He grinned wryly. "I guess she keeps me on my toes."

"I hope you will be very happy, Ned, but . . ."

"But?" He raised his eyebrows in a question.

Lily was suddenly very afraid of losing him. "Don't abandon me, will you? Promise you will always be my friend. Promise me you will be there if I need you. I'm so lonely. So alone."

"I'll be there," he promised.

The following week Lily went into labor. It was six o'clock in the evening and John was not home. The doctor came and she swore to him that the baby must be premature, even though both of them knew perfectly well it was full-term. But it was not his place to comment, and when John finally arrived and worriedly asked if his wife would be all right even though the baby was so early, he said reassuringly that everything was going well and there was no need for concern.

John paced the library floor all night while Lily bravely gritted her teeth, fighting the waves of pain until ten hours later Finn's son was born.

John peered proudly at him, swaddled in a lacy woolen shawl in his mother's arms. "He looks like you, Lily," he exclaimed. But she knew he did not. He looked just like Finn.

One evening a week later at around eight o'clock, the doorbell rang and the parlormaid told John that Mr. James had come to see him. "Show him in, show him in," he cried, pleased.

"This is a surprise," he said, coming forward to shake hands. "To what do I owe the pleasure?"

Finn ignored his outstretched hand. He said, "I'm sorry, Mr. Adams, but I have not come here to see you. I have come here to see my son."

Puzzled, John stared at him, and then his face turned gray. He needed no explanations, he had only to remember Lily's lengthy visits to New York, her irritability with him, her seduction of him, and then the "premature" birth. He had been made a fool of and it struck at the very core of his honest, upright being.

"I cannot allow you to see Lily or the child," he said quietly to Finn. "Would you please leave? No doubt when Lily is well enough she will be in touch with you."

"I'm sorry, sir," Finn said, eyeing him sadly. John was an unintentional victim; he had not wanted to hurt him, but it was the only way.

He watched John walk to his favorite chair by the library fire and sink into it. He sat, staring blankly at the flames. His face was expressionless and he held out his hands to warm them.

Finn walked from the room, leaving him alone with his misery. He let himself out and walked around the corner to his own house on Louisburg Square. It was the end for Lily. Now he would wait for her to come to him. And he was certain she would.

Later that night John Adams walked quietly upstairs to his wife's room. She was sleeping and he stood looking at her for a while. He told himself he had been an old fool ever to think that anyone as desirable as Lily would not be stolen away from him, a man who knew and understood so little of the ways of women; a man in his sixties, set in his routine, wrapped up in his work the way he was. He had neglected her, expected her, so young and so vital, to stay cooped up here alone with no friends, no parties, not even another woman to gossip with. What could he expect but that she would fall for the first handsome young man she met?

But he still could not forgive her. He put the letter he had written on the bedside table. In it, he told her that he was going away for a while and that when she was well enough he wanted her to leave his house with her child. *"The baby's father came here to claim him and no doubt you will both go to join him,"* he had written finally.

He walked over to look at the dark-haired infant sleeping as soundly as his mother in the crib beside the bed, and he sighed a bitter, regretful sigh that it was not his. When a son had been born he had counted it the highest of his achievements, of more value to him than all his learned theses and rare manuscripts, because his son was a living part of himself.

He walked back downstairs again and shut himself in the library. He sat for a long time, thinking of the happiness Lily had brought him and he counted himself a lucky man ever to have called her his own. She had given him more companionship and pleasure the past few years than he remembered having in his whole life. And now it was over.

His hand trembled as he poured himself another glass of port, and as he sipped it the pain in his heart spread through his chest and along his left arm. His throat tightened and he felt as though he were choking. The glass dropped from his hand, spilling the wine and staining the beautiful pale rug a deep red. As he gasped for air he thought of Lily sleeping upstairs and he struggled to his feet. He wanted to take the letter back, he wanted to keep her at all costs. He just couldn't bear to lose her, no matter what she had done. The pain gripped harder and blackness was all around him and he fell to the floor, unconscious.

The maid discovered him the next morning when she went in to clean. She screamed when she saw him lying on the floor and at first she thought the stain on the rug was blood. The other servants came running and they sent for the doctor. When he arrived he confirmed that Mr. Adams had died of a heart attack and that he had been dead for several hours.

Lily had woken earlier and read John's letter telling her that Finn had been to see his son and that he expected her to leave his house. Now John was dead and she knew, because he had told her so years ago, that he had left everything he owned, including the house, to her. She cried bitter, guilty tears for him and she cried for herself. John had been a good, gentle man; he had been her anchor, her security, her lifeline. And now, because of her, he was dead.

All of Boston turned out for John Porter Adams's funeral. All those who had refused to receive him and his wife when he was alive paid their respects to him now he was dead—though they studiously ignored the veiled, aloof widow, who did not even bother to look their way. And rumors ran rife about the reason for his sudden death, especially with a son and heir just born. The servants had gossiped about Lily's absences in New York and many of those at the funeral put two and two together, though they did not know who "the other man" could be. And Lily was twice condemned by the ladies of Boston.

CHAPTER
42

DAN O'KEEFFE WAS ONE OF THE YOUNGEST CONGRESSMEN in Washington. Grover Cleveland was in the White House for the second time, and he was still embroiled in an ongoing fight with the powerful Tammany Hall Democrats. Cleveland's independent streak was turning his own party against him, but Dan O'Keeffe was also an individual who spoke his own mind and nobody else's; a man who fought not only for the Irish, but for all the downtrodden immigrants' rights, and a man as against graft and excessive tariff protection as Cleveland was himself. The president had taken a shine to him and he was often invited to dinners at the White House, both official and unofficial.

Dan thought the White House the most sublime edifice ever built. He was not born in America, so he knew he could never be President O'Keeffe and master of all its splendor, but he nurtured the hope that maybe, one day, when he got married and had children, his son might.

Congress sat for only four or five months of the year, and when the summer's heat struck Washington like a blow, Dan went back to Boston to take care of his constituents and his business. It was growing almost faster than he could keep track of. He demanded two things from his employees: honesty and loyalty. "A few brains wouldn't go amiss either," he would tell his shop managers, and he could tell the men with get-up-and-go by the eagerness in their eyes, the proud way they'd carried themselves, and the determination not to take "no" for an answer.

He paid them well and expected them to work hard and those who shirked their duties or attempted to unburden their load onto another were promptly fired, even though it meant hardening his heart to their pleas that they had a wife and nine children to support. "Maybe you'll think of that next time somebody gives you a good job," he would say coldly.

Dan's philosophy was that if a man was only ninety-nine percent on his side, then he could not be counted on for his support. One hundred percent was his yardstick, both for his employees and his friends, though it was different in politics, where points and friends were traded over the carved desks and brass spittoons on the House floor as easily as gossip.

Thanks to his brains and his own hard work he now had stores in forty large cities from the East Coast to the West. Wherever there were Irish immigrants there was also a Daniel's store. He gave the rich uptown areas employing Irish servants and cooks the same smart claret-colored uptown stores as Beacon Hill, and in the poorer areas he offered shamrock-green grottos filled with bargain goods at bargain prices, counting on mass-marketing methods to make him his profits.

He had it going both ways and he thought himself a pretty smart fellow who had come a long way from peddling watches at county fairs, though he always wore the red suspenders that had become his trademark. Any picture of him in the newspapers, or any political cartoon, inevitably showed big Dan O'Keeffe with his thumbs hooked through his suspenders and his derby hat on the back of his head and a confident grin on his face.

There had been no time in his life to find a wife and no time even to buy himself a house. He still called the two rooms over the Beacon Hill shop his residence, and like most of the other congressmen, for the few months he was in Washington he took a room at a boardinghouse. He had a substantial sum of money in the bank, his business was turning over a small fortune, and his political career was well established. And in all his life he had never had a place he could properly call his home.

As a congressman from Boston, Dan read all the Massachusetts newspapers every day and it was impossible to miss the coverage on the sudden death of one of Boston's most eminent scholars, who also happened to be a member of one of Boston's best families. He read enviously of John Porter Adams's academic achievements, of his degrees from Harvard and Oxford and the tributes from his colleagues, because the one thing that always plagued him was his own lack of education.

He read about the funeral in the *Boston Herald* and he saw that the widow, Mrs. Lily Adams, headed the list of mourners, and that the famous actor Ned Sheridan had been there to support her. And later he read in one of the tabloids that Mrs. Adams, who had given birth to a son just a few days before her husband's death, was the former Lily Molyneux from Ireland, and that she was also his former housekeeper. And that she had inherited the vast Adams fortune.

Dan pushed back his battered leather chair, propped his feet on the desk, pushed his derby to the back of his head, and stared thoughtfully in front of him. *So. Lily Molyneux has come back to haunt me again, has she?* He picked up the newspaper and read again about her fine home on Mount Vernon Street and the fact that her late husband was sixty years old when he died, and that his son had been born just a few days before.

He remembered Finn's house was just around the corner from Mount Vernon Street and he pondered the coincidence. Surely his brother could not have been so near to Lily and failed to see her? Yet he had never mentioned her. Finn lived his own busy life in New York. As far as Dan knew there were a succession of fancy ladies keeping him occupied, and Lily's name had not passed his lips in years. He didn't know whether the flame of love had turned to hate and then gone out, but one thing he did know. *He* was going to see Lily.

No matter how Lily filled the big silent house on Mount Vernon Street with flowers and kept bright fires burning in the grates, when she ate her supper alone by candlelight in the dining room it still felt like a shrine to all the dead Adamses, and not like a cheerful home for the new son and heir who would carry on their name. And, as Finn had so succinctly put it when he had reduced her life to zero again, there was no way to prove the child was not her husband's. And, as much as she had not wanted her first son, she adored her second. Sometimes, as the long lonely days dragged endlessly by, she thought that if it were not for her baby, she would have nothing to live for.

She had named her son Liam, the Irish version of her brother William's name, and John for her husband. She was getting back at the Boston Brahmins by giving the son of one of their grandest families an Irish name. She knew they would think it a great comedown in the world, while she, proudly, thought it was a leg up. *Those poor lily-livered prissy old dames could do with a bit of good Irish blood roaring in their veins,* she told herself over her untouched supper, talking to herself as she often did nowadays because there was no one else to talk to. Except the baby, and right now all he needed her for was nourishment. His nurse was an uppity woman from Philadelphia who thought herself better than her notorious employer. Lily would have sacked her but she was good with the baby, and Liam was her prime concern.

Liam was her stake in the future. She had someone else to think of now besides herself. She would take her time with him, plan his life out carefully: his schools, his college, his career, and his social life, though how he was ever going to have one with her for a mother, she didn't know. Unless she achieved a miracle between now and then.

But that was all in the future. She put it to the back of her mind and pushed away her uneaten plate of food and took her glass of wine with her into the library.

She sat opposite John's old chair with her feet on a little embroidered footstool that reminded her of her mother, sipping her wine and staring into the flames, listening to the silence and thinking how different it would have been with John sitting opposite her, planning their son's life.

She leapt to her feet at the sound of the doorbell. "Whoever can that be?" she asked out loud, because no one, unless it was the doctor, ever called at her house. She listened to the maid's footsteps crossing the hall. She heard the door open and a man's voice, and the maid asking him to step inside. She heard her cross the hall and tap on the library door.

If it is Finn, Lily told herself bitterly, *I'll kill him.* The parlormaid offered her a silver tray with the calling card of Representative Daniel O'Keeffe.

Astonished, Lily stared at the maid. "He is here to see me?"

"Yes, ma'am. He's waiting out in the hall."

"Ask him to come in." Lily patted her hair into place and nervously smoothed her skirt. She told herself that if Dan had come to plead for Finn's forgiveness she would tell him exactly what she thought of his unscrupulous brother. She would tell him that her father had been right, that all the O'Keeffes were nothing but a bunch of blarney-mouthed blackguards. With her temper rising she waited for the maid to escort Dan into the library.

He seemed to fill the room with his presence as he walked toward her, both hands outstretched and an expression that was a mixture of sympathy and delight on his handsome red-bearded face. She had forgotten how tall he was, and how big: massive-shouldered and powerful-looking. With his red hair and his beard and his commanding presence, he was as handsome as his brother, in a different way.

"Lady Lily, Mrs. Adams . . . forgive me for calling so late, and without writing or telephoning first," he said as though they had seen each other just the other day. "But I read about your sad loss in the *Herald* and I felt compelled to seek you out again and convey my sympathy."

"Spoken like a true politician, Dan," she said, reluctantly offering him her hand. He bowed over it with such social aplomb that she laughed. "The last time I saw you, you were covered in coal dust. You looked like a gargoyle on a cathedral parapet."

He smiled reminiscently. "I haven't forgotten. And you looked like a waif. A lost, lonely girl. You were only a child yourself then, Lady Lily."

"Seventeen. Old enough to know better," she said bitterly.

"Not the way you were brought up. Sheltered from the world and real life as most of us knew it, by your family's position and wealth. Bad things just didn't happen to girls like you."

She eyed him warily. "Was it your silver tongue that got you to be a congressman?"

"Sure and it was. That and the fact that I promised to fight for better working conditions and shorter hours and higher wages, and because I helped people out with their problems and their kids. You've not heard of the Dan O'Keeffe Summer Camp then? It gives poor children who live in the slums, the way I did myself, a couple of weeks of fresh country air and good food. I support it mostly myself and I raise the extra from other Irishmen who have been lucky enough to come to America and make their fortunes. In a way," he said, leveling a glance at her that left no doubt he considered himself her equal, "in a way, I have a lot to thank you for."

She remembered Finn saying the same thing and she said, flustered, "It sounds like a very worthy cause."

"Sure and now you have a son of your own you'll know what it means to be a mother, to be able to bring him up properly, and to give him the good things in life."

Her chin shot up and she glared at him, waiting for him to say it. To say that he had come here because Finn wanted forgiveness, and he wanted his son.

Dan hesitated, choosing his words carefully. "The other child, Lady Lily," he said delicately, "was it . . . ?"

"Dead," she lied quickly, turning her face away and blushing.

"I'm sorry, though I daresay you were not. And of course it was no child of my brother's."

"No," she said bitterly. "It was not." He still had not gotten to the point of his visit and she said abruptly, "Why are you here, Dan? What do you want from me?"

"The truth is, I wanted to see you again. I've never forgotten you, and I forgave you years ago for any injustice you did to me. After all, look at me now." He laughed a big, booming, jolly laugh that filled the room and she laughed, too, in relief.

"But I won't be keeping you now, Lady Lily, for I can see I'm interrupting your peaceful evening. And it's so soon after . . . afterward. Only tell me that I can come and visit you again, and I shall leave a happy man." He took her hands in his big paws again and beamed at her, and despite herself Lily found herself smiling back at him. She wasn't sure whether she was inviting trouble in by the door, but she found herself saying yes, of course she would like to see him again. She thought of Finn and added quickly, "But as I'm in mourning and not really supposed to be receiving visitors, it must be our little secret. Promise you won't tell a soul."

"Not a single soul," he said, putting his finger to his lips to seal them, and she smiled.

When he had gone she sat in front of the fire again, wondering whether she had finally gone out of her mind. She had agreed to see Dan O'Keeffe. She, his brother's ex-mistress with his brother's son asleep in the crib upstairs in the nursery. She stared into the flames, a dozen different thoughts and ideas flying through her mind about Finn and Dan, but none of them made any sense and she went tiredly to feed her son, and then to her lonely bed.

DAN WENT HOME TO HIS TWO ROOMS over the shop that night a happy man. He looked around him at the cheap, garish rugs and the ugly secondhand bits of furniture, amazed that somehow he had never noticed before how small and shabby it was. And how poor, compared with Lily's grandeur, and his own brother's. He told himself it was no place for a man in his position to be living, and it was certainly no place for a man like him to entertain a lady.

Early the next morning he went out to buy himself a home. He wanted it immediately and he wanted it complete with furniture and staffed with servants, to whom, of course, he would pay more than the minimum wage and who, he would make sure, worked only the hours prescribed by the new laws he himself had helped legislate.

It was more difficult than he thought: Irishmen, and especially nouveau riche Irishmen, were looked upon with disfavor by the upper-crust residents of the smarter areas of Boston, and even more so when they were also politicians. And Democrats. Lily had married into Beacon Hill and Finn had inherited his way in, but there was no way Dan could buy his way into it.

Back Bay was a possibility, they told him, and by the end of the day he had purchased a newly built redbrick house on a pleasant tree-shaded street. It had six bedrooms and he thought that would be plenty to accommodate his future children. He paid the large amount demanded in cash and hired someone to fix it up with the proper sort of curtains and antiques. "And make sure it's in good taste," he told them, though he wasn't exactly sure what that meant. He just knew he wanted it.

He went to see Lily again that evening and he told her about his new purchase and his instructions to the decorator, and she eagerly offered to help him. "That'll be just grand," he said, pleased. "And it'll maybe get you out of the house a bit. There's too much sadness in here, too many memories." And besides, he told himself happily, it meant now he had an excuse to call on her whenever he was in Boston.

Dan had never allowed himself to think there was ever the smallest chance with Lily, first because she was unattainable, and second, she had always belonged to Finn. Now he was a rich man. Now he was "somebody," and she was a widow with a child who badly needed a father. She was alone and vulnerable, and he was head over heels in love with her. He always had been.

He thought, happily, they were a long way from Ardnavarna. Lily had come down in the world and he had come up and now they were equals. And one day, strange as it seemed, he intended to ask Lady Lily to become Mrs. Daniel O'Keeffe.

CHAPTER
43

MAUDIE

Ardnavarna

WE WERE SITTING HALFWAY UP a hill looking out over the flat brown peat bogs to the Atlantic Ocean. An icy stream fell from some unseen point far above, tumbling past us down the hill, carving its way through piled-up rocks to join a confluence of similar baby streams in a rushing peaty-brown little river that ran parallel with the road below.

Shannon was lying on her back with her hands behind her head, gazing at the sky—blue today and dotted with puffs of cotton-wool clouds, tinged with gray at the edges, promising showers later. Eddie was lying next to her, propped on one arm, watching her, and I daresay he could see as many fleeting expressions on her pretty young face as she could see cloud changes in the sky. The dogs were circling around, enjoying the sunshine and sniffing exciting rabbit scents, and they were the only ones of us who did not appear sad.

I felt sad today, thinking of Mammie and Lily and what was to come, and I told myself briskly it was only a touch of the melancholy, a disease we Irish are prone to. George Bernard Shaw understood it, and I quoted from his play *John Bull's Other Island* to them.

"But your wits cant thicken in that soft moist air, on those white springy roads, in those misty rushes and brown bogs, on those hillsides and granite rocks and magenta heather. Youve no such colors in the sky, no such lure in the distances, no such sadness in the evenings. Oh, the dreaming! the dreaming! the tortured, torturing, heart-scalding, never satisfying dreaming, dreaming, dreaming, dreaming!"

I said, "Ciel often used to come to this place after William died, when she was left to look after Pa. And years later she brought me here to tell me about it. She said that she would come here to be alone. There would be nothing but the sky and the wind, and the occasional cry of the gulls in the distance and the flutter of a hawk overhead, and she would know she was trapped. Trapped by Pa, trapped by Ardnavarna and all its memories, and trapped by her own melancholy.

"She would gaze at the peaty bogs, the white springy roads, the misty rushes, dreaming and dreaming, just the way Shaw said. Of escape.

"And, as if to emphasize her solitude, Lily's letters were so exciting. First they had been full of Finn, how she had met him by chance, how he had come up in the world and that now he was her neighbor. And after that the baby and the terrible news that John was dead. And then Dan O'Keeffe, who was 'as handsome and charming as can be,' had come calling."

The next thing Ciel knew Lily had married him. She said she had closed up the house on Mount Vernon Street, "with all its sad memories," and she and the baby had moved into Dan's new home in Back Bay.

I thought there was no point in prolonging the mourning and making myself unhappy. And my first thought was of what was best for the baby. Dan is so kind and helpful, and he's a great success in business as well as in politics, though they are not the "right sort" of politics for my grand neighbors, the Old Guard Republican Boston Brahmins. But when he came calling in that terrible period after John's sudden death, he was like a rock I could lean on. I came to depend on him more and more, until I found I just could not manage without him.

It must seem strange to you, darling Ciel, locked away at Ardnavarna all these years with your only memories of the O'Keeffe brothers as our family servants, to think of your sister married to one of them. But this is the land of opportunity and now Dan is as rich if not richer than Pa and is helping govern his new country. What more can I say to explain?

I'm afraid that my marriage has caused a scandal on Beacon Hill, but what do I care? I laugh at their silly, fussy old-fashioned ways, and besides, why shouldn't I be happy? After all, poor John is dead and there is nothing I can do about that.

After that, she said little about Dan in her letters; they were all about her son, Liam. She said he was a beautiful boy with hair as black as her own, but that he was delicate and she worried about him in Boston's icy winters.

But Ciel didn't have much time to contemplate her sister's strange marriage, because Pa was becoming increasingly fragile. He hated to let her out of his sight even for a minute. "Where are you going?" he would demand loudly whenever she got up to fetch a book, or to walk the dogs, or to exercise the horses. "Make sure you hurry," he would call anxiously after her.

He depended on her completely: it was her shoulder he leaned on now instead of his stick; her eyes he used to read the *Times* to him every morning; her young legs that raced to fetch his forgotten spectacles, or his book, or his lemonade to be sipped in the shade of a tree on a fine hot afternoon. He had dismissed the butler, saying there was no need for the man because he did not intend to do any more entertaining, and so now it was Ciel who decanted his port and placed it on the little round Italian marquetry table by his chair in front of the study fire of a cold, dark evening, and afterward she would read to him.

She was twenty-one years old. She had many friends, but she never invited them to Ardnavarna now, with Pa the way he was. She was held fast at her father's side by invisible bonds of love and loyalty, and his fears and selfishness.

But despite his fragility Lord Molyneux had no intention of dying. One spring day he got up from his chair and said firmly, "I'm tired of Ardnavarna. I need a change. Have our bags packed, Ciel. We are going to London."

The long-neglected but still-sumptuous town house in Belgrave Square was swept and dusted and refurbished for their return, and then Pa took off for his club. He ordered new spectacles and began to read his own newspapers again; he ate lunch at the club promptly at one and then he played bridge all afternoon. He would have drinks there with his old cronies before dinner, which he always ate alone at his own special table at the club, by the window overlooking Green Park, and then, leaning on his blackthorn cane, he would hobble around the corner to a private gaming house where he would lose consistently at cards.

While Pa gambled away a great deal of his money, Ciel spent it. She threw parties and gave dinners, spending lavish amounts in the true Molyneux tradition of giving their guests only the best. Of course, it was a scandal that she was never chaperoned, but with Lily's disgrace embedded in her memory she always behaved herself, even though she was as bad a flirt as her notorious sister.

She was what the French call *jolie-laide,* a girl who was not pretty but who nevertheless was attractive. She had spirit and a joyfulness about her that attracted people to her. She had a good figure and dressed extravagantly, if not exactly in good taste. She had style; she was witty and amusing and fun to be with. She was never short of suitors, but she still hadn't met one she could think of spending the rest of her life with. Whenever Pa asked about them, looking hopefully at her and thinking of a grandson to carry on his name, she would complain that one was "too bookish," another "too horsey;" or one would be "too old," another "too young."

"There's always something wrong with them, Ciel," he roared, with a spark of his old spirit. "Dammit girl, they are all from good families, they all have houses and land and money. They are all *gentlemen.* What more does a woman want?"

Ciel looked him sadly in the eye. She said wistfully, "Oh, Pa, I don't know. I think I want love."

Freed from the melancholy of Pa and Ardnavarna, her naturally bubbly spirits suddenly rose again. "Jayzus, Lily," she wrote joyously, "I'm after kicking over the traces and having myself a wild old time, party after party after party. There are more good-looking eligible young men in this city than you can count, and quite a few of them seem interested in your little sister. But I'm not ready for marriage yet. I'm only just tasting my first freedom. Remember, I did not have a debut at seventeen like you, and ever since I left the school I've been shut away at Ardnavarna like a cloistered nun."

She spent every day happily shopping, buying all the pretty clothes she had been deprived of for so long. She even took a quick trip to Paris, where she ordered a dozen gowns from Worth and a red fox floor-length coat from Revillon that almost matched her hair; the vendeuse thought she was crazy, but Ciel loved it. She had her fizzy red curls cut by Paris's most fashionable coiffeuse and bought a dozen little hats to perch on top of her newly elegant head. She scattered her mother's heirloom diamond brooches across her bosom like glittering confetti and stuck a couple onto her hat for good measure. And she always wore her mother's famous rope of pearls, large as quail's eggs and with a massive diamond clasp, which had been a wedding present from her husband. She would waft into a party or a ball, all aglitter in her brightly colored silks and satins with a big eager smile on her

charming little monkey-face, and she would be immediately surrounded by young men.

They spent that Christmas in London and Pa was as spry and chip-
per as a sixty-year-old, despite the winter's chill. "I've finally got Ireland's damp mists out of my bones," he told Ciel on New Year's Day,
stepping firmly down the street and barely leaning on his cane. He
looked better than he had in years: there was a sparkle to his eyes and
a purpose to his step as he strode down Belgrave Square, heading for
his club, his morning coffee, and the *Times.*

It was a surprise therefore when a few hours later his friend, Dr.
Barnett, a man as old as Pa himself, called at Belgrave Square. "I'm
afraid it's bad news," he told Ciel. She stared at him, white-faced,
knowing before he even said it that Pa was dead.

"It was sudden," he said comfortingly. "He's always had high blood
pressure and I suspect it was a coronary occlusion."

Tears poured down her face. "At least he enjoyed himself these last
few months," she said. "That's something to be grateful for." And if he
had to die, then she was glad it was at his club among his friends, and
not alone at Ardnavarna with only his bad memories.

Ciel accompanied her father's body on the ferry to Dublin, and on
the long train journey to Galway and then by road back to Ardnavarna.
She had sent instructions that the house was to be cleaned until it
sparkled; that all the rooms were to be made ready for guests; that
fires were to be lit in every grate and enough food prepared to feed the
family's hundreds of friends who all showed up for the funeral two
days later. There were so many, they spilled over into the neighboring
country houses and the funeral took on a party air. The weather was
dry and crisp for once, and Pa's leave-taking was accomplished with
much lusty singing of hymns in the church and reminiscences over
tumblers of whiskey in front of a roaring fire later at the Big House.

Everyone ate and drank and talked of Pa and gossiped about their
friends, and Ciel thought, pleased, that he would have been delighted.
The house looked almost the way it used to, filled with people and
noise and snatches of laughter. Any moment she expected to see Pa
striding into the room in his shooting jacket with his favorite Purdy
shotgun slung over his shoulder, calling everyone to attention and reminding them that it was time for the shoot.

But when they were all gone it settled back into its old somber
silence and she paced from room to room in her black mourning dress,
for once without jewels. She folded her arms, wrapping them close to
her body to keep away a chill that came from inside herself, looking

around at everything, seeing it with new eyes. She, Ciel Molyneux, was now mistress of Ardnavarna. And she was all alone there.

She dashed the tears from her eyes and ran upstairs to her room. She tore off her black dress and flung on a pink woolen robe trimmed with white fur that made her look like a cross between a Russian princess and Queen Elizabeth the first, and sat down at her desk and wrote a letter to Lily.

> *Dearest Lily,*
>
> *Today we buried Pa with all the love and pomp and circumstance he would have liked and about a thousand friends as well as all the tenants and the villagers to see him off in grand style. I think he probably enjoyed it because I am sure he was there in spirit, if not in the flesh.*
>
> *And now I am left alone here at Ardnavarna and, Lily, I cannot stand it. Do you realize what Pa's death means? It means that I am free to see you again. We can be together. Oh, darling Lily, you will never know how much I've missed you. I shall book a passage on the first liner sailing from Liverpool and I shall be with you before the end of the month. I cannot wait to see you and my dear little nephew, and Dan, of course.*
>
> *Oh, and by the way, I had better tell you that Pa left everything to me, including the houses and the land. I know you won't mind because you are such a rich woman now yourself, and besides I don't even know how much the estate is worth yet, but I do know that this past year Pa was gambling heavily, so I am expecting the worst.*

A week later, with fifteen cabin trunks of clothes, two dozen hatboxes, and an immense black leather jewelry case crammed with her 'stuff,' as Ciel called it, she set sail on the liner *Etruria,* for New York, where she had instructed Lily to meet her.

CHAPTER
44

THE DAY HE HAD MARRIED LILY, Dan thought he would burst with pride and love, even though the wedding was not in St. Stephen's where he would have liked it to be because Lily was not a Catholic.

So, to avoid gossip, because it was after all only six months after John's death, they had settled on marrying in a judge's chambers in a small New England town. For the sake of discretion they drove separately to the ceremony, and to Dan's delight his brother Finn had managed to find time from his hectic schedule to act as his best man.

"Let's not tell, Lily," Finn had said when he had called with the news. "Let it be a surprise."

Dan looked ruggedly handsome in his brand-new custom-tailored gray cutaway, and Finn looked just as handsome, though solemn and weary, in black. Dan said jocularly, "I hope you're not overdoing it, brother. All work and no play makes a man dull. And anyhow, when can we be expectin' yourself to marry? It's time you and I produced a brood of young ones of our own. Imagine the Christmases we would have together, Finn, your wife and mine, your children and mine, all playing happily in front of the fire on Christmas Day, and sitting around the table together for Christmas dinner, just like they used to at the Big House."

"Don't be a fool, Dan," Finn said coldly. "It'll never be like Ardnavarna and you know it. No matter how much money we make, we shall never be like them."

Lily wore a tailored dress and jacket in her favorite color, a deep pinkish-violet. She wore an extravagant Paris hat trimmed with pink silk roses, the Adamses' heirloom five-strand pearl choker and pearl-and-diamond earrings, and she carried a posy of sweet-smelling pink roses and violets. As she drove to her wedding she went over in her mind every detail of her affair with Finn.

She knew he had seduced her to get his revenge and she knew he would think she was just getting back at him when he heard about her and Dan. But it wasn't true; Dan had restored her sanity when she was crazy with grief and disillusionment. He was kind and unselfish and he was a rock to cling to in the stormy seas of life. And she was just so tired of those stormy seas. With Dan and her son, and maybe even more children, she would settle for peace and contentment. It was her private bargain with God. She would be a good and dutiful wife and mother, and she hoped God would forgive her her trespasses the way the prayer said, and grant her contentment and companionship, if not great love. And she hoped that Finn would keep out of her life and keep their secret.

Still, as she drove to her wedding, she couldn't help wishing that when Finn found out she had married his brother it would feel like a knife twisting in his guts, because that was the way she had felt the night he had thrown her out of his apartment. "I only took what I already paid for," he had called after her, and she had turned at the door and glared at him. "Oh, no, you did not," she had snarled. "You haven't paid enough. Not nearly enough yet, Finn O'Keeffe."

Well, now he was about to pay, and then it would all be over.

Waiting for Lily in the anteroom of the quiet little New England courthouse, Dan thought that she was like a girl in a fairy tale; even as a child she had been an enchantress, with her wild beauty and flashing blue eyes and her imperious ways that made everyone run to do her bidding. Lily had entwined herself around his heart then, just as she had his brother's, and now the best man had won her. And strangely enough, because the odds had seemed set against it, that man was himself.

He heard her quick, light footsteps in the hall and he rushed out to meet her, beaming with delight when he saw how beautiful she looked.

"Are you nervous, Lily?" he said anxiously, because she was shivering.

She thought, panicked, *There's still time. You can go now. Run away. Think about it this time, Lily. Think about what you are you doing.*

"Dan," she said desperately, "I—I think . . ."

"Well, well, the beautiful bride has arrived," Finn said mockingly.

She saw him standing in the doorway and she stared at him like a mesmerized rabbit at a fox.

"Finn agreed to be my best man," Dan explained quickly, because he had broken his promise not to tell anyone about their marriage until it was over. "After all, he's my only family, and I knew you wouldn't mind old Finn."

He looked hopefully at them, but Lily and Finn were staring silently at each other. There was a strange glint in Finn's eyes as he looked at her. Dan thought for a minute it was contempt, but he laughed that away as ridiculous.

He took Lily's arm and said jovially, "This is a wedding, not a funeral. Come on, you two, the judge is waiting."

"Dan," Lily said desperately. Then she caught Finn's eye and saw the little satisfied smile on his lips and she knew why he had come. He had thought that when she saw him she would not be able to go through with it. Well, he was wrong. "I'm ready, Dan," she said.

The ceremony was over in minutes; the groom placed a gold ring on the bride's finger and kissed her gently, and then the best man called for his own traditional reward of a kiss.

"Congratulations, Mrs. O'Keeffe," Finn whispered as he took her in his arms and kissed her boldly on the lips. She froze and he let go of her. "Well, sister-in-law," he cried, "on to the celebration wedding lunch."

Even though his bride was silent for most of the lunch and on the drive home afterward, Dan thought his wedding day was the happiest day of his life. He took her on a honeymoon trip to Washington, where he introduced her to his colleagues, and they said, "That old son-of-a-gun has done well for himself. Lily O'Keeffe is a classy lady. And a beauty." They were invited to dine with President and Mrs. Cleveland at the White House, and it was the only time on her entire honeymoon that Lily felt at home.

Washington was a small, unsophisticated city and she hated their hotel. She hated the food, the wine, the service. She loathed the mosquitoes and the surrounding countryside. The heat gave her a headache and she missed her baby. Dan was a passionate, loving man, but no matter how often she reminded herself of her bargain with God, every time he made love to her she wished it were Finn.

On the last day of her honeymoon she admitted to herself she had made a mistake. She locked herself in the bathroom and cried until her eyes were puffed and red and her face blotchy, and she still had not got the despair out of her system. But as usual it was too late to turn the clock back. She would keep her bargain.

Finn took to visiting them at their Back Bay house whenever he was in Boston, but he was always careful to make sure first that Dan was home. He didn't trust himself alone with Lily and he didn't want to hurt his brother. He wanted to see his son.

"He's a fine boy," Dan said, hefting the baby up onto his shoulder. "Looks like Lily, too, though she says he is going to take after the Adamses and become an academic."

He grinned happily at the child. "There's no chance your mother would let you start out in life selling red suspenders," he chortled, and Lily glared at him. She was getting tired of Dan's homespun philosophies and his tales of "how he got started." Finn caught her look and she glared at him, too, daring him to say something about the child. But he did not. For whatever reason, Finn's lips were as sealed as hers, though he did spoil the boy, bringing him armloads of expensive presents every time he came to visit.

"One toy would be sufficient," Lily told him icily, but he just laughed and said mockingly, "I have a right to spoil my own 'nephew,' don't I?"

"He is not your nephew, he is Liam Adams," she reminded him, coldly.

"Well, my stepnephew then. Anyway, he's the only kid I know, and a fine little fellow he is too." He added provokingly, "I can even see a bit of the O'Keeffe in him somewhere, even though we are only 'step.'"

Life with Dan in Back Bay was very different from being married to John on Beacon Hill. When Dan was in Boston the house was constantly full of people: ward bosses, state senators, politicians of all kinds and from every level. They were polite, burly men, Irish for the most part, and there always seemed to be a parade in the offing, with brass bands and balloons and fireworks and horses, or a charity picnic, or a campaign to be fought.

Whenever Dan left for Washington the house would fall silent and Lily didn't know whether she was relieved to see him and all his cronies go or at a loss to know what to do with herself now they were not there. Finn never came to visit when Dan was away and she thought despairingly that she was the loser after all.

Maudie

"AND THAT, MY DEARS," I said to Shannon and Eddie, "was the state of affairs when Ciel arrived in Boston."

"Explosive, I'd say," Eddie said, helping me up from the rock where

I had been sitting. My bones creaked as usual; age is not kind in taking away the coiled tensile springs of youth, when everything slides and turns like clockwork, lubricated by secret oils and cushioned by new, unworn cartilage. But once I'm on my feet I can still hike up and down this hill with the best of 'em.

"Step this way," I called, sounding like Dan O'Keeffe selling those blasted red suspenders. "I want to show you something."

They scrambled after me up the hill to a place where the little stream fell from an outcropping. Behind it was a cave tall enough to stand up in. I edged my way into it, brushing away spiderwebs, and beckoned them to follow.

We stood in the cave with the crystal stream tumbling in front of us and the sunlight turned it a dozen different colors. "It's exactly like being inside a rainbow!" Shannon exclaimed as Eddie brushed a spider from her hair. We stood for a few minutes listening to the lovely rushing sound of the water and the mysterious rustling noises coming from the shadows at the back of the cave.

"Bats, probably," I said briskly, and Shannon was out of there like a shot from a gun.

"Ciel and Lily used to come here as children," I explained. "Mammie told me it was their secret place. They would make wild plans to run away and live in it, and they would carry food up here and hide it, but of course when they came back it was always gone. Lily told Ciel the fairies had taken it, though she knew perfectly well it was just mice and small wild creatures. But a fairy story was always better than the truth anytime for Lily, and I suspect that that was part of her trouble. She only ever saw things the way she wanted to see them.

"Anyhow, my dears," I said as we reached the road again and Shannon's waiting red Fiat, "tonight after dinner I shall tell you what finally happened to them all."

I could see they were agog to know finally how it all turned out, and as I soaked myself leisurely in the bath I felt sad because this was the part that had hurt Mammie most to tell.

I almost never wear black anymore because I find it does nothing for an older skin; just look at all those sallow black-veiled widows and you'll see what I mean. Still, tonight, because I thought the story suited it, I wore black. Lace, of course, early Valentino with a tight waist and one of those flirty bell-skirts over pink satin. Far too grand for dinner at home, but I felt like it. I rubbed up the diamonds and flung them on and added a touch of lipstick and scent, and I was ready again to tell my story.

Boston

THEY CALLED THE LUXURY LINERS the "grayhounds of the ocean" because they made the crossing in a speedy seven days, and Ciel flirted and danced her way across the Atlantic, having herself a great old time.

When the liner finally docked she hung excitedly over the rail, searching for her sister in the milling throng below. And then she saw her: a tall, wonderfully elegant woman in a little fur jacket and hat who turned every head as she strolled toward the liner. People parted to let her pass, stopping to look at her, wondering who she was, because she certainly looked like "a somebody." Ciel laughed. Nothing had changed. Lily was the same beautiful, autocratic Lily; people still stepped back to let her pass, and stopped to look at her, and Ciel was sure, still rushed to do her bidding.

"Lily," she yelled, waving frantically. Their eyes met and Lily's face lit up with happiness and relief. "Thank God, you're here at last. I'm coming on board."

They ran into each others arms, oblivious of the curious stares of the departing passengers; they only cared that they were together again.

Lily stepped back, holding her at arms' length, staring at her with tears in her eyes. "Oh, Ciel, you look wonderful." She inspected Ciel's russet Paris suit and little tip-tilted hat with the russet feathers and added, surprised, "And with such style."

"And you must be the most beautiful woman in New York. It was like the parting of the Red Sea when you walked down the pier, Lily. Nothing has changed."

"Oh, how I've missed you," Lily said, and they hugged each other again. "Promise me you'll stay forever."

They followed Ciel's mountain of baggage onto the pier, and soon they were on their way to the Fifth Avenue Hotel. They held hands like children while Ciel talked nonstop about Ardnavarna, and Lily said hopefully, "I thought I had been banished forever, but maybe one day soon I can go home again."

Ciel said sadly, "It's not the same anymore. It's lonely now, without them all. But being without you was the worst." Remembering, she began to cry, and Lily put a comforting arm around her shoulders.

"All that matters is that we are together again now," she said reassuringly. "And now we're going to have some fun. Tonight we are going to see my friend Ned Sheridan in his new play on Broadway, and afterward he is taking us to dinner at Delmonico's."

That night Ciel wore deep-green panne, cut high at the neck and tight at the waist, with her usual clutter of diamond brooches as well as her mother's huge pearls. She wore diamonds in her hair and her ears and her long red fox-fur coat. And Lily was her usual elegant self in blond lace, low-cut with long tight sleeves, and the Adamses' sapphires, and her black fox cape.

Ned Sheridan told them he was the proudest man in New York because he had the city's two most beautiful women on his arm, and Ciel felt giddy with happiness as they toasted each other in champagne at Delmonico's. She whispered to Lily that he was the most handsome man she had ever seen, and the nicest, and maybe Lily should have married him after all.

"Maybe," Lily said, and Ciel caught the touch of sadness in her voice. But she thought it was obvious to anyone watching that Ned Sheridan was head over heels in love with her sister.

They took the train to Boston the following morning and drove through Beacon Hill so that Lily could point out her old house, closed and shuttered, on Mount Vernon Street, and Finn O'Keeffe James's house on Louisburg Square, and then finally to Dan's house in Back Bay.

"Don't bother to look around," she cried, dashing up the stairs like a homing pigeon. "Come and see Liam."

The little boy heard them coming; he hurled himself at his mother, and Lily swept him, laughing, into her arms, raining kisses on his face, his hair, his arms, anywhere she could find a place to put one.

He was almost two years old and tall for his age with a slender, wiry body, dark hair, and cool gray eyes. But his face was pale and he was coughing.

Worried, Lily stared at him. "How long has he been coughing like this?" she asked the nanny.

"Only since yesterday, Mrs. O'Keeffe. Sure and it's nothing but a little tickle in his throat. The boy is fine; he's been playing quietly with his bricks and his toys."

"Liam never plays quietly," Lily said angrily. "Haven't you been here long enough to know that? If he is quiet, then he must be ill." She put her hand to his forehead; it felt cool, but maybe it was too cool. Maybe he was cold. "Put him to bed at once," she ordered, "and wrap him up warmly. I'm calling the doctor."

She turned and saw Ciel standing in the doorway. "Oh, Ciel," she said, "I'm so worried about him. He always gets this cough; the doctor told me he had a weak chest. . . ."

"He's a grand boy, Lily," she replied, "and he seems fine enough."

He was peeking at her from behind his mother's skirts and she laughed. "I'm your aunt Ciel," she said, sinking onto the rug next to him. "I'm here to play games with you and spoil you."

She grinned at him and he grinned back. He had a thin, cheerful little face and a sweet expression and she thought he was adorable, though he did not look in the least bit like Lily. He sat on the floor beside her and took up his bricks and said, "Let's play."

"No," Lily said firmly. "You're going to bed. And I am calling the doctor."

The nanny whisked him away and a little while later the doctor called. He told them there was nothing to worry about, that the boy had no fever and his throat was just fine. "But Nanny said he was so quiet," Lily objected.

"I daresay he just felt like playing quietly. Sometimes children do, you know," the doctor replied wearily. He was only too used to Lily's frantic calls, sometimes in the middle of the night, and almost all of them unnecessary.

Ciel said, "You worry too much, Lily. He looks like a fine strong boy to me."

"Oh, what do you know," Lily shouted, stamping her foot. "I'm the one who has to look after him. I have to be so careful. He's *everything* to me. *He's all I've got.*"

Astonished, Ciel stared at her. "But you have your husband, Lily," she said. "And your lovely home, and your life with Dan."

"I just meant that Liam is all I have left . . . of John," she explained. "I just love him so much, Ciel, I couldn't bear it if anything were to happen to him."

Dan had promised to be home that evening and Lily paced the house like a nervous cat, wondering what Ciel was going to think of her diamond-in-the-rough husband. Ciel was upstairs getting changed for dinner when he arrived, his derby on the back of his head as usual and a spotted kerchief knotted around his throat. Lily took one look at him and groaned, wondering why he must always look like an Irish street politician heading for the nearest saloon. She urged him upstairs to change and then went to check that the dinner table was set precisely as she had instructed.

Dan loved his little stepson dearly and was heading to the nursery to say hello when he bumped into Ciel on the stairs. They looked each other over, smiling. "Can this vision really be little Ciel Molyneux?" he demanded, taking her hands in his big paws.

"And can this handsome man-of-the-world really be Daniel

O'Keeffe, son of Padraig?" she demanded back, and he threw his arms around her in a great bear hug.

"Did y'ever think we would be doing this? Huggin' each other and kissing? Brother- and sister-in-law?" he asked, beaming at her.

"I'm only glad it's true," she retorted. "I can't think of anyone I would rather have for my brother-in-law. Except maybe Finn," she added with a touch of her old mischief-making.

"Sure and didn't I ask myself, on my very wedding day, why it was *me* your beautiful sister was marryin' and not my brother? When the two of them had been thick as thieves when they were kids? But I'm glad to say I was the fella she chose and I'm proud to tell you, sister-in-law, that she has made me a very happy man. And I hope to put many more little fellas in that nursery before too long." He winked conspiratorially at her. "I only wanted to take a peek at the wee lad and then Lily told me I have to change into something 'respectable' for dinner with her sister."

Laughing, Ciel watched him tiptoe exaggeratedly along the corridor to the nursery. She thought what a nice man he was and how good-looking, and she thought her sister was a lucky woman to be his wife.

Dinner was a jolly affair; the wine flowed and, despite Lily's withering glances, Dan told his stories of how he got his start. He talked to Ciel about Washington and the White House, and promised her a visit there before too long. Then the conversation veered back to Ardnavarna and a look of sadness crossed his face.

"I've never told you how much I've wanted to go back there," he said to Lily. "When I first came to Boston and Finn and me were living in a windowless hovel, I used to dream of Ardnavarna. I dreamed of the greenness of its gardens and the rustle of the rain on the leaves of the alder trees and the sweetness of the air filling my lungs, instead of the gray, stinking, filthy streets of the North End. How many times did I imagine myself wading in the peaty river, fighting a salmon, or striding the fields with a shotgun after the pheasant. The only trouble with those dreams was that they were in the past, and being where I was then, I had only the terrible present, and no dreams or even hopes of any future that I could see.

"It just goes to show how a man can be proved wrong," he added triumphantly. "And if we think Ireland is God's own country, then America is surely God's *chosen* country, because I'm not the only poor ignorant Irishman to make it big here. As I tell my voters, 'It's the land of opportunity, and all y'have to do is get off yer lazy backsides and grab those opportunities.'"

"Dan," Lily protested frostily.

"I'm sorry for my earthy talk, Lily," he said calmly, "but I'm a man who calls a spade a spade, and a backside is what it's always been. A backside."

Ciel laughed at her sister's scandalized face. "I seem to remember you using worse words, Lily," she reminded her, and Lily laughed, but she was wondering how she could ever go home to Ardnavarna again, with Dan O'Keeffe her husband.

"Well, well. A happy family reunion," Finn said from the doorway, and their heads swung around to look.

"Finn O'Keeffe!" Ciel leapt to her feet and ran toward him. She grabbed his hands. "Can it really be you?" she demanded, looking him up and down. He was lean and darkly handsome and immaculate. "The last time I saw you, you were in a green striped vest and riding breeches, with two days' stubble on your handsome face and a wicked gleam in your eye that was the scourge of every maiden from Galway to Westport."

He grinned back at her. "The gleam's still there, only the suit is different," he said. "And maybe what's inside, too, now I've had a chance to learn how to behave myself properly in good society."

"And how to make money," Ciel exclaimed, never one to hold back what she was thinking. "They tell me you are a rich man, maybe richer than Pa." She grinned at him. "That wouldn't be too difficult—the old boy was gambling away a fortune at the end. I've come down in the world, and you have gone up."

"We were not expecting you, Finn," Lily said coldly.

"Dan told me Ciel would be here. How could I miss the opportunity to see my tormentor again?" He grinned at her. "Just don't expect me to dance like a bear for you, little Miss Ciel."

She laughed and he took a seat next to her, throwing Lily a mock pleading glance. "Can you spare a plate of food for a poor fella who has just made the long journey from New York City, and who's starvin' and in need of a jar or two?"

"Oh, stop with that silly brogue," she said impatiently, signaling the maid to set another place.

Dan poured the wine and said, "I'm surely glad you are here, Finn. Now it's the four of us together. A family. And that's just the way it should be."

Finn sipped the claret and looked admiringly at Ciel. "Nobody told me you had grown into a beauty," he said.

She threw him a sceptical look. "Now stop with your blarney, Finn

O'Keeffe. No one in their right mind would ever call me beautiful. So either you're out of your mind or you're a terrible flatterer."

"Both," he said firmly, and they laughed. "You look just grand," he said sincerely. "So elegant, and so, so . . . carrot-headed and lively. I always liked you, Ciel."

Lily quickly rang the bell for the maid to clear their plates. "If you are too busy talking to eat your dinner, Finn, then we shall just go on to dessert," she snapped.

Surprised, Ciel stared at her; after all, Finn had only been there ten minutes.

"Do we get to see young Liam tonight?" he asked after dinner when they were back in the drawing room.

Lily threw him a venemous glance and he smiled sweetly back at her. "It's too late," Lily said. "He's sleeping."

"Oh, come on, Lily, you can't keep a man away from his own *nephew,*" he said cajolingly. "After all, I don't see him that often."

"Sure you can see him." Dan was always ready to show off his boy. "Why don't we all go and take a peek at him."

"He was coughing today. I had to send for the doctor," Lily objected, and Ciel stared at her. She knew perfectly well the doctor had said there was nothing wrong with Liam.

"Oh, please, Lily," she begged.

Lily led the way upstairs, resentment showing in the stiffness of her back and the flounce of her skirts. Liam was asleep. "Did you ever see anything so innocent and sweet?" Ciel whispered, glancing at her sister, thinking what a lucky woman she was. She had it all: a handsome rich husband who adored her, a beautiful home, and a son everyone loved.

"He's surely a handsome little fellow," Dan whispered. "And he's so nearly mine now that, looking at him, you might almost think there was a bit of genuine O'Keeffe blood in him."

"You might at that," Finn agreed.

Lily's cheeks burned as she bent over her son and pulled the blanket up to his neck. "He must be kept warm," she admonished the undernurse, waiting outside the door. But the tremor in her voice was not from worry. It was fear of Finn and the power he had over her. And there was nothing she could do about it.

Back downstairs again, Finn said to Ciel, "I shall be in Boston for a couple of days. Why not let me show you around."

"I had planned to show Ciel the sights myself," Lily protested, trying to keep him out of her life. "After all, we haven't seen each other in years."

"Then maybe you both can spare time to come and take tea with me tomorrow afternoon. And maybe later I can be the one to show you New York."

"Maybe," Ciel replied, walking him to the door. He turned to wave as he strode away, and with a sinking heart Lily noticed the little smile on her sister's face as she watched him go.

Maudie

"SO THERE THEY ALL WERE, TOGETHER AGAIN, only this time they were equals," I told Shannon, sitting next to me on the big blue brocade sofa with the broken springs that grab you when you sit down, causing unsuspecting ladies to imagine someone might have pinched their bottoms.

Shannon slid onto the rug where Eddie was already stretched full-length in front of the fire, his hands behind his head and his eyes closed, and I swung my legs thankfully up onto the sofa. I propped a couple of cushions behind my head, admiring my black suede high-heeled pumps and wishing that my ankles were not quite so skinny. I have been eating so much, with my two visitors to encourage me every night, that I thought I might have put on a bit of weight. But no such luck. The older I get, the thinner I get, and that's just the way it is.

"Anyway," I said, "Ciel told me that Finn was the best-looking man she ever saw: tall and broad-shouldered with a strong, wiry body, piercing gray eyes, and a lean jaw. He had thick black hair with a tendency to wave, which he wore brushed straight back. And he looked like the million dollars or more he was worth, in custom-tailored suits and fur-collared overcoats, and he certainly knew how to treat a girl.

" 'Obviously from experience,' she told me, a little bitterly I thought, but that was before I heard what happened. Well, of course, he wooed her. He pursued her with telephone calls and surprise visits and flowers until Ciel said Lily was tearing her hair out with anger, and she couldn't understand why, so she asked her."

Boston

"HE'S JUST SUCH . . . SUCH A PEASANT," Lily exclaimed with snobbish venom.

"Then you are a peasant's wife, because you are married to his brother," Ciel retorted. "And I can see no reason why I shouldn't go to New York to see him."

Lily flounced away up the stairs. "Oh, go if you must," she called angrily. "But I'm warning you, you have to watch out for a man like that. He has a bad reputation with women." She turned to look at her. "You have led a sheltered life, Ciel. You know nothing about men like him. I'm just looking out for my little sister, that's all."

She had no need to worry; Ciel wasn't about to let herself be seduced by Finn, but she *was* falling in love with him. How could she not? He met her in New York and he treated her as though she were the most precious creature on earth; he filled her hotel room with apricot roses—to match her hair, he told her. He bought her jeweled trinkets: tiny parrots and bees and horses and spotted dogs in diamonds and onyx. They made her laugh and she said she didn't know where she could pin such a large menagerie because her bosom was already so full of Mammie's glittering stuff.

He showed her the city and dazzled her with the somber, monied splendor of his offices and the deference with which everyone from the doorman upward greeted him. He took her to see the Statue of Liberty and the latest musical show; he wined her and dined her at all the smartest restaurants, and he bombarded her with telephone calls even when he had only just left her and she had her head on her pillow, ready to go to sleep.

"Just to say I miss you, Ciel," he said in that low voice that sent a shiver down her spine.

"Silly man," she told him, "you've only just left me half an hour ago."

"The longest half hour of my life," he murmured, and she laughed as she hung up the receiver.

Finn O'Keeffe James was showing off for her and she knew it, and she loved it. And despite Lily's uncalled-for objections, she went as often as she could to New York to see him, and he came to Boston more frequently than he ever had before.

"I don't know what you see in the man," Lily fumed.

"And I don't know why you are so against him. He's just fun to be with, Lily, that's all," Ciel said, afraid for some unknown reason to confess to her sister that she was in love with him.

He kissed her for the first time exactly three months to the day after he had remet her. "An anniversary kiss," he told her, only somehow it felt like much more than that, and it sent unexpected quivers through Ciel's veins and tingling little messages to nerve ends she hadn't known she possessed.

"I'm afraid I'm falling in love with you," he murmured, and she hung her head, shy for once, unwilling to admit to herself that she was falling in love with him, because she was too worried about what Lily might say.

A month later Finn invited the sisters to dinner at his Louisburg Square house. Lily wanted to kill him because of the way he was romancing her sister. She just knew he was doing it to torture her, to show her how little he cared about her. And to flaunt his power over her. And she was sure poor little Ciel was falling for his blarney, no matter how she tried to put her off him. She told herself he would soon be bored of his game, and she tried to think of some suitable men for her sister.

The week of the dinner party Lily came down with a bout of influenza and the doctor forbade her to set foot out of bed, so Ciel went alone.

The butler showed her into the drawing room where Finn was waiting. The weather had turned springlike; all the windows were open and a pleasant breeze ruffled the curtains, bringing the scent of the blossoming lilacs from the garden.

"Am I the first to arrive?" she asked, unaware that she was repeating her sister's exact words, and that Finn had staged exactly the same performance.

"You are the only guest," he told her. "I canceled everyone else when I heard Lily couldn't come, because then I knew I should have you all to myself. It's all right," he assured her when she glanced nervously around, "the servants will chaperone us. Don't worry, I won't try to seduce you."

"Jayzus, Finn James," she said with a laugh. "You are an impertinent old fellow to imagine you could even do such a thing."

He took a ring box from his pocket and she stared, dazzled, at the enormous emerald surrounded by diamonds. Then he went down on one knee and said solemnly, "Ciel, I know I'm not worthy of you. You know my humble background only too well, but I hope you'll see I've risen above it. My heart is in my mouth with fear you'll refuse me, but I'm asking you to do me the honor of becoming my wife."

She stared at him, smiling, pink-faced with pleasure. "That must be the longest proposal of marriage ever spoken. *And* the biggest ring." She tapped him jokingly on each shoulder, the way a queen did when knighting her subject, and said, "Arise, Sir Finn O'Keeffe James. I have just promoted you to the aristocracy so you can ask me to marry you properly, and away with all that 'humble' nonsense."

He threw his arms around her, laughing. "Dear God," he demanded, casting his eyes questioningly to heaven, "why didn't I meet her before—"

"Before what?" she asked. But he just shrugged and said, "You haven't given me an answer."

"You haven't asked properly yet."

"Ciel, will you please marry me?" he shouted.

"Yes, dammit," she yelled, and they fell, laughing, into each others arms.

Ciel put her engagement ring on a ribbon and hung it around her neck, hiding it under her dress until she could pluck up the courage to tell Lily she was going to marry Finn.

A few days later, the time seemed right. Finn was in New York, Dan was in Washington, and she and Lily were alone.

Ciel put on her ring and went with her sister and Liam for a walk on the Common. She watched Liam kicking a ball around and her sister trying not to rush to pick him up every time he fell. "I can't bear it when he gets hurt," Lily said. "Dan always tells him, 'Buck up, old fella, there's nothing to cry about. It's only a scratch,' and I always rush for iodine and bandages, thermometers and kisses."

"That's love," Ciel said philosophically. "And talking of love . . ."

Lily looked suspiciously at her. "What about it?"

Ciel held out her left hand. The emerald glinted like green ice in the sunlight. "Finn asked me to marry him," Ciel said, her eyes as starry as the diamonds on the ring.

Lily felt the blow to her heart; she turned without a word and ran after Liam. She picked him up and held him close, fighting back her tears. "The bastard, oh, the treacherous bastard," she repeated over and over to herself. "How could he do this to me? How could he push it this far?"

"Lily," Ciel said pleadingly, but she ignored her, clutching her son closer.

"Lily, I don't understand. Why are you so upset? What's wrong with my marrying Finn? After all, you married his brother. I hoped you would be pleased for us."

Lily swung around. She was too hurt to cry anymore. If Finn didn't care what weapons he used against her, then neither did she. All was fair in love and war. She said desperately, "You can't marry Finn."

Bewildered, Ciel shook her head. Liam was crying, but for once Lily didn't seem to notice. "But whyever not," she begged. "Just tell me one good reason."

"You are looking at him," Lily said in a dead little voice. "This is Finn's son."

Ciel stared at her sister and then at Liam. She could see Lily was speaking the truth.

"Well, you did it again, Lily," she said bitterly, trying to stop her heart from jumping into her throat and choking her. And then she turned away and walked quickly back across the Common.

Maudie

CIEL SAID HER TRUNKS WERE PACKED and she was out of the house and on her way to New York by train that very evening without so much as a good-bye.

Lily had locked herself in her room, but Ciel did not want to see her anyway. She never cared if she saw her sister again. She left for England the following morning on the *Etruria,* the same liner she had sailed on so joyfully just a few months earlier. And two weeks later she was back home at Ardnavarna again, licking her wounds.

Now, Ciel, my own darling mammie, was by her own account a passionate woman. She loved life and she loved men and she loved love. But she had never been in love the way she was with Finn, and she confessed to me when she told me this story that she never was again. Not even with Jack Allerdyce, the man she finally married, and who became my father.

Oh, she loved him all right; he made her laugh and they were great companions and they liked all the same things, horses and country living and foreign travel, and fast motor cars and parties. But she never felt for anyone again that heart-stopping excitement she felt for treacherous Finn.

She kept his ring, of course, as a souvenir. "To remind me of what a blitherin' fool I almost made of myself," she said.

I waved my hand under the lamplight and Finn's emerald glowed and the diamonds sparkled, and Shannon and Eddie oohed and aahed over it.

"It's a little part of history," Shannon said breathlessly.

But clever Eddie said, "Did he really set her up just to get back at Lily? Or did he really love her?"

"Ah," I said mysteriously. "Unfortunately, my dear boy, that is something we shall never know. Mammie said that when she analyzed it years afterward—'when she was sane again,' was how she put it—she thought maybe he had loved her after all. But of course there was no turning back the clock, and anyway maybe it was all for the better, because it was all getting a bit like a Greek drama, with all those tangled family relationships.

"So we shall never know if Finn loved Ciel. I've always thought that he did, but you must make up your own minds what you choose to believe."

CHAPTER
45

BOSTON

DAN O'KEEFFE THOUGHT IT VERY ODD that his sister-in-law had left so suddenly, even though Lily tried nervously to play it down, saying she just suddenly got homesick. "I suspect it's London's bright lights and a certain young man she was yearning for," she told him.

"London? With all of New York her playground?" Dan said, astonished. "And Finn to keep her amused and introduce her to a dozen handsome eligible young fellas. Though now I think of it, I'm not so sure Finn wanted to do that." Dan remembered the way Finn had sought out Ciel's company and the way Ciel had looked at him, all starry-eyed, the way he always wished Lily would look at him. He thought maybe his brother had wanted to keep Ciel all to himself.

"Finn's at the bottom of this," he said positively. "Any fool could see she was falling for him and his blarney. Do you think maybe they've had a fight? By God, if he has treated her badly, I'll beat the livin' daylights out of him."

"I'm sure it had nothing to do with Finn," Lily protested too quickly.

"Well, I am not." Dan marched over to the sideboard and poured himself a generous tumbler of whiskey. "Goddamm it," he roared, knocking the drink back in a single gulp. "I'm tellin' you, Lily, if it's Finn has caused her to leave, he's in trouble all right. All these years you've waited to see her again, and now the young bastard sends her fleeing home. He just can't keep his hands off any woman, that's Finn's fault. He has a string of 'em in New York. 'Fillies,' he calls them. And I guess he thought it would be a feather in his cap to add Ciel to his 'stable.' "

"He's always been jealous of you, Dan," Lily said, suddenly egging him on. If she couldn't do it herself, then she wanted Dan to beat Finn up. She wanted to see Finn's nose bloodied, maybe a tooth or two knocked out to wipe that self-satisfied grin from his handsome, lying face.

"Jealous?" Dan poured another tumbler of whiskey, staring at her, surprised.

"For marrying me. The daughter of the Big House. You know he always thought I liked him. Well, I chose you, so he made a play for my sister instead. He's jealous of you, Dan, don't you see it? With all your success—and marrying me as well? He wanted to marry Ciel so he could be like you. . . ."

"And didn't I think it was a grand idea myself!" He clapped his hand to his forehead in an agony of remorse as he downed another whiskey. "Wait!" He suddenly thought of something. "Are you telling me he made a play for you as well, Lily?"

He stared at her, his face red and his big fists clenched. "No. Oh, no, he never did that," she said hastily. "He always knew I preferred you, Dan."

"I didn't know you had seen him before you met me," he said, suddenly suspicious.

"Well, I . . . only once or twice," she admitted reluctantly. "He came to speak to John about the rare books he had inherited from Cornelius James."

"You never told me about that," he said, staring hard at her.

Lily knew she was getting into deeper water than she had intended, and in the impatient, haughty tone she always seemed to use with him these days, she said, "It was nothing. It just wasn't important, that's all."

His eyes followed her as she walked briskly to the door. She said, "None of it is important. Ciel will be back soon. She just needed to go home to Ardnavarna for a while. Pa's death affected her more than she showed."

"Where are you going?" he demanded, stalking after her to the door.

"I'm going to change for dinner. Jayzus, Dan, you're acting as if the world just fell apart because Ciel suddenly went home. I've told you, nothing's wrong."

She flounced from the room, skirts rustling, and he stared thoughtfully after her. Then he went back to the sideboard and poured himself another drink. He glanced at his watch. Seven-thirty. Finn would be here at eight. *He couldn't wait to see him.*

At eight on the dot Finn bounded eagerly up the front steps and rang the bell. He smiled, surprised when his brother opened the door to him instead of the parlormaid. "Staff problems, Dan?" he asked, striding past him into the hall. "Surely not in this house. Isn't everyone paid more than any other establishment in Boston? And with better hours and working conditions?" He laughed, tossing his coat over a chair and flinging a friendly arm around his brother.

"You look as though you've beaten me to a drink," Finn said, walking into the dining room, and then glancing closer at him. "And by quite a few, I'd say."

"Not that many I don't know what I'm saying," Dan said stonily.

Finn looked surprised. "I'm glad to hear that, old son; I'm here for an evening of civilized conversation, not the ramblings of a drunken Irish politician."

"What the hell d'ya mean by that?"

Dan stepped menacingly toward him and Finn said, hastily, "It was just a joke, Dan, that's all."

Dan poured himself another drink without offering Finn one and Finn watched him warily. Tension crackled between them and his scalp prickled warningly. Something was up and he hoped it wasn't what he thought it was.

"Where is Ciel?" he asked, glancing at his watch, trying to defuse the situation. "She's usually waiting for me."

"Not anymore, 'ould son.' Ciel packed her bags and left this afternoon. Gone home to Ardnavarna. Or more likely, she's run away from you."

"You can't mean that," Finn said quietly. Puzzled, Dan thought he looked like a man who had just been dealt a body blow.

"Sure I do. Ask Lily. And maybe she'll tell you the real reason she's gone, though she's not telling me."

"We were engaged to be married," Finn said. "I had bought her a ring—"

"She never said anything about that to me. Nor as far as I know to her sister. But then, I'm suddenly finding out there's a lot I don't know about Lily."

Lily appeared on cue in the doorway. She was perfectly turned-out in blue silk and pearls, with her hair swept back in an immaculate chignon. Their eyes were fixed on her she walked nonchalantly across the room and sank into a chair by the window. "It's so warm tonight, for spring," she said, fanning herself.

"Lily, what have you been up to?" Finn demanded.

"I don't know what you mean." She flinched as he stalked nearer, seeing the bitter anger in his eyes. She said quickly, "Ciel said she was sorry not to say good-bye. She just had a longing to go home again. It's perfectly understandable, so soon after Pa's death."

"That's not true and you know it," he yelled angrily. "Ciel loved me. We were engaged to be married. She would never have left without speaking to me first." She looked up at him with frightened blue eyes. "Unless you had a hand in things, Lily. Stirring them up as usual."

"I don't know what you mean," she repeated. "Only *you* know what happened between Ciel and yourself. Dan said you have a string of 'fillies' in New York, and Ciel knew about it and she just didn't want to be counted among your 'trophies.' "

"Did you tell her that?" he demanded, standing threateningly over her.

"Dammit, no, I did not. I don't know how she found out. But how do you expect a lady, *a Molyneux,* to behave over something like that? Do you expect her to just sit there and smile like a good little peasant wife and say it doesn't matter?"

"You are lying, Lily," Dan roared. He was standing with his feet apart and his arms folded, staring angrily at them. "Ciel did not know about Finn's women, and neither did you, until I told you just now. So exactly what did happen between you and Ciel? Come on, Lily, why don't you tell us? Put us both out of our misery, because there's something going on here and I'm determined to know what!" He banged his fist into the table, sending a pretty meissen dish flying to the floor, where it shattered into a hundred pieces.

"You've done it again, Lily, haven't you?" Finn said bitterly to Lily. "You thought the game was still going on and now it was your turn to win. Well, let me tell you, my dear Lily, you will never win. You will always be the loser. I thought Ciel was the one person you really loved. But I was wrong. Even precious little Ciel could not stand in your way."

He turned and strode to the door, but Dan blocked his way. "What was that all about?" he demanded angrily.

"Ask your wife," Finn said, shouldering him aside. He strode into the hall and across to the stairs.

"Where are you going?" Dan yelled after him.

"Ask your wife," Finn repeated, heading up the stairs.

Lily ran after him. She saw him on the landing and she knew where he was heading. "No," she screamed, running after him. "No, Finn."

"Where is he going?" Dan asked, bewildered. "What's going on?"

"Stop him, Dan, stop him," Lily cried. "He's going to get the baby."

Dan leapt up the stairs after them. He grabbed Lily by the shoulders. "Why does he want Liam?" he demanded, but he had no need of an answer, he read it in her eyes.

He flung her away from him and ran down the upstairs hallway after his brother. Finn was standing by Liam's bed, gazing at the sleeping boy. His shoulders drooped and he looked like a man who has just lost everything he ever cared about.

"Get away from that boy," Dan whispered through gritted teeth. "Get out of the nursery, you bastard."

Finn shrugged wearily. So now Dan knew. He had his revenge and it was not sweet. He walked past him out the door and along the hall. With a great roar, Dan ran after him. "By God, I'll kill you," he yelled. "I said I'd do it for Ciel, but now it's for Lily."

"Why not do us both a favor, brother, and kill Lily instead," Finn called, standing at the top of the stairs, waiting for him. "She's the one who should pay for this mess. Not you or me."

Dan stripped off his jacket and put up his fists, circling him angrily. Finn flung off his coat. "Come on, you drunken old sod," he called. Dan charged at him like an enraged bull, his great fists were knotted and his face was purple with rage.

Blood spurted from Finn's broken nose and a cut over his eye. He knew he couldn't win; Dan was drunk enough and wild enough to kill him. "All right, Dan, all right," he said, mopping the blood and walking backward down the stairs, afraid to take his eyes off him. "You win. The honors, such as they are, are yours. And so is Lily. But one day I shall be back for my son."

Dan let out a howl of pain. He launched himself at his brother and Finn heard Lily scream as he flung himself quickly out of his way, watching, horrified, as Dan hurtled past him, arms outstretched, falling over and over, down the beautiful staircase, until he landed with a thud at the bottom and lay still.

Finn walked down the stairs and looked at his brother. Then he looked at Lily standing silently on the first floor landing, a hand clutched anxiously to her breast. He picked up the phone and called the doctor, saying there had been an accident and it was urgent. He looked sadly down at his unconscious brother and then he strode to the door. "Good-bye, Lily," he said coldly. "And don't forget," he added, "one day I shall be back for my son."

Lily watched him go. She knew he had meant it when he said good-bye this time. It was all over between them, but now the war over the boy was about to begin. She looked at her husband lying at the bottom of the stairs, and she suddenly realized that he had not moved.

"Dan," she screamed, hurling herself to her knees beside him. His eyes were rolled up in his head, he was very pale, and he was breathing rapidly. Filled with foreboding, she knelt beside him and took his cold hand in hers, waiting.

At the hospital she sat numbly in the stuffy little waiting room while they did what they could for her husband, thinking about Finn and wondering what was going to happen to her now.

WHEN DAN REGAINED CONSCIOUSNESS he found he had multiple fractures of his left leg and a suspected fracture of the spine, and even though he was very ill he remembered clearly what had happened and he burned with anger against Lily.

"That woman does not enter my door," he told the terrified nurses.

A week later, encased from neck to toes in a plaster cast, he had a long conversation with Father O'Byrne from St. Stephen's and he thanked heaven he had not married Lily in the Catholic Church. He employed a man to make some enquiries about his wife's past, and what he discovered surprised him because he was not a reader of the gossip columns. A few weeks later civil divorce proceedings were entered against his wife, citing her adultery.

Lily received the papers from the hands of a smirking sallow-faced young process-server who had pushed his way past her parlormaid into the hall. Telling him coldly to get out or she would send for the police, she took the papers to her room and stared aghast at the name of the corespondent. She knew why Dan had done it; as a politician he was avoiding even more scandal and he was keeping his own family name clean by not naming his brother. Wondering what her mother would think if she could see her now, she burst into tears asking herself what she had done wrong.

The next day her maid packed her things and, with the nanny and Liam, she returned to her own house on Mount Vernon Street. "After all, it's better that Liam should grow up in his father's own home," she told herself comfortingly, eliminating his true father from her mind with a single master stroke, just the way she had managed to eliminate Dermot Hathaway and his son all those years ago. Liam was hers. He belonged to her now and no one else. She would put her wicked past behind her and devote her life to him. She would be an exemplary mother, just like her own darling mammie. She would put his name down for the right schools and he would follow in his father's brilliant academic footsteps to Harvard.

Lily pictured herself as the mother of the brilliant young professor, entertaining his colleagues at dinner the way John used to, and she told herself fiercely that now she had picked up the pieces, maybe life wasn't so bad after all. She had this beautiful house, she had money and her freedom, and she had her son to plan for. And nobody was going to take him away from her.

She paid a visit to her attorney to make sure that Liam's birth was properly registered and she said that she wished to make her will. She was leaving everything in trust for her son, and eventually his children, and so on in perpetuity.

She had lost everyone she loved, except her son, and now she was making sure that Finn could never claim Liam was his and take him from her.

Ned was the only friend she had left. She hadn't seen him in ages, and she didn't know where he was, but she knew his manager, Harrison Robbins's habit of breakfasting at Delmonico's when he was in New York, so she telephoned him there.

Harrison groaned when he heard her imperious voice; he had thought he had gotten rid of her when she got married. "Ned's a family man now," he told Lily coldly. "He has a wife and a child to look after and another on the way, as well as a new tour coming up that's going to be pretty damned grueling, even for a man of Ned's stamina. He's taking a well-earned rest and no one knows where he is."

"I must see him. Something's happened . . . I must talk to him, Harrison. It's urgent."

He groaned. When Lily wanted something, she always got it. He promised to give Ned the message.

"What's wrong?" Ned asked worriedly when Harrison called him in Nantucket.

Harrison shrugged indifferently. "I don't know, and if you want my opinion you're a damned fool if you intend to go and find out."

He should have saved his breath: Ned went anyway.

She was alone in her big house, looking calm and serene and not at all at her wits' end, as she had told Harrison. Ned was tensed up with anxiety about her; all the time on the train he had been thinking maybe she was ill or maybe something had happened to her son. He was sure it was going to be something terrible and he felt weak with relief that she seemed all right.

Lily poured tea into pretty flowered china cups. "I needed someone to talk to, and you are my only friend," she said. "Besides, there's something I have to tell you." She was going to say "before the process-server finds you." But her nerve failed, and instead she said, "How is your wife?"

"Fine. The baby is due in a couple of months. She swears it'll be another girl." He helped himself to a sandwich.

"Lucky Juliet," she said sadly. She knew she couldn't put it off any longer. She said, "Dan is suing me for divorce. He's accusing me of adultery and I'm afraid he's named you as corespondent."

Astonished, he looked at her. "But it's not true. You and I were together before you married him. Never after."

"Are you prepared to go into court and testify to that?" she cried. "Because I can tell you, Ned, I am not. Dan intends to divorce me and he will use any means he has to achieve it. He's the injured party, and if he blames me the scandal will roll right off his back. If you and I defend ourselves we shall have to testify in an open court. You know what the tabloids are like, every salacious detail of your life and mine will be splattered across the headlines."

She turned pleadingly to him. "Think of our children. How can we do this to them? Why not just let Dan have his divorce quietly? It will be a one-day wonder. I shall take Liam away on holiday for a while and by the time we get back it will all have blown over.

"Please, Ned." She took his hand and held it to her cool cheek. "Please. If you still love me."

Ned thought of the scandal he would have to face because he was who he was, a star in the public eye. He thought of his wife and children and what it would cost them. And then he looked at Lily, alone and helpless, with no one to turn to. His heart was filled with love for her and, as he always had, he knew he would do as she asked.

Lily breathed a huge sigh of relief. Now people would think it was Ned who was her lover. They would never link her name with Finn, and Liam would be safe.

Ned returned to New York and told Harrison what was happening. "The case will be uncontested," he added, not looking him in the eye.

"Uncontested? But goddamm it, Ned, you haven't been near the woman. . . ."

Ned shrugged. "That's the way it's going to be," he said, tight-lipped. "The case will probably come up when I am out of town with the show, so I want you to take care of Juliet for me."

"Tell her, you mean? You must be out of your mind. She'll kill me instead of you."

Ned grinned at him. "Isn't that what managers are for?"

DAN SPENT FOUR MONTHS IN THE HOSPITAL and when he came out he was in a wheelchair. It took another four or five months of teeth-gritting determination and pain and hard work before he walked again, and even then it was with a stick. His cronies and colleagues and the people of the North End who had given him their votes shook their heads pityingly as he limped by. " 'Tis a sad thing, and himself such a fine strappin' fella," they said sympathetically, "and handsome and successful with it. And now he has himself a trollop of a wife to deal with also."

Finn read about the divorce in the newspapers. He couldn't miss it —it was splashed all over the front pages of every scandal sheet in the city, with Ned Sheridan's handsome face staring at the world, branded as the scoundrel who had stolen another man's wife. There was no picture of Lily, though they did mention that she had been Mrs. Adams, a wealthy Boston widow, when she married Dan.

He thrust the newspapers into his wastebasket and put his head in his hands, thinking about Lily, and about his brother, crippled by that stupid drunken accident. Dan had refused to see him. He had not spoken to his brother since that night, and he doubted he ever would again.

CHAPTER
46

MAUDIE

Ardnavarna

WE HAD TAKEN AN OLD BOAT out into the bay, just a little outboard motor vessel, held together with spit and string, but it had lasted me half a century and I saw no reason it shouldn't last another. "Safe as houses," I said cheerfully to Shannon when I saw the doubt on her face. "Besides, we're only going a little way out and you could always swim back."

"What about you?" she asked worriedly.

"I look at it this way," I told her. "If God is going to send for me, then he'll do it when *he* chooses, and not me. Besides, I know this boat and these waters as well as I know my own face, and there's the same amount of choppy little waves and crinkles on both of 'em."

"You're a fatalist," Eddie said with a smile. "But there's no need to worry, God's not going to get you in his clutches today. I'm a Californian and I've been swimming since I was one year old. I'll save you."

He tinkered with the motor and it grumbled once or twice, then it sputtered into life and we were off to fish for our suppers in a sheltered spot I knew to the east of the bay, leaving the dogs sitting disconsolately on the rocks, howling into the breeze like a couple of spotted sirens attempting to lure sailors to their doom.

The morning was pleasantly warm with the sun half in and out and the water a lovely deep blue, pretending it was the Mediterranean with baby wavelets all a-sparkle.

Shannon propped her long legs on the edge and tilted Mammie's old straw gardening hat over her face to protect it from the bad rays. My own hat is solely for vanity because it's too late for preservation.

It's blue, that sort of darkish aquamarine color that I thought toned well with the color of the sea that day, and it has a broad brim, upturned at one side and pinned back with a big floppy pink silk flower. I bought it years ago for one of Molly's weddings, must have been about 1950, I suppose, though you'll be pleased to know I wasn't wearing the rest of my wedding outfit on the boat. I was suitable dressed in white sailor pants bought in Saint-Tropez in 1966. I forget how old I was then, and don't you dare to even try to calculate, but it was during the time of the "youthquake," and believe me I did not intend to be left behind.

I told Shannon and Eddie the story of how I was staying on a famous person's yacht: he was a great racing man and I often met him in Ireland, at Punchestown and Leopardstown, and at his wonderful stud farm. He once sold me a mare and that's always a great bond between horse people, and I daresay I was invited onto his yacht for a cruise around the Med as much for my entertainment value as for my fashionable appearance. Because, as I told you before, we Irish are never short of a story. In fact we often have to be held back in civilized company lest we monopolize the conversation.

Anyhow, in 1966 I was older than I would have liked to be, which seems to be the story of my life, and of the firm belief that no woman over the age of thirty-nine should show more than two inches of leg above the knees, even though I still had pretty legs.

Of course, all the saucy little girls were in skirts the width of curtain rods, which showed their thighs and sometimes more, and I decided I couldn't possibly compete so I went shopping in those smart little boutiques in the back streets and bought myself these wonderful sailor pants. They fit like a second skin and I wore them with a thin-as-air white voile shirt with the sleeves rolled up, and the tails tied in a big knot at my bare midriff. I had a big straw hat and the biggest darkest sunglasses and the local cheap espadrilles, and believe me I started a fashion. Soon everyone in that little town was into voile shirts and white sailor pants, all except the saucy little girls who weren't about to abandon thighs for fashion.

I was with a man, an Italian industrialist and a great charmer. He was, to put it delicately, "a special friend," and he was handsome in the macho way power and money has of endowing looks on an older man, but he also possessed an unbeatable charm and a terrific sense of humor. I had known him, on and off, for ten years and we always enjoyed each other's company. I spoke his language and he spoke some of mine, and we got along just fine. Until this little miss arrived. I think someone on a neighboring boat met her sitting at a café on the port, sipping Pernod and greedily eyeing life and men on the grand yachts moored opposite.

Anyhow, before she knew it she had been picked up and was on board one of the grandest of them all, and she was brought along to have cocktails on our boat. She recognized my friend from his frequent appearances in the world's gossip columns and she made a beeline for him. She was eighteen, blond and, goddamm it, gorgeous and the Italian was no match for her wide-eyed breathless admiring wiles.

Now, I had never had an "exclusive" on him, nor he on me, we just had an ongoing "friendship," but she and her escort stayed on board for dinner and she elbowed me ruthlessly aside and took a seat next to my Italian, while I was fobbed off with her escort, a perfectly nice man with whom I had nothing at all in common. The little minx snuggled up to my Italian, with her hand resting lightly on his thigh, gazing adoringly at him and all the while casting triumphant glances at me, while I tried to keep a civilized conversation going.

I admit to a little sulk and maybe a bit too much champagne, and was it entirely my fault that later, on her way back down the gangplank, she should "accidentally" slip and fall, plop, into the rather tired waters of the port? We gathered at the rail to watch as her escort dived in to rescue her, though she could have swam perfectly well if she hadn't been so angry, and I was satisfied to see that she didn't look nearly so gorgeous with her mascara sliding down her face, spitting old cigarette butts from her pouting little mouth.

But there's a happy ending to this little saga; a year later I read about her marriage to a racing car driver she had met at a disco, the son of a German tycoon, and she ended up as grand a lady as they've ever seen in Munich, complete with Bavarian castles and a yacht of her own. She had four beautiful children and became quite well known for her charity work, especially for underprivileged girls.

Eddie laughed so hard at my little story that he almost fell into the bay himself, but I can be forgiven anything because I am a woman, and old.

There was nothing on our fishing lines, so we lazed about, admiring the scenery and the distant glimpse of Ardnavarna through the trees, and it was odd seeing the strand from the water instead of as we usually did from horseback as we galloped along it.

"If you are bored," I suggested, "I can tell you what Lily did next."

Shannon sat up. "I'm not bored," she said eagerly, "but I can't wait to hear. I mean, did she see Finn again? And what about Ciel?"

"All in good time," I said, holding up a restraining hand and admiring my new coral nail polish.

"Well, now," I said. "Lily adored that son of hers and she nearly smothered him with affection and mothering. He was a nice little boy, if a little subdued, and he was handsome in rather a delicate sort of way. And you have to wonder if he really was that delicate or if that was the way she liked it to be, because it meant she kept him to herself. She devoted her days to him, always looking to the future, planning his schooling, and of course there was no question but that he would go to Harvard. Even so, one small boy was not enough to fill a woman's daily life, and especially those long nights, and Lily was lonely. And she was also filled with guilt.

"In an effort to redeem herself, in her own eyes as well as the Lord's, she took up her charity again. Remember the Porter Adams ten thousand a year for the benefit of poor Irishwomen in the North End? Well, she contributed a lot more, and this time, with memories of her mother taking baskets of food to the sick and needy, she put on a plain simple dress and went to work, visiting hospitals and schools and soup kitchens, deciding for herself how the monies from her charity should be distributed. And the Irish people liked her; she was a grand lady and they knew it, but she gave herself no airs, and she understood them. Education was her priority because she knew without it those ragged ghetto children were as doomed as their parents. And she brought in teachers, endowed scholarships, and she counted it a personal achievement whenever one of 'her children' made it through school into college."

Boston

STIFLED BY BOSTON'S SUMMER HEAT, Lily bought a country mansion on the northern shores of Long Island in an area near Manhasset known as the "Irish Channel" because so many rich Irishmen maintained estates there. She named it Adams Farm and she moved there with Liam and her staff and began to entertain her neighbors.

Of course it wasn't a proper "farm"; there was a chicken coop somewhere on the edge of their fifty acres for fresh eggs, and there was a donkey in the paddock to keep Liam's pony company, and to her joy she finally had stables again and she stocked them with the finest horseflesh the Adams money could buy. She rode across her acres with six-year-old Liam at her side on his pony, and she felt happy again, and free. But she never allowed herself to forget Finn's threat.

She was in her early thirties and still beautiful; she was always perfectly turned out, whether it was for a ride through the woods or a grand dinner, and when she entertained she was the perfect hostess.

She read in the *Boston Herald* that Dan had sold his house in Back Bay and had built himself a mansion outside Washington, in Maryland. They said it was a miniature White House, and that Dan was running for the senate. They also said that he was often confined to a wheelchair these days, from the old injury to his back. Tears stung her eyes as she remembered that fateful night, and as always she wished she could turn back the clock. She remembered her exasperated mother telling her again and again: "If only, Lily, if only," she would say. "Those words are the story of your life. When will you ever learn there is no such thing as 'If only'? You did what you did and it's your own fault." And she thought sadly that when she died, the words "If only" should be carved on her gravestone.

They were back in Boston when she was surprised one evening to hear the doorbell ring. She was in her little sitting room upstairs working on a piece of needlepoint, trying to fill in her time, the way she filled the canvas with colored wools. Liam was getting ready for bed and she would go to kiss him good night, and then she would be alone again in the big silent house until another lonely morning dawned.

The parlormaid came and told her there was a young man to see her. He looked "rough," she said nervously, so she had left him outside on the steps. "He says his name is John Wesley Sheridan, ma'am," she added.

"Sheridan?" Lily repeated, shocked.

"He's a big lad, ma'am, about sixteen years old, I'd say."

Lily knew her worst nightmare had come true. Her son had come to find her. She ran to the window and peered into the street, but there was no sign of him.

Frightened, she told herself that the boy had nothing to do with her. He had no part in her life. He was in the past. A picture of Dermot Hathaway's ruthless face swam before her eyes and she remembered his body on hers, his cruel hands and the pain and the humiliation. She wanted to scream. She told herself again that the product of such a union had no right to a mother. "Tell the boy I do not know who he is and I will not see him," she told the maid.

Her voice trembled and the maid glanced worriedly at her.

"Just tell him what I said," Lily hissed, "and see that he goes or I shall send for the police and have him arrested."

The girl scuttled, terrified, from the room, onto the first floor landing.

Liam was leaning over the banister looking down at the hall. "Who is that fellow down there?" he asked curiously.

Boy Sheridan was there, staring up at them. He had let himself in, even though the maid had asked him to wait outside, and she quickly ran down the stairs afraid he meant to steal something. Liam followed her. Boy waited, a strange little smile on his lips.

He stared at Liam. "Who are you?" he asked roughly.

"I'm Liam Porter Adams. And who are you?"

"Porter Adams, eh?" The boy strolled casually through the hall, peeking in the library, noting the rich furnishings and the expensive treasures. "So, all this is yours, is it?"

Liam nodded, puzzled. "I guess so."

"Madam says she doesn't know you and you are to leave at once or she will send for the police," the maid said frantically. He was a big lad and there was a look in his eyes that frightened her. "You shouldn't be in here," she added nervously. "I'm going to tell madam to call the police right now."

He shrugged indifferently, staring at Liam, the son who had it all while he had nothing. "Just tell her she knows me all right. And that I'll be back," he said, strolling to the door. He turned and grinned at Liam. "Good-bye, brother," he called as he left.

Liam ran upstairs to tell his mother. She was standing at the window watching Boy Sheridan walk away down the street. Liam told her what the strange fellow in their hall had said, and she sent him quickly to bed. And then, sick with fear, she telephoned Ned.

She told him what had happened and that she had decided to leave Boston in case he came back. "I'll take Liam to New York," she said. "I'll be at the usual hotel."

Ned called Nantucket to find out what had happened. His mother told him there had been some new trouble and Boy had been accused of beating up another lad, badly enough for him to be hospitalized. He was always restless and angry and he wanted to get off the island. He had disappeared, taking fifty dollars of Mr. Sheridan's money with him, and they didn't know where he was, but somehow they knew he wasn't coming back.

"All these years they've cared for him," Ned said sadly, "and he repays them like this."

"We all did our best," Lily replied angrily. "What he *is* has nothing to do with them, or with me."

SHE BOUGHT A SMALL TOWN HOUSE on Sutton Place with views of the East River, and she enrolled Liam in a good private day school until he was old enough for St. Paul's. It occurred to her, with a tiny buzz of fear, that she was in the same city as Finn. But she thought that since the new friends she would make through Ned would be in the theater world and the opera, of which she intended to become a patron, it would be unlikely that their paths would cross. But she couldn't help wondering about him; what he was like now, whether he was married. And if he had forgotten her.

CHAPTER
~~~~~~~~~~~~~ 47 ~~~~~~~~~~~~~

CIEL MOLYNEUX'S FRIENDS WERE PUZZLED as to why she was on the shelf. After all, she was attractive and vital, witty, charming, and full of fun and, despite her father's lapse into gambling before he died, she was still rich.

Yet the years went by and though she went to all the parties and knew "everyone," she still had not married.

"It's her own choosing," the gossips said, because they knew all her friends adored her and so did the men, who found her less of a challenge and a lot more fun than some of the famous "beauties."

Ciel was twenty-eight years old; she spent a fortune on clothes, she loved hunting and fishing, she adored the theater and parties, and yet she had not yet met a man who could take the place of the treacherous Finn O'Keeffe. She tried bravely not to think about him, pushing him to the back of her mind along with the memories of her wicked sister. They deserved each other, she told herself, wishing William were alive to share Ardnavarna with her.

She was in Dublin, walking down Molesworth Street heading for tea at Buswell's Hotel after an energetic afternoon's shopping, when she bumped into Jack Allerdyce. She had met him years before in London, but their paths had only crossed occasionally since, and on an impulse she asked him to join her for tea.

Jack was really Major John Howard Allerdyce, an ADC at Dublin Castle. He was an Englishman in his middle-thirties with steady brown eyes, brown hair cut short and brushed neatly back, and a dashing mustache. He was not a handsome man the way Finn was, but with his upright military bearing and his pleasant features, he was attractive. As they sat over hot buttered teacakes and scones in Buswell's, Ciel thought he had style, and besides, he made her laugh, and she was pleased when he told her he would also be at the supper dance given by mutual friends that evening.

She arrived deliberately late, searching eagerly for him in the crowd, pleased when she finally spotted him. He looked debonaire in his dress uniform, a short scarlet mess jacket with gold epaulets and gold buttons, and black trousers with a red silk stripe down the side.

He shouldered his way through the throng to her side. "I'm booking all your dances," he said authoritatively.

"Whatever will people say?" she asked, amused.

"I don't care." He wrote his name with a flourish across her entire dance card and said, "I didn't think you could look any prettier than you did in that little hat with the spotted veil this afternoon, but you do. I like you in pink."

"Even with my carrot hair?" she demanded.

"*Because* of your carrot hair," he said firmly, and she knew then that she *really* liked him.

They danced every dance and went in to supper together, and she knew everyone was watching them and speculating, but she was having a wonderful time. Still, always wary of scandal, she did not permit him to take her home.

His nice steady brown eyes and his laugh were the last thing she thought about as she fell asleep that night and the first thing she remembered when she woke up. She thought of Finn and all the pain rushed back again. Then she told herself that Jack Allerdyce was a fine-looking man, well-read, cultivated, and from a very good family, and she laughed, thinking rebelliously he was exactly the kind of man her father would have wanted her to marry. But when the first bouquet of flowers from him arrived with breakfast, she leapt from the bed and packed her bags and fled in a panic back to Ardnavarna.

Jack telephoned her that evening. "Why did you run away?" he asked, sounding so hurt and bewildered that she began to melt.

"It wasn't your fault," she said. "It's just me. I don't know, I can't explain. Maybe it's that you are just too eligible."

"Don't hold it against me," he said, laughing. "And anyhow, I'm not half as eligible as you. I'm only a second son, with no inheritance and the army as a career."

"Thank God," she said, relenting. And she asked him out to Ardnavarna that weekend.

He arrived laden with flowers, champagne, chocolates, and books like a summer Santa Claus, putting the sparkle back in her eyes and a new lightness in her heart. He was so different from Finn she soon forgot to make comparisons.

It was a quick romance and she married Jack at a quiet ceremony in Dublin a few months later. One of the conditions of her father's will was that her husband must agree to take on the Molyneux name. So Jack became John Howard Allerdyce Molyneux. He swept her off for an extended honeymoon in France and when they returned they threw an enormous reception at the house in Fitzwilliam Square for all their friends. The friends smiled, satisfied, seeing that they doted on each other and that they were always laughing. "The perfect couple," they said.

They were based at Ardnavarna but Jack was an army man and Ciel followed happily wherever he was posted; to India, Borneo, or Hong Kong. She threw herself into whatever new environment they were currently in, making friends and enjoying life because, as she told Jack, with him she would be happy in a jungle or a desert and anything in between.

"It doesn't matter, as long as I'm with you," she said, coping gamely with servants who spoke only Hindi or Urdu, or Cantonese or Malay. She swatted away mosquitoes the size of dragonflies and swept away cockroaches the size of mice, and shot rats the size of rabbits, and screamed at spiders as big as her hand. And she prayed she would never come face-to-face with a snake because it was the one thing she knew she couldn't cope with. "I'll simply go all to pieces," she told Jack, so he bought her a pair of mongooses who became so devoted to her they refused to leave her side and had to be forcibly restrained from climbing onto the bed with them at night.

"You see, everybody loves you," Jack said, laughing at her as he shoved the little mongooses out onto the veranda where they belonged.

The only trouble was that the years were passing and there were still no children. "Maybe it's the hot climate," Jack said, because he knew she was worrying about it. And maybe he was right, because the minute they found themselves back in England, where Jack was given a desk job at the War Office, Ciel became pregnant.

They had been married for eight years when Maudie was born. "Another rousing redhead," Jack said with a grin, enchanted to have a second little imp to brighten up his household.

Whenever she looked at her little girl, Ciel thought wistfully about Lily. She remembered trailing devotedly after her elder sister and she desperately wanted little Maudie to have a sister of her own to keep her company, but no matter how hard they tried, it was not to be.

Ciel took Maudie to Ardnavarna for the summer months and Jack joined her as often as he could get away, but she was alone when Finn returned to his homeland.

She noticed the maids with their heads together, gossiping excitedly and thinking maybe there was to be more "trouble," she asked what was happening.

"It's Finn O'Keeffe. Padraig O'Keeffe's son," they added, as though the name had not been indelibly imprinted on the brain of every Molyneux. "He's come home to visit the old country. And with a million dollars in his pocket, so they say. And lookin' it also."

Ciel's heart sank to her boots. She had put Finn out of her mind and out of her life, and that was all very well as long as she never saw him again. Now he was here, she wasn't so sure. She told herself that he would never dare come to see her. But she was wrong.

The excited maids let him in and the dalmatians charged toward him, barking their heads off, wagging their tails as though he were an old friend. Walking slowly down the great sweeping staircase toward him, Ciel thought if they had any sense they would have bitten his head off.

She walked past him into the uncomfortable little anteroom off the great hall. He followed her and she sat down on a hard little upright chair because she did not trust her wobbly knees. She did not offer him a seat. He looked just the same, handsome, well dressed, rich. Only he was older, his nose was crooked now as though it had been broken, and there were more lines on his face.

"I heard you had been in the village, throwing your money around," she said coldly.

He shrugged. "I wanted to do something for my old friends. Is there anything wrong with that?"

"Why are you here? What right have you to come to my house?"

"Would you believe me if I said I had come to apologize?"

"I don't want to hear it. I'm a married woman now."

"I heard. I'm glad you're happy, Ciel."

She glared at him and he said, "But there's another reason I've come to see you. I want to buy Ardnavarna."

"Ardnavarna is not for sale," she said. "And if it were I would never sell it to you."

She strode past him into the hall and he followed her. "I'll pay any sum you ask. Just name it."

Ciel walked up the stairs, not looking at him. She said, "Go back to New York, Finn, where you belong. Because you have never belonged at the Big House and you never will."

She went to the nursery and told the nanny to pack little Maudie's trunks, they were returning to London for the rest of the summer.

She thought the long journey by train and ferry and then train again would never end. She was in such a fever to see Jack again, and when she finally saw him pacing the train station, eagerly searching the row of carriages for her, her heart filled with love for him and she breathed a huge sigh of relief. She had just proven to herself that Finn did not matter one bit to her anymore. It was Jack she loved, and she put Finn out of her mind and out of her life at last.

CHAPTER
48

MAUDIE

Ardnavarna

WE WENT FOR A LONG WALK, Brigid and I, two old women clumping over the hills in ancient Wellington boots, wrapped in dark-green shooting jackets with a dozen different pockets meant to hold everything from a brace of pheasant to pipe and tobacco. They used to belong to my own pa, about 1930, and they still keep out the thin drifting Irish rain and the wind. Brigid wore one of those Sherlock Holmes style tweed hats with the little earflaps and I had my old black felt; and with one of us as big and round as a butterball and the other as little and skinny as a jackrabbit, we made as odd a pair as you are ever likely to see tramping Connemara's lanes, mismatched as an Irish wolfhound and a Jack Russell terrier.

Brigid knew I was upset, telling the tale of my own mammie's unhappiness. "Don't y'go dwelling on it again," she warned me, giving me a hand over a treacherous bit of loose rocks and rubble. "Ye know there's no point in upsettin' yerself. It's all over and done with long ago, and there's precious little ye can do about it now."

"I know, I know." I sighed. "It's just that I always think up to this point in the story I can forgive Lily anything, because after all, what happened was not really her fault. She just never got over that first terrible mistake. But y'see, Brigid, I believe that Finn really fell for my mammie. Not lock, stock, and barrel maybe, the way he had fallen for Lily, with all the mad passion of youth and first love. But he really liked Mammie; they made each other laugh, they enjoyed being together."

"She wasn't sexy like Lily," Brigid said, striding ahead, her tiny feet twinkling so fast through the springy grass I had almost to run to keep up with her.

It was true, I know. Even when she was only seventeen and too young and ignorant of what it was all about, Lily had lured men. And that was what had got her into trouble in the first place, with Dermot Hathaway, and it was what had continued to cause trouble throughout her life, with Finn and Dan and Ned. And even, in a way, with her own son, though I'll tell you what I mean by that a bit later.

"Don't be frettin' about yer mammie," Brigid cautioned again as we stood at the top of the rise, gazing through the gray, misty landscape, smelling the sea on the air and listening to the silence. There wasn't even a bird cry and when it's like this I always think the land must have looked exactly this way for centuries. Nothing has changed and nothing ever will. Ireland is like that.

We walked slowly back down the hill with the dogs dashing ahead of us, and on an impulse I suggested we walk into the village. It's nothing but a straggle of low cottages, washed in the same bright greens and yellows that my grandfather had painted them, and which I saw to it were repainted every year. The gardens are not fit to be called such because the Irish in these parts are not much for flowers, except those like myself, of course, with big estates and a passion for it. But the hydrangeas grow wild in a riot of blues and pinks and the wild fuschia form fine colorful hedgerows as you walk through, and with all the brightness around you might almost think you were in India or the tropics, if it were not for the gray, misty skies overhead. There are two saloons, O'Flaherty's and Burke's, good Connacht names both, one at each end of the street and loyalty is divided fairly between them. Burke's is also the general store, serving flour and eggs and soap along with the foaming black Guinness pulled by the pint.

We stopped in and I ordered a couple of jars while Brigid puttered about, prodding tomatoes and peaches with a discriminating forefinger that left little bruises on them, picking out the best for our suppers tonight; and the dalmatians curried favor with Moura Burke who had seen the movie *One Hundred and One Dalmatians* some years ago and who has been a pushover for their big-eyed wiles ever since. I pretended I didn't see the surreptitious biscuit she slipped to each of them while I sipped my Guinness and passed the time of day with the other customers. You know there's something convivial about combining a shop and a bar, and maybe it takes away a woman's guilt at having a Guinness midmorning instead of a cup of tea.

"Sure and it'll take the mist out of yer lungs," Moura said cheerfully, while the dogs hovered hopefully around her. "And how're your young guests? The girleen was in yesterday, buying postcards, and the young fella bought himself one of Dessie O'Flaherty's finest hazelwood walking canes. He asked where he could find a bit of poteen and I said to him, "Yer asking me when y've the finest source right there in yer own house?"

I grinned knowingly. "Sure and I don't know what you're talking about Moura," I said, for poteen is one of the great secrets of Ireland. It can be good—strong enough to knock your socks off—or it can be lethal. It's an illegal hooch made from a mixture of sugar, yeast, barley, and water and boiled over a peat fire, but anyhow the Gardai will be after me if I tell you more.

"If he's after poteen, he'd better be careful," I said.

"Sure and didn't I tell him that meself." Moura grinned back at me. She's half my age and a fine-looking woman, black-haired and pink-cheeked with flashing dark eyes, and I've known her since she was born, the way I have most of Ardnavarna's villagers, except for the oldies like me and Brigid, and there are not too many of us left anymore.

Brigid finished her shopping and the dogs their begging and we all finished our Guinness and off we strolled back along the lane. We climbed over a broken bit of wall and took the shortcut through the old parklands of the Big House and, thinking of Mammie, we made a little detour to the family chapel. We went in and said a little prayer for her, and for Pa and all the rest of them, including Lily, while the dogs curled like faithful hounds at the foot of the statues of a recumbent knight and his lady. After that little communication with God and my loved ones, somehow I felt better, and I stepped briskly out on the path to home, looking forward to a snooze by the fire and the return of my "grandchildren," as I like to call them, this evening.

They came back bearing presents: a magnificent brightly colored silk scarf for Brigid and one of those photographs of themselves, taken in a photo booth, that they had had put in a silver frame for me. Brigid blushed a fiery red to match her scarf, she was so pleased and embarrassed, and I saw from the glitter in her eyes she was touched almost to tears by their unexpected gift. My own present could not have been a more perfect memento. I inspected it eagerly again. Eddie had his arm around Shannon and their faces were pressed close together and they were both laughing. The tiny silver frame enclosed the moment for me forever and I kissed them both warmly. "I shall put it on my night table," I told them, "where I can see your happy faces first thing when I wake."

They had even bought chocolates for the girls who help in the house, and doggie treats for the "boys," so no one was left out, and it felt almost like Christmas as we quaffed a bottle of good red wine and ate hearty platefuls of Irish stew while they, for a change, since it's usually myself who does all the talking, chattered nonstop and flirted.

I could see how matters were progressing between them and I smiled with satisfaction. Now to be sure, it's none of my doing. I may be a busybody and a pushy old woman, but romance takes its own course, as you will have noticed from this story. And as I said before, Ardnavarna is conducive to romance.

Shannon had bought herself a silky hand-knit sweater the color of the fuschia hedgerows and she wore it with a flowing black silk skirt. "I thought if you could get away with red hair and pink frocks, so could I," she said, teasing.

"And very nice it looks, too, dear girl," I said approvingly, though I did look askance at Eddie, still in blue jeans. I'm beginning to worry the lad has nothing else. Perhaps I should offer him something from Pa's wardrobe. I bet he would look wonderful in plus-fours with one of those checked jackets with the pleats in the back. Pa used to look superb in it, a bit like the young Duke of Windsor, only with a mustache and a stronger chin.

I myself was in soft panne silk velvet, one of Mammie's own dresses from Vionnet, in a subtle grayish-green that looked silvery under the lamplight, with long sleeves and a pair of leaf-shaped diamond clips pinned at the corners of the low, square neckline. It had a tasseled sash and I had wound a gauzy silver scarf around my neck to disguise its scrawniness, and I had placed a frivolous little green velvet bow atop my curls. My long fake emerald-and-ruby earrings were St. Laurent from his gypsy period, about 1968 I think, and they clanked and rattled with every movement of my head. Why is it that earrings like that make a woman feel so feminine and flirtatious? I bet Lily knew the secret.

AT THE TIME WE PICK UP THE STORY, Liam was seventeen years old. He was built like his father, tall and slender with a wiry body, but in temperament he was more like Lily's brother, a dreamer who preferred music and painting to sports. He had the sculptured refinement of Lily's features, but he had his father's clear gray eyes and black hair.

If you knew Finn was his father you would have said, of course, he looks exactly like him. But if you did not, then you would have said, well of course, he looks like Lily. Liam had the best of both their looks, and the best of both their temperaments. He was calm and easygoing, he was clever enough in school, but to Lily's chagrin he was not academic like John Porter Adams, the man he thought was his father.

Boston

"IF ONLY YOU WOULD TRY A LITTLE HARDER, you could become as renowned a scholar as your father," she would say, irritated by his dreaminess, and ignoring the fact that he was not the slightest bit academic.

Liam didn't want to go to Harvard. He wanted to go to Florence and study art, and after that he wanted to wander through southern Europe with an easel and paints and a single bag with his few belongings, just painting anything that inspired him; the red earth hills in Provence, the horizon blending into the sea in Venice, the ochre and umber and terra-cotta villages of Tuscany, and the silver-green Mediterranean olive groves. But he was wise enough not to divulge these plans to his mother just yet.

He was a loner at school, not because he was unpopular with the other boys but because he preferred it that way, and since he was good at all the usual subjects, he was well thought of by his teachers. It was generally expected that he would follow in his father's footsteps, and in any case Lily planned to endow a John Porter Adams library at Harvard and to donate a great many of her husband's rare volumes, along with a vast amount of money.

Liam knew there would be trouble when he told his mother he had no intention of going to college, but he put the problem out of his mind to be faced later, exactly the way Lily always did, and he lived each day as it came.

The years were passing and Finn was a very rich man, much richer than he had been when Cornelius James left him his inheritance, and probably even richer than his brother Dan, whose stores now stretched from coast to coast and who was reaching new markets in the remote farming settlements on the wheat plains of the midwest and the isolated forests and lakes of the north, through his innovative mail-order catalogues. The brothers had never spoken since the night of the fight, but Finn had followed Dan's progress in the financial pages as well as the political pages of the newspapers.

Dan was a senator now. He lived alone but for the servants in his fine white-pillared mansion in Maryland, and except when a grand occasion or an important speech made it necessary and a large dose of painkiller made it possible for him to get to his feet, he was confined to a wheelchair. From the news photos Finn saw that his brother had gained a little weight, but he was still the same handsome Senator Dan, with his derby and his red suspenders, his tousled curls and his cheery grin. "Honest Dan" the media had dubbed him, and the name had stuck because, as Dan often said himself, it was true.

Finn, too, lived alone, but in a vast fourteen-room apartment on Fifth Avenue. He rarely went out, always worked late, and was at the office early again the next morning before the world markets opened. Any spare time was filled reading his way through all the books Cornelius had left him in his library, as well as the ones John Porter Adams had recommended. He had also sought out a professor of literature at Columbia University and got him to draw up a reading list, and he conscientiously read one a week from his list.

Finn kept track of Lily; he knew where she lived, who she saw, and what she was up to. He had bided his time and now he wanted his son.

Liam was seventeen when Finn O'Keeffe paid a visit to his prep school, ostensibly looking it over for a future son.

After he had been shown around, he mentioned casually that John Adams had been a neighbor of his in Boston, and that he had heard his son attended the school. "I thought I might say hello to him," he said, nonchalantly waving away their suggestions that they ask Liam to join them for tea in the headmaster's study. "No, no. Just tell me where I might find him, and I'll stroll by," he said easily.

Liam was sitting on the riverbank sketching. Finn watched him silently for a few moments, choking back the tears as he gazed at his son, a boy he barely knew. The raw emotion of paternal love struck him for the first time, and he wondered why he had wasted all these years.

"That's a very clever sketch," he said admiringly, when he could manage to speak.

Liam scrambled respectfully to his feet. "Thank you, sir," he said, embarrassed at being observed.

Finn held out his hand. He said, "I'm Finn O'Keeffe James. I knew your father. He was a neighbor of mine, and he was kind enough to help me with my library."

Liam was surprised, he rarely met anyone who had known his father, and he shook Finn's hand eagerly. "Good to meet you, sir. And you are luckier than I am because I never knew my father."

"He was a good man. And a great scholar."

Finn was surprised when Liam said, "Yes, I know. And it's hard to live up to such standards."

"Why don't we walk along the riverbank and you can tell me what you mean," he suggested.

It was odd, but Liam felt he could unburden himself to this stranger in a way he never could to his mother, and he told Finn his dilemma. He said that what he wanted most in the world was to be an artist. He added guiltily, "My mother would be angry if she knew what I just told you, even though you were my father's friend. You see, I haven't told her. Not yet."

"I understand," Finn said quietly.

"My mother is devoted to me," Liam said suddenly. "She's had my life planned out since the day I was born. Maybe it's because my father died so soon afterward and she just transferred all that extra love and caring to me." He glanced hopefully at Finn. "I'm sorry, Mr. James, if I'm out of line, talking like this. Only sometimes it gets on top of me. She just smothers me with so much caring. Since I was a kid every meal was planned for its nutrition, I even had to come away to school to taste my first candy bar. Every class I took: riding, dancing, fencing, swimming, ice-skating, was not just for pleasure but to fulfill some function, social or physical, I don't know. And I've been stuffed with books and learning like a force-fed goose since I was old enough to read."

"And how old was that?"

Liam grinned. "Four years old, sir."

Finn laughed. "I was fourteen before I could read properly, and now I'm the one who's like a force-fed goose, stuffing myself with books and knowledge in an attempt to catch up on all I missed." He looked thoughtfully at his son. "Let me ask you something, Liam. Have you ever questioned your artistic talent? Have you asked yourself how good you are? Or is painting just a pleasant pastime that you are clever at and that you enjoy?"

Liam said eagerly, "I don't know how to explain it, sir, but it's as though I'm thinking with my fingertips. The idea is there in my mind, the shapes, the colors, the light, and it just somehow translates itself through my brush onto the canvas. I don't know how good I am, and

I'm certain I have a lot to learn. All I know is that I'm willing to give up everything to do it."

Finn raised a quizzical eyebrow. "Everything? Your home? Your position in life? Money?" He paused and then added cleverly, "Your mother?"

"Everything, sir, except the last one."

"Think about it, Liam," Finn said as they strolled back to the school. "Because it seems to me that if you did, your mother would be the first thing you would lose. Ask yourself if your art means that much to you."

"Will you be visiting the school again, Mr. James?" Liam asked eagerly as they shook hands and said good-bye. "I've enjoyed talking to you."

Finn smiled and slapped his shoulder genially. "Then we must talk again. And next time we shall have lunch. How about Saturday? Only let's not tell your mother. From what you've told me, she probably wouldn't approve."

Liam sighed as he watched him walk away. He knew he was right and of course he wouldn't tell his mother, but for the first time in his life he had met a man to whom he could talk about matters close to his heart. Almost like a father, he thought wistfully.

CHAPTER
49

FINN WENT TO SEE LIAM the following Saturday and over lunch they got to know each other better. He told Liam that he had come to America from Ireland when he was Liam's age, just seventeen, and how he had worked for Cornelius, and the events that had made him a rich man.

And after that, whenever Liam was free, Finn was there. They discussed his talent and his future endlessly and Finn saw an easy way to get back at Lily and take her son from her. If Liam went to Italy to become an artist, she would cut off his money, leaving him with no choice but to do as she said. But if he offered to finance him, Liam would be free to do whatever he wanted, and he would also be alienated from his mother.

Finn was tempted, but for the first time there was another emotion besides his desire for revenge. He loved his son and, like a true father, he wanted the best for him. He wanted Liam to go to college.

"You are young," he said. "There is time for everything you want to do. Study the history of art and architecture. You can travel abroad in the summer vacations, maybe you can take courses in drawing in Florence or Sienna. I'll find the best tutors for you. And if there's any financial 'difficulty' "—he grinned at Liam, who knew he meant "trouble with his mother"—"then I shall be delighted to underwrite your expenses."

He held up his hand to stop his protests. "I wouldn't have gotten where I am today without help," he said firmly. "And I consider it my duty to help you now. Besides, I rather fancy being a patron of the arts. When you're famous I can tell everyone I was the first to recognize your talent."

And so, to Lily's relief, Liam went to Harvard without protest the following year, and though the subjects Liam chose to study were not the ones she would have preferred, at least he was dutifully following in his "father's" footsteps.

Boy

MEANWHILE, LILY'S OTHER SON, John Wesley "Boy" Sheridan, was a grown man of twenty-eight. Since he had run away from Nantucket he had crisscrossed the country a dozen times, traveling in railroad boxcars and sleeping rough with other vagrants, huddled around bonfires to keep out the cold in derelict city yards, or hiding in country haystacks and barns, stealing food and money wherever he could, and spending most of that on cheap booze. His face was lined and battle-scarred from too many barroom fights, and he looked older than his years. He was a bitter, angry young man, easily pushed to violence, and there were at least two hobos who had not survived his brutal beatings or his quickness with a knife.

Every now and again he would find himself a temporary job. Sometimes it was rough work tidying up yards in pleasant suburban neighborhoods, where the ladies of the house were sympathetic to his story of how he had fallen on hard times, and so fed him and paid him a little more than they had meant to. For some reason Boy had an allure for women; there was a boldness in his eyes when he looked at them that made them blush and fuss with the necklines of their blouses.

More often he worked on farms, reaping the corn and picking apples and peaches. He found that in the country areas the women were lonelier and the comforts they offered along with the job were easier to come by than with suspicious city women. And often, when he left them, he managed to take a trophy or two with him: a ring or a bracelet, or a stash of money from under the mattress, to ease the next phase of his endless journey.

On one of the remote farms he met a widow, a woman fifteen years older than himself. She was tall and thin and flat-chested and not his style, with hair already graying at the sides and faded blue eyes with crinkles at the corners from peering out at the endless flat wheat fields she owned, all the way to the horizon. Hundreds and hundreds of rich acres, as Boy was quick to notice. The farmhouse was weathered gray clapboard like all the others, and when he came calling his first task was painting the white trim.

"I like to keep things nice around here, even with Ethen long gone," the woman said proudly. "I have no sons and I still run this farm myself. Ethen, my husband, was caught in the grainstore, y'know. He was up the ladder shoveling it down the chute when something got stuck and he jumped down onto the grain to see what had happened. And that whole mountain of grain just slid right over him, burying him. It was a week afore we found where he was, and the grain was ruined by then."

Boy stared at her, imaging the decomposing body in the grain.

"He shoulda known better," she commented grimly.

As the weeks passed she gave him more and more tasks to do—cleaning the machinery, helping with the plowing and the fertilizing, grooming the horses, cleaning the storage barns. Gradually Boy realized she did not want to let him go. She was a rich lonely widow and she liked having him around.

"You're better company than the usual farmhands," she said, offering him a cold beer at the kitchen table with his dinner of fried chicken and grits. "How'd y'like to stay on permanent, as my manager?"

Their eyes met across the table and Boy knew that all these acres of wheat fields and this farmhouse and all it contained, including Amelia Jane Ekhardt, were his for the taking. All he had to do was ask.

He thought about it and six weeks later he proposed marriage. The ceremony was performed at the nearest town without invited guests. Boy found his husbandly duty tiresome, but Amelia liked it well enough and she didn't expect too much anyway. As master of the house, he shared her bedroom and strode his acres, and his dinner was set, steaming hot on the table, every night at five-thirty, with a bottle of beer to wash it down.

A few months later, when he could no longer stand the monotony of the daily routine and the boredom of the open plains, he cleaned out Amelia's bank account of several thousand dollars and hopped the train to Chicago. He bought himself a fine suit of clothes and took a room at the grandest hotel and inquired where the best women and the nearest poker game could be found. With money in his pocket, he aimed to become a gambling man, but he wasn't clever enough to beat the real pros and was soon reduced to zero again. He hocked his fine clothes and, back in the nondescript hobo's outfit of worn jacket and pants, hit the road again.

And all the time, the knowledge of who he was and what might have been burned like acid into his brain. Every night, he sat hunched over a makeshift fire with a bottle of the cheapest hooch to ease the pain in his soul and the hunger in his belly, remembering the stories the Sheridan women had told him. Of how his mother was the daughter of a rich and titled Irishman whose family owned vast estates. Of how she had abandoned him because she was too young and too hurt to take care of him herself, though she had always sent money for his keep. Of how she never wanted to see him.

Boy had checked out the facts of the matter. He had gone to the library in Boston and found a volume of *Burke's Peerage,* which revealed what they said was true. Since then he had asked himself the same question a thousand times over: was he not entitled to his share of all those rich Irish acres? And the money? And maybe even the title too? It had been easy to find his mother's whereabouts and he had gone there intending to confront her, but she had refused to see him and threatened him with the police. And since he'd had stolen money in his pockets he could not afford a run-in with the law.

But there was something else that burned him even more than that: it was the memory of her other son standing on the fine staircase in their grand house, asking him coolly who he was, as though he had no right to be there, and the fact that that kid was lord and master instead of him.

Shivering around those makeshift bonfires on icy winter nights when the wind cut right through a man, in company with other derelicts and drunks and the dregs of a society down on their luck, Boy promised himself vengeance on them one day, and he knew just how to do it.

It happened that Boy found himself back in Boston the first semester Liam was at Harvard. He was broke and even in the slums he was dirtier and shabbier than most. He spent his nights in a charity hostel where they gave him a bowl of soup for his supper, and tea and bread for breakfast and a few coins in his pocket to get him through the day and on to his next destination.

In the refined streets and squares of Beacon Hill, he stood out like a sore thumb. Watchful eyes noticed him loitering along Mount Vernon Street and reported the matter to the police, and he found himself hustled into a paddy wagon, so named for the many Irish policemen. He was thrust into a cell and allowed to cool his heels and his temper for a couple of days, and then allowed out with a warning to stay away from Beacon Hill and get the hell out of town.

Instead he drifted back to Beacon Hill and robbed at knifepoint a smart grocery store called Daniel's. It was easy; people didn't expect things like that to happen in places like Beacon Hill, and he got away with over four hundred dollars. He fled across the Charles River to

Cambridge, where he bought himself some clothes, had his hair cut short, and shaved off his mustache. He rented a cheap room on Massachusetts Avenue and went back over the bridge to Beacon Hill and Mount Vernon Street again. This time no one seemed to notice him and he was able to observe the daily comings and goings of his mother, and also of her son.

The first really big fight Liam had with his mother was about whether he should be allowed to live on campus like the other students, or whether he should go home to Beacon Hill every night, the way she wanted. Lily had stormed and wept, saying if he loved her he would never leave her all alone. She reminded him of how much she had given up for him, and how hard it had been for her to let him attend boarding school.

In the end he had given her the choice: he would stay home with her and not go to college, or else he would go to college and live on campus. She had been forced to give in but she never let him forget it, and she was always coming around, bringing unwanted home treats and offering unwanted advice. The only respite came when she went to New York.

Liam understood that despite her charity work, she was an unfulfilled, lonely woman. She was forty-six, still youthful-looking and very beautiful, and he wished she would meet some nice man and get married and be happy. Then maybe she would let him get on with his own life. But he knew it was unlikely; Lily seemed uninterested in men.

Finn still visited him as often as he could; they were good friends, though his mother still didn't know it. He was meeting him at a café on Harvard Square that night and he was running late. He was hurrying down Dunster when he became aware that he was being followed. It was a moonless night with black ice glinting on the sidewalks and long stretches of darkness in between the spluttering gas lamps. Thinking it must be a fellow student, Liam slowed down to see who it was.

Finn had grown tired of standing around in the cold and he was walking from the other end of Dunster to meet him. He saw Liam turn and look behind him and then stop and talk to someone, but he was too far away to see who it was.

"Wait a minute," the stranger called.

Liam peered at the stranger as he came closer to the pool of lamplight. There was something familiar about him, but he couldn't quite remember what.

"Hello, brother," the stranger said. "I told you I would be back."

Then he recalled the night, years ago, when an unknown boy had come to their house. "Good-bye, brother," he had called as he left, and somehow it had stuck in his memory. And now he had just called him "brother" again.

"What do you want? And why do you call me 'brother'?"

"What do I want? Why, to talk to you, of course. And why do I call you brother? Why, because we have the same mother, Liam. Mrs. Lily Porter Adams, the former Lily Molyneux."

Liam's thin young face flamed with fury. "Don't you dare even mention my mother's name, or I shall call the police."

Boy grabbed Liam's arms and twisted them behind his back; then he pressed a knife against his ribs. "That's what your family always does, isn't it, when there's something they don't want to hear, or someone they don't want to see? Send for the police and have them removed. Well, you can't have me removed now, brother, so you will just have to listen to what I have to say. Even if you don't like it. And you might as well know your mother is my mother all right, only she abandoned me in Nantucket after the shipwreck. When I was born she left me there, like so much unwanted baggage, and took herself off to better things. To Mr. John Porter Adams and the good life. Which you, dear brother, so far have had sole enjoyment of. Only now I am back and I intend to claim my share."

The knife nicked Liam's flesh and he felt the blood begin to trickle. He wondered, terrified, how Boy knew so much about his family. But it wasn't true about his mother and he'd kill him for saying such a thing.

"You cheap bastard," he roared, pushing Boy away. The knife clattered to the ground between them and they both stared at it.

Boy grinned menacingly at Liam. "Go on, brother," he whispered. "I dare you. Pick it up and then let's see the best man win."

But before Liam could move, he grabbed the knife. He was through with talking. He stared at Liam. He just wanted to cut out all those years of hate. And he thrust the knife into him, again and again.

Finn ran the last few yards. He brought his stick down hard on Boy's hands. Boy howled with pain, staring at his broken fingers, and then, spitting curses and insults, he leapt for his attacker's throat. Finn whacked his silver-topped malacca cane down on Boy's skull. There was a sickening crack, like a cue striking a billiard ball, and Boy fell stunned to the sidewalk.

Finn saw the blood seeping through Liam's clothes and he groaned. He took off his overcoat and covered him, and then he removed his jacket and made a cushion for his head. He ran to the end of the street and told some passersby to get help, then he ran back to Liam. He had only been gone a few minutes but when he got back the would-be assassin had disappeared. He cradled Liam in his arms, tears trickling down his face. "Dear God," he prayed, "don't let him die. He's so young. And I've only just found him."

The ambulance came and took Liam to the hospital, where he was sent immediately to the operating room. The surgeon told Finn that he had multiple stab wounds and that he must operate right away. Finn told the police what had happened and they sent for Liam's mother.

Lily flung through the door, wild-eyed with fear. She stopped dead when she saw Finn.

"I'm sorry, Lily," he said gently. "Liam is still in the operating room. There is no news yet. It's lucky I was there to help him."

"*You* helped my son?" She sank into a chair, her eyes wide with disbelief.

"Don't forget who he is, Lily. I care as much as you do."

"How can you care?" she cried. "You don't even know him. I brought him up. I'm the one who cares, I'm the one who loves him, I saw him through all the childhood illnesses, saw that he got good grades. I'm the one who's always been there for him." She glared murderously at him. "How dare you suggest that you *care* as much as I do? *That boy is my life.*"

She paced the corridor, terrified. "Who was it?" she cried. "Where is he? I'll kill him myself. Oh, why, why. *Why* did he do it?"

"Maybe he was a thief. Maybe he demanded money and Liam refused to give it to him."

Lily stared at him suspiciously. "And you just happened to be there, walking up Dunster. Just as Liam was walking down. That's a remarkable coincidence, Finn. A bit *too* remarkable, it seems to me."

He shrugged. "Just luck, I guess. But this is not the time or the place to be picking up our old fight. Let us just think of Liam."

They sat silently opposite each other, waiting. Half an hour later the surgeon came to tell them that a deep stab wound had collapsed Liam's right lung. Another had penetrated the abdomen, thankfully missing the vital organs, though it had caused severe internal bleeding. They had done what they could: now it was up to Liam.

He said they could see him for a few moments and they stood on either side of him, staring at his ashen face. He looked so young and so vulnerable, like a child again, Lily thought sadly. "Sleep well, my darling," she said, bending to kiss him.

Finn took her home to Mount Vernon Street and she invited him in. "I think we have a few things to discuss," she said.

They sat in John's library on either side of the dying fire, looking at each other, both of them remembering the night when he had come here to see her under the pretext of speaking to John, and remembering how their love affair had begun.

She rested her head against the cool dark-red leather of the wing chair, watching as Finn poured glasses of brandy.

"Drink it," he said. "You will feel better."

"I want to know why you were meeting my son," she said.

He sighed. "We have known each other for some time. We are, I suppose, good friends."

Her face was the color of the ashes in the grate. "And why do you choose to be friends with him now? After all these years?"

"He is my son too."

She looked at him sadly. "Did you ever stop to think of what might have been? Don't you remember when I told you I was pregnant? Can you really not recall what happened, what you said, what you did that night? You disowned your son, Finn. You gave up all rights to him. You said he was not yours and that no one could ever prove he was. Well, let me tell you now, Finn, that what you said was the truth. Liam is John Porter Adams's son and no one can ever prove he isn't. You forfeited any claim to him that night. I am his mother and you will never get him away from me, even if I am forced to tell him the truth." She stood up and walked to the door. "And now you can leave my house, and my life, and my son. I never want to see you again."

She walked away from him, up the stairs, but she did not look back. He knew it was finally over. They had both lost and now they had lost each other forever.

He walked out of her house and went back to the hospital. He gazed at the face of his son. "Get well soon, my dear boy," he said, kissing his cheek for the one and only time in his life. And then he left.

CHAPTER
50

In a way, Lily was almost pleased when Liam decided he did not want to return to Harvard. Three months in the hospital and a further two recuperating at home had turned him into the perfect invalid, and she was able to dote on him and spoil and pamper him as much as she wished. He had no memory at all of his attacker and he puzzled over the reason. "Why me, mother?" he asked, and she told him, equally puzzled, that it must have been a robber. And when spring came, and Liam told her he wanted to go to Italy, she agreed. She thought it would be good for him and it would also keep him away from Finn just in case he decided to come back. But Finn had made no further attempt to see him, and Liam didn't even know it was Finn who had saved his life.

They sailed for Naples a few weeks later, and then traveled in a chauffeured motorcar all the way to the lakes. Liam was living his dream; he devoured the colors and the landscapes with his eyes, storing them in a special compartment in his brain, to summon up later when he was back home in Boston.

They had taken a suite of rooms at the luxurious Villa d'Este and he was up at dawn, wandering along the lakeside with his sketchpad and watercolors. And for once Lily was able to relax and enjoy herself. She was, as always, beautifully turned out in the latest fashions, still beautiful, and still able to draw men's eyes.

"Your mother is the most gorgeous woman I have ever seen," a girl said to Liam, peeking over his shoulder at the watercolor sketch of the little boats bobbing by the pier at the lakeside. "And my, you are certainly a fine artist, anyone can see that."

He turned, embarrassed, to look at her. She was petite, sweet-faced, and American. He liked her shiny gold-blond hair and her amber-brown eyes and peach-colored skin. He thought she was the color of an early autumn landscape and he smiled back at her.

"Thank you for both compliments, though the last one is not true. At least not yet. I've a lot to learn."

"You already know more than most of us," she replied, laughing and showing small, even white teeth. "But you really should paint your mother's portrait. Isn't she just gorgeous?" She sighed exaggeratedly. "Oh, what I wouldn't give to look like that."

"You shouldn't want to change anything about yourself. You look perfectly fine the way you are," Liam said, amazed by his daring. He thought it must be something in the Italian air that made him so bold.

"Well now, thank you, sir," she said, dropping a mock curtsy. "But there are those women who are different from the rest of us, and your mother is one." She held out her hand. "I'm Jennie Desanto from Chicago. And who are you?"

"Liam Porter Adams. From Boston." He wiped the yellow ochre and burnt sienna from his fingers and took her hand. It was small and soft as a kitten's paw and he smiled delightedly.

"Oh. Boston," she said, pulling a face. "City of prudes and snobs. Not like Chicago." She laughed. "Anything goes in the Windy City."

She sank onto the warm wooden boards of the jetty next to him and hooked her hands around her knees, staring across the blue lake, sparkling under the early morning heat haze. "We're here on vacation," she said. "But my family originally came from Italy. My father and mother are in Milan now, but I couldn't stand the heat and the city fumes, so they sent me to the lake to wait for them. They'll be back next week." She grinned mischievously at Liam. "To tell you the truth, I'm enjoying my freedom without them. What about you? Aren't you a bit old to be traveling with your mama?"

Liam felt himself blushing. "I'm nineteen," he said quickly. "And I would have preferred to be alone, like you, but I had an—an accident, and I'm recuperating. So that's why my mother is with me."

"Oh, I'm sorry." Her amber eyes inspected him curiously. "Is that why you have that interesting scar on your cheek?" She laughed. "I thought maybe it was a dueling scar, fought for the honor of a damsel in distress."

"No such luck. I was attacked in the street by a madman with a knife."

Her eyes widened with horror. "Oh, gosh, I am sorry. Does it upset you to talk about it?"

Liam thought about it. The only thing that upset him was that Mr. James had not been to see him. When he had recovered consciousness he had looked for him every day, but he had not even sent a message. He had not heard another word from the man he had called his friend and he was hurt and bitterly disappointed. He just couldn't imagine any reason why his mentor would drop him so abruptly, and he thought it was his fault, and that he must have offended him. He had agonized for weeks over what it might be but he still had no answer, and he knew he could not contact him at his office. If Mr. James chose not to see him, that was his privilege.

"I don't mind talking about it," he said. "But that's in the past."

"I guess we should always look to the future," she said solemnly. "Being so young, we don't have much past anyway."

Liam packed up his paints and they strolled companionably along the lakeshore, keeping to the shade of the sweeping cedars while Jennie chatted amiably about home—a large house also on the shores of a lake, just outside Chicago. She told him about her sisters and brothers, "all older and much cleverer than me," she assured Liam. "I'm the spoiled baby of the family and nobody really expects very much of me."

She looked wistfully up at him and Liam felt a dizzy sense of pride that she had chosen him to talk to. She was petite and pretty and she was his exact opposite. He was introverted and lonely and artistic, and Jennie was outgoing and joyous and fun to be with.

On an impulse, he invited her to lunch with his mother. "At one o'clock. On the terrace," he said, as they walked back to the hotel.

"I'll be there," she promised.

The girl was so admiring at lunch that Lily responded graciously. After all, she told herself, Liam needed a young friend on his holiday, and Jennie was an innocent enough companion, though certainly not "top drawer." Besides, she was rather caught up with a Count Crespoli, a handsome, gray-haired older man, who was involved in shipping and the automobile industry, and who flattered her with stylish compliments and was only too happy to escort her on little excursions, or to sweet romantic little restaurants, and even for a pass at the gaming tables. It all made her feel quite young again.

Left alone for once, Liam spent all his free time with Jennie and he was so absorbed in her he quite forgot about the strange defection of his old mentor, Finn James. He bought her a sketch pad and charcoal and they tramped the hills together, sketching the views down to the lake. When she grew tired of it, she would lie back on the grass with her hands pillowing her head, gazing at the sky, while he painted. Sometimes she would sing and he told her admiringly she had a beautiful voice.

"Don't be silly," she said, laughing. "It just sounds good out here in the fresh air. In the music room it sounds like a tin whistle."

"I like everything about you," he said, catching her hand and kissing it, Italian style. She leaned forward and kissed him on the lips and he slid his arms around her and they clung together, breathing each other's breath, not wanting to let go.

"Would you think I'm a fool if I said I loved you?" he asked humbly.

She looked at him solemnly. "No. Oh, no. I wouldn't think you foolish at all, Liam," she replied.

Her parents returned the following day and when Liam introduced them to Lily, she shook hands with them, frozen-faced. "They are vulgar and nouveau riche," she said angrily to Liam, back in their rooms. "Why, the woman was wearing a diamond necklace at lunch!"

"And why shouldn't she, if that's what she likes?" Liam demanded, equally angry, because whatever Jennie and her family did was all right with him.

But Jennie's family looked down on Lily too. "She's no better than she ought to be," Mrs. Desanto fumed, still burning from Lily's dismissive stare. "Going around with the count like that, all alone, 'on excursions to look at the ruins,' she says, so loftily. What ruins? I'd like to know. There are none worth looking at around here."

She was a stout, motherly-looking woman with a liking for bright colors and shiny jewelry. Her husband had made a great deal of money importing Italian olive oil, and supplying Italian sausages to delicatessens across the United States. He was a brusque, angry little man who worried constantly about his business and the activities of his children, but who doted on his wife. Whatever she said was law as far as the family was concerned, but in his business, he was king. If she did not approve of their daughter seeing Liam Porter Adams, then that was fine with him. "You will not see him anymore," he told Jennie sternly.

"But Papa, he's only a friend I've met on holiday," she pleaded. "What harm can it do to see him? After all, there's no one else here for me to talk to."

"She's right," Mrs. Desanto said, relenting a little. "There are no other nice young girls and boys for her to pass the time with." Jennie beamed at her, scenting a reprieve. "But only for the holiday," she said, wagging a warning finger.

Liam and Jennie spent their time kissing and hugging and promising eternal devotion, and when they weren't doing that he painted her portrait. At first just pencil sketches, then watercolor, and then oils. "I'll never have time to finish it before you leave," he said, staring anxiously at the half-finished painting. Jennie peered over his shoulder at it. "I'm not half as pretty as that," she said.

"Oh yes, you are." He grabbed her and pulled her close to him. "You are beautiful, wonderful. And I want to spend the rest of my life with you. Will you marry me, Jennie?"

"Oh yes, of course I will," she said impetuously. "But it will have to be our secret for now." She frowned, thinking worriedly of her parents. "What will your mother say?" she asked Liam.

"She'll probably go crazy, but I don't care. What about yours?"

She made a little face. "The same. But I don't care either. But when shall we see each other, Liam? I shall be in Chicago and you will be in Boston."

They contemplated the thousand or so miles that would separate them, and their hearts sank as they realized they would not be together.

"I'll write to you every day," she promised.

"Me too," he said, holding her close again.

The day Jennie departed with her parents was the saddest day of his life. He watched their car chugging off down the white road until it disappeared in a haze of dust. And then he walked back along the lakeshore to the place they used to go together, and he sat down and wrote a letter to her, the first of hundreds he would write over the next two years.

Lily was happy in Italy. She decided to stay for a while longer and allow Liam to attend art school in Rome while she enjoyed the new life she had found, with Count Amadeo Crespoli as her entrée into Roman society. She took a palatial villa on a hill, with fountains and gardens filled with lemon trees and statues and lily ponds, and with a distant view of St. Peter's.

She bought her clothes in Paris and wore the Adams jewels and entertained her new friends lavishly, happily showing off her handsome young son, the artist, and forgetting all about how she had wanted him to follow in his father's footsteps, because now his tutors told her that Liam had real talent.

"One day my son will be famous," she told her new friends proudly, in fluent Italian, because she had always had an aptitude for languages.

Liam studied hard and avoided her parties whenever he could. His companions were his fellow students at the institute and he felt more at home with them in the shabby cafés in the artists' quarter, drinking cheap red wine and arguing over models and girlfriends. But in his heart was the knowledge that one day he would see Jennie again. He reread her letters until the ink faded into an indescipherable blue blur, but it hardly mattered; he knew every word of them by heart. He knew that when he was twenty-one he would come into a small amount of money, ten thousand dollars left him by his grandfather Adams. With that in his pocket, he intended to go to Chicago and marry Jennie. And if her parents refused to accept him, then he would carry her off into the night. And then they would be together always.

Liam's twenty-first birthday coincided with Lily's falling out with the count and her sudden boredom with Europe. She booked passages for both of them on the *Michelangelo,* to New York. They celebrated his coming of age with a bottle of vintage Krug. "As old as yourself," she told him proudly at a quiet dinner for two in the ship's palatial dining room.

"This is just the way I like it," she said, squeezing his hand across the table. "You and I together, Liam. That's the way it's always been, hasn't it? And naturally, that's the way it always should be."

Back in Boston, the papers were signed and Liam finally had money of his own; money he did not have to ask his mother for. He was free.

He told his mother he was taking a little trip. "I need to get away, to think things out," he said while she watched him nervously.

"But where are you going?" Lily demanded. "I'll come with you. You can't just go off alone like that."

"I shall be back in a couple of weeks," he said, picking up his bag and striding to the door.

"Liam," she cried. "Come back here at once."

"See you soon, mother," he called, opening the door.

"At least tell me where you are going," she said, bewildered.

"To Chicago," he said, looking her in the eye. "To see old friends."

Liam took the train to Chicago. He hung out of the window as it pulled into the station and, emerging from the clouds of steam, he saw Jennie anxiously searching the carriages for him.

"Jennie. Over here," he cried, and her face lit up. She ran toward him and he was out of the carriage before the train even stopped. They stood and looked at each other, assessing the difference two years and new experiences had made on them, and she heaved a huge sigh of relief. "Oh, thank God. You haven't changed."

"And neither have you. Except you've gotten even prettier."

They stepped into each others arms and he knew it was all right. Time had passed, but nothing had changed between them.

"Will you marry me?" he murmured in her ear, dropping kisses all over her dear little face.

"Of course I will," she breathed happily. "We shall never be apart again. No matter what anyone says."

She said that because she knew what her parents had planned for her. Her father knew exactly who she was going to marry: he had chosen the fellow himself. Italian, of course, from a family similar to her own, only vastly richer and more successful. It was the way things had always been done in Italian families, and no matter how educated and liberated they were in the new country, a daughter was expected to follow the old ways when it came to marriage.

They went to the Edgewater Beach Hotel because Liam was only used to staying at the best places and he didn't know about money and economy. Jennie told him about her father's plans for her and said, desperately, "You only just got back in time, Liam. I just can't marry him. He's twice my age and I don't even like him. Besides, I'm in love with you. Everything I said to you in my letters is true. I've thought of you every single day, and every night before I went to sleep. I even dreamed about you. It was destiny that brought us together, and once that happens you are together forever."

She looked miserably at him. Her golden hair was swept up at the sides and her cheeks were pink from the cold and her amber eyes round with sincerity. He squeezed her hand, thinking about what to do. "I shall ask your father's permission to marry you," he said firmly. "If he says no, then I'll take you home with me."

"And what about your mother" she asked, apprehensively, remembering Lily's possessiveness.

"Don't worry about a thing," he replied. "When I tell my mother I'm going to marry you, she will have no choice but to agree. And anyway, she's sure to love you because I do."

Jenny didn't quite believe it, but she hoped for the best, and they took a cab across town to her home. "Mama, Papa," she said, holding Liam's hand and pulling him into the parlor. "This is Liam Adams. You remember, we met in Italy, at Lake Como."

"So? What's he doing here in my house now?" Mr. Desanto asked, looking suspiciously at them.

"We were just about to have dinner," Mrs. Desanto said, bustling forward. "Maybe you'd like to join us."

"Wait." Mr. Desanto held up a commanding hand. "I wanna know why he's here. Como's a long way from Chicago, and a long time ago."

Liam said, meeting his gaze squarely, "The fact is, sir, that I have come to ask your permission to marry Jennie."

"My daughter? Marry you?" Mr. Desanto's face turned the color of beets and his eyes almost disappeared into slits of fury.

"And what does your mother think of this?" Mrs. Desanto demanded, remembering Lily only too well.

"She doesn't know yet," Liam admitted. "But I'm sure she will be pleased to gain such a beautiful daughter-in-law. I have money of my own, sir," he added hastily, lest they think him penniless and unable to look after her.

"Money? How much money?" Desanto took a menacing step closer.

"Well, ten thousand dollars, sir."

"Ten thousand dollars?" Desanto turned to his wife and laughed scornfully. "The aristocrat has money. *Ten thousand whole dollars.* Bah, the man my daughter is marrying can buy and sell your family ten times over. To him ten thousand dollars is chicken feed. Now get outa my house and stay away from my girl. Y'hear me?" He stepped closer, his face now magenta with anger. Jennie dragged Liam hurriedly into the hall.

"Go now," she whispered. "Wait for me at the Edgewater Beach." She pushed him out the door and closed it firmly, and Liam stood undecided on the steps. He wanted to go back in and argue his case, but he knew it was useless and so he returned to the hotel to wait.

Jennie arrived three hours later, carrying a small bag. "They locked me in my room," she said breathlessly, "but they forgot about the balcony and the steps leading onto the terrace. It was easy to escape." She leaned her elbows on the table and smiled at him. "What now?"

"The next train out of here." He grabbed her bag and his own and they fled to the station and just caught the train leaving for New York.

They huddled, exhausted, in their compartment, their arms around each other. They were together again and that was all that mattered.

"What will your father do?" he asked her worriedly while they were in New York waiting for the Boston train.

"He will have disowned me by now," she said somberly. "I have dishonored his name and that's the end of it."

He glanced anxiously at her. "I'm sorry, Jennie."

She shrugged and said philosophically, "It's better to be disowned than be forced to marry a man I don't love."

It was dusk when they finally arrived in Boston. The lights were on in the house on Mount Vernon Street and Liam took Jennie's hand as he led her inside. She stared around, amazed by its grandeur. "If Papa had known you were this rich he would maybe have said yes," she whispered.

"I'm not rich, my mother is," he whispered back. "Don't worry, he'll be all right once we are married though. I'm sure of it."

"Liam," Lily said from the top of the stairs, and they both looked up at her. "Who is that with you?" she asked, surprised.

"An old friend, Mother. It's Jennie Desanto. Remember, we met at Lake Como?"

"Of course I remember." She glided, soft-footed, down the stairs. "And what is Miss Desanto doing in Boston?"

"I brought her to see you, Mother. All the way from Chicago," Liam said eagerly.

"Chicago? So that's why you went there." She turned and walked into the library. "You might as well come in here," she said over her shoulder. "This is where all the dramas occur in our household. And I have the feeling that there is going to be a drama tonight. Am I correct, Liam?"

She sat in the big red leather wing chair and they stood in front of her. She inspected Jennie quickly up and down, and Jennie's cheeks burned as she saw the look in her eyes. Liam gripped her hand tighter as he said, "I've brought Jennie here to meet you again, Mother, because I love her and I'm going to marry her. And I'm sure you'll love her, too, once you get to know her."

"Would you mind leaving us alone," Lily said. Jennie glanced anxiously at Liam and then hurried from the room and closed the door. She went to sit on a chair in the hall, staring at the family portraits, straining her ears for the sound of their voices. She knew Lily hated her for taking Liam away from her, but she had burned her bridges and she prayed Liam would be strong enough to stand up to his mother and burn his.

Lily looked at her son and anger welled up inside her. All she had worked for all these years was being stolen from her by a little girl from an upstart Italian peasant family. How dare they, she asked herself, staring at her son, standing with his hands clasped behind his back like a naughty boy waiting for his sentence.

"You will not marry that girl," she said decisively. "She is completely unsuitable. Do you forget, Liam, that you are a Porter Adams? You have a family name and tradition to uphold. This liaison is impossible. Send her home to Chicago. Tell her I will pay her, five, no, *ten* thousand dollars to leave you alone. There are a hundred beautiful girls in Boston and New York, from good families like your own, who would be only too pleased to marry you. Oh, I admit maybe I've been selfish keeping you all to myself, but now things will change. We shall go tomorrow to New York, we shall open up the house there, and we shall start to entertain again. We'll invite young people for you, Liam."

"Mother, please . . ."

"Do not argue, Liam. I shall call the bank manager at home now, and tell him to send ten thousand dollars around right away. You will give it to the girl and she will be on her way, well pleased, I have no doubt."

"Mother, are you crazy?" Liam said, white-faced. "You haven't even listened to what I said, have you?" he shouted angrily. "You never have. All these years you have just gone on doing exactly what you want to do, running my life as well as your own. Or maybe *instead* of your own. Yes, that's the truth of it, isn't it, Mother? You tried to use my life to make up for the inadequacies of your own. Well, no more. I'm marrying Jennie, and that's all there is to it."

"Think of what you're leaving, Liam," she cried. "Your inheritance, the houses, the money. You have no idea how wealthy you will be one day."

"Keep it," he said scornfully, striding to the door. "Buy yourself a new life with it, Mother."

"Wait." She ran to the cabinet near the door that held a pair of beautiful old Purdey shotguns. She took one out and checked the chamber while he watched her, stunned. Then she opened the door and walked past him into the hall. Ignoring Jennie, sitting on a chair by the door, she walked slowly up the stairs, carrying the loaded shotgun.

She paused on the landing. "If you leave this house for that girl, Liam, I will kill myself," she said, her voice trembling. "The choice is yours."

She walked along the landing toward her room, stopping when she heard the door open. She leaned over the banister and saw Liam take Jennie's hand.

He looked up at her white-faced. "I refuse to be blackmailed," he said curtly. "Good-bye, Mother."

Lily watched her life, her love, her reason for being, walk to the door and something seemed to snap inside her head. All she had fought to achieve in her shattered life was suddenly reduced to nothing again. "You bastard," she hissed. "Yes, that's what you are. You're no

Porter Adams. You are an O'Keeffe, through and through. Exactly like your bastard of a father."

Liam stared at her with horror. He turned to Jennie and put his arm around her. Then they walked out of the house and closed the door.

Lily dropped the shotgun and ran down the stairs after him. She sped across the hall and flung open the door and ran down the steps into the street. But the darkness had already swallowed him up, as if he had never existed.

LILY DID WHAT SHE ALWAYS DID when she was in trouble. She called Ned. "You must stop him," she cried, hysterical with fear. "He cannot marry her. You must get him back, Ned."

"But Lily, I'm in New York," he said worriedly. "What can I do?"

"That's exactly where he's going, I'm sure of it. At this time of night there's only the last train to New York."

"I'll go to the station," he promised. "I'll do what I can, Lily. But Liam is twenty-one now. He's of age, and he's a man in love. You know how that is, Lily. It's a tough thing to fight."

"You *must*," she said desperately. "Just stop him, Ned, whatever you have to do."

WHEN NED HAD BEEN NAMED CORESPONDENT in Lily's divorce all those years ago, Juliet had screamed and stormed and raged through their wonderful country house, and through their spectacular Manhattan apartment, threatening suicide and murder, or both, but she had known she was fighting a losing battle. It was the way it always had been: when Lily wanted Ned, he was there. Their stage career continued together as successfully as it always had, but the rows left their fellow players gasping, while at home their children scrunched up their eyes so as not to see their parents' angry faces and clapped their hands over their ears so as not to hear their bitter words.

Finally, Juliet had left him. She kept the country house and Ned kept the Manhattan apartment and every summer Ned took the children to Nantucket for the holidays. He had bought Sea Mist Cottage next door for Lily so that there would be no scandal about her staying alone with him in his house, but she had only gone there occasionally; she was too restless for so much peace and quiet.

Ned was giving a dinner party in his splendid Manhattan apartment for the backers of his new show when she called. He apologized to them, pleading an emergency, and left immediately for Grand Central. He strode the cold platform waiting for the train, and when it finally came he saw that Lily's guess had been right. Liam was with a small blond girl, and he looked tired and grim-faced. He glanced up at Ned, surprised.

"Your mother called me," Ned said.

Liam shrugged resignedly. "I might have guessed. But don't think you can talk me out of this, Ned, because you can't. But maybe you can tell me what she meant," he said, looking puzzled. "Maybe you know. She said I was not a Porter Adams. That my real father was an O'Keeffe. Is that true?"

Ned hesitated. "Well, yes, but let me explain. . . ."

Liam stared blankly at him. He was twenty-one years old and he had just learned that he was not the person he thought he was. He suddenly remembered the night when the man had stabbed him, what he had said about his mother, and now he realized with horror it was all true. He grabbed Jennie's hand and began to run.

Ned followed them through the barrier and out into the street. There was a cab cruising outside and they leapt into it, slamming the door as it sped off. Ned ran out into the street to try to stop them, and an oncoming cab hit him, tossing him onto the sidewalk. A crowd gathered around, exclaiming when they saw it was the famous actor. He was rushed to the hospital, where he was pronounced "as well as can be expected" to the waiting press, and kept under the constant vigil of around-the-clock nurses.

Ned was lucky to be alive. He had broken limbs and a fractured skull. Lily, distraught, moved back to New York and came every day to see him, bringing him baskets of fruit and flowers and the latest books to read, but even as he got better, Ned seemed disinclined to open them. A terrible lethargy had overtaken him, and he lay in his hospital bed, staring at the wall.

When he was finally allowed out of the hospital, Lily took him back to Nantucket to recuperate. But he was no longer the old vibrant Ned. He leafed disinterestedly through the scripts awaiting him, and the truth soon became apparent. His powers of concentration and his memory had been affected by the accident. He could no longer remember the lines. Ned Sheridan was finished as an actor.

Lily remained with him, living next door at Sea Mist Cottage, blaming herself and waiting for Liam to come back to her. Though in her heart, she knew he never would.

〜〜〜〜〜〜〜〜〜 51 〜〜〜〜〜〜〜〜〜

MAUDIE

Ardnavarna

"So THERE YOU HAVE IT, my dears," I said to Shannon and Eddie. "The story of the past. Or almost all of it. There is just one more episode and I am only sorry I was not there personally to witness it. Because you see, Lily did come home again to Ardnavarna. But she came home to die.

"I was away at school in Paris when it happened. My pa was in China on army business and Mammie was all alone. She said it was a glorious day of pale sunshine and soft breezes and Ardnavarna was looking its best. Late roses were in bloom and the scent of them was on the air. Mammie was returning from a ride; her red hair was blowing in the breeze and her chestnut mare looked very much like Lily's old horse, Jamestown. It might have been a scene from the past."

LILY STEPPED FROM THE BATTERED OLD CAR that had brought her from Galway. The two sisters stared at each other while the mare danced and skittered and the barking dogs leapt toward them. For a long minute they just looked at each other, then Lily said, "I've come home, Ciel," in a trembling little voice.

"Am I welcome?" she asked, looking apprehensively at her sister.

"As the buds in May," Ciel cried, leaping from the horse and throwing her arms around her. They stepped back and held each other at arms' length, searching for changes, seeing the passing of time, and on Lily, the marks of her illness. The two had always been more like twins than sisters; they always knew everything about each other and there was no need for Lily to tell Ciel that she was dying.

"Why, oh, why didn't you come home earlier?" she cried tearfully.

Lily shook her head. "I'm home now, and that's all that counts, isn't it?" She smiled, her head tilted in her old coquettish way. "Am I forgiven?" she asked hopefully.

"Aren't you always." Ciel grinned, and in an instant they were back into their old relationship; the adoring younger sister and the beautiful, confident older one.

They walked into the house, arms around each other's waist, and Lily told the sad story of Liam leaving her. "He'll come back," Ciel cried. "I'm sure of it. There's still time."

But Lily just shook her head and said, "I'm afraid time has run out for me." There was so much sadness in her voice and Ciel knew it was not for herself. Whatever else she was, Lily had always had courage and she was not afraid now. Ciel knew she was mourning for her lost son, and she was glad her own daughter Maudie was away, because their happy relationship would have only emphasized Lily's loneliness.

Lily wandered around the drawing room, touching remembered objects: a family photograph in a silver frame; a tapestry footstool worked by her mother; the binoculars William always used for bird-watching, and a beautiful rosewood humidor. She lifted its lid, smelling the aromatic odor of Monte Cristos, closing her eyes as the scent conjured up a vision of Pa, clearer than any photograph.

She could see herself as a small girl, sitting on his knee while he chose his cigar, as he went through the slow luxurious ritual with the special gold clippers and the long wooden matches that she always got to blow out. And then, best of all, he would put the cigar band on her finger like a ring. She could see Mammie sitting with her needlework and Pa with his newspaper and she savored again the special atmosphere of peace and security she had known as a small child, privileged to creep downstairs and curl up beside those two wonderful beings, before being sent scuttling back to bed.

"If only, oh, if only . . ." she thought longingly for the very last time in her life.

The news that wicked Lily Molyneux had come home flashed through the household and then the village with the speed of a brushfire; the servants gathered to stare curiously and soon everyone knew that Lily had come home to die. "It's written on her face" they told each other solemnly, and all the old stories and rumors were brought out and rehashed again in the crowded village store, and over a jar or three in the saloon.

Lily was content just to be home, riding alone through the bracken-fronded trails and along the strand. She sat quietly by the fire in the evening, smiling as they talked over old memories, old times. And the dogs, just as they always had done in times past, lay at the foot of Lily's bed, gazing adoringly at her as though they were her own best-beloved dalmatians from forty years ago. When she grew too weak to ride anymore, she walked slowly around the gardens, leaning on Pa's old silver-headed malacca cane. She refused the large doses of morphine prescribed by the doctor, because with so little time left she was not going to waste it in a drugged haze.

"I want to savor every last minute of my time at Ardnavarna," she said quietly to Ciel. "Because I know that *this* is paradise, and when I die I shall have to leave it all behind. Again." She glanced pathetically around her and said, "Do you think Pa has finally forgiven me? Will he turn in his coffin if you bury me beside him?"

"Of course he has forgiven you," Ciel lied, choking back her tears. "He told me so a hundred times. And you're not going to die for a long time yet." But Lily just smiled at her.

On those long evenings alone together by the fire, she told Ciel the truth about John and Finn and Daniel; about her two sons and her hatred for one and her overwhelming possessive love for the other. "Liam just never came home again," she said sadly. "I did it again, you see, Ciel. I just didn't think about anybody but myself. I tried to find him, to ask his forgiveness, but it was no good. He simply disappeared."

"Did you never think about how different life would have been if you had never met Dermot Hathaway?" Ciel asked.

"Did I?" Lily laughed, a sad, bitter little laugh. "Only every day of my life, that's all. But I've learned the hard way that there is no going back. You can't change the past, Ciel, though heaven knows I tried."

She took the diamond necklace from her pocket and gave it to Ciel. "Remember?" she asked, smiling. "When I was seventeen and had the world at my feet. Now I want your daughter to have it, when she is seventeen and all life lies before her, and everything is possible."

She spoke about Ned, whom she had been forced to leave behind in Nantucket in the care of a local woman. "He is my only friend, apart from you, Ciel," she said. "Now his poor mind wanders, but he is as handsome and gentle and charming as ever. Why, oh, why did I not love him enough to marry him? Life would have been so simple then.

But his old theater friends are loyal; they still make time to visit him and in the summers there's often a crowd of them at the white house to keep him company. I knew it was better to say good-bye to him while I was still myself, and not let him see what I have become." She glanced ruefully down at her hands, just a thin bunch of bones covered in blue-veined parchment skin. "An old woman's hands," she sighed regretfully, "and yet I shall never grow old."

The day finally came when Lily could not get up. Ciel had her bed moved to the window so that she could gaze at the lovely gardens and the alder trees planted by their great-great-grandfather, and glimpse the silver sea and the broad opalescent sky and see the horses trotting by. Even though the late summer air was balmy, Lily felt cold and a fire burned constantly in the grate. The dogs remained devotedly by her side, their heads on their paws, and the orange cat sat on the window ledge, watching and waiting.

A week passed, and then another, and Lily could no longer eat. She took liquid through a straw, though she told Ciel there was no point. "It doesn't matter anymore, darling Ciel," she said. "I'm home now." Her eyes were like dark glowing sapphires and her thin, wasted face seemed all bones, but Ciel saw that the yearning and sadness had finally left her.

Lily moved her hand and let it lie on the dog's big head. With a sigh of contentment she closed her eyes and Ciel knew that she would never open them again.

The tenants came, as they had always done, to decorate the cart that would carry her coffin with mosses and ferns and all the scented Gloire de Dijon roses from the garden. They walked behind Ciel to the family chapel and then to the tomb where Lily was finally reunited with her beloved pa and mammie, and this time they removed their caps in respect at the passing of Lily Molyneux.

Maudie

I GLANCED AT MY TWO LISTENERS. Their heads were lowered and they were gazing at me solemnly as they thought of Lily. "She died happier than she lived," I reminded them gently. "At least she was home again, where she had always wanted to be."

"Ned must have died a few years after that," Eddie said. "I still have the old newspaper clippings about his funeral and the big memorial service later. Everybody who was anybody in the theater went to say good-bye to him and pay their respects."

I looked at Eddie and said, "So now you know what happened to your great-grandfather. He gave up everything he was for the woman he loved, bit by bit, then he almost gave his life, and finally she cost him his career. He was a fine man and a great actor, and he was a fool for her.

"Before Lily died she asked Ciel, 'Was I really a wicked woman?' And Ciel told her what I think is the truth. 'You were never wicked,' she said loyally. 'You were silly and headstrong. You always regretted things afterward, but by then it was too late.'

"And that is what *I* feel is the truth about Lily. But as I said in the beginning, you must make up your own minds about her."

"Poor Lily," Shannon said compassionately. "I don't believe she was wicked; it was just that bad things happened to her."

"But she brought them on herself," Eddie said, and I could tell he was thinking of Ned, whose life had been ruined because of her.

"That is not quite the end of my story," I said, and they picked up their heads and took notice again. "Because the next visitor from the past to come in search of Ardnavarna was Shannon's father, Bob Keeffe.

"It was around 1980, if I remember correctly, when he appeared on my doorstep and when he told me his name I knew right away he belonged to Finn. He had a 'look of him' as they say around here: dark and handsome. Oh, he was Finn's grandson all right and nobody around here would have disputed it."

Shannon propped her chin on her hands, gazing eagerly at me as I told her the story, exactly as her father had told it to me.

BOB KEEFFE HAD TRACKED DOWN his past, just the way his daughter was doing twenty years later. He had found Lily's portrait and the letters at Sea Mist Cottage on Nantucket. Then he checked the orphanage records, and, with what I was able to tell him, we deduced the rest.

LIAM AND JENNIE WERE MARRIED twelve years before their son, Robert, was born, adding to their happiness. Liam had taken his real father's name, O'Keeffe, and changed the Irish "Liam" to William, so the couple were now known as Mr. and Mrs. William O'Keeffe, and that was the name he signed on his paintings. And it was probably the reason that all the detectives Lily employed over the years were never able to trace him.

They lived in northern California in a small remote cottage near Mendocino and they kept to themselves, though they were always pleasant when they met their neighbors on the village street or in the store. The locals said that, though they were "artistic types," Jennie O'Keeffe kept her house clean as a new pin, with starched gingham curtains at the windows and good food on their table. Their boy was too young to attend school and no one knew much about them except that they had settled there after years of wandering the country, stopping whenever Liam found someplace he wanted to paint. Every three months Liam would make the trip to San Francisco to sell his paintings so he could pay the rent, and after his death the gallery owner said that though he had not yet come into his own, he had had true talent and the world had lost a fine artist.

They were making a rare trip East—who knows, maybe to try to reconcile with Lily, and Finn, and show them their grandchild. Then, in the early hours of a foggy morning, the express collided with a freight train. Among the names of the dead listed in the newspapers were William O'Keeffe and his wife, Jennie, survived by their five-year-old son, Robert. Relatives were requested to contact the Catholic children's orphanage where the boy had been taken into care.

Young Bob had been found wrapped in his father's arms, protected from the impact by his body. At the orphanage he waited impatiently for his father to come and get him, and when he asked why he did not, the nuns hushed him softly and told him his father had gone to Paradise, where all good men aspire to go.

"I wish he'd come here for me instead," he cried resentfully.

They told him that soon his relatives would be found and they would come and claim him, like a lost parcel. But no one came and Bob wondered why. As he grew older his wondering turned to anger and resentment that no one in the whole of America wanted him. He determined that when he became a man, he would show them all. He would become rich and famous and successful and everybody would want to know him, and then he would track down those relatives who had rejected him and show them he didn't need them anyway.

It was many years before he went to the cottage on Nantucket, where he found Ciel's letters and Lily's portrait. He went to the address he found on the envelope, his grandmother's house on Mount Vernon Street, but it was closed and the neighbors told him that Mrs. Adams had returned to Ireland many years ago.

And then, years later, already a rich man, he came here to find Ardnavarna, and his roots. He told me that all his life he had suffered, thinking that nobody cared enough to rescue him from the orphanage, and that he had never really known who he was. I told him, "You are Lily's grandson all right, and Finn O'Keeffe's all right, and if either of them had known it was you in the railroad crash they would have been there in a flash to claim you." And when I told him he was also the legitimate heir to Lily's fortune, he just shrugged and said, "It's too late now. Let the dead stay dead and I'll just get on with my own life."

Anyhow, I gave him the necklace—"For your daughter," I told him, just the way Lily had said to Mammie. "When she has all life still in front of her, and everything is possible." There were tears in Shannon's pretty gray eyes and I saw the depths of her grief. I said gently, "Your father chose to let the past alone, but maybe there are others who have not. And that, I am sure, is the reason he was killed."

She looked at me with puzzlement and I said, "No man of the caliber of Bob O'Keeffe is going to kill himself over mere money. A woman, maybe. The Molyneuxes have always been an emotional lot, sentimental over dogs, horses, and women. But money? Never. Besides, if his business had failed and he was broke, he knew he had Lily's inheritance, several millions of dollars, just for the taking. And it's still there today, sitting in the Bank of Boston awaiting an heir."

"But he knew no one from the past," Shannon said. "No O'Keeffes. No Molyneuxes. Who do we know who would do such a terrible thing? And *why*?"

Eddie put his arms comfortingly around her. "We'll find who did it, Shannon," he said quietly. "I'll help you. We'll go back to Nantucket, where it all began. Maybe if we look harder, we'll find the final clue that will give us an answer."

I told them there was an old Irish saying: "To find his enemy an Irishman looks first at himself, and then at another Irishman." I said I thought there might be a lot of truth in that. And that Brigid, who knows about these things, would tell you there are three basic motives for murder: money, passion, and revenge. "One thing I'm sure of," I said. "Where families are concerned, particularly one with such a turbulent history, you must look carefully at those close to the victim. That's where you will find your killer."

SHANNON AND EDDIE DECIDED they would return to Nantucket, and to cheer them and myself up I decided to throw a farewell party. I phoned everyone I knew and told them to show up Saturday night dressed in their finery to meet and say good-bye to my newfound "granddaughter."

The long-disused ballroom at the rear of the house was swept and polished and the little gilt chairs burnished. Help was summoned from the village to shift furniture around, and a band was ordered from Dublin. Brigid was in her element in the kitchen, planning and organizing a buffet supper for a hundred and fifty, and a dozen women rushed around to her orders, chopping and simmering and baking.

But before the great event happened, we had another surprise visitor to Ardnavarna.

CHAPTER
52

I WAS ON MY KNEES pulling up weeds from the flowerbeds under the drawing room windows when I heard the car crunching up the gravel driveway. It was a sunny morning and I pushed my hat to the back of my head and put my hand over my eyes, squinting at the white Mercedes stretch limousine bouncing over the ruts toward the house. Such a splendid automobile had not been seen at Ardnavarna since my own pa's beloved Rolls and I wondered if maybe it was a rock star who had lost his way to Ashford Castle.

The chauffeur pulled up at the front door and I grinned as I saw him take off his cap and wipe his sweating face. He threw an apprehensive glance at his paintwork, thinking of the bracken fronds and the brambles, and I thought how angry he was going to be when I told him he had come to the wrong place. Throwing me a disdainful glance, he hurried to open the door for his passenger.

The legs emerged first: impossibly long and elegantly slender, and wearing, if I am not mistaken, Manolo Blahnik red suede shoes. The rest of the lady followed, as tall as you would expect from such legs, with, as they say, curves in all the right places, emphasized by her well-cut white suit. Her long blond hair fell about her shoulders like a lion's mane and her face was pretty rather than beautiful. She flung a smile of incredible sweetness in my direction and said in a New York accent, "Pardon me, could you direct me to your mistress?"

I clambered to my feet, wiping my muddy hands on the seat of my jodhpurs, just as the dogs discovered something was going on and hurled themselves at her, leaving decorative paw prints all over her immaculate white skirt.

"Oh, the darlings," she exclaimed. Naturally, I liked her.

"Forgive my dogs their exuberance," I apologized. "They are not used to such splendid motorcars nor to such glamorous visitors." I held out my still-grubby hand and said, "I am Maudie Molyneux, mistress of Ardnavarna." She blushed at her mistake.

"Oh, I'm so sorry," she gasped. "I thought you were the help . . . well, a sort of gardener."

"No problem," I reassured her. "I'm that too: gardener, stablehand, chauffeur, housekeeper. And who do I have the pleasure of meeting?"

"Joanna!"

We turned as one at the sound of Shannon's voice. She was standing in the doorway staring at the stranger and I remembered that she had told me her father's mistress was Joanna Belmont. I glanced interestedly at her, and I could see why Bob Keeffe had chosen her. She was a man's woman; pretty and voluptuous, yet with a healthy outdoor all-American-girl quality about her. I knew she would have made Shannon a better stepmother than that cold socialite, Buffy, and I felt sorry for her, losing the man she loved.

"Shannon!" Joanna replied, a little nervously I thought, and I understood why. Here was the father's mistress confronting his daughter, and for reasons we did not yet know.

"I had to come," Joanna said. "And after that sweet letter you wrote me, I thought maybe you wouldn't mind." She looked hopefully at Shannon, still worried that she might ask her angrily how she dare intrude on her, because after all, she was just the mistress and not the wife. But Shannon did not.

She walked toward her and put her arms around her. "I don't know why you are here," she said, "nor how you found me. But I'm glad you came. I know in my heart that Dad loved you and that's all that matters to me."

Joanna Belmont burst into tears. She stood there, tall and glamorous with paw prints all over her white skirt and mascara tears running down her pretty face, while the chauffeur stared, and Shannon hugged her and cried too.

I knew it was good for them to share their grief, so I said sympathetically, "When you are ready, I shall be in the kitchen. I'll ask Brigid to fix some coffee and we'll talk."

A little while later they came into the kitchen. I introduced Eddie and Brigid and we sat around the table, drinking coffee and assessing each other, while the dogs settled themselves at Joanna's feet, gazing at her raptly. Is this breed a sucker for beauty or what? I asked myself, nudging them with my foot and hissing the word "traitor" at them. But they took no notice and continued to gaze at Joanna, pawing her occasionally for another caress.

"J.K. gave me the address," Joanna said. "He told me you were here but he wasn't sure why. To tell the truth I was a bit afraid to call him because your father and I . . . well, he had always kept his business life separate from his 'personal' one, and I wasn't sure J.K. even knew who I was. Anyhow, I guess he did because he asked no questions, he just told me you were at Ardnavarna. And so here I am."

"But *why* are you here?" Shannon asked. "Surely not just to see me?"

Joanna took the black leather attaché case she had been carrying and pushed it toward Shannon. "Your father gave me this for safe-keeping," she said, "just before he was killed."

Shannon stared at her, surprised. "Then you think he was *killed*?"

"I *know* he was." Joanna leaned forward and grasped Shannon's hand across the table. "The night before your party, Bob told me he was going to ask Buffy for a divorce. He asked me to marry him. He said it might take a while before he was free and that there was a lot to sort out first. I thought he meant the settlement, you know—alimony and all that—but he didn't.

"Your father didn't steal all that money," she said. "He was being robbed."

Brigid and I glanced at each other and then back at Joanna again, and then she told us what had happened.

New York

JOANNA HAD BARELY LEFT HER APARTMENT since Bob's death. She roamed the apartment overlooking Central Park, remembering how they had chosen it together, and how happy she had been, furnishing and decorating it for them. Now, without him, it was just another set of rooms.

She went into the dressing room and stared at his clothes, still hanging next to her own. She looked at the watch she had given him for his birthday two years ago, and at the enamel cuff links that were a first-anniversary present. Whenever he came to the apartment he would always change his watch and put on the one she had given him, and he always wore her cuff links when they went out together.

She would never in a million years have thought that she could accept being Bob Keeffe's "undercover woman," but she had not really minded it. Sometimes, sitting at home waiting for him, she had felt more like the "wife" than the "other woman," because she knew his wife, Buffy, never sat at home and waited for him.

She lifted the sleeve of Bob's favorite old tweed jacket, the one he always wore weekends, and pressed it to her cheek. She closed her eyes, seeing the two of them walking across the park on a Sunday morning to pick up the *New York Times,* maybe going for croissants and coffee at a café. Then they would come home and read the news-papers and maybe climb back into bed again. God, he was a sexy man, and oh, how she had loved him.

Tears blinded her as she stumbled from the dressing room, tripping over his black attaché case standing by the dresser. It fell open and papers spilled across the black and white zebra-striped rug. She picked them up and quickly pushed them back in and closed the case again. She put it on a shelf in the closet and straightened up, then paused and looked doubtfully at it.

She had read every word about Bob in the newspapers. She knew they were calling him a crook and that he was being investigated for fraud and she didn't believe any of it. She remembered watching the FBI agents and the representatives of the SEC and the IRS on televi-sion, removing all the documents and files from Keeffe Holdings's offices. Except the ones in the attaché case sitting right here in her closet.

Picking up the case, she carried it into the room Bob had always called the den. She sat on the white sofa, clutching the attaché case to her chest, staring out of the window at the circling pigeons, thinking. She had never pried into Bob's business world, though she had always listened when he wanted to talk about things. He was excited about his new skyscraper, and he had talked about every phase of the construc-tion. She knew it wasn't the monument to his ego that the media were making it out to be. Bob was a man who had found success the hard way, and Keeffe Tower was meant to be the pinnacle of his successful career. Instead, it had become his epitaph.

She thought about their conversation the night before the night he died, when he had asked her to marry him, remembering how ex-hausted he had seemed. "I'm getting too old," he had said bitterly. "Too old to keep my dreams and illusions. Suddenly they are all fading away."

She remembered him handing her his attaché case and asking her to keep it somewhere safe for him, and the sad, wistful look in his eyes as he had returned to kiss her a second time before taking the elevator and leaving her forever. And she knew without a shadow of doubt that Bob had not killed himself. Someone had stolen those missing millions, and Bob had found out about it. And the thief, whoever he was, had killed him.

She thought of the papers in the attaché case he had asked her to keep safely for him, and she knew Bob must have found some evidence of the fraud, and that she must be holding it.

She opened the case and studied the documents. They were all contracts for the purchase by Keeffe Holdings of building plots in a dozen major American cities. They were all exactly the same legal format, with the name of the vendor and the purchaser, the description of the plot of land with attached maps and diagrams, the purchase price, and lots of legal clauses. The name of the vendor was different on each one, but she noticed that written in small type underneath it was "a subsidiary of the ExWyZe Fund," and that each was signed for the vendor by a man with a foreign name, Jean Michel Zymatt, and for the purchaser, Keeffe Holdings, by two of the partners, Brad Jeffries and Jack Wexler. Not one of them was signed by Bob.

People never expected it of an actress, but Joanna was good at math. She quickly added the purchase prices in her head and knew in an instant that she was looking at over four hundred million dollars' worth of contracts.

She put the documents carefully back in the case and closed it. She stared at it, wondering if this was what all those fraud-squad guys were looking for. But they were talking about much more than four hundred million. Nine hundred they said, maybe over a billion dollars, and share manipulation and false collateral. She thought of all those bankers waiting for their money. Well, she could certainly tell them where some of it was. In M. Jean Michel Zymatt and the ExWyZe Fund's bank account, that's where.

She wondered what Bob had meant about keeping his illusions? Was it because Brad and Jack had been cheating him all these years? But *four hundred million dollars' worth*? She shook her head; it was hard to believe. As far as she knew, Brad lived a simple life in a nice redbrick house on a few acres at Kings Point, Long Island. He drove a Mercedes and he spent his vacations alone, fishing in Canada. Wexler was flashy, it was true, but he had owned the Sutton Place house for a long time. Sure, he drove an Aston-Martin, but Bob said it was all for show, and that Jack needed to impress the girls, and anyway the man was a bachelor and what else was he going to spend his money on?

Maybe they had both acted in good faith and it was the ExWyZe

Fund that was crooked. Joanna sighed as she carried the attaché case back in to the dressing room and tucked it safely into a drawer and locked it. She put the key in the pocket of her robe and began to get dressed. She didn't know what had been going on, but she was afraid to go to the police because of the scandal, and she was afraid to confront the partners and demand the truth because . . . her knees suddenly turned to jelly . . . because maybe Brad Jeffries and Jack Wexler had murdered Bob.

She pulled herself together quickly, and put on a black dress and did her face. Because she was tall and striking people always assumed she wore a lot of makeup, but in fact she was strictly a touch of powder, a brush of mascara, and a hint of lipstick person, and she had never bought anything other than dime store cosmetics. A legacy of her poorer days as a struggling actress. But now, thanks to Bob, she was a comparatively rich woman. He had bought her this apartment, he had put money regularly into her bank accounts and paid all her bills. "You need never work again," he had told her cheerfully, because he knew she wasn't even trying to get work because of him. She wanted to be free whenever he could manage to see her.

She thought of the four hundred million paid over to Jean Michel Zymatt and the ExWyZe Fund for all those plots of land, wondering if they even existed. There was only one way to find out.

She took two contracts out of the case: one for a property in New York, and one in Boston. She put on a black-and-white houndstooth jacket, a large black straw hat with a wide brim, and tucked the contracts safely in her purse. The doorman handed her her mail on the way out and she pushed the letters into her purse and took a cab to Second Avenue.

It was an area of shabby buildings that looked as though no one had touched them since the day they were jerry-built in the early nineteen hundreds. There was a minimarket on the ground floor and next to it a Laundromat and a dry cleaner. Telling the driver to wait, Joanna stepped inside and asked to speak to the manager or the owner.

The Haitian youth behind the counter of the minimarket gazed at her like she was visiting from the starship *Enterprise,* and she said briskly, "Be quick, young man, I'm in a hurry."

He wandered into the back regions and returned with an old man with greasy hair and hostile eyes. "Waddya want?" he snarled.

"I want to know who owns this building," she said as he stepped intimidatingly closer.

"Waddya wanna know for?"

"I might be interested in buying."

"Huh?" He walked around her, looking her up and down, and she thought about running for the cab, but she had to know. Her eyes followed him as he came back and stood in front of her again. "He's a landlord," he said indifferently. "I dunno his name. I just pay my rent lady, thatzall."

She thanked him hurriedly and went to the Laundromat next door. The African-American girl behind the counter was pretty and bright and she told her the landlord's name was Marks and that he sent a man to collect the rent every Friday. And no, she had not heard of any plans to develop the site. "Who'd want to build anything here?" she asked with a mocking laugh. "We're all just trying to get out."

Joanna told the cabdriver to take her to La Guardia Airport and she caught the shuttle to Boston. The cabdriver at Logan Airport looked oddly at her when she gave him the address and asked her if she was sure. And when they arrived she knew why. The area was a grim slum of semiderelict buildings and she didn't even bother to get out to inspect the boarded-up old warehouse that Keeffe Holdings had paid thirty-two million dollars for. She just told the cabdriver to take her back to Logan and caught the next shuttle back to New York.

On the flight she reread the contracts for the two sites she had just seen and she knew she was looking at fraud. But something told her this was just the tip of the iceberg. There was more, lots more. Bob had found out what was going on and he knew who had done it. And that's what he had meant by "losing his dreams and his illusions." Whoever it was, it was somebody close to him, and when he had confronted them, the same person or persons had killed him. She looked at the two signatures again, Brad's and Jack's, and asked herself the question. She shook her head; they just didn't look like murderers. But how was a murderer supposed to look? Like a gorilla with staring eyes and a menacing smile? My God, she thought, shocked, it might even have been Buffy for all she knew.

She stuffed the documents securely back in her purse and looked through the letters the doorman had given her on the way out. One was postmarked Nantucket and she glanced curiously at it. No one she knew ever went to Nantucket. She opened it and glanced, astonished, at the signature, *Shannon Keeffe,* and when she read the sympathetic message, tears came to her eyes.

When she glanced at the address, Sea Mist Cottage in Nantucket, she wanted to ask the pilot to turn the plane around and go right back to Boston so she could go and thank this lovely girl for even thinking about her. For even caring that her father's mistress might be grieving her heart out more than his wife was. She remembered what she had read in the newspapers about Buffy leaving for Barbados where she was staying incommunicado, waiting for the scandal to subside, leaving her stepdaughter alone to face whatever mud was thrown at her.

"The bitch," she said vehemently, and the woman in the next seat glanced at her, startled. Joanna apologized and put the letter back in her purse, thinking about what to do.

When she got back home, she flung off her shoes and paced the floor of her apartment, wondering whether she should tell Shannon Keeffe her suspicions that her father was murdered, and show her the fraudulent documents? Then she told herself Shannon had been through so much, she had probably just accepted her father's suicide, and to tell her would be like rubbing salt into an open wound. She wondered about telling her best friend, but she didn't want to involve her: this was too dangerous a game. She was talking *murder* here.

She prowled around a bit more and then she went to the phone and dialed a number. When they answered she ordered a mozzarella and tomato pizza with extra cheese and went and sat in front of the TV. When the pizza arrived she ate one slice, staring at the news on CNN, relieved that for once there was no mention of Bob.

She pushed the rest of the pizza into the box and shoved it into the garbage and took a shower. Then she lay down on the bed and closed her eyes. "What shall I do, Bob darling?" she asked, and clear as a bell the answer came into her mind, as though he were speaking to her. "Tell Shannon." Joanna sighed with relief. She would do just that.

JOANNA FINISHED HER STORY and looked expectantly at us. "So here I am," she said in a small, apologetic voice, in case we wished she were not. She pushed the case with the documents across to Shannon. "I thought about going to the police, but then I reminded myself who I was. I knew the media would have had a second field day if Bob Keeffe's mistress had showed up with an attaché case full of documents left in her closet, which she claimed was proof his partners had murdered him." She gave us a wry little smile and I admired her courage for admitting that she was only "a mistress," even though she knew she had been much more than that.

"It's up to you, Shannon, to decide what must be done," she said quietly.

Shannon stared helplessly at Eddie and then at me. We took out the documents and passed them around, inspecting the partners' signatures, and staring puzzled at the name of the vendor, ExWyZe Fund, and the man with the foreign name who had signed on its behalf.

"Maybe it's one of those fancy foreign tax-dodge companies, in Switzerland, or Liechtenstein, or somewhere," Eddie said thoughtfully.

"If that's true, then there will be no way we can check it," I said. "They're always confidential and I doubt we would even be able to find out exactly who ExWyZe's proprietor is."

"But Mr. ExWyZe is sitting on at least four hundred million dollars of Bob Keeffe's money. Surely, if it's stolen, they have to tell."

Remembering recent similar cases that had hit the headlines, I shook my head. "We shall have to find out another way."

Shannon ran her hands distractedly through her long copper hair as she thanked Joanna for bringing her the documents and for not going to the police. "I don't know what to do," she said soberly. "How can I believe they would steal all this from my father? How can I believe they would kill him? And yet . . ." She looked at us with frightened gray eyes. "And yet, they were both at the party that night. And they were both behaving strangely. They were very subdued—I mean they didn't dance or come over to talk to me, not even to wish me happy birthday. I noticed Brad was drinking a lot, and Jack looked sort of dark and moody, and I remember his girlfriend looked bored. But they had been close to my father for years. How could they kill him? And besides, what did they have to do with the past?"

"Maybe they didn't kill him," Eddie said, more to calm her than because he believed it. "And maybe when we get back to Nantucket, we shall find the vital clue that will point the way to the criminal."

Joanna looked mystified at them, and I patted her hand. "You'll hear all about Bob's past before too long," I told her. "Meanwhile, I insist that you stay here at Ardnavarna with us. There's a farewell party Saturday night you just won't want to miss."

Now, THE MOLYNEUXES HAVE ALWAYS BEEN GREAT party-givers and I intended Shannon and Eddie's farewell bash to be one of the best. I had invited everybody I knew, old and young, and we all helped to decorate the house, robbing the garden for flowers and plants, ferns and boughs until we had turned the ballroom into a leafy bower. A band arrived from Dublin and set themselves up on the little podium at one end, and Brigid tore around like a tinker's coat, setting out an amazing buffet of smoked salmon and trout, oysters and mussels, shrimp and lobsters, and a seafood bisque that made your mouth water just to smell it. There were hams and turkeys and loins of pork, smoked chicken and wild duck, glistening fresh salads and vegetable soufflées, and cakes and desserts that she had spent hours decorating with filigree spun sugar and a feather-light touch, until they resembled miniature works of art.

Brigid had outdone herself, and a few minutes before our guests were to arrive, she hovered anxiously in the dining room, whisking away the eager dogs and cats, dressed in her finest black silk with a gardenia corsage, but with no apron because she was also a guest at this ball. She had slicked her hair down with a drop of water and anchored it firmly behind her ears with my diamond arrows, and she was wearing black stockings and her little high-heeled boots.

"You look dazzling, Brigid," Eddie said approvingly. "And the table looks even more dazzling!" Hand in hand, he and Shannon inspected the buffet, while I observed both of them with satisfaction. I had delved deep into my wardrobes and dressed them both in the family's finest. Shannon was in a Fortuny velvet that had belonged to Mammie, a long simple tunic whose myriad tiny pleats clung to her tall, slender body like molten silver. Her hair was a vibrant coppery cloud and Lily's diamond necklace glittered at her throat. Eddie, who was holding her hand, looked as though he never wanted to let go.

If ever a man looked good in evening clothes, he did. Forget Molly's Ralph Lauren lover: handsome Eddie wore Pa's old Savile Row dinner jacket as though he had been born to the aristocracy. It might have been tailored especially for him.

It had not failed to cross my mind, and I'm sure Brigid's also, that this might be our own "farewell party," as well as Shannon's and Eddie's. Not that we are expecting the worst, but at our age you tend to savor each moment, just in case it is your last. Besides, who knew when we might have another excuse for such a shindig? Hence Brigid had outdone herself with her buffet, and I had brought out the last of Pa's old wines and vintage champagnes from the cellar.

I had decked myself out in tulip-red chiffon from Valentino 1970. It moved sensuously around the body to the hips and fell in a delicious many-layered flutter around my silly sparrow-boned ankles. I wore red satin sandals to match and a load of worthless but spectacular jewelry: a wide gold-mesh necklace, bracelet and earrings studded with "gemstones" in red and blue and green, which Pa had bought Mammie in a bazaar when they were in India. The bracelets jangled satisfyingly when I moved and the earrings swished around my face the way I liked them to, and I had tucked a gardenia in my red curls. I'd splashed on a large amount of L'Heure Bleue, rouged up my cheeks and my lips, flung on my matching chiffon stole edged with a ruffle of red feathers, and now I was ready to greet my guests.

We stood in the hall, admiring each other and looking anxiously at our watches, thinking Joanna was late just as she floated downstairs toward us, a lofty goddess in a simple black Calvin Klein floor-length silk shift, without a single jewel. We drew in our breaths in admiration and I thought how proud Bob Keeffe would have been of his women, if only he had been able to see them tonight.

The guests began arriving at the appointed hour of nine, because no one comes politely late for a party in Ireland. They just can't wait to get there and begin enjoying themselves. The four of us formed a little receiving line and I happily introduced my new loved ones to my old cronies, and to the dozens of young people who had come all the way from Dublin and Cork and Galway for the party, staying locally with friends and relatives in their chilly "Big Houses."

But there was nothing chilly about Ardnavarna that night. Like us, it looked its glorious best, with fires blazing cheerfully in every grate. Even the dalmatians wore red satin bows, though the clever orange cats would stand for no such fripperies. Soon the champagne was flowing, and so was the conversation, and the sound of music lifted to the old rafters. I stood to one side, watching them all, dancing, laughing, chattering, and I thought about how many parties Ardnavarna must have seen.

There's something about a party that goes to my head like strong wine; a heady excitement that I want everyone around me to share. I wanted them to take this memory of Ardnavarna home with them so that, many years later, they would look back and say to each other, "Do you remember that magical night at Ardnavarna? And old Maudie Molyneux? How beautiful the old house was, and how stylish old Maudie was, and how Brigid had prepared a feast fit for the gods?"

Speaking of a feast, it was time for supper. I picked up the hunting horn that had belonged to Lily and Ciel's Pa when he was Master of the Hunt, and placed it to my lips. The piercing "view halloo" ricocheted from the walls as my triumphant playing summoned them all to eat. The band stopped in mid-chord and headed for the bar. Amid the laughter, the guests flocked to devour Faithless Brigid's feast, though they all said it was almost too beautiful to spoil by eating. Brigid stood proudly by her table accepting their compliments, red of face and with an anxious smile as she watched them fill their plates. I thrust a glass of champagne in her hand and said, "Brigid, my old darlin', isn't this the best party we ever gave at Ardnavarna?"

"You always say that, Maudie," she says, grinning at me.

"And isn't it always true?" I reply, smiling back at her.

But this time it really was the best party ever given at Ardnavarna, for no one wanted to leave, even with the dawn, and hadn't I my lovely "grandchildren" with me? And who knew when I would see them again?

CHAPTER
53

I MOPED AROUND THE HOUSE like a lost dog after they left, and even those darned creatures were miserable, following me, ears down, tails drooping, their claws clattering on the oaken floorboards as we roamed the house, trapped by the incessant rain and *nostalgie de la vie.*

"How many years has it been," I asked myself, staring out at the gray-green rain-drenched garden, "since I last traveled? Ten? Fifteen maybe? Jayzus!" I shouted triumphantly, quoting the notorious Lily, as I came up with the solution to my melancholy, if not the murder.

Hurrying back upstairs, I took my sapphires from the top dresser drawer, remembering Eddie saying that if I ever wanted to sell them they would fetch enough to live out my life in comfort, and I laughed out loud. "The hell with comfort," I cried. "I'm for adventure!"

Still chortling, pleased with myself, I swept downstairs, back in my old sparkling form. "Brigid," I yelled authoritatively so that she wouldn't argue. "Pack our bags. We're off to New York. *And* we're flying Concorde."

I felt like a three-year-old filly at the starting gate when the plane took off a week later, though I have to admit the poor ground crew quailed when they saw my luggage. I suppose a steamer trunk is not seen too often anymore, especially on air travel. Plus all my other ancient bits and pieces of solid leather valises and gladstone bags and Paris hatboxes. My theory was that everyone else these days travels light, so there would be plenty of room for my stuff, and besides, I've discovered that one of the few advantages of being old is that no one likes to say "no" to you. And I have to say that British Airways took us in their expert stride.

Brigid was wearing her best black and her trotty little boots (I had forbidden the Wellingtons though I would not have put it past her to have secreted them somewhere in the luggage) and without, thank heavens, the ankle socks. She was wearing a sweeping feathered hat that put my own neat felt chapeau to shame, but my navy suit, Chanel 1964, with its gold buttons and white braid trim, looked as up-to-date as anything in the shops now, and my white gloves, high-heeled navy pumps, and pearls were exactly what a lady should wear. Oh, we looked a grand pair, Brigid and I, setting off together on our adventure. She crossed herself, closing her eyes and clutching my hand as we took off, and I grinned as that old familiar whoosh of excitement rippled through me, and we headed into the unknown in search of Bob Keeffe's murderer.

Now, I've always liked New York. It's flamboyant and you know I'm partial to that, and I also adore grand hotels. We swept up to the portals of the Ritz-Carlton in grand style in a black-windowed stretch limo. I tilted my hat to exactly the right impish angle and patted my red curls into place, tipping the doorman extravagantly as he summoned a relay of bellboys to deal with our baggage. And then, feeling in my element, I swept into the foyer like a queen. The manager hurried toward us. In an instant, he took in the mounds of good old leather luggage spattered with labels from times and hotels and ships and trains long since past: Raffles and the White Star Line, Cunard and Claridges, the Cipriani and the Orient Express, the Pera Palace, Istanbul, and the Cascades in Egypt and the Blue Train and the Negresco.

"It is a pleasure to have you both staying with us, Madame Molyneux," he said, recognizing class when he saw it.

"Faith, 'tis an age since I've been travelin'," I said, slipping into the brogue I can do so well when it suits me, and which never fails to charm a man, and he immediately upgraded us to his best suite, a delightful bower of luxury and comfort that was soon filled with bouquets and chocolates and bottles of champagne. I gave the valet my riding boots to be shined and hung up my hunting jacket, just in case, and I told the sweet little maid sent to assist me, the details of every garment as she hung them in the closet; where it was bought and the date and where it was worn. I'm an old chatterbox, I know, but beneath it all my brain was fizzling with ideas.

Brigid looked tired; she was never used to the travelin' the way I was, and I tucked her up in bed and sent to room service for strong black tea, to be served in a mug and not a cup, just the way she likes it, and cinnamon toast. "It's my turn to pamper you, Brigid," I told her firmly. "And on this trip, *you* are going to be waited on."

She sighed happily, spreading herself out in the enormous king-size bed, switching channels on the TV as though she had been used to it all her life. I patted her hand and kissed her quickly on the cheek and told her she need not get out of bed the whole time if that's what she wished, and then I left her to her cinnamon toast, and took myself off to the lavish sitting room to think things out.

I kicked off my shoes and sat on the elegant sofa, nibbling on a biscuit while I tallied up Lily's legacy of disasters and victims.

Somewhere in that list was the answer to the mystery. But where to begin?

I picked up the phone and placed a call to Shannon in Nantucket.

"Hello," she answered, sounding surprised that anyone should be telephoning her.

"Maudie here," I yelled, because I've never been able to bring myself to quite believe they can hear you all those miles away unless you shout. "I'm in New York. I just checked into the R.C."

"The Church?" she asked, bewildered.

I laughed. "The Ritz-Carlton, silly. Brigid and I have come to help you solve the mystery, and I think I've got a headstart on where to begin to look. What about you? Any clues turn up yet?"

"I wish," she replied wistfully.

"Well, I've been going through the list of Lily's victims, and I have decided that if the murder is connected to the past, as we believe it is, then we must find the descendants of those victims. I've got my list all ready, so why don't you and Eddie get yourselves back here to New York, and we'll get started?"

They arrived the next morning and my heart thrilled at the sight of their eager faces. They seemed to light up the room when they strode into it, so young and beautiful, so confident and at the same time so tremulously insecure, as only the young and those in love can be.

I greeted them and said briskly, "It's a good thing Brigid and I are here to help you, since you don't seem to be getting very far on your own. Now, let's get down to business.

"First, I think we should find out what happened to Daniel and Finn O'Keeffe."

It didn't take Eddie long to find out that the brokerage house James and Company was still very much in business, and that a Mr. Michael O'Keeffe James was its chairman. And it took only a little longer to discover that the famous multimillion-dollar chain of Danstores was one and the same as the original Daniel's started in Boston at the turn of the century. And that the man who was now its head was the popular Senator Jim O'Keeffe.

I placed a call to Mr. Michael James, told him who I was and that I was visiting from Ireland, and that I believed our families used to know each other "in the old days."

"They surely did," he replied with a laugh and he invited us around right away to see him.

Shannon and I gussied ourselves up, powdering our noses, and brushing our curls. She was in jeans and a short fitted red jacket, and I was wearing a little bottle-green St. Laurent suit from 1975, and a hat with a tiny veil and a silver feather, and I found myself trotting along like Brigid in my heels, to keep up with Shannon's long-legged lope.

The offices of James and Company were even more palatial than when Finn O'Keeffe had first started working there. The original building had been torn down long ago and a modern skyscraper erected in its place, though it wasn't one of Bob Keeffe's. Michael James came out from his office to greet us. He was a tall sandy-haired man, older than I expected, in his sixties. He had brown eyes and he didn't look anything like "black Irish" Finn, except maybe for the wide smile and the easy charm. "I feel I already know you," he exclaimed, taking my bony hand in both of his, and beaming down at me. "Or at least, I know most of the Molyneuxes, from the stories my dad told me." His eyes twinkled as he added, "My father was Finn O'Keeffe, you know."

"I didn't know," I said, astonished, and I heard Shannon gasp. "I must introduce you to Shannon Keeffe," I added with a matching twinkle in my eye. "She's by way of being a relative of yours."

I explained that she was Finn and Lily's great-granddaughter. He flung back his head and laughed. "Is there no end to the old man's surprises? I'm sorry," he apologized quickly to Shannon. "I didn't mean to be rude, but old Finn was known to have a roving eye and he was as full of charm and blarney as most Irishmen, right to the end." He paused and added with a frown, "But wait, aren't you Bob Keeffe's daughter?"

"I am," she said, lifting her chin proudly.

"I'm really sorry," he said, taking her hand and patting it kindly. "He was a fine man and none of us here at James and Company can believe what's happened. Bob Keeffe was no more a crook than the Queen of England. It's scandalous, the way the media are after him like vultures."

"Thank you," Shannon said with a wavering smile, because sympathy is the one thing that triggers her tears. "My father is really the reason we are here." She glanced appealingly at me, and I took over, briskly telling Michael James that we believed Bob had been murdered, and we wouldn't rest until we found out who had done it.

"I won't go into why, because it's too long a story," I said, "but we believe the murderer is connected with the past in some way, and with Lily Molyneux."

"Ah, the famous Lily," he said thoughtfully.

"Notorious, more likely," I added briskly.

Michael nodded. "I guess maybe you're right. My father told me the whole story when I was eighteen. I had just graduated from high school and was heading for Yale. He had retired and was living in the house on Louisburg Square where he had once worked as a stableboy. He called me into his study and he said to me, 'Michael, there's a lot about me you don't know, and maybe there's some things about me I'm never going to tell you, but I want you to know where I came from. I want to tell you about our roots in Ireland. And about the woman I loved more than any other, and how a man's stupid pride can do more damage than a bullet. In fact, there were times, after I had lost her, when I might have preferred the bullet.'

"That was in 1951, I guess, and he was a man in his eighties, still upright and handsome, with silver hair and those fine gray eyes I always wished I had inherited. But I'm like my mother, Madeline Whittier James. Mom was tall and fair-haired and nice-looking, and she was always laughing and easy to be with, and after I heard about Lily, I guessed that's why Dad liked her. He said she was as straight as a die and he always knew exactly where he was with her.

"Mom was much younger than he was; he met her at a Fourth of July picnic at a friend's house out at Southampton. He was sixty-five then, though he told me proudly he looked nearer fifty. He was handsome and he was rich, and he could have had his pick of a dozen women, but he said he knew right away she was the one.

"Mom died when I was fourteen, and my father was like a lost dog. He didn't know what to do without her. He took to going back into the office again, but his mind wasn't on it. I was away at prep school and he was lonely and he would show up at odd times, and drag me out for lunch, or to a football game. I suppose gradually he got over the shock and the loss, but he said he would miss her to the end of his days. 'She was my favorite companion,' he told me soberly. 'I never wanted any other woman when your mother was alive.'

"Anyhow, the day he called me into the study, he told me for the first time about where he was born, in that little earth-floored hovel in Connemara. 'I know I haven't revealed any of this before,' he said, 'but it's not because I'm ashamed of it. It's just that it all became so complicated. But now that I'm an old man, I guess you had better hear about it from me, and then there'll never be any surprises sprung on you in the future. And just so nobody can ever accuse your old dad of keeping things from you.'

"And then he told me the story, about him and Lily and Liam. The whole thing. And about his brother Daniel whom I never knew existed until then.

" 'We O'Keeffe lads did well for ourselves in the new country,' he told me proudly. 'Only along the way, we somehow lost each other.' He looked me piercingly in the eye and said, 'So now you know all about your long-lost relatives, and the half-brother who disappeared. Odds are they'll never show up to haunt you, but if they do, you now know the truth.'

"I asked him if he had ever tried to find Liam, and he admitted guiltily that he had, but that it was too late. Liam had disappeared and he never saw him again."

Michael looked at me and said thoughtfully, "Lily must have been some woman."

"She was," I admitted. "But now you know that Bob Keeffe was Liam's son, and that makes Shannon your cousin. So you see," I said triumphantly to Shannon, "you are not alone in the world anymore."

Michael James laughed. "You can count on me for any help you need," he told her kindly. "And I'd like you to come and meet my family, any weekend you are free. It's all pretty casual and easygoing out at Sag Harbor, and there's always room for one or two more."

Shannon blushed with pleasure and thanked him prettily, and I told him that since she was Lily's heir and had come into a considerable amount of money, she might be in need of his business advice as well.

"And now we have eliminated you from our list of murder suspects, we must get on to the next one," I said, and he stared at me with astonishment.

"Murder suspect?" he repeated. "You thought maybe *I* had killed Bob Keeffe?"

"It was just a thought," I replied airily. "But now we've met you, we know you didn't do it."

"*How* do you know?" he asked curiously.

"Gut reaction," I said firmly, "or else woman's intuition. Either way, I'm sure."

We said good-bye and promised to be in touch soon, and went off in search of our next suspect, Senator Jim O'Keeffe.

CHAPTER
54

WASHINGTON

Now, I've always loved trains; there's something about them that offers more glamour and excitement than a mere plane ever can. I remember chugging and steaming through London to Dover, and the choppy gray ferry crossing, and then being back on the train where suddenly all of Europe is stretched before you. You could have dinner and then curl up like a pampered pet in your elegant little berth and wake up in any one of half a dozen countries, steaming through snow-capped mountain passes and green valleys, bustling cities and verdant forests. I would be wild with anticipation, as the passport officials would stride the swaying corridors, checking papers and looking like something out of a Sidney Greenstreet movie. And we would end up in Baden-Baden or Transylvania, Vienna or Venice, Istanbul or Moscow. Oh, it was an experience all right, and one I'm glad not to have missed.

And that's why I was pleased when Shannon suggested we take the train to Washington to meet Senator Jim O'Keeffe. Brigid was with us, thrilled at the thought of the tour of the White House she was going to take while we visited the senator.

Jim O'Keeffe was a popular man, massive like his grandfather; a bachelor with a reputation for enjoying the company of women. He had thick dark hair growing back from a wide forehead, and it was streaked with silver at the temples. His eyes were as silver-gray as the streaks in his hair, and his smile could, as they say, charm the birds from the trees.

He looked us appreciatively up and down as we were ushered into his office in the Senate building. "Two beautiful redheads," he said, striding toward us and holding out his hand. "My lucky day." Need I tell you I was immediately won over?

It was obvious within the first few minutes that his tongue was as silver as the other parts I have already mentioned, but the man was sincere when he told Shannon how sorry he was about her father. He sat next to her on a large green sofa, patting her hand, and telling her just as Michael James had that he had never believed for a minute Bob Keeffe was a crook. "And I've seen enough of those in my business to know," he added, a touch grimly.

I glanced at Shannon, staring at him, misty-eyed, and I sighed. I knew from that old gut reaction that Senator Jim O'Keeffe was no murderer either, but then I thought hopefully, maybe what he had to say might lead us to the man, or woman, we wanted.

I explained briskly what we had discovered so far, and that Shannon had come to me searching for the story of the past, so we could make sense of the present.

"You mean the story of Lily Molyneux," he said, just as Michael James had. It seems that both O'Keeffe brothers had carried their memories of her in their hearts as well as their heads, right to the end, passing her legend down from generation to generation, the way I had done with Shannon.

He said, "I can't help you much with the present, except to offer my assistance if you need it, but let me tell you what I remember about my grandfather."

Now, there's something about those tall, bearlike bearded men that has always appealed to me. They look somehow more solid and dependable than the rest of us, and I could understand his appeal to the voters, and his popularity with the media. Senator Jim O'Keeffe, like most Irishmen, was a born raconteur with a voice as smooth and hypnotic as the sound of waves on the shore, and we listened eagerly to his memories.

"GRANDFATHER DANNY O'KEEFFE WAS QUITE A CHARACTER," he said, looking at us and smiling. "He was already an old man when I was born, but you know, he never lost that booming voice, and that vitality. And even though he was a cripple, he never developed the fraility that old men do. I'd bet that when he died, he didn't look that much different from when Lily Molyneux married him, except for the extra weight and the white hair, of course. And the wheelchair.

"He maneuvered that chair like it was a tank, charging around the house like a battle commander, flinging orders right and left as he went, to the servants, the dogs, the secretaries, because he never relinquished his control of Danstores. He kept on working right to the end, and I was with him on the day he died.

"We were at his villa in Portofino; he had married an Italian woman he met there in 1919. He had fallen in love with the country and with her and she was everything Lily wasn't: sweet, gentle, and from a family who worked for a living. Her mother and father ran a little trattoria patronized by the locals and the occasional tourists or the people from the grand yachts that cruised the Mediterranean waters in the summer, though Portofino was still tiny and unspoiled then.

"When Dan had the fight with his brother, he wanted nothing more to do with him. After he quit politics, like many newly rich men of that era, he bought himself a beautiful gleaming white yacht and sailed the seas for months on end with a bunch of friends, exploring the world and enjoying himself. He ruled his empire from it, just as he had from his office in D.C.

"He had been one of the most popular senators in Washington, just the way I am myself." Jim smiled at us with an engaging lack of modesty. "But Dan's business was taking more and more of his time, and as he became even more dependent on the wheelchair, he decided to give up politics. They said it was a sad day in Washington when Senator Danny O'Keeffe stepped down from office. He had pushed many a law through, helping the immigrants and the poor and he was truly 'a man of the people.' He must have had a million friends and well-wishers and they said the party he threw at 'the mini White House'—his home in Maryland—was one of the best ever seen in this city.

"Anyway, he met and married Maria Annunciata, whom he always called Nancy, within the space of two months. The ceremony was at the local church in Positano, and a year later their son, my father Patrick, was born. And soon after that, two sisters. He bought a spectacular spur of land on a bluff overlooking the water, and built a splendid pink villa on it.

"It may have been the most beautiful house I ever saw." Jim smiled at me and added, "but then I have never been to Ardnavarna, and Grandfather Dan told me it couldn't hold a candle to that. He said there was no place in the world as beautiful as Connemara. I remember asking him why he never went back there if it was so special, and that was when he told me the story.

"I was nine years old and I was spending my summer at the Villa Favorita with my grandparents, as I always did. They divided their time between the Maryland house in the winter months and the yacht and the villa in spring and summer. I loved those long hot summer days.

God, even now I can feel the sun on my back as I scampered down to the rocks to fish, and I can smell the wild rosemary and thyme crushing beneath my sandaled feet. I can tell you, I was a lucky little boy to have known those golden Italian summers, all those long hot blue days and sparkling warm nights, when I was allowed to stay up late like the rest of the Italian kids, and wander the streets of the village with them, hanging out at my other grandpa's trattoria. It was a taste of freedom I never had back at home. In Washington, my dad helped run Danstores, though he was always the crown prince and never the king, because Grandpa Dan never abdicated in his favor, and Dad only got to take over control after he had died.

"Over the years, because of his lack of mobility and his fondness for good Italian food, Grandpa Dan had gained a lot of weight, and I remember they rigged up this special hoist to get him from his wheelchair onto the yacht, slinging him across in a sort of canvas bos'n's chair, yelling and cursing and shouting commands, and looking like an enraged bear. It always made me laugh to see him, and when he was safely on board he would grin at me and say, 'All right then, son, now it's your turn.' And he would have them sling me across, too, telling the crew to let me drop almost into the water so that I screamed and yelled, half-afraid and half-delighted, while he laughed his head off at me.

" 'Now you know what it feels like,' he said every time we did it, and he knew I loved it, just as I loved being with him, even more than with my own mom and dad.

"He was always fun to be with; he was full of stories and bonhomie, and the villa and the yacht were always crammed with a mixture of friends, new ones as well as old, because he collected people as easily as he acquired money. And through the same talents—a way with words and an enjoyment of life.

"He told me the story of Lily and his brother, 'Just in case the truth ever surfaces,' he said. 'Because with you following in my footsteps and going into politics, you can't afford any skeletons in the closet.'

"Now, don't forget, I was only nine years old and the only thing I wanted to be at that moment was a fisherman, right there in Positano, going out with the boats in the morning on that hazy blue sea and returning in the evening with a glistening catch, and carousing later in the bars and trattorias, the way I saw my friends' fathers doing. They were my preferred role models in life, but Grandpa Dan had other plans.

" 'I see the marks of a politician on you,' he said, studying my face.

'And I'm going to see to it your education points you in the right direction. And maybe all the way to the White House.'

"I could see his eyes gleaming as he thought of an O'Keeffe sitting in the Oval Office. I didn't understand until much later how much it would have meant to him to triumph over his background, his brother Finn, and over Lily and all the Molyneuxes.

"I've always thought it sad that he and Finn were not reconciled before they died, but the bad blood went too deep, I guess. And I always wondered, even though I know he adored my grandmother Nancy, whether he secretly hoped one day Lily would come back to him.

"So, there you have it. He died the following year when I was ten, without ever seeing Lily, or Finn, again. And I followed his instructions and became the second O'Keeffe to become a senator. I'm glad I did, and I'm really glad I had him for a grandfather." Jim looked at us, shaking his head reminiscently. "He was the tops," he said. "A fine man.

"My own father died five years ago, and as far as I know he never went to Connemara. We may be the only Irish who have never been back to visit 'the old country,' maybe because the past was always shrouded in mystery and unhappiness, and because the Villa Favorita where Grandma lived alone for years until she, too, died was always the family 'home' and the place where we all congregated in the summer."

WE SMILED OUR THANKS at him for telling us his story. "Well, now you know the Molyneuxes are not all bad, maybe you'll come and visit us," I said warmly, liking him for his openness as well as his good looks and charm. "I'm invitin' you now, Jim O'Keeffe. I'll be expectin' to see you and I can guarantee Ardnavarna will welcome you like a long-lost son."

With that he laughed and swept us off for lunch at a grand restaurant, where Shannon and Brigid and I were so busy gaping at the famous political faces and all the celebrities, we almost forgot to eat the delicious food, though I could tell Brigid was savoring every detail, and probably comparing it unfavorably to her own cuisine.

Senator Jim took us back to the railway station in his limousine and we parted in a flurry of hugs and kisses, like old friends. "See you in Connemara," he called as we waved from the train, and somehow I was sure we would.

"What next?" Shannon said, back again at the Ritz-Carlton. Brigid had retired to her lavish bed with more cinnamon toast and tea and I could hear a game show blasting from her television set. Eddie was sitting next to Shannon and we were drinking a restorative glass of champagne and thinking out our next move.

I heaved a sigh. "The partners are next, I'm afraid," I said, because I honestly couldn't think of anyone else. "First Brad, and then Jeff."

"Okay, then this time I'm coming with you," Eddie said, "because I'm sure they did it." We stared at him with surprise. "Well," he said, "who the hell else can it be? We've eliminated the O'Keeffes, and we know the partners were robbing him."

"Or we know that it looks that way," I said, because I had long ago learned that nothing is the way it seems.

Brad Jeffries lived out on Long Island, and we drove off in our hired limo to beard the lion in his own den. We had not telephoned ahead because we wanted to catch him offguard, but as it happened we were the ones who were surprised.

CHAPTER
55

A SMARTLY DRESSED HOUSEKEEPER answered the doorbell and let us in. A few minutes later Monica Jeffries came hesitantly down the stairs to greet us. She was an older woman, though I never like to use that phrase when speaking of another lady—and I could see she *was* "a lady." But she must have been well into her sixties and natural with it; by that I mean she was as nature had made her, unlifted and untucked, and still pretty in a pale, discreet sort of way. Pale hair, pale skin, and pale eyes behind almond-shaped tortoiseshell spectacles.

"Shannon honey," she said in a lovely Southern accent, "what a surprise." I thought she sounded as nervous as she looked and my hackles rose like the dalmatians when they scented a rabbit. Monica Jeffries had something to hide, I just knew it.

Shannon introduced me and then Eddie, and southern gentlewoman that she was, Monica offered us tea.

"We should be delighted," I said, waiting until the Earl Grey was served in pretty Wedgwood cups and the social talk was out of the way before saying abruptly, "What we really came for is to see your husband."

"Brad?" she said, blushing a fiery red. Her hands shook as she replaced her cup hastily in its saucer.

"We want to talk to him about Daddy," Shannon said hurriedly. "If he happens to be around?" She looked questioningly at Monica and all of a sudden the poor woman burst into tears.

"Brad's gone," she said between sobs. "He's left me. After forty years together. There's another woman, younger than me, and pretty. She trains horses down at her farm in Kentucky, and that's all I know about her. I suppose it must have been going on for some time, but the first I knew of it was just after your father died. Brad came home one night, all tense and silent, but he'd been that way ever since . . . well, ever since it happened and the business collapsed, so it wasn't anything different. And then he told me there was this other woman. He said he was packing his bags and going to live with her, and that I could keep this house and everything in it, and he would make sure I was taken care of financially. He said our children were all grown-up and so there was no need for him to worry about them, and he was going to start a whole new life and enjoy himself for once." She glanced at us through her tears, and tender-hearted Shannon took her glasses and held them while Monica attempted to dry her overflowing eyes.

"Oh, dear, now I've embarrassed you," she sniffed, struggling to regain her composure, while I looked for anything she might inadvertently reveal about her errant husband. But it soon became obvious that she knew little more than where he was and nothing at all about his business and Bob Keeffe's death.

I gathered up Shannon and Eddie, ready to leave. "I'm sorry to have upset you, Mrs. Jeffries," I said, "but if you'll just give us his address, we intend to go and interview him. And make no mistake, I shall tell him what I think of him, leaving a fine gentlewoman like yourself for a little horse-mad hussy." And as she hurried to get the address for us, I wondered why she hadn't gone after the silly man herself and horse-whipped him, the way he deserved.

The next morning we were on a flight down to Louisville where we were picked up by a limo and driven to Bradlee Farm. On the way there, we stopped in the nearest little township, a mere straggle of feed stores and minimarkets dominated by a gigantic Mobil gas station at the intersection of two main roads. Eddie sauntered into the feed and grain store on the pretext of asking directions to Bradlee Farm, and with his easy friendliness, learned in no time at all that Bradlee Farm was owned by Brad Jeffries and had been for the past ten years. Fedora Lee had been hired to run it for him and she was a real whizz with horses, and not a bad-lookin' woman either. And she'd had Mr. Jeffries twisted around her little finger from day one. Everybody knew it, but it had been going on for so long now, nobody even talked about it anymore.

"Interesting," I said thoughtfully, wondering how Brad Jeffries had come by the large amount of money needed to purchase a beautiful and obviously very expensive farm in the best bluegrass country. Acres and acres of immaculate paddocks and corrals were dotted with shade trees and Thoroughbreds of such quality that I burned with envy. In the distance, we could see a sprawling white ranch house surrounded by flowerbeds and lawns, and to one side the extensive stables.

We were stopped at the gate by a guard. He came out of his cute little white-clapboard guardhouse to give us a once-over and then, impressed by the limo if not its passengers, he telephoned the house to let them know we were here. He pressed the button that lifted the barrier and let us through and we bowled down a mile or so of perfectly kept roadway, past all the lovely horses and the ranch hands busy about their business, and I longed to stop and explore but I knew I could not. I had Brad Jeffries to deal with first.

He was waiting on the steps to greet us and he looked as nervous as his wife had. He wore dark glasses, so I couldn't see his eyes as he shook my hand and welcomed me. "This is unexpected, Shannon," he said, putting his arm around her shoulders as we walked indoors into the hall. "But I guess you spoke to Monica."

"We did," she said, shrugging him off and sounding colder than I could ever have imagined. But then I remembered that it wasn't just on Monica's behalf she was angry at Brad: she knew from Joanna that he had been stealing from her father, and that this fancy farm was probably paid for with that stolen money. And maybe Brad had even killed for it.

Brad took us into a comfortable den with a bar in one corner and a huge stone fireplace in another, and we arranged ourselves cautiously on the edge of the huge squashy sofas refusing his offer of a drink, and looking stonily at him.

"Well?" he said, glancing apprehensively at us, "what can I do for you?"

"We've come about these," I said, taking the ExWyZe Fund contracts from the attaché case and opening them one by one at the pages with his incriminating signature. The color left his face as he stared at them. He said, "But how did you get those?"

"My father found them and gave them to Joanna Belmont for safe-keeping," Shannon said icily.

"It's not the way it looks," Brad protested. "They were just regular transactions, nothing more than usual. Bob bought the land and he had us take care of the details and sign the documents. You know how little he cared for that side of the business." He looked appealingly at Shannon. "He liked working out the deals and talking the bankers into giving him the financing, but after that he always left it to us. . . ."

"I understand you bought this farm ten years ago," I said briskly. "But even then it must have cost a great deal of money. I haven't yet had the pleasure of visiting your stables, but I'm a fair judge of horse-flesh and those Thoroughbreds I saw out there in your beautiful pad-docks are a major investment. But in any case, we know you were stealing and we have the evidence to prove it."

Brad's face turned ashen as Shannon said bitterly, "My father took you into his business. He helped you up the ladder. I *know* how well he paid you, and all those generous 'bonuses' he gave you, and the trips and the lavish presents at Christmas. You took his generosity and his simple trust and you abused it. You stole from him so you could leave Monica and come here and live in splendor with a younger woman who probably thinks you're nothing but an old fool anyway."

"Do you mean me?" a sharp voice said from the doorway, and we all swung around to look at the woman who was standing there watching us. She was tall and elegant in cream riding britches that fitted like a second skin, a white cotton shirt and perfect riding boots that I ad-mired briefly before reminding myself that this was "the other woman." She had an oval face, dark eyes, and a firm mouth, and her black hair hung down her back in a braid. I guessed she was in her middle-thirties. She was in perfect shape, and I knew she must be a good horsewoman.

There was a cold expression in her dark eyes and a tightness around her mouth as she strode into her den and said, "Am I 'the other woman' you are looking for?"

"At a guess, yes," I said, standing up and drawing myself to my full height. "That is if you are Fedora Lee?"

"I am," she said, pulling off her riding gloves and throwing them and her riding crop onto a chair. "And who might you be?"

"This is Mrs. Molyneux," Eddie said, making the introductions. He put an arm around Shannon. "And this is Shannon Keeffe."

"Keeffe? Oh, I get it." She shrugged dismissively. "That's pretty good, the daughter of one of the country's biggest thieves coming here and accusing Brad of stealing." She laughed, a short, brittle sound as she went to sit next to Brad. I saw him glance helplessly at her and I knew instantly that she was at the bottom of things, or at least of his stealing. Brad was a weak man. He had never had what Bob Keeffe had; the get-up-and-go that makes a man a winner. And it had taken someone like Fedora Lee, a tough pill in a glossy sugar coating, to set him up and encourage him to cross the border from minor treachery to major fraud. And I would be willing to bet that most of what he had stolen was now in her neatly numbered little bank account in Switzer-land. Or else in Liechtenstein with the ExWyZe Fund.

The man was a fool but I knew he was no murderer. I quickly pushed the contracts back into the attaché case and saw Brad glance wildly at Fedora. She leapt across and grabbed the case from my hands, staring triumphantly at me. "I think these belong to Brad," she said silkily. Enraged, I stared at her, and then I gave her a swift karate chop just below her elbow. She screamed with pain and dropped the case and Eddie leapt to pick it up.

"You bitch," she snarled at me, and I smiled.

"Just a little something I learned at karate class of a winter's evening in the village hall," I said in explanation. "And now we shall say goodbye. But you have not heard the last of us, Miss Fedora Lee."

CHAPTER

〜〜〜〜〜〜〜〜〜〜〜 56 〜〜〜〜〜〜〜〜〜〜〜

JACK WEXLER DID NOT LOOK SURPRISED to see us, standing on the doorstep of his smart East Side brownstone. "Shannon," he said, nodding coolly in our direction as she introduced us. He didn't invite us in, he just turned and walked back into the house. We glanced questioningly at one other and then followed him in.

I couldn't say the house was beautiful with the all-embracing, protective intimacy that I expect from a home, the way Ardnavarna is for instance. But I suppose it had a sort of bleak architectural grandeur. Walls and floors had been ripped out to create new volumes and spaces, and winding staircases linked the different galleried levels where splashy, colorful works of art were displayed. I stared around me interestedly. I'm not one to dismiss anything new simply because I am old and do not understand it, and I would have enjoyed spending some time studying his collection in more detail. But that was not what we were there for.

It was eleven o'clock in the morning and I watched Jack refill his glass with whiskey. He slumped into a hard-looking black leather sofa, staring at us, and I knew this was not his first drink of the morning. I was looking at a worried man, maybe even a frantic man.

He did not offer us a drink, he just sat there silently. Shannon said coldly, "Do you know why we are here?"

"Brad called," he said sullenly.

"Then you know we have the contracts that you and Brad signed, for the purchase of the worthless properties. Dozens of them . . ."

"Those properties were all hand-picked by your own father, probably to bury tax money he didn't want to disclose. He bought those properties and then he had us do the dirty work and sign the documents. There's no way you can pin anything on me."

I wandered around the large room, peering at the signatures on the paintings, though even I knew that the series of three immense abstracts were Rothkos. And even in the wilds of Connemara we know what sort of price a Rothko commands.

"Very nice," I said crisply, sitting myself down next to Jack on the hard leather sofa. I winced and wondered why it is that architects always choose such bleak furnishings. Is there no softness in their souls? Looking into Jack Wexler's eyes I knew there was certainly no softness in this particular architect's soul. Nor in his heart. My gut instinct told me I was looking at a bitter, frustrated man. It showed in his disillusioned eyes, in the tight lines around his mouth and the flicker of apprehension, or even fear, that passed across his face as he watched me, wondering what I was going to say next.

"Such museum quality art must cost a great deal of money," I said pleasantly. "Shannon was able to tell me exactly what your yearly salary was with Keeffe Holdings, and I doubt it would buy one of these masterpieces, let alone three. As well as all the rest of your wonderful collection. And this very smart town house. To say nothing of the Aston-Martin and the other 'toys' you own, Mr. Wexler."

He tossed the remainder of his drink down his throat and slammed the glass down on the minimalist glass coffee table. "It's none of your business, you interfering old busybody," he snarled.

Quite suddenly that smooth, handsome man had disappeared and Jack Wexler's background was showing. The tough street fighter who had learned to cover his cheap soul—and his tracks—using his smooth, easy good looks and practiced charm. I felt I was looking at a man who rehearsed his lines and his smile in the bathroom mirror every morning, a man who had learned to use people, who knew how to tell them what they wanted to hear and how to take what he wanted. And I pitied any woman foolish enough to get involved with him.

Jack was a user and now the whole self-centered glossy world he had created for himself was about to fall around his ears, and he was panicked. I could almost smell the scent of it on him, the way dogs can, and I smiled my most guileless smile and said, "Mr. Wexler, did you murder Bob Keeffe?"

"Are you out of your mind," he yelled, leaping agitatedly to his feet. He strode across to Shannon and put his arm protectively around her shoulders.

"How can you accuse me of killing him?" he yelled, red-faced with fear and anger. Then, pulling himself together with an effort, he said more calmly, "I'm not perfect, I admit, but goddam it, I'm no killer."

He turned abruptly away and went and poured himself another drink. He hands were shaking and I wondered how much he had been drinking these months since Bob died. But I knew he was speaking the truth because Jack's only concern was the way he seemed to other people; his "presentation" was everything. He was a show-off. Hence his smart town house in the grand neighborhood, the expensive art collection and the flashy cars. Jack was all facade and no content. For some reason I didn't yet understand, he had thought he could steal from the company without being caught. He had done it to fuel his extravagances and bolster his ego and his image, but I didn't think he had killed for it. We were looking at a man who was worried about going to jail for fraud, not murder, and I sighed regretfully as I stood up to leave.

"Of course, you are a thief, Mr. Wexler," I said pleasantly, because I hate being rude when I am a guest in someone's house. "And now, as you look around your grand house and grand possessions, you must ask yourself if it was worth it. I wonder just how many years a man gets for grand larceny. Or will it be considered fraud?" I shrugged, smiling. "But that's for the judge to decide. And we must say good morning and be on our way."

Jack glared at me and then said appealingly to Shannon, "Honey, I know how you're feeling. Believe me, I've shed my own tears for your dad. We worked together all those years. He was my friend. How could you believe that I would steal from him? I promise you it's not true."

He was using all his smooth charm on her. He even looked like himself again: a lean, attractive, expensively dressed man, with just a hint of a little-boy-lost that some women are such suckers for. Not Shannon.

He put his hands on her shoulders, pulling her closer, staring deep into her eyes, and I saw Eddie bristle and gather himself together, ready to punch him if he made one wrong move. "Don't touch me," Shannon said in a voice so tipped with ice it made him shudder. "Don't even talk to me. You cheated my father and for all I know you shot him when he found out. You ruined that fine man, and even if you didn't kill him, you killed everything he had worked for. His company and his good name."

We walked from the room without saying good-bye, leaving Jack staring after us with the panic in his eyes.

~~~

"THERE'S ONLY ONE PERSON LEFT," Eddie said. "J. K. Brennan."

Shannon sighed as we drove back to the Ritz-Carlton. "He's the only one I believed when he said he was sorry. He was the only one who helped me. I still have his credit line of fifty thousand dollars at the bank. I just can't believe he was stealing. Of all of them, he was the one who owed most to my dad, and from what he told me he felt it right to the heart."

We located J.K. out at his farm in Montauk, and Shannon phoned him to say we were coming to visit. I've found that surprise is always a good weapon and I didn't approve, but she said it was a long way to go and then not find him there.

I had thought we would be taking a commercial airliner, but Shannon had other ideas. "Dad gave me flying lessons for my twenty-first birthday," she said with a confident grin. "I shall be your pilot today."

The rented plane was a sweet little red-and-white four-seater Cessna and Shannon handled it expertly. Eddie sat up front next to her and I sat behind them, staring excitedly out of the windows at the green-and-blue landscape dotted with sunshine and cloud-shadows drifting away beneath us. I was glad Brigid had decided to spend the day in Bloomingdale's and not come with us, because she would have had the rosary beads out and been crossing herself and making us all nervous. I just hoped she wouldn't squander her life savings in one gigantic shopping spree.

J.K. was waiting for us at the little airfield and he was exactly as Shannon had described: middle-height and stocky with smooth brown hair brushed straight back and mild brown eyes behind gold-rimmed spectacles. He was wearing well-pressed jeans and a blue shirt with the sleeves rolled up, but even at the wheel of his white Range Rover, he looked uncomfortably like a man who should be sitting behind a desk. "Casual" was not a word that could ever be used to describe J. K. Brennan. My guess was that he was a man who lived by his own set of daily rules and regulations, and it's my experience with people of that sort, who operate within a restrictive little framework, that whenever they step out of it they are likely to fall to pieces.

He was more than pleasant, he was welcoming. And deferential toward Shannon. There was none of the familiarity I had expected, since he had been the one to comfort her and help her out by lending her money. He shook hands with her as formally as he did with Eddie and me, and he pointed out the places of interest like a good host as he drove us to his "farm" on the shores of Long Island Sound.

I smiled when I saw it—it was more like an Irish farm than an American one; a couple of fields fenced in, a carefully tended vegetable plot, a few token flowers and a low white house clinging to the landscape in perpetual fear of being blown away by the fierce Atlantic gales.

"It's nothing much," J.K. said apologetically, "but it's a great place to get away from the rat race."

"A refuge," Shannon said quietly and they smiled at each other, remembering when he had offered it to her for just that reason.

I thought it was odd that a man like that should want to get away from the rat race, but Shannon had told me about his early life on the farmstead in South Carolina and I thought maybe he was just going back to his roots, with his neat little "play farm" that didn't have to work for a living, the way the farm in his youth had.

It was decorated in a charmingly casual fashion, easy and comfortable with green-shaded lamps and masculine plaid throws on the old sofas, and logs piled to one side of the big stone fireplace, and you could just imagine cozying up at night in front of the glow. My estimation of him went up, and then he told us he had bought it complete with furnishings from a writer who couldn't stand the solitude. I laughed. It was hard to get a fix on a man who seemed to be wearing another man's clothes and living in another man's house.

He said he hoped we would stay for lunch but I quickly declined, knowing that the real reason we were there was not social.

Shannon took the initiative this time. She said firmly, "Maudie and Eddie and I, *and* Joanna Belmont, think my dad was murdered. No, let me correct that. We *know* he was. And we are determined to find out who did it."

"I thought you had gotten over that idea," he said, looking puzzled.

She shook her head. "Now I'm even more sure. Especially as we have evidence that Brad and Jack were stealing from him."

She took out the contracts and handed them to J.K. "Have you ever seen these before?" she asked, and he scanned them quickly and shook his head.

"Nope. But that doesn't mean they are not legit. The partners often signed contracts, even major ones, though with Jack it was usually with the suppliers and contractors—you know, for the girders and the marble and the elevators. But Shannon, you know your dad hated what he called 'office work.' That was one of the reasons he hired me, to take all that day-to-day grind of contract reading and letter writing and following up, off his hands. He was an engineer and that's what he liked doing. He spent three quarters of his time at the building sites, and the other quarter wining and dining bankers and talking them into giving him more money. And he was damned good at it too."

"Surely the contracts were always checked by his lawyers before they were signed," I said as the thought suddenly occurred to me.

"Always," he said firmly. "But as far as I can tell, there's nothing wrong with these contracts anyway."

"Except that the land is worthless," Eddie said bluntly, and J.K. glanced at him with surprise.

"That's the partners' department," he said with a shrug. "You'll have to talk to them. I know nothing about it."

"And what exactly was 'your department,' Mr. Brennan?" I asked curiously, wondering why this inocuous young man had proven so indispensable to Bob Keeffe.

"I guess I was a kind of a 'man Friday.' I just took care of all the things Bob didn't want to. It varied from day to day, month to month. Maybe he would send me to Italy to check why the marble shipment was delayed, or to London to talk to a banker. Or Pittsburgh to talk money with a new supplier of steel girders. Or Hong Kong to see what the building action was, or to inspect building sites in Sydney or Timbuktu. I was everything to him that he wasn't himself. It got so that sometimes I would think of things before he did and then he would say them a minute afterward. He said sometimes we were just like terrible twins. We knew too much about each other."

I wondered whether Bob had known too much about J.K. that night he was shot and I said suddenly, "And did you kill your employer, Mr. Brennan?"

He looked at me with shock. Then he turned to Shannon and said, "My God, how can you even think such a thing? Bob Keeffe gave me my start. He literally took me from the street when I knew nobody else would have." He walked across to the window, staring out at the pale sea lapping the rugged coastline, his shoulders hunched miserably.

"I'm sorry if we've upset you, J. K.," Shannon said quickly. "It's just that we had to ask. We're just investigating, you know."

"Amateur sleuths," I said, beaming. The man looked genuinely upset and though I could not get a reading on him, I did not have the feeling he was a killer. "Maybe we could change our minds about lunch," I suggested to jolly things along. After all, he had been kind to Shannon, and her father had cared about him.

His face lit up and he hurried to light the barbecue, and I saw that a salad had already been prepared and that fresh swordfish steaks were already marinating, and I knew he had hoped we would stay.

Eddie and Shannon relaxed and we drank a bottle of California wine with our pleasant meal and afterward we went for a walk around the garden, inspecting his neat soldierly rows of onions and carrots and potatoes, and the regimented ranks of beans and peas climbing up over trellises, and the rampant over-size squash. "If you take your eye off them for a day or two, they just go wild," he said apologetically, as though we might care that he had allowed his zucchini to take over their own destiny.

After lunch, he drove us back to the airstrip, and as we took off I could see him, sitting straight-backed in his white Range Rover, one hand shielding his eyes from the sun as he watched us soaring off into the distance. And I wondered about him.

We were silent on the flight back to Manhattan, each thinking gloomily that we were no further ahead than when we had started. I apologized to them both as we drove back through the choking traffic to the hotel. "Maybe I've been leading you up the wrong path," I said. "I'm an interferin' old woman, and you probably know best, after all."

They laughed and told me not to be silky, we were all just floundering around, searching for the truth. And after all, thanks to Joanna, we had already proven Brad and Jack were the thieves.

"Let's go back to Nantucket," Eddie suggested to Shannon. "Let's search the white house and Sea Mist Cottage from top to bottom, end to end, for clues."

I waved good-bye to them as the limo dropped me at the Ritz-Carlton and then turned around to take them back out to the airport again. I was sad, but glad to see them go, because it gave me a little time on my own to think things out.

I opened the door to my suite and stopped in my tracks, staring with astonishment at the litter of tissue paper and glossy carrier bags, and I groaned. The worst had happened. Brigid, who had never shopped further away than Galway in her life, had gone mad with consumerism in Bloomingdale's.

I followed the trail through the foyer into the sitting room. Garments of all sorts were draped over the sofas and chairs. There was silky lingerie, and packets and packets of black stockings, some with glittery stripes and others with stars or lace, strewn on the floor. There were colorful skirts and blouses and sweaters, and at least half a dozen black dresses. And, ranged in front of the marble hearth, were six identical pairs of black, high-heeled trotty little boots. Italian and, I could see, very expensive.

Brigid appeared in the doorway of her room, flushed with triumph and the excitement of it all. She was wearing a long quilted housecoat in hot Florida colors, orange, fuschia, and lime-green, with the label still dangling from the sleeve, and she beamed proudly at me.

"What d'ya think, Maudie?" she cried excitedly. "Isn't it all wonderful? Sure and there's nothin' they don't have in New York. And those salesgirls are a miracle, y'just tells 'em what you want and they find it for you. 'No problem,' they say, and 'Six pairs? Of course, madam.' And 'How about this one, too, it's exactly right for you.' God bless 'em, for they made me a happy woman today. I've never had so much fun in me whole life."

"In that case, Brigid, it was worth every cent," I said approvingly, because I'm all for a woman having a good time, whatever it takes to make her happy.

She glanced apprehensively at me and then slowly lifted the hem of her robe. She was wearing lizardskin cowboy boots with Cuban heels and fluffy tassels and her plump pink knees stuck out over the top like a pair of Florida grapefruits. "What d'ya think?" she asked cautiously.

"Brigid, I love 'em," I said enthusiastically, and I went over and gave her a great big kiss. "And I love you too," I added.

"I was thinking of getting them in another color also," she said thoughtfully, and I laughed. "Well, there's still plenty left from Mammie's sapphires to pay for them," I said, because what was mine was hers, even though she had her wages for the past thirty years tucked away in the Bank of Ireland.

"I'll niver accept that," she said, shocked. "Yer mammie's earrings are rightly yours, and you should only have been there spending along with me today instead of 'investigatin',' as you call it."

"Sleuthin' " I said, flinging myself wearily onto the sofa and the piles of clothes. I sighed. "And no nearer we are to a solution either, Brigid."

I told her the results, or lack of them, of today's encounter with J. K. Brennan, and she looked thoughtfully at me and said, "But all you know about J.K. is what he's told you himself."

She was right, and it was so obvious I don't know why I hadn't thought of it myself. Yet the story he had told Shannon about his past had had the ring of truth about it: the poor boy from the wrong side of the tracks whose mother was a bad lot and whose father was a drunk.

And about the grandmother who had been the only person to love him and give him dreams.

Dreams of what? I wondered. The past? Or the future? There was only one way to find out.

"Put on your new clothes, Brigid," I said, springing to my feet again. "We're going on a little trip."

I remembered Shannon telling me that J.K. came from South Carolina and that he had gone to college in a small town there, and I called down to the concierge and asked him to book us on the next flight.

"To what city, madam?" he asked me.

"Wherever the planes go, just as long as it's South Carolina," I replied, forgetting all about the vast distances of the American continent.

We arrived in Charleston late that night and checked tiredly into the airport hotel. We sent down to room service for sandwiches and tea and sat, each in our own queen-size bed, munching silently and gazing at the TV like a pair of zombies. It had been a long day and half an hour later we were both fast asleep.

I was on the phone the next morning at nine sharp, and I soon had a list of all the small-town colleges in the state. There were so many I feared it would take me a week to check them all, but I began at the top of the list with *A,* and struck lucky paydirt with *B.* Jonas Brennan had attended Boonespoint Valley College from 1980 to '83. That was all the information they would give me, but Brigid and I had our bags packed again in a flash and with me at the wheel of a hired Cadillac convertible, we set out for Boonespoint.

It was one of those ugly, sprawling little towns that you never seem to find the center of: just a series of long straight roads lined with used car lots and gas stations, and McDonald's arches and Wendy's chains. There were cheap-looking supermarkets and tired minimalls with closed-down yogurt parlors, and beauty salons with grubby windows and old-fashioned hair dryers that had seen better days. A creek ran across the middle of town and on the bluff on the far side we could see rows of larger houses, with trees and gardens and smart cars in the driveways, and we knew that must be on "the right side of the tracks." The part of Boonespoint where we were in was J. K. Brennan's territory.

We found the college and took a look at the straggle of prefabricated concrete buildings that no architect had ever had a hand in creating. The kids were mostly wearing T-shirts and baseball caps, back to front, chewing gum and chatting up the short-skirted cute-looking girls. They stared curiously at the two old biddies in the big Cadillac, cheering as we roared past. "Go, dude," they shouted after me, and I grinned with delight.

I remembered from the movies and detective novels that if ever you want to find out something about somebody, you go to the local newspaper offices and ask to check their archives. And we did just that.

The *Boonespoint Echo,* a weekly rag, covered everything from high school graduation ceremonies to funerals, from golden wedding anniversaries to arrests for car theft and brawls, and a myriad other crimes of which there seemed to be a great many for such a small town. It showed the latest fashions to arrive at Elite Style in the Boonespoint Mall, and the cheerleaders in action at the Boonespoint Valley College football games, and it had been in existence for fifty years.

"Must be one of the oldest in the state," the middle-aged perky little woman at the front desk told us, showing us into the gloomy airless dungeon where copies of all the newspapers dating back to its beginnings were housed. "Anything you want, just holler now," she said, leaving us staring hopelessly at the files, wondering where to begin.

Remembering the graduation pictures, I started with the year Jonas Brennan had graduated from Boonespoint Valley College. And there he was in the photograph, half-hidden in the second row from the front among forty or so youths and girls, Class of '83.

Brigid and I peered excitedly at the photograph and I decided he had changed very little since then; he was still smooth-faced and smooth-haired and bespectacled and stocky. Only now he looked rich. Richer than any of his fellow classmates of '83, I'd be willing to bet.

Just how rich was J.K., I wondered? And how truly "poor" had he been? I remembered his grandmother had died a month before he had graduated. Poor though she was, surely the *Echo* would have reported her death. I searched carefully, page by page, through every newspaper for the two months before J.K.'s graduation, while Brigid sifted through even earlier issues looking for a report of his mother's death. I found nothing, and heaved a disappointed sigh.

"Glory be to God, will y'only be lookin' at this, Maudie," Brigid exclaimed, shocked, peering over her spectacles at me. Her finger shook as she pointed to the photograph above a headline. LOCAL BARMAID FOUND MURDERED IN ALLEY.

There was a picture, horrifying even by tabloid standards, of a bloodstained body lying amid a litter of trash and garbage cans. And next to it was a photograph of a hard-faced, flashy-looking woman with a big smile on her face and none at all in her calculating eyes. And her name was Alma Brennan.

"I thought he said she had died of cirrhosis," Brigid said indignantly. She forgets nothing, and that was exactly what Shannon had told us J. K. had said. That they had *"scooped her up from the sidewalk one night, hemorrhaging from the mouth."*

"It seems J.K. must have been lying, Brigid," I said, busily reading the report of how the body had been found by a store owner arriving early to open up his shop. And that Alma Brennan had worked for years as a barmaid in the Red Rooster Saloon on First and Main, *"and she was a well-known woman about town."*

"And what will they be meanin' by that?" Brigid asked.

"You know. A tart," I replied, reading on.

It said the body had been taken to the county morgue and an autopsy was being carried out that very afternoon. And police inquiries were underway for her assassin. Meanwhile her mother-in-law and her son, Jonas Brennan, who lived out at Jekyll's Farm, had been informed.

We glanced apprehensively at one other as we pulled out the next edition of the *Echo*. BARMAID SHOT FIVE TIMES BY UNKNOWN ASSASSIN the headline said. I could just imagine young Jonas flinching as he read that, along with the report on her private life, or, more aptly, her "public life," because Alma Brennan had been known as a woman with plenty of men friends. "Could have been any one of 'em killed her" was the indifferent consensus of those on the street who were interviewed about her death.

We found the next *Echo* and this time there was just a short report. MURDERER STILL AT LARGE it said, over a three-line statement that Alma had been buried the previous afternoon.

I looked disappointedly at Brigid and she said, "Don't give up yet. Maybe they found who did it." So we went on scanning a couple of months of newspapers until our eyes glazed over from fatigue. But we couldn't have missed the headline anyway. SON HELD FOR QUESTIONING IN BRENNAN MURDER.

"God save us," Brigid gasped, crossing herself while I quickly read the report of how the police had taken eighteen-year-old Jonas Brennan into custody "for questioning," and how he had been held overnight at Boonespoint P.D. The police had searched Jekyll's Farm but had failed to find the weapon, though they had found several shotguns on the premises.

I sighed with relief as I saw the headline in the next edition. JONAS

BRENNAN RELEASED it said, in letters much smaller than before, as though people were already losing interest in Alma's death and J.K.'s fate. But it was the line beneath that riveted my attention. It said that Jonas Brennan's grandmother, Mrs. Iris Sheridan, had made a statement to the press that it was "a crime against her grandson that he had ever been accused of such a terrible thing." And that "whoever had shot Alma, it certainly was not him." She said that "the police had better smarten up a little and find out who the real culprit is, though by now so much time has passed, he probably skipped town long ago."

"Mrs. Iris Sheridan," I repeated, staring at Brigid.

"Did y'ever stop to wonder what the *K* in Jonas K. Brennan stands for?" she asked, thoughtfully.

"Keeffe?" I asked, and she nodded.

"I'll bet my cowboy boots on it."

I'll tell you we were out of that dungeon like a couple of bats from hell, throwing a quick thanks to the woman at the counter. "Y'all want copies of anything?" she asked and I dashed back again, waiting impatiently while she slowly photostated the articles I needed. And then we were back in the convertible and speeding toward Charleston and the plane back to New York.

I thought worriedly of Shannon and thanked God she was safe in Nantucket with Eddie, because now I was convinced that J. K. Brennan was Bob's murderer, and that the past had caught up with the present, just the way we knew it would.

CHAPTER
57

BACK AT THE HOTEL, I tucked the exhausted Brigid into her bed and telephoned Shannon on Nantucket to tell her what we had discovered. I let the phone ring but there was no reply, and disappointed, I replaced the receiver and prowled the suite restlessly. I took a leisurely bath, filling the tub with the expensive bath oil Brigid had bought in Bloomingdale's, lying there with a moisturizing pack slathered on my face while I contemplated what to do. Finally, I put on my makeup, brushed my curls, and changed into a mannish dark-blue pinstripe St. Laurent 1980 suit that might have been designed specially for "sleuthing."

AND THEN THE PHONE RANG. It was Shannon and I sighed with relief. There was a lot of background noise and she said she was calling from the plane. They were on the shuttle flight from Boston back to Manhattan, and they would be here within a couple of hours.

She said, "J.K. called me. He sounded really excited. He said he thought he had the evidence I needed. Oh, Maudie, I'm not supposed to tell you or Eddie, but I'm going to meet him later tonight so he can show me what he's got."

"And did he say what that was?"

My voice was sharp and she said quickly, "He'll tell me when I get there. But he did say he knew what the ExWyZe Fund really was."

I thought of J.K. sitting like a spider at the center of the complex web he had created, waiting for her, and I was filled with the sort of deep anger I haven't felt since I heard my Archie had been killed by the Nazis. "And where is it you're to be seein' him?" I enquired.

"It's odd, but he wants me to meet him at the new Keeffe Tower on Park Avenue. He said to take the freight elevator to the penthouse and he would meet me there at eleven. There was something important I had to see."

"You are not to go," I said strongly. "Meet me here and we shall all go along to meet Mr. J. K. Brennan at eleven."

"He said it was important I told nobody. Not until I had seen what he had to show me, and then the choice was mine." She hesitated and then said, "You know, Maudie, there was something in his voice, a kind of 'sympathy.' Do you think maybe he has evidence that my dad did kill himself, after all? That he wasn't murdered, and we have all been rushing around looking for suspects when there are none."

"I'm sure that's not true," I said, wondering exactly what J.K. had up his sleeve. And as I put down the telephone receiver, I was determined that I was going to find out.

I thought the next hour would never pass. I looked in hopefully on Brigid but she was snoring peacefully, and I didn't have the heart to wake her and tell her the new developments. I stood in front of the TV, switching channels the way she did, but nothing interested me and I went to the window and looked down at the breathtaking view of the magical city. The nighttime skyscrapers were lit like a forest of Christmas trees and I thought of J.K. waiting at the Keeffe Tower for young Shannon, and my stomach churned.

At ten o'clock I scribbled a note, pulled on a slouch-brimmed navy felt hat and sensible-heeled shoes and tucked a camellia from the flower display into my lapel. I picked up Pa's old hazelwood walking stick, checked my hair and new Paloma red lipstick and took the elevator down to the lobby.

Everyone in the hotel knew me by now, for haven't I stopped and had a chat with each and every one of them, from the night manager and the concierge to the bell captain, the waiters and the receptionists, and they all gave me a smile and a greeting as I stepped briskly by. The doorman called me a cab and asked where I wanted to go, looking surprised when I said the new Keeffe Tower on Park. "That building's not yet finished, Mrs. Molyneux," he said doubtfully. "Are y'sure that's where you want to go?"

"Certain, thank you, Patrick," I said, stepping into the cab while he gave the driver the address.

There was a security guard at the entrance to the foyer and he looked at me with astonishment, as I hurried toward his brightly lit glass cubicle. From his badge I saw his name was Mulligan. Wondering how I ever became so devious, I put on an anxious face and a brogue and said breathlessly to him, "Oh, thank God, 'tis a fellow Irishman y'are, and sure isn't the whole of New York Irish anyways?" I clung to his little window ledge, trying my best to look pale, and I must have suceeded because he said, "Are you all right, ma'am?"

"I'm being followed," I gasped, summoning up old memories of Ingrid Bergman in similar situations. "He's lurking around the corner now, waiting for me. . . . I would have called a cab but there wasn't one in sight and I was too frightened to wait around."

"I'll check him out for you, ma'am," he said, coming out from his little office and placing one hand menacingly on the revolver in the holster at his hip. "You just wait right there, honey," he said, "and then I'll get you a cab."

He walked out of the foyer and into the street and I saw him glance from left to right and then turn and look inquiringly at me. I pointed urgently to the left, and he strode off, out of sight to the corner. Grinning wickedly, I fled through the still-unfinished foyer to the back and the big, open-sided freight elevator. I quickly pushed the button, and I closed my eyes as it lumbered slowly past floor after empty unfinished floor, mere levels of concrete illuminated bleakly with work lights. It looked frightening, and I thought of Bob and all he had gone through to build his unfinished tower: all the long negotiations on prices and contracts, planning permission and tax concessions, all the bureaucracy and wheeling-dealing that went into the construction of a major building in one of the world's most important cities. And I thought how sad and frightening it looked. It was still only a skeleton and I wondered whether there would ever be any "flesh" on its steel-girder bones.

The elevator lurched to a stop and I stepped out into a different world. The floor of the entry hall was highly polished parquet, and a crystal chandelier, old Waterford if I'm not mistaken, sparkled from the ceiling. I walked cautiously over the soft silk rug in subtle blues and faded bronzes, wondering if J.K. had arrived yet. I peeked through the open double doors and drew in my breath in amazement as I saw more beautiful rugs, and expensive sofas and antique furnishings, and as I tiptoed into the room I noticed that each piece had a sticker on it. A lot number from an auction sale.

And then I saw the painting dominating the wall opposite the windows. Van Gogh's "Avenue" glowed like an icon under the special low directional lights, and I realized that all this now belonged to J.K. He had bought all of Bob's things, his furniture and rugs and antiques, just the way he had bought the writer's Montauk house with all his furniture. He was taking on Bob's identity, and Bob's van Gogh, the symbol of his success, was the final touch. It was living proof that he had made his dreams come true.

"Maudie," J.K. said behind me, and I swung around from the painting, blushing like a guilty schoolgirl caught cribbing from someone else's notes.

"Did Shannon send you?" He sounded surprised and I shook my head.

"No, she did not, J.K. I've come here because I need to discuss some things with you."

"Can I ask how you knew to find me here?"

"Shannon told me she had an appointment with you." He nodded and went to the graceful little Sheraton sideboard. "Would you care for a drink?" he asked, pouring himself a glass of brandy.

I couldn't share a jar with a killer and I said a polite no, thank you. He sat in what they call a French concierge's chair, one of those hooded boxlike chairs you still find in French hotels or in antiques shops. The high sides cut off the light from his face, leaving him half in shadow, and I wished nervously he had sat opposite me on the sofa.

I'm a curious old biddy, but my curiosity had never placed me in such a strange situation before, and I was never known to be subtle, so I got right to the point. "Why don't you tell me why you killed Bob?" I asked, because, apart from being concerned about Shannon, that was the one reason I had come to speak to him myself. I had to hear from his own lips why he did it, just so that I would know my theory was right.

"Maudie, why ever would you say such a thing?" he said, sounding pained. He took a sip of his brandy and as he leaned forward I could see he was smiling.

"Because your grandmother was married to Lily's son, 'Boy' Sheridan. And because your mother, Alma Brennan, didn't die of cirrhosis the way you said she did. She was shot dead in an alley and you were arrested and questioned for her murder. And your name is not Jonas K. Brennan, you only added the K after you had decided to become Bob Keeffe. To take over his life, his work, his money, and his name, because you felt it rightfully belonged to you."

"That's very clever of you, Maudie," he said. "But then I knew when I met you you were too clever for your own good. Don't you think it's interesting that we are cousins?"

I have to admit I had not even thought of that, and my jaw dropped at the idea of being kin to a murderer and a madman. "It wasn't so clever," I said. "All we had to do was look into the past. And that's the trouble at the bottom of it all, isn't it, J.K.? The past."

He downed the brandy in one gulp and sat twirling the fragile glass in his fingers, staring down at it. "My life was always a series of wounds, you know," he said in a polite conversational tone, as though he were talking about something he had read in a newspaper. "All the insults and the jibes, the humiliation and rejection. Nobody wanted the dirt-poor Brennan kid whose grandma lived with a black, and whose mom had slept with every guy in town and more besides. It was only Gran's tales of the past that had any beauty to them. She told me the stories Boy Sheridan had told her, of his glamorous rich mother, Lady Lily Molyneux, who lived in a Beacon Hill mansion, and about her family back in Ireland. About how many thousands of acres of land they owned, with castles and houses, and their own lakes and rivers. And a hundred servants to do their bidding so they need never lift a finger their whole lives. I used to dream about them, when I was out in the fields picking corn under the broiling sun. Or lying in bed at night, sweltering and mosquito-bitten in summer and half frozen with cold and damp in winter. I would think of them when I put cheap food into my mouth, and cheap clothes on my back, and I thought of them when I was alone in the schoolyard and the other kids taunted me or ignored me. It was always one or the other. And those stories became like legends to me, glowing fables with a cast of glamorous people who never had a care in the world, and who had rejected my grandfather, Boy Sheridan, because Lily had gotten herself into trouble.

"I used to think of the lordly Molyneuxes, back in their castle with their acres and their money, and they haunted me. I was obsessed with the fact that they were still living their wonderful lives, and I was locked out from it all.

"When I was a teenager, I began to investigate the past. I went to the library; I looked up the history of Ireland, and at encyclopedias and maps. I discovered a volume of *Burke's Peerage* and found the names of my own ancestors in there. I spent as much time researching the Molyneux family tree as I did on my schoolwork, and I knew that, but for circumstance, I would have been a young Lord living in my Irish castle with money to burn.

"I even took a summer job in Boston so I could find out more about Lily. I delved into the city's archives, the records of births, marriages, deaths, names, dates, places. I found out about Lily's other son, Liam Porter Adams. And, just like Bob did, I tracked them down, and I

guessed that Bob Keeffe was Lily's grandson. And that burned me
deeper than any wound I'd suffered before. We were both descended
from Lily's sons, but Bob was still the legitimate heir. And he was so
rich he didn't even want to claim Lily's money. Bob had everything
and, as always, I had nothing.

"I pinned his picture on my wall at college and every night as I
ground through the long, hard hours of study and loneliness, I told
myself that one day I would have everything he had gotten, everything
that should, by rights, be mine. One day I would be Bob Keeffe. I
would become him."

He paused and I could tell he was looking at me, though I couldn't
see his face, and I said, "And now you think you have succeeded?"

"Almost. There was just one thing left."

I knew in a flash what he meant. "Shannon," I said, and he nodded.

"I have everything to offer her, everything her father had. She
wouldn't even look at me before, but now I know she will. I was going
to ask her to marry me tonight."

"And then it would be complete. You would have everything you
considered legitimately yours. Everything Bob Keeffe had, including
his daughter."

"Right, Maudie, that's exactly the way it's going to be. Only now
you've come along, asking questions and interfering, just when everything was going so smoothly." He sighed deeply. "I really wish you
hadn't."

I smiled at him, summoning up a modicum of the old charm. I
glanced apprehensively at my watch and saw it was still only a quarter
of eleven. Shannon wouldn't be here for another fifteen minutes and I
had to stall him. "Before I go," I said, trying not to think how ambigu-
ous that word "go" might turn out to be, "Before I go, why don't you
tell me how you stole Bob's money?"

He laughed as he told me. "I'm a clever man, and Brad and Jack
were easy pawns to manipulate. I knew what they wanted, and I offered it to them, and then more. Much more. And they couldn't resist
the bait.

"For ten years I worked hard. I began as Bob's protégé and I became his right-hand man. I took care of everything he didn't want to,
and then more. There was nothing I didn't know about the Keeffe
business and Bob would have trusted me with his life."

I thought how ironic that statement was, but he seemed to see nothing strange in it and he went on. "In order to manipulate a man, to

bend him to your will, you have to really understand him. You have to know what he wants, what he longs for, what he would die or kill for."

"His Achilles heel," I said helpfully.

"Exactly. Jack Wexler was not a talented architect, he was just darn lucky to find himself in an easy job. Bob trusted everybody and Jack took full advantage of it. He had a big ego, he wanted to be the rich successful playboy bachelor, but without money he would have ended up a suburban husband, commuting to Westchester with a middle-class house and a pretty blond wife with an expensive taste in clothes and two-point-four children needing braces and college tuition fees. He had been helping himself from Keeffe Holdings for years before I joined the company. He took kickbacks on every contract for every item that went into a Keeffe construction, and he made himself a nice few bucks in the process.

"And Brad was the same; he had had his hand in the Keeffe till right from day one, starting with a little here and a little there. But it wasn't until he met Fedora Lee at a country club polo match that he really needed more. There's nothing like a woman to fuel a man's ambitions, and Fedora was a woman who knew exactly what she wanted.

"So, once I knew about them, it was a fait accompli. I just showed them how easy it would be to make big bucks instead of little ones. I told them that grand larceny was just as easy as minor theft, except you make a lot more money. Millions of dollars more. And when I explained to them that you went to the same jail whether you stole five thousand or five million, and that I had the power to turn them both in and send them to that jail, they came to heel like a pair of eager dogs, ready to do their master's bidding.

"I had already formed ExWyZe Fund in Liechtenstein with money from the sale of stocks and bonds Bob kept as collateral for the bank loans, and now I used a little of it to buy up cheap worthless properties across the States. Without Bob's complete trust, and because he was so wrapped up in what he was doing, this would never have been possible, but he did trust me and he was busy and I kept him happy, and it was all simple. ExWyZe Fund bought the properties and then sold them at a vastly inflated price to Keeffe Holdings, who bought them with more money from the sale of collateral.

"Brad and Jack took care of the contracts and the money was paid to Liechtenstein and their share went into secret numbered Swiss bank accounts. I never signed anything, so nothing could be pinned on me. Brad bought his farm and his woman; Jack bought his Rothkos and paid for his house and his flashy life-style; and I sat on my millions and waited for the ax to fall, because I knew one day it had to, and that when it did I would have to kill Bob Keeffe. And that was exactly the way it happened."

He emerged from his hooded chair like a snake from its lair and walked back to the sideboard and poured himself another brandy. "Sure you won't have one, Maudie?" he asked, like the perfect host.

I said, "That wasn't the first time you killed, though, was it J.K.?"

"You mean my mother?" He dismissed her with a shrug. "She didn't deserve to live. She was a blot on the landscape of my youth, a cheap woman who made a mockery of my grandmother's dignity. And she stood in the way of the future I was planning for myself. Besides, if I hadn't done it one of her pickups would have before too long."

He came and stood over me and I looked up at him and for the first time I was afraid. He took a sip of his brandy and said thoughtfully, "And now there's you, Maudie."

He was too close for comfort and I glanced under my lashes at my watch, hoping he wouldn't notice, but he missed nothing. "It's five minutes before eleven," he said calmly. "There's just time before Shannon gets here. You will be gone, and then I shall be here to help her get over her grief."

"Just the way you were when Bob died," I reminded him, and he smiled.

"I really wish I didn't have to do this, Maudie," he said as I eyed him warily. "You should never have interfered. Everything was so neat and tidy, there were no flaws. No one need ever have known."

"You'll never get away with it, not a second time," I said, standing up and gripping Pa's hazelwood stick tightly as he walked away from me again to the sideboard. He opened the drawer and took out a gun. "Shannon will never believe I killed myself," I warned him, wishing my silly old voice didn't sound so high-pitched. After all, we Molyneuxes had always had a reputation for being brave in battle. But this wasn't a battle I was facing, this was a psychopath.

"I'm not going to shoot you," he explained, smoothing back his hair with one hand and adjusting his gold-rimmed spectacles. "I'm just going to escort you down to the next floor."

"Why not just do it here in comfort," I said, thinking of the bleak concrete spaces and steel girders and the windowless walls shrouded in plastic sheets. It was no place to spend my final moments and I would have preferred the soft silky Persian rug. *Whatever are you thinking of, woman?* I asked myself. *Choosing a place to die, like a sick old dog, when there's fight left in ye yet? The fightin' Irish, that's what Bob used to call us, and dammit, he was right.* Besides, I knew Shannon would be here any minute and I thought that maybe with the diversion, I would be able to turn the tables on J.K.

And then the phone rang. J.K. turned and picked it up and I was across the room and out the door in an instant, just as I heard him say, "Shannon!"

She was on the phone and I thought, gosh darn it, she's not coming because I told her not to and now I'm on my own and it's up to me. I pushed the elevator button but no little lights flashed on and I guessed J.K. had switched off the current, and then I heard his footsteps on the parquet and I pushed open the door to the stairway and fled downward.

My heart was pounding as I reached the next floor and then I heard the door slam and his footsteps as he hurried after me. *Jayzus,* I thought, *you had better get a move on, Maudie,* and I fled down another flight.

It was hard going for a woman my age. The stairs were only dimly lit and I was afraid of breaking my leg or my neck, though I don't know why, since J.K. was about to do it for me. If he could catch me, that is.

I dodged sideways into the dark morass of girders and struts and plastic sheeting, stumbling over cables and coils of metal and stray buckets, and almost falling. I found a concrete pillar and hid behind it, listening to the silence, hoping he hadn't seen me, and that he could not hear my silly old heart pounding away like a teenager's, as loud as an express train.

I looked around me and realized I was on one of the empty unfinished floors I had seen from the elevator on my way up, and that my only way out was down those long flights of stairs, all the way to the street, a hundred floors below. I could hear the sound of traffic wafting faintly upward, and where the wind had caught a piece of the plastic I saw black emptiness and the lights of the building across the street. I shivered. The place was freezing, and the wind whipped gustily through the unfinished walls, then over the noise I heard the sound of a soft footfall.

"Maudie," J.K. said calmly. "I know you're here. Don't make this hard on yourself. After all, you're an old woman. It's time for you to go."

I felt a flash of heat and adrenaline and I grasped my hazelwood stick angrily. How dare he call me an old woman, and how dare he decide when I should depart this world. I was damned if I was going to let him. I had my stick and I was a black belt at karate, and we'd see who won if it came to a fight—though I rather hoped Shannon and Eddie might arrive, like the cavalry, just in the nick of time.

My hope faded fast as a shot rang out. It whistled past my pillar in a quick flicker of orange and I gasped and shut my eyes, telling myself he wouldn't dare to shoot me because then he would be stuck with my body with a bullet in it, and there was no way he could get away with that because too many people knew about Bob Keeffe now.

"Gotcha," he said, grabbing me from behind, and I jumped like a surprised eel in his arms, whacking him backward with my finest elbow chop and giving him a firm crack with my stick. I ran, tripping and stumbling, back toward the door and the stairs, but he caught me again. And then the lights flickered as the current was switched back on and I heard the sound of the elevator thundering upward toward us.

Help at last, I thought, just as J.K. realized he had no time to lose. Gripping me in a headlock, he dragged me, kicking like a mad thing, toward the yawning windows and the abyss outside, and I knew what he meant to do.

I whacked him with my stick, yelling as loudly as I could, and he tightened his grip on my neck. There was a whooshing sound in my ears as my air was being choked off. In the distance I thought I heard the elevator stop, but I was fading and I told myself it was already too late. I kicked feebly backward but there were purple patches floating in front of my closed eyes and I feared I was losing the battle.

"Maudie," I heard Shannon scream, and then J.K. dropped me and I fell all in a heap, like a bag of old bones, to the hard cement floor. There was the sound of running footsteps and a scuffle and then a shot rang out. And, as they say, I knew no more.

CHAPTER
58

THEY WANTED TO KEEP ME IN THE HOSPITAL, but I wasn't having it. "If I have to lie in bed all day, then I'm going to do it in luxury," I said, and, as you know, when I make up my mind there's no moving me.

Back at the Ritz-Carlton, I lay there in my splendid super-king-size bed in blissful comfort, waited on hand and foot; with flowers and presents, and everyone from the chambermaid to the waiters and the concierge as well as the manager popping in for a cup of tea and a gossip.

Joanna came to see me every day, bearing gifts of books and magazines and pretty bed jackets, smiling her lovely Doris Day smile that makes her look like a very glamorous girl-next-door. And now that her mind was at rest about Bob I hoped for her happiness in the future.

Later, Eddie told me what had happened, and poor Shannon was so distraught I felt tears of sympathy in my own eyes as she wailed, "It's all my fault. I should have realized earlier that it was J. K. It's all so obvious when you think about it."

"Nonsense, dear girl," I replied soothingly. "It was my own curiosity that got me into it, and my own silliness that got me a few cuts and bruises. And I'm only glad you both showed up when you did."

"In the nick of time," Eddie said with an affectionate grin. He was holding one of my hands and Shannon the other, and I laughed and said to the hovering Brigid, "What about a glass of champagne, Brigid?"

"Roederer Cristal," she said firmly, dialing room service. She's a quick learner, my Brigid.

I was rescued by Shannon and Eddie's quick thinking after they found my note and Brigid told them of our suspicions. They had called the cops and so had the security guard, who had been looking for me. And with five cars of New York's finest, how could I not be saved?

In return I had sent a generous donation to the Police Pension and Christmas Fund and a note of thanks, with an invitation for any one of them, should they be passing through Connemara, to come and visit me at Ardnavarna. And I meant it.

The champagne arrived with a complimentary bowl of caviar, courtesy of a fellow guest who had heard about my exploits, and I preened myself in my little pink marabou bed jacket, wondering who he was and whether we shouldn't ask him to share our champagne.

"Another admirer, Maudie," Shannon exclaimed, because there had been so many cards and gifts from well-wishers who had read the story in the newspapers and seen us all on television. We were famous and I have to admit I was enjoying all the attention.

"We must drink a toast," Brigid said, looking solemn, because she still hasn't gotten over the fact that she almost lost me. But instead it was that nasty J. K. who lost out. He shot himself before the police could do it for him. He knew that it was his "time to go."

"A toast to Lily," I said, raising my glass, "because without her, we might never have met."

"And to my great-grandfather, Ned Sheridan," Eddie said.

"And to my father," Shannon said softly. "May he rest peacefully now."

There were tears in her eyes as we drank the toast and Brigid sniffed noisily. She can cry buckets at the drop of a hat and I told her briskly to drink up and not be a silly old woman, and for once she didn't argue with me.

And I looked at the two young things, smiling at me and at each other, and I wondered if they knew yet that they were in love. Maybe that's one thing it doesn't take age and experience to recognize and understand. But one thing is certain, I surely love them.

I refused to allow them to accompany us to the pier when we sailed the following week, back to England on the *QE2*. I knew it would be too sad a leavetaking, and instead we said our good-byes at the hotel, in privacy, so we could all cry as much as we wanted. Though in fact not one of us shed a tear. We laughed and joked and hugged and kissed and swore we loved each other and that we would stay in touch and see each other soon.

My last view of my dear "grandchildren" was their smiling faces through the windows of the limousine as I waved good-bye. I threw them a kiss and that was that.

Our stateroom on the lovely liner was a bower of blossoms, and looking at them, I thought of Lily on the old *Hibernia* and how she would have enjoyed present-day travel, whisking between continents in speed and luxury. It would have been just her style.

Brigid and I hung over the deckrail, staring at the Statue of Liberty disappearing into the dusk and then, with a regretful sigh that it was all over, we went down to join our fellow passengers for dinner.

But the last thing I thought of that night as I fell asleep, lulled by the movement and with the infinity of the Atlantic Ocean in front of us, was of their dear, young, smiling faces that I had come to love so much.

EPILOGUE

Ardnavarna, Connemara

KNOWING ME AS YOU DO by now, you will understand that I always have to have the last word. Even after "the finale."

I've just come back from a long ride along the strand, the same one Lily used to take with Finn, and the one you know so well by now. I'm sitting in my chair by the window with the dogs tucked in beside me, as always, and they are twitching in their sleep as they chase rabbits through the leafy woods of dreamland. The petals of the Gloire de Dijon roses are falling and those that remain are curling brown at the edges, but their scent is still beautiful as it drifts toward me, and there's the smell of the ever-present peat fire and the wonderful fresh-ness of the air.

Brigid is in the kitchen cooking up a fresh batch of scones for tea and regaling the girls with her tales of America. She is quite the celeb-rity in the village, with her stories of the high life in New York and Washington, smart in her Bloomingdale's dresses and her cowboy boots, which, thank heavens, have replaced the old green Wellingtons as her favorites.

It has surely given both us old ladies something to talk about on the long dark autumn evenings that are fast approaching, and we shall warm our hearts with the memories as we toast our toes by the kitchen fire. In fact I've enjoyed myself so much sleuthin', maybe I'll take it up as a profession. "Maudie Molyneux, Private Investigator." That would be a first for the Molyneuxes!

I think often about my dear "grandchildren." They telephone me every week, and send me letters. Eddie from Los Angeles, where he has a role in a new movie. Not a big one, he told me, but "significant" and all our high hopes go with him that he will achieve the success Ned Sheridan did. Shannon is in L.A. too. She has decided to follow in her father's footsteps and maybe revamp the fortunes of his company, and with that in mind and Lily's fortune in her bank account, she is studying architecture at a very advanced school there. The darlings are both planning to visit me in the spring and I can't wait.

I dream about them, you know. I can see their wedding now, here at Ardnavarna. Shannon a beautiful bride in white silk and lace and Eddie the handsomest groom since my Pa's day.

Maybe they haven't thought of it themselves yet because, for the young, there is always plenty of time. But I am planning on a guard of honor made up of locals mounted on their horses and dressed in their best hunting pink, with their riding crops raised to form a triumphal arch, and even the darling dogs will be wearing smart red ribbons. And all the guests will come from miles around, dressed in their best; the sun will shine, the sea will glitter, the Gloire de Dijon roses will be in full bloom and their scent will mingle, as it always does, with that of the peat smoke and good food and the dust of ages, here at Ardnavarna.

Ah, my dear friends, laugh if you will, but an old lady is entitled to her dreams, isn't she? And who knows, maybe you and I shall see each other again. Sometime.